Sustainability Management
Strategies and Execution to Achieve *Responsible* organizational goals

About the Author

Dr. Deb Prasanna Choudhury has been working in the areas of project and supply chain management for over 30 years in the oil & gas, construction and service industries and held numerous senior management positions in renowned private and public sector organizations in USA, India and Gulf countries. He is also a founder and director of an NGO in India which he completely funds himself. Dr. Choudhury has a record of innovations and business process improvements and has also authored books and articles on management.

Dr. Choudhury is also a professor of MBA, ACCA and CIPS programs in various universities in UAE and India. While his postgraduate study on organizational sustainability at Harvard university (USA) prepared him and brought appreciation about sustainability advantages, it is his practices of sustainability in his own organization and profession which helped him to experience first-hand the tremendous scope and benefits of sustainability management. He has used his extensive academic knowledge and practical professional experience in running both profit and non-profit organizations in writing this book.

Dr. Choudhury has a Bachelor's degree in Mechanical engineering, a Bachelor degree in Economics, a Master degree in Business Administration, a Master degree in law, a Doctorate degree in Business Administration, a Doctor of Philosophy (Ph.D.) in Management, a Doctor of Medicine degree in Alternative Medicine and a postgraduate qualification is sustainability from Harvard university. He is also a professional corporate member of the following:

Fellow of the Chartered Management Institute
Fellow of the Chartered Institute of Procurement and Supply
Fellow of the Institute of Directors
Member of the American Society of Mechanical Engineers

Dr. Choudhury has been recipient of many awards and honours such as "Glory of Bengal" award, "TATA Inspire" award and a road has been named after him called the "Dr. Deb Prasanna Choudhury Road" in Bolpur, India.

Sustainability Management

Strategies and Execution to Achieve *Responsible* organizational goals

Dr. Deb Prasanna Choudhury

ZORBA BOOKS

ZORBA BOOKS

Published in India by Zorba Books, 2018

Website: www.zorbabooks.com
Email: info@zorbabooks.com

Copyright © Dr. Deb Prasanna Choudhury

ISBN Print Book - 978-93-87456-60-0
ISBN eBook - 978-93-87456-61-7

Zorba Books Pvt. Ltd.(opc)
Gurgaon, INDIA

Printed at Repro Knowledgecast Limited, Thane

This book is dedicated to all the destitute and underprivileged children, women, and men who have allowed me to serve them and made my life worthy of living by visiting my charitable organization in India, Deb Kalika Choudhury Charity & Development Center— as well as to my parents without whose motivation, support and effort, this service would not have been possible.

Acknowledgment

I would like to acknowledge the contribution of the following person and organization in writing this book:

Harvard University (USA) where I learned about sustainability and its implications at global, national, community and individual level. Prof. Dr. Robert Pojasek from whom I learned about application of sustainability in its three imperatives of environmental, social and economics at organizational level. I would also like to thank all other authors who have been mentioned in the Bibliography and had a direct or indirect contribution in my writing this book.

Preface

Sustainability is perhaps the most important term in the area of management today and indeed in all areas of organizational survival and progress as well as its influence on the environment and society at large. Sustainability is relevant to all levels of human activity, from the global level to the national, regional, community, organizational, and individual levels. Continuous economic growth is desirable but no longer considered inevitable at the cost of harm to the environment and society, and such economic growth must be without the use of non-renewable natural resources as much as possible. Therefore, the terminology is sustainable development or growth and not just growth or development per se. In sustainability, the pursuit of growth and profit blends seamlessly with the pursuit of the common good.

I decided to write this book after completing my post-graduate study in sustainability at Harvard University, USA but it is not until I started practicing sustainability in my own organization in India (The case study of my organization, DKCCDC is part of this book) that I realized the profoundness of this concept in everyday organizational life and its immense impact on the environmental, social and economic domain of our world. Further, I realized that there is limited understanding of sustainability and even more limited appreciation about climate change and its adverse effects among people at large though this is a concept which is equally important at the organization and people level.

This book is unique as it presents and covers not only the environmental, social and economic aspects and impacts of sustainability but organizational sustainability from the aspect of being able to meet its mission, vision, and goals and managing the risks and governance issues while being held accountable by its stakeholders. It also addresses how we at the individual level can practice sustainability and take responsibility towards a greener and safer planet. It is important to recognize that sustainability is different from the environmental movement alone and greenwashing in that it recognizes the need for a healthy economy and social conditions too. It is in the context of sustainability and climate change that the world has become so interdependent as damage to the climate caused in one country affects another country and therefore, damage to the climate and controlling emission of the Green House Gases are becoming a joint effort by all countries. The 2015 Paris Climate agreement is a prominent example of that. It is to be noted though that this book is not about sustainable development at a policy level but a practical book on attaining sustainability at organizational level and addresses all areas of sustainability management including sustainability strategy and risk, how to calculate and meet the GHG reduction goals, sustainability in different industry sectors and management functions together with sustainable finance, procurement, marketing and sustainability reporting are also explored. Sustainability reporting, measurement and metrics are also widely covered. In fact, there is mounting evidence that there is real ROI advantage to companies that include ESG / Sustainability as an integral part of competitive, capital and operational strategy. The sustainability books that are in the market today address certain specific areas of sustainability however; this book is a comprehensive book on sustainability and applies sustainability to most areas of management.

The book provides a global perspective on sustainability and therefore, provides ample examples and cases to demonstrate the benefits of practicing sustainability as well as cases from Indian companies from both profitable and nonprofit sectors which can be applied by both businesses and on a personal level. Therefore, this book and the examples are relevant and applicable in the global as well as Indian context. Ultimately, the purpose of the book is to trigger sustainable action from the organization and individual point of view. The book is intended for sustainability management studies at undergraduate and postgraduate levels as well as can be used a reference book on sustainability for professionals and amateurs alike. Upon completing the reading of the book, the reader will possess the understanding and experience to integrate environmental and social sustainability with commercial and economic success. The book also addresses the global issues surrounding sustainable management and reviews the framework of sustainability that provides the scientific foundations and economic principles of how sustainability can help managers to achieve a natural competitive advantage. An understanding of the basics of social and environmental sustainability is critical to successfully managing an organization in today's world. Businesses, governments, and nonprofit organizations face a world in which life-supporting systems are threatened by climate change, the loss of major ecosystem services, and significant social, and economic disparity. The majority of Fortune 500 companies have a sustainability officer at the VP level or higher, and leading businesses are coming to see sustainability as a driver for the next wave of innovation and profitability and growth. Local governments are leading the charge to make our cities and infrastructure more resilient and livable. Yet few graduates of business schools are given the tools to manage companies, governments, or organizations sustainably. This book addresses this gap adequately.

The book is divided into four parts. PART I (Chapters Nos. 1 to 7) of the book addresses sustainability from the aspects of definitions, strategies, benefits and measuring and controlling the GHGs whereas PART II (Chapters 8 to 19) discusses the organizational and governance aspect of sustainability including how to imbed sustainability in to an organization and its various functions such as marketing, finance, supply chain and sustainability metrics. PART III discusses two case studies, PART IV includes Appendices, and PART V covers Bibliography.

I sincerely hope that the book will not only provide a good practical foundation for sustainability management to students and practitioners of sustainability but also trigger in-depth sustainable action at individual and organizational level.

Contents

PART I

Contents

PART II

Contents

PART III
Cases

PART IV
Appendices

PART V

Chapter Summary

Chapter 1 provides an introduction to sustainability and the business case for pursuing sustainability together with how business should engage with sustainability. For proper understanding, the chapter discusses the contrast between a sustainable and unsustainable company. It also discusses sustainable framework, difference between CSR and sustainability, climate change and sustainable development as recognized by the United Nations. This chapter also covers the personal reasons as well as practice of sustainability at an individual level.

Chapter 2 provides details of sustainability benefits and opportunities as well as avoiding risks with numerous examples. This approach maximizes sustainable profit.

Chapter 3 defines the sustainable strategies and steps in sustainable strategy formulation as well as sustainability planning. It also discusses unsustainable and sustainable business models. Impact assessment discusses the relationship that an organization has with the environment. The relationship between sustainable development and renewable energy is also addressed.

Chapter 4 discusses the approach to sustainability process as well as the efficient and effective processes and the process control.

Chapter 5 covers sustainability assessment by various industry sectors and management functions level. This self-assessment is quite detailed and done in a manner where the sustainability practice for various sectors and functions are also stated and the reader can also add to it based on his/her experience and knowledge and improve on the existing level based on such assessment.

Chapters 6 and 7 discuss Lifecycle analysis and carbon footprint together with calculating Green House Gas emissions. This will help in measuring and controlling greenhouse gases emitted by an organization to meet various standards and mitigating measures required to be deployed to reduce GHG quantities. It also addresses carbon emission trading and carbon tax for proper GHG management.

Chapters 8 cover the nature of organization, internal and external context of the organization and scanning the environment and context of sustainability in the organization.

Chapter 9 addresses sustainability risk management issues as well as different types of risks and risks mitigation and how risks to revenue can be captured.

Chapter 10 covers embedding sustainability in an organization, attributes of organizational sustainability, the five-stage journey to a sustainable enterprise as well as sustainable business model innovations.

Chapter 11 covers identification, engagement and management of various stakeholders as well as the social license to operate which is granted by the stakeholders in the community.

Chapter12 addresses the organizational governance and leadership for sustainability change management as well as behavior changes and factors required for successfully implementing sustainability-related changes.

Chapter 13 and 14 address developing sustainability metrics including leading and lagging indicators with many practical examples. It also looks at performance measurement methods and models and performance framework for proper sustainability management.

Chapter 15 discusses sustainability resilience and its various dimensions.

Chapter 16 addresses Sustainability marketing strategies and mix, benefits of sustainable marketing, sustainable consumer behavior and customer segmentation

Chapter 17 covers sustainable procurement, key objectives for sustainable specifications, and benefits of sustainable procurement. It also discusses strategies for a sustainable supply chain.

Chapter 18 discusses sustainable finance and sustainable investing together with case studies on how financial organizations practice sustainable finance.

Chapter 19 addresses sustainability reporting and sustainability reporting frameworks

PART I

Chapter 1

Introduction to Sustainability

1.1 What is Sustainability?

Sustainability is relevant to all levels of human activity, from the global level to the national, regional, community, organizational, and individual levels. Sustainability and sustainable development have been described in many ways: "Meeting our needs or needs of the present generation without compromising the ability of future generations to meet their own needs" or "Living well within the limits of nature." In another word, sustainability refers to a state of the global system with a focus on the environmental, social, and economic subsystems, in which the needs of the present are met without compromising the ability of future generations to meet their needs. Sustainable development is needed to meet the needs of both present and future generations and is essential to sustainability. The Harvard Business Review compared what it called the "Sustainability Imperative" to other game-changing business megatrends of the past generation, such as the rise of the quality movement, the personal computer, and the Internet. Such game-changing trends profoundly affect the competitiveness, and even the survival, of organizations.

Sustainable management takes the concepts from sustainability and synthesizes them with the concepts of management. From this definition, sustainable management has been created to be defined as the application of sustainable principles and practices in the categories of businesses, society, environment, and personal life by managing them in a way that will benefit current generations and future generations and achieve synergistic goals and benefits for organizations. Sustainable management is needed because it is an important part of the ability to successfully maintain the quality of life on our planet. Sustainable management can be applied to all aspects of our lives. For example, the practices of a business should be sustainable and linked to the social, environmental and economical imperatives if they wish to stay in businesses, because if the business is unsustainable, then by the definition of sustainability they will cease to be able to compete. Communities are in need of sustainable management, because if the community is to prosper, then it must apply the sustainability framework. Forest and natural resources need to have sustainable management if they are to be able to be continually used by our generation and future generations.

Sustainability is important to address the following concerns:

i) Growing environmental pressures related to increasing population

ii) Resource scarcity and rising costs for energy and materials as billions of people aspire to join the middle class in places such as India, China, and Brazil

iii) Increasing consumer demand for safe and natural products

iv) Unprecedented levels of transparency arising from the Internet and social media

v) Stronger demands for accountability and engagement among the "millennial" generation of workers, and stronger demands for improved governance by boards and other stakeholders

vi) Our personal lives also need to be managed sustainably for our sustenance and growth. This can be by making decisions that will help sustain our immediate surroundings and environment, or it can be by managing our emotional and physical well-being.

True sustainability has, therefore, three co-equal components:

- *Social* (acting as if other people matter): Actions and conditions that affect all members of society (e.g. poverty, violence, injustice, education, public health, and labor and human rights)

- *Economic* (operating profitably): Actions that affect how people and businesses meet their economic needs – for example, securing food, water, shelter, and comforts for people and for businesses turning a profit so that they will be able to continue for years to come.

- *Environmental* (protecting and restoring the ecosystem): Actions and conditions that affect the earth's ecology (e.g. climate change, preservation of natural resources, and the prevention of toxic wastes)

In line with the above, businesses have long referred to this as the "triple bottom line." Instead of trading these realms off against one another (jobs or the environment; economic growth or environmental health; development or habitat), sustainability aims to optimize all three to achieve synergistic goals. The triple bottom line 3 Ps are:

i) Economic sustainability **(Profit)**

ii) Environmental sustainability **(Planet)**

iii) Social sustainability **(People)**

In the long term, you can't have one without the others. China, for example, has been reporting 9% economic growth or more over the last decade but is beginning to recognize that the environmental costs of that growth (e.g. flooding, pollution, health problems and resource depletion) wipe out most of these gains. Pan Yue, deputy director of China's State Environment Protection Administration, figures that environmental injury costs China 8 to 15% of its annual GDP.

Without a healthy economy, unemployment is high, leading to a host of social problems; and without a healthy economy, governments don't have the revenue to handle these social ills. Without a healthy environment, we deplete the resources upon which our economy depends and contribute to human illness. Without a vibrant community, we don't have the employee to work in businesses, and people in crisis don't have the luxury of being concerned about environmental degradation. When we don't exactly understand these interdependencies, we often make poor decisions and tend to focus on one realm over the others.

Sustainability is different from the environmental movement in that it recognizes the need for a healthy economy and social imperatives too. Sustainability is also no longer a fringe issue. Consider the fact that the fastest growing segment of the energy sector is wind power with solar in hot pursuit; in the travel industry, it is eco-tourism; in the investment community, it is socially responsible investments; in agriculture, it is organic farming. In venture capital, clean-tech is in the top three. These trends all point to the same direction, towards sustainability. In fact, sustainability is becoming ubiquitous and affects both human life and organizational life.

The foundation of sustainability as stated above implies that all human activity needs to stay within the ecological carrying capacity of the planet, and it must not consume natural resources in excess of the ability of ecosystems to regenerate them. Anything else compromises both the ability of the present generation to meet its needs and the ability of future generations to meet theirs.

The Natural Step, an international non-governmental organization, espouses four scientifically based system conditions that echo the fundamental components of sustainable development.

- Nature's functions and diversity must not be subject to increasing concentrations of substances extracted from the earth's crust.
- Nature's functions and diversity must not be subject to increasing concentrations of substances produced by society.
- Nature's functions and diversity must not be impoverished by overharvesting or other forms of ecosystem manipulation.
- Resources must be used fairly and efficiently in order to meet basic human needs worldwide.

We are part of the whole, not separate from it. We cannot exist sustainably without the ecosystem services provided to us free of charge by clean air, clean water, clean soil, and fully functioning habitats. Preservation of those (even at current levels, as degraded as they are, based on what we know existed from historical record) is the big challenge that sustainable development attempts to address. As we have lost our way with nature by recklessly damaging it over the past few centuries, environmental sustainability, in particular, is about connecting back to nature through the aforementioned steps.

The Profit element of the 3Ps is easily understood and accepted by companies — it is about the long-term financial health of the enterprise. The Planet dimension reminds companies to not only "do no harm" to the environment with their operations and products, but also to help restore the environment from harm already done. This requires reducing the amount of energy, water, and materials consumed in the manufacture of products, plus reducing waste and remediating contaminated sites. The People element encompasses how the company treats its employees, the working conditions and labor relations in its own operations and those of its suppliers, adherence to business ethics, and investment in communities it touches. In business journals like The Economist, environmental, social, and governance (ESG) is the preferred label for sustainability. Do ESG, CSR, CR, sustainable development (SD), and "green" all mean the same thing? Not quite, but they are close enough to capture the common essence of sustainability.

The use of business terminology helps companies recognize their direct or indirect dependence on natural capital for their energy, materials, food, and water. The term "natural capital" reinforces the wisdom of living off the Earth's interest, not its capital. Human capital is the company's engaged workforce. Social capital is the good reputation the firm has with its important stakeholders, like customers, communities, regulators, suppliers, and investors.

1.2 Sustainability and Responsibility

Acting responsibly is at the very core of the practice of sustainability. Organizations must address three responsibilities of environmental, social and economic and take the following actions to meet these sustainability responsibilities:

Environmental Stewardship:
- Reduce the use of all resources
- Eliminate waste
- Prevent pollution
- Respect the need for climate change mitigation and adaptation
- Protect natural habitat and biodiversity
- Consider each of these items throughout the value chain

Social Well-Being:
- Protect human rights
- Ensure fair operating practices
- Assess labor practices, including health and safety
- Evaluate consumer issues associated with product and services

- Optimize community involvement and awareness
- Consider each of these items throughout the value chain

Economic Prosperity:

- Create top-line growth (brand)
- Ensure bottom-line growth (profits)
- Improve governance and maintain the organization's "license to operate"
- Contribute to community development
- Consider each of these items throughout the value chain

1.3 Business Case for Pursuing Sustainability

- *Customers are asking for it:* A sustainability coordinator in a multinational engineering firm began tracking how many times request for a proposal (RFPs) asked about its environmental management systems and sustainability. This data pushed the firm into this field.
- *First Mover Advantage:* Often the first to market with an innovation gets the recognition and competitive advantage while others in the industry may match or surpass their efforts. BP gets most of the attention even though other oil companies have engaged in similar efforts. Some companies and communities recognize the benefit of being known as the first and the best. For example, Portland, Oregon, was featured in a sustainability documentary, in part because it was the first city in the USA to have a Climate Action Plan.
- *Getting left Behind*: It only took a couple of years for LEED (Leadership in Energy and Environmental Design) to become the de facto standard for commercial buildings. Architects who were not certified have been scrambling to catch up lest they look hopelessly out of touch.
- *Legal compliance:* Focus on legal compliance to avoid liabilities such as compliance with environmental standards and codes have become an important reason to pursue sustainability.
- *Saving Money/Increase profit:* Pursuing sustainability can save money in terms of cheaper and better products and services and reducing wastes which can lead to competitive advantage and a higher level of profit.
- *Protecting one's image:* Nike became interested in sustainability after being lambasted for the treatment of workers in its supplier's operations. It asked the question: what might hit us next? Environmental sustainability was the answer.
- *Longevity:* Pursuing sustainability is the best way to ensure business survival and prosperity

- *Investment:* Investors worldwide are increasingly becoming aware of the environmental, social and governance (ESG) footprint of companies. The expanding field of ESG investing applies a set of agreed criteria to select companies on the basis of corporate sustainability. Examples of common criteria include those agreed at the UN Global Compact, the UN Principles for Responsible Investing (PRI) and the Sustainability Accounting and Standard Board. There is much evidence that the incorporation of ESG factors does not impose additional costs from an investment return point of view.
- Figure 1.1 shows the Business case and sustainability benefits

Capture Opportunities	Increased revenue and market share
	Reduced energy expenses
	Reduced waste expenses
	Reduced materials and waste expenses
	Increased employee productivity
	Reduced hiring and attrition expenses
PLUS	
Avoid Risks	Reduced Strategic and Operational Risks
Business Case	**Benefits**

Figure 1.1

- A Virtuous Cycle: Sustainability Fosters Engagement, Which Fosters Sustainability
- Building a long-lasting business with an overarching Sustainability goal can provide a greater purpose beyond profits. It can give employees an opportunity to serve something larger than themselves

Sustainability provides a fresh conversation for soliciting employee input, unleashing employee creativity, surfacing, and recognizing leadership talent, and driving innovation—all of which further engage employees. Chances are, your shipping crew or warehouse front line can figure out how to reduce packaging costs. Or a truck driver can recommend how to save gas or cut other transportation costs. Or an administrative assistant can advise you on cutting printing, postage, paperwork, or office maintenance and management costs. Or a cashier can help figure out how to bag a watermelon more cost-effectively. Therefore, the innovation related to sustainability can come from practically anybody at any level in an organization with a flexible organizational mindset. Therefore, businesses may want to be able to create a winning proposition for all key stakeholders while ensuring that their operations are able to build long-term values and also impact global challenges, going forward. Some key fundamentals assumptions and principles on which sustainability management is based include:

- Sustainability is a good business
- Sustainability is not just a change in the process but a change in mindset
- Sustainability is a good model for social value creation
- Community participation is a key to drive sustainability agenda
- Voluntary sustainability policies and codes of conduct ensure greater transparency
- Product responsibility and sustainability makes a good business case
- Leveraging technology and programme innovation for scale and efficiency
- Extending sustainability to supply chain is equal to shared value approach
- Global Compact's Ten Universal Principles are driving sustainability agenda globally. This is discussed more in detail in Chapter 3.
- State incentives can help businesses escalate their sustainability initiatives
- Adoption of bottom-up approaches will fast-track social license to help facilitate operational advantage
- Robust internal mechanisms are key to increase operational business efficiency, and
- Sustainability initiatives deepen business brand value and its reputation

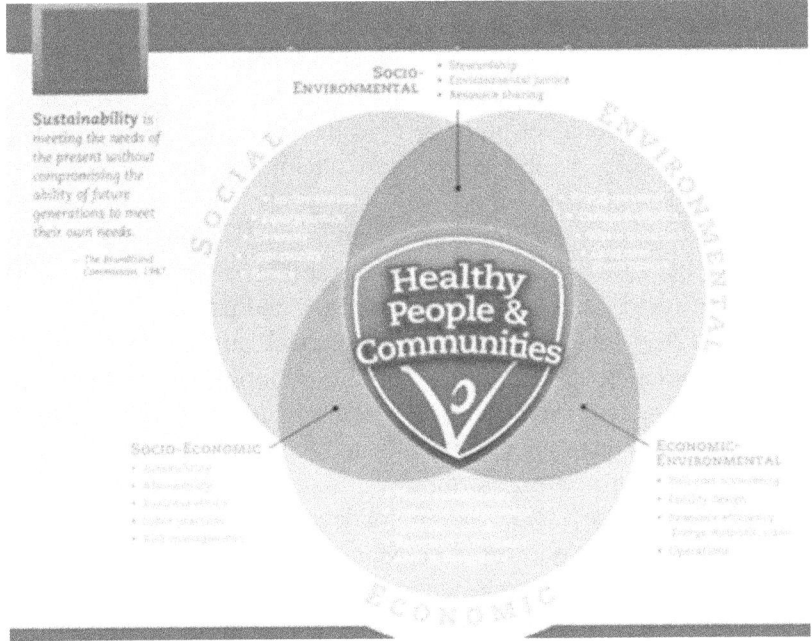

All the above assumptions have been proved to be correct as the benefits derived from practicing sustainability is immense as discussed more in detail in Chapter 2.

Sustainability as a consequence of corporate action on key constituents and major stakeholders including its efforts to gain a deeper connection with the community and more deepened approaches to operating with a clear social license to operate has begun to get clear calls within the boardrooms and no longer remains a mere statement of purpose.

1.4 Sustainability Framework

The starting point for any measurement of the sustainability of companies should be the work of the Brundtland Commission Report (1987) which in effect held that we need to find a way to meet the needs of the current generation without jeopardizing the ability of future generations to meet their needs.

There are many sustainability frameworks and tools available which are discussed in detail in Appendix 1. However, the following guideline will help in thinking about sustainability in different areas:

The main sustainability factors are the environment, social, governance, financial and quality of management. A company that fails on any one of these factors may fail completely as a business. Figure 1.2 shows the three main areas of sustainability. This proposed method is therefore overarching and of equal relevance to mainstream and socially responsible investing. Investors and asset owners who ignore it would do so at their peril.

To break down these factors a bit further:

E - Environmental impacts, risks, and opportunities. For example, Trucost impacts data showing companies with the largest environmental damage costs per dollar of profit or revenue, and HSBC climate change index, which looks at companies' best attempting to find innovative environmental solutions.

S - Social risks and opportunities. Arguably, social metrics are the hardest to quantify, but firms like KLD take a stab at that, reviewing issues such as employee relations, human rights, diversity, and product safety among many others. Any company failing to perform well on these issues runs the risk of not attracting or retaining the best and the brightest employees, nor retaining shareholders who focus on specific issues such as involvement in Sudan, and not retaining customers who focus on lifestyle choices and their consumption patterns accordingly. On the plus side, plans have been forwarded for establishing the likes of a Social Stock Exchange, as funded by Rockefeller, whereby companies would need to demonstrate the best social attributes to retain exchange membership. This sort of "exchange plus" is already in place in Brazil and South Africa and has been successful.

G - True governance risk, as performed best by the likes of The Corporate Library, which highlights situations of overcompensation, board composition and related conflicts of interest. For example, The Corporate Library had flagged Bear Stearns and Lehman Brothers as Ds and Fs in its scoring system, which if used in an overall true sustainability risk system, as proposed, would have protected investors accordingly. We now know that both Lehman Brothers and Bear Stearns went bankrupt and closed in 2008 during the financial crisis at that period. On the positive side, companies that reward all employees, shareholders, and investors equally, and have full checks, balances and incentives, arguably represent an ideal which few firms achieve -- but those that come closest may well outperform. Private equity firms increasingly recognize that to best maximize their assets, they need to be top performers in these areas; there are increasingly creative and thoughtful short-term investors who see that this is the way forward.

F - Traditional financial criteria. Even for passive investors, sustainability risk is essential to consider. And it should go without saying that combining positive financial criteria with sustainability risk should offer the best of all possible worlds.

Q - Quality of management is something that can be achieved only by direct interaction and investor judgment. Hence, sustainability inevitably needs human interaction, face-to-face dialogue, and understanding that management is committed to the full integration of sustainability by walking the walk, not just talking the good talk.

In order to continually improve its sustainability performance, an organization may seek to establish, implement, maintain and continually improve the sustainability framework according to the sustainability principles and processes. The organization determines:

- How it will satisfy its three responsibilities (Social, economic and environmental) within the sustainability program
- How it will embed this framework into its operations – part of how the organization operates each day
- The interests of its stakeholders

1.5 Sustainable vs. Unsustainable Company

Unsustainable	Sustainable
1. It contributes directly or indirectly to the systematic increase in the concentration of waste from the earth's crust such as heavy metals, fossil fuels, and byproducts from their use.	1. Radical resource productivity: Companies stretch natural resources by increasing productivity for a given amount of a resource by factors of 5, 10, or 100. This addresses the issue of overharvesting and depletion.
2. It contributes directly or indirectly to systematic increases in concentrations of hazardous and nonhazardous waste from substances produced by society such as over 70000 chemicals, dioxins, and PCBs.	2. Ecological Redesign: Companies are closed-loop production systems so that any waste from production and end-of-life disposal is treated as a resource and reused.
3. It contributes directly or indirectly to systematic over-extraction and degradation of nature by physical means, such as deforestation, over-harvesting of fisheries and depletion of farmlands	3. Service and Flow economy: Companies replace their goods with services. They lease products and their solutions instead of selling them. When the product becomes obsolete or is unable to produce its service, the company takes it back and recycles or remanufactures the returned product.
4. It contributes directly or indirectly to abuses of political or economic power in society so that human needs are not met for such things as clean air, potable water, nutritious food, adequate shelter and quality of life.	4. Investment in natural capital: Companies restore, maintain, and expand ecosystem to sustain society's needs and avoid social upheaval and costly regulations.

TABLE 1.1

1.6 How should business engage with sustainability?

Most business firms, especially small and medium enterprises, probably see doing nothing as the smart strategy. They view their mandate as serving customers and generating returns for the shareholders. Managing the impact on society is out of the scope of their activity and thought better left to the government and/or NGOs. In any case, the problems of sustainability seem too large and expensive for any individual firm to tackle, or even make a difference.

More astute business leaders, especially of large organizations, recognize that demands from important stakeholders require sustainability to be incorporated within their corporate agenda. In one Accenture survey, 97% of industry CEOs said that sustainability is critical for the future success of their business. On further reflection, business leaders realize the pursuit of sustainability can have some of the following benefits for their firms:

- Build corporate reputation (i.e., license to operate)
- New growth opportunities (e.g., hybrid cars for Toyota)
- Cost reduction (e.g., energy conservation by Walmart)
- Employee engagement (e.g., Tata with the largest corporate volunteering program)
- Resonance with a specific segment of consumers (e.g., Body Shop, Whole Foods)
- Access to specific pools of capital (e.g., socially responsible funds, impact investors)

Five steps for successful engagement in sustainability

1. Start with your own leadership passion. Simply put, people follow leaders who have a passion that guides others. Sustainability develops leaders who:
   - Understand how to deal with a changing world
   - Approach outside resources and seek their reach across organizational silos to find and implement solutions,
   - Can coordinate and cross-manage finance and communications issues.
2. Tell your own stories. Start your conversations by telling people what got you started.
   - Talk about what you love. Share your stories and invite others to share their own; ask how they became interested in sustainability and what it means to them. Good stories have specifics and drama. So, ask them hard questions about how their efforts fit into their home life, their family, their everyday worries.
   - Challenge yourself to go long. The best North Star goals and Personal Sustainability Practices (PSP) are long-term and not just episodic. Picking up trash once at the beach is good, but it's not a practice unless it's something that you do regularly to improve your life, your community, and the planet. Practices, like sports, yoga, or playing the piano, steady the mind by providing a consistent structure that allows you to excel. Remember to think across social, economic, environmental, and cultural impacts.
3. Support early adopters and latecomers. Be on the Lookout for your early adopters. They will teach you so much about how the project will work and will probably become your leadership for far beyond your first Phase. What engages them? How does It solve their problems? Make sure that most of your early adopters are not executives since

executives do not generally represent the entire employee population. Equally important, do not discount your late bloomers, perhaps those with longer tenure, who take longer to understand new technologies and new opportunities but who embrace them fully and drive forward.

4. Stay positive. There will always be people who say that your Personal Sustainability Project is impossible. But, stay your course which means getting the most people possible engaged in the larger project. If people want to participate, then let them-but regularly check in with them on their workload.

- Act Now: Choose Your Own PSP
- As a leader, you make a difference with your own actions. Here are some steps you can take to start your own Personal Sustainability Practice:
- Identify an area that enhances your life, for example, friends, family, and being in nature.
- Think of a personal sustainability practice that would improve your day, even in the smallest way.
- Ask yourself; is it repeatable, inspirational, sustainable, and enjoyable?
- Start small, start now, and share what you are doing with peers, family, and friends.
- Ask the people closest to you in your life to develop their own PSPs. Recall that a core quality of engaged employees is that they have an engaged manager and an engaged support system.
- Commit to it publicly and start sharing stories of setbacks and successes.
- The best ideas come from where real social, economic, environmental, and cultural problems are actually solved, which is not necessarily at the top. Engaging a workforce in a strategy for sustainability is an innovation strategy.

  In its Global Innovation Metrics Survey, McKinsey found the most common metrics that leading companies use to track innovation:

  1. Revenue growth due to new products or services (16 percent)
  2. Customer satisfaction with new products and services (13 percent)
  3. Number of ideas or concepts in the pipeline (10 percent)
  4. R&D spending as a percentage of sales (8 percent)
  5. Percentage of sales from new products or services in a given period (8 percent)
  6. Number of new products or services launched (8 percent) 12

But Will a Strategy for Sustainability Truly Engage Employees?

- People become engaged when their workplace activities connect to what matters in their lives and what makes them happy. And yes, most people want to work at a company with a purpose that goes beyond the next quarter's earnings, and that is larger than themselves and the organization.
- Just as sustainability does not work for businesses unless it serves business needs first, sustainability does not engage individuals unless it first and foremost solves the problems they experience in their lives. A strategy for sustainability can provide a strong sense of purpose and greater meaning to the company's mission can connect people to their own job goals and can speak to the next generation of workers. But it cannot be bolted on: just as it is core to your strategy, it must be integral to their lives. And so, to execute a strategy for sustainability, it is important to engage individuals personally.
- A great tool of sustainability—small actions anytime, anywhere that are good for the actors, good for their organization, and good for our planet. It can be as simple as biking to work, serving vegetables and turning off the TV, and giving thanks for the miracle of your food. Look for daily or recurring practices that can express an individual's values.

1.7 Climate Change and Global Warming

Presently, the term "climate change" is of great interest to the world at large, scientific as well as political discussions. Climate has been changing since the beginning of creation, but what is alarming is the speed of change in recent years, and it may be one of the threats facing the earth. The growth rate of carbon dioxide has increased over the past 36 years (1979–2014). For more than a decade, the objective of keeping global warming below 2 °C has been a key focus of international climate debate.

Climate change caused by the global increase in temperatures triggers multiple negative effects on the planet. These effects interrelate with each other putting at risk the species that inhabit the Earth, including the humans.

The entire world, or almost all of it, is feeling the effects of global warming – increase in temperatures, changing rainfall, the rise in sea levels and damage to the ecosystem.

Global warming is the term used to describe a gradual increase in the average temperature of the Earth's atmosphere and its oceans.

The planet's average surface temperature has risen about 2 degree Fahrenheit (1.1 degree Celsius) since the late 19th century, a change driven largely by increased carbon dioxide and other human-made emissions into the atmosphere.

The rise in temperatures caused mainly by greenhouse gas emissions affects multiple scenarios:

Three main levels of climate change impact are:

The global increase in temperatures can influence the physical, biological and human systems.

First, variations in the physical systems of the planet can be observed in the melting of the poles, which at the same time cause glacial regression, snow melting, warming and thawing of permafrost, flooding in rivers and lakes, droughts in rivers and lakes, coastal erosion, sea level rise and extreme natural phenomena.

In the biological systems, there is death of flora and fauna in terrestrial and marine ecosystems, wildfires and flora and fauna displacement searching for better life conditions.

In human systems, climate change affects and destroys crops and food production, causes disease and death, destruction and loss of economic livelihoods and migrations of climate refugees.

In addition, these negative consequences feed each other back and increase their magnitudes; for example:

—Droughts frequently cause wildfires, which then destroy crops.

—The melting of glaciers, snow, and ice causes sea level rise, which erodes the coast and involves the destruction of many economic means of subsistence.

—Droughts, rising sea levels, extreme natural phenomena and floods cause climate refugees.

Link between climate change and Sustainable development:

Climate change does not yet feature prominently within the environmental or economic policy agendas of many developing countries. Yet evidence shows that some of the most adverse effects of climate change will be in developing countries, where populations are most vulnerable and least likely to easily adapt to climate change, and that climate change will affect the potential for development in these countries. Some synergies already exist between climate change policies and the sustainable development agenda in developing countries, such as energy efficiency, renewable energy, transport and sustainable land-use policies. Despite limited attention from policy-makers to date, climate change policies could have significant ancillary benefits for the local environment. The reverse is also true as local and national policies to address congestion, air quality, access to energy services and energy diversity may also limit

GHG emissions. Nevertheless, it is encouraging that in the United Nations Climate change conference in Paris in 2015; nearly 200 countries have signaled an end to the fossil fuel era, committing for the first time to a universal agreement to cut greenhouse gas emissions and to avoid the most dangerous effects of climate change. Impact of climate change affecting business strategies are considered in Chapter 3.

1.8 Sustainable Development

The world population is expected to grow from the 7.5 billion currently (5 billion in 1987) to 10 billion by 2050. This increase is driven by a combination of enhanced life expectancy and high birth rates. While the former has been a global phenomenon, the latter is primarily restricted to the Asian and African continents. Projections beyond 2050 are more varied. Some projections see declining, while others seeing increasing, world population. Regardless of the longer-term picture, the anticipated near-term growth in population will put considerable stress on the planet in the coming three decades.

There is widespread consensus in the scientific community that increased human emissions of greenhouse gases (GHG – carbon dioxide, methane, and nitrous acid) has caused global warming and climate change. The average temperature has increased by 1.3 degrees centigrade between 1910 and 2015. GHG emissions were 60 percent higher in 2014 compared to 1990, showing an accelerating trend compared to the slower increase since the industrial revolution. As stated above, the 197-nation Paris climate treaty, inked in 2015, vows to halt warming at "well under" 2 deg C compared to mid-19th century levels, and "pursue efforts" to cap the rise at 1.5 deg C. UN Secretary-General Antonio Guterres said climate change was "the most systemic threat to humankind". With only one degree of warming so far, earth has seen a crescendo of droughts, heatwaves, and storms ramped up by rising seas due to the melting of ice caps. For example, the average annual temperature for the globe between 1951 and 1980 was around 57.2 degrees Fahrenheit (14 degrees Celsius). In 2015, the hottest year on record, the temperature was about 1.8 degrees F (1 degree C) warmer than the 1951–1980 base period. That calculation comes from NASA. India is the world's third-largest carbon polluter, behind China and the United States. However, India plans to cut carbon emissions by 33 to 35 percent from 2005 levels by 2030.

Accounting for a quarter, fossil fuel consumption is the single largest source of GHG emissions. Hence, the push for energy conservation and the move to alternative sources of energy, especially renewable energy.

Agriculture, forestry, and other land uses, account for 24% of GHG emissions. Rising population and increasing standards of living are expected to raise, substantially, the demand for food. For example, one expert argued that the planet must produce more food in the next four decades than all farmers have harvested over the past 8000 years. To avoid hunger and starvation, it is imperative to increase yields, reduce wastage, while conserving consumption of water and energy as well as minimizing the use of chemicals and antibiotics.

Increasing population combined with urbanization will put great pressure on cities. The United Nations report on urbanization envisages an increase of 2.5 billion in the world's urban population by 2050. Given that the overall global population is also expected to grow by 2.5 billion, the deleterious effects of the increased population will be concentrated in the urban areas. Since 90% of this urban growth will be in Africa and Asia, they will see enormous demand for urban infrastructure, particularly, affordable housing, large public transportation networks, and health care access.

On 25th September 2015, recognizing the challenges above, the United Nations adopted 17 goals stated below related to people and planet. Associated with these goals, 169 specific targets were set as part of the "2030 Agenda for Sustainable Development" to end all forms of poverty, fight inequalities, and tackle climate change. While not legally binding, all global leaders committed to progress in meeting these goals as stated below:

- **Goal 1** End poverty in all its forms everywhere
- **Goal 2** End hunger, achieve food security and improved nutrition and promote sustainable agriculture
- **Goal 3** Ensure healthy lives and promote well-being for all at all ages
- **Goal 4** Ensure inclusive and equitable quality education and promote lifelong learning opportunities for all
- **Goal 5** Achieve gender equality and empower all women and girls
- **Goal 6** Ensure availability and sustainable management of water and sanitation for all
- **Goal 7** Ensure access to affordable, reliable, sustainable and modern energy for all
- **Goal 8** Promote sustained, inclusive and sustainable economic growth, full and productive employment and decent work for all
- **Goal 9** Build resilient infrastructure, promote inclusive and sustainable industrialization and foster innovation
- **Goal 10** Reduce inequality within and among countries
- **Goal 11** Make cities and human settlements inclusive, safe, resilient and sustainable
- **Goal 12** Ensure sustainable consumption and production patterns

- **Goal 13** Take urgent action to combat climate change and its impacts
- **Goal 14** Conserve and sustainably use the oceans, seas and marine resources for sustainable development
- **Goal 15** Protect, restore and promote sustainable use of terrestrial ecosystems, sustainably manage forests, combat desertification, and halt and reverse land degradation and halt biodiversity loss
- **Goal 16** Promote peaceful and inclusive societies for sustainable development, provide access to justice for all and build effective, accountable and inclusive institutions at all levels
- **Goal 17** Strengthen the means of implementation and revitalize the global partnership for sustainable development

If we distribute the goals among the 3 main areas of sustainability, then we can categorize them as follows:

Economic Goals: 8,9,10 and 12

Social Goals: 1,2,3,4,5,7, 11 and 16

Environmental Goals: 6,13,14 and 15

Overall Goal: 17

Example of Sustainable Development:

Why biotech innovator Novozymes uses the SDGs as a catalyst for growth?

(https://www.greenbiz.com/article/why-biotech-innovator-novozymes-uses-sdgs-catalyst-growth)

Novozymes president and CEO Peder Holk Nielsen is optimistic that the world has the willingness and the technology to tackle climate change.

But he worries that too many well-intentioned companies are wasting time taking action because they're looking for perfect solutions for the long-term rather than embracing good ones that have the potential to make a smaller impact more quickly.

Nielsen's own company, Danish biotech firm Novozymes — which develops enzymes used for bioenergy, food and agricultural applications, household care products and production processes — has taken that sentiment to heart. And then some.

Since 2015, the company's business strategy has been explicitly aligned around catalyzing technologies that will play a role that exploits the "inventory of business opportunities" embedded into the U.N. Sustainable Development Goals (SDGs) into reality. Using the SDGs as a talking point helps Novozymes put it strategies into context for national governments, cities, investors and other key stakeholders, such as its roughly 6,200 employees.

Indeed, a "significant" portion of the compensation for Novozymes' top 200 executives is tied to the company's ability to grow revenue related to catalyzing a low-carbon future, while meeting its own corporate sustainability targets, Nielsen said.

Sustainability is not a corporate department in Novozymes; but it's a part of what they do, it's the strategy, and that's an important distinction to make.

To be clear, the company isn't trying to tackle all 17 SDGs. It has honed its focus to five that explicitly play into its business:

- No. 2 – Zero Hunger
- No. 4 – Quality Education
- No. 6 – Clean Water and Sanitation
- No. 13 – Climate Action
- No. 17 – Partnerships for the Goals

Novozymes is the global leader in industrial enzymes, controlling an estimated 48 percent of the market and holding more than 6,500 granted and pending patents, according to the company's annual report. The organic revenue growth for its bioenergy business was 11 percent in 2017, while its food and beverage business grew 9 percent. Right now, about 65 percent of its business comes from developed economies and Nielsen views the SDGs as a way of starting more serious dialogues in emerging nations.

One example of how the SDG lens shapes Novozymes's strategy is its partnership with the NICE Group, one of China's largest detergent companies — and one of the biotech company's biggest customers. In 2017, two companies began collaborating on a research and development project to help NICE create far more concentrated formulas of its products which will save huge amounts of energy in terms of transportation and packaging which will be a leap forward for sustainable development.

Another example of how Novozymes uses the SDGs for guidance on investment decisions is its BioAg Alliance with Monsanto; an initiative focused on developing new pesticides and herbicides that are made from naturally occurring microbes. The products are already being used on more than 80 million acres of farmland; the goal is to reach 250 to 500 million acres worldwide by 2025.

1.9 Personal Reasons and Practice for Pursuing Sustainability:

- *Children:* Perhaps the most common reason people have an interest in sustainability is their concern for the future of their children or grandchildren.
- *Illness:* Some people have a family member or friend with a disease that is suspected to be related to environmental triggers e.g. asthma, cancers, cholera
- *Love of Nature:* Many who enjoy the outdoors may or may not identify themselves as an environmentalist and yet care for the clean and healthy environment and earth.

- *Personal Experience:* People may have been the recipient of discrimination or had other experiences that left them feeling empathy for the plight of others.
- *Travel:* Often travelers return home with an appreciation of the world's problems and exposure to different ways of addressing societal changes.

The Practice of Sustainability at Individual level

Sustainability can be practiced at the individual level in the following ways:

Travel and leisure

1. Plan journeys to use the most efficient means of travel and the optimum route
2. Walk or cycle rather than drive short journeys thereby reducing C02 emissions (environmental), getting a great workout (social), and potentially cutting health-care costs and health-club fees (economic). Or at least park in the spot farthest from the entrance of the workplace to get some daily exercise. See your neighborhood in a whole new way (cultural). Or share a ride or take a bus instead of taking your own car to minimize GHG emission
3. Go by train or bus for medium/longer journeys (but note that empty buses or trains use more energy than a car, so provision of more public transport is not always the best long-term solution)
4. Holiday nearer to home, to reduce demand for air travel in particular
5. Work from home (even one day per week worked from home reduces the environmental impact of commuting by 20%)
6. Live nearer your workplace
7. Use a more economical car (but note that because a lot of resources and energy go into making cars, the lifecycle energy cost is not necessarily reduced by buying a new, more efficient car when an older one is still serviceable)
8. Drive more slowly (most cars are much more fuel efficient at 40-60mph than at 70mph)
9. Choose pastimes/hobbies that don't require large amounts of fuel, electricity or material resources

Goods and Food

1. Reuse carrier bags and other containers rather than obtaining new ones
2. Complain to retailers and manufacturers when goods are supplied with excessive amounts of packaging

3. Insist that goods are properly labelled regarding origin, environmental standards, etc. (look for recognized and audited environmental assurance schemes; ask for carbon footprint information)
4. Buy local wherever practicable (look for 'food miles' information – but note that buying seasonal food may be better than buying local food out of season if it is energy-intensive to grow)
5. Adopt a lower meat content diet (there are environmental arguments for and against a vegetarian diet, but it is clear that a high meat content diet is less sustainable than a low meat one)
6. Repair rather than replace items where possible
7. When buying appliances that use water or energy, look for efficient models (but note that the environmental cost of manufacturing an item may outweigh any reduction in the environmental impact when in use; also, some efficient devices may have so much energy 'embedded' in their manufacture that overall it may be better to use a simpler model)
8. Skip a fast-food meal once a week and prepare one at home instead, thereby reducing saturated fat and sodium in your diet (social) and the packaging—the paper-wrapped burger; cardboard container for fries; plastics for lids, straws, and ketchup; and oh so many napkins—that ends up in a landfill (environmental). If you typically idle your vehicle in the drive-through lane, then skipping a fast-food meal could cut your fuel costs (economic). Perpetuate your family's recipes (cultural).

Governments

1. Individuals can lobby their representatives to persuade the government to put measures in place that will improve sustainability.
   • Such measures include: Financial incentives for individuals and organizations to reduce their environmental impact and penalties for those who don't.
   • Awareness campaigns to highlight the real environmental costs of things that people and companies do.
2. Legally binding regulations regarding environmental labelling
   • Auditable environmental and energy efficiency standards
   • Increased emphasis on sustainability in education
3. Removal of environmentally perverse incentives (both taxation and government benefits/grants, etc, sometimes have the perverse effect of encouraging the environmentally unsustainable behaviour. This needs to be pointed out and corrected.)

At Home

1. Insulate the building to the best practicable standards (in the UK high insulation standards for new buildings are specified in the building

regulations, but insulation of older buildings can often be improved. Sometimes this is prohibitively expensive, though upgrading loft insulation is usually cost-effective.)

2. Stop draughts, keep windows and doors closed during the heating season (but ensure sufficient ventilation to avoid condensation)
3. Turn off lights and appliances when not required
4. Use low energy bulbs (high-efficiency bulbs typically use less than 20% of the electricity for an equivalent light output compared to old-style (incandescent) bulbs). Change lights bulbs to highly efficient CFLs (compact fluorescent lights) or LEDs (light-emitting diodes) to reduce electric bills (economic) and slow global warming (environmental).
5. Draw curtains or close shutters at night to reduce heat loss (daytime heat gain during hot weather can be minimized in a similar manner)
6. Set heating thermostats to the minimum comfortable temperature (similarly, set the air conditioning to the highest comfortable temperature in hot weather)
7. Set heating system timers to operate only when the heat is required
8. Use natural ventilation rather than air conditioning whenever possible
9. Dress appropriately rather than heating the building more than necessary (note that in climates such as in the UK, a small reduction in heating temperature results in a proportionally large reduction in heat demand)
10. When cooking or making hot drinks, do not heat or boil more water than necessary
11. Take showers as these generally use less water and heat than baths (but power showers have a high flow-rate and may use more water than a bath if run for more than five or ten minutes). Avoid unnecessarily deep or frequent baths.
12. Use low water flush WCs
13. Use water efficient techniques for garden watering (plenty of tips can be found on the internet)
14. Consider rainwater harvesting and grey-water recycling
15. Use renewable energy (but check out the overall 'lifecycle' energy costs of the equipment, supply, and transport of renewable fuel, etc.)
16. Compost organic waste (check local regulations to avoid creating health hazards or other nuisances)
17. Explain the importance of sustainability to your family and friends 3 population matters

At Work

1. Individuals, as well as employers, can contribute to sustainable practice in the workplace. The best way to do so can be summarised very simply.

2. Treat your environmental impact at work as you would do that at home (in particular, treat your consumption of resources – water, heat, power, etc. – as if you were paying for them yourself)
3. Encourage your employer to invest in efficiency and support any workplace initiative to do so.

1.10 Calculate Your Own Carbon Footprint

Calculate your own carbon footprint through the carbon footprint calculator in the following website: https://www.carbonfootprint.com/calculator. aspx.

You can take an active effort to reduce your own footprint by replacing high emission activities with lower ones.

1.11 Five steps for successful engagement

Sometimes you might accept the idea of engaging others toward sustainability, but in practice, you might not know where to start. What follows are descriptions of specific steps you can take, and traps you should avoid, on your way to encouraging others:

1. Start with your own leadership passion. Simply put, people follow leaders who have a passion that guides others. Sustainability develops leaders who
   - Understand how to deal with a changing world
   - Approach outside resources and seek their
   - Reach across organizational silos to find and implement solutions, and
   - Can coordinate and cross-manage finance and communications issues.
2. Tell your own stories. Start your conversations by telling people what got you started, what you're happy about. Talk about what you love. Share your stories and invite others to share their own; ask how they became interested in sustainability and what it means to them. Good stories have specifics and drama. So, ask them hard questions about how their efforts fit into their home life, their family, their everyday worries.
3. Challenge yourself to go long. The best North Star goals and PSPs are long-term and not just episodic. Picking up trash once at the beach is good, but it's not a practice unless it's something that you do regularly to improve your life, your community, and the planet. Practices, like sports, yoga, or playing the piano, steady the mind by providing a consistent structure that allows you to excel. Remember to think across social, economic, environmental, and cultural impacts.
4. Support early adopters and latecomers. Be on the lookout for your early adopters. They will teach you so much about how the project will

work and will probably become your leadership for far beyond your first Phase. What engages them? How does it solve their problems? Make sure that most of your early adopters are not executives since executives do not generally represent the entire employee population. Equally important, do not discount your late bloomers, perhaps those with longer tenure, who take longer to understand new technologies and new opportunities but who embrace them fully and provide deeper institutional insights for driving them forward.

5. Stay positive. There will always be people who say that your Personal Sustainability Project is impossible. They'll want to argue with you and bring you down. Ignore them. That's their process for creating connection. Stay your course. Your job is not to massage your ego or theirs, but to listen and to serve, which means getting the most people possible engaged in the larger project. If people want to participate, then let them-but regularly check in with them on their workload.

- Act Now: Choose Your Own PSP
- As a leader, you make a difference with your own actions. Here are some steps you can take to start your own Personal Sustainability Practice:
- Review and reflect on your responses to the basic Gallup poll questions and happiness questions discussed in this chapter.
- Identify an area that enhances your life, for example, friends, family, and being in nature.
- Think of a personal sustainability practice that would improve your day, even in the smallest way.
- Ask yourself; is it repeatable, inspirational, sustainable, and enjoyable?
- Start small, start now, and share what you are doing with peers, family, and friends.
- Ask the people closest to you in your life to develop their own PSPs. Recall that a core quality of engaged employees is that they have an engaged manager and an engaged support system.
- Commit to it publicly, and start sharing stories of setbacks and successes.

1.12 Walk the Talk on Sustainability

Let us not just talk sustainability – Let's do it! Advancing the Sustainable Development Goals together.

Everywhere one looks nowadays--from Wall Street to Walmart--'Sustainability' is becoming mainstream and familiar. Therefore, we need to move past talking about sustainability, and accelerate ACTION!

The UN Sustainable Development Goals (SDGs) stated above, provide a golden opportunity to embrace globally agreed upon language and a framework to "end poverty, protect the planet and ensure that all people enjoy peace and prosperity." And while many organizations are already on their SDG journey, the rate of progress is far slower than needed to meet the 2030 targets.

Today's consumers have technology and social media to show them what is really happening at the origin of their products.

As a result, many companies are turning to certified sourcing programmes as one of the key tools to achieve their sustainability goals – and to help them demonstrate independently verified results. Several large companies are sourcing 100% certified commodities already.

However, as the Economist Intelligence Unit recently reported, while four in five companies say they have responsible supply chains, fewer than a quarter are actually addressing key issues such as climate change or child labour. In fact, 30% have decreased their focus on supply chain responsibility over the last five years.

It's time to act! Every person, organization, and community has a role to play and needs to be a part of bringing solutions. As Sustainability concerned citizens, we are on the front lines to lead and make courageous commitments - and then ACT on those commitments! We, as sustainability professionals need to "up our game" and demand that our colleagues do the same. We need to increase knowledge, skills, and abilities, change corporate culture, and integrate systems thinking into operations. We need to innovate and collaborate - across departments, companies, communities, and industries. We need to work faster and bolder - together.

The question is what are you and your organization doing to advance the SDGs?

What's working? What are the challenges and how are you overcoming them?

1.13 Difference between Corporate Social Responsibility and Sustainability

1. Objective

The concept of CSR has been around since the 1950's and has been called so many other names including; Corporate Responsibility, Corporate Ethics, Corporate Citizenship, Corporate Sustainability, and Responsible Business. CSR is based on the premise that a business can only thrive if it operates within a thriving society. In that way, the business depends on the community it operates within, and as such, has an ethical and moral responsibility towards that community.

Business sustainability takes this a bit further, and explicitly encompasses other factors of environment and economics. It is based on the premise that businesses operate in such a way that it uses limited resources to meet its needs today, while still ensuring that these resources are still available to meet the needs of future generations.

So right off from these premises, we see some differences between CSR and business sustainability:

2. Vision

Corporate Social Responsibility (CSR) looks backwards, reporting on what a business has done, typically in the last 12 months, to make a contribution to society. Business Sustainability is futuristic while CSR is antiquated

CSR involves deeds that have been done in the past to support one community project or the other like building a library to support literacy in a community or providing a health care centre for a community. Major oil companies in Africa are very good at initiating CSR projects basically because they are mandated to give back to the communities where they extract their resources from.

Sustainability looks forward, planning the changes a business might make to secure its future (reducing waste, assuring supply chains, developing new markets, building its brand). Business Sustainability talks a lot about the future, forward-thinking plans to sustain a business and improve targets, for instance, waste reduction and innovative brand development are examples of business sustainability projects.

3. CSR doesn't have to align with your business, but Business Sustainability does

Many businesses carry out their CSR initiatives by identifying an issue in the community and providing something to help ease the issue. But these initiatives don't always align with the strategy of the business. This increases the risk of the initiative being perceived as greenwashing, or as short-term with no long-lasting positive implications. For example, Etisalat Nigeria has a Fight Malaria Initiative where they provide insecticide-treated mosquito nets in Kano state. The project is not integrated into Etisalat's business model, so it's easy for them not to be invested in the long-term impacts of the project. Yes, this initiative is responsible, but it's not necessarily sustainable. On the other hand, if Etisalat analyzed their business to see where they could better utilize resources (like how they collocate towers) or partner with others to send health educational messages along with their standard status SMSs, then these could be seen as business sustainability initiatives as they are more integrated into their core business.

4. Targets

CSR tends to target opinion formers – politicians, pressure groups, and the media.

Sustainability targets the whole value chain – from suppliers to operations to partners to end-consumers.

5. Business

CSR is becoming about compliance and to manage the reputation of the company in the eyes of the public and other stakeholders. CSR is mostly external

Sustainability is about business leading to profitability and cost savings. Business Sustainability is both internal and external

6. Reward

CSR investment is rewarded by politicians.

Sustainability investment is rewarded by the City ('Finally, we provide evidence that High Sustainability companies significantly outperform their counterparts over the long-term, both in terms of stock market and accounting performance').

Indian Context:

CSR: 2014 saw the Companies Act with the mandatory CSR provision coming into effect.

The Act makes it mandatory for companies meeting certain thresholds to spend 2% of their net profits on CSR. The Indian act largely focuses on philanthropy and certain key areas. The focus is on giving back to society over and above the ordinary course of business. Even as the Indian law looks at a philanthropic, community-centered approach, it is also true that smart strategies have been developed by industry leaders that look at CSR while creating far-reaching positive business impact.

Sustainability: Most large firms in India and internationally have been focusing on developing sustainable business practices and reducing environmental impact of their activities. These activities include a reduction in emissions to diminish the impact of climate change, waste and water management and a move towards renewable sources of energy.

This is particularly important now since India has committed a 35% reduction in emissions by 2030.

A report titled "India's Top companies for CSR and Sustainability, 2015" provides sustainability efforts and results by some top Indian companies, https://www.iimu.ac.in/upload_data/main_containts/about/Social-Responsibility/IIMU_CSR_REPORT.pdf

1.14 Current Major Sustainability Trends and the questions you should ask

What are the sustainability trends?

A number of key sustainability trends will continue to influence organizational practice. Some of these sustainability trends are of course not new. However, there is often a lag between the recognition of an issue and that issue being translated into corporate management priorities which might give rise to changes in behaviour.

Below, are overviews of some issues which will grow in relevance for business sustainability in the coming years, as well as highlighting some questions to consider when focusing upon the sustainability of your organization:

- Carbon reduction
- Plastics & ocean pollution
- Global mega trends
- UN Sustainable Development Goals (SDGs)
- Sustainability Reporting
- Taxation

1.14.1 Carbon reduction is stepping up

Despite the US Government exiting the Paris Agreement in 2018, it looks like many US states and companies and countries worldwide are moving forward with plans for action both on carbon emissions reduction but also accelerating renewable energy production.

Alongside this, investors are getting in on the act, increasingly moving away from fossil fuel funding. For instance, at the One Planet Summit on 12th December 2017, the World Bank committed itself (among other things) to cease funding new oil and gas exploration from 2019. It was joined in this declaration by announcements from both the insurance company AXA and the bank ING, that they would be divesting from fossil fuel projects, with a particular focus upon reducing their exposure to coal.

Beyond company undertakings, some countries are also making commitments to reduce fossil fuel dependency. The UK Government made the headlines in 2017 with its decision to ban the sale of diesel and petrol cars from 2040. Some commentators have suggested that this simply allows the UK to appear progressive while essentially delaying a problematic transition for future governments. It could also be said that their commitment provides a clear picture of the need for more sustainable transport over coming decades. In contrast to the UK Government's rather mixed approach to new fossil fuel discovery (the 2017 UK Autumn Budget also gave tax breaks to new North Sea oil exploration), in December 2017 the French Government passed legislation to ban all exploration of oil and natural gas in its territories by 2040. However, while 2040 still feels a long way off, France has also pledged that existing drilling permits will not be renewed when they expire, and no new exploration licenses will be granted, with immediate effect.

Questions to consider

- The world is moving to renewables – what is your dependency on non-renewable energy and what are your plans to go fossil free?
- Do you use diesel and what are your plans to ensure a transition to cleaner fuels or the latest technologies?
- Solar and wind generation is becoming cheaper and more reliable, especially when combined with energy storage solutions, how is your company exploring the opportunities to generate your own energy or to contribute towards local or distributed generation capacity?
- How exposed is your business model to climate change risks? If you depend upon global supply chains, and especially if you have biological supply chains (food, drink, natural yarns etc.), the countries you source from will be increasingly impacted by water availability, social and demographic shifts and political instability arising from accelerating climate change.

1.14.2 Plastics and ocean pollution

The issue of plastic pollution is gathering pace. BBC's Blue Planet 2 provided a shocking insight into the sheer scale and extent of how plastics have entered ecosystems even in the most remote parts of the world. Plastics are entering food chains, with birds and animals mistaking plastic for food and it being found in the guts of animals even at 36,000 feet down, at the bottom of the Mariana Trench. Governments are starting to respond: in the UK, a ban was introduced on plastic microbeads in cosmetic products, with an extension to other products.

Companies have also been engaging in activities to tackle the issue, from Adidas' plan to make more than 1 million shoes from ocean plastic, to Interface's work with fishing communities in the Philippines to provide them with additional income in collecting ocean plastic waste for use as a recycled feedstock for their 'Net Effect' floor tiling products. Other corporate focus for ocean plastics is upon the development of circular industrial and economic processes. Plastics are extremely useful, high-performing and lightweight components in many technologies, products and infrastructure. With something so vital to modern life as we know it, wouldn't it make more sense to retain such material within our systems of production, so that they can be recycled and remanufactured, rather than giving rise to pollution on such a vast scale?

Questions to consider
- How do you use plastic and do you know what happens to it once it leaves your control?
- Are there opportunities to innovate your approaches to make use of recovered plastic, how might this help reduce your impact and create new product differentiation?
- Beyond just reducing your use of plastics, what can you do to play a role in wider, societal, waste plastics recovery?

1.14.3 More global mega-trends

Companies will be increasingly required to understand how global mega-trends such as climate change, demographic shifts, increasing inequality, water issues and biodiversity loss have relevance to their business models and strategic plans.

Such investigation should become a standard aspect of their strategic analysis and planning, representing key elements of their strategic context. Beyond a simple acknowledgement that the world is changing fast, companies will need to disclose the implications of such changes for their business and demonstrate how their strategies seek to minimize their contributions to the acceleration of negative trends and maximize their positive impacts through core business.

Questions to consider
- Do you understand how global mega trends provide new sources of risk and opportunity for your business?
- Have you conducted strategic analysis to quantify these risks and opportunities?
- How are you communicating the impacts of megatrends? The UN Sustainable Development Goals (SDGs)

For the UN Sustainable Development Goals, companies will increasingly need to understand and prove how their activities and strategies are located against the SDGs. In practice this will involve highlighting which of the SDGs have particular relevance to the business and how the company intends to contribute towards the achievement of the Goals while ensuring their activities do not undermine them.

Questions to consider
- Do you acknowledge the UN SDGs in your strategic approach to sustainability?
- Which specific SDGs have particular relevance to your business… which of them do you directly impact, either positively or negatively, and what can you do differently to play an active role in delivering the future we want?

1.14.4 Sustainability Reporting

Sustainability reporting is maturing. With the Global Reporting Initiative's (GRI) move from guidance to standards in 2016, companies using the standards will have to ensure that their approach to reporting makes the grade.

Reporting is also, slowly, making progress in getting on investors' agendas. Carbon and water remain areas of primary focus. However, there's an ongoing evolution of approach, moving from a requirement for companies to disclose their environmental and social impacts, investors are increasingly asking companies to tell them how these trends and impacts manifest as risk and exposure.

Four recommendations on climate-related financial disclosures that are applicable to organizations are structured around four thematic areas:

- **Governance**: The organization's governance around climate-related risks and opportunities.
- **Strategy**: The actual and potential impacts of climate-related risks and opportunities on the organization's businesses, strategy, and financial planning.
- **Risk Management**: The processes used by the organization to identify, assess and manage climate-related risks.
- **Metrics and Targets**: The metrics and targets used to assess and manage relevant climate-related risks and opportunities.

Another trend in reporting we will see in 2018 is a move towards the further development of disclosure on social and natural capital impacts through more meaningful indicators of performance. At present companies tend to focus upon lagging indicators (this is how much we emitted last year) but will need to start adding some leading indicators (here is our relationship to the state and health of the natural capital we depend upon and to the resilience of the communities and societies we rely upon and sell to). Look out for our thinking on moving from lagging to leading indicators of sustainability in early 2018.

Questions to consider

- Are you focusing your reporting upon material business impacts?
- What best practice approaches do you use to guide your reporting -GRI Standards, IIRC or SASB?
- How are you dealing with multiple capitals reporting, and do you understand your dependence upon healthy natural and social capital?
- How are you engaging your investors in your sustainability activities, can you demonstrate to them how sustainability minimizes your risk and maximizes your value creation?
- How are you acknowledging and integrating the TCFD recommendations on climate change risk disclosure and

communicating with investors how you understand, mitigate and manage your climate risks?

1.14.5 Taxation

Responsible tax has become ever more prominent recently, with news stories on corporate tax management grabbing headlines around the world. Judging how much tax a business should pay is of course immensely difficult, and the activities of the vast majority of companies is legal. However, in the public mind, there is a difference between legal and acceptable, and the more complex approaches adopted by some companies (e.g. placing company Intellectual Property in 'conveniently' low tax territories) is increasingly seen as artificial and ethically problematic. The challenge though, is that it is tax revenue that allows countries to build social capital (roads, healthcare, education – useful stuff like that) which in turn supports the work forces, consumer base and intellectual capital that companies rely upon. Aggressive tax planning is more likely to be seen as evidence of an *extractive* approach – taking the benefits without paying the costs of doing business. Companies which can demonstrate how they provide genuine social utility should be the ones that can genuinely demonstrate that they are socially sustainable.

Questions to consider
- How do you tell your tax story, can you justify that your arrangements are appropriate and justified?
- Can you demonstrate your social utility, how do you balance the value you get from stable and functional societies with the tax you may to support their health and future viability?

Questions:

1. Define sustainability and sustainability's three responsibilities.
2. Discuss the business case for sustainability and how a business should engage in sustainability.
3. Discuss the difference between sustainability and corporate social responsibility.
4. What are your personal reasons for pursuing sustainability and how do you practice sustainability at the individual level?
5. Discuss United Nations Sustainable development goals.
6. Discuss the current major sustainability trends.

Chapter 2
Benefits of Sustainability

When 'sustainability' is used as a business strategy, we must be able to define and quantify the business benefits that can be derived from adopting this model. These then become the criteria against which success can be measured, because just as with any other business strategy, return on investment will be the ultimate measure of success.

Each of the above benefits as shown in Fig. 1.1, Chapter 1 are described more in detail below:

2.1 Benefit 1: Increased Revenue

Reducing expenses is one way to improve profits, but as the saying goes, you can't save your way to prosperity. That is why business strategy is often driven by bolstering revenue more than by cutting costs. Therefore, the first sustainability benefit that can be examined is increased revenue and market share.

Sustainable enterprises disconnect revenue growth from depletion of natural resources by drastically reducing the amount of natural resources required to make their products and by using resource- and energy-efficient manufacturing processes. They decouple revenue growth from waste, pollution, and the depletion of natural capital by taking back their products at the end of their useful lives and ensuring they are responsibly disposed of, or reused.

Three innovative revenue streams that help ensure higher profits for sustainability leaders are:
1. More business-to-consumer (B2C) and business-to-business (B2B) revenue from a more sustainable brand
2. New revenue from new green products
3. New revenue from services and leasing

More B2C and B2B Revenue from a More Sustainable Brand:

A sustainable brand makes a difference in the B2C sector. Increasingly, people prefer to do business with companies that are doing good things and take some responsibility for the society too. The responsible image of the company builds loyalty with customers who identify with the values of the company — such customers are more loyal to the company than to its products.

There are many ways a company can improve its image as a responsible corporate citizen. It can lighten its carbon footprint by using less energy from fossil fuels. It can conserve water to ensure the most precious natural resource on the planet is available for future generations. It can enforce strict sustainability standards for suppliers. It can be a better steward of its waste. It can "green" its buildings. It can respect employees and support communities by say, creating jobs or building schools and hospitals.

These are all company-level initiatives. The company is still producing the same products, but it has improved its overall track record and polished its image as an entity that cares about society's environmental and social challenges. Consumers who share those concerns are more inclined to do business with kindred corporate spirits.

Within the last few years, there has been growing evidence that a company's sustainability image is important in the B2B sector as well. Suppliers can capitalize on this huge B2B market if their operations and products satisfy their business customers' sustainability criteria, especially if their competitors' do not. As a company pays attention to the life cycle footer prints, of its products and reduces its social and environmental impacts, it earns" the right to be retained as a valued member of its current customers' sustainable supply chains. If competitors are dropped from their customers' supply chains because they are sustainability laggards, more sustainable companies can pick up that business.

Following is a questionnaire that Walmart uses to gauge its Supplier Sustainability Index:

A. Energy and Climate

1. Have you measured your corporate greenhouse gas emissions (GHGs)?
2. Have you opted to report your GHGs to the Carbon Disclosure Project (CDP)?
3. What is your total annual GHGs reported in the most recent year measured?
4. Have you set publicly available GHG reduction targets? What are they?

B. Material Efficiency

1. What is the total amount of solid waste from facilities that produce a product(s) in the most recent year measured?
2. Have you set publicly available solid waste reduction targets? What are they?
3. What is the total water use from facilities that produce a product(s) for Walmart?
4. Have you set publicly available water use reduction targets? What are they?

C. Natural Resources

1. Have you established public sustainability purchasing guidelines for your direct supplier(s)?
2. Have you obtained third-party certifications for any of the products that you sell to Walmart?

D. People and Community

1. Do you know the location of all the facilities that produce your product(s)?
2. Do you evaluate the quality of, and capacity for, production at all supplier facilities?
3. Do you have a process for managing social compliance at the manufacturing level?
4. Do you have a process for managing social compliance with your supply base to resolve compliance issues?
5. Do you invest in community development in markets you source from/ operate within?

Gaining B2C and B2B revenue from a more responsible brand is the first of three ways that sustainability strategies bolster revenue. Next, we'll look at new revenue from new green products.

New Revenue from New Green Products:

The sustainability attributes of a company's products are differentiators to B2C and B2B customers who seek "green" solutions.

Figure 2.1 shows the consumer demand for green products is still strong in the USA, although surveys indicate that consumers will not pay much extra for them. However, by applying creative approaches to manufacturing and design, environmentally friendlier products need not be more expensive or lower in quality. When green and non-green products achieve price equity, there is evidence that consumers choose the greener one. Green products may also open up new markets.

There are parallel B2B revenue opportunities. GE is the classic example of a company determined to dominate the B2B market for green products. As explained by GE's ecomagination 2009 annual report, the ecomagination portfolio of products and services, which includes "green" appliances, aviation, energy, healthcare, lighting, oil and gas, transportation, and water products, grew from 15 in 2005 to over 90 by 2009. When GE first launched its ecomagination thrust in 2005, it quickly generated 6.4% of the company's sales — $10.1 billion toward GE's overall revenue of $157.2 billion in 2005. Four years later, GE's ecomagination revenues had grown to $18 billion, even in a challenging global environment, and accounted for about 10% of GE's revenue. In 2011, GE pledged that ecomagination

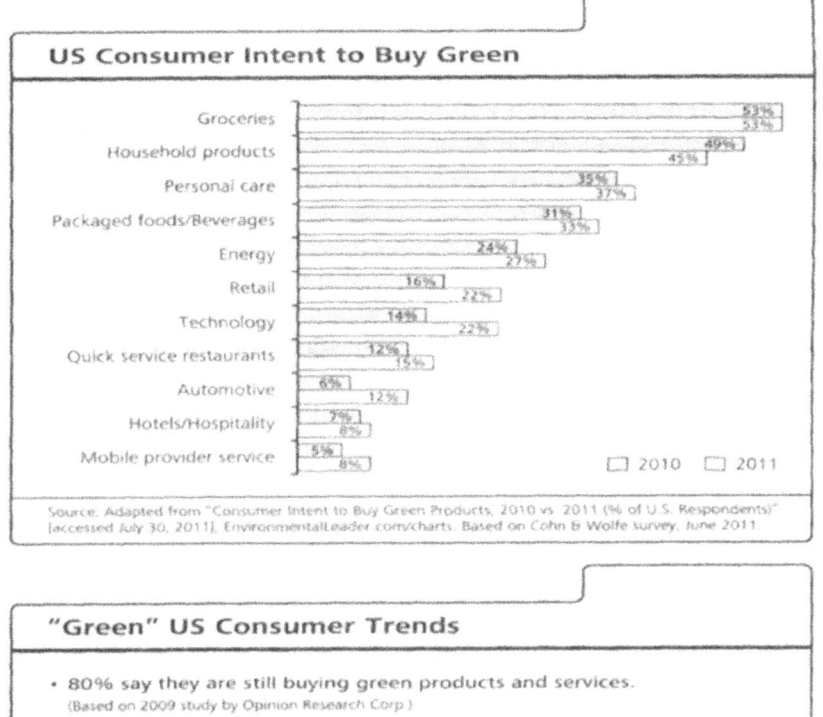

Figure 2.1

revenue will grow at twice the rate of total company revenue between 2010 and 2015, making ecomagination an even larger proportion of total company sales.

Siemens has a similar aggressive green product strategy. Its environmental portfolio includes products used in renewable energy; power transmission and distribution; green solutions for transportation; building technologies; lighting; environmental technologies; and healthcare. In the fiscal year 2010, Siemens' environmental portfolio accounted for around €28 billion, or 37%, of the company's total revenue of €76 billion.

Siemens and GE want to be the go-to companies for green products in their market sectors. Companies like them thrive on the upper-left-hand quadrant of Figure 2.1. They "creatively destruct" their own product lines to produce exciting new green products before their competitors do.

We have looked at two ways in which sustainability strategies can boost the top line. Next, we'll look at a third sustainability-enabled revenue stream.

2.1.1 New Revenue from Services and Leasing

There are four new revenue streams that companies exploit when they focus on selling services instead of producing goods that deplete natural capital.

- Lease the product instead of selling it. Value is delivered as a flow of services. For example, Interface FLOR's Evergreen Lease® system leases flooring rather than selling it. A company that leases products will take them back at the end of their useful lives and recycle their components. The steady flow of monthly lease payments stabilizes the peaks and valleys of income from more volatile sales. Leasing also reduces the need to maintain manufacturing capacity to meet peak demand, another source of waste and risk.

Interestingly, leasing reverses the motivation behind the throw-away society. Instead of using planned obsolescence to boost sales, manufacturers are encouraged to make more durable and easily upgradeable products. The longer the product lasts, the more profit for the company. Happily, for the environment, longer durability avoids waste and overflowing landfill sites.

- Use economies of scale to provide off-site outsourcing for non-core customer functions. An example of this approach is computer companies that provide computing services for companies which previously had their own in-house IT departments.
- Grow revenue by creatively supplementing current product revenue with associated contract services.

So, companies benefit from leasing, outsourcing, contracting, and consulting revenue streams, while the environment benefits from less waste and resource depletion.

Some examples are as follows:

i. Interface Flor's Evergreen Lease system allows customers to choose from the complete range of Interface FLOR products, but rather than buying the floor covering, customers pay a monthly leasing charge. In return, Interface FLOR supplies and installs its carpet tiles, replacing worn tiles as necessary.

ii. Dow Chemical's CHEMAWARE program supports the concept of chemical leasing — a complete shift in paradigm. Using this innovative system, companies can drastically increase their efficiency (up to 80% reduction in solvent use) while seeing emissions decrease. This is possible because customers are charged per square meter of product cleaned or by the time needed to clean the parts. Therefore, the supplier "leases" the product and also sells a service, providing a win-win situation for all parties.

iii. VeriForm's "greening experiences" with its metal fabrication process in 2007-8 helped it launch an independently owned energy management company, VeriGreen, to advise companies on how real-world, practical solutions can quickly reduce energy costs and increase profits.

2.1.2 Potential Top-Line Totals

More B2C and B2B revenue from a more sustainable brand. The 5% growth in revenue over three to five years resulting from a more sustainable company image is a conservative estimate. It is driven by the reputation of the company as an environmentally and socially responsible corporate citizen. A company can quickly improve its overall energy, water, and waste footprints, and its social responsibility track record, through continuous improvement techniques when it decides to embark on its sustainability journey. Reaping the low-hanging fruit of eco-efficiencies to save expenses has the co-benefit of greening the company image. All these dynamics could easily produce more than 5% additional revenue by the fifth year.

1. New revenue from new green products. When the company invests in research and development (R&D) dollars to create new eco-effective products, the additional revenue generated by the new green products easily recovers the R&D investment. For example, GE invested $1.5 billion on eco-imagination R&D in 2009; in 2010 it committed an additional $10 billion to eco-imagination R&D over the next three to five years — $2 billion per year. As described above, GE is earning 10% of its revenue from new green products. Siemens is earning 37%.

2. New revenue from services and leasing. When products are leased instead of sold, they become accessible to customers who could not otherwise finance their purchase. As the company builds a base of stable revenue from customers' lease payments, it can add creative value-added service, consulting, and support offerings. A conservative 2% increase in revenue from the leasing/service part of the business is assumed, which again allows time for the orderly launch of the new lines of business in the five-year timeframe.

2.2 Benefit 2: Reduced Energy Expenses

2.2.1 The Lowest-Hanging Fruit

Even if a company does not really care about the environment per se, there are substantial savings to be derived by using less energy, water, and materials in the manufacturing process. These are the "low-hanging fruit" of eco-efficiency associated with sustainability programs.

The quickest and most cost-effective way to save money is to reduce unnecessary energy use. Energy savings are the lowest-hanging eco-efficiency fruit for businesses of any size. They drive fast and significant expense reductions, are eligible for government incentives, and enhance public image. By implementing energy efficiency measures, the United States could avoid wasting $300 billion each year.

It is easy to improve the energy efficiency of a facility with little expertise or money. A company can capitalize on myriad proven, simple, low-risk, high-return, energy-efficiency actions, many of which require little or no capital investment. If resources permit, undertaking a comprehensive energy audit and efficiency program — with the assistance of an outside consultant if needed — may yield even greater savings.

Examples of Energy savings:

i. **Deloitte's resources** 2011 survey polled 400 business decision makers responsible for their companies' energy policies. It found that 90% of companies have set specific goals for their electricity and energy management, and 76% have or are setting goals to reduce electricity cost and consumption. Companies are targeting, on average, a 25% reduction in their energy consumption or cost, often within a two- to three-year time horizon. The survey also found that 71% have set or are in the process of setting goals for improving buildings' energy efficiency and 56% of companies have or will have goals that aim to improve profitability by reducing electricity use.

ii. **US Postal Service (USPS):** USPS reduced facility energy use by 29.4%, or 9.9 trillion BTUs, from 2003 to 2010, and accumulated over $400 million in avoided energy costs from 2007 to 2010. The Morgan mail processing and distribution facility in New York City saved more than $1 million in energy costs in two years. Its green roof reduced energy use by 40% in the first year it was in place. In its Annual Sustainability Report for 2010, USPS reported a 132.7% increase in postal vehicle alternative fuel use from 2005, beating a 10% per year goal for 2015.

2.2.2 Saving Energy in Buildings: An Inside Job

In the United States, buildings account for 72% of electricity consumption, 39% of energy use, and 38% of all carbon dioxide emissions. Sustainability champions look for energy savings in buildings all the time.

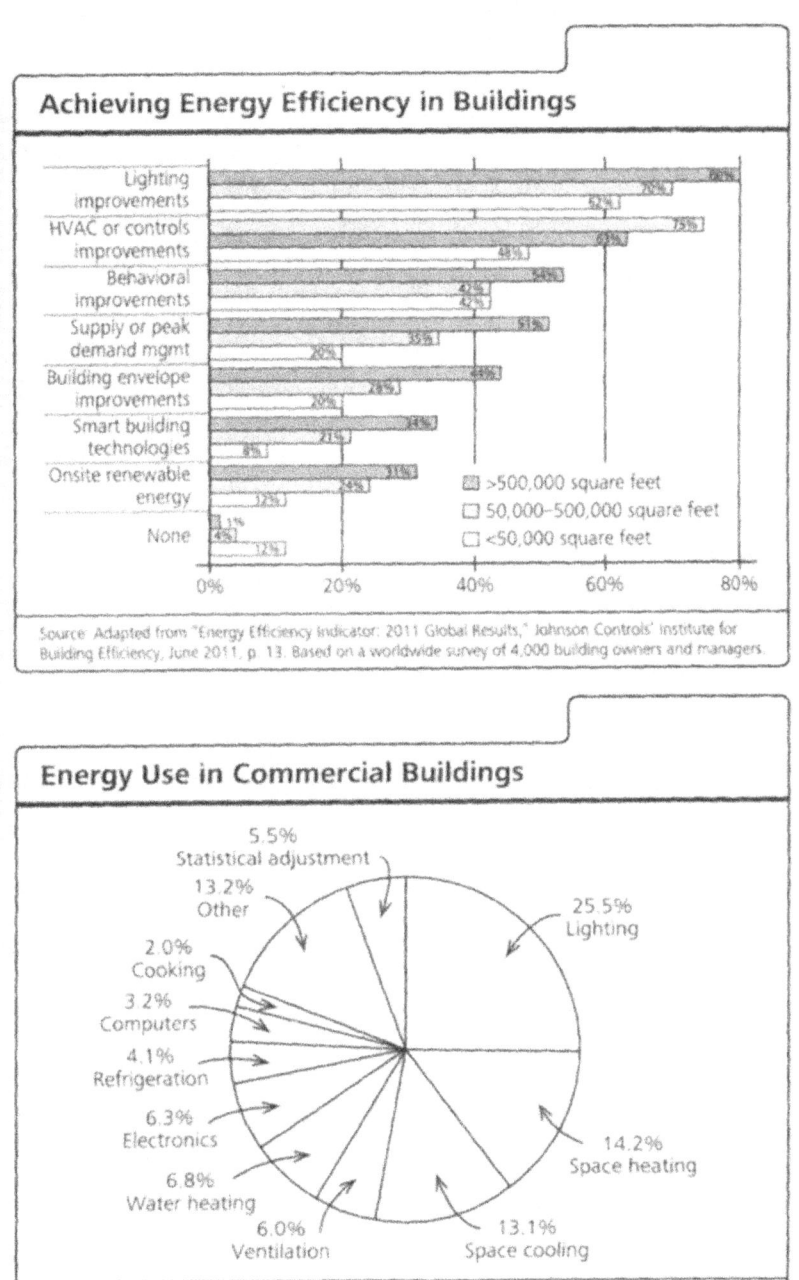

Figure 2.2

Although many developers assume green buildings must cost more to build, green design can actually decrease construction costs, chiefly by reducing infrastructure expenses and by using passive heating and cooling techniques that make costly mechanical equipment unnecessary. Using the seven approaches listed in Figure 2.2, some buildings already achieve net-zero energy. New energy-efficient buildings are no longer a technical challenge. Retrofitting old buildings to save enormous amounts of energy is also becoming common. As shown in Figure 2.2, heating, ventilation, and air-conditioning (HVAC) systems account for about 23% of energy use in commercial buildings. Every degree of heating and cooling can increase energy consumption by up to 10%. Lighting accounts for just over 25% of energy use in commercial buildings. Installing readily available, proven lighting technologies can reduce a building's energy use by 50% to 70%. It is easy to do, and it pays back quickly — no wonder it is called the low-hanging fruit. These data are based in US industry.

2.2.3 Driving Energy Savings in Transportation

Companies pay shipping costs for their raw materials and/or their finished goods. If companies do not cover transportation costs overtly, they usually are buried in the buying or selling price. That means companies are looking for ways to reduce the amount of fuel used in transportation, even if they do not have their own company fleet of cars or trucks.

Savings in resource-efficient transportation and snipping are achieved through:
- Reduced fuel costs from more efficient modes of transportation
- Increased cost-effectiveness due to lighter, smaller, and more efficiently packaged products
- Fewer vehicles or loads due to smarter combinations of shipments by batching loads
- More efficient routing algorithms

We are primarily concerned with the first option here.

For a company like Chiquita, which sells fresh fruit and vegetables, the price of bunker fuel is an important variable component of its transportation costs. As they have for most companies, Chiquita's fuel costs have increased substantially in recent years. It offsets the effect of these increases through fuel surcharges and mitigates the effect of fluctuating fuel prices by purchasing bunker fuel forward contracts that lock in fuel prices for up to 75% of its expected core shipping needs for up to three years. In addition, diesel fuel and other transportation costs are significant components of what Chiquita spends on the produce it purchases from growers and distributors. If the price of any of these items increases significantly, there is no assurance that Chiquita will be able to pass on those increases to its customers. The price of fuel is critical to such companies.

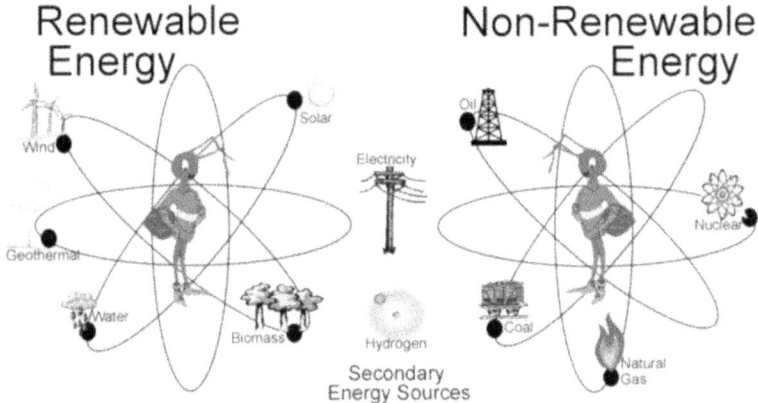

Figure 2.3

Further, many shipping companies are willing to put time and effort into sustainability, even if there is no return on investment (ROI), while 11% of retail and third-party logistics shippers want a considerable ROI. Danish shipping company Maersk Line plans to build a fleet of container ships that it describes as the world's largest and most energy efficient. Maersk's new fleet will use smaller engines, a waste-heat recovery system, and economy of scale to achieve its fuel savings. The fleet will also use 35% less fuel per container than thousands of ships being delivered to Maersk's competitors, transforming fuel consumption used in transportation into a competitive advantage.

2.2.4 Renewing Energy Savings with Substitutions

Companies are discovering amazing opportunities for energy savings and are driving down their energy requirements. That makes them good candidates for the other part of the energy pincer movement namely that they can create renewable energy onsite for their remaining energy requirements.

Renewable energy alternatives are becoming more cost competitive. In 2011, wind power was down to 4.2 cents/kWh, making it competitive with traditional non-renewable energy sources. The photovoltaic (PV) industry is reducing the cost of solar energy at a breakneck rate. Prices on solar panels have dropped over 50% in just two years. The US Department of Energy said in February 2011 that it would spend $27 million to reduce the cost of solar power by 75% by 2020 in a bid to make the renewable power source as cheap as fossil fuels — about 6 cents/kWh. If the cost of PV energy achieves par with conventional sources, it will continue flourishing even if government incentives are withdrawn.

Other renewable energy projects that seemed unprofitable two years ago are beginning to look good from an ROI perspective. Companies use combined heat and power (CHP) technologies to capture wasted heat from their industrial processes and use it to generate electricity. The company can use the resulting power onsite and feed excess electricity into the electrical grid to generate a credit on the company's bill from the local electrical utility. For example, Campbell's makes both soup and electricity from the steam in its cookers and generates revenue from both.

It would be nice if the billions of dollars in fossil fuel subsidies were converted to support renewable energy. To help cover the price differential in the meantime, there are government incentive programs available from most levels of government in most jurisdictions. They include grants, tax breaks, loan guarantees, and technical assistance for green building and renewable-energy components of commercial, residential, and industrial projects. Additional financial and technical assistance may be available from utilities, nonprofits, and faith-based organizations.

2.2.5 The Secret Mantra of Eco-Efficiency Savings: Engaged Employees

Educated, caring employees can make a critical difference to energy conservation in their day-to-day discretionary activities at work. Employees can save energy by turning off lights when they leave offices and conference rooms, using stairs instead of elevators when going up or down a few floors, using the power-saving settings on their computers, and turning off their computers when they are out of the office.

Encouraging employees, especially the purchasing department, to use systems thinking helps them see how long-term operational costs are much more significant than one-time purchase prices for things like transformers, wire, and motors.

- It is more energy efficient and more cost effective to spend more money to acquire efficient transformers and then save money on energy. Purchasing cheap, inefficient distribution transformers wastes $1 billion in electricity per year in the United States.
- Electricians usually bid the thinnest and cheapest allowable wire to save money on materials.
- Pumping is the most common application for motors, and motors use 75% of all industrial electricity. Manufacturing requires motors and pumps — lots of them. Interface Inc. discovered that using big straight pipes with small pumps, instead of small crooked pipes with big pumps, cost less, even before the ongoing energy savings from the lower electricity use of the smaller pumps, motors, motor controls, and electrical components. By first laying out the pipe route and then positioning the tanks, boilers, and other connected equipment, Interface discovered it could use 7-horsepower pumps instead of 95-horsepower pumps, a 92% reduction.

Turned-on employees, energized by an opportunity to reduce the environmental footprint of their company, astound their managers with good ideas. Figure 2.4 gives a few examples of how technology-based ideas can provide fast and substantial returns on investment. Add "green

Energy Savings at VeriForm

VeriForm, a steel fabricating company located in Cambridge, Ontario, invested $46,186 between 2006 and 2008 to reduce electricity costs by more than 58% ($89,152 annually) and increase its profit by 76%. The average payback period for its 42 energy saving projects was 6.3 months. As can be seen from the table of projects below, some projects paid for themselves in just weeks. The company also reduced its natural gas consumption by 90% and its CO_2 emissions by over 45% annually.

Project	Initial Cost (Can$)	Annual Savings (Can$)	Payback Period (Years)
Replace HID plant lighting with T5 lights in the old plant ($6,000) and in the new, expanded area ($2,000)	$8,000*	$20,916	0.38 (4.5 months)
Install equipment capacitors to raise power factor to above 90 to avoid surcharge on electrical bill for inefficiencies	$11,285	$24,118	0.46 (5.5 months)
Install a single tamper-resistant, programmable thermostat in the plant to replace multiple manual thermostats	$1,200	$13,911	0.08 (1 month)
Install wire heating disconnects on five bay doors so when the bay door goes up, the heat turns off in the whole shop (This encourages staff to chase shippers to unload faster)	$1,200	$7,893	0.15 (1.8 months)
Turn off printers/monitors/ computers at night	$250	$2,978	0.08 (1 month)
Install software to print multiple pages per sheet	$320	$1,200	0.26 (3.1 months)

* An additional $1,000 grant from the local electricity utility helped defray the initial cost. All other projects listed were self-financed, without any assistance from subsidies or grants.

Source: "Manufacturer Finds Lighting Energy Efficiency Convenient, Truthfully" [accessed July 30, 2011], GreenManufacturer.net.

Figure 2.4

teams" into the mix, and behavior-based eco-savings are even more impressive — see Figure 2.4 for examples of green teams' efforts to reduce waste expenses. Employees' innovative ideas, firsthand knowledge of workflows, and passion to help the company solve its sustainability puzzle are the underpinnings of eco-efficiency savings. Engaged employees trump technology.

2.2.6 Potential Energy Expense Savings

Despite the primary focus on energy savings in many companies these days, energy costs are still only a small fraction of total costs in most industries (a conservative estimate is that the cost of electricity and fuel represents 2% of company revenue, although this amount is growing as the cost of energy increases). As a result, executives may not pay them the attention they should. They forget that energy savings go straight to the bottom line, whereas only 5% to 15% of revenue typically does. That is, you'd need about 7 to 20 times the value of energy savings in additional revenue to generate the same amount of profit. If you were the CEO, would you rather improve profit by saving $100,000 on your energy bill or by somehow generating $2,000,000 more revenue?

Some companies already save over 100% of their energy bill. How? If a company can generate more energy onsite than is required for its internal use, in some jurisdictions it can sell the excess power back to the grid, the resulting revenue is counted within these energy savings.

2.3 Benefit 3: Reducing Waste

Companies buy raw materials with the aim of turning them into marketable products. While a certain amount of the purchased material and energy ends up embodied in products, more of it ends up as "non-product output" or waste — material that was purchased and paid for but that was ultimately thrown away. If the term "waste" were replaced with "squandered corporate assets," shareholders would pressure corporations to pay more attention to this opportunity for cost savings. And the business imperative to stop squandering these assets has environmental co-benefits.

Waste is embedded in processes, a direct result of inefficient systems and procedures that are, perhaps unwittingly, designed to produce waste. Solid waste, water waste, and air emissions are indicative of production inefficiency. Process redesign saves embedded waste costs. (We will see, under Benefit 4, how dematerialization, substitution, recycling, and product take-back save materials costs and further reduce waste.)

If business leaders were asked how much material is wasted by industry each year, most would admit that a certain percentage is wasted, but not a great deal. Actually, we are more than 10 times better at wasting resources than we are at using them. A study by the US National Academy of Engineering found that about 93% of materials that companies buy and "consume" never end up in saleable products at all.

However, it is also important to recognize that not all waste is equal. When the waste stream consists of many different materials or commodities, as in the case of food waste, the economic values and environmental footprints of the waste components can vary widely. In a typical paint shop, about 39% of the value of the raw materials ends up in useful products, while the other 61% is wasted. That is still high, but more hopeful than the 12% to 88% split by weight. In today's take-make-waste business model, waste has become an accepted by-product of doing business. The wake-up call comes when the costs of wasted materials, capital, and labor are added to arrive at the total cost of waste.

2.3.1 The Four-Factor Formula for the Full Cost of Waste

Too often, the cost of waste is equated with the cost of waste handling. To more accurately account for a company's waste bill, we need to rethink waste and tally four factors described in the UN document Environmental Management Accounting Procedures and Principles, illustrated in Figure 2.5

1. Cost of materials purchased but later wasted (60%). This includes raw materials, auxiliary materials, operating materials, packaging, and water.
2. Cost of processing the material before it is wasted (20%). This includes the wasted energy and labor consumed working on the material before it becomes scrap.
3. Cost of waste prevention and environmental management (10%). This includes any external services for environmental management, personnel for general environmental management activities, research and development on waste issues, extra expenditures for cleaner technologies, and other environmental management costs such as environmental monitoring, environmental assessments and audits, and wildlife habitat protection.
4. Cost of end-of-pipe waste treatment and waste disposal (10%). This includes storage, haulage, disposal, and tipping fees; depreciation for related equipment; related personnel costs; any fines and penalties; insurance for environmental liabilities; and any provisions for cleanup costs, remediation, reclamation, and decommissioning.

These costs "are offset by any revenue realized from selling sorted waste streams or selling new products created from previously discarded waste.

The term "environmental management" is sometimes used to refer to the third and fourth factors. In Canada in 2008 the cost of environmental

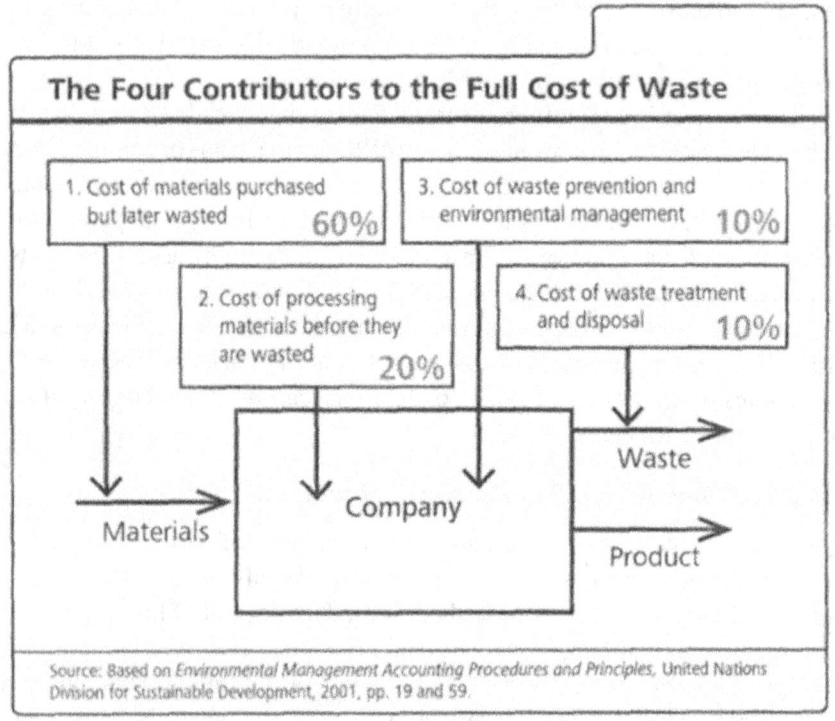

Figure 2.5

management totaled $5.2 billion, up almost 10% from 2006. These expenditures were mostly directed toward waste management and sewage services ($1.6 billion), followed by pollution abatement and control ($1.3 billion). The costs related purely to disposal (e.g., waste disposal fees, external waste transport) account for 1% to 2% of the total expenses, not just the waste costs, for a manufacturing company. We estimated 10% as the proportion of waste costs for both waste prevention and waste treatment/disposal.

2.3.2 Company Efforts to Avoid Waste

Companies in the United States dispose of 7.6 billion tons of industrial waste each year. Much of this industrial waste is made up of reusable non-hazardous materials. No wonder some companies are taking aggressive measures to stop wasting their waste.

Lockheed set a goal of reducing the amount of waste sent to landfills by 25% by the close of 2022, based on 2007 levels. The targets are absolute reductions, not reductions in intensity, where consumption, waste, and emissions are typically measured in comparison to other factors such as revenue, units of production, or number of employees. By the end of the first quarter of 2011, the firm had cut waste-to-landfill by 30%, exceeding the targeted reduction.

In 2010, Boeing diverted 73% of its non-hazardous solid waste from landfill, compared with 68% in 2009. From 2007 to 2010, the company's diversion rate improved by 26%. In April 2011, the Boeing 787 assembly plant in North Charleston, SC, became the company's fourth zero-waste-to-landfill site and its first major commercial airplane production facility to attain "zero waste" status. Boeing's other zero-waste sites are a helicopter plant in Philadelphia, a Salt Lake City factory where commercial airplane parts are fabricated, and a strategic-missile-and-defense-systems facility in Huntsville, AL.

Continuous improvement of old manufacturing processes to prevent embedded waste eventually hits a wall when the cost of squeezing out additional waste savings exceeds the savings that would be gained. The biggest savings breakthroughs occur when companies adopt a fresh approach to process design that considers industrial systems as a whole, rather than as a collection of isolated parts. Rather than battling the law of diminishing returns while fine-tuning existing processes, designers use whole-system thinking to discover that saving a large fraction of resources can actually cost less than saving a smaller fraction of resources.

Procter & Gamble: In 2010, Procter & Gamble's manufacturing facility in Auburn, ME, became the company's first in North America to achieve zero-waste-to-landfill status by recycling or reusing more than 60% of the overall waste produced and incinerating the rest for energy production. The company's Global Asset Recovery Purchases (GARP) team found a beneficial use for the nearly 40% of factory waste that could not be recycled or reused. The excess materials were incinerated and used to power the facility; any excess power was sold back to the local utility. The GARP team calculated that the program diverted over 10,000 tons of waste from the landfill and saved the company tens of millions of dollars in cost recovery over the year. Auburn is the ninth P&G plant to earn the distinction of zero-waste-to-landfill, which P&G says fits its goal of having zero waste going to landfills globally and instead of being beneficially reused in its value stream.

Source: "P&G Announces Its First North American Manufacturing Plant to Achieve Zero Waste to Landfill" press release [accessed July 30, 2011], PGinvestor.com, December 6, 2010.

Interface: Interface Inc. has an objective to eliminate all waste in the manufacture of carpet. This zero-waste strategy led to a corporate-wide treasure hunt under its QUEST™ program to engage employees in identifying, measuring, and eliminating waste in its manufacturing processes. As a result of employees' valuable suggestions to minimize material usage and improve the efficiency of equipment and processes, Interface achieved a 50% reduction in waste cost per unit, resulting in $372 million in avoided waste costs by 2010. Interface waste reduction efforts have resulted in a 76% decrease in total waste to landfills from its carpet factories since 1996,

Source: "Waste" [accessed July 30, 2011], Interfaceglobal.com.

Walmart: "During the recession, [Walmart] did not cut back on its sustainability spending at all because it is driving bottom-line benefit. [The company] has a goal of zero waste from its operations by 2025, and one Canadian store has achieved 97.6% diversion."

Source: Jim Harris, "What You Don't Know about Green Tech — But Should" [accessed July 30, 2011], Backbonemag.com, May 13, 2011.

2.3.3 Bonus: Revenue from Selling Waste

Each year it costs US companies $22 billion to put their waste into landfills. The materials in that landfilled waste are worth an estimated $20 billion. The real waste is not the materials; it is the lost opportunity.

Valuable materials such as cardboard, boxboard, mixed paper, glass, ferrous metals, copper, aluminum, plastics, organics, and construction and demolition materials in useful concentrations are embedded in waste streams. However, most companies have limited knowledge of the composition of their waste and know even less about how to separate the marketable portion from the waste stream. Innovative services such as Recycle Match provide marketplaces where waste can be traded as valuable raw material. The RecycleMatch website gives the following examples:

- Instead of paying $1.5 million to put used materials into a landfill, IBM found a way to sell those "waste" materials for $1.5 million, resulting in a net $3 million improvement.
- GM's various recycling activities generated more than $2.5 billion in revenue between 2007 and 2010. It now earns $1 billion a year from selling scrap. That is on top of the value the company has achieved by reusing and repurposing materials within its own operations.[10]
- Recycling made the US Postal Service (USPS) $13 million in revenues last year, while saving $9.1 million in landfill fees...in 2010 it recycled more than 222,000 tons of material, almost 8,000 tons more than in 2009.[n]

Using the waste from one company as the food for another is called "industrial ecology' illustrated in Figure 2.6. One of the first examples of industrial ecology comes from Kalundborg, Denmark, where companies conveniently located near each other in the city's eco-industrial park trade

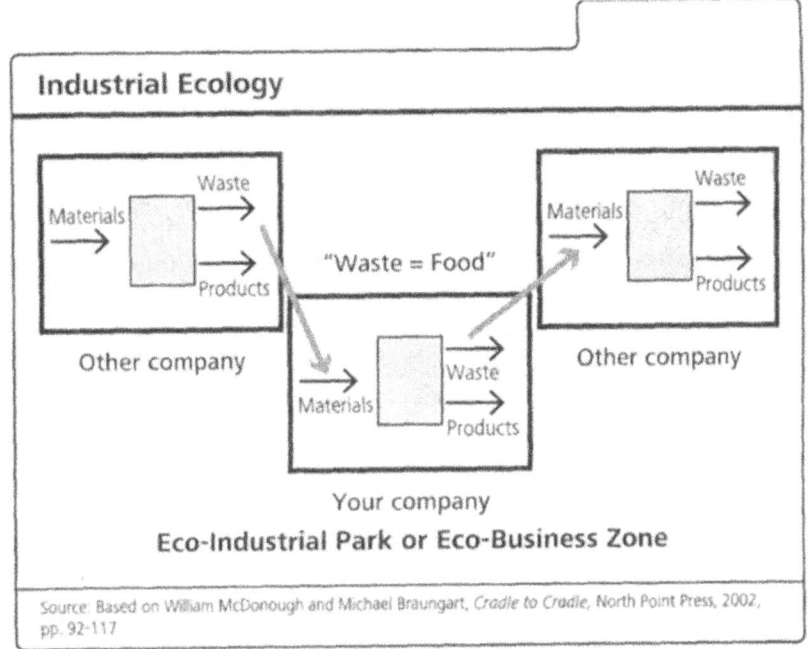

Figure 2.6

various by-products: steam and heat, water, refinery gas, gypsum, biomass, liquid fertilizer, fly ash, and sludge. They invested $60 million over five years on the infrastructure to support these exchanges and have reaped over $120 million in cost savings. This increased efficiency benefits the bottom lines of all participating partners.

There are eco-industrial networks across Canada, the United States, and Europe, referred to as eco-industrial parks, industrial ecosystems, zero emissions clusters, and sustainable technology parks. The closed-loop systems in these industrial ecosystems benefit the companies, the communities, and the environment. They profit from each other's waste.

2.3.4 Potential Waste Savings Help Build a Sustainability Capital Reserve

The cost to industry of environmental protection, including pollution reduction, waste management, monitoring, regulatory reporting, legal fees, and insurance, has risen rapidly in the past 20 years, with increasingly stringent environmental regulations worldwide. Waste reduction makes a surprisingly high contribution to potential bottom-line benefits from sustainability strategies.

What should we assume as the potential waste reduction factor within the next three to five years? PepsiCo's UK and Ireland division has set a goal to achieve zero waste across the supply chain within 10 years. Walmart's California operations have diverted more than 80% of their waste from landfills, and the retailer's goal is to create zero waste. In 2010, GM announced that 52% of its worldwide facilities were landfill-free, and it aimed to grow that figure continuously.

2.4 Benefit 4: Saving Natural Capital Saves Financial Capital

All companies use materials. Companies that manufacture goods take raw materials and parts, which are the finished product from the supplier's raw materials, and combine them to produce finished goods for customers. Wholesale and retail companies buy materials in the form of products for resale. Commercial establishments purchase materials in the form of office consumables, especially paper, arid often food for their cafeterias. Packaging materials are used in all sectors, as is water, another material.

We use the word "materials" as an umbrella term to include raw materials, parts, finished goods, consumables, packaging, and water. Materials arrive at the receiving dock or through a pipe, are processed by the company, and leave the shipping dock as finished goods for sale to another company or to be sold directly to the consumer. They also go down the sewer, up the chimney, or into the dumpster as waste. Under Benefit 3 we looked at savings opportunities involving waste. However, from a sustainability perspective, using fewer materials is even better as it minimizes the extraction and consumption of increasingly scarce natural capital. In fact, a truly sustainable enterprise would use and waste no new raw materials.

Manufacturing, construction, wholesale, and retail companies use the most materials. Material purchase costs can make up from 50% to 80% of total expenses for an American manufacturing company and 70% of expenses for its German counterpart. Another study pegged the cost of materials for German manufacturers as 57% of overall expenses.

As illustrated in Figure 2.7, there are four ways to save money on materials.

- Dematerialization: Reduce the amount of material used per product to reduce the material intensity of goods.
- Substitution: Use less expensive, more environmentally friendly, raw materials.
- Recycling onsite waste: Reduce, reuse, and recycle scrap materials, turning them into useful raw materials for products instead of throwing them away.
- Product Take-Back: Reuse and recycle components and materials from returned products in a closed-loop, cradle-to-cradle system.

We consider each approach in this chapter.

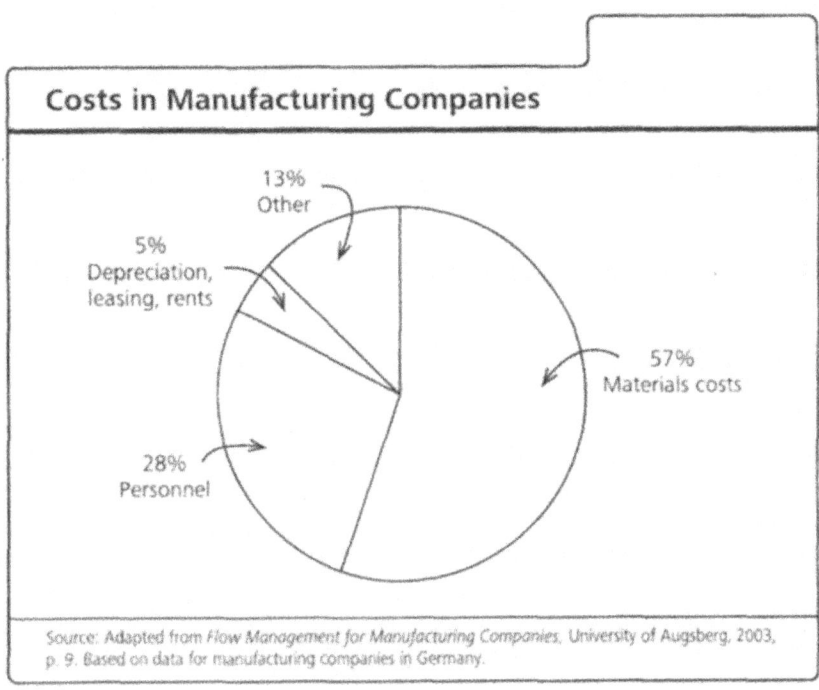

Costs in Manufacturing Companies

13%
Other

5%
Depreciation,
leasing, rents

57%
Materials costs

28%
Personnel

Source: Adapted from *Flow Management for Manufacturing Companies*, University of Augsberg, 2003, p. 9. Based on data for manufacturing companies in Germany.

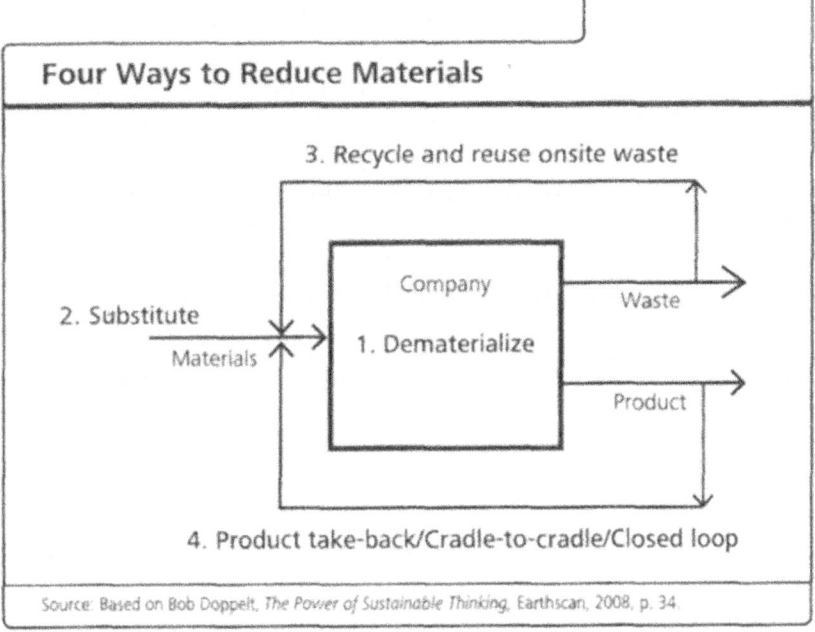

Four Ways to Reduce Materials

3. Recycle and reuse onsite waste

Company

Waste

2. Substitute

Materials

1. Dematerialize

Product

4. Product take-back/Cradle-to-cradle/Closed loop

Source: Based on Bob Doppelt, *The Power of Sustainable Thinking*, Earthscan, 2008, p. 34.

Figure 2.7

2.4.1 Savings from Dematerialization

Dematerialization is doing more with less. Using less means the company buys less. Buying less saves money. Dematerialization saves money. That is the bottom-line benefit. The sustainability-related benefit is that we raze less natural capital.

In some ways, sustainability is a reframing of traditional approaches to lean manufacturing and running an efficient organization. Dematerialization helps streamline operations and increase organizational effectiveness. Minimum-material design not only minimizes the material intensity of the finished product; it also has labor productivity benefits. There are reduced handling costs because there are fewer components or less material, and there is less overtime because of more efficient processes.

The idea is to reduce the total material that goes into a product or its packaging without sacrificing quality or benefits to customers. Efforts to optimize material intensity lead companies to design and manufacture smaller or lighter products. Well-documented examples include using less metal in thinner beverage cans and using fewer materials in automobiles without reducing quality or safety. The WellMet2050 program at the University of Cambridge points out that most products could use one-third less metal without loss of performance.

Enthusiasm for dematerialization has often focused on the use of digital technologies to provide information services without other media — e.g., "the paperless office" with online newspapers, electronic directories, and e-books. Their intended co-benefits are resource savings in material extraction; improved eco-design of products; and technological innovations in the organization and management of production processes. However, we must use a life-cycle lens to consider these changes to ensure that the required electronic equipment for digital music, for example, does not have a greater material burden than the replaced media.

Packaging optimization projects can often result in 100% ROI after the very first year. RG Barry's payback period for its packaging savings was six months.

This resource-productivity model reduces the price of production, which increases competitiveness and lays the foundation for a higher bottom-line return. Business strategies built around radically increasing the productive use of natural resources can solve many environmental problems at a profit.

Examples of Dematerialization

Apple: Materials conservation was a key requirement in the design and manufacture of the Universal Motherboard Architecture (LIMA) for Apple's Power Mac G4 Desktop Computer. Apple wanted to reduce materials because of the costs of the actual materials, warehousing, and associated labor for installing components. Material savings were made through the substantial integration of parts and the use of larger chips. The dematerialized UMA used 50% fewer components than the previous Power Macintosh G3 logic board design and fewer than 1,000 components compared to over 2,000 for the G3. This resulted in time, resource, and cost savings by eliminating administrative and procurement efforts, logistics, and the actual installation of components onto the printed circuit board.

Source: A. Sweatman et al., "Design for Environment: A Case Study of the Power Mac G4 Desktop

Computer," Proceedings of the 2000 IEEE International Symposium on Electronics and the Environment,0

IEEE Computer Society, Technical Committee on Electronics and the Environment, 2000, p. 13.

RG Barry: Slipper and footwear giant RG Barry reduced its shipping carton choices and saved more than $2.5 million in 18 months. The company replaced cartons made from five sheets of paper glued together with ones made from two sheets of paper surrounding a corrugated core. That format results in a stronger but thinner carton. The company also changed its,' standard box arrangement per carton from six wide by two deep to four by three. "Deeper is cheaper," since deeper cartons require less material for flaps than shallow ones. RG Barry also ensured that cartons used the entire pallet; footprint, to save storage space. As a result of optimizing and dematerializing its shipping processes, the company spent 15% ($200,000) less on packaging, lowered inbound freight costs by 20% ($1.6 million), reduced the need for ocean containers, and trimmed storage expense by 25% ($1 million).

2.4.2 Savings from Substitutions

Despite notions of market- or customer-driven corporate strategies, consumers do not choose the materials used in goods. Corporations do. Companies that wish to be sensitive to the environment consider what it takes to produce the raw materials they are purchasing. This "cradle-to-grave" perspective encourages them to look back to the cradle of the raw materials themselves — the energy and materials consumed in extracting, preparing, and transporting the purchased resources. There are a couple of ways to substitute less expensive, more environmentally friendly, more benign raw materials.

First, use materials with smaller "ecological rucksacks." Ecological rucksacks contain the total quantity of materials moved from nature to create products or services, including the hidden material flows that occur during the life cycle of the product. These rucksacks are a proxy for the environmental strain and resource inefficiency of the product or service.

Big rucksacks may equal higher prices, although "perverse subsidies" in many natural resource and fossil fuel industries distort this free market assumption. Such subsidies are "perverse" because they make citizens pay twice to encourage environmentally destructive behavior: their taxes pay for the subsidies, and then they pay the direct and indirect costs of environmental restoration and health care. By choosing raw materials that have smaller ecological rucksacks, companies will be in a better competitive position when subsidies are dropped. They will directly save money while indirectly contributing to the health of the planet.

Second, 'replace hazardous materials and chemicals with non-hazardous ones, as suggested by the two examples in Figure 2.8. As with dematerialization, this switch has a sometimes overlooked benefit in the form of labor savings from reduced handling costs due to use of

Examples of Substitutions

Wood preservatives: For decades, wood was preserved with PCP (a fungicide) and lindane (an insecticide). Both preservatives were the focus of environmental protests in the 1970s and 1980s as a result of accidents during production and use; the persistence of the two chemicals in soil, food, and human tissues; and their contamination with ultra-toxic dioxins. They were classified as dangerous chemicals, and consumers rejected them for use in home projects. Producers in this market reacted to consumer demands for less-toxic products by replacing lindane with Pyrethroides and PCP with Dichlofluanid.

Rechargeable batteries: In the mid-1980s, the growing use of camcorders, household appliances, power tools, etc., fuelled an increased demand for smaller rechargeable batteries. At the time, nickel-cadmium batteries (NiCd) were favored, but due to their 15% cadmium content, these batteries are considered hazardous waste. When they were buried in landfills, cadmium leached into groundwater; when they were incinerated, cadmium was emitted into the atmosphere. In the 1990s, battery producers, mainly in Japan, anticipating a shortage of cadmium, developed nickel-metal–hydride (NiMH) and lithium ion (Li-ion) substitutes. NiMH cells have approximately twice the capacity of NiCd batteries. In many markets, such an improved technical performance, rather than environmental considerations, drove the introduction and acceptance of the new batteries.

Source: Joachim Lohse and Lothar Lißnar, "Substitution of Hazardous Chemicals in Products and Processes," Ökopol GmbH and Kooperationsstelle Hamburg, 2003, pp. 78–79 and 83.

Figure 2.8

less hazardous materials, and reduced staff time to monitor and report compliance with hazardous materials regulations.

Unfortunately, because of inequitable subsidies and short-term costing of traditional energy and materials, suggested substitutions often cost more today than their less benign alternatives. In some cases, the cost of recyclable materials exceeds the cost of raw materials. For example, virgin plastic resin costs 40% less than recycled resin. We also need to consider the life-cycle energy requirements of substituted components to ensure we are not trading off a materials rucksack for an energy rucksack. Systems thinking are a must when evaluating alternatives.

2.4.3 Savings from Recycling and Reusing Onsite Waste

Reduce. Reuse. Recycle. The 3Rs of waste reduction lead to a materials-saving opportunity as companies source materials from what would otherwise be disposed of as waste. Many waste materials generated during the production process can be reused or recycled onsite in the plant or on the plant property, as shown in Figure 2.8. Executives are delighted when a firm does not waste materials and can make more products without buying more raw materials.

2.4.4 Savings from Product Take-Back/Closed-Loop Systems

The ultimate reduction of material occurs when companies take back their product at the end of its life (see examples in Figure 2.7). Customers enjoy the use of the product but do not own it. When they are finished with it, for whatever reason, the company takes back the materials, which it still owns, and uses them again. Rather than creating and selling products, the firm creates a service that provides the same benefit.

In business, the best way to make sure the company retains its asset after the consumer is finished using it is to lease it, the way people lease cars or computers. There is a subtle but profound difference in what consumers are purchasing. People are not buying a car; they are leasing personal transportation. They are not buying a computer; they are leasing computing capability. Interface Flor's Evergreen Lease have attractive floors without buying a carpet.

Government "take back" regulations make this flow mandatory, but once a company understands the value of taking back its own products, it flips from fighting such regulations to insisting on them. Take-back, or extended producer responsibility (EPR), makes producers responsible for the environmental impacts of their products at the end of their products' useful life. As such, EPR shifts to private industry the responsibility for taking back, recycling, and ultimately disposing of any discarded material that would otherwise be managed by local governments. This incorporates the cost of product disposal or recycling into product price. Companies implement voluntary EPR initiatives when they are able to make a profit or gain a marketing advantage by taking back products, components, or extracted materials. In such cases, take-back is a proactive, financially attractive example of corporate social responsibility.

The real benefit of taking back "products of service" is the producer mindset it encourages. The company uses design for disassembly (DFD) so that it is easier to take the product apart to reuse its components. It uses different and fewer fasteners. It stamps plastic components with part numbers and other information instead of using gummy labels that require more labor and time to remove. It gets serious about using nontoxic materials in order to simplify handling processes.

Examples of Product Take-Back

Maersk: "Maersk Line will implement the most comprehensive cradle-to-cradle passport ever seen" for its new giant ships. They are completely recyclable. "The materials of the ships will all be marked and numbered — separating high and low grade steel, copper wiring, hazardous materials and waste ... The cradle to cradle passport will identify each and every nut and bolt of the giant 60,000 ton ships ... Based on the sorting it will be possible to reuse nearly all materials for new ships, making dangerous and polluting ship scrapping a thing of the past."

Source: "Maersk Line Triple-E: Total Vessel Recycling" [accessed July 30, 2011], C2Cportal.net, April 5, 2011.

Sprint: In 2010, Sprint recycled 36% of all phones it sold. In 2011, the company announced a series of ambitious goals to reduce its e-waste streams, including a goal of collecting 100% of Sprint's own electronic waste for reuse and recycling by 2017, and collecting 90% of all phones sold for reuse or recycling by 2017.

Source: Matthew Wheeland, "Sprint Sets Ambitious Zero E-Waste Goal for 2017" [accessed July 30, 2011], GreenBiz.com, May 26, 2011.

Nike: "Nike established a consumer-take-back program to recycle shoes, turning them into sport-courts ... Their executives publicly explain that if they were to continue to meet earnings and growth predicated on a business-as-usual industry standard model, they would literally require more natural resources than the earth has within our lifetimes."

Source: Brooke Farrell, "Debunking Six Myths about the Materials in Your Company's Dumpster" [accessed July 30, 2011], EnvironmentalLeader.com, March 2011.

Figure 2.9

Product take-back requires collaboration among manufacturers, retailers, users, and municipal governments. These players engage third-party recyclers to help with the logistics and recovery processes. A full cost analysis should be done to ensure the ongoing benefits of the closed-loop system outweigh the costs, but even a product as gigantic as a container ship can use cradle-to-cradle design, as explained in Figure 2.9.

2.4.5 Water Sustainability:

Water is a very special material. Even if a business does not use a lot of water, it is likely to face some restrictions on its use, and an increase in its cost. If a business relies on water and operates in a drought-affected area, it is already acutely affected.

In industrial facilities, water is used in a wide range of activities.

- Incorporation in the final product
- Washing or rinsing of raw materials, intermediates, or final products
- Preparation of solvents or slurries
- Cleaning of equipment and space
- Removing or providing heat
- Meeting hygienic and domestic needs
- Irrigation of landscape space

Every good contains what is called "embodied water" which is a measure of the total amount of water used to produce that good or service. For example, it takes about 60 liters of water to make a typical ream of paper weighing 2.5 kilograms.

Water prices vary between cities or regions because of the range of water tariffs or sources of supply, but PepsiCo has found that even in places where water is inexpensive, the costs of treating it, using it, filtering it, and discharging it adds up. In some cases, PepsiCo sees a tenfold increase in the fully measured cost of water between the time it enters a facility to the time a process is complete.

Reducing the amount of water used in manufacturing can yield substantial savings. For example, sewage costs are usually based on the what-goes-in-must-come-out theory — they reflect the amount of water metered at the plant intake. If the company purchases less fresh water from the local utility, there is a corresponding reduction in sewage charges. Companies can reduce their need to purchase water by treating it themselves and reusing it in a closed-loop system.

A naturalized landscape that does not use pesticides and greatly reduces water consumption is a daily reminder to employees and passersby that the company cares. About 40% to 80% of a water utility's peak demand in the summer is driven by landscape watering, which can be reduced by

Examples of Water Savings

Fluke: Fluke Corporation in Seattle, which manufactures industrial testing equipment, found it paid for water four times: when it purchased the water in the first place, when it treated the water to production standards, when it treated the water prior to discharge, and when it paid its sewage fees. Over two years, Fluke reduced water use from 2.5 million gallons per month to 400,000 gallons per month, resulting in bottom line savings of $138,000 per year.

Source: Scott D. Johnson, "Identification and Selection of Environmental Performance Indicators: Application of the Balanced Scorecard Approach," *Corporate Environmental Strategy* 5, no. 4, Summer 1998, p. 40.

Lockheed Martin: In 2008, Lockheed Martin set goals of reducing water use by 25% by the end of 2012, based on 2007 levels. The targets are absolute reductions, not reductions in intensity (in which consumption, waste, and emissions are measured in comparison to other factors, such as revenue, units of production, or number of employees). By the end of 2010 the company had implemented efficiency and conservation measures that cut water use by 22%. In the first quarter of 2011, the firm surpassed its goals by bringing the reduction in water consumption to 27%.

Source: Leslie Guevarra, "Lockheed Saves $2.6M in IT Energy Costs; Tops Water, Waste Targets" [accessed July 30, 2011], GreenBiz.com, April 20, 2011.

Figure 2.10

about 50% by relatively modest improvements: using water-frugal grasses, growing flora indigenous to the region, and converting lawns into diverse native grasslands, bushes, and trees.

Figure 2.10 below shows how Fluke and Lockheed Martin saved water during its operations.

2.4.6 Savings on Consumables and Paper

Every employee is a resource gatekeeper. Suppose a company educated its employees to be more aware consumers, and they started to look for more enviro-friendly actions in their homes and workplaces. There is evidence that employees become more careful about consumables at work if they are trained to be more frugal without sacrificing quality. The forestry company Weyerhaeuser, for example, participated in a program, based on Vicki Robin's book Your Money Or Your Life, that taught employees better money management and more conscious spending practices. In a follow-up survey of employees a year after they had taken the workshop, 28% said they were 'more frugal with company resources than before.

One of the most basic materials in business is paper, used in everything from billing to photocopying, marketing, and reporting. According to US Environmental Protection Agency data, the average US office worker uses 10,000 sheets of copy paper each year, which contributes to an annual consumption of about 5 million tons of paper and paperboard. According to ForestEthics, a member of the Environmental Paper Network, the number of pages of paper consumed in US offices is growing by about 20% each year. Meeting the demands of this great paper chase within today's corporations requires a resource-intensive manufacturing process that is dependent on forests, water, and energy.

As shown in Figure 2.11, paper and cardboard constitute over half the waste from a typical office. Paper waste can be avoided in two ways. First,

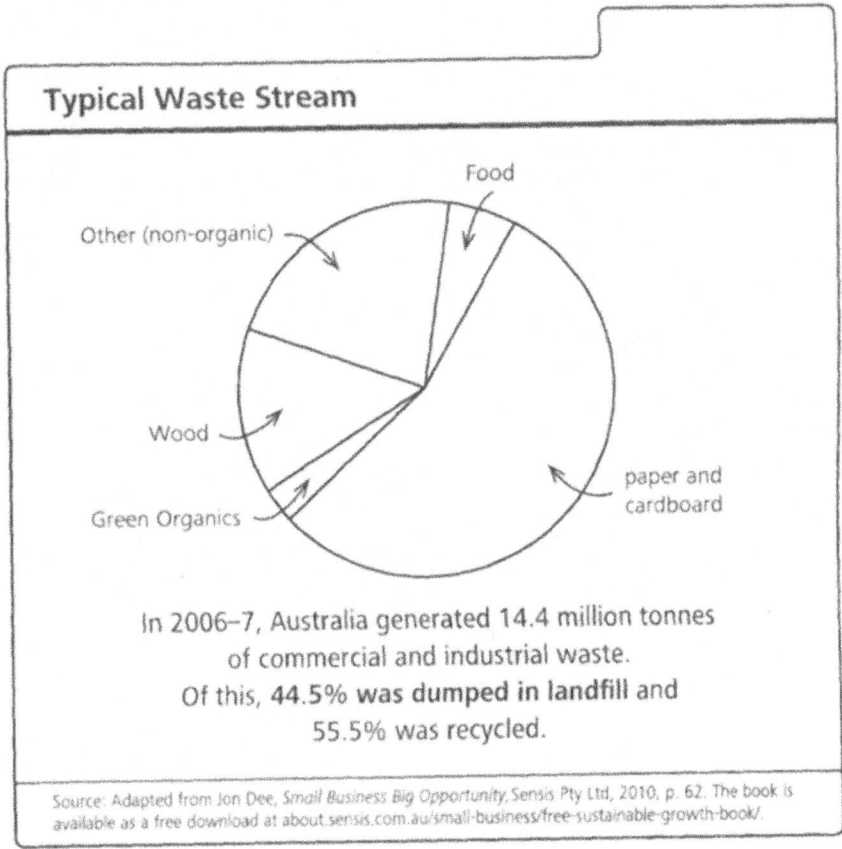

Typical Waste Stream

Other (non-organic)

Food

Wood

paper and cardboard

Green Organics

In 2006–7, Australia generated 14.4 million tonnes of commercial and industrial waste.
Of this, **44.5% was dumped in landfill** and 55.5% was recycled.

Source: Adapted from Jon Dee, *Small Business Big Opportunity*, Sensis Pty Ltd, 2010, p. 62. The book is available as a free download at about.sensis.com.au/small-business/free-sustainable-growth-book/.

Figure 2.11

use less by converting to electronic documents, invoices, bills, and copies. Reducing paper usage avoids forest depletion and shrinks the company's environmental footprint. It also helps the bottom line. Second, sort the paper waste so that it can be sold to recyclers instead of thrown into a landfill. This helps to convert an expense into a revenue stream, further helping the bottom line.

As with energy savings, avoiding paper waste depends on employee cooperation and engagement. Without that cooperation, policies and proclamations are futile. With it, companies can save tons of unwanted or unneeded paper and paper waste.

2.5 Benefit 5: Increased Employee Productivity

The team-consulting company Belgrade-Fisher-Rayner created an engagement model (see Figure 2.12) that shows how four factors combine to yield employee desire to strive above and beyond their defined role. Employees are committed to a project or overarching goal when

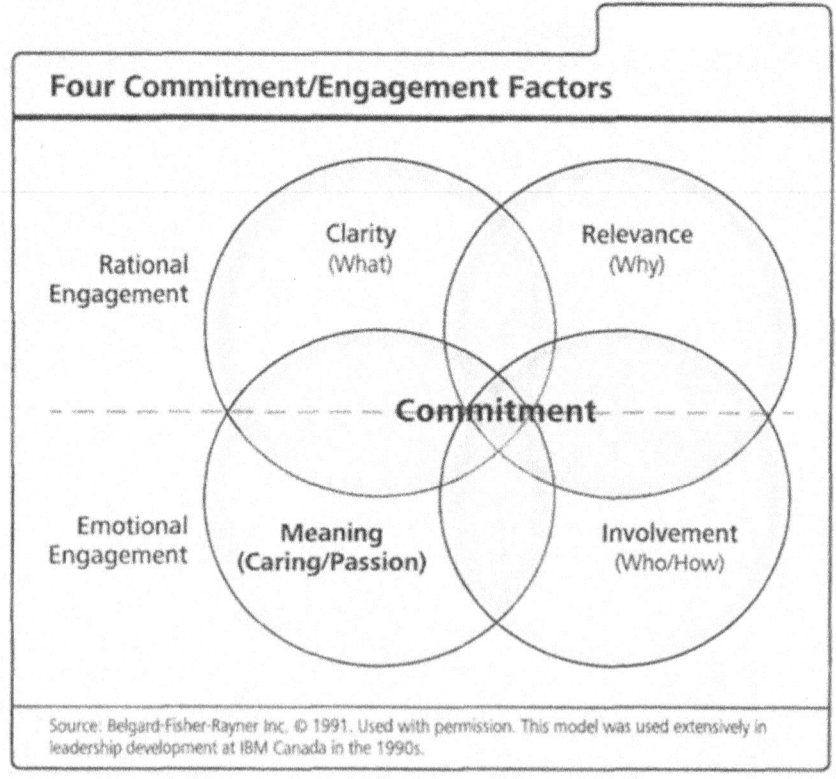

Figure 2.12

they understand what it is (Clarity); see how it benefits the company (Relevance); have a personal opportunity to shape and implement the initiative (Involvement); and find that it resonates with their personal values as a worthwhile goal (Meaning). Meaning is the energy source for the commitment. Through our work, we seek a sense of purpose, contribution, value, and hope. When we achieve fulfillment at work, we become fully engaged and innovate beyond our wildest dreams.

Visions related to sustainable development contain economic, social, and environmental dimensions — it would be difficult to find a more powerfully inspiring trio of aspirations. A company taking on an ambitious sustainability mission creates an energized, committed, and motivated workforce that is more productive and innovative. Zero emissions, self-sufficient energy production, zero waste, and restoration of the social and environmental health of the planet are powerful vision elements for a company.

2.5.1 Engagement Drives Business Results

The reason companies want engaged employees is that they want better business results. Happy employees are a convenient by-product. As shown in Figure 2.13, there is clear evidence that high employee engagement is related to improved organizational results.

A Gallup Consulting study of data from over 152 organizations contrasts the upside of having an engaged workforce with the downside of having a disengaged workforce. As shown in Figure 2.13, Gallup compared the performance of companies in the top quartile of companies with engaged employees with the performance of companies in the bottom quartile with disengaged employees. There was a dramatic difference between the top and bottom quartile companies' track records in safety incidents, employee turnover, and absenteeism. More importantly, Gallup found that companies with highly engaged workgroups have 18% greater productivity and 12% higher profitability than organizations with lower engagement in their same industry, as well as 2.6 times the earnings-per-share growth rate.

Companies that connect people to their passions and enable them to make a significant contribution to causes they care about as human beings will see a direct correlation to higher levels of engagement and significant business benefits. According to a WorkUSA survey, companies with engaged employees experience a 26% higher revenue per employee, 13% higher total returns to shareholders, and a 50% higher market premium.

Companies want lower absenteeism, lower employee turnover, and fewer safety incidents. They also want higher customer satisfaction, higher employee productivity, greater profitability, and faster growth. These benefits come from more engaged employees and sustainability efforts contribute to that higher level of engagement. CEOs who want to improve their companies' hard business results would be well advised to focus more on soft, meaningful, impactful sustainability efforts.

Before sustainability-related contributors to employee productivity and innovation is explored, we set the stage by elaborating on how:

- Engagement enables productivity and innovation
- Sustainability programs promote productivity and innovation
- Volunteerism vaults employee engagement and productivity

2.5.2 Engagement Enables Productivity and Innovation

If we are to assess the connections between purpose and employee engagement, between employees' engagement and productivity, and between innovation and business results, we need to know how we would recognize an engaged employee if we saw one.

Hewitt Associates provides a helpful definition of engagement, as shown in Figure 2.14: The "Say" behavior helps to attract top talent to the organization through word of mouth; the "Stay" behavior mitigates attrition of top talent who are already working in the company. The "Strive" behavior drives productivity and innovation as employees "strive to achieve above and beyond what is expected in their daily lives." It is the "Strive" behavior that is of interest, since it connects with motivation, engagement, productivity, and innovation.

A survey by Greenomics in 2010 confirmed that 97% of executives believe innovation is important to becoming sustainable. It is essential in creating future value for the firm. When innovation is mentioned, many of us equate it with technological breakthroughs. It is softer than that.

Organizations do not innovate; inspired people to innovate, at all levels in the organization. A high-performance culture unleashes the creativity of people who are intellectually and emotionally committed to clear, relevant, and meaningful work that they helped shape. Whether the goal is to deliver greater value through innovative new products and services or to reinvent an entire business model, engaged and committed employees to figure out the best answers faster and more efficiently than external experts. All we need to do is provide a culture and environment within which human ingenuity can flourish.

Innovation and productivity are increasingly paired. By elevating engagement, we raise both. It's a two-for-one deal.

Engagement Helps Business Results

- Companies with engaged employees **grew profits three times faster** than competitors.
- Highly engaged organizations have **87% less staff turnover** and **20% better performance** than average.
- **Operating income** of companies with engaged employees **improved by 19% in one year** vs. a decline of 33% for companies with low levels of employee engagement.
- **59%** of engaged employees say their job brings out their most **creative ideas** vs. 3% of disengaged employees.

Source: "Engage: Inspiring Employees about Sustainability," World Business Council for Sustainable Development, August 2010, p. 6.

Engagement Drives Business Results

Difference between the top quartile of companies with actively engaged employees and the bottom quartile of companies with disengaged employees

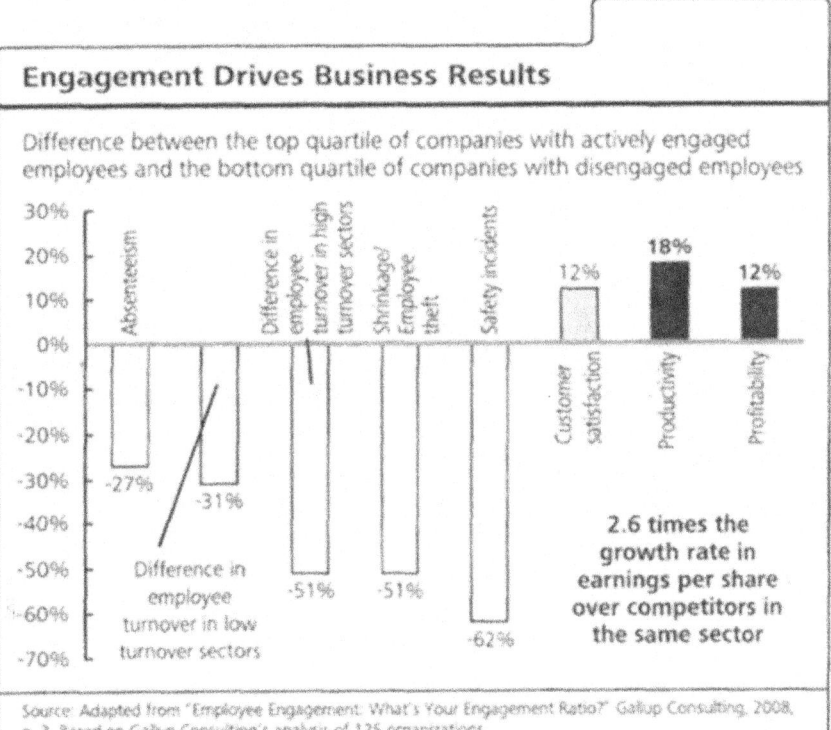

Source: Adapted from "Employee Engagement: What's Your Engagement Ratio?" Gallup Consulting, 2008, p. 3. Based on Gallup Consulting's analysis of 125 organizations.

Figure 2.13

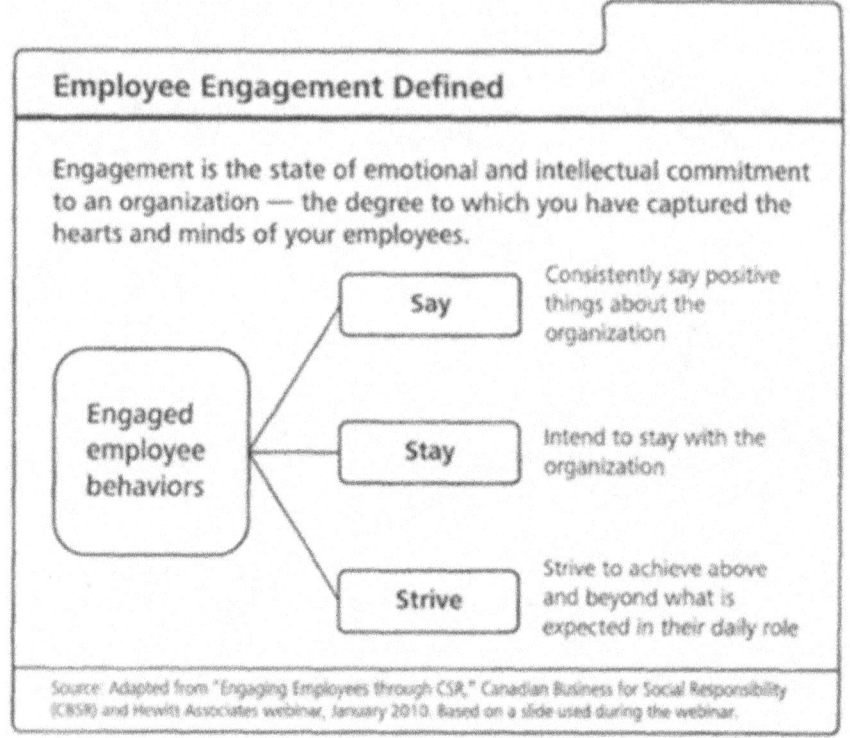

Figure 2.14

2.5.3 CSR Programs Promote Productivity and Engagement

In 2010, Hewitt Associates, the global human resources consulting company, partnered with Canadian Business for Social Responsibility (CBSR) to understand the relationship between employees' perceptions of their companies' corporate social responsibility (CSR) efforts, their level of engagement, and other work-environment factors. Hewitt and CBSR gathered opinions from over 100,000 employees send 2,000 leaders from more than 230 workplaces. A good CSR reputation is one of 21 factors that Hewitt has identified which correlate positively with employee engagement. The straight-line correlation (see Figure 2.15) shows that the more employees agree that their company is proactively pursuing worthy environmental and social activities, the more they are engaged. It is hard to prove a cause-and-effect relationship but, at a minimum, it is a happy correlation.

Hewitt's research found that CSR programs encompass the seven dimensions shown in Figure 2.15. In a sustainable enterprise, every employee is engaged, and sustainability efforts are measured, rewarded, and aligned throughout the firm, a reality addressed by the corporate

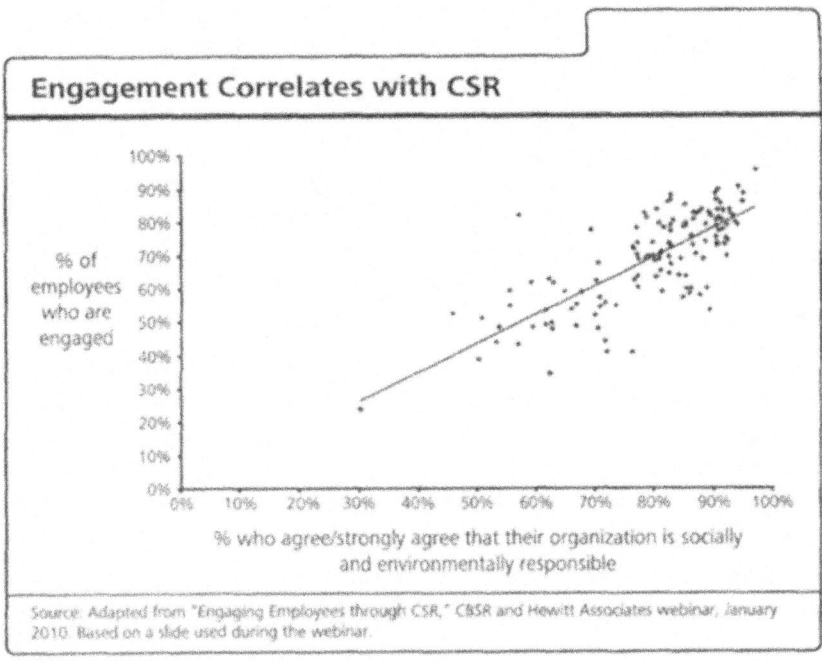

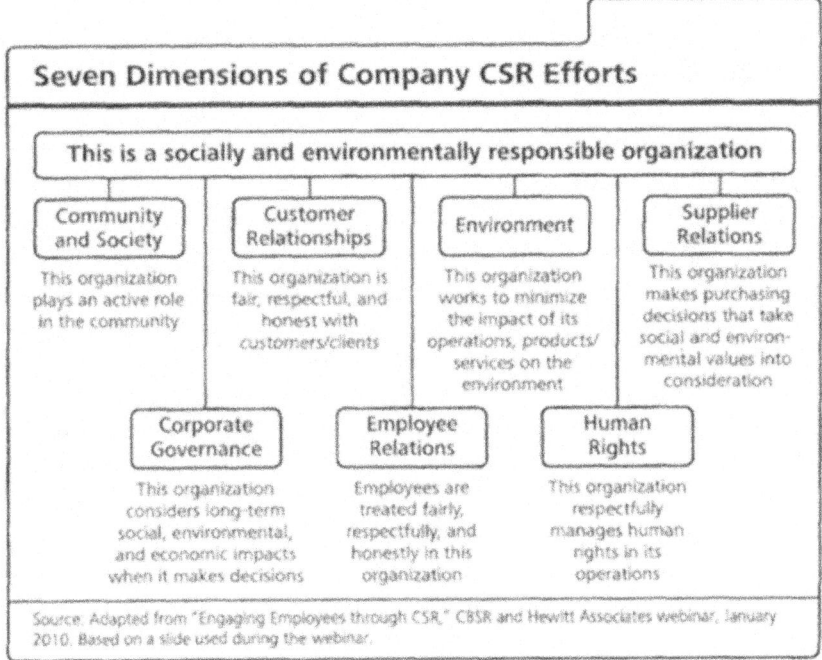

Figure 2.15

governance and employee relations dimensions. Equally important is the company's relationship with its customers and suppliers, including human rights issues within the firm. Programs that address the company's impacts on the environment and on the community provide opportunities for employee volunteerism (which we cover next).

Hewitt's seven dimensions provide a wonderfully holistic template for corporate CSR programs. They show that there is no magic silver bullet. A company needs to be strong in all seven areas to be deemed a good corporate citizen by its own employees.

Gallup has done extensive surveys and identified 12 factors that drive employee engagement. Most of the factors are about the job itself, such as opportunities to do what the employee does best every day and access to tools required to do the job well. Another factor is relationships at work — for example, being recognized in the last week by the managers.

Gallup's research, like Hewitt's, suggests that CSR is only one of many factors that drive engagement. However, it is gaining in importance, in concert with society's concern about sustainability issues and the role of corporations in helping to address them.

2.5.4 Volunteerism Vaults Employee Engagement and Productivity

Employee volunteer programs are an important part of the social dimension of a company's sustainability efforts. A surprise co-benefit when the company allows employees to give their talent, time, and energy to causes that they personally care about, and which align with the company's mission, is the volunteers' higher level of engagement and productivity back in the workplace. Two-thirds of workers surveyed in the UK said that having paid time off during working hours to commit to charity work would "significantly improve" motivation. In Ireland, a recent study found that 87% of employees who volunteered with their companies reported an improved perception of their employer. More importantly, a whopping 82% felt more committed to the organization they worked for.

The cause could be Habitat for Humanity, helping the homeless, tutoring

- Disadvantaged school children, a neighborhood cleanup campaign, helping a village abroad — anything worthy that allows employees to volunteer to help. Employees' engagement is fueled by their caring for the program's outcomes;

People find personal meaning when making a difference. Volunteers also feel fulfilled and energized when they see they are making a difference, and that energy transfers back into the work environment. In Corporate Karma, Peggie Pelosi tells about her experience at USANA, same employees, same customers, and same products — double the sales after the volunteer program was implemented. Pelosi cautions that the recipe for success is important.

When establishing a volunteer program, the cause must be carefully chosen. The company should ensure the purpose of the non-profit organization it allies with meshes with the firm's values and mission. The CEO, the board, even customers should participate, to reinforce its importance. Such an alliance needs to be a strategic initiative, more profound and enduring than a one-time intervention like helping the food bank at Christmas. Progress should be tracked and reported against declared meaningful goals to emphasize that this is a serious company focus.

In addition to increasing productivity, volunteer programs also develop employees' leadership capability, build new transferable skills, enhance loyalty and retention, stimulate innovation, engender trust in leadership, build a sense of camaraderie with interdepartmental colleagues, improve the business's community relationship, and reduce absenteeism. When the whole company becomes inspired by giving back, volunteer programs create employee engagement and improved business results.

2.6 Benefit 6: Increased Productivity from Reduced Absenteeism

Unplanned absenteeism costs much more than most companies realize and is often not well tracked or managed. There are large direct and indirect costs of high rates of absenteeism. When employees do not come to work, co-workers experience lost productivity, and there are costs associated with finding and paying for temporary replacements. We conservatively assume absenteeism costs 2% of payroll today.

Studies suggest 60% to 70% of employee absenteeism is due to reasons other than illness. The following are common reasons employees tend to miss work:

- Employees are stressed or preoccupied with personal matters, such as parental concerns, marital problems, community involvement, family well-being, care for elderly relatives, care for severely ill immediate family members, and so on.
- Employees are overwhelmed with their current working situation, or they are overworked due to workforce reductions and voluntary turnover.
- Employees are dissatisfied with their current working conditions, position, team performance, supervisor, or overall organization.
- Employees are not committed to their team, department, or organization,
- Employees are not challenged by their position and have increased feelings of burnout.

Employers can influence the approximately 60% of employee absenteeism, and the resulting loss of productivity, that results from personal matters by giving employees flexible work schedules and work-at-home options. These approaches help employees juggle stressful demands on the home front with workplace requirements. An employer can also directly influence the other main causes of absenteeism in the list by taking steps to improve employees' intrinsic motivation. For example, an employer might ensure production goals are realistic, increase desirable job responsibilities, and improve working conditions.

Governance policies that treat employees with respect and care make a difference to absenteeism rates, as do sustainability-related personnel policies. As just discussed, employees who volunteer through their workplace report improved physical and emotional health, as well as more positive attitudes toward their colleagues and company. We assume sustainability-related human resources policies and programs could create a high-performing company culture that will reduce absenteeism by 20%.

2.6.1 Increased Productivity from More Telecommuting and Less Travel

Exploiting the potential of e-business, e-mail, and secure intranets can significantly reduce the environmental impact of doing business. Telecommunications eliminate the need for many office workers to commute every day. Working from home offers benefits for the environment, the company, and employees.

The environment benefits from a reduction in vehicular emissions, less pavement, and more green spaces.

The company benefits through financial savings. Figure 2.16 shows that 40% of employees have jobs that are compatible with telecommuting and outlines, the financial benefits if just 100 employees work from home half the time It is assumed that 10% of employees could telecommute.

Employees benefit by eliminating the time, expense, and hassle of commuting. They may also experience a more enjoyable and relaxed working environment. Surveys show that 30% of employees would take a pay cut in order to telecommute and enjoy an improved, more discretionary balance between their work and personal lives. Employees who work half of their time out of the office save about two workweeks of commuting time and anywhere from $2,000 to $6,800 because they are using less gas and reducing parking, food, clothing, and other expenses. The needs of disabled workers are also often better addressed through telecommuting.

The icing on the cake is the potential for increased employee productivity. IBM Canada has seen teleworker productivity improvements of up to 50%. Reducing business travel to meet with clients or colleagues, or to attend conferences, and replacing it with teleconferencing and video conferencing also frees up more productive time during the workday. For most businesses, teleconferencing via the phone is already here. Videoconferencing, which uses digital video cameras connected to

Telecommuting Savings

At least 40% of employees have jobs that are compatible with telecommuting, but less than 2% of employees work from home the majority of their time. If the 80% of workers who want to telecommute did so — even if it was only half of the time — businesses could save $124 billion in real estate, electricity, and related costs; they could also increase productivity by more than $235 billion. Letting one employee work half of their time out of the office saves their company about $10,000 per year. Businesses that let 100 employees work half of their time from home can save about $1.1 million a year.

- $576,000 would come from increased productivity as employees experienced fewer interruptions, practiced better time management, and put in more hours by working when they would have been commuting.
- $304,000 would come from savings in electricity, real estate, parking lot leases, furniture, supplies, maintenance, and space consolidation.
- $113,000 would come from fewer unscheduled absences and less sick time, and from employees working while sick or waiting for personal appointments (cable installation, parcel delivery, etc.) that would normally result in a full day off work.
- $76,000 would be saved due to lower employee turnover.

Source: Kate Lister and Tom Hamish, "Workshifting Benefits: The Bottom Line," TeleworkResearchNetwork.com (TRN), May 2010, available at www.workshifting.com. The benefits are based on TRN's telework savings calculator, which assumes 50, 100, or 500 employees are teleworking half the time, as well as the total savings for the United States.

Figure 2.16

home and office personal computers, is widely available and effective, with potentially huge travel and pollution savings. A Carbon Disclosure Project study calculated that businesses in the United States and the United Kingdom could save $19 billion on travel costs between 2010 and 2020 by deploying 10,000 video conference/telepresence units. A co-benefit is a saving of 5.5 metric tons of carbon.

2.6.2 Increased Productivity from Green Buildings

Green buildings provide surprising increases in employee productivity. Paul Hawken, Amory Lovins, and Hunter Lovins, authors of Natural Capitalism, quantify productivity gains of 6% to 16% from people working in well-designed, energy-efficient buildings. The Green Building Council of Australia estimates that occupants are 1% to 25% more productive in green buildings. Joseph Room, the author of Cool 'Companies, calculates that productivity benefits due to workplace green design range from 7%

to 15%. In addition, Room notes a drop in sick leave and absenteeism. Since a typical office pays about 100 times as much for people as it does for energy, this increased productivity in people is worth 6 to 16 times as much as eliminating the entire energy bill.

Figure 2.17 shows how this productivity gain should be factored into the business case for green buildings. Gregory Kats at MIT found that four of the attributes associated with green buildings — increased' ventilation control, increased temperature control, increased lighting control, and increased day-lighting — positively and significantly correlate with increased productivity. Increases in tenant control over ventilation, temperature, and lighting each provide measured benefits ranging from 0.5% to 34%.

Mail sorters at the main US Post Office in Reno, NV, became the most productive and error-free in the western United States after a green energy and lighting upgrade in their building. The $300,000 upgrade produced $50,000 in yearly energy and maintenance savings and a whopping $400,000 annual productivity gain from employees.20 After VeriFone renovated its building, beating California's strict Title 24 building code by 60%, employees were 5% more productive, and absenteeism dropped by

Green Building Business Case

Financial Benefits of Green Buildings
Summary of Findings (per ft²)

Category	20-Year Net Present Value
Energy Savings	$5.80
Emissions Savings	$1.20
Water Savings	$0.50
Operations and Maintenance Savings	$8.50
Productivity and Health Benefits	$36.90 to $55.30
Subtotal	**$52.90 to $71.30**
Average Extra Cost of Building Green	**(-3.00 to -$5.00)**
Total 20-Year Net Benefit	**$50 to $60**

Source: Gregory H. Kats, "Green Building Costs and Financial Benefits," Massachusetts Technology Collaborative, 2003, p. 8. Data from Capital E Analysis.

Figure 2.17

45%. These benefits reduced the payback period from 7.5 years to less than a year, for a return on investment of more than 100%.

Given the 0.5% to 34% range of estimates of increased productivity for employees working in green buildings, we conservatively assume a 10% gain. Some employees may already be working in such facilities; some may never be able to. We very conservatively assume another 10% of the workplace can be greened within the next five years, so the resulting productivity gain is the product of those two percentages: 1%. We further conservatively assume only 10% of this 1% productivity gain is in addition to gains already counted, as explained later.

2.6.3 Increased Productivity and Innovation from Improved Collaboration

The whole is greater than the sum of its parts: success in the new economy is dependent on creative collaborative relationships. Successful companies collaborate with a broader network of interdepartmental colleagues and external stakeholders to invent breakthrough ideas so they can thrive in today's more complex economy.

In many large organizations, working relationships between departments verge on dysfunctional. Misaligned goals cause internal rivalry between organizational silos, wasting attention and energy that should be used to challenge the company's external competitors. The more opportunities interdepartmental staff have to get to know each other and work together for common purposes, the better they develop interdepartmental esprit de corps. Training programs, like the one for Marks and Spencer, help overcome interdepartmental friction as employees work together to accomplish worthy sustainability-related objectives. These cohesion-building opportunities have a beneficial spillover effect: departments continue to collaborate outside sustainability projects and innovate together to transform the firm's products, services, processes, and culture.

Wiki-savvy employees can tap into more possibilities of peer- and cyberspace-connected collaboration, sharing fresh and radical thinking through platforms that enable self-organized mass teamwork among internal and external stakeholders. The networked world provides new ways of navigating the white waters of change and complexity for the benefit of all. Employees find it is fulfilling to innovate and collaborate their way through the necessary transformation.

When sustainability is at the core of business and is connected to the conscience of an organization, it can be a platform for greater business growth and innovation, and an essential pillar of creative business partnerships. Now more than ever, strategic partnerships between industry and governments, academia, and non-government organizations (NGOs) are critical to finding solutions to challenges such as supply chain footprints, access to clean water, and harnessing renewable energy sources. The seeds of multi-stakeholder collaboration blossom in wonderfully innovative solutions to business challenges, with exciting co-benefits for our collective sustainability challenges. The resulting productivity gain from improved company-wide collaboration could be significant.

Marks and Spencer (M&S), the United Kingdom's largest clothing retailer, which has stated publicly that sustainability is critical to future business success, took top prize in the 2011 Guardian Sustainable Business Engaging Employees contest with its Plan A initiative. Plan A ("there is no Plan B") is designed to make M&S the world's most sustainable retailer. The company claims it is "the most successful motivational and change management programme ever delivered within M&S, enabling people from different parts of the business and functions to work together for a common goal."

By early 2011, Plan A had improved energy efficiency in stores by 19% and fuel efficiency for clothing deliveries by 30%. Carbon emissions were down by 20% per square foot. M&S had raised levels of sustainably sourced wood and fish to 72% and 62%, respectively.

The panel of judges for the Guardian award described the plan as "a solid mix of inspiration, incentives, and measurement" that would be embedded deeply into the M&S culture. For example, a proportion of director bonuses is based on their Plan A achievements and leadership, and "employee engagement" is one of 180 measurable sustainability commitments the company wants to achieve by 2015. Each of M&S's 690 UK stores has a Plan A champion, a volunteer who encourages colleagues to cut electricity consumption, reduce paper use,-and recover more waste. Stores are ranked each month to foster a sense of competition. On team days, champions meet to share ideas.

The company also seeks to engage its 76,000 staff at home by offering discounted solar technology, bikes, train fares, and eco-holidays. Employees could also claim a free energy monitor worth $50 and free attic insulation worth $400. Every employee can take one day a year, with pay, to work for a charity, and the company recognizes outstanding volunteer work.

New recruits often cite Plan A as the reason they're applying for work at the company, and store-level Plan A champions are increasingly moving into the company's management development program, allowing M&S to retain good, motivated talent.

In addition to enhancing employee engagement and interdepartmental relationships, Plan A generated $82 million additional profit in 2009-10, which M&S invested back into the business.

2.6.4 Increased Productivity and Innovation from Higher Engagement

Productivity improves when a company gets more and better results from the same workforce. Productivity also improves with innovation, as employees or others come up with more efficient ways to do the same work.

As discussed earlier, engaged employees are more productive and more innovative. This is good for business. When the current cohort of employees generates more output, the company avoids the cost of adding additional employees to the payroll in order to reap the same benefits. It also avoids the cost of hiring consultants to help find and capture the benefits. Less absenteeism, more telecommuting, and less business travel provide direct sustainability-related productivity benefits by allowing more time on the job and eliminating the need to hire more people to fill in for the lost time.

2.6.5 The War for Talent Still Rages

If only accountants agree with this CEO maxim: People are our most important asset. Employees are too often pigeonholed as an expense in income statements, rather than as assets on the Balance sheet Nevertheless, employees are vital human capital supporting company success, and companies compete fiercely to attract and retain the best and brightest talent.

In 1997, McKinsey, a management consulting firm, did a landmark study of 77 companies and almost 6,000 managers and executives to assess the importance of this issue. They found that the most important corporate resource over the next 20 years would be talent: smart, sophisticated business people who are technologically literate, globally astute, and operationally innovative. In 2001, McKinsey updated the study and found that, despite the economic slowdown, the war for talent was intensifying dramatically. Their update showed that 89% of those surveyed thought it was more difficult to attract talented people than it had been three years earlier, and 90% thought it was more difficult to retain them. McKinsey concluded that attracting and retaining talent was not just a valid desire — it was a business imperative.

In 2008, a third McKinsey report confirmed that the war for talent still rages. The report summarized findings from two studies. The first, in 2006, indicated that executives regarded finding talented people as the single most important managerial preoccupation for the decade. The second study, conducted in 'November 2007, revealed that nearly half of the respondents expect intensifying competition for talent — and the increasingly global nature of that competition — to have a major effect on their companies over the next five years. No other global trend was considered nearly as significant. Executives need to create strategies that nurture talent at all levels. Those value propositions should reflect what prospective employees seek.

2.6.6 A Sustainable Enterprise Is a Talent Magnet

Hiring top talent is one challenge; keeping it is another. Many employees have their periscopes raised to keep an eye out for more attractive corporate shores. However, employees who are highly committed to an organization work hard, are absent less often and are less likely to leave for a new job. A UK survey found that nearly half that country's workers were more likely to stay with an employer that allowed its workforce to "donate time or raise money for charities during working hours."

Survey after survey shows that the best people stay when they feel like valued contributors to company success, when their innovative ideas are solicited, when a profit-sharing scheme helps them reap personal benefits from their efforts to help the company do well, and when they are empowered, have career opportunities, and feel the company respects work-life balance issues as well as care for and contribute towards environmental and social causes. This is about the G in ESG. Exemplary governance includes human resources policies and practices that bring out the best in people.

For example, LoyaltyOne, the company that operates the Air Miles reward program, was selected as the Best Employer in Canada in 2011 by the Globe and Mail "Report on Business" because

- Its rate of staff turnover had dropped from 23% in 2008 to 11% in 2009
- The company's "associate engagement score," which measures "the extent to which [employees] are committed, motivated and actively involved in helping the company be successful," had improved from 79% to 85%
- 85% of employees had said they would recommend their employer "as one of the best places to work," up 6% from 2008.

Loyalty One attributes its culture of engagement to visible senior-leadership support for its sustainability initiatives; regular broadcasting of sustainability news using internal communication channels; contests with environmentally friendly products as prizes; education to help employees live greener at home; an annual environmental fair where external vendors bring in their catalogues and showcase their green products to staff; management support for grassroots green ideas; and a regular survey on employee engagement to ensure feedback opportunities. Publicity about these efforts helps attract top talent to the company.

2.6.7 Paying the Price for Voluntary Turnover

Involuntary turnover happens when companies downsize or encourage employees to find a better fit for their skills somewhere else. Voluntary turnover occurs when good people decide to leave, sometimes moving to competitors who lure them away. Voluntary turnover costs a company dearly. To calculate the cost, we multiply the number of employees who leave voluntarily each year by the costs associated with their leaving and replacement.

According to Comp data surveys of 5,300 participating HR departments, the average turnover rate in 2008 in the United States was 16.5% for the manufacturing sector, 24.4% for the distribution and warehousing sector, and 19.8% for the services sector, with an average of 18.7% for all sectors.

A company's sustainability strategies, behaviors, and reputation can save it a considerable involuntary turnover expense.

2.7 Benefit 7: Reduced Risks

There are only two reasons a company changes: it wants to capture opportunities and/or it wants to mitigate risks. That is, it is attracted to the carrot and/or it wants to avoid the stick. Convincing a company to fully embed sustainability into its strategies and operations therefore requires a compelling two-part business case. This case must include the risks of what might happen if the company does not take action, as well as the benefits it can reap if it does.

A successful company's carefully crafted strategies, operational processes, and product lines have served it well. There have to be very good reasons to mess with success. Sustainability champions need to show what the company will gain if it embraces sustainability-related strategies — which is what we have done with the first six Benefits — and they need to articulate the threats to the company if it does not.

Figure 2.18 shows the benefits reaped from smart sustainability strategies aligned with the "Capture Opportunities" part of the business case. The benefit of avoiding the risk of not being proactive on sustainability issues is aligned with the "Avoid Risks" component.

In financial reports, the income statement and balance sheet provide a rearview mirror snapshot of past performance. Management's discussion and analysis (MD&A) in the annual report is where management looks at future prospects. The risk section of the MD&A explains how various uncertain non-financial factors could significantly impact future success. In a sales situation, we sometimes use the FUD factor — planting seeds of fear, uncertainty, and doubt about what could happen if the proposed solution is not adopted. The risks help show that the Status quo is not a viable option.

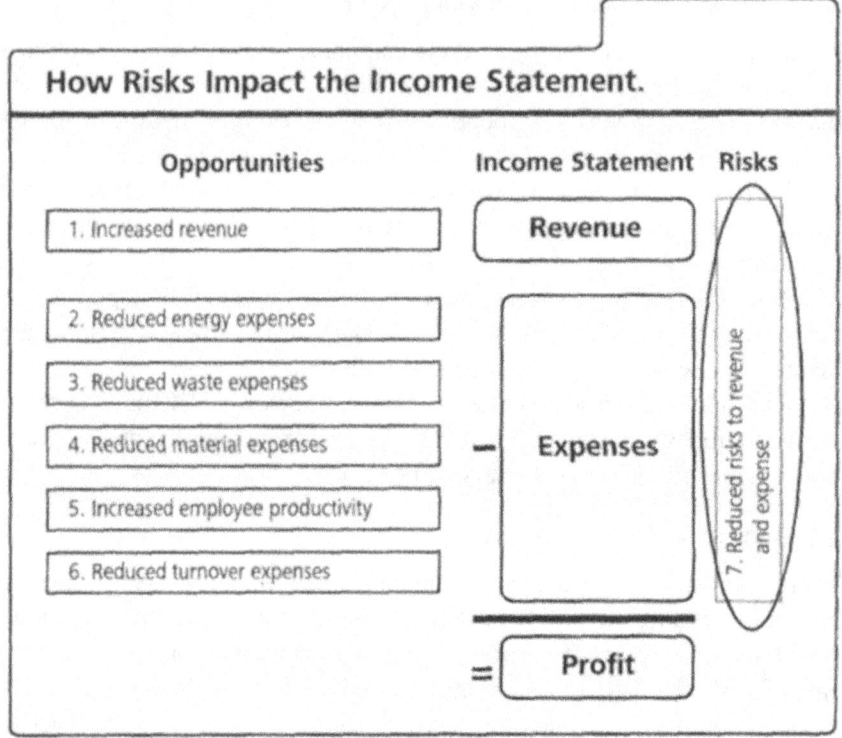

How Risks Impact the Income Statement.

Opportunities	Income Statement	Risks

Opportunities:

1. Increased revenue

2. Reduced energy expenses

3. Reduced waste expenses

4. Reduced material expenses

5. Increased employee productivity

6. Reduced turnover expenses

Income Statement: Revenue, − Expenses, = Profit

7. Reduced risks to revenue and expense

Figure 2.18

2.7.1 Aligned with the Standard Value Chain Framework

Figure 2.19 shows a standard, generic business value chain. It is based on several other value chain frameworks and captures the most important elements from each. Its components are what it takes for any company to be successful. It is generic — it applies to any for-profit company, in any industry, anywhere. Do you want to start a company? Do you want it to be successful? Be good at each link in the value chain, and you will succeed.

Following the chain from left to right, the company takes guidance from the market and develops the vision, goals, values, strategies, and systems that enable its success. If it is a manufacturing company, it makes quality products from raw materials, energy, and water. Companies in every sector want to attract, retain, and engage talented employees to produce and deliver their goods and services and to support customers. An unfortunate by-product of the company's operations is waste. On the other hand, if the company's products and services delight customers, the resulting revenue stream leads to the goal on the right-hand side — bottom-line profits.

Executives are continuously looking for ways to make the company's value chain more robust and resilient. Smart sustainability strategies and

The Standard Value Chain

Source: Based on Maurice Berns et al., "The Business of Sustainability," *MIT Sloan Management Review* Special Report, 2009, p. 21.

Value Chain and Sustainability Benefits

Source: Based on Maurice Berns et al., "The Business of Sustainability," *MIT Sloan Management Review* Special Report, 2009, p. 21.

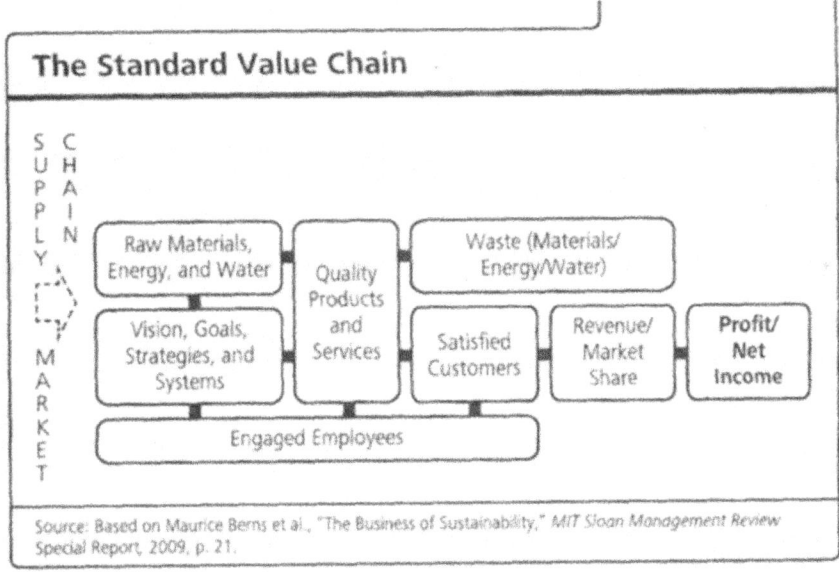

Figure 2.19

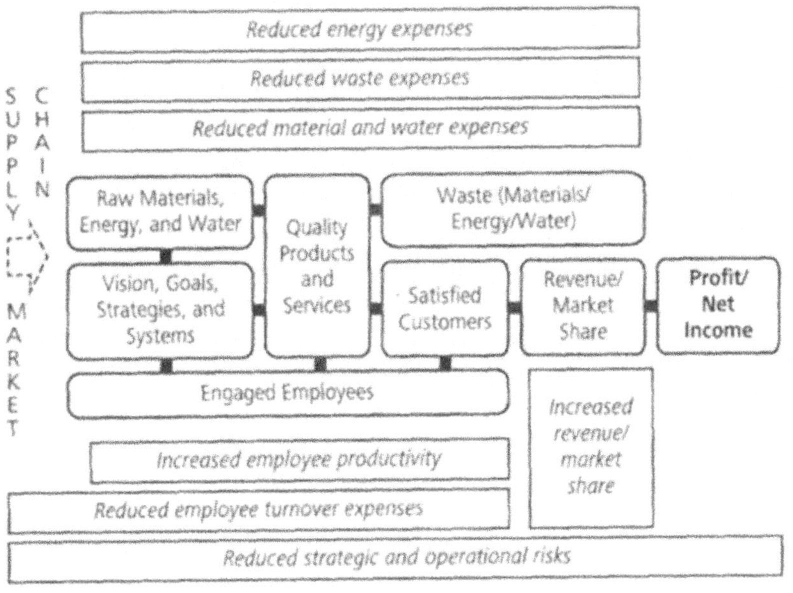

programs can help strengthen key links in the chain. Each of the seven benefits associated with strategic sustainability programs can be arrayed beside the link in the value chain that it most promotes, as shown in Figure 2.19.

Aligning sustainability-related benefits with the value chain framework makes it evident how and where each benefit strengthens important links. Being' able to relate the "so what?" of sustainability benefits to the standard value chain enhances their business importance. By showing how sustainability-related strategies lead to benefits that are helpful to key elements in their current business model, we gain executives' support and accelerate their adoption of sustainability-based approaches. We make sustainability relevant.

Figure 2.19 reinforces a fundamental insight: social and environmental initiatives are not something a typical company pays attention to out of the goodness of its heart — they are business imperatives if a firm wants a winning value chain in today's game of business. The benefit of sustainability initiatives is that they strengthen the links in the value chain. Their co-benefit is that they are also good for the environment and society.

2.8 Sustainable Consumption:

Sustainable consumption is the consumption of goods and services that have minimal impact upon the environment, are socially equitable and economically viable whilst meeting the basic needs of humans, worldwide. Sustainable consumption targets everyone, across all sectors and all nations, from the individual to governments and multinational conglomerates.

In the last 50 years, the global population has consumed more goods and services than the combined total of all previous generations (Tillard 2000). This growth in consumption has fostered economic growth, environmental degradation and improved the quality of life for many. However, consumption patterns differ significantly between developed and developing nations. Tillard (2000) notes that the richest one fifth of the world accounts for 86% of consumption whilst the poorest one fifth account for about one percent of consumption.

Current unsustainable consumption patterns are destroying the environment; depleting stocks of natural resources; distributing resources in an inequitable manner; contributing to social problems such as poverty; and hampering sustainable development efforts. Focusing on the demand side, sustainable consumption compliments sustainable production practices and achievements. At individual level, one should take responsibility for sustainable consumption in line with the recommendations at Section 1.9.

Sustainable consumption requires a multidisciplinary and multinational approach. Teams composed from various disciplines are required to create and implement policies. Developed nations need to assist rather than exploit developing nations.

The main barriers to sustainable consumption include: lack of awareness and training; lack of support from the community, government and industry; reluctance to include the true environmental and social costs in the price of goods and services; ingrained unsustainable thinking and behaviours patterns; and lack of alternative sustainable products and services.

Therefore, sustainable consumption requires the effort of everyone - individuals; government; non-government organizations; industry associations; educators; research institutions; decision makers; economists; business; industry; etc

2.9 Costs related to Sustainability benefits

Enormous benefits are possible when sustainability-related strategies are employed. But what the costs are in this cost-benefit analysis? Costs associated with sustainability initiatives are addressed in various.

First, funds for many sustainability efforts are already in line items in many companies' operating budgets. Companies have budgets for communication, maintenance, advertising, and education. New ways can be found to use those existing allocations, rather than suggesting that more money is required.

Second, sustainability projects requiring capital can be self-funded from savings from the reduced materials and waste benefits and can be used as a rotating pool of capital to fund sustainability projects. Many beneficial sustainability-related projects require amounts of capital too small to warrant board-level attention.

Third, companies can also take advantage of government grants and incentives for many sustainability projects. Early movers usually get the most grants.

Fourth, some capital projects may exceed the available funds through aforementioned savings, so they need to compete for the company's overall pot of available capital. Sustainability capital projects are approved the same way any capital project is approved. Companies only undertake capital projects that meet stringent payback periods and yield at least a minimum rate of return — the hurdle rate. If the capital has to be borrowed from an outside lending institution, loans for sustainability projects may receive a preferential rate. The business case assumes that the realization of the net benefits from sustainability-related projects is staggered over five years, to allow for various payback periods, so allowance for the impact of capital costs is built into the business case.

Fifth, many sustainability projects should be considered as investments rather than as costs. Other ways of enriching the bottom line pale in comparison to high-yield, low-risk investments in sustainability projects, especially when compared to how much more top-line revenue would have to be generated to have an equivalent impact.

Questions:

Discuss the many benefits of sustainability.

Chapter 3
Sustainability Strategies

3.1 Sustainability Strategies

As sustainability moves up the boardroom agenda, it is increasingly being integrated into corporate-level strategic planning. Management now needs to balance increased regulation, protecting the brand and ensuring stable supply chains with seeking opportunity for enhanced performance and using the sustainability agenda for strategic advantage.

Developing and integrating a detailed sustainability vision into your long-term strategic plan in a way that creates lasting value whilst also building public trust is a common challenge for all types of organizations.

The following should be considered for strategic sustainability:

- Identify your issues and goals to determine where the pressures are likely to be and raise awareness of what needs to happen to make your business more sustainable.
- Prioritize these issues from both a sustainability and commercial point of view. This will help you recognize and better manage risk, improve efficiency, revenue potential, growth and other opportunities.
- Map the short and long-term ambitions for your sustainability vision, assess the risks, and address any gaps in delivery.
- Support the alignment and integration of your sustainability vision into your overall corporate strategy.
- Develop and deliver a robust sustainability programme that includes prioritized initiatives, enablers, milestones, key performance indicators, and measurable targets.

What is becoming increasingly evident is that a sound sustainability strategy protects a company's reputation; it drives innovation and employee engagement, it satisfies consumers and attracts and retains top talent; it demonstrates compliance and leads to market differentiation - all key ingredients for long-term growth and profitability.

Among the key components of any successful sustainability strategy are:

- Elevate sustainability in company governance, including direct board oversight and accountability over environmental and social issues, more diversity and special expertise on boards, and linking executive and other employee compensation to sustainability goals;

- Robust regular dialogues with key company stakeholders on sustainability challenges, including employees, investors, NGOs, suppliers, and consumers;
- Open reporting on sustainability strategies, goals and accomplishments;
- Systematic performance improvements to achieve environmental neutrality and other sustainability goals across the entire value chain, including operations, supply chains and products.

Comparison of a Built-to-Last strategy with a strategy for Sustainability

Built-to-Last	Sustainable
Definition of Visionary	
A premier organization in its industry and one that (i) maintains a strong reputation (ii) contributes positively to society (iii) concentrates on building an enduring organization (iv) pursues core ideology and not just profit (v) adapts without compromising is core ideals (vi) commits to its mission and goals (vii) grows its own management (ix) hires according to its core ideology and (x) experiments strategically	An organization that (i) forms groups, that is, supports families and communities, not just employee and customers (ii) "right sizes" adjusting its resource consumption and production to be as small or large as necessary (iii) embraces diversity of all kind (iv) turns waste in to profit and does not dump in its neighborhood (v) evolves with generation of products, processes, and people (vi) does not buy on credit, using resources only to the level and at the rate that they can be renewed (vii) optimizes systems and not just its individual component (viii) has good metrics, and information symmetry and (ix) adapts quickly to changes to the environment, resources, and competition
Type of Leadership	
Clock builders, not time keepers, people who build on the organization's core value system instead of relying on great product ideas or their own charisma to achieve short-term results	Servant-leaders who are on both clock builders and time keepers, but who recognize how today's actions will serve the next generation
Leadership Focus	
Manage to the founder's core values, balancing quarterly profitability with perpetual viability	Connect with and manage to core values of broader global challenges (societal, economic, environmental and cultural) and not just those of the founder of the organization

Driving Business Goals	
Goals are clear, compelling, imaginative, tangible, achievable and bold, take revolutionary steps forward; guide strategy development and unify efforts, fuel progress, rally staff and require a real stretch. Trade-off goals are possible based on prioritization	Goals are optimistic, aspirational, achievable in five to ten years and personally actionable; connect to the core business and larger purpose; ignite individuals' passion in the organization; are incremental steps to solve a global human challenge and align with organizations' strength. No trade-off of goals as all four elements of sustainability – social, economic, environmental and cultural are essential
Organizational Culture	
Cult-like, wherein employees believe strongly in the company's core ideology and managers indoctrinate, or fire employees who do not fit; elitist, an arrogance of membership in such a visionary company, information held tight	Open, welcoming, transparent, and driven by a larger purpose; employees experience a confluence between personal and work lives; employees understand organization's roles in obligation to a larger world
Tools for Constant	
Product lines, profit strategies, cultural tactics, and organization structure can change but a core ideology should not	Ongoing STaR (Society, Technology, and Resources) mapping of changes; ongoing TEN (transparency of information, engagement of employees; and a network of suppliers; customers, investors and local and global community) cycle management; scenario analysis of how potential changes in STaR will effect SEEC (Social, econ omic, environmental and cultural) goals of one's strategy relative to organizational behavior.

Werbach, Adam, "Strategy for Sustainability," 2009, Boston, Harvard University Review

TABLE 3.1

3.2 Steps In Sustainable Strategy Formulation:

STAGE 1	STAGE 2	STAGE 3	STAGE 4
Viewing of Compliance as Opportunity	**Making Value Chains Sustainable**	**Designing Sustainable Products and Services**	**Developing New Business Modules**
Central Challenge	**Central Challenge**	**Central Challenge**	**Central Challenge**
To ensure that compliance with norms become an opportunity for innovation	To increase efficiencies throughout the value chain	To develop sustainable offerings or redesign existing ones to become eco-friendly	To find novel ways of delivering and capturing value which will change the basis of competition
Competency Needed	**Competency Needed**	**Competency Needed**	**Competency Needed**
i)The ability to anticipate and shape regulations	i)Expertise in techniques such as carbon management and life-cycle assessment	i)The skills to know which products or services are most unfriendly to the environment	i)The capacity to understand what consumers want and to figure out different ways to meet those demands
ii)The skill to work with other companies including rivals to implement creative solutions	ii) The ability to redesign operations to use less energy and water, produce fewer emissions and generate less waste	ii) The ability to generate real public support for sustainable offerings and not be considered as "greenwashing"	ii)The ability to understand how partners can enhance the value of offerings
	iii)The capacity to ensure that suppliers and retailers make their operations eco-friendly	(iii) The management know-how to scale both suppliers of green materials and the manufacture of products	
Innovation Opportunity	**Innovation Opportunities**	**Innovation Opportunities**	**Innovation Opportunities**
Using compliance to induce the company and its partners to experiment with sustainable technologies, materials, and processes	i)Developing sustainable sources of raw materials and components	i)Applying techniques such as biomimicry in product development	i)Developing new delivery technologies that change value-chain relationships in significant ways
	ii)Increasing the use of clean energy sources such as wind and solar power	ii)Developing compact and eco-friendly packaging	ii)Creating monetization models that relate to services rather than products
	iii)Finding innovative uses for returned products		iii)Devising business model that combines digital & physical infrastructure

TABLE 3.2

3.3 Steps in Sustainability:

Steps towards Sustainability:

Figure 3.1 *Steps toward sustainability*

The Figure 3.1 above shows steps towards sustainability. On the low end are organizations that are still focused on regulatory compliance and primarily concerned with avoiding legal liabilities and may view environmental issues as a source of additional costs and headaches. Organizations focusing on eco-efficiencies have discovered that saving resources not only helps the environment but also a financial bottom line. The focus of these two perspectives is internal. At some point, many organizations realize that being green can attract new customers or make their community more attractive. They use green marketing to differentiate themselves from their competitors. Both green marketing and eco-efficiencies focus on doing better. When organizations reach the level of sustainability, they balance their demand with what nature can provide. But some organizations can go beyond sustainability towards restoration and rebuilding what they have degraded.

3.4 Sustainability Planning

3.4.1 What It Is

Sustainability plans are plans developed by an organization or government to achieve goals that foster environmental, community, and financial sustainability. These plans set goals that are particular to the organization in question. The plan will also establish guidelines for achieving and measuring the impact of these objectives.

3.4.2 Why It Matters

Sustainability plans create a template for creating and implementing sustainability goals and measures. This plan will allow you to formalize and solidify what sustainability will look like at your organization.

Every organization is different, and so your goals and implementation will necessarily be tailored to your particular organization. Your goals should reflect the kind of work your organization performs. For instance, a vegetable processing company might find that they could make the biggest environmental and financial impact by reducing their water usage. This same goal would make less sense for a clothes retailer, who might instead focus on sourcing sustainable and ethically produced merchandise.

Similarly, your steps and timelines for meeting your goals should match the personnel and financial resources of your organization. While many sustainability measures will yield cost savings over time, they may require up-front funding that does not make sense for your organization in the near future. These goals might still be included, but will have a longer timeline and greater attention to financial impacts.

The measurement dimension of your plan should provide a way to account for the financial, environmental, and community impacts of the changes your organization undertakes.

Steps in Planning

- **Step One:** Write a vision or mission statement.
- **Step Two:** Research other organizations' sustainability plans and projects.
- **Step Three:** Identify areas that the organization can have a positive environmental, social or economic impact.
- **Step Four:** Outline specific goals and targets based on your review of your organization.
- **Step Five:** Determine how you will implement these goals.
- **Step Six:** Determine timelines for each goal.
- **Step Seven:** Decide what metrics you will use to measure your goals.
- **Step Eight:** Create a reporting plan.

Step One – Write a vision or mission statement

Consider what your overarching goal is in pursuing sustainability measures. What do you hope to achieve? How do your goals relate to your business operations and your strategic plan? Will your plan focus more on your organizational processes or its products, or will it do both? How do you imagine these plans will impact your employees and your community?

Another way to approach this is to identify the environmental issue that concerns you and build your sustainability mission statement around this. A paper company, for example, might have the following mission statement:

"Deforestation around the globe has serious environmental consequences. It can lead to a loss of wildlife habitat, accelerate climate change, and degrade local water systems. As a leading paper production company, Organization X is uniquely positioned to help address these problems. Organization X is committed to minimizing our impact on ancient forests worldwide. We will achieve this by sourcing responsibly, reducing processing waste, and working to change our customer's relationship with paper products."

This statement recognizes a serious environmental problem, acknowledges the role that the organization plays in this problem, and suggests three broad areas where the organization can make changes. Protecting ancient forests is the orienting view for the entire plan. The sourcing, production, and customer arenas that are identified in the next statement are essentially an outline or preview of the implementation portions of the plan.

Step Two – Research other organizations' sustainability plan and projects

Research what other similar organizations have done to green their operations. This can include both sustainability plans and specific projects they've undertaken. This will help you get a sense of what's achievable and provide templates that are specific to your industry. You can use your local chamber of commerce and other professional networks as a resource to for identifying these organizations.

Step Three – Identify areas that the organization can have a positive environmental impact

To better understand where you can take steps to reduce your environmental impact, sketch out your organization's processes, inputs, and outputs. This will require a broad knowledge of your organization's operations. You might also consult with middle managers and employees to get a more detailed sense of how your resources are being used, as well as where and how waste is generated. Also, include employee behaviors relevant to the organization (such as commuting) whenever possible.

You might also consider performing an energy audit, a waste audit, and measuring the carbon footprint of your business to see where changes are most needed. These evaluations could also be included as the first steps in your sustainability plan.

Step Four – Outline specific goals and targets based on your review of your organization

Review what you've learned about your organization's environmental footprint and consider what goals make the most sense for your operation. Having a mix of short and long-term goals will make your sustainability plan a living document that your organization can return to and revise over time.

You might decide to choose goals that tackle a broad spectrum of issues at your organization—everything from using reusable plates in the break room to installing solar panels – a scattered approach. Or you could tackle one or two large issues from different angles. Both approaches have their advantages – a thematic approach.

The scattered approach will improve your environmental impact on a number of fronts but may seem disconnected and hard to rally around. A more thematic approach can lend some coherence to discrete measures. For instance, your plan might set an umbrella goal of dramatically reducing energy usage, and then attack that problem from a variety of vantage points.

Step Five – Determine how you will implement these goals

Now that you have your goals, how will you achieve them? Consider the upfront costs of making these changes, potential future cost savings, and the time and labor that will be required. Estimate as best you can the environmental benefits of the changes you're considering. Compare the costs and time investment to the potential social and environmental benefits. Draft guidelines for meeting your goals. Be as specific as possible when deciding what steps need to be taken and who will guide their implementation.

Prioritize the goals that you find most compelling. These might be the goals that have the biggest impact, are easiest to implement, best fit your vision statement, or will save your organization the most money.

Step Six – Determine timelines for each goal

Develop timelines for each goal. For easily realizable goals, these may be short and concrete, while more complicated goals might have longer and more suggestive timelines. Regardless, it's good to start with some sort of schedule, and stagger goals based on your resources and their level of priority.

Step Seven – Decide what metrics you will use to measure your goals

You need to be able to determine whether or not you've achieved a goal. Review your goals and implementation steps to ensure that you have both a measurable goal and a means of measuring it. For example, if one of your goals is to reduce your organization's paper usage, you'll need to know 1) how much paper your organization uses now, 2) have a strategy for reducing that use, 3) a realizable and specific target for reduction, such as a 20% reduction, and 4) a way of determining if you've achieved that goal by your deadline.

While measurement is important, you may have some goals that have impacts that are hard to measure. Employee and customer education is one example. These are still important goals and may be measured in the alternative, less conclusive ways. For instance, you can track attendance numbers at sustainability training, or through more qualitative evidence.

Step Eight – Create a reporting plan

Include a plan for reporting your goals and achievements to employees and customers, if relevant. Decide on a direct and straightforward way to present a summary of your achievements. This might be as simple as assigning each goal one of three statuses: "achieved," "in progress," or "not on target."

This summary can be a powerful way to communicate to stakeholders your commitment to the environment and your community. It demonstrates that you've taken the time and resources to commit to your pledges. Be prepared to back up your reporting with facts about specifics goals. This will shield you from charges of greenwashing.

Going Further

- **Step One:** Create a sustainability or green team.
- **Step Two:** Communicate the plan and progress on goals to employees and stakeholders.
- **Step Three:** Evaluate, revise, and amend your plan.
- **Step Four:** Seek out local partners.
- **Step Five:** Continue to seek out inspiration and innovations.

Step One – Create sustainability or green team

Consider organizing a team of employee volunteers to manage and perhaps even write your sustainability plan. This will help you to engage employees in the process and make it easier to communicate those goals and guidelines to the entire organization. For more complicated plans, it's likely that you will need a team of people to implement your plan's guidelines. Using volunteers rather than assigning a team will make it easier to identify the people in your organization who are passionate about this topic.

Step Two – Communicate the plan and progress on goals to employees and stakeholders

Communicating your plan to your employees is key. Having a solid mission statement will help them to understand the rationale behind specific measures and their role in implementing those measures. Keep employees updated on progress towards goals and revisions to the plan. It may also help to solicit feedback, particularly for goals that the organization has trouble meeting.

Consider also communicating your plan and progress towards goals to outside stakeholders. This could be one piece of a larger marketing strategy.

Step Three – Evaluate, revise, and amend your plan

It's likely that your plan will not be perfect in its first iteration. This is not a problem in and of itself; it is a problem if you persist with a plan that clearly isn't working. This suggests to employees and other stakeholders that your commitment to sustainability is not serious. Identify areas that need improvement. Some goals may simply not be realizable and will need to be bracketed for the time being. Other goals may need revised timelines or more modest targets. In some areas, you may be doing better than expected and can set more aggressive goals. Seek out feedback on how to meet goals that are lagging.

Step Four – Seek out local partners

You are probably not an expert on environmentalism, and that's fine! Seek out people who are. You might find that the best way to meet your goals— or even to define those goals—is by partnering with relevant community organizations that can collaborate with you on specific projects.

Step Five – Continue to seek out inspiration and innovations

Be open to researching new strategies, technologies, and products. The fields of green technology and environmental science are constantly changing. If you've identified a problem you don't have a solution for, don't simply strike that problem from your list of goals. Keep it on the back burner. A few years from now, there might be a more affordable or easier to implement a solution than is available now.

3.5 Sustainability Strategies are smart business strategies:

Sustainability strategies give companies a sustainable competitive advantage. The business benefits are quantifiable and real — the return on investment from aggressively improving company-wide sustainable development knowledge and initiatives makes other traditional investment opportunities seem trivial. Whichever company captures these benefits soonest has a significant competitive edge. Companies that ignore this reality are squandering easily achieved bottom-line benefits. Sustainability is a race to the top.

Corporations handle sustainability quite differently than organizations (facilities and suppliers). Corporations place sustainability into strategy; organizations place it into the work tasks that people do every day. Corporations depend on "initiatives," but facilities measure the processes that have sustainability built in, not bolted on. Corporations write reports, facilities look at their sustainability results and seek to continually improve. Their perspectives are quite different and will always be different. The trick is to see how a corporation can get its facilities, suppliers and other departments at the corporate level to work together.

The larger the group (corporations), the more they need to use a common management system that is transparent to all and measured with true leading indicators (e.g., Baldrige Program) and maturity matrices. This has been proven at the City level. Examples are posted on the Internet (Coral Springs, FL and Irving (TX). Sustainability should not be managed separately from the rest of the business but part of the total corporate strategy.

Saving the world and making a profit is not an either/or proposition. It is a both/and proposition. Good environmental and social programs make good business sense. Benefits from more aggressive and creative attention to environmental and social projects create a win/win/win approach for the corporation, society, and the planet.

Addressing environmental and sustainability issues in a systematic way provides new opportunities to focus on core business objectives such as reducing hiring and retention costs, improving productivity, reducing expenses at manufacturing and commercial sites, increasing revenue and market share, reducing risk, and increasing profit. That is why CEOs want to fully embed Sustainability into their company's strategies and operations, as shown in Figure 3.2. It is smart business.

Significant CEO Mindset Shift

CEOs Agree /Strongly Agree that sustainability should be	2010	2007	2010 Increase Over 2007
... fully embedded into company strategy and operations	96%	72%	24%
... discussed and acted on by boards	93%	69%	24%
... fully embedded into subsidiaries' strategies and operations	91%	65%	26%
... embedded throughout the global supply chain	88%	59%	29%
... the basis for industry collaborations and multi-stakeholder partnerships	78%	56%	22%
... incorporated into discussions with financial analysts	72%	51%	21%

Source: Adapted from UN Global Compact-Accenture, "A New Era of Sustainability," June 2010, p. 32. Based on findings from a survey of 766 CEOs worldwide, including 50 in-depth interviews.

Figure 3.2

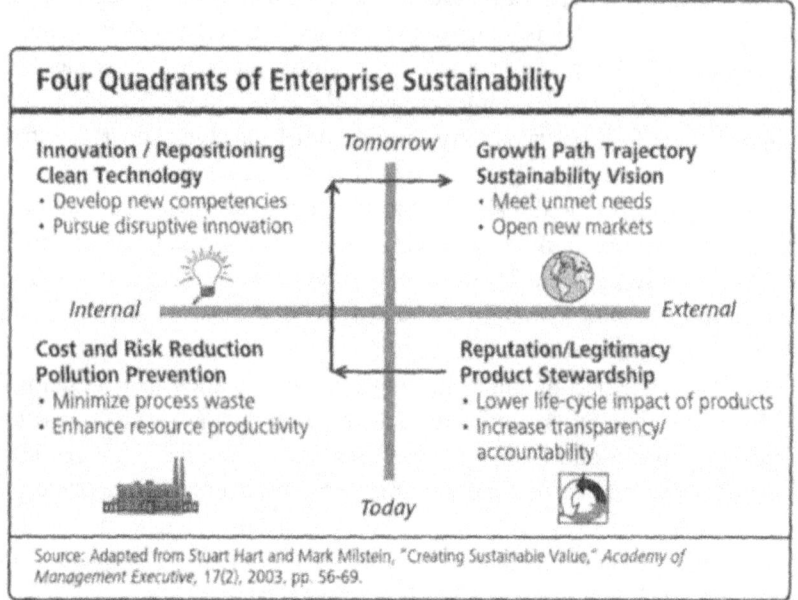

Four Quadrants of Enterprise Sustainability

Innovation / Repositioning
Clean Technology
· Develop new competencies
· Pursue disruptive innovation

Tomorrow

Growth Path Trajectory
Sustainability Vision
· Meet unmet needs
· Open new markets

Internal ———————————————— *External*

Cost and Risk Reduction
Pollution Prevention
· Minimize process waste
· Enhance resource productivity

Reputation/Legitimacy
Product Stewardship
· Lower life-cycle impact of products
· Increase transparency/
accountability

Today

Source: Adapted from Stuart Hart and Mark Milstein, "Creating Sustainable Value," *Academy of Management Executive*, 17(2), 2003, pp. 56-69.

Figure 3.3

One way to portray the evolution of company attention to sustainability is shown in Figure 3.3 Companies begin improving their legitimacy and image simply by ensuring they and their suppliers comply with human rights, environmental, and health and safety regulations in all their operations. Then they capitalize on eco-efficiencies to save money on their energy, water, materials, and waste bills. The exciting part is in the upper two quadrants. Companies practice disruptive innovation, reinvent their products and processes to improve their green attributes, and then take them to current and new underserved markets in the top right-hand quadrant.

In this chapter, we expand these four quadrants into a more granular five-stage journey. First, we set the table for the buffet of Sustainability benefits by clarifying terminology, frameworks, and our premise.

3.5.1 The Premise

Because companies are "for profit," they are required to ensure their bottom lines are healthy enough to allow them to continue operating. We need to equip enlightened executives with compelling numbers that show that sustainability-related strategies are smart business — that the company can do, better by doing good; that a more responsible form of capitalism generates higher profits. They know that superior environmental and social performance leads to more goodwill with the company's important stakeholders listed in Figure 3.4. They also know that sustainability strategies improve revenue and reduce costs.

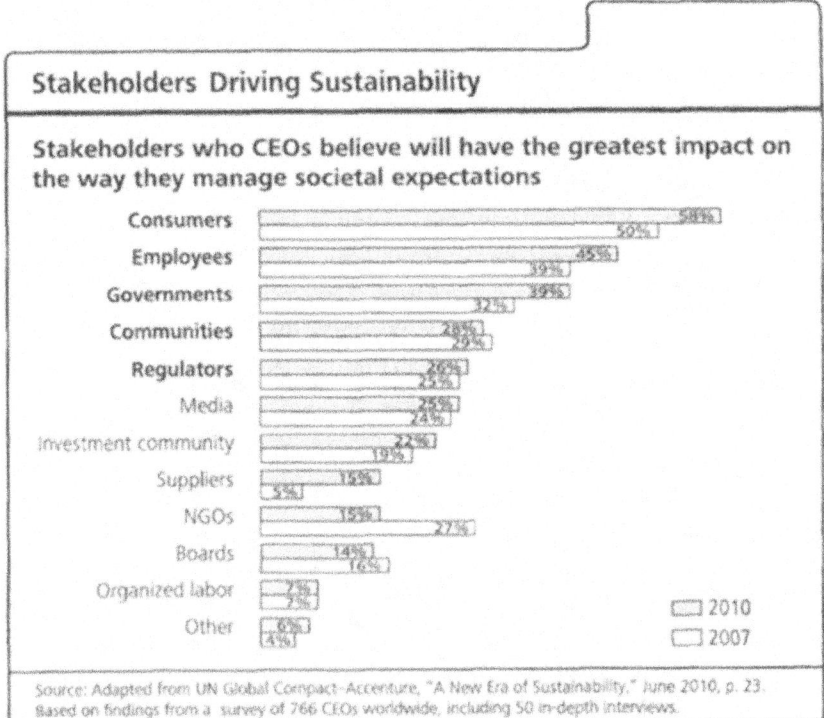

Stakeholders Driving Sustainability

Stakeholders who CEOs believe will have the greatest impact on the way they manage societal expectations

Consumers
Employees
Governments
Communities
Regulators
Media
Investment community
Suppliers
NGOs
Boards
Organized labor
Other

☐ 2010
☐ 2007

Source: Adapted from UN Global Compact-Accenture, "A New Era of Sustainability," June 2010, p. 23. Based on findings from a survey of 766 CEOs worldwide, including 50 in-depth interviews.

Sustainability Drivers for CEOs

Top drivers of CEOs' action on sustainability issues

Brand, trust, and reputation	72%
Potential for revenue/ growth/cost reduction	44%
Personal motivation	42%
Consumer/customer demand	39%
Employee engagement and recruitment	31%
Impact of development gaps	29%
Regulatory environment	24%
Pressure from investors	12%

Source: Adapted from UN Global Compact-Accenture, "A New Era of Sustainability," June 2010, p. 20. Based on findings from a survey of 766 CEOs worldwide, including 50 in-depth interviews.

Figure 3.4

To be convincing, we need to ensure we are talking the language of senior executives. We must quantify the benefits of a revolutionary transformation to a more sustainable and profitable business model in the new economy. We need to meet the executives where they are, use familiar frameworks to show the relevance of sustainability-related strategies to today's priorities, and show how the company can position itself to capitalize on going further on its sustainability journey.

The time has come to dispel the notion that being green is bad for business. If saving the planet is not reason enough, there's another incentive for companies to contribute to sustainable development — it boosts profits.

3.6 Unsustainable Take-Make-Waste Business Model

Overconsumption and poor resource management have resulted in the unsustainable use of natural and social capital. Climate change puts further pressure on natural systems, upon which all our social systems and economies depend. We have limited time to avoid a global tipping point that could impact all of humankind, including future generations, adversely and permanently.

Today's business model encourages companies to relentlessly deplete the natural capital that companies and communities require for their food, water, energy, and materials. Companies contribute directly or indirectly to systematic over-extraction and degradation of nature by physical means, such as deforestation, overharvesting of fish stocks, and depletion of farmlands. Nature is resilient and self-regenerative, but there is an ecological tipping point beyond which it cannot recover from this abuse. We are eating and fouling our own nest.

Excessive waste accumulates from things we dig up. Extractive businesses like mining and oil-and-gas companies notoriously leave tailings and other waste behind. Refineries, smelters, and manufacturing plants create more air, water, and soil pollution. When we burn natural resources for fuel, more waste is produced. Further, Earth's air, water, and soil are treated as dump sites by companies and their customers. Nature cannot absorb our pollutants fast enough to avoid their buildup. We must do a better job of managing those waste thresholds, or we risk drowning in our own garbage.

Moreover, the current business model interferes with peoples' needs being met. Many business models today contribute — directly or indirectly — to abuses of political or economic power that mean people don't have access to the clean air, potable water, nutritious food, adequate shelter, and quality of life they need. Today's business model encourages overconsumption by the haves at the expense of the have-nots. It is unsustainable.

Therefore, today's take-make-waste business model, shown in Figure 3.5 is no longer feasible. It violates all four of The Natural Step's system conditions for a sustainable society stated above.

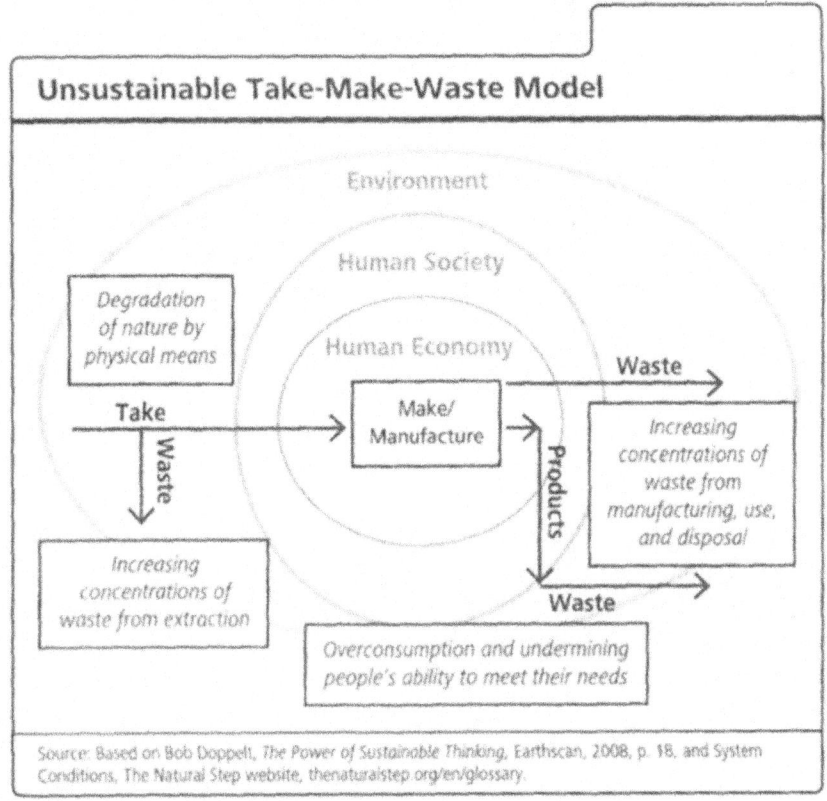

Figure 3.5

3.6.1 The Curse of Growth

Prosperity without Growth? was the title of a 2010 report from the Sustainable Development Commission that offers creative alternatives to continuous growth. As outlined in Peter Victor's book 'Managing Without Growth' shows how the growth imperative has failed us. According to him, rich countries should turn away from economic growth as the primary policy objective and pursue more specific objectives that enhance well-being:

   i.   Continued worldwide growth is unrealistic due to environmental and resource constraints

  ii.   Rising income increase happiness and well-being only up to a level that has since been surpassed in rich countries.

 iii.   Economic growth has not brought full employment, diminished poverty or reduced the burden of the economy on the environment.

Richard Heinberg's book 'The End of Growth' goes further and shows why continuous growth is blocked by resource depletion, environmental impacts, and rising levels of debt.

In today's conventional business model, growth is a given, an imperative. "Grow or die" is the maxim of business leaders. The stock market punishes companies that do not meet growth expectations. Growth is good. Since growth is synonymous with progress and with winning in today's game of business, we need to show how sustainability strategies are relevant and support companies' growth goals.

Continuous growth is at odds with sustainability principles. We know that it is inherently unsustainable, given the finite carrying capacity of the planet. In medicine, continuous growth is called cancer, but this analogy is the elephant in many board rooms, something managers don't talk about. Passionate, principled champions of sustainability find it repugnant to help companies grow, because it is against their core values to do so. That is why some shy away from the "sustainable development" label — development implies growth, and continuous growth is unsustainable. So, "sustainable development" is an oxymoron?

Not necessarily. Sustainable, enterprises decouple revenue growth from depletion of natural resources and creation of waste and pollution. Their products and services improve the quality of life for their employees, customers, and the communities they serve. They grow while decreasing their ecological and social footprints. Their rate of material throughput — the metabolism of the industrial system — does not endanger society, prosperity, and quality of life.

Sustainable companies can nudge unsustainable competitors off the playing field because they spend less on resources and grow their revenue faster. That is a good thing. However, at some point, even the continuous growth of more sustainable companies will be problematic. The planet cannot sustain the growing demand for its non-renewable natural capital nor can it continue to absorb more and more waste. Unless companies are resource, energy, and water neutral, and produce zero waste and zero pollution, we overshoot the carrying capacity of the planet.

3.6.2 The Curse of Overconsumption

Consumption is the root cause of growth since companies grow when the demand for their products grows. However, overconsumption is the second elephant that no one in the board room is talking about. A UN report warns that by 2050, humans could triple the amount of natural resources they consume unless economic growth is decoupled from resource use and current consumption rates. Warning that global population growth and rising economic prosperity could drive resource consumption far beyond what is sustainable on a finite Earth, the report states that nations must improve their rate of resource productivity — in other words, do more with less.

When consumption takes on a life of its own, we risk overshooting the carrying capacity of the planet.

3.7 A Sustainable Business Model

It is one thing to criticize the dominant take-make-waste business model a sustainable; it is another thing to design a model that is sustainable. As sustainability champions, we need to have a positive vision of the pot of gold at the end of a sustainability rainbow — a vision that does not depend on continuous growth and overconsumption. Here are five characteristics of a sustainable, cyclical, borrow-use-return business model that is better for the environment, society, and the company (illustrated in Figure 3.6).

1. Radical resource productivity. Companies stretch natural resources by increasing productivity for a given amount of a resource by factors of 4, 10, or even 100.
2. Investment in natural capital. Companies protect and restore ecosystems to sustain societal and business needs. They decouple economic growth from depletion of the global commons.

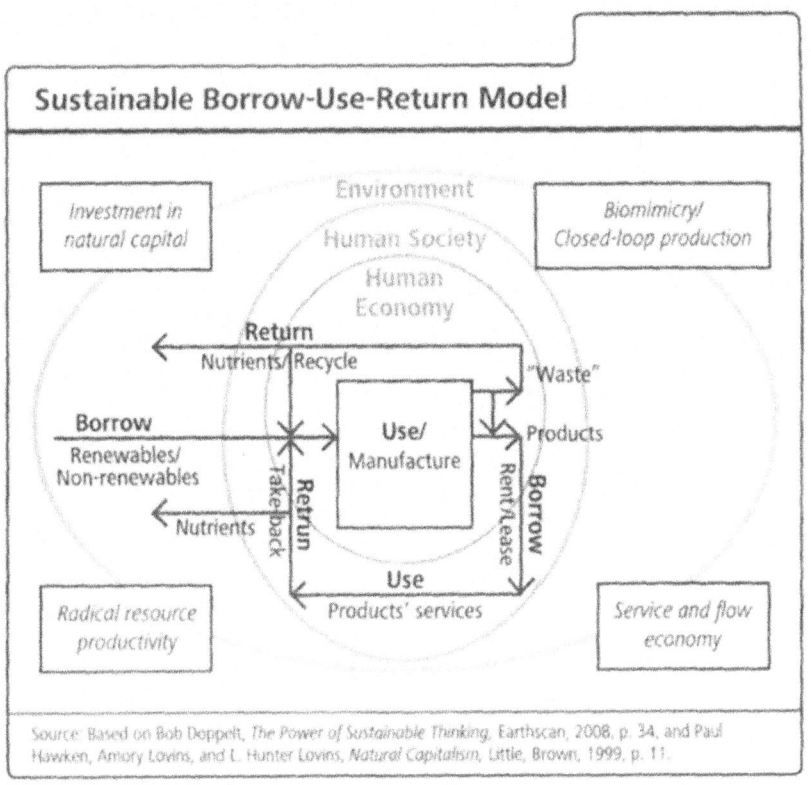

Figure 3.6

3. Ecological redesign. Companies eliminate human-made toxic chemicals from their production processes, minimize the use of resources and energy, use closed-loop production systems, and decrease waste and harmful emissions.
4. Service and flow economy. When products become obsolete or unable to perform their intended service, the company takes them back and recycles or remanufactures the returned products.
5. Responsible consumption. Responsible consumption reduces the demand for stuff and its associated pollution. Consumers make better-informed decisions based on a product's place of origin, the labor conditions under which it was made, its ingredients, it's packaging, its life-cycle ecological footprint, and other sustainability-related criteria.

New forms of company ownership and profit-sharing ensure company success is more equitably distributed. Resilient, locally owned enterprises-are more accountable and devoted to serving community needs. Ethics, fairness, and transparency are baked into day-to-day governance systems, partnerships, community relations, and employment practices. Employees are treated like valuable contributors to the company's success, and reward and recognition systems are aligned to encourage environmentally and socially responsible decisions and behaviors. Figure 3.6 above shows Borrow-Use-Return Model.

Such a model is a win-win-win for the environment, society, and the company. The company helps restore the economic, ecological, and social health of the planet. And it makes more profit. The business case for sustaining the planet is stronger than the business case for trashing it.

Energy Savings at IBM

In 2010, IBM had 2,100 energy conservation projects at 299 locations that delivered savings equal to 5.7% of the company's total energy use versus the corporate goal of 3.5%. These projects avoided more than 139,000 metric tons of CO_2 emissions and saved $29.7 million in energy expenses.

Between 1990 and 2010, IBM saved 5.4 billion kWh of electricity consumption, avoided nearly 3.6 million metric tons of CO_2 emissions (equal to 52% of the company's 1990 global CO_2 emissions), and saved $399 million through its annual energy conservation actions.

Source: "Energy and Climate Programs" [accessed July 30, 2011], IBM.com.

Figure 3.7

Top 10 Business Priorities for 2011

Category	Top Two Priorities by Category	Percentage Selecting
Growth	Grow overall company revenue	64%
	Acquire and retain customers	54%
Efficiency	Lower the firm's overall operating costs	44%
	Improve quality of products and/or processes	37%
Innovation	Improve our ability to innovate as an organization	32%
	Drive new market offerings or business practices	28%
Talent	Acquire and retain talent	38%
	Improve workforce productivity	31%
Transparency	Comply with governance regulations and requirements	14%
	Improve corporate environmental sustainability and social responsibility	10%

Source: Christopher Mines, "Sustainability Doesn't Sell ... or Does It?" [accessed July 30, 2011], GreenBiz.com. Based on Forrester's survey of 2,691 executives in Europe, North America, and Asia, in "Forrsights Business Decision-Makers Survey, Q4 2010."

Figure 3.8

3.7.1 Aligned with the Income Statement Framework

We need to make it easy for CEOs, CFOs, and other numbers-oriented executives to see how sustainability strategies contribute to the firm's success. That is, we need to connect the dots between a typical financial statement and the benefits that can be realized from smart environmental, social, and governance (ESG) approaches and programs. Aligning sustainability benefits with income statement elements helps executives see how sustainability initiatives are relevant to their current financial priorities.

Figure 3.8 shows the basic elements of an income statement, also known as a profit-and-loss (P&L) statement. Accountants use three categories of expenses.

- Cost of goods sold (COGS), which includes the costs of acquiring and producing the inventory of goods/products that the company sells
- Selling, general, and administrative (SG&A), which include the costs of running the company
- Interest, tax, depreciation, and amortization (ITDA)

A manufacturing company would realize the biggest savings from sustainability initiatives in its COGS expenses, which include the cost of labor, energy, water, and material to acquire and produce the goods it sells. A services company would see most of the savings from sustainability initiatives in its SG&A expenses since COGS are much less significant

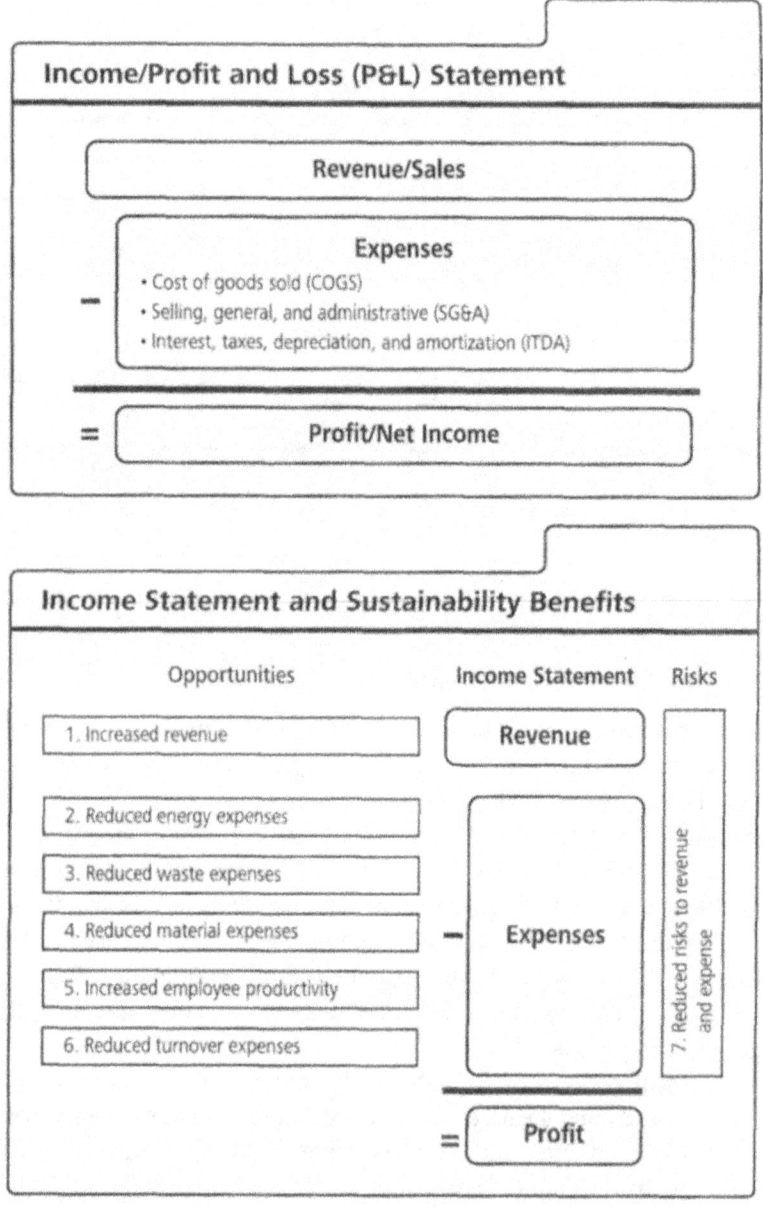

Figure 3.9

for a non-manufacturing company. For our purposes, we do not need to differentiate between COGS, SG&A, and ITDA, so we combine them into one group of "Expenses."

Each of the seven benefits associated with smart sustainability strategies can be aligned with the element of the income statement that it most affects, as shown in Figure 3.9. The graphic makes evident how each benefit contributes to a more positive profit. Being able to relate the "so what?" of sustainability benefits to the income statement enhances the credibility of sustainability champions.

The income statement is the framework that we use in the business case for sustainability. It determines the flow of the benefits that we examine. We start by looking at how sustainability-strategies improve top-line revenue opportunities; then we monetize, the benefits of reducing expenses and mitigating risks that might jeopardize profit.

3.8 Impact Assessment

Impact assessment examines the relationship that your organization has with the environment, the society within which it operates, your customers, suppliers and other members of your industry. In short, it is an examination of what you take from the environment and society, what you do with what you take, and what you contribute in the end (both good and bad) to the environment, society, and your industry.

Some organizations, especially those in the service or non-profit sector, don't often think of themselves as having environmental or social impacts. After all, there are no belching smoke stacks on top of their offices, no trucks unloading precious resources at their doors, nor any raggedly dressed children working in the back office. Nonetheless, conducting an impact assessment, even on a service organization, can be very revealing. Every organization, for instance, makes use of energy and materials, moves documents and people and makes choices that have rippling effects beyond their office doors. Service organizations, in particular, shape the behaviour of the customers whom they serve. Insurance companies, for example, may not be the biggest consumers of natural resources, but they have a huge impact upon how sustainably their customers behave. They influence whether people locate homes in floodplains or fire zones, what kinds of cars people choose to drive and how they drive them, and what health-impacting lifestyle choices they make. All service-sector businesses (e.g. banks, architects, restaurants and law firms) influence the behaviour and choices of their customers and can, through their own practices and policies, determine whether or not people make more sustainable choices.

In addition, every organization participates in an industry sector (e.g. manufacturing, government, service and high tech). Many of its impacts are determined by the conventions and practices inherent to that industry. In addition to cleaning up its own act and helping its customers to behave more sustainably, an organization should consider how it can influence its industry to bring policies, practices and, where appropriate, legislation. Multilevel approach to analyzing impacts:

An impact analysis can be done at several levels. If you are just beginning the process, we recommend starting with one of the high-level processes described below. These macro-level assessments take a broad look at your operations and identify the major categories of impacts. Once this is done, you will have a better idea of where you need to drill down a level to gather more specific data to support the educated guesses you make at the higher level or gather baseline data in preparation for action items. As your sustainability efforts mature, you may find it useful or necessary to conduct a detailed life-cycle-assessment of one or more of the products that you make or use. This level of analysis can give you the information you need to malice choices-for material procurement or product/service design.

If you look beyond the obvious sometimes an activity has more of an impact than is immediately apparent. For example, a legal firm, understood that it was a big consumer of paper (in fact, if you stacked the reams it used each year, the stack would be as tall as a 22-storey skyscraper!). It knew that paper consumption was one impact it could reduce through a variety of changes in employees' work habits. Upon further investigation, however, it began to realize that saving paper was just the tip of the benefits iceberg. In addition to saving an estimated US$20,000 on paper purchases each year, the firm discovered that by migrating to electronic file management, it would save on rent (file cabinets take up a good deal of valuable real estate), support time (all of the staff hours dedicated to retrieving and re-filing documents after they passed through attorney's hands) and process inefficiency (by working electronically, a file never got lost or was unavailable because it was checked out by a single person; in fact, multiple people could simultaneously work on an electronic file magnifying everyone's productivity).

Viewing activities through the lens of sustainability also reveals waste that has gone unnoticed. An engineering firm also sought to reduce its paper consumption. When it examined its processes, it discovered that most of the printing was done in association with the creation of check sets' - sets of documents that were printed for quality checks. Some projects went through as many as 35 check sets before the project was completed. This represented more than a waste of paper: it represented a process flaw and a lack of standardization around the points where it was necessary to check for accuracy. By establishing project conventions, the firm could save a good deal of billable staff time as well as paper by systematizing the process.

Go beyond your gates:

When assessing their footprints, organizations often overlook the impact of their products after they are shipped to customers. In many cases, use and disposal of products dwarf manufacturing impacts. Electrolux, the maker of home appliances, discovered this when conducting a life-cycle analysis of its washing machines. The biggest impact was not in production or delivery, but in the millions of gallons of water - much of it hot - that their machines used during their lifetime. While at first, it may seem as if you don't have control over how customers use your products, you actually have two opportunities to influence them. Consider the informational, educational or marketing strategies used by many manufacturers to influence the behavior of their customers. For example, Charmin toilet paper uses its TV ad campaign to demonstrate (delicately, with animation) that it takes fewer sheets of its product than competitors to 'get the job done.' Every communication you have with a customer (through instructions, marketing, advertising, etc.) is an opportunity to help them make the best use of your product.

The biggest opportunity to diminish a product's impact however, is in design. Electrolux's recognition of washers' impact led it to innovate its designs in order to create machines that use significantly less water. Not only did this reduce the products environmental footprint, but gave it a tremendous market advantage. Similarly, Nature Works, the Cargill subsidiary that makes polylactic acid (PLA) plastic, not only designed its product to make use of organic materials instead of petroleum, but can make much of the fact that unlike traditional plastic, its product will biodegrade.

Tips for getting the most out of your impact analysis

- Involve a broad enough group of people in this process that you have all die major functions and operations of your organization represented. This will enable you to identify the most informed and comprehensive list of impacts. At a minimum, consider involving whoever manages your purchasing function, your facilities, your core manufacturing or service delivery operations, and your shipping and receiving
- Use the framework you employed to create your vision to help you set the criteria how each aspect of your operation should operate. In other words, translate your vision into the specific actions and materials that your organization will need to employ in order to be sustainable.
- You will also need to decide how much of your organization to analyses: just your facility; just manufacturing or the office;

the entire organization? If you choose to address your entire life cycle, you will necessarily have to consider customers and suppliers as well.

- Use existing data where you have it to inform your analysis. Purchasing records, for example, provide a rich source of information about consumption. If your records are not easily sorted by purchase types, ask your key vendors to provide summaries of your purchases for the year. If you reimburse employees for work-related trips, then you likely have a record of transportation energy consumption related to the plane and car trips.

3.8.1 Resources

Reporting and metrics
- The International Society of Sustainability Professionals has a webinar recording on Mapping Your Impacts that provides a demonstration on how to do impacts assessment (see www. training.sustainabilityprofessionals.org).
- Spark™, the Sustainability Planning and Reporting Kit, includes an Excel version of the high-level impacts assessment described below (see www.axisperformance.com for more information).
- Lean and Environment Toolkit published by the US Environmental Protection Agency shows how and where to integrate environmental factors in a process diagram (see www.epa.gov/ lean/toolkit/ LeanEnviroToolkit.pdf).

METHODS AND INSTRUCTIONS

In this chapter, three ways are proposed for conducting an impact assessment (see Table 3.3).

High-level impact assessment

When to use. This high-level approach is a good way to quickly understand your organization's major impact areas and to begin to see what pursuing Sustainability would mean to your organization.

How to prepare. Convene a cross-representational group from your organization so that all the critical functions are represented. Make sure that the members of this group have

TABLE 3.3 *Overview of methods for identifying priorities*

Process	*when to use*
High-level impact:	assesses simple approach to conducting an impact analysis is quick and easy, while still resulting in the critical information that you need to launch a sustainability effort. This can also be a useful precursor to the aspects and impact process below.
Aspect- and impact-weighted	This approach is useful when you want a more detailed approach to your impact analysis and when you are considering a large number of impacts. It will likely appeal to organizations with an environmental management system. Unlike the version above, it provides quantifiable results.
Process Mapping	The process mapping approach is appropriate if you are focusing on your core processes and want to find efficiencies in addition to impacts a good understanding of sustainability and are familiar with the framework or guiding principles that you have chosen for your organization.

How to conduct this activity is shown in Figure 3.10

- *Energy* includes all of the power (electricity, natural gas, propane, etc.) needed to run your operation, as well as the fuel used to transport people and products.
- *Materials* are all the inputs and products that go into your products and are consumed by your administrative functions.
- *Processes* refer to the major activities that occur within your organization. If you are a manufacturing organization, then certainly this includes your production processes. If you are a service organization, then at the very least this would likely include meetings, document creation, customer interactions and the like
- *Facilities* refer to your physical plant or the buildings that you occupy.
- *Employees* are meant to include the work environment and your key human resources policies. *Waste* is all the 'non-product' that leaves your facility.
- *Product or service* is obviously what you deliver to your customer along with unintended side effects.
- Community (local and or global). *Community* refers to the relationship that you have with the community within which you operate,
- *Industry* is meant to address your involvement and influence over your industry

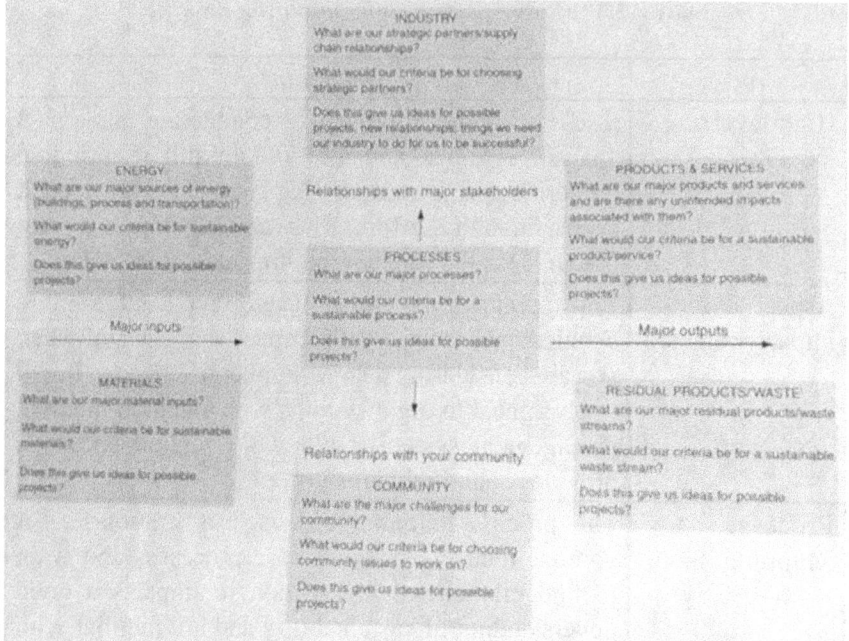

Figure 3.10

How to conduct this activity. Once you are clear on your criteria, generate a list of your organizations key activities and/or aspects. You can pull these from the high-level impact assessment diagram (see Figure 3.10), a process flowchart or, in simple operations, you can brainstorm them from scratch. You will need to determine the level of detail that you want to take with this analysis. Your list might be limited to the key activities of the organization and their biggest inputs, or you can drill down into each activity to identify the detailed aspects and sub-steps. If you are doing an impact assessment for the first time, it is probably sufficient to stay at a high level.

Create a matrix using your two lists: the list of your aspects and activities, and the list of your criteria. Enter the aspects and activities down the first column and the criteria in the fields across the first row. To give nuance to your analysis, consider whether all of the criteria you have chosen are of equal importance. If there are some that seem more important to you than others (either because of their impact or because of special relevance to your industry), assign a higher weight to them. For most organizations, we recommend keeping the rating system simple, using a scale of 1 to 3 (equivalent to a low/medium/high scale), with 3 being the most important or largest impact.

Now you are ready to conduct your analysis. For each aspect or activity listed in the first column, rate it based on how serious an impact it has — for example, a scale of 1 to 3 or a scale of 1 to 5, as in Table 4.2's scoring worksheet. If the aspect or activity is in extreme violation of the criterion, give it the highest number. If it doesn't violate it at all, give it a 1 or 0. Then multiply each rating by the weight for that criterion to obtain a score for entry into the cells in your matrix. You can then calculate a total score for each aspect to quickly arrive at high-priority issues. The example in TABLE 3.4 below is a sample, abbreviated. It uses criteria derived from The Natural Step system conditions.

Weighted criteria matrix						
Criteria	Carbon Neutral	Non-toxic	Locally sourced (within 300km)	Zero waste	Fair Labor Practice	Total score
Weight Aspect/activity	3	2	1	2	2	
Source ingredients For pizza	2	1	2	1	3	18
Cook pizza	3	1	1	1	1	16
Deliver pizza	3	3	1	2	1	23

Table 3.4

3.9 Renewable Energy and Sustainable Development

Sustainable development has become the center of recent national policies, strategies and development plans of many countries. The United Nations General Assembly's Sustainable Development Goals (SDGs) which included 17 goals stated above are key targets to be achieved by the signatories of the SDGs. In addressing climate change, renewable energy, food, health and water provision requires a coordinated global monitoring and modelling of many factors which are socially, economically and environmentally oriented. Replacing fossil fuel-based energy sources with renewable energy sources, which includes: bioenergy, direct solar energy, geothermal energy, hydropower, wind and ocean energy (tide and wave), would gradually help the world achieve the idea of sustainability. Governments, intergovernmental agencies, interested parties and individuals in the world today look forward to achieving a sustainable future due to the opportunities created in recent decades to replace petroleum-derived materials from fossil fuel-based energy sources with alternatives in renewable energy sources. Renewable energy supplies reduce the emission of greenhouse gases significantly if it replaces fossil fuels. Since renewable energy supplies are obtained naturally from ongoing flows of energy in our surroundings, it should be sustainable. There is a close link between renewable energy and sustainable development. For renewable energy to be sustainable, it must be limitless and provide non-harmful delivery of environmental goods and services. For instance, a sustainable biofuel should not increase the net CO_2 emissions, should not unfavourably affect food security, nor threaten biodiversity happening today. However, this is not what exactly happening today.

In spite of the outstanding advantages of renewable energy sources, certain shortcoming exists such as the discontinuity of generation due to seasonal variations as most renewable energy resources are climate-dependent, that is why its exploitation requires complex design, planning, and control optimization methods. Fortunately, technological advances are helping to do that. Another example is Hydropower which is an essential energy source harnessed from water moving from higher to lower elevation levels, primarily to turn turbines and generate electricity. Hydropower generation does not produce greenhouse gases and thus mostly termed as a green source of energy. Nonetheless, it has its advantages and disadvantages. It improves the socio-economic development of a country; but, also considering the social impact, it displaces a lot of people from their homes to create it, though they are sometimes compensated but are not enough. The exploitation of the sites for hydropower such as reservoirs that are often artificially created leading to flooding of the former natural environment. In addition, water is drained from lakes and watercourses and transported through channels over large distances and to pipelines and finally to the turbines that are often visible, but they may also go through mountains by created tunnels inside them. Hydroelectric structures affect river body's ecology, largely by inducing a change into its hydrologic characteristics and by disturbing the ecological continuity of sediment transport and fish migration through the building of dams, dikes. In countries where substantial plants or tree covers are flooded during the construction of a dam, there may be formation of methane gas when plants start rotting in the water, either released directly or when water is processed in turbines. Therefore, though hydropower may largely be environmentally sustainable, it is not always socially and economically sustainable.

Renewable technologies are considered as clean sources of energy and optimal use of these resources decreases environmental impacts, produces minimum secondary waste and are sustainable based on the current and future economic and social needs. Renewable energy technologies provide an exceptional opportunity for mitigation of greenhouse gas emission and reducing global warming through substituting conventional energy sources (fossil fuel based).

In spite of some of the adverse effects in implementing renewable energy discussed above, renewable energy has a direct relationship with

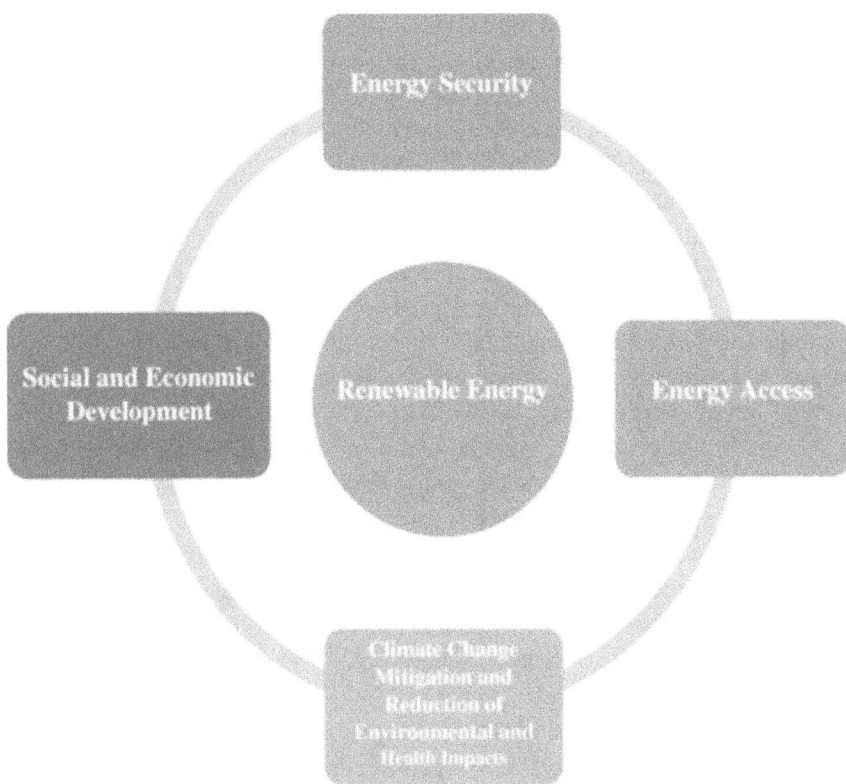

Figure 3.11

sustainable development through its impact on human development and economic productivity. Renewable energy sources provide opportunities in energy security, social and economic development, energy access, climate change mitigation and reduction of environmental and health impacts. Figure 3.11shows the opportunities of renewable energy sources towards sustainable development.

In addition to largely reducing the impact of GHG emission, renewable energy sources are largely evenly distributed around the globe as compared to fossils and in general, less traded on the market. Renewable energy reduces energy imports and contribute diversification of the portfolio of supply options and reduce an economy's vulnerability to price volatility and represent opportunities to enhance energy security across the globe. The introduction of renewable energy can also make a contribution to increasing the reliability of energy services, to be specific in areas that often suffer from insufficient grid access. A diverse portfolio of energy sources together with good management and system design can help to enhance security. It also creates employment; a renewable energy study in 2008, proved that employment from renewable energy technologies was about 2.3 million jobs worldwide, which also has improved health, education, gender equality and environmental safety

(Edenhofer et al., 2011Edenhofer, O., PichsMadruga, R., Sokona, Y., Seyboth, K., Matschoss, P., Kadner, S., ... von Stechow, C. (2011). Renewable Energy Sources and Climate Change Mitigation. Cambridge: Cambridge University Press.

The sustainable development goal seven (affordable and clean energy) and thirteen (action to combat climate change and impact) seeks to ensure that energy is clean, affordable, available and accessible to all and this can be achieved with renewable energy. Therefore, all organizations should try to use renewable energy as a business strategy and part of risk management against future energy shortage as well as GHG emission.

Investing in renewable energy is taking the stage like never before. Following are some reasons why businesses are taking the concept of using renewable energy seriously:

i. Consumers are evaluating and prioritizing companies that are committed to reducing and/or eliminating dependence on fossil fuels.

The Apple brand isn't only loved for its great technology. Recently, the company illustrated its dedication to sustainability planning by announcing goals for 100% clean energy reliance.

ii. Government regulations will likely soon have an even bigger impact on companies and their energy usages.

In the US, the EPA's Clean Power Plan may have a significant role in putting the pressure on businesses for clean energy use.

iii. Companies are seeing the advantage of investing in renewable energy initiatives, and the possibility of financial savings.

A major player in this effort is the Renewable Energy Buyers Alliance (REBA), which is an organization that helps businesses understand the advantages of moving to renewables, and has over 100 major corporate buyers on its roster.

3.10 Implications of Climate Change on Business Strategy

There are many adverse effects of climate change such as i) increases extreme weather events (droughts and flooding of agricultural lands) ii) increases moisture loss to the atmosphere iii)reduces the level of natural water reserves iv)increases temperature levels in temperate areas v)lack of soil moisture increases dust bowl events vi) overgrazing occurs due to decreasing natural grasslands vii) loss of groundwater due to increased irrigation viii) millions of acres turned to desert each year ix) reduced food supply which will increase food price reducing availability to the poorest causing poverty, x) adverse health outcome xi) effects on human behavior.

Therefore, climate change presents companies with significant risks, uncertainties, and an increasing number of market opportunities. Companies now confront a patchwork of regional regulation. In addition, most companies expect federal regulations to limit GHG emissions within the next decade. The unknowns of potential regulation create uncertainty, and therefore risk, for businesses making strategic decisions. Volatile energy prices wreak havoc on cost structures, severely impairing the ability to accurately forecast profitability. Large storm events have caused companies to think differently about the physical risks of climate change. Accumulating scientific evidence, coupled with these large storms, has boosted public awareness, leading to changing consumer preferences. Companies are looking at these changing preferences and identifying market opportunities, broadening the traditional risk-mitigation centered approach to climate change. Therefore "climate-related strategies," defined as the set of goals and implementation plans within a corporation that either aim to reduce GHG emissions, or that significantly reduce GHG emissions as a co-benefit. This includes strategies and measures for achieving near-term emission reductions from a company's own operations; research, development, and investment in low-carbon production and process-related technologies; alternative products that have a more attractive carbon profile; energy-efficiency initiatives; reductions obtained through offsets and emissions trading; and activities to reduce "upstream" or "downstream" GHG emissions along their value chain.

Leading companies are taking action both inside and outside their fence lines to reduce their own emissions and become more resilient to inevitable climate impacts. C2ES (Center for Climate and Energy Solutions) has found that, internally, companies are seeking a deeper understanding of the risks and opportunities of a changing climate, and are taking steps to reduce their carbon footprints (the emissions from producing their products) and their handprints (emissions from the sales and use of their products). Externally, they are engaging suppliers, customers, key stakeholders and policymakers, and are publicly reporting emissions and energy-usage data, climate-related risks and management strategies. Companies are also demonstrating their commitment to climate action by partnering with other companies and stakeholders on solutions and by publicly supporting policies like the Paris Agreement. Around the world, many businesses are demonstrating their commitment to solving the problem of climate change. Not only are companies speaking out on the severity of the problem, they are setting and meeting corporate targets to reduce greenhouse gas (GHG) emissions from their businesses. A number of underlying themes emerged regarding companies' motivations for setting targets. Among the most salient are these: companies that set

GHG reduction and energy efficiency targets do so because they believe that setting and meeting the targets will improve their bottom line and drive innovation. They believe that over the long term, the world will have to deal with climate change, so their climate-friendly investments will pay off. They also believe that by taking the initiative, they can help the government to create a climate change policy regime that works well for business. It is one thing to advocate policies such as reasonable targets and timetables and flexibility for businesses to use various means (such as emissions trading) to implement clearly defined goals. It is another thing to actually demonstrate via corporate action that these measures work.

Greenhouse gas inventory – or carbon footprint – and a cost curve for greenhouse gas reduction can assist business to quantify the cost and potential of various responses to reduce its greenhouse gas emissions, thus helping climate change policy development.

The Greenhouse Gas Inventory

A Greenhouse Gas Inventory provides a company with an understanding of its greenhouse gas emissions over a period of time. The inventory is typically broken down by source – for example, electricity, natural gas, and petrol as discussed in more detail in Chapters 6 and 7. A typical process for developing an inventory includes:

1. Determining boundaries: For example, should the emissions associated with waste to landfill be included or excluded? Are taxis treated in the same way as employee cars used for business purposes? Should the electricity used for building HVAC being included? Many of these questions can be resolved via reference to international greenhouse gas standards such as ISO 14064. However, there is flexibility in the way that the rules can be applied.
1. Data gathering: Emissions data are sourced from invoices, interviews, and interrogation of information systems. It is often the case that, during data gathering, opportunities to reduce emissions, energy use and/or energy cost become apparent.
2. Analysis: The raw data are converted to CO2-e (CO2 equivalent) using established methodologies, then aggregated to create a chart similar to that shown below.

The effort involved in producing a greenhouse gas inventory varies, depending on:

- The number of sources that are deemed to be inside the boundary. For example, including the full lifecycle emissions of products is more difficult than including emissions from electricity use and direct emissions from fossil fuels.

114

- The quality of data available: for example, electricity consumption data may be readily accessible and centralized, or contain gaps and be distributed across several functional areas.
- The level of detail required. For example, a full breakdown of electricity use to show the various usages – lighting, kitchen, office equipment, etc. – will take longer than a single category of "electricity."
- The level of accuracy required. For example, invoices for diesel use may show total purchases of fuel, but there may be no way of knowing how much diesel was used over a particular period. A rough estimate may be quick but will be less accurate than probing for more accurate data.

The accuracy or granularity of the inventory can also be improved by including a larger range of "optional" emissions sources, such as the embedded emissions associated with copy paper, office furniture, etc.

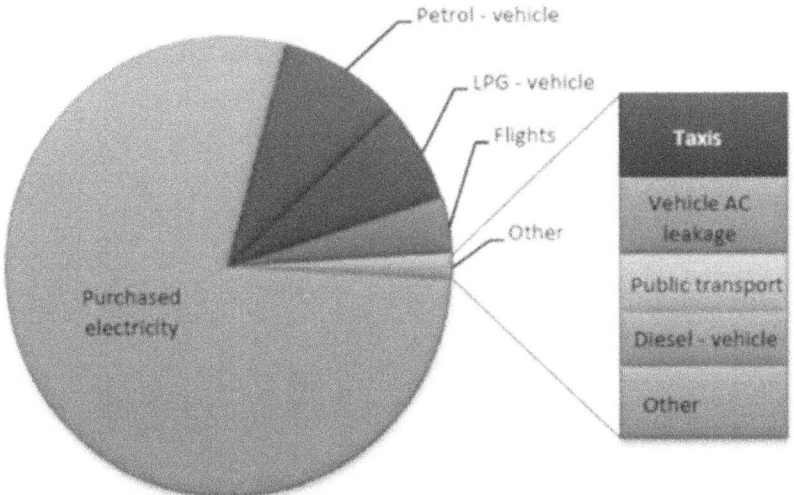

Figure 3.12 (Emissions Sources)

The Cost Curve

While a greenhouse gas inventory can inform the size of the effort required, a cost curve will complement the inventory by providing a company with the information it needs to prioritize its GHG reduction activities. A typical process involves:

1. Identifying candidate projects: The methods of generating projects vary, but it is sometimes worthwhile holding workshops, in which employees are asked to come up with ways to reduce

emissions, thereby simultaneously educating and gaining the benefits of their engagement on the issue.

2. Evaluating projects: Projects are coarsely screened to determine those most viable. Each project in the shortlist is then evaluated on its merits, using a "baseline and

3. credit" methodology, to determine the cost per tonne of abatement.

4. Charting the results: Although the results can be presented in tablature form, the clearest representation is that of a cost curve, similar to the hypothetical curve shown below. The benefit of this type of representation is that the marginal cost of abatement for a given reduction goal is intuitive.

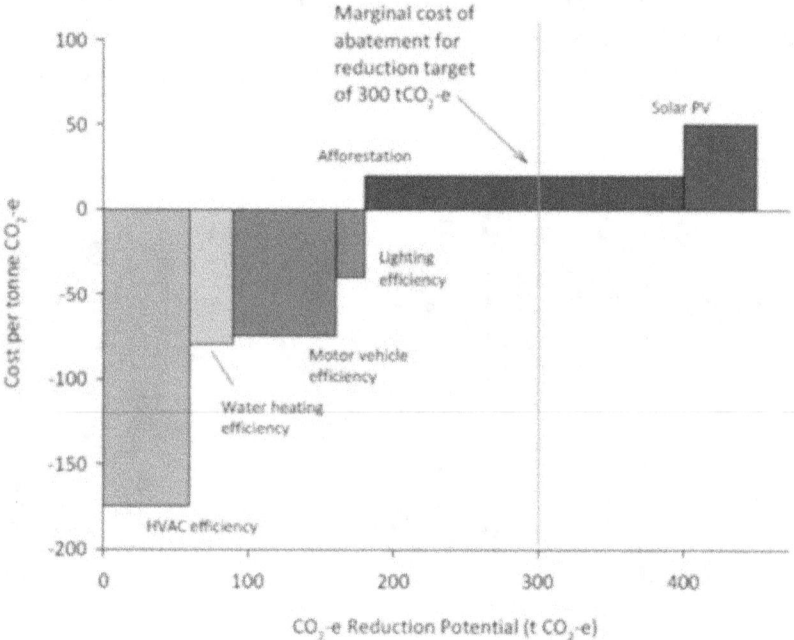

Figure 3.13: The Cost curve for Green House Gas Reduction

Putting It Together

The purpose of all of this is to provide senior management with a rational approach to climate change policy development. Ultimately, the information provided by these tools can be used to assist with the overall integration of climate change into corporate strategy. For example, for many office-based organization, which usually have low emissions intensity but use quality rather than cost as a competitive advantage, it may be viable to become carbon neutral. If this option is tabled as part of strategy development, the cost curve will be critical to understanding the likely cost associated with this approach.

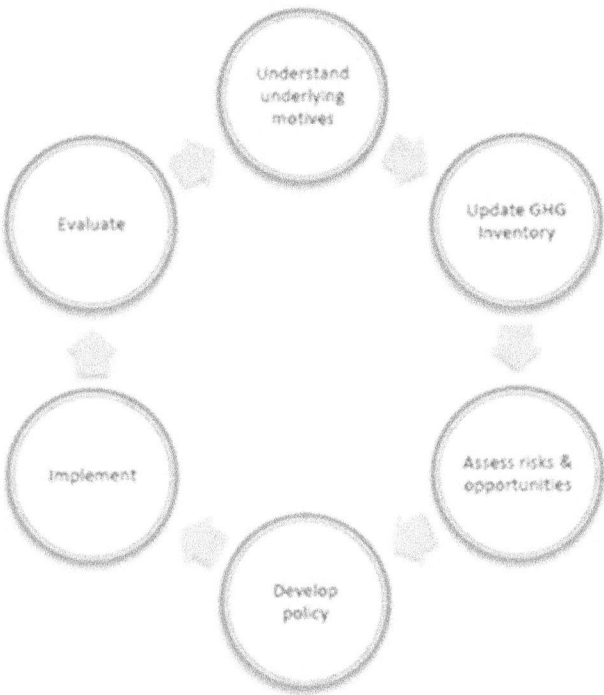

Figure 3.14 Process Cycle

The process cycle shown in Figure 3.14 above illustrates how the two tools can be used in policy setting; the GHG Inventory is shown in the diagram, while the Cost Curve is an important input to the assessment of risks and opportunities. Other considerations that might be covered as part of a climate change policy include:

- Overall position on climate change (i.e. is it real? Is it serious?)
- Approach to managing contribution to climate change (e.g. emissions reduction target, direct and indirect emissions reductions prior to offsetting)
- Position on emissions boundaries (i.e. which sources are included or excluded from the inventory)
- Organizational guidelines on emissions reduction activities (i.e. what types of activities are encouraged versus those that are considered undesirable). This will likely draw heavily on the cost curve and may involve consideration of procurement processes, travel policies, product development, community-based programs, verification and monitoring and external communications.
- Organizational guidelines on offset procurement (i.e. whether or not offsets will be procured, what types of offsets are acceptable)
- Extent of staff engagement and participation in the process

For most organizations, climate change is viewed as a deeply confusing area that is not a part of core business. However, more and more businesses are finding that its implications are appearing in unexpected places.

Crafting a comprehensive strategy with complementary policies is an important first step in the journey to integrate climate change into corporate strategy. Those that move swiftly to embrace its potential will find themselves with a competitive advantage over their rivals.

Some case studies of businesses adapting to climate change strategies are as follows:

Coca-Cola

The soft drinks giant made a pledge in 2007 to return all of the water it uses, back to nature.

The goal has led to increased water efficiency and recycling as well as a number of conservation projects.

As well as the obvious cost savings and environmental benefits, the company has also helped to protect its own water supply during periods of drought, as well as that of the communities living in the vicinity of its bottling plants.

Starbucks

Working with Conservation International and a number of NGO partners, Starbucks has been helping coffee farmers in Mexico to adapt to changing growing conditions.

It has also worked with academics to develop a number of vulnerability assessments and to model the effects of a number of climate scenarios on coffee cultivation.

By acting early, the company believes it can protect its own supply of coffee and prolong the benefits of its cultivation for communities in Mexico.

GlaxoSmithKline

In partnership with the UK blackcurrant juice drink Ribena and the Scottish Crop Research Institute, GSK has developed new climate-resilient varieties of blackcurrant.

With the majority of blackcurrants grown in the UK, the lack of alternative sources made Ribena's supply chain was particularly vulnerable to erratic weather patterns. Two varieties of Blackcurrant are already on the brink of disappearing from key agricultural regions.

Two new, more hardy varieties have been developed and grown commercially, protecting Ribena's supply, and benefitting UK farmers.

Microsoft

The software giant funds access to relevant environmental journals in 107 developing countries through its Research4Life programme.

In collaboration with the European Environment Agency, Microsoft's Eye on Earth delivers real-time environmental data to all users to monitor the progress of adaptation programmes.

The company is looking to build all of this data into a single "cloud-based" storage facility, making it fully transparent and accessible to all.

3.11 Linking Sustainability to Corporate Strategy Using the Balanced Score Card

The balanced scorecard uses four strategic perspectives complementary but distinct lenses for looking at organizational strategy and performance as follows:

i)   Financial: Owners, investors, and analysts view the organization as a financial system that provides a return on investment.

ii) Customers: Customers and stakeholders see the business' products and services as a way to satisfy needs and desires at an appropriate price.

iii) Internal Processes: Internal management and staff work on business processes to efficiently turn resources into outputs that can be sold to satisfy customer needs.

iv) Organizational capacity: is the foundation of the others – the physical infrastructure, culture, tools and technology, knowledge and skills, and information systems required to plan, design, and deliver products and services to customers and stakeholders.

Sustainability becomes strategic when it is integrated into the fabric of the organizational planning and management process.

Sustainability can be described by each of the four perspectives of the balanced scorecard, for example:

- From a financial standpoint, sustainability means staying in business and creating an acceptable return for investors.
- From a customer and stakeholder standpoint, sustainability means satisfying and providing value for the growing number of safety and sustainability-conscious consumers.
- From a process standpoint, sustainability means managing materials, energy, and waste in the most ecoefficient way possible.
- From an organizational capacity standpoint, sustainability means creating a culture that values sustainability, reflected in the choices that employees make every day.

When building an integrated strategy-based scorecard system, we build a "Strategy Map" for each theme. A strategy map shows the cause and effect links among strategic objectives, across the four perspectives, in

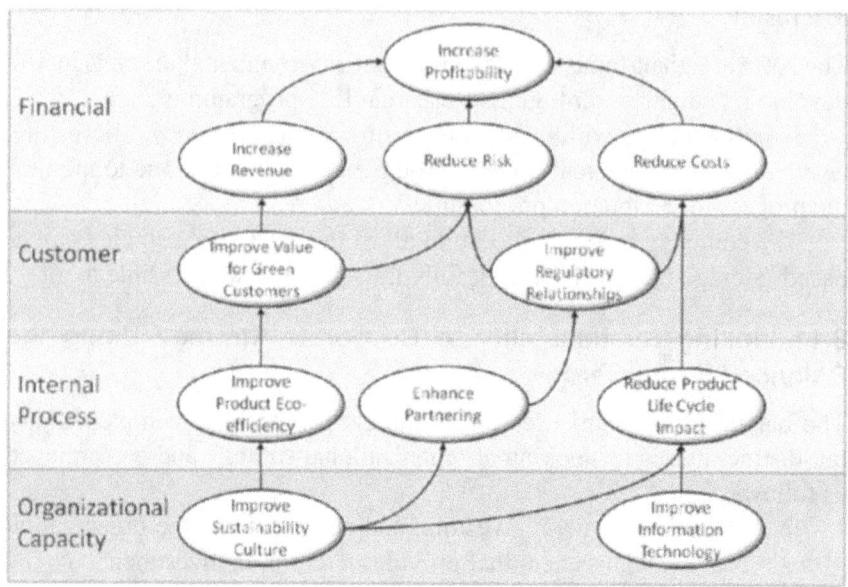

Figure 3.15

a visual map that tells the "Story of the Strategy." Figure 3.15 is a typical strategy map for a "Sustainability" theme.

The strategy map says that by creating a strong focus on sustainability in our corporate culture, we will align our people to develop more eco-efficient products, partner with regulators more effectively, and reduce the life cycle impact of our operations. In addition, we build new information technology capabilities that help us track life cycle impacts more effectively. By producing more eco-efficient products, we will provide value for the increasing number of "green" customers in our market, which will lead to increased sales. Our capability for partnering will enable us to communicate more pro-actively with the regulatory community, allowing us to be an active player rather than responding reactively to government directives. This will reduce business risk. Ecologically safe products will reduce potential product liability risk. Reduced risk will have a positive impact on our cost of capital. Reduced life cycle impacts will lead to direct cost savings on fuel, water, electricity and waste disposal. Taken together, increased revenues, reduced risks, and reduced costs will increase our profitability. Building a strategy-based scorecard planning and management system will lead to a high performance sustainable organization and accomplishment of the sustainability Mission.

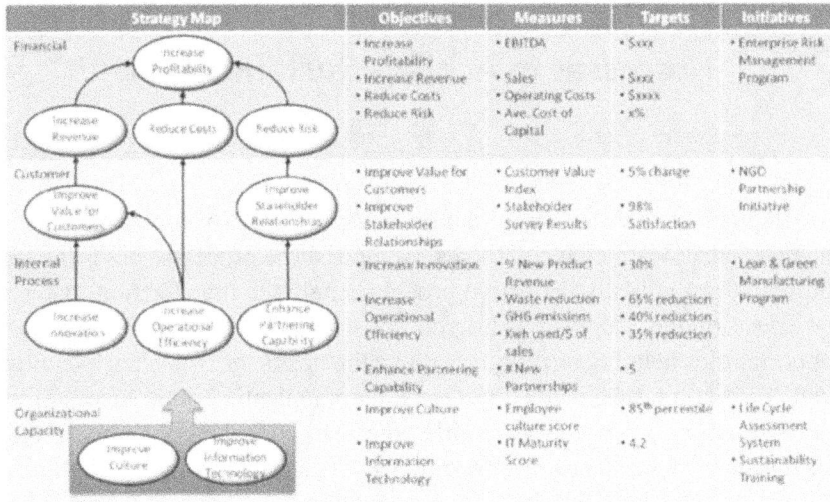

Figure 3.16

As you can see from the Figure 3.16, each strategic objective is supported by one or more measures. As you can see, the company is tracking life cycle impacts, has set targets for reducing them, and has identified initiatives to achieve that reduction. This set of measures can still support conventional sustainability reporting requirements and initiatives but is now linked explicitly to the broader competitive and financial strategy of the firm.

Questions:

1. What are the key components of sustainability strategy? Discuss the steps in sustainable strategy formulation.
2. Differentiate between built-to-last and sustainability strategy
3. Discuss sustainability planning
4. Distinguish between Unsustainable Take-Make-Waste Business model and Sustainable Borrow-Use-Return business model
5. What is impact assessment? Discuss multi-level approach to analyze impacts. How do you conduct impact assessment?
6. Discuss how renewable energy contributes to sustainable development
7. Discuss the implications of climate change on business strategy with examples.
8. How can you link Sustainability to Corporate Strategy Using the Balanced Score Card?

Chapter 4

Processes to Achieve Sustainability

To achieve sustainability, sustainable processes need to be practiced to meet the mission and strategic objectives, whether these processes are followed implicitly or explicitly. Effective processes help the organization manage the effects of uncertainty in its internal and external operating environment. Opportunities help organizations achieve the upside of risk when executed well. To become sustainable over time, an organization must successfully identify and act on the opportunities that can contribute significantly to the upside of risk. The most effective way for an organization to optimize its opportunities is to first, assess all elements of uncertainty with a focus on the organization's environmental, social, and economic responsibilities. These responsibilities form the foundation for meeting the intent of the sustainability policy. Second, the organization must affirmatively address the significant opportunities through the operational processes that were designed to support the strategic and operational objectives. Only in this way can the organization become more sustainable in the long, term.

The delivery of efficient operations requires not only diligence in the management of significant opportunities and threats posed by the effects of uncertainty in the internal and external operating environments but also the recognition of the interests of the stakeholders through both the engagement process and participation in the uncertainty assessment efforts.

Efficient operations and processes are necessary to ensure the organization is capable of achieving its mission and strategic objectives. Efficient processes, effective operations, and an efficacious sustainability strategy can be created and embedded in the way work is accomplished in the organization (i.e., the work instructions and operating controls). These processes and operations can then become a major contributor to the sustained success of the organization.

Process Approach

An organization can achieve consistent and predictable results when its operations are understood and managed as a set of interrelated processes. This approach to managing operations aligns all the processes to meet objectives.

It is called a "process approach." A process is a set of interacting activities that use inputs to deliver a product or service. This process approach helps the organization1

- Understand the process and be able to consistently meet customer and stakeholder product and service requirements
- Understand how the processes will add value
- Achieve effective processes and efficient operations
- Improve its processes based on the evaluation of data and information, collected in the monitoring and measurement activities

The process approach is a management strategy for its product and service operations. By using this strategy, the organization can develop, implement, and control its operational processes. Here are some ways to establish a process approach for an organization's operations:

- Determine and document product and service requirements.
- Establish a process to design and develop products and services.
- Monitor and control external processes, products, and services.
- Manage and control production and service provision activities.
- Implement arrangements to control product and service release.
- Control nonconforming outputs and document all actions taken.

While this list states what needs to be addressed, the organization can tailor the procedures to determine how they will be addressed.

4.1 Working with Processes and Creating Process Map

There are a number of widely used methods that help organizations understand processes so the process approach can be put to good use. In the smallest organizations where operations are still implicit in nature, these methods, can be used qualitatively to understand processes. Other organizations can use these methods to begin creating an explicit process approach when meeting the objectives in the face of uncertainty becomes more urgent. Four such methods are described next.

4.1.1 Process mapping

When to use: This approach examines your key processes and is most appropriate for those organizations where it is clear that one or two processes have the biggest impact. It may also be helpful for particularly complex processes with many different steps, as is often the case in manufacturing. It is also useful for identifying process waste and inefficiency that, in addition to revealing ways of reducing your environmental and social footprint, also create an opportunity for productivity gains. Manufacturing, for example, may want to initially ignore its support functions, such as administration and marketing, in order to focus on its primary manufacturing process.

If you do not already have a process map, you may choose to create one by following these steps:

1. Define the beginning and end points of your process.
2. Then brainstorm steps on sticky-backed notes so that you can move them around until you get them in the right order.

3. Then go out onto the shop floor or wherever the work is done to observe the degree to which your map matches the territory. Adjust it as appropriate.

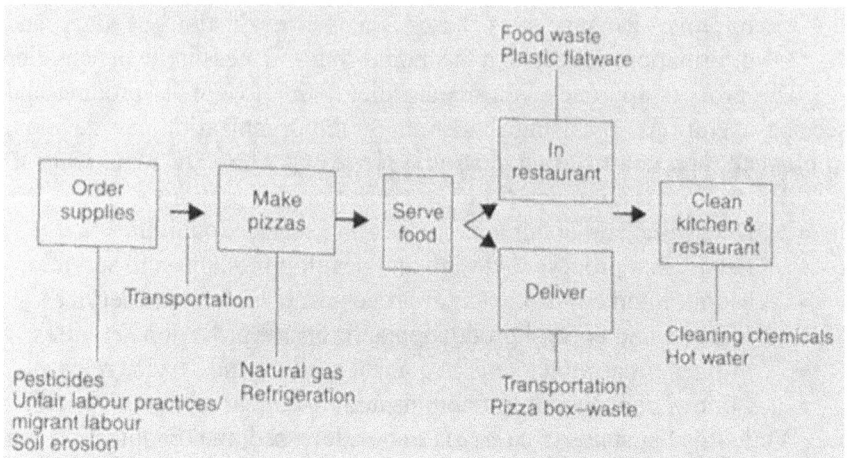

Figure 4.1 provides a simple process diagram of making a pizza.

How to conduct this activity:
1. Go through your process map and flag any steps that use a lot of energy, involve toxic chemicals or make heavy demands on natural resources, such as water.
2. Identify the highest priority impacts based on a set of criteria that may include urgency (regulators are breathing down your neck, or costs are escalating) and feasibility (fixes are available and cost-effective).

How to debrief. Review the priorities and do a gut check Are these really the best things to focus on? Can you make a significant difference? Then build a plan to reduce the impact that comes to the top of your priority list.

4.1.2 Turtle Diagram

A little diagram provides a useful means for understanding a single process (Figure 4.2) This diagram tracks the inputs and outputs of a single Turtle diagram for describing a single process—generic concept.

Process. It also includes some of the important dependencies that the process relies on:

- What are the required technology, machines, maintenance, materials, infrastructure, and work environment?
- How will it be measured and how often?
- Who are the people and their requisite skills?
- What are the methods and procedures?

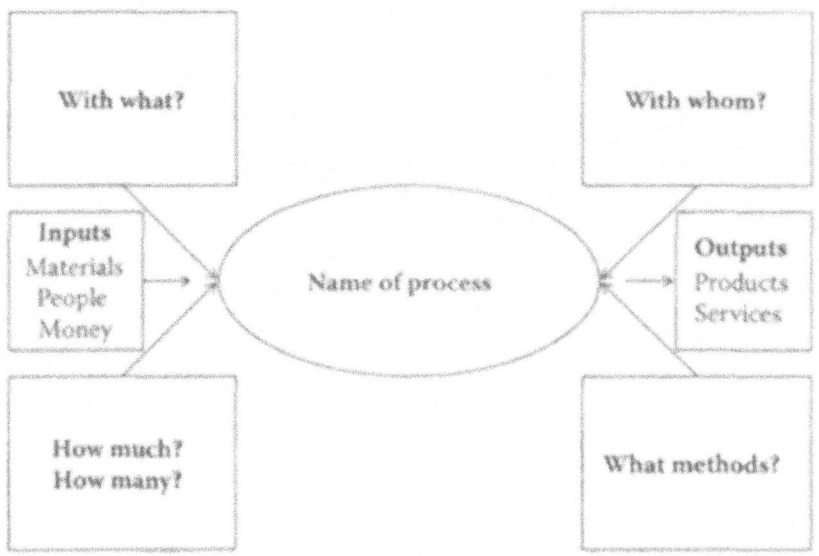

Figure 4.2

Many organizations prepare simple turtle diagrams to use for simple work Instructions. Many variations of the turtle diagram in Figure 4.1 can be easily found on the Internet.

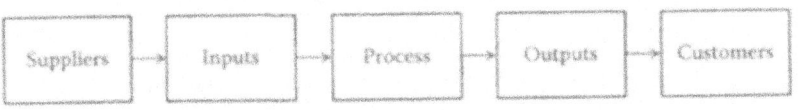

Figure 4.3

4.1.3 SIPOC diagram—generic concept.

Entire value chain for a process (Figure 4.3). In today's global economy, every organization uses materials from many locations in the world. Sustainability demands that every organization pay attention to the environmental, social, and economic responsibilities of their suppliers. Many organizations are creating "supplier codes of conduct" for suppliers for this purpose.

Managing the Processes

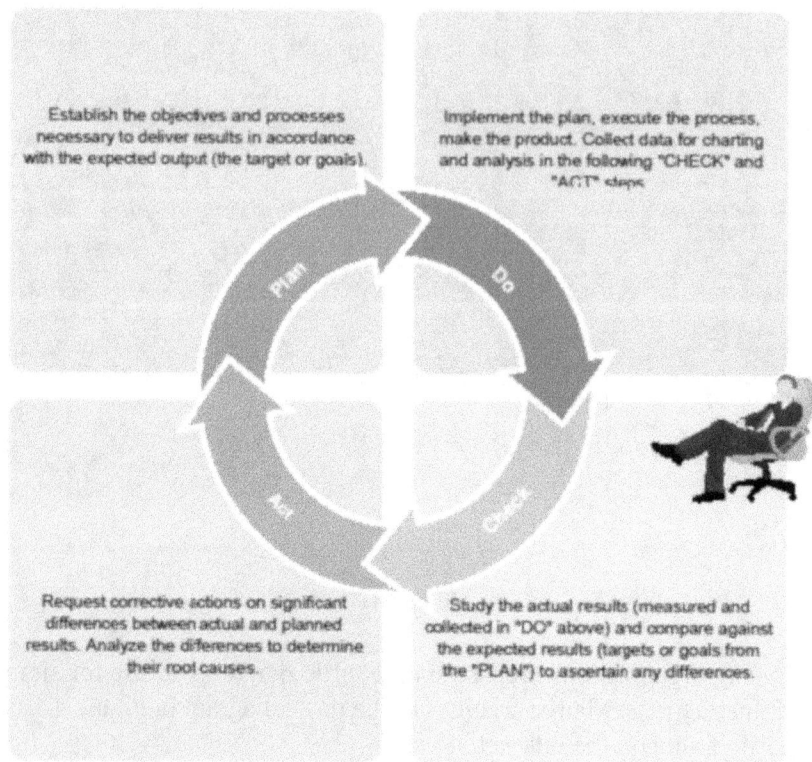

Establish the objectives and processes necessary to deliver results in accordance with the expected output (the target or goals).

Implement the plan, execute the process, make the product. Collect data for charting and analysis in the following "CHECK" and "ACT" steps

Request corrective actions on significant differences between actual and planned results. Analyze the differences to determine their root causes.

Study the actual results (measured and collected in "DO" above) and compare against the expected results (targets or goals from the "PLAN") to ascertain any differences.

Figure 4.4

4.1.4 A plan-do-check-act

(PDCA) (Figure 4.4) method is used to manage processes and the organization's operations as a whole. The PDCA method can be described as follows:

- Plan: Establish the system of processes, along with the resources needed, to meet the mission, strategic objectives, and operating goals of the organization as it seeks to meet the customer requirements. planning must also be sensitive to the interests of the stakeholders and the opportunities and threats that were found to be significant in the uncertain analysis.
- Do: Implement the system of processes as were planned.
- Check; Monitor and measure the processes, along with the products and servicesagainst the organization's policies, objectives, and requirements. The results of these checks need to be reported in a manner consistent with the organization policies.
- Act: Take actions to improve process performance, as necessary. the interests are aligned. These same organizations are also receiving.

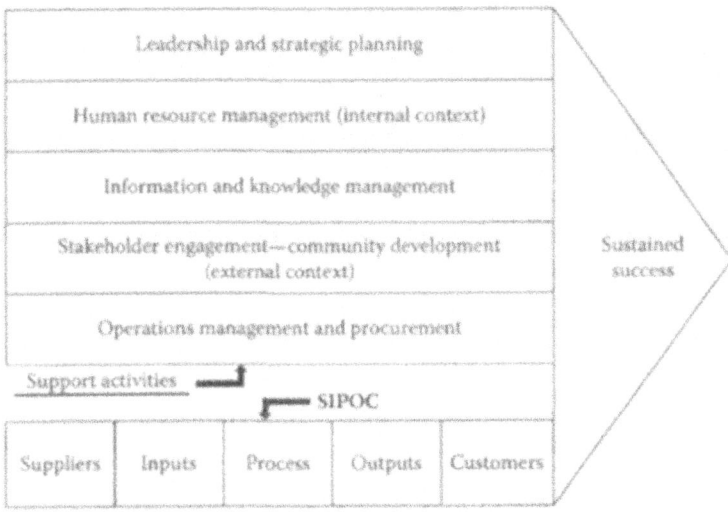

Figure 4.5

Supplier codes of conduct from their customers. There is an expectation that these codes of conduct will be followed, and that each organization will use in the sphere of influence to give meaning to sustainability throughout the entire value chain.

4.1.5 Value Chain Diagram

The- concept of the value chain conveys the message that processes and activities are universal to all organizations, whether they are business or have some other purpose. An organizational value chain diagram depicts. the organizational processes, at the bottom of the diagram and the functional areas that can drive the performance of the processes at the top (Figure 4.5)

It takes the combination of and interactions between processes and people to create value and continually improve the processes so that the organization can meet its objectives.

According to the principles of risk management, every organization needs to proactively manage its processes so it can have more effective processes and efficient operations. Organizations can use the process approach to establish formality in the more complicated processes, making it easier to determine any interdependencies between processes, look for constraints, and see where resources can be shared. Processes need to be reviewed on a regular basis. When there are problems, suitable actions need to be taken to improve the processes to make them more effective.

4.2 Process Approach and Control

Growth in organizations creates. the necessity to accurately determine and plan the processes by which the organization will define the functions necessary for providing the product and services that will meet the need and expectations of customers, organization members, employees, and other stakeholders on an ongoing basis. It becomes important to plan these processes in light of the organization's strategy, mission, and objectives. This planning enables the control of the processes by which the organization secures the provision of resources, facilitates the delivery of a product or service, monitors the activities, measures the performance of the process, and reviews the operating activities for ways to continually improve them. Process planning and control within an organization help an organization in

- Watching for changes in the external operating environment
- Forecasting the need for the outputs over the short and medium term
- Determining the interests of the stakeholders
- Understanding the objectives of the processes and how they get translated into the overarching strategic objectives
- Paying attention to the regulatory and legal requirements, as well as the three responsibilities of sustainability
- Managing the uncertainty by managing the opportunities and threats
- Controlling process inputs and outputs, including the use and loss (waste) of resources
- Paying attention to all interactions between processes
- Managing resource productivity and information and knowledge
- Monitoring activities and procedures, along with the people that are competent to perform the activities
- Maintaining records and other documented information required for transparency and accountability
- Conducting proper monitoring, measurement, and analysis of the process outcomes
- Taking corrective action when something does not work as planned
- Continually seeking improvement, innovation, and learning that benefit the outcomes of using the processes

Process planning must be attentive to the determined needs of the organization for developing or acquiring new technologies or developing new products or services, or both. This planning is how organizations add value that enables them to meet their strategic objectives.

Someone must be responsible for the processes. Members or employees of an organization must be provided with defined responsibilities and authorities to get the work completed. A "process owner." Could be a person or team of people, depending on the nature of the processes, and the culture and principles of the organization.

Processes need to be changed from time to time. These changes need to be carefully planned to make certain that they meet the requirements expected of the previous process, while also determining if there are any new requirements or old requirements that will no longer exist after the change. Just as changes in the external operating environment create new opportunities and threats, internal changes also introduce new opportunities and threats. Some internal changes may influence the external context as well. The information gathered by this process of managing change would be kept in the uncertainty (risk) register.

Many organizations restrict their planning activities to operations in a "normal" operating state, but what about emergencies and other uncertain operations or risk events? In an uncertain world, organizations are paying more attention to establishing procedures for determining how to respond to an internal incident, such as a fire, explosion, or accident. Organizations need to pay attention to how to

- Respond to emergency situations and accidents not covered by the characterization of the external context
- Take action to reduce the consequences of many different kinds of emergency situations, appropriate to the magnitude of the incident and the potential for impacts to the external stakeholders and the community at large
- Periodically test the procedures developed for managing these potential situations
- Periodically review and revise the procedures, where necessary, or do this after the occurrence of accidents, emergency situations, or tests of the emergency planning system

4.3 Resource Management

An organization must consider the internal and external resources that are required to achieve its strategic objectives in an underlain world. These resources include facilities, equipment, materials, energy, water, knowledge, finances, and people. Resources must be used efficiently so the operations can accomplish "more with less." An organization should identify and assess the uncertainty associated with the securing of certain materials and people when they are needed. This might include the scarcity of available resources, as well as mass sickness affecting the members or employees in the organization. The processes need to be optimized in a way that would cover some level of contingency for these and other similar considerations. At the same time, the organization should be vigilant in its search for alternative resources and new technologies. This will lead to a more agile and resilient organization.

Financial resources are reviewed periodically with the organization's financial advisors. This is part of the requirement to maintain sufficient financial resources to support activities required to meet the organization's strategic objectives. Improving the effectiveness of the processes and the efficiency of the operations can improve the financial situation by

- Reducing process, product, and service failures and eliminating materials, waste, and lost employee time
- Eliminating the costs of compensation associated with any guarantees or warranties, legal costs (including mediation and litigation costs), and the costs of lost customers, markets, and reputation

Human resources are very important to the long-term success of an organization. Leaders need to create a shared vision and shared values within the internal context, which will enable people to become fully involved in helping the organization meet its objectives. It is also critical to the success of the organization to provide people with a suitable work environment that encourages personal growth, learning, knowledge transfer, and team work. Every organization needs to have a means for managing people through a planned, transparent, ethical, and socially responsible approach. It is important that the members or employees of the organization understand the importance of their contributions and meeting organizational objectives.

Infrastructure must be managed with effective processes so that its operations helps the organizations become more efficient. Such an effort includes

- Maintaining the dependability of the infrastructure needed by the organization
- Ensuring its safety and security
- Providing infrastructure elements needed for products and service provision
- vigilantly pursuing efficiency, cost, capacity, and effects on the work environment
- Lowering the impact of the infrastructure and assets on both the work environment and the natural environment
- Identifying and assessing the opportunities and threats associated with the infrastructure to make certain that these uncertainties are included in the scan of the internal and external operating environment, and in the creation of potential contingency plans for dealing with events that may disrupt the infrastructure

The work environment must be suitable to achieve and maintain the sustained success of the organization, as well as the competitiveness of its products and services. The work environment should encourage productivity, creativity, and a sense of well-being for the people who are working in or visiting the organization's premises. It must also meet applicable statutory and regulatory requirements and address all applicable local standards. A suitable work environment is derived from a combination of human and physical factors that include

- Opportunities for greater involvement in creating processes that help develop the potential of people in the organization
- Safety compliance standards
- Ergonomics
- Dealing with stress and other psychological factors
- Location of the organization
- Proper facilities for members or employees
- Maximization of efficiency and minimization of wastes
- Adequate control of heat, humidity, light, and airflow
- Proper hygiene and cleanliness, while diminishing noise, vibration, and pollution
- Access to nature, preferably physically but at least visually

Attention to the built environment is an important component of an organization's sustainability. In a sustainable organization, the built environment should be designed not only for cost efficiencies but also to provide physical and emotional health benefits and to preserve and protect the environment.

Knowledge, information, and technology need to be treated as essential resources for the organization. The organization needs to identify, obtain, maintain, protect, use, and evaluate its continual need for these resources. It should also share knowledge, information, and technology with its stakeholders, as appropriate. Leaders need to determine the organization's current knowledge and information base and seek to protect that knowledge and information. The need to meet future knowledge and information requirements should also be determined. Reliable and useful data needs to be converted into information for use in decision-making leaders also need to consider technological options that may enhance the organization's performance in all areas of its operating system

Natural resources need to be protected to ensure availability of materials the future to meet the requirements of customers and stakeholders. The organization needs to identify the opportunities and threats associated with the availability and use of energy and natural resources in the short and longer term. Appropriate consideration should be given to the stewardship of its products and services, as well as to the development of designs and processes to address these opportunities and threats. It is important to minimize the environmental, social, and economic impacts over the full lifecycle of its products and services, from design, manufacturing, and service delivery to product distribution, use, and end of life.

4.4 Efficacious Strategy

The organization's strategy consists of how the organization seeks to meet its objectives in an uncertain world, along with the plans to achieve these objectives. The strategy should be clearly stated in a "looking forward" document. To be efficacious, the strategy must have the power to achieve the desired outcomes. If clear strategic options are created and vetted through stakeholder engagement and uncertainty analysis of each of the operational objectives, goals, and action plans, then the result will be an efficacious strategy. The analysis of uncertainty helps prioritize all the identified opportunities and threats found within the operating system, elsewhere in the internal context, and in the external operating environment. Stakeholder engagement and the effective management of uncertainty provide a means for ensuring that the strategy will be efficacious and that strategic decisions will reliably deliver the desired outcomes. Uncertainty analysis and management are critical tasks for creating an efficacious strategy. Uncertainty in the internal and external environment may produce a wide range of different opportunities and threats. The nature of the uncertainty can change almost without notice in a highly dynamic situation. Organizations must be vigilant to capture all the factors from the PESTLE and TECOP analyses and use strengths, weaknesses, opportunities, and threats (SWOT) and other tools to determine and assess the consequences associated with opportunities and threats. Paying close attention to the uncertainty analysis and the development and veiling of the strategy provides the best available information needed by the organization to improve its decision making and its capability to manage effectively. In an uncertain world, changes, events and other circumstances can reduce the success of the strategy. But if they are included in the uncertain analysis, then changes in the strategy can be initiated when the sense making activity detects change in the context, Then organization can determine what controls need to be put in place to optimize the consequences of these challenges

4.5 Effective Processes

Effective processes mean that the processes are the correct ones for delivering what is required by the customers and stakeholders. While processes may be efficient, this does not mean that they are correct or the most effective processes that the organization could employ. Developing more effective processes is the way organizations can satisfy customers and stakeholders. The operational system, and its processes and activities provide the means by which the organization will translate the efficacious strategy into the successful attainment of its objectives. The importance of the operating system in meeting strategic objectives makes it very clear that it is critical to have effective processes. Correct processes are built into the operating system and should never be managed by a set of independent sustainability initiatives.

The uncertainty analysis can help the organization determine the proper response to significant opportunities and threats. Having this information can help identify the necessary operational controls. When implemented, these operational controls must also be evaluated for effectiveness. If the uncertainty management is not comprehensive, the processes will not be effective. The overall intention is to ensure that processes are effective and that operations are efficient at all times. Effective processes provide the means by which operations are changed, and strategy is realized.

4.6 Efficient Operations

All organizations need to have efficient operations. The best way to ensure the ability of the organization to meet its objectives is to improve the efficiency of the operations. Especially in difficult times, it is important that the operating system continue to be executed as efficiently as possible. As mentioned, delivering more efficient operations can be ensured by developing processes and activities so that they require fewer resources. There is no point in operating efficiently if those operations are based on incorrect processes or separately operated sustainability initiatives. Uncertainty management is also relevant to the continuity of an uninterrupted, efficient operating system. This continuously is a critical component of any sustainability program.

Questions:

1. Why is it important to manage the operations of an organization using the process approach?
2. How does an organization create effective processes throughout its operations?
3. How does an organization ensure that its operations are efficient?
4. Why does the sustainability strategy need to be efficacious?

Chapter 5

Sustainability Self-Assessment
by Sectors and Functions

For sustainability to be successful, it must infiltrate all aspects of the organization. Sustainability change agents, in the form of a Sustainability Coordinator, can come from any part of the organization. The SCORE (Sustainability Competency & Opportunity Rating & Evaluation) self-assessments can be done for each industry sector, and function should lead to actions you can take within your span of control. If your organization is already well versed in sustainability and has been actively working towards it, these assessments can help you identify missing elements in your sustainability strategy. If not, it can help you to undertake sustainability action. The maturity of an organization's system of management is determined through the use of self-assessment which is defined as a comprehensive and systematic review of the organization's activities and its sustainability performance in relation to its degree of maturity. In the self-assessments Tables provided below, "Incubator" is the least matured whereas "Integrated" is the most matured.

5.1 Sustainability Coordinator/Director of Sustainability

Sustainability Coordinator/Director of Sustainability				
Practice	Incubator 1 point	initiative 3 points	Integrated 9 points	points
Sustainability management system (SMS): Have in place a process to routinely set priorities for sustainability improvements, monitor the results and institutionalize best practices.(see related practices under senior Management and Environmental Affairs.)	Implement a formal (but perhaps temporary) structure and process to identify and make sustainability improvements (e.g. a steering committee)	Implement an environmental management system that contains the elements prescribed by ISO 14001	Implement an SMS with sustain-ability policies, criteria and targets embedded.	

Vision: Have a clear vision for how sustainability relates to your organization's mission (See related practices under Leadership/Senior Management.)	Develop a business case and obtain executive support for pursuing sustainability initiatives.	Conduct a back casting-like process to develop a clear long-term vision of sustainability and interim goals. Get the support of Leaderships to communicate these 'audacious long-term goals.'	Catalyses the organization in developing a long-term vision of your organization's role in a fully sustainable society. Assumptions of your mission or business model and engage in long-term efforts to transform your of generation and sector.	
Implementation Plan: Develop a realistic plan for implementing sustainability in the organization	Develop and implement a plan for a pilot-level initiative.	Develop and implement a plan to spread sustainable thinking and actions across the organization.	Develop and implement a plan to embed sustainability into the fabric of the organization and into other strategic relationships.	

Sustainability Coordinator/Director of Sustainability				
Practice	Incubator 1 point	Initiative 3 points	Integrated 9 points	points
Performance Metrics: Develop and track a set of sustainability metrics. (See related practices under senior Management and finance/accounting.)	Develop and track metrics to show a return on investment and other benefits of sustainability projects.	Develop a holistic set of sustainability performance metrics to track the performance of the organization.	Develop metrics and methods for tracking the sustainability performance of strategic partners (e.g. major suppliers) and major externalities associated with the operation.	
Reporting: Regularly report on the results of sustainability efforts (see related practices under senior Management and Finance/Accounting)	Report to management and employees at least annually about the benefits and costs of sustainability projects.	Report to management on progress toward sustainability performance metrics. Develop and publish an internal sustainability report.	Report to management and other stakeholders on sustainability performance via a publicly available sustainability report.	

Role shift: Evolve the role of sustainability coordinator over time so that responsibility for sustainability is spread throughout the organization.	Lead the sustainability effort.	Show all management how to support the sustainability effort.	Educate others outside your organization on how to lead the sustainability effort (e.g. through public speaking, site visits).	
			total	
			Average	

If your average score is	Then you are
Less than 1	Lagging: you are beginning to fall behind others who are implementing sustainable practices and should look for ways to catch up. You may need to develop a more compelling business case for pursuing sustainability. We recommend beginning with projects that make good business sense from a traditional perspective.
1-3	Learning: you have made good progress but have a lot more the you can do. Look for ways to build on your existing success of choose projects that are timely for other reasons.
Over 3	Leading: you are out in front, blazing the trail for others. Keep innovating and share your lessons learned through speaking and writing

Sustainability by Industry Sector

5.2 Sustainability in Services and General Office Practices.

Service organizations often struggle to understand how they can participate in the sustainability movement. Since they have no smokestacks coming out of their offices and they dutifully recycle their paper, they question their impact. While it is true that the direct impact of their own operations will be less compared to manufacturing, they need to appreciate the impacts they indirectly cause or influence through the delivery of their services and the pattern of the customer behavior they create. Every service organization occupies a facility, uses various forms of transportation and consumes paper which by themselves suggest improvement opportunities. However, many service organizations also gave production components such as accountants produce reports, hotels and hospitals wash laundry, restaurants cook food; nonprofit organizations host fund-raisers; rental car companies, rent their fleet; retail stores sell goods. Therefore, sustainability opportunities can be found in all these areas. It is important to consider three other areas:

1.The ripple effects of the service you offer. The biggest effect of a service organization is not what it does itself but how it affects the behavior and choice of its customers. When architects design a building and specify materials, their impacts go far beyond their blueprints. When bankers decide to fund a home or business, their impact far exceeds the paper the loan is printed upon. Their decision may affect the quality of life in the community, pollution level, traffic congestion, etc.

2. Strategic threats: The second area services should consider is the impact of sustainability on matters key to their business: their customers, their images and also the foundation factors for their businesses. Aspen and many other ski resorts are concerned that global warming might eliminate snow from their mountain tops or dramatically shorten the season

3. Emerging opportunities: You don't have to be a nonprofit organization to have a mission to contribute to society. Starbucks, while vilified sometimes for the proliferation of stores, is trying to create a reliable market for fair trade, shade-grown coffee. Through Conservation International, they provide premium price, long-term contracts with responsible growers who can prove they are living up to Starbuck's sourcing guidelines. Their guidelines include environmental requirements (e.g. Shade-grown, bird-friendly practices), social elements (e.g. Fair labour practices) and economic expectations (e.g. transparency and fair pay) i.e., addressing all the three areas of sustainability namely, environmental, economic and social. Therefore, you can use the following sustainability strategy:

1. Clean up your own operations
2. Manage your ripple effects
3. Evaluate strategic threats
4. Explore emerging threats.

You can use the following Table to assess your progress towards sustainability.

Services				
Practice	Incubator 1 point	Initiative 3 points	Integrated 9 points	points
Strategy: Develop a business strategy related to sustainability that identifies your opportunities and threats.	Develop a formal business case for adopting sustainability and take initial steps to implement the insights.	Sustainability is part of formal strategic and business planning processes sustainability is seen as an important element of your organization's competitive advantage	Actively work to affect customers, suppliers and others in your industry to solve sustainability-related problems.	
Service Delivery: Embed sustainability into the core service.	Conduct a sustainability analysis of your core service and identify sustainable targets for all major impacts. work on at least on sustainability initiative per year.	Redesign service to eliminate or offset all major external impacts and engage in activities to mitigate common, negative side effects from the delivery of your product or service.	Change the service delivery such that customers change their behavior to support sustainability.	
Office Supplies and Equipment: Minimize impacts associated with office supplies, furnishings, and equipment.	Select a couple of targeted purchasing categories and identify more sustainable options.	Have a system in place for routinely assessing the impacts of purchases and are working on finding better options.	80% or more of office supplies and equipment come from sustainable sources (i.e. from a certified sustainable source, 100% post-consumer waste, recyclable, product take-back).	
Energy: Improve energy efficiency and transition to renewable. (See related practices under Facilities).	At least every three years, conduct an energy audit on office operations and act on the results.	Have a system in place for monitoring and communicating energy efficiency, including behavioral changes. Purchase 25% or more renewable power (or the equivalent carbon offsets).	Achieve climate neutrality for electricity, heating, and cooling (e.g. via generating energy, purchasing 100% green power and/ or purchasing carbon offsets).	

Transportation: Actively promote the reduction of climate impacts associated with the transportation of people and documents/ materials. (See related practices under Human Resources)	Encourage alternative transportation for commuting through incentives and other means (e.g. parking fees. Car-share). For correspondence, freight and business travel, use the lowest impact carrier that will meet the needs of the parties involved.	Offer incentives to contractors and customers to reduce fossil fuel use.	Be climate neutral for all organizational transportation and for at least 25% of commuting impacts.	
Contract services: Use contractors that share a commitment to sustainability (e.g. banks, janitorial, landscaping, courier, catering, etc.).(See related practices under purchasing)	Notify all major contractors/ suppliers of your commitment to sustainability	Implement a tool for evaluating contractors on their sustainability practices. Write sustainability criteria and requirements into contract language for all contractors.	Actively influence the selection of contractors not hired directly (e.g. work with the building owner or create collaborative purchasing programmers with building tenants).	
Food Services: Ensure access to healthy, sustainable food and minimize waste (cafeterias , vending machines, etc.)	Use non-disposable tableware and energy-saving devices.	Label and promote the sale of healthy foods (organic produce, low-fat, etc.) Use green of sustainable cleaning products.	Only provide locally sourced, in season sustainable food items. All food items. All food waste is composted.	
Remodels: Employ green building principles when choosing a new site or remodeling an existing one. (See related practices under Facilities.).	Achieve LEED certified or equivalent.	Achieve LEED silver or equivalent.	Achieve LEED platinum or equivalent.	
Total			Total	
Average			Average	

5.3 Sustainability in Manufacturing and Product Design

NOTE: Manufacturing businesses should also take the services assessment to capture their office and service-related activities.

Sustainability movement is affecting the manufacturing movement first as manufacturing often deals with hazardous chemicals, uses a lot of energy, depletes natural resources, and generates tons of wastes. Manufacturing companies are implementing sustainability and herein below are some of the benefits they have realized:

(i) Uncovering innovations that provide a competitive advantage: When you examine a product through the lens of sustainability, you unleash creative thinking that often results in startling innovations. C&A Floorcoverings, for example, was getting complaints from their customers about end-of-life issues associated with carpeting, since construction waste is a significant percentage of what goes into landfills and carpeting may last many years there. Therefore, they set a goal of making new carpets from old carpets through recycling by separating the vinyl backing from the nylon nap. They found that the resulting carpet performed better and cost less. Now they are eager to take back old used carpeting instead of sending to landfills.

(ii) Saving energy in the manufacturing process and reducing costs

(iii) Improving product reliability by improving lifespan of products

(iv) Reducing hazardous materials in manufacturing materials

(v) Eliminating waste.

Manufacturers also pursue sustainability to reduce risk such as losing customers, bad press, shut out of large markets, harassed by NGOs and Government agents, pressured by customers, proliferation by regulations, losing insurance coverage and being sued.

Strategies you can use: As you can see that there are many sustainability-related issues affecting the manufacturing sector. To counteract these threats and take advantage of the opportunities, the industry is pursuing a number of activities that can be organized into two activities namely product design and operations.

Product Design: Most of the impacts of a product are determined in the design stage, and therefore strategies for producing the sustainable product are related to design. It may include considering such factors as recycled content, recyclability, embodied energy (how much energy it took to create the material), more abundant materials especially metals, toxicity, and harvesting practices. Design also considers efficiency and eco-effectiveness of the manufacturing process. How much energy is required? How can we use waste heat? Can water be reused? Are the most benign chemical/materials being used? Do we need it? Can we do without it? Can we borrow, rent or get it gently used? Is the product designed to be durable or multifunctional? Is the product designed to minimize waste? Can it be smaller, lighter or made from fewer materials? Is it available in a less toxic form and made with less toxic materials? Does it use renewable resources? Is reuse practical and encouraged? Is the product or packaging recyclable, refillable or repairable? Is it made locally? Is it made from socially or environmentally responsible company? Often trade-offs must be made between one criterion and another.

Life Cycle Assessment (LCA): LCA is a process of examining the impacts of a product's emission over its entire lifetime: where do the raw materials come from? How are they transported? How is the product manufactured? How is the product transported and sold to a customer? How does the customer use the product? What happens at the end of its useful life? LCA quantifies the environmental impacts at each step in this life cycle, and you can use LCA to design products so that they have the least negative environmental and social impacts.

Life Cycle Costing (LCC): examines the costs (as opposed to the environmental impacts) over the life cycle of a product from research and development and manufacturing to maintenance and disposal.

Operations: While much of the product's impact is decided during design, everyday operational decisions also have an impact. Here are some of the most common strategies to improve your sustainability performance:

(i) Energy and Greenhouse gases: Your manufacturing process may directly create CO_2.

(ii))Collaborate with Supply Chain: Managing your supply chain has become increasingly important as a business strategy, not only to reduce environmental impacts but also to manage costs and uncertainty.

(iii) Product Certification: A number of third-party certification systems intended to give purchasers certain assurances about the products they buy are being developed for natural-resource based products. If you do not opt for certification, it may lock you out of certain markets especially in the European Union or Asian market. The construction industry has LEED which stipulate tiers of building performance.

(iv) Zero Waste in operations means efficient operation without any waste

(v) Extended producer responsibility, product stewardship and product take back: Product stewardship is basically synonymous with EPR (extended producer responsibility in the EU or extended product responsibility in the USA) and involves taking responsibility for your products for its entire lifetime.

Self-Assessment can be done as follows:

Manufacturing				
Manufacturing	**Incubator** **1 point**	**Initiative** **3 points**	**Integrated** **9 points**	**points**
Design				
Design for environment (DFE)/sustainability (DFS): Redesign your product to maximize sustainability using the best available technology.	At least every five years, redesign one product with sustainability in mind. Disseminate lessons learned from other related products. Apply DFE designing any new products.	At least every five years, review and redesign most products to 'push the envelope' of sustainable performance. Use DFS techniques that incorporate social as well as environmental criteria for all new products.	Have significant products third-party certified as sustainable.	
Packaging: Minimize packaging and its associated impacts.	Conduct a cursory life cycle analysis on packaging and take appropriate action.	Reduce packaging by at least 20% (weight and/or volume).	Convert to packaging that is 100% reusable, recyclable and/or compostable.	
Supplier influence: engage suppliers in a formal process for redesigning products and processes.	Engage at least one first-tier supplier.	Engage all first-tier suppliers (e.g. materials declaration, supplier workshops, technical support).	Work to change the entire supply chain to achieve sustainability.	
Life cycle thinking: Apply life cycle thinking to your products, processes, packaging, and distribution.	At least every five years, conduct a life cycle analysis (LCA) on prevalent product components and/or packaging.	At least every five years, conduct and publish a life cycle assessment paper on one or more products.	Make available independent LCA comparisons available on your and your competitors' products.	

Operations				
Energy efficiency and renewable:Conduct a process energy audit and implement the best available technology.	Reduce energy usage by 10-15% per unit of production.	Reduce energy usage by at least 25% and get at least 25% of your electricity from renewable or cogeneration.	Reduce energy usage by more than 50% with at least 75% of energy (electricity and other fuels) coming from renewable sources.	
Climate change: conduct a process greenhouse gas (GHGs) audit and take appropriate action to reduce GHGS.	Reduce GHGs to 1990 levels.	Exceed Kyoto protocol standards.	Be climate neutral (through reductions and offsets).	
Resource efficiency; conduct a (non-energy) resource process efficiency audit and act on the results.	Reduce inputs of raw materials (water and other natural resources) by 10%	Reduce inputs by more than 10%	Reduce inputs by 25% of more, and source at least 75% (by volume of weight) from certified sustainable sources.	
Transportation and distribution: Reduce impacts associated with moving raw materials and products.	Factor in the distance when sourcing supplies. Install the best available technology to enhance fuel efficiency.	Switch to at least 50% befouled made form feed stocks.	Redesign the distribution systems and logistics to minimize transportation. Use at least 75% alternative fuels.	
Social impacts: Ensure fair working conditions.	At least every two years, conduct an internal work climate survey and act on the results.	Conduct social audits of your major suppliers.	Require all suppliers to adhere to SA 8000 or equivalent standards.	
Chemicals: Reduce exposure risks to all toxic chemicals.	Complete a chemical inventory that ranks or rates them by toxicity and volume. Reduce toxic and hazardous materials by 25% Assure that all MSDSs are available, easy to access and up to access and up to date.	Eliminate all hazardous chemicals and persistent bioaccumulative toxins (PBTs). If appropriate, implement a chemical pharmacy system.	Eliminate all toxic chemicals on all customer grey lists.	

Product steward-ship: Implement a product steward-ship strategy.	Take responsibility for your product at the end of its useful life (e.g. reverse distribution sys-tems). Dispose of any waste respon-sibly.	Work with indus-try to eliminate waste.	Turn product into a service; cradle to cradle	
Waste manage-ment: Eliminate the concept of waste	Reduce soil waste by 20-50%	Reduce solid waste by 50-89%	Achieve zero waste to landfill (90-100% reduction)	
			total	
			Average	

5.4 Sustainability in Government Agencies:

The government has a large role to play in sustainability. Their decisions determine to a large extent the livability of our communities and the environmental impacts of our lifestyles. For example, China has been heralded as having dramatic economic growth, but the world recently estimated that they are losing 8% of GDP in environmental costs. Governments must see their communities as a whole system and make decisions that simultaneously improve the health of the community, the economy, and the environment.

SCORE GOVERNMENT

NOTE: This assessment focuses on the larger impacts government has on its community. This assessment is intended to be used at a municipality, regional or national level, although an individual agency may want to score itself on a practice that directly relates to its mission. Governmental agencies should also take the services assessment to capture their internal impacts and the appropriate functional assessments.

Government				
Practice	Incubator 1 point	Initiative 3 points	Integrated 9 points	points
Energy policy: promote energy efficiency, conservation and renewable.	Offer and promote free energy audits to the constituency.	Have a system of incentives that encourages organizations and individuals to conserve energy and switch to renewable.	Have set a renewable standard of at least 50% renewable by 2050. Have a viable plan and are on track to reduce greenhouse gases by at least 80% by 2050.	
Land Use: promote sustainable land use practices.	Use smart growth and associated principles and policies in new development and redevelopment projects. Provide outreach and education.	Have in place long-term land use plans that protect important natural services (clean water, carbon sequestration, recreation, biodiversity, wild lands, esc.) and natural resources (agriculture/ forests/ fisheries).	Base the long-term land use planning on an estimate of population growth and carrying capacity such that if needed, the community could provide for 80% of its critical needs (food, water, fibred, etc.)	
Transportation: Actively promote the reduction of climate, air-quality and congestion impacts associated with transportation.	Transportation planning is integrated with land use planning. All public transportation vehicles use clean fuels. Provide outreach and public education.	Give preference and alternative transportation through investments, incentives, and regulations.	Require major employers to rebuke one-person-per-cat- commuting through a variety of incentives.	
Contract services: Use purchasing power to influence the marketplace.	Include sustainability as a selection criterion in all requests for proposals.	Write sustainability criteria and requirements into contract language for all contractors hired.	Develop systems to help others identify vendors/ suppliers with effective suppliers with effective, sustainable practices	

Buildings: promote green building practices.	Set a better-than-code standard for all new government buildings (LEED-silver or equivalent); use green building principles when remodeling existing facilities.	Actively promote green building practices in the community through education, incentives, technical assistance, etc.	Increase building code requirements to LEED silver or equivalent.	
Waste management: move toward a 'zero waste' society.	Provide convenient recycling services for organizations and the public for all recyclable/compostable materials.	Build markets for recyclable materials through economic development incentives, technical assistance, and provide convenient hazardous waste collection systems for all toxic products including electronics, batteries, pharmaceuticals, paints, pesticides, etc.	Implement product stewardship/EPR legislation for all toxic materials, requiring some form of product take-back such that it creates incentives for the manufacturers to create more sustainable alternatives.	
Economic Development: Encourage sustainable development.	Use sustainability as a criterion for selecting targeted industries.	Educate existing businesses about sustainability and provide services to develop effective business clusters.	Create legislation, regulations and other mechanisms to eliminate unsustainable practices in the community. Give a Tax credit for implementing sustainable technologies	
Human Health: Promote human health and well-being for all citizens.	Ensure all citizens have access to basic health care and basic services (shelter, food, drug/alcohol prevention, mental health services, etc.)	Actively promote healthy lifestyle choices (diet, exercise, stress management, etc.) through education, events, labeling, and incentives.	Adopt the precautionary principle as policy.	
Tolerance and Diversity: Promote practices that enable all citizens to reach their potential.	Actively recruit and hire from disadvantaged populations. Provide job and literacy training.	Have programmes that teach tolerance and conflict resolution. Provide mediation and arbitration services.	At least every five years, systematically evaluate the community's well-being and have effective systems in place to increase social capital and civic engagement (e.g. neighbourhood associations, citizen advisory committees).	

Education: Ensure all citizens have the knowledge and skills necessary to participate in a sustainable society.	Include some sustainability content in primary and secondary educational materials ,including systems thinking. Assess schools on their sustainability performance and act on the results.	Embed sustainability into the curriculum of primary and secondary education and create sustainability demonstration and community service projects. In higher education, develop strong academic and research programmes.	Sustainability education is required in high school and higher education, linked to social, economic and environmental subject matter. Ensure that every citizen (children and adults) receives regular messages about how to be more sustainable and gets meaning feedback on the overall performance of their community.	
Global Peace and Prosperity: Promote practices that avoid war, de-escalate tensions, and prevent mass migrations due to famine natural disasters, or political strife.	Provide outreach and education to help local citizens understand global sustainability challenges and the impacts their decisions can have on other peoples.	Screen purchases and investments to avoid supporting regimes or organizations that contribute to world problems. Give preference to organizations that actively work to prevent world problems.	Actively support sustainable economic development throughout the world through education, exchange programmes, participation in sustainability-related organizations technical assistance, aid , and trade.	
Emergency preparedness: Have effective plans in place to protect citizens. Property and the environment in the case of natural or man-made disasters.	Regularly educate the community about potential threats and what to do to protect themselves. Have programmes that help them put together an emergency preparedness plan and kit.	Have an effective network of trained disaster relief workers spread throughout the community and a robust communication system; have a well-tested plan for foreseeable disasters.	Have systems for handling sewage and containing hazardous materials without electricity or other major infrastructure elements such that there will be no harmful releases into the environment.	
			Total	
			Average	

Sustainability by Organizational Function

5.5 Senior Management

Sustainability can be a particularly useful tool for top management to organize their thinking. Top management must juggle the competing interests of different stakeholders groups: customers who want good value, shareholders who want quarterly profits, employees who want meaningful work and regulators who want safety for employees and the environment. One misconception that prevents many executives from pursuing sustainability is the assumption that it will end up costing more. In fact, sustainability actions often save money, yielding unanticipated benefits as well and becomes a source of competitive advantage.

The self-assessment for senior management is as follows:

SCORE SENIOR MANAGEMENT

Executives				
Practice	**Incubator 1 point**	**Initiative 3 points**	**Integrated 9 points**	**points**
Sustainability Management system: Have in place a process to routinely set priorities for Sustainability improvements, monitor the results and institutionalize best practices.	Have a formal (but perhaps temporary) structure and process to identify and make Sustainability improvements (e.g. a steering committee)	Have implemented an environmental management system that contains the elements prescribed by ISO 14001	Have an ISO – compliant EMS with Sustainability policies, criteria, and targets embedded.	
Vision: Have a clear vision for how Sustainability relates to your organization's mission.	Establish a vision and framework for Sustainability that clearly defines the business case for pursuing it.	Conduct a back casting-like process to develop a clear long-term vision of Sustainability and interim goals.	Have a long-term vision of your role in a fully Sustainable society. Question basic assumptions of your mission or business model and engage in long-term efforts to transform your organization and sector.	

Strategy: Integrate Sustainability into the strategy and mission.	Create a strategy to spread sustainable thinking throughout the organization.	Embed Sustainability into the strategic and business planning process of the organization.	Have a plan for transforming your industry or supply chain.	
Communication and Education: Clearly, communicate the importance of the vision and strategy to all affected employees.	Explain the need for pursuing sustainability and take symbolic action to back up the rhetoric.	Train all employees in sustainability and your chosen framework(s). Provide frequent updates and ways to reinforc Sustainability thinking.	Speak regularly to other groups about your efforts, encouraging them to adopt sustainable practices and learn from your experience.	
Commitment; demonstrate a commitment to sustainability through accountability and resources.	Form a steering committee and/ or create sustainability coordinator position	Require each department to work on sustainability initiatives and goals.	Build sustainability into budgets, reviews, selection criteria, and compensation. demonstrate your commitment externally.	
Implementation: embed sustainability into the organization.	Implement pilot efforts and achieve some measurable results.	Embed sustainability in business processes (planning, budgeting, appraisal, rewards, procedures, etc.) and make it every department's and person's responsibility.	Undertake efforts to move sustainability into your supplier's customers and other stakeholders operations	
Transparency and stakeholder involvement; operate in a transparent and involving manner.	Provide ready access to complete and accurate performance data to investor regulators and the public.	Provide mechanisms to solicit input from all major stakeholder groups.	Conduct regular, formal assessment of stakeholder expectations and satisfaction levels.	
Sustainability Reporting: annually produce and review a sustainability report reflecting your goals your goals and progress.	Produce an internal document used by managers and employees that reports on goals, projects, and sustainability metrics.	Produce reports available to the public.	Produce reports that meet standards such as the global reporting initiative or the greenhouse gas protocol and are audited by a third party.	
			Total	
			Average	

5.6 Facilities: How to save energy and water, improve productivity and reduce waste

Because of the potential for cost savings and the relative size of the impacts, many organizations begin their sustainability efforts with a focus on their facilities. Following is the self-assessment:

SCORE FACILITIES

FACILITIES				
Practice	**Incubator** **1 point**	**Initiative** **3 points**	**Integrated** **9 points**	**points**
Energy: reduce environmental and social impacts associated with energy use through conservation, and renewable	At least every five years, conduct an energy audit and act on the results.	Have in place systems for monitoring and reducing impacts from both equipment and human behavior (e.g. turning off lights and computers). Purchase at least 25% renewable energy.	Purchase or produce at least 80% renewable energy (electricity and other fuels) Demonstrate significant overall reductions in energy consumption.	
Waste: Move toward a zerowaste facility.	Conduct a waste audit and act on the results. Educate staff about reducing consumption. Have systems in place for waste reduction (e.g. recycling is easier, monitoring and feedback systems, signage).	Provide incentives for employees and haulers to divert resources from the waste stream.	Achieve zero waste (at least 90% reduction in solid waste going to the landfill) while directing residual products to the 'next best use 'whenever practical.	
Landscaping: Provide landscaping that maximizes ecological benefits.	Conduct a chemical assessment of landscape products and eliminate any that qualify as 'high concern.'	Minimize use of synthetic chemicals through a formal integrated pest management system. Design landscaping to minimize water use and avoid pesticides and maximize ecological value (e.g. xeriscaping, native plants).	Restore or replace natural features of significant ecological value on your property (e.g. daylight a stream, provide habitat on an eco-roof).	

Parking and Transportation Facilities: Create incentives for alternative transportation.	Provide free parking only for carpoolers. Provide bike parking and shower facilities.	Subsidize bus passes and / or provide other incentives for alternative transportation.	Consistently choose sites that permit commuting choices, including convenient alternative transportation.	
New construction and Remodels:\n\nUse green building principles and practices.	Achieve LEED certified or equivalent, Use life-cycle costs, not first costs, as the basis of decision-making.	Achieve LEED silver or equivalent.	Achieve Living Building standard or equivalent.	
Building Operation: Use green building principles and practices in building operation and maintenance.	Achieve LEED EB (existing buildings) or equivalent.	Achieve LEED EB silver or equivalent.	Achieve LEED EB platinum or equivalent.	
Janitorial; Use cleaning products and pest control methods that minimize toxins.	50% or more by volume are green cleaning products (green seal, green cross, UGCA or equivalent). For janitorial paper products, source those with high post-consumer recycled content.	75% of cleaning products are green/sustainable and use non –toxic pest control methods. Apply integrated pest management practices.	100% of cleaning products are green/ sustainable, and all pest control methods are non-toxic.	
Fleets; Minimize the impacts of the fleet through the selection, maintenance and use of vehicles.	Implement a maintenance programme that minimizes hazardous waste maximizes recycling and uses bio-based and non-toxic alternatives (e.g. the Ecological certification programmed).	Assess the needs of the drivers and select vehicles with the best of efficiency and emissions that will meet the needs. Develop systems to minimize driving distance.	Use alternative fuels (biodiesel, ethanol, hydrogen) for all fleet vehicles.	

Water; mini-mize the use of water and reduce storm water run-off.	Conduct a water conservation assessment and act on the results. Eliminate any wasteful uses of water (e.g. single pass cooling towers). Have in place a storm water pollution prevention plan.	Have a formal system in place for reducing water use and have methods for capturing and treating some of the storm water that falls on the property.	Eliminate the need for water other than what falls as precipitation on the property (e.g. through recycling, water treatment) and keep at least 90% storm water run-off on site in normal rain years.	
			Total	
			Average	

5.7 Human Resources: How to Support the Change Process and Bolster Employee Commitment

Human resources professionals are in a good position to influence the sustainability of an organization. Following is the self-assessment process:

SCORE Human Resources

Human Resources				
Practice	Incubator 1 point	Initiative 3 points	Integrated 9 points	points
Promote sustainability concepts	Expose executives to sustainability through articles and other methods.	Provide executives with formal training on sustainability an incomparability and incorporate discussions of its relevance in planning meetings.	Make sustainability knowledge and commitment a selection and performance criterion for executives.	
Promote sustainability projects	Launch sustainability pilot project(s).	Help to manage a formal, organization-wide sustainability –wide sustainability initiative.	Embed sustainability into all business systems (planning, budgeting, reviews, rewards, etc.)	

152

Sustainability Culture	Develop an empowered culture where employees routinely come up with ways to impose performance; sustainability is one of the areas employees focus on.	Have a formal system for recognizing employee contributions to sustainability.	Demonstrate through word and action, both internally and externally, that sustainability is a core value of the organization.	
Sustainability Training	Provide training to employees involved with suitability efforts.	Train the entire staff on sustainability concepts, frameworks, and tools relevant to their jobs.	Routinely offer training on advanced sustainability practices.	
Innovation: Promote innovation culture and process	Have a formal process to help employees discover how to apply sustainability to their everyday work.	Rewrite job descriptions and selection criteria to include sustainability for all appropriate employees and promote innovation	Incorporate sustainability into performance evaluations and reward innovation	
Compensation: refiners fairness and creates incentives for sustainability performance.	Provide a fair living wage and adequate benefits to all employees.	Provide incentives and remove disincentives for sustainability performance.	Have a policy for marinating a fair ratio (less than 50:1) between the highest and lowest paid employee.	
Organizational climate; provide a respectful and productive workplace.	Conduct an employee survey at least every two years and act on the results (including such elements as employee involvement, diversity, work/balance, living wage jobs).	Actively recruit form and provide jobs for people from disadvantaged populations (e.g. people with disabilities, minorities, at-risk youth).	Be listed as one of the best places to work in the state, province or country.	

Commuting: provide effective incentives to encourage the use of alternative transportation and/ or reduce the need to commute.	Only provide paid parking for car-poolers. Promote the use of alterna-tive transportation. Site takeoffs such that it can be eas-ily accessed by at least one alterna-tive transportation method.	Provide assistance for al-ternative commuting (e.g. subsidized bus transpor-tation savings accounts, ride share assistance, personal use of shared vineries)	Provide financial incentives to encourage attentive transportation including bonuses, carbon offsets, etc.; and/or provide financial assistance for employees to purchase the most environmentally responsible car model available.	
Volunteering and charities: support the communities in which you operate of which you affect.	Have systems that encourage employ-ees to donate to charities and to volunteer.	Allow employees to volunteer during paid work time.	Select certain charities of the social/environmen-tal issue(s) that are strategic to your organization and provide at least 40 hours per person of pro donor services per year.	
			Total	
			Average	

5.8 Purchasing: How to Determine What to Buy and How to work with Suppliers

SCORE Purchasing

Purchasing				
Practice	Incubator 1 point	Initiative 3 points	Integrated 9 points	points
Policy: have a purchasing policy related to sustainabil-ity.	As a matter of prac-tice, evaluate major purchases based on sustainability and other criteria but have no formal policy in place.	Have a formal sus-tainable or environ-mentally preferable purchasing policy that incorporates waste reduction. Shun sup-pliers that contribute to human misery, war, or environmental deduction.	At least 80% of purchases (by weight, volume or cost) are from environmentally preferable or sus-tainable sources (e.g. third-petri-fied eco-labels)	

Audits: conduct purchasing audits against goals to assess the impacts of your purchases including items with a short lifespan, toxic materials, and social impacts.	At least every five years, conduct an assessment against sustainable criteria on the largest categories of purchases and act on the results.	Conduct an assessment on the majority of purchases and routinely seek out more sustainable options.	Use life cycle assessments or life cycle thinking to determine the impacts of major categories of purchases.	
Supplier influence: choose suppliers based in part on their sustainability performance.	Send out letters and/or surveys to suppliers to express your commitment to sustainability and your intent to give preference to sustainable suppliers with positive environmental and social practices.	Actively work with suppliers to develop the most sustainable solutions.	Engage in processes to transform the industry.	
Contracting: include sustainability criteria in the selection of contract services.	Include sustainability caritas and language in RFPs. Make sustainability at least a minor selection criterion (e.g. worth up to 15%)	Include in contracts requirements to perform sustainability-related functions of tasks (e.g. construction waste recycling, green cleaning products).	Transform your relationship with major suppliers to provide incentives for stainable performance.	
Reinforcement: have meaningful systems for assessing progress toward sustainable purchasing.	Have purchasing systems that automatically give preference to more sustainable options (e.g. the first choice presented in your online purchasing system is the preferred one) but may not prevent people from purchasing less sustainable options. No feedback is provided on purchasing choices.	Measure and report progress toward goals and targets on major categories of purchases, broken down by individual or group so as to provable meaningful comparisons.	Provide the employee with training and incentives (via compensation, performance appraisals or the formal means) to encourage purchasers to see out sustainable options.	
			Total	
			Average	

5.9 Information Technology: How to Save Energy, Reduce Waste and Facilitate to Low impact Operation:

There are two broad-based aspects to consider when planning your strategies for making IT more sustainable: the operation of the system and its equipment and the opportunities for IT to facilitate energy and resource efficiencies throughout your organization's operations.

Following is the self-assessment for information technology.

Practice	Incubator 1 point	Initiative 3 points	Integrated 9 points	Points
Data centre management; Ensure the most efficient operation of all information and communications technology.	The energy consumption of data centers and related IT equipment is tracked and reviewed by IT MANAGER.	There are efforts to reduce the energy consumption of IT (using sleep modes, turning off idle equipment, upgrading cooling systems, replacing old inefficient equipment, etc.)	Data centre efficiency is maximized through continuous power monitoring / balancing, server virtualization, efficient rack and room layout and similar strategies. The operation is powered by renewable energy.	
Equipment; purchase only the most efficient and sustainable products.	30% of equipment meets EPEAT standard for design and construction.	60% of equipment meets EPEAT standard for design and construction.	100% of equipment meets EPEAT standard for design and construction.	
E-waste; Develop systems and policies for appropriate managing of electronic equipment at the end of its useful life.	Send at least 50% of e-waste to recyclers or reuse centres.	Responsibly manage the –of-life handling of at least 80% of computer-related equipment; monitors, keyboards, PDAs, etc.	Recycle all technology-related consumables (batteries, printer cartridges, PDAs, cell phones, etc..). Achieve zero e-waste.	
Dematerialization; contribute to the transition to reduce material contents	Make video-conferencing technology available, support electronic document management.	Make an electronic document the norm.	Over half the meetings with people at a distance and done using electronic conferencing. More than half of employees telecommute at least part time. Achieve a virtually paperless office.	

156

Process support; support the efficient management of (transportation logistics, manufacturing processes, facilities use, etc.)	Assure the efficiency of program design to minimize unnecessary use of server energy. Help facilities, shipping, and other departments monitor energy use.	Support use of best available technology (e.g. digital metering, routs demand response energy software, process design, and simulation tools) to optimize the performance of the entire organization and provide useful data on sustainability metrics.	Through the strategic use of best available technology, optimize the performance of the entire supply chain. Apply applications to create solutions to environmental and social problems.	
Product Design and selection support; Maintain the data necessary to sustainable design.	Provide material tracking systems to measure and monitor the types and amounts of materials used in product design or in materials consumed.	Manage product content information for reporting and certification.	Maintain sophisticated databases of life cycle information for use in product design or materials purchase.	
			Total	
			Average	

157

5.10 SCORE Environmental Affairs

EH&S and pollution prevention professionals all have an important role to play in sustainability. Following is the self-assessment.

Environmental Affairs				
Practice	Incubator 1 point	Initiative 3 points	Integrated 9 points	points
Sustainability Management systems; convert your existing environmental management system (EMS) into a sustainability management system (SMS). [note; if you don't have an EMS, see sustainability management system under leadership/senior management]	Have an EMS that has many elements of ISO 14001.	Have an ISO 14001 conformant EMS. Sustainability clearly is reflected in the policy and targets. A long-term plan is in place to reach sustainable levels of all significant impacts. The SMS includes goals associated with customer and supplier impacts.	The SMS has become part of the overall management of the organization and is no longer a discrete, separate system. The SMS takes responsibility for the full lifecycle of your product or service.	
Chemicals and toxics; Eliminate chemicals that adversely impact human health and the environment.	Complete a chemical inventory and rate them based on toxicity and volume. Eliminate all use of persistent bioaccumulative toxins (PBTs).	Reduce use of hazardous materials to below the level needed for permits. Complete a grey; and 'black' list of chemicals to eliminate from the workplace and your products. If appropriate, implement a chemical management system.	Use the precautionary principle for purchasing, products. Have phased out all grey and blacklisted chemicals. Have implemented a cradle-to-cradle system for technical and biological nutrients.	
Water quality and conservation: minimize the use of water, keep water on site, and treat discharges/ run-off.	Conduct a water audit at least every five years and act on the results. Assess water discharge and develop a conservation plan.	Provide on-site water treatment for majority of storm water. Reuse water where practical.	Water discharged is as clean or cleaner than the source; no discharge of storm water off the site. Maximize water reuse and conservation opportunities.	

Natural resources: protect natural resources on your own properties.	Conduct an assessment of natural resources and act on the results.	Consider natural resource impacts in decision-making.	Restore habitat to replace natural resources lost by development.	
Air Quality: protect the air-shed inside and outside your facilities.	Conduct air quality testing in all work areas and take appropriate them within all government regulations.	Switch to low-VOC (VOLA-TILR ORGANIC COMPOUNDS) PRODUCTS FOR ALL COATINGS, SOHESIVES, etc.	Switch to benign alternatives (e.g. plant-based, biodegradable).	
Emergency response; have effective plans in place for all serious contingencies.	Have effective crisis response plans foreseeable problem. Give higher priority to protecting public health and the environment than protecting your short-term financial interests and image.	Actively engage stakeholders in identifying ways to prevent and deal with foreseeable crises.	Actively promote industry-wide practices and standards that protect public health and the environment.	
Role shift: redistribute responsibility for environmental issues and sustainability across the organization.	Sustainability coordinator and/or environmental affairs is the main source of sustainability leadership.	Sustainability leadership is fully integrated into management	The organization has evolved to one of disseminating sustainability information to the broader community information to the broader community (e.g. lectures, supplier workshops).	
Hazardous waste: manage hazardous waste to protect human health and the environment.	Have an inventory plan that is fully compliant with all government regulations and OHSAS 18000.	Systematically find replacements for hazardous chemicals.	Eliminate all hazardous chemicals from the site.	
			Total	
			Average	

5.11 SCORE Marketing and Public Relations

Marketing and public relations professionals have critical skills to support a sustainability initiative. They can use their understanding of their market place and stakeholders to design more sustainable products and services as well as frame their organizations' messages effectively. Marketing people are key to creating demand for more sustainable products. Following is the self-assessment in this area:

Marketing				
Practice	Incubator 1 point	Initiative 3 points	Integrated 9 points	Points
Marketing strategy; have a strategy in place that encourages to choose the more sustainable options.	Assess market segments for their understanding and opinions about sustainability. Use this information to target the green market segment.	Develop a message that will resonate with each market segment choice (e.g. take-back opportunities as a marketing strategy).	Develop an aggressive customer education customer education campaign around sustainable products and services.	
Product positioning: make all products more sustainable.	Assess all your major product lines for their sustainability impacts.	Eliminate or redesign lines with the worst sustainability performance. Seek credible eco-labeling of certification for some of your products.	All products are sustainable (e.g. third-party certified). Demonstrate significant innovations that push the limits of existing 'green' practices and move the industry forward.	
Internal marketing: Educate all employees about the organization's sustainability efforts.	Incorporate sustainability into employee communications on an ad hoc basis.	Communicate at least quarterly via two types of media or more.	All employees are fully aware of sustainability activities.	
Marketing materials and giveaways: Make sustainable choices about collateral.	When printing, use high post-consumer recycled content paper and soy-based inks. Reduce the use of give-aways and choose products that exemplify sustainability. Make it easy for customers to eliminate duplicate mailings or get off your mailing list. Honour do-not-call lists for telemarketing.	Minimize the use of printed marketing materials through the use of technology where life cycle assessment indicates this would be preferred.	Promote the concepts of sustainability in marketing materials to educate customers.	

Public Relations				
Practice	**Incubator** **1 point**	**Initiative** **3 points**	**Integrated** **9 points**	**points**
PR/Outreach strategy: Educate stakeholders about your sustainability efforts.	Assess your stakeholders' opinions of sustainability.	Show how the organization has taken significant initiative in sustainability	Produce a publicly available, formal annual sustainability report that honestly portrays your progress as well as your areas for improvement.	
Stakeholder engagement: provide mechanisms for stakeholders to express their expectations, priorities, and concerns.	Identify your major stakeholders and actively assess their trust, perception, and ideas for improvement.	Conduct formal stakeholder audits and involve key stakeholders in major, sensitive decisions.	Partner with key stakeholders on projects to shift the sustainability performance of your industry (e.g. aggregating purchasing power, setting standards, creating political pressure for change).	
Incident/ Emergency response and media communications; ensure everyone has the best information.	Provide timely, accurate and complete information to authorities and the public when a crisis does occur (e.g. bad press, accident, high-profile mistake). Give higher priority to protecting public health and the environment over protecting your short-term financial interests and image.	Proactively provide ready access for the media and the public about incidents and responses (e.g. via website, press releases, etc.)	Operate with integrity and transparency, avoiding the temptation to spin bad news in your favour. Take full responsibility for your actions and move quickly to sustainable solutions.	
			Total	
			average	

161

5.12 Score Finance and Accounting

The area of finance and accounting are the least developed in terms of incorporating sustainability into their practice. Following is the self-assessment

Finance				
Practice	**Incubator 1 point**	**Initiative 3 points**	**Integrated 9 points**	**points**
Financial analysis: use tools to provide a more complete assessment of options that take sustainability into account.	In addition to traditional financial methods for determining return on investment, include an assessment of risks and intangible benefits when assessing options.	Use total cost of ownership (versus first cost) and identify externalities radiated to the life cycle of the product or investment.	Make full life cycle analysis available and take responsibility for all identifiable extensities when making major decisions; choose discount rates that don't unfairly discount the needs of future generations.	
Sustainability reporting: make available and use qualitative/ quantitative data on your progress toward sustainability.	Produce an internal report highlighting accomplishments and areas for improvement.	Include sustainability reporting as part of existing public reports.	Publish a separate, detailed and audited sustainability report.	
Investments: factor in sustainability when making investment decisions (e.g. pension plans, stock purchases, bonds).	Employ negative screens for such criteria as tobacco, arms, child labour; etc.	Give preference to investments that demonstrate a commitment to sustainability practices.	Only invest in sustainability-related investments.	
Your systems so that people are encouraged to optimize the sustainability performance of the entire organization rather than their own budgets.	Sustainability as one of the criteria that should be assessed before money is spent.	Accounting for benefits that accrue to different budgets (e.g. capital versus operations/ maintenance; operations versus customer service department).	Systemic barriers exist that inhibit sustainability, provide a way to return some of the department (s) that indirectly created the savings.	

Metrics; develop a set of sustainability metrics.	Develop a set of metrics to assess the progress toward your sustainability projects and goals.	Develop a complete set of sustainability metrics for the organization and report on them at least annually.	Regularity conduct sustainability best-practices studies with other organizations to uncover opportunities for improvement.	
			Total	
			Average	

Accounting				
Practice	Incubator 1 point	Initiative 3 points	Integrated 9 points	points
Budgets: modify your systems so that people are encouraged to optimize the sustainability performance of the entire organization rather than their own budgets.	Include sustainability as one of the critical that should be assessed before money is spent.	Provide a method of accounting for benefits that accrue to different budgets (eg capital versus operations/ maintenance; operations versus cushions versus customer service department).	Where significant systemic deterrents exist that inhibit sustainability, provide a way to return some of the savings to the department (s) that indirectly created the savings.	
Metrics: Develop a set of sustainability metrics.	Develop a set of metrics to assess the progress toward your sustainability projects and goals.	Develop a complete set of sustainability metrics for the report on them at least annually.	Regularity conduct sustainability best-practices studies with other organizations to uncover opportunities for improvement.	
			Total	
			Average	

Questions:

1. Why should an organization consider using self-assessment as a means for measuring the performance of its sustainability program?
2. Conduct self-assessment of any 2 sectors and any 3 functions of your choice based on your experience

Chapter 6

Life Cycle Analysis, Carbon Footprint, and Green House Gas Quantification

6.1 Life cycle assessment / analysis

Using the established methodology of Life Cycle Assessment (LCA) your company can measure the carbon footprint of your suite of products and/ or services.

Life Cycle Assessment (also known as Life Cycle Analysis, Ecobalance, and Cradle-to-Grave Analysis) is an accurate technique to determine the volume of carbon dioxide emissions connected to your company's products and/or services. LCA involves measuring the volume of carbon emissions during the full life cycle of a product / service. From the initial start point when the requisite raw materials are processed and converted into a product / service — to the final, conclusive point in the life cycle — when that product becomes waste.

What is Life Cycle Assessment?

First developed in the 1960s, Life Cycle Assessment (LCA) is the most widely used and highly regarded tool for quantifying the environmental impacts of products and services. Despite being conceptually quite straightforward, LCA can be very complex with many important, often material-specific, assumptions that can significantly influence the outcome. LCA is the tool that is used to develop Environmental Product Declarations (EPD) which are a standardized set of environmental information based on a common set of rules called Product Category Rules (PCRs). EPD are increasingly being used by construction product manufacturers in the UK and the EU to provide robust, quantified environmental data for their products.

LCA involves the collection and evaluation of quantitative data on the inputs and outputs of material, energy and waste flows associated with a product over its entire life cycle so that its whole-life environmental impacts can be determined.

An LCA essentially comprises three steps:
1. Compiling an inventory of relevant energy and material inputs and environmental releases (outputs) associated with a defined system. Releases can be solid wastes or emissions to air or water
2. Evaluating the potential impacts associated with these inputs and releases, e.g. the global warming impact from CO_2 emissions
3. Interpreting the results to help make informed decisions.

An important first step in any LCA is to clearly define the goal and scope of the study. The goal and scope of the study should define key details of the study including:

- The functional unit of the product or system to be assessed, e.g., a tonne of structural steel, 1m2 of external wall or a whole building, etc
- The system boundaries, i.e., what is included/excluded from the scope of the assessment
- Any specific assumptions and limitations of the study
- The allocation methods used to partition the environmental load of a process when several products or functions share the same process, e.g. blast furnace slag is a valuable by-product of steelmaking from iron ore and therefore should carry a proportion of the environmental impact from steelmaking to the product in which it is used. Allocation is used to 'allocate' a proportion of the environmental impact from steelmaking to the blast furnace slag

The environmental impact categories chosen, e.g. if only the climate change impact is included within the scope of the LCA, then the assessment is, in fact, an embodied carbon assessment.

LCA methodology is flexible in terms of the goal and hence the scope of assessment. However, a robust LCA of a construction product (or a building) should include the impacts of:

- Extraction of the relevant raw materials, e.g. quarrying, mining
- Refinement and conversion to process materials, e.g. steelmaking or cement production
- Manufacturing and packaging processes, e.g. steelwork fabrication or making precast concrete products
- Transportation and distribution between each stage
- Waste at each stage
- On-site construction impacts, e.g. water and energy use, temporary works, shuttering, worker commuting, etc
- Operation during the lifetime of the building including maintenance, refurbishment, replacement, etc. At the end of its useful life, demolition, final transportation, waste treatment and disposal.

Any recycling or recovery operations built into the life cycle should lead to a proportionate reduction in the adverse environmental impact and should be accounted for.

6.2 LCA impact categories

The impact of the inventory of flows or outputs from a system is assessed and interpreted by linking them to environmental impact categories through a process known as characterization. The environmental impact categories generally considered in an LCA study are shown; the most common categories are shown in bold.

Climate change	Ecotoxicity to land
Water extraction	Waste disposal
Mineral resource extraction	Fossil fuel depletion
Stratospheric ozone depletion	Eutrophocation
Human toxicity	Photochemical ozone creation
Ecotoxicity to freshwater	Acidification
Nuclear waste (high level)	

A very good case study on "Comparative Life Cycle Assessment (LCA) of streetlight technologies for minor roads in United Arab Emirates" can be seen from the following link:

**https://ac.els-cdn.com/S0973082613000380/1-s2.0-
S0973082613000380-main.pdf?_tid=ec0bd3f6-ce0e-460a-a704-baf34
966cc2c&acdnat=1529501742_466b11e7a82edfeb992dcfee7b5e6621**

6.3 LCA environmental impact categories

Environmental impacts in one category can be caused by many different emissions and therefore characterization factors are used to combine the impact of different substances. A good example of this, which is also relevant to embodied carbon assessments, is the impact category of climate change.

Climate change is caused by a number of different greenhouse gases each which have a greater or lesser impact on the climate over time. In LCA therefore (and in robust embodied carbon studies) climate change characterizations factors (or global warming potentials (GWP) - see table below) are used to combine the global warming potential of different greenhouse gases to derive a single metric, in this case CO2e or carbon dioxide equivalents. Similar characterization processes are undertaken for other LCA impact categories.

Greenhouse gas	GWP – 100 year timeframe (kgCO2e)
Carbon dioxide (CO2)	1
Methane (CH4)	25
Nitrous oxide (N2O)	298
Sulphur hexafluoride (SF6)	22800
Perfluorobutane (C4F10)	8860
HFC 134a (tetrafluoroethane)	1430

Characterization (or GWP) factors for common greenhouse gases

Having established quantitative measures for each of the impact categories within the scope of the LCA, a further step undertaken in some LCA methodologies is to weight the different impact categories to produce a single value of environmental impact. Although this approach is not endorsed in LCA standards, it can be used to produce a single metric scoring system that is easy to understand for users.

LCA takes into consideration the total volume of CO_2 emitted:

1. While mining / extraction;
2. Transporting raw materials;
3. Production;
4. When selling and then;
5. Using the product, and finally;
6. During the waste management process.

In the cyclical course of a LCA it is also possible to measure, not only total emissions, but also emissions during certain specific production phases; that the manufacturer is responsible for (for example, throughout the specific phases comprised in the operation of sourcing raw materials: to the point of placing the product on the market shelf).

Life Cycle analysis is highly recommended, if your company

i.   wants to assess and reduce energy and raw material consumption for both its products and services;
ii. intends to take advantage of Environmental Awareness because you view it as conferring a competitive edge;
iii. searches for strategic business solutions that distinguish its product range from other competing products;
iv. wishes to attract green shoppers (who are loyal, have more money to spend and who have been growing in number);
v.   Your company want the ZeroCO2 trademark and would like to exploit the business potential in Carbon Neutrality.

6.4 Carbon Footprint

A total product carbon footprint is a measure of the direct and indirect greenhouse gas (GHG) emissions associated with all activities in the product's life cycle. Products are both goods and services. Such a carbon footprint can be calculated by performing (according to international standards) a LCA that concentrates on GHG emissions that have an effect on climate change.

The World Resources Institute (WRI) and the World Business Council for Sustainable Development (WBCSD) have partnered to develop The Greenhouse Gas Protocol: A Corporate Accounting and Reporting Standard. The framework gives business and organizations an internationally accepted methodology to help quantify and report the GHG emissions associated with their operations. Businesses often have multiple objectives in developing such an inventory, but a primary objective is frequently to support the identification of GHG emission reduction opportunities. The accounting framework looks at both direct (Scope 1) and indirect emissions (Scopes 2 and 3), which are explained further below:

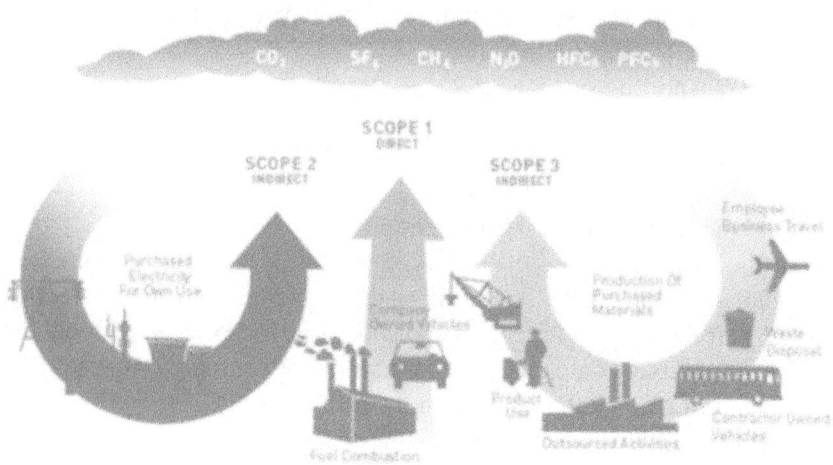

Source: Bahtia and Ranganathan, 2004

- Scope 1 – Direct GHG emissions – these occur from sources that are owned or controlled by the company, for example emissions from combustion in owned or controlled boilers, furnaces, vehicles, etc. or emissions from chemical production in owned or controlled process equipment.

- Scope 2 – Electricity and heat indirect GHG emissions – this accounts for GHG emissions from the generation of purchased electricity and heat consumed by the company. Purchased electricity is defined as electricity that is purchased or otherwise brought into the organizational boundary of the company. Scope 2 emissions physically occur at the facility where the electricity is generated.

- Scope 3 – Other indirect GHG emissions – this is a reporting category that allows for the treatment of all other indirect emissions. Scope 3 emissions are a consequence of the activities of the company, but occur from sources not owned or controlled by the company. Some examples of Scope 3 activities are the extraction and production of purchased materials, the transportation of purchased fuels and the use of sold goods and services.

The current corporate GHG standard has defined detailed criteria for the accounting and reporting of Scope 1 and 2 GHG emissions. The WRI and the WBCSD are now developing new standards for product and corporate value chain GHG accounting and reporting. To develop the new guidelines, the GHG Protocol Initiative is following the same broad, multi-stakeholder process used to develop the previous standards, with participation from businesses, policymakers, NGOs, academics and other experts and stakeholders from around the world. The new standards and guidance will cover both product life cycle and corporate level value chain accounting and reporting. Building upon existing methodologies, the standards and guidelines will provide a harmonized approach for companies and organizations to inventory GHG emissions along their value chains and better incorporate GHG impacts into business decision-making.

Carbon Footprint Analysis

Carbon Footprint Analysis, referred as Greenhouse Gas Emissions Assessment, analyzes the greenhouse gas emissions by the production of a product or any given activity that contributes to global warming. First of all, the emissions of carbon, sulfurhexafluoride, and methane are assessed. After the emissions are found, the assessment converts the output into carbon dioxide equivalents (CO_2e). Three core standards around carbon footprint analysis are the GHG Protocol, ISO DS 14067, and PAS 2050. The GHG Protocol is the most commonly used international tool for business leaders and governments to comprehend, quantify and control GHG emissions.

It includes four different standards:

Product Life Cycle Accounting and Reporting Standard: This standard involves understanding product life cycle GHG emissions, including raw materials used, production, distribution, and disposal akin to a Product LCA.

Corporate Value Chain Accounting and Reporting Standard: This standard is intended for organizations or businesses to evaluate their entire value chain and calculate the environmental impacts of the GHG emission by the value chain.

The standard also involves identifying possible ways to lessen GHG emissions.

Project Accounting Protocol and Guidelines: This standard is used to assess reductions of GHG emissions by any given projects.

Corporate Accounting and Reporting Standards: This is more or less the same as an organizational LCA. It is intended for organizations/businesses and is used to assess GHG emissions from business operating and activities.

Everything has a carbon footprint. So, carbon footprint can be assigned to a product, a production plant, and an organization or a business.

6.5 Hand printing:

Many companies are already changing the world for the better—by greening their products, launching programs for sustainability in their communities, or improving the lives of employees and their families. Each of these initiatives is a positive business impact—what is called a "handprint." We compare a company's handprint to its footprint (which is an adverse impact of an organization's operations), and when its handprint is larger than its footprint, the company becomes a *Net Positive Enterprise*. Hand printing concept has been applied in Case Study No. 2.

6.6 Similarities and Differences between Carbon Footprint and Life Cycle Analysis

With the buzzword "Sustainability" flying everywhere, it has become tough to distinguish between numerous environmental assessments available around us. Life cycle assessments, carbon footprint analysis, water footprint analysis, CSR reports, VOC testing, environmental risk assessments, the list goes on and on. Life cycle assessment and carbon footprint analysis are two of the most common of these assessments.

The carbon footprint of a product, or the inventory of its life cycle GHG emissions, represents its impact on climate change. Hence, it is a subset of the life cycle assessment.

In fact, the LCA measures the potential environmental impacts of a product, process or service over its life cycle. In addition to GHG, the LCA takes into account all other material and energy inputs and environmental releases and assesses their potential impact on the environment.

The spectrum of impact categories is broad and includes human health, ecosystem degradation, climate change and natural resource depletion. LCA is therefore a "multicriteria" analysis that assesses multiple impacts.

The carbon footprint is essentially "monocriterion" as it focuses on a single environmental impact, climate changes.

Both methods rely on functional approaches for impact assessment. In fact, a "functional unit," or quantified performance of a studied product, serves as the basis for analysis and enables comparability between products with similar functional units.

There are a number of similarities and differences between these two.

Such approaches are central to green claims as well as to understanding greenwashing. Let's have a clear understanding of both of these two assessments to understand the similarities and differences:

6.7 Life Cycle Assessment (LCA)

LCA systematically assesses multiple environmental impacts of a product, activity or a process over the life cycle of that product, activity or process. It has been around for more than 30 years now. Carbon footprint analysis thus is a subset of a complete life cycle assessment of a product, activity or process. The core standards around LCA are ISO 14044 and ISO 14040. Just like a carbon footprint, LCA can be done for a product, service, project, and an organization. The multiple assessment categories under LCA include impacts on natural resource depletion, climate change, ecosystem degradation and human health.

LCA, in addition to GHG, takes environmental releases and all other material inputs throughout the life cycle into account and assesses all the potential direct and indirect impacts on the environment. Thus, LCA is a "Multi-Criteria" analysis that assesses multiple environmental impacts. On the other hand, the Carbon footprint is basically a "Mono-criterion" analysis as it focuses on only one environmental impact, climate change by GHG emission.

Both analyses depend on functional approaches to impact measurement. In effect, a "functional unit," or the environmental impact output of a studied product, process or activity, serves as the foundation for assessment and facilitates comparability between products, process, and activity or any other above mentioned items with similar functional units.

These days, there are various online carbon footprint and LCA assessment tools that can be used to have some general ideas about the possible environmental impacts of any product, process, activity, business or project. http://www3.epa.gov/carbon-footprint-calculator/and http://www.lcacalculator.com/ are two most popular calculators available online.

6.8 Carbon Emission Trading

Carbon emissions trading is a type of policy that allows companies to buy or sell government-granted allotments of carbon dioxide output. In another word, trading the rights of greenhouse gas emissions. The idea is a response to the Kyoto Protocol. Both countries and companies can reduce their emissions below designated levels and sell this amount to a business or country with greenhouse gas emissions that are too high.

Governments distribute a finite number of CO_2 "credits" to companies. That's the "cap" part. The companies can only emit as much CO_2 as they have credits for. Those below their CO_2 limit can sell credits to companies that exceed the limit. That's the "trade" part. It equally works for countries. Basically, each country has a cap on the amount of carbon they are allowed to release. Carbon emissions trading then allows countries that have higher carbon emissions to purchase the right to release more carbon dioxide into the atmosphere from countries that have lower carbon emissions.

The goal is to slow down global warming. Industries, like utilities, are the biggest traders. They burn coal and other fossil fuels that emit too much carbon dioxide into the air.

How did this come about? The International Energy Agency recommended that no more than a third of the world's reserves of fossil fuels should be burned by 2050. If more is burned, the CO_2 will heat up the atmosphere to a dangerous level of 2 degrees Celsius above pre-industrial levels.

Scientists agree that the resultant climate change causes flooding, drought, and hurricanes. (Source: "The Coming Carbon Asset Bubble," The Wall Street Journal, October 30, 2013.)

Cap and Trade Makes Carbon Trading Possible

Carbon emissions trading really took off when the European Union instituted a cap and trade program in 2005. This set a cap on the total the amount of CO_2 that heavy industries and utilities could emit.

The cap must be low enough to actually reduce the greenhouse gases that cause global warming.

If the cap is too low, then it will make the cost of doing business too high, and slow economic growth. If the cap is too high, then it won't impact the pace of global warming.

In November 2017, the EU reduced the carbon cap by 2.2 percent each year through 2030. The cap was 1.74 percent annually. The cap's goal is to reduce carbon emission by 43 percent by 2030.

It affects 11,000 energy and industrial plants.

The Carbon Trading Market

The market for carbon trading was $176 billion in 2011. It could exceed $1 trillion by 2020. At least 84 percent of this is the EU's Emission Trading Scheme. It caps emissions for any company doing business in the EU. (Source: "Existing and Planned Carbon Markets," Ernst & Young.)

As of 2017, there is no cap and trade program in the United States, despite some attempts at legislation. Some other countries are creating their own markets. As part of the United Nations Framework Convention on Climate Change, all countries agreed to the Durban Platform in 2011. This said they would negotiate the details of a comprehensive global cap and trade program by 2015. (Sources: "The Future of Global Carbon Markets," Ernst & Young, "What a Gas!" Global Finance, July 2008.)

How Trading Works

The cap allows each company to emit a certain amount of CO_2. The EU issues about two billion of these European Union Allowances each year. To comply with the EU mandate, companies may either:

1. Take measures to emit only what they are allowed.
2. Reduce their emissions below the allowed amount and sell or bank the surplus EUAs.
3. Continue emitting above their allowance and buy EUAs in the marketplace to cover it.

Carbon Emission Reductions Credits

Certified Emission Reductions credits are also traded. These were created by the Kyoto Protocol. They are credits issued to projects in developing countries that reduce emissions.

There are also greenhouse gas emission credits, which cover more pollutants than just CO2. They can fulfill nation-specific caps in the United States, UK, Canada, New Zealand and Japan.

Is Carbon Emissions a New Form of Currency?

This ability to buy and sell EUAs, CERs and other units on a freely traded market has created a new form of "currency." Traders include not only the emitters themselves but also banks, hedge funds, and other investors. They provide liquidity and increase market efficiency. A unit of carbon trading equals the reduction of one metric ton of carbon dioxide or its equivalent in other greenhouse gasses.

(Source: Cantor CO2 web site.)

The idea of a tradeable market based on something that is just a concept takes trading to a new level. Even if the value of a mortgage-backed security is far removed from its underlying asset, you can still trace it back to something tangible: a loan made by a bank to a person who owns a house. Increasingly abstract forms of currency are on the rise. The 2008 financial crisis was created by new types of derivatives. The value of these collateralized debt obligations and MBS expanded far beyond that of the hard assets upon which they were based. Creation of new forms of currency is bound to continue.

In some ways, carbon trading is a new form of currency. The value of EUAs, CERs and the like can only be traced back to a colorless, odorless gas. But the monetary value assigned to a unit of this gas is based on how much damage it can do the climate systems that affect all aspects of our lives Like gold, but unlike a house, it doesn't really have a "useful" value other than what the market says it has. But the market didn't assign that value arbitrarily. It was assigned to address a threat to stability and safety of life on Earth.

6.9 Carbon Tax

A carbon tax is a fee imposed on the burning of carbon-based fuels (coal, oil, gas). In another word, a carbon tax is the core policy for reducing and eventually eliminating the use of fossil fuels whose combustion is destabilizing and destroying our climate. A carbon tax is a way — the *only* way — to make users of carbon fuels pay for the climate damage caused by releasing carbon dioxide into the atmosphere. If set high enough, it becomes a powerful monetary disincentive that motivates switches to clean energy across the economy, simply by making it more economically rewarding to move to non-carbon fuels and energy efficiency.

For example, Singapore Budget 2018 announced that a Carbon tax of $5 per tons of greenhouse gas emissions is to be levied from 2019 to 2023.

6.10 Carbon footprint of different diets

Even since the FAO announced that 18% of global emission result from livestock people have talked about the climate benefits of reducing meat consumption.

More recent studies show that food system emissions could account for as much as quarter of all human emissions. That is 12% from agricultural production, another 9% from farming induced deforestation, and a further 3% from things like refrigeration and freight.

Such studies beg the question, what is the impact of meat on an individual's foodprint?

This analysis tries to answer that question using data from the US. In it we compare five different diets:

Meat Lover, Average, No Beef, Vegetarian and Vegan

For each diet we look solely at the emissions associated with the food supply, so we do not include those from consumer's transportation, storage or the cooking of food. Nor do we consider land use change emissions.

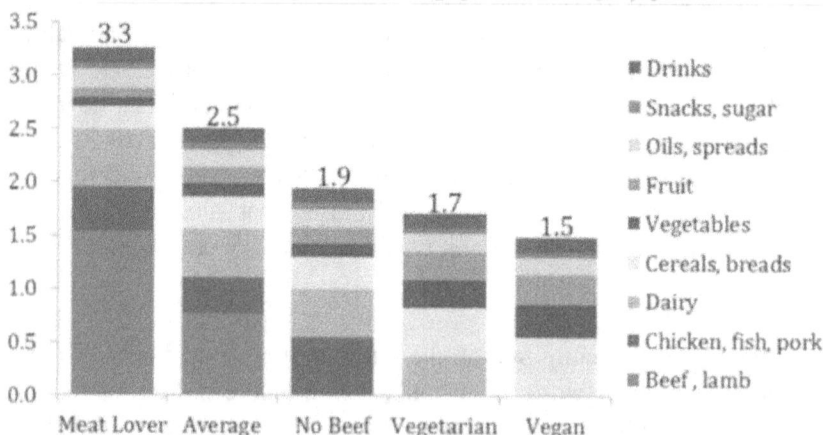

Foodprints by Diet Type: t CO2e/person

Note: All estimates based on average food production emissions for the US. Footprints include emissions from supply chain losses, consumer waste and consumption.. Each of the four example diets is based on 2,600 kcal of food consumed per day, which in the US equates to around 3,900 kcal of supplied food.

Sources: ERS/USDA, various LCA and EIO-LCA data   Shrink That Footprint

A Vegetarian's footprint is about two-thirds of the average American and almost half that of a meat lover. For a Vegan, it is even lower. But perhaps most interestingly, eating chicken instead of beef cuts a quarter of emissions in one simple step.

Food production is responsible for about 25 percent of the greenhouse-gas emissions heating up the planet. And scientists have long known that meat has a bigger climate footprint than fruits and vegetables do — partly because meat takes more energy to produce, but also because cows tend to burp up a lot of methane. (Cows, in turn, have a larger impact than pigs or chickens.)

An Average American's diet has a footprint of around 2.5 t CO2e per person each year. For a Meat Lover this rises to 3.3 t CO2e, for the No Beef diet it is 1.9 t t CO2e, for the Vegetarian it's 1.7 t CO2e, and for the Vegan, it is 1.5 t CO2e. Each of these estimates includes emissions from food that is eaten, wasted by consumers and lost in the supply chain.

In the average diet, animal products make up 60% of emissions despite accounting for just a quarter of food energy. For the Meat Lover, beef consumption causes almost half of emissions from just a tenth of food energy. In the No Beef diet, all the reductions from the Average footprint come by switching from beef to chicken. The difference between the Vegetarian and Vegan diets arises from dairy consumption being switched to a mix of cereals and vegetables.

Perhaps the most fascinating thing is that although the footprints vary greatly, three-fifths of each diet is identical. In other words, 60% of food energy consumed is the same in each of these four diets.

The share that is constant accounts for 1550 kcal of food energy per day and about 0.7 t CO2e of each foodprint. So all the variation depends on the remaining 1,000 kcal per day. The Vegan gets these 1000 kcal for 0.8 t CO2e, the Vegetarian for 1 t, No Beef for 1.2 t, Average for 1.8 t and the Meat Lover for 2.6 t.

Carbon neutrality, or having a net zero *carbon* footprint, refers to achieving net zero *carbon* emissions by balancing a measured amount of *carbon* released with an equivalent amount sequestered or offset or buying enough *carbon* credits to make up the difference.

Questions:

1. Describe Life Cycle Assessment and impact categories
2. Discuss when LCA is recommended to be carried out.
3. What is carbon footprint? Discuss similarities and differences between carbon footprint and LCA
4. What are the direct (Scope 1) and indirect (Scope 2 and 3) emissions?
4. What is GWP and where is it used?
5. Discuss Carbon emission trading and Carbon Tax.

Chapter 7

Green House Gas Emissions Quantification

7.1 Global Greenhouse Gas Emissions Data

It is imperative that Green House Gases emitted by the organizations are measured and quantified so that they can take effective measures to reduce such emissions. As the cliché goes, that what is not measured can not be managed.

Main Green House Gases are water vapour (60%), the four principal greenhouse gases are carbon dioxide (CO_2) (26%), methane (CH_4)/ nitrous oxide (N_2O) (6%), O_3 (8%) and the halocarbons or CFCs (gases containing fluorine, chlorine, and bromine). These gases can remain in the atmosphere for different amounts of time, from months to millennia, and affect the climate on very different timescales.

The lifetime in the air of CO_2, the most significant man-made greenhouse gas, is probably the most difficult to determine because there are several processes that remove carbon dioxide from the atmosphere. Between 65% and 80% of CO_2 released into the air dissolves into the ocean over a period of 20–200 years. The rest is removed by slower processes that take up to several hundreds of thousands of years, including chemical weathering and rock formation. This means that once in the atmosphere, carbon dioxide can continue to affect the climate for thousands of years.

Methane, by contrast, is mostly removed from the atmosphere by chemical reaction, persisting for about 12 years. Thus, although methane is a potent greenhouse gas, its effect is relatively short-lived.

Nitrous oxide is destroyed in the stratosphere and removed from the atmosphere more slowly than methane, persisting for around 114 years.

Compounds containing chlorine and/or fluorine (CFCs, HCFCs, HFCs, PFCs) include a huge number of different chemical species, each of which can last in the atmosphere for a specific length of time – from less than a year to many thousands of years. The IPCC has published a comprehensive list of the atmospheric lifetime of the various CFCs and other greenhouse gases.

Water vapour is a very effective absorber of heat energy in the air, but it does not accumulate in the atmosphere in the same way as the other greenhouse gases. This is down to it having a very short atmospheric lifetime, of the order of hours to days, because it is rapidly removed as rain and snow. The amount of water vapour that the atmosphere can hold increases as the atmosphere gets warmer, so the greenhouse properties of water vapour are usually considered to act as part of a feedback loop, rather than a direct cause of climate change.

176

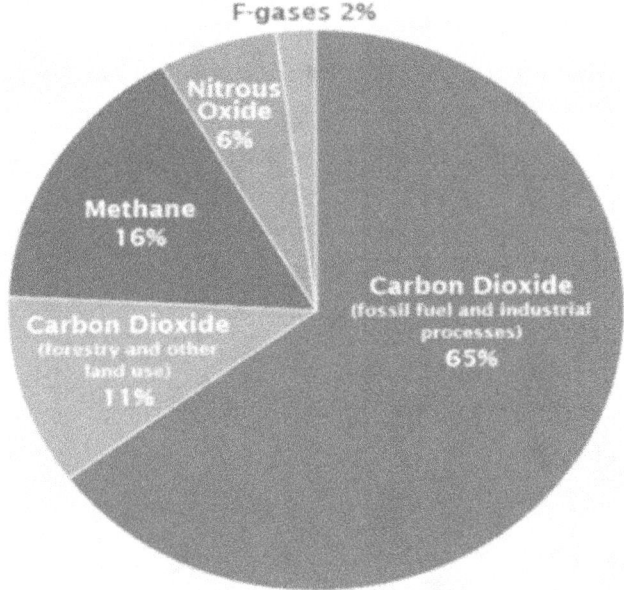

Figure 7.1

Source: IPCC (2014) based on global emissions from 2010. Details about the sources included in these estimates can be found in the *Contribution of Working Group III to the Fifth Assessment Report of the Intergovernmental Panel on Climate Change.*

- **Carbon dioxide (CO2)**: Fossil fuel use is the primary source of CO2. CO2 can also be emitted from direct human-induced impacts on forestry and other land use, such as through deforestation, land clearing for agriculture, and degradation of soils. Likewise, land can also remove CO2 from the atmosphere through reforestation, improvement of soils, and other activities.
- **Methane (CH4)**: Agricultural activities, waste management, energy use, and biomass burning all contribute to CH4 emissions.
- **Nitrous oxide (N2O)**: Agricultural activities, such as fertilizer use, are the primary source of N2O emissions. Fossil fuel combustion also generates N2O.
- **Fluorinated gases (F-gases)**: Industrial processes, refrigeration, and the use of a variety of consumer products contribute to emissions of F-gases, which include hydrofluorocarbons (HFCs), perfluorocarbons (PFCs), and sulfur hexafluoride (SF6).

Black carbon is a solid particle or aerosol, not a gas, but it also contributes to warming of the atmosphere.

Global Emissions by Economic Sector

Global greenhouse gas emissions can also be broken down by the economic activities that lead to their production

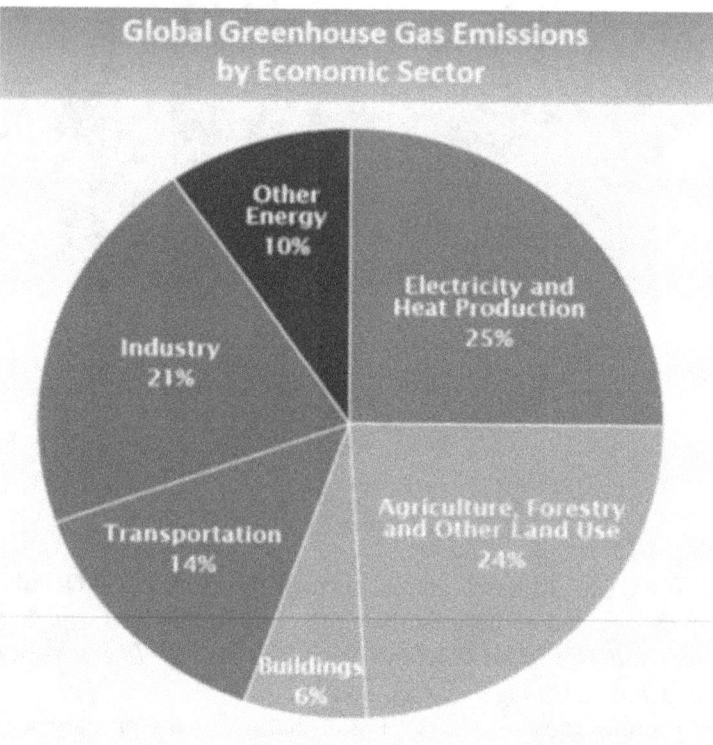

Figure 7.2

Source: IPCC (2014); based on global emissions from 2010. Details about the sources included in these estimates can be found in the *Contribution of Working Group III to the Fifth Assessment Report of the Intergovernmental Panel on Climate Change*.

- **Electricity and Heat Production** (25% of 2010 global greenhouse gas emissions): The burning of coal, natural gas, and oil for electricity and heat is the largest single source of global greenhouse gas emissions.
- **Industry** (21% of 2010 global greenhouse gas emissions): Greenhouse gas emissions from industry primarily involve fossil fuels burned on-site at facilities for energy. This sector also includes emissions from chemical, metallurgical, and mineral transformation processes not associated with energy consumption

and emissions from waste management activities. (Note: Emissions from industrial electricity use are excluded and are instead covered in the Electricity and Heat Production sector.)

- **Agriculture, Forestry, and Other Land Use** (24% of 2010 global greenhouse gas emissions): Greenhouse gas emissions from this sector come mostly from agriculture(cultivation of crops and livestock) and deforestation. This estimate does not include the CO_2 that ecosystems remove from the atmosphere by sequestering carbon in biomass, dead organic matter, and soils, which offset approximately 20% of emissions from this sector.
- **Transportation** (14% of 2010 global greenhouse gas emissions): Greenhouse gas emissions from this sector primarily involve fossil fuels burned for road, rail, air, and marine transportation. Almost all (95%) of the world›s transportation energy comes from petroleum-based fuels, largely gasoline and diesel.
- **Buildings** (6% of 2010 global greenhouse gas emissions): Greenhouse gas emissions from this sector arise from onsite energy generation and burning fuels for heat in buildings or cooking in homes. (Note: Emissions from electricity use in buildings are excluded and are instead covered in the Electricity and Heat Production sector.)
- **Other Energy** (10% of 2010 global greenhouse gas emissions): This source of greenhouse gas emissions refers to all emissions from the Energy sector which are not directly associated with electricity or heat production, such as fuel extraction, refining, processing, and transportation.

Note on emissions sector categories.

Trends in Global Emissions

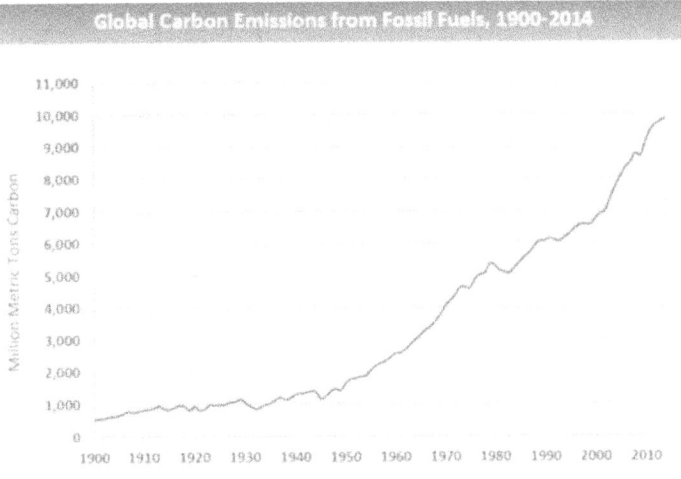

Figure 7.3

Source: Boden, T.A., Marland, G., and Andres, R.J. (2017). Global, Regional, and National Fossil-Fuel CO_2 Emissions. Carbon Dioxide Information Analysis Center, Oak Ridge National Laboratory, U.S. Department of Energy, Oak Ridge, Tenn., U.S.A. doi 10.3334/CDIAC/00001_V2017. Global carbon emissions from fossil fuels have significantly increased since 1900. Since 1970, CO_2 emissions have increased by about 90%, with emissions from fossil fuel combustion and industrial processes contributing about 78% of the total greenhouse gas emissions increase from 1970 to 2011. Agriculture, deforestation, and other land-use changes have been the second-largest contributors.

Emissions of non-CO_2 greenhouse gases have also increased significantly since 1900. To learn more about past and projected global emissions of non-CO_2 gases, please see the EPA report, *Global Anthropogenic Non-CO2 Greenhouse Gas Emissions: 1990-2020.*

Emissions by Country

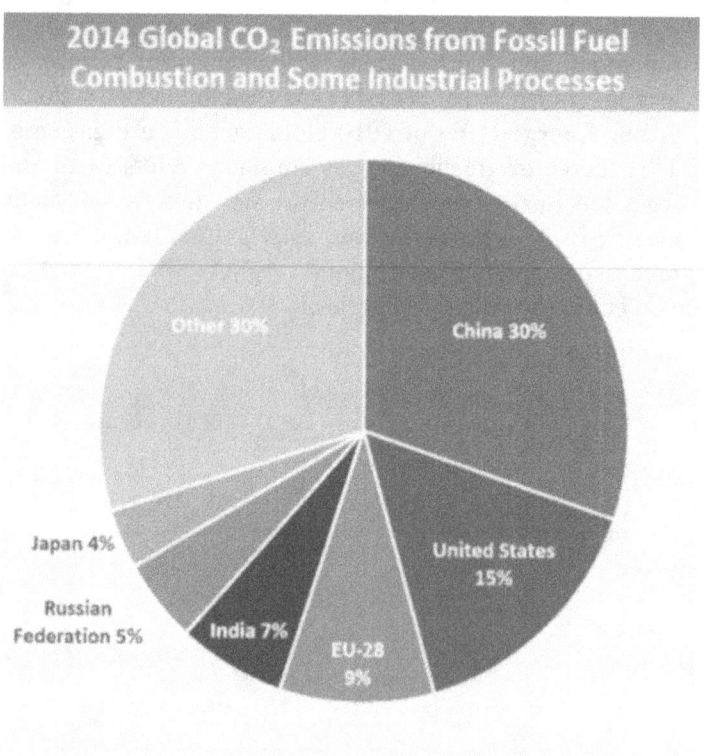

Figure 7.4

Source: Boden, T.A., Marland, G., and Andres, R.J. (2017). National CO_2 Emissions from Fossil-Fuel Burning, Cement Manufacture, and Gas

Flaring: 1751-2014, Carbon Dioxide Information Analysis Center, Oak Ridge National Laboratory, U.S. Department of Energy, doi 10.3334/ CDIAC/00001_V2017.In 2014, the top carbon dioxide (CO_2) emitters were China, the United States, the European Union, India, the Russian Federation, and Japan. These data include CO_2 emissions from fossil fuel combustion, as well as cement manufacturing and gas flaring. Together, these sources represent a large proportion of total global CO_2 emissions. Emissions and sinks related to changes in land use are not included in these estimates. However, changes in land use can be important: estimates indicate that net global greenhouse gas emissions from agriculture, forestry, and other land use were over 8 billion metric tons of CO_2 equivalent,[2] or about 24% of total global greenhouse gas emissions.[3] In areas such as the United States and Europe, changes in land use associated with human activities have the net effect of absorbing CO_2, partially offsetting the emissions from deforestation in other regions.

7.2 The Climate Registry

("The Registry") envisions a world on a measurable path to sustainability. www.theclimateregistry.org

The Climate Registry's General Reporting Protocol is divided into three parts:
1. Determining what to report
2. Quantifying emissions
3. Reporting emissions

This chapter gives guidance on quantifying GHG emissions.

The GHG Protocol corporate standard provides standard and guidance for companies and other types of organizations preparing a GHG emissions inventory. It covers the accounting and reporting of the six greenhouse gases covered by the Kyoto protocol – carbon dioxide (CO_2), methane (CH_4), nitrous oxide (N_2O), hydrofluorocarbons (HFCs), perfluorocarbons (PFCs), Sulphur Hexafluoride (HF6) and Nitrogen Trifluoride (NF3). The standard and guidance were designed with the following objectives in mind:
- To help companies prepare a GHG inventory that represents a true and fair account of their emissions, through the use of standardized approaches and principles
- To simplify and reduce the costs of compiling a GHG inventory
- To provide business with information that can be used to build an effective strategy to manage and reduce GHG emissions
- To provide information that facilitates participation in voluntary and mandatory GHG programs
- To increase consistency and transparency in GHG accounting and reporting among various companies and GHG programs.

Identifying the Organizational Boundary:

The organizational boundary is the sum of the operations that make up an organization. There are two general approaches to defining the organizational boundary, the "equity share" approach and the "control" approach.

- Equity share approach: Members reporting under this approach must report all emissions sources that are wholly owned or partially owned according to the member's equity share in each. When reporting to the Registry, members using this approach do so in addition to the control approach i.e. financial or operational control.

- Control Approach: Under this approach, members must report 100% of the emissions from sources that are under their control, including wholly owned and partially owned sources. Control can be defined in either financial or operational terms.

After a company has determined its organizational boundaries in terms of the operations that it owns or controls, it then sets its operational boundaries. This involves identifying emissions associated with its operations, categorizing them as direct or indirect emissions, and choosing the scope of accounting and reporting for indirect emissions.

To help delineate direct and indirect emission sources, improve transparency, and provide utility for a different type of organizations and different type of climate policies and business goals, three "scopes" (scope 1, scope 2 and scope 3) are defined for GHG accounting and reporting purposes which have been discussed in the previous chapter.

Calculation of Direct Emission from Stationary Combustion for Total CO_2 emission as follows:

1. Determine the total annual quantity of fuel consumed
2. Calculate the CO_2 emissions total, as given below
3. Calculate the CH_4 emissions total as given below
4. Calculate the N_2O emissions total as given below
5. Convert the CH_4 and N_2O emissions to units of CO_2e (by multiplying with GWP factor) and determine the total emission

Calculating CO2 Emissions from Stationary Combustion:

Fuel A CO_2 Emissions = Fuel consumed x Emission Factor ÷ 1,000
(Metric Tons)   (gallons)   (kg CO_2/gallon)   (kg/metric ton)

Calculating CH_4 Emissions from Stationary Combustion:
CH_4 Emissions = Fuel Use x Emission Factor ÷ 1,000
(metric tons)   (MMBtu)   (g CH_4/MMBtu)   (g/metric ton)

Calculating N2O Emissions from Stationary Combustion:
N2O Emissions = Fuel Use x Emission Factor ÷ 1,000
(metric tons)   (MMBtu)   (g N2O/MMBtu)   (g/metric ton)

Converting to CO2e and determining total emissions:
CO2 Emissions   = CO2 emissions x 1
(metric tons CO2e) (metric tons)   (GWP)

CH4 Emissions   = CH4 emissions x 21
(metric tons CO2e) (metric tons)   (GWP)

N2O Emissions   = N2O emissions x 310
(metric tons CO2e) (metric tons)   (GWP)

Total Emissions = CO2   +   CH4   +   N2O
(Metric Tons CO2e) (Metric Tons CO2e) (Metric Tons CO2e) (Metric Tons CO2e)

Emission factor can be found from either Fuel Density approach or Heat Content Approach.
Fuel Density Approach:
Emission Factor = Fuel density x Carbon Content x % Oxidized x 44/12
(kg CO2/gallon) (kg/gallon)   (kg C/kg fuel)   (CO2/C)
Heat Content Approach:
Emission Factor = Heat Content x Carbon Content x % Oxidized x 44/12
(kg CO2/gallon) (Btu/gallon)   (kg C/Btu)   (CO2/C)

Emission Factor for Greenhouse Gas Inventories can be obtained from the following link:
https://www.epa.gov/sites/production/files/2015-07/documents/emission-factors_2014.pdf

Emission factor is defined as Measure of the average amount of a specific pollutant or material discharged into the atmosphere by a specific process, fuel, equipment, or source. It is expressed as number of pounds (or kilograms) of particulate per ton (or metric ton) of the material or fuel. The default emission factors are averages based on the most extensive data sets available, and they are largely identical to those used by the Intergovernmental Panel on Climate Change (IPCC), the premier authority on accounting practices at the national level. However, the GHG Protocol recommends that businesses should use custom values whenever possible. This is because the industrial processes or the composition of fuels used by businesses may differ with time and by region.

Global Warming Potential: **Global warming potential** (GWP) is a relative measure of how much heat a greenhouse gas traps in the atmosphere. It compares the amount of heat trapped by a certain mass of the gas in question to the amount of heat trapped by a similar mass of carbon dioxide. GWP is expressed as a factor of carbon dioxide (whose GWP is standardized to 1). Converting emissions of non-CO2 gases to units of CO2 equivalent i.e. CO2e allows GHGs to be compared on a common basis i.e. on the ability of each greenhouse gas to trap heat in the atmosphere. GWP factors represent the ratio of the heat-trapping ability of each GHG relative to that of carbon dioxide. For example, the GWP of methane is 21 because 1 metric ton of methane has 21 times more ability to trap heat in the atmosphere than one metric ton of carbon dioxide.

Energy Efficiency and Conservation	Economy-wide carbon-intensity reduction (emissions/$GDP)	Increase reduction by additional 0.15% per year (e.g., increase U.S. goal of reduction of 1.96% per year to 2.11% per year)	Can be tuned by carbon policy
	1. Efficient vehicles	Increase fuel economy for 2 billion cars from 30 to 60 mpg	Car size, power
	2. Reduced use of vehicles	Decrease car travel for 2 billion 30-mpg cars from 10,000 to 5,000 miles per year	Urban design, mass transit, telecommuting
	3. Efficient buildings	Cut carbon emissions by one-fourth in buildings and appliances projected for 2054	Weak incentives
	4. Efficient baseload coal plants	Produce twice today's coal power output at 60% instead of 40% efficiency (compared with 32% today)	Advanced high-temperature materials
Fuel shift	5. Gas baseload power for coal baseload power	Replace 1400 GW 50%-efficient coal plants with gas plants (4 times the current production of gas-based power)	Competing demands for natural gas
CO₂ Capture and Storage (CCS)	6. Capture CO₂ at baseload power plant	Introduce CCS at 800 GW coal or 1600 GW natural gas (compared with 1060 GW coal in 1999)	Technology already in use for H₂ production
	7. Capture CO₂ at H₂ plant	Introduce CCS at plants producing 250 MtH₂/year from coal or 500 MtH₂/year from natural gas (compared with 40 MtH₂/year today from all sources)	H₂ safety, infrastructure
	8. Capture CO₂ at coal-to-synfuels plant	Introduce CCS at synfuels plants producing 30 million barrels per day from coal (200 times Sasol), if half of feedstock carbon is available for capture	Increased CO₂ emissions, if synfuels are produced without CCS
	Geological storage	Create 3500 Sleipners	Durable storage, successful permitting
Nuclear Fission	9. Nuclear power for coal power	Add 700 GW (twice the current capacity)	Nuclear proliferation, terrorism, waste
Renewable Electricity and Fuels	10. Wind power for coal power	Add 2 million 1-MW-peak windmills (50 times the current capacity) "occupying" 30x10⁶ ha, on land or off shore	Multiple uses of land because windmills are widely spaced
	11. PV power for coal power	Add 2000 GW-peak PV (700 times the current capacity) on 2x10⁶ ha	PV production cost
	12. Wind H₂ in fuel-cell car for gasoline in hybrid	Add 4 million 1-MW-peak windmills (100 times the current capacity)	H₂ safety, infrastructure
	13. Biomass fuel for fossil fuel	Add 100 times the current Brazil or U.S. ethanol production, with the use of 250 x10⁶ ha (1/6 of world cropland)	Biodiversity, competing land use
Forests and Agricultural Soils	14. Reduced deforestation, plus reforestation, afforestation and new plantations.	Decrease tropical deforestation to zero instead of 0.5 GtC/year, and establish 300 Mha of new tree plantations (twice the current rate)	Land demands of agriculture, benefits to biodiversity from reduced deforestation
	15. Conservation tillage	Apply to all cropland (10 times the current usage)	Reversibility, verification

Table 7.1

To convert emission of non-CO2 gases to units of CO2e, multiply the emissions of each gas in units of mass (e.g. metric tons) by the appropriate GWP factors (as shown above). See Case Study No.2 for detailed example of calculation of Green House Gases.

7.3 Stabilization Wedges to Reduce Carbon Emissions

Pacala and Socolow proposed 15 ways to reduce carbon emission which they called "stabilization wedges". A wedge represents an activity that reduces emissions to the atmosphere that starts at zero (2005 base) and increases linearly until it accounts for 1Gtc/year of reduced carbon emissions in 50 years. There are 15 possible stabilization wedges, each one with the potential to reduce carbon emissions by 1 giga tonne/year by 2054. The wedges are shown in the following TABLE 7.1

The following are the description of these wedges:

Wedges 1-4: Efficiency and Conservation

1) **Efficient vehicles: increase the fuel economy for 2 billion cars from 30 to 60 miles per gallon**. Or, increasing it from 13 to 26 kilometers per liter. When they wrote their paper, there were 500 million cars on the planet. They expected that by 2054 this number would quadruple. When they wrote their paper, average fuel efficiency was 13 kilometers/ liter. To achieve this wedge, we'd need that to double.

2) **Reduced use of vehicles: decrease car travel for 2 billion 30-mpg cars from 10,000 to 5000 miles per year**. In other words: decreasing the average travel from 16,000 to 8000 kilometers per year. (Clearly, this wedge and the previous one are not additive: if we do them both, we don't save 2 gigatonnes of carbon per year.)

3) **Efficient buildings: cut carbon emissions by one-fourth in buildings and appliances**. This could be done by following "known and established approaches" to energy efficient space heating and cooling, water heating, lighting, and refrigeration. Half the potential savings are in the buildings in developing countries.

4) **Efficient coal plants: raise the efficiency of coal power plants to 60%**. In 2004, when they wrote their paper, "coal plants, operating on average at 32% efficiency, produced about one-fourth of all carbon emissions: 1.7 GtC/year out of 6.2 GtC/year." They expected coal power plants to double their output by 2054. To achieve this wedge, we'd need their average efficiency to reach 60%.

Wedge 5: shifting from coal to gas

5) **Shifting from coal to natural gas: replace 1400 gigawatts coal-burning power plants with gas-burning plants**. Natural gas puts

out half as much CO_2 as coal does when you burn them to make a given amount of electricity. After all, it's mainly methane, which is made from hydrogen as well as carbon. Suppose by 2054 we have coal power plants working at 90% of capacity with an efficiency of 50%. 700 gigawatts worth of coal plants like this emit 1 gigatonne of carbon per year. So, we can reduce carbon emissions by one 'wedge' if we replace 1400 gigawatts of such plants with gas-burning plants.

That is four times the 2004 worldwide total of gas-burning plants.

Wedges 6-8: carbon capture and storage

6) **Capturing CO_2 at power plants: 800 GW of coal plants or 1600 GW of gas plants** . Carbon capture and storage at power plants can stop about 90% of the carbon from reaching the atmosphere, so we can get a wedge by doing this for 800 GW of baseload coal plants or 1600 GW of baseload gas plants by 2054. One way to do carbon capture and storage is to make hydrogen and CO_2, burn the hydrogen in a power plant, and inject the CO_2 into the ground. So, from one viewpoint, building a wedge's worth of carbon capture and storage would resemble a tenfold expansion of the plants that were manufacturing hydrogen in 2004. But it would also require multiplying by 100 the existing amount of CO_2 injected into the ground.

7) **Capturing CO_2 at plants that make hydrogen for fuel: 250 megatons/year made from coal, or twice as much made from gas**. You've probably heard people dream of a hydrogen economy?. But it takes energy to make hydrogen. One way is to copy wedge 6, but then ship the hydrogen off for use as fuel instead of burning it to make electricity at power plants. To capture a wedge's worth of carbon this way, we'd have to make 250 megatons of hydrogen per year from coal or 500 megatons per year from natural gas. This would require a substantial scale-up from the 2004 total of 40 megatons of hydrogen manufactured by all methods. There would also be the task of building the infrastructure for a hydrogen economy. The challenge of injecting CO_2 into the ground would be the same as in wedge 6.

8) **Capturing CO_2 at plants that turn coal into synthetic fuels: 1.8 teraliters of synfuels per year**. As the world starts running out of oil, people may start turning coal into synfuels, via a process called coal liquefaction. Of course, burning these synfuels will release carbon. But suppose only half of the carbon entering a synfuels plant leaves as fuel, while the other half can be captured as CO_2 and injected underground. Then we can capture a wedge's worth of CO_2 from plants that produce 1.8 teraliters of synfuels per year. For comparison, total yearly world oil production in 2004 was 4.7 teraliters

Wedge 9: nuclear power

9) **Replacing 700 gigawatts of coal-fired power plants with nuclear power**. As Pacala and Socolow already argued in wedge 5), replacing 700 gigawatts of efficient coal-fired power plants with some carbon-neutral form of power would keep us from burning one gigatonne of carbon per year. To do this with nuclear power would require 700 gigawatts of nuclear power plants running at 90% capacity (just as assumed for the coal plants). The means *doubling the world production of nuclear power*. The global pace of nuclear power plant construction from 1975 to 1990 could do this! But of course, there's still a downside: we can only substantially boost the use of nuclear power if people become confident about all aspects of its safety.

Wedges 10-13: renewable energy

10) **Replacing 700 gigawatts of coal-fired power plants by 2000 gigawatts of peak wind power**. Wind power is intermittent: Pacala and Socolow estimate that the 'peak' capacity (the amount you get under ideal circumstances) is about 3 times the 'baseload' capacity (the amount you can count on). So, to save a gigatonne of carbon per year by replacing 700 gigawatts of coal-fired power plants, we need roughly 2000 gigawatts of peak wind power. Wind power was growing at about 30% per year when they wrote their paper, and it had reached a world total of 40 gigawatts. So, getting to 2000 gigawatts would mean *multiplying the world production of wind power by a factor of 50*.
The wind turbines would 'occupy' about 30 million hectares, or about 30-45 square meters per person — some on land and some offshore. But because windmills are widely spaced, land with windmills can have multiple uses. To increase something by a factor of 50 in 50 years, it's enough to maintain an annual growth rate of slightly more than 8%.

11) **Replacing 700 gigawatts of coal-fired power plants by 2000 gigawatts of peak photovoltaic solar power**. Solar power is also intermittent. Pacala and Socolow estimate that to save a gigatonne of carbon per year, we need 2000 gigawatts of peak photovoltaic solar power to replace coal. Like the wind, photovoltaic solar was growing at 30% per year when Pacala and Socolow wrote their paper. However, only 3 gigawatts had been installed worldwide. So, getting to 2000 gigawatts would require *multiplying the world production of photovoltaic solar power by a factor of 700*.
In terms of land, this would take about 2 million hectares, or 2-3 square meters per person. To increase photovoltaic power by a factor of 700 in 50 years, it's enough to maintain a 14% annual growth rate.

12) **Using 4000 gigawatts of peak wind power to generate hydrogen for powering automobiles**. Renewable energy can be used to produce hydrogen for vehicle fuel. 4000 gigawatts of peak wind power, for example, used in high-efficiency fuel-cell cars, could keep us from burning a gigatonne of carbon each year in the form of gasoline or diesel fuel. Unfortunately, this is twice as much wind power as we'd need in wedge 10, where we use wind to eliminate the need for burning some coal. Why? Gasoline and diesel have less carbon per unit of energy than coal does.

13) **Making 5.4 gigaliters of bioethanol per day to replace gasoline**. Fossil fuels can also be replaced by biofuels such as ethanol. To save a gigatonne per year of carbon, we could make 5.4 gigaliters per day of ethanol as a replacement for gasoline — provided the process of making this ethanol didn't burn any fossil fuels! Doing this would require *multiplying the world production of bioethanol by a factor of 50*. It would require 250 million hectares committed to high-yield plantations, or 250-375 square meters per person. That's an area equal to about one-sixth of the world's cropland. An even larger area would be required to the extent that the biofuels require fossil-fuel inputs. Clearly, this could cut into the land used for growing food.

Wedge 14 and 15

14) **Stop deforestation, start reforestation**. We could stop half a gigatonne of carbon emissions per year if we completely stopped clear-cutting tropical forests over 50 years, instead of just halving the rate at which they're getting cut down. For another half gigatonne, plant 250 million hectares of new forests in the tropics, or 400 million hectares in the temperate zone!

To get a sense of the magnitude here, note that current areas of tropical and temperate forests are 1500 and 700 million hectares, respectively. Pacala and Socolow also say that another half gigatonne of carbon emissions could be prevented by establishing approximately 300 million hectares of plantations on nonforested land.

15) **Soil management**. When forest or grassland is converted to cropland, up to one-half of the soil carbon gets converted to CO_2, mainly because tilling increases the rate of decomposition by aerating undecomposed organic matter. Over the course of history, they claim, 55 gigatonnes of carbon has gone into the atmosphere this way. That's the equivalent of two wedges. (Note that one wedge, ramping up linearly to 1 gigatonne/year for 50 years, adds up to 25 gigatonnes of carbon by 2054.)

However, good agricultural practices like no-till farming can reverse these losses — also reduce erosion! By 1995, these practices had been adopted on 110 million of the world's 1600 million hectares of cropland. If this could be extended to all cropland, accompanied by a verification program that enforces practices that actually work as advertised, somewhere between half and one gigatonne of carbon per year could be stored in this way. So: maybe half a wedge, maybe a whole wedge!

7.4 Example: Sustainability in construction and civil engineering.

Sustainability in construction and civil engineering is the optimization of construction activities in a way that does not have harmful effects on resources, surroundings, and living ecosystem. It is a way of minimizing the harmful environmental impacts of construction projects.

Construction involves activities like use of building materials from various sources, use of machineries, demolition of existing structures, use of green fields, cutting down of tress, etc. which can impact the environment in one or more ways.

Why is sustainability important in construction?

Construction has a direct impact on the environment due to the following reasons:
1. Generation of waste materials
2. Emissions from vehicles, machineries
3. Noise pollution due to use of heavy vehicles and construction machinery.
4. Releases of wastes and pollutants into water, ground, and atmosphere.

Sustainability assessment of construction projects is essential to the fact that it does not create any harmful effects on the living ecosystem while optimizing the cost of construction. This is to ensure the availability of resources for the future generations. Following are the important construction activities which have large impacts on sustainability in construction and civil engineering:

1. Wastes from the demolition of buildings and structures:

Over billions of tonnes of construction and demolition waste are generated worldwide annually. These wastes can be hazardous to the environment is not disposed off at a suitable place without environmental impact assessment of such wastes. The other alternative is to recycle and reuse the demolished building materials to minimize the risk of harmful impacts.

How to make construction waste sustainable?

Following are the steps which need to be followed to make construction waste more sustainable:

- Eliminate – avoid producing construction waste in the first place.
- Reduce – minimize the amount of waste you produce.
- Reuse – reuse the construction wastes in other works.
- Recover (recycling, composting, energy) – recycle what you can only after you have reused it.
- Dispose – dispose of what is left in a responsible way.

Use of durable construction materials and quality control at site for durability of structure is one step towards minimization of construction waste generation.

2. Use of Sustainable Building Materials:

Building Materials such as sand and gravel have been used for thousands of years in construction. The demand for these is increasing day by day as demand for infrastructure development is increasing.

Uses of construction materials such river sand and gravels also have negative impact on environment. Excessive sand-and-gravel mining causes the degradation of rivers. Instream mining lowers the stream bottom, which may lead to bank erosion. This results in the destruction of aquatic and riparian habitat through large changes in the channel morphology. Impacts include bed degradation, bed coarsening, lowered water tables near the streambed, and channel instability.

There are many harmful impacts of using river sand and mining of gravels and a detailed study is required to list all the negative impacts. The use of alternate building materials can reduce the impact of this on environment.

The alternate to river sand is Manufactured Sand (M-Sand) which can be used in construction works reduce impacts of mining river sand.

3. Energy Consumption and Green House:

Around 40% of total energy consumption and greenhouse gas emissions are directly due to construction and operation of buildings. The best way to reduce this impact is the use of green buildings construction techniques. The use of transparent concrete in buildings also helps to reduce the use of energy for lighting during daytime.

How to Ensure Sustainable Construction?

Following steps should be taken for better sustainability of construction activities:
- Reduce the supply chains to reduce transport costs
- Exercise waste minimization and recycling construction
- Building orientation – Choose the building orientation in a way to reduce energy utilization.

- Durability and quality of building components, generally chosen to last for the appropriate refurbishment or demolition cycle.
- Use construction materials which are locally available.
- Design buildings and structures as per local topological, climatic and community demands.
- Select appropriate construction methods – prefabrication, wood or concrete structures.
- Reuse of existing buildings or structures can reduce the construction waste. Reutilizing by strengthening and rehabilitation of buildings can also save construction cost.
- Make site waste management plans not only during construction but also during use or operation.
- Minimize energy in construction.

A very good case on sustainable construction engineering and technology can be viewed from the following: "DESIGN AND DEVELOPMENT OF SUSTAINABLE CONSTRUCTION STRATEGY FOR RESIDENTIAL BUILDINGS: A CASE STUDY FOR COMPOSITE , Chetan S. Dhanjode1 , R. V. Ralegaonkar2 , Vaidehi A. Dakwale, International Journal of Sustainable Construction Engineering & Technology:

https://www.researchgate.net/publication/257886102_Design_and_ Development_of_Sustainable_Construction_Strategy_for_Residential_ Buildings_A_Case_Study_for_Composite_Climate

Questions:

1. What are the main Green House Gas emissions and how do you calculate it?

PART II

Chapter 8
Sustainability Perspective of Organizations

8.1 Nature of an Organization

An organization is a social entity that has objectives (whether explicitly stated or not), a deliberate operating structure, and a coordinated activity system and is linked to its external operating environment. Organizations come in many sizes and kinds: sole proprietorships, microbusinesses, companies, corporations, partnerships, not-for-profits, nongovernmental organizations (NGOs), government departments and agencies, houses of worship, families, and institutions. These organizations can be a single unaffiliated operating unit or operating as part of a large multinational corporation. The term organization does not typically apply to government acting in its sovereign role to create and enforce the law, exercise judicial authority, and carry out its duty to establish policy in the public interest or honor the international obligations of the state.

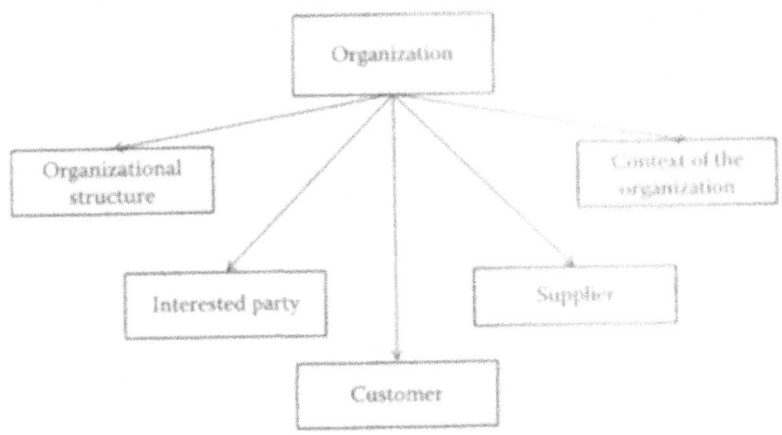

Figure 8.1

Relationship diagram for an organization. (Adapted from ISO, Quality management systems-Fundamentals, and vocabulary, ISO/DIS 9000, ISO, Geneva, 2014.)

Organizations are made up of people in a structure with an arrangement of responsibilities, authorities, and relationships. Leaders create a structure and commit resources to achieve the organization's purpose—its strategic objectives. An organization interacts with its customers, suppliers, and external stakeholders. All this is true whether the organization is unaffiliated or a part of a larger organization. Every organization has an internal and external context that it operates within. A relationship diagram helps to illustrate the organizational relationships covered by topics in this book (Figure 8.1). Organizations shape our lives in many ways, and each of us belongs to multiple organizations.

The point of studying organizations is to enable us to find ways to improve their performance and effectiveness. To be effective, an organization needs clearly articulated overarching objectives and an appropriate strategy for achieving these objectives. Increasing an organization's effectiveness is not always a simple matter. Different people want different things for an organization, and when change is needed, people often establish change initiatives that are not embedded into how the organization operates. Superimposed on this is the demand that an organization constantly adapt to changes in its external operating environment, cope with increasing size and complexity, and create the right kind of culture needed to help it meet its objectives.

Organizational theory classifies an organization's design on a scale ranging from "mechanistic" to "organic." Mechanistic design is characterized by a centralized operating structure, specialized tasks, formal management systems, vertical communication, and a strict hierarchy of authority. On the other end of the scale, organic design is characterized by a decentralized structure, empowered roles, informal systems, horizontal communication, and collaborative teamwork and more geared towards a sustainable organization structure for speed of decision making and flexibility. The complexity of the external operating environment in the world today is causing many organizations to shift to more organic designs. Mechanistic designs are more effective when the change in the external operating environment is changing at a slower pace.

8.2 Strategy and Organization's Objectives

Objectives are defined as "results to be achieved. Some people use the terms goals, targets, and aims and sometimes use them interchangeably with each other and with the term objective, it is important to be consistent with terminology when attempting to understand the hierarchy and Relationship diagram for the strategic objectives of an organization. (Adapted from ISO, Quality management systems—Fundamentals and vocabulary, ISO/D1S 9000, ISO, Geneva, 2014.) Organizational components of a top-down, bottom-up process approach by which sustainability is embedded into the day-to-day operations of an organization.

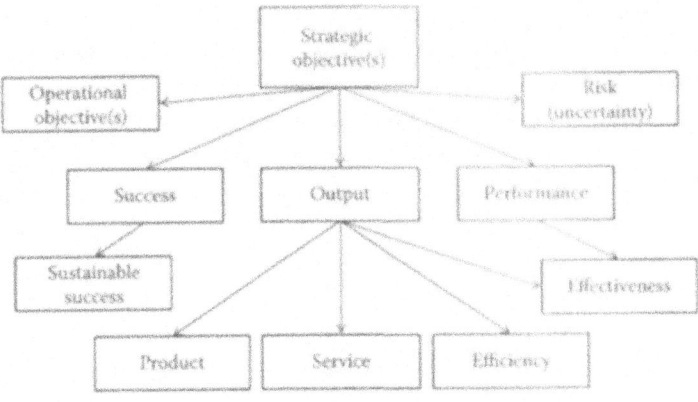

Figure 8.2

Objectives can be strategic, tactical, or operational. As previously mentioned, strategic objectives relate to the organization's purpose. Tactical objectives are set for each operating unit of the organization, from the top of the organization to the bottom. All the objectives must be linked to the strategic objectives. At the operational level in an organization, objectives can relate to different functions (e.g., financial; environmental, health and safety; assets management; and quality). A relationship diagram of how an organization addresses objectives and other related issues is provided in Figure 8.2.

An organization is deemed to be successful when it meets its objectives. Sustained success involves meeting objectives over a period of time—typically on a 5- to 10-year horizon. To accomplish sustained success, an organization needs to establish a balance between economic and financial interests and those of the social and environmental elements of its external operating environment .Sustained success also involves a range of stakeholders of an organization, such as leaders, owners, members, employees, suppliers, bankers, unions, partners, neighbors, the community, and society in a larger sense than the community.1-' Sustained success is possible when organizations consistently address the interests of these stakeholders over long term.

An organization typically has control over the operations found within its internal operating environment. It has some level of influence in its external operating environment. The sphere of influence is defined as the "extent of political, contractual, economic or other relationships through which an organization has the ability to affect the decisions or activities of individuals or organizations outside of its internal context."

An organization can exercise its influence with others either to enhance positive impacts on sustainable development or to minimize negative impacts—or both. When assessing an organization's sphere of influence and determining its responsibilities, an organization needs to exercise "due diligence." Different methods for exercising influence may include

- Establishing contractual provisions or incentives
- Public statements by the organization
- Engaging with the community, political leaders, and other external
- Stakeholders
- Making investment decision
- Sharing knowledge and information with other

Whether conventional, sustainable, or resilient, it is important to remember that all organizations consist of people and to further understand how people, principles, and culture work within an organization.

Organizational culture is part of the internal context of the organization and consists of the attitudes, experiences, and values of the people within the organization. *Organizational culture* is a system of shared assumptions, values, and beliefs, which governs how people behave in organizations. These shared values have a strong influence on the people in the *organization* and dictate how they dress, act, and perform their jobs. This culture is acquired through social learning and determines the way people interact within the organization, as well as with society outside of the organization. All organizations have a culture, whether it forms organically or is strategically created by leaders. In order to create an organizational culture that supports the organization's mission and strategic objectives, the leaders must understand how culture is formed within organizations. There are a number of attributes that influence an organization's culture such as attitudes, beliefs, customs, and written and unwritten rules that have been developed over time and are considered valid. By identifying these attributes, organizations can see which can be managed to help implement and sustain a constructive social change within the organization. None of the components can influence an organization's culture on its own, and none can individually deliver the desired improvements. Regarding the organization's external operating environment, what matters to the organization, and what resources it has to use as it operates and grows. This knowledge can be used to make the organization more resilient and capable of operating more effectively and confidently in our increasingly volatile, uncertain, complex, and ambiguous world. People say that organizational culture determines how things get accomplished in an organization—what happens and what does not happen.

8.2.1 What is Strategy

Strategy is defined as the determination of the basic long-term goals of an enterprise, and the adoption of courses of action and the allocation of resources necessary for carrying out these goals which will provide a competitive advantage.

Strategic management is the management of an organization's resources to achieve its goals and objectives. Strategic management involves setting objectives, analyzing the competitive environment, analyzing the internal organization, evaluating strategies and ensuring that management rolls out the strategies across the organization. At its heart, strategic management involves identifying how the organization stacks up compared to its competitors and recognizing opportunities and threats facing an organization, whether they come from within the organization or from competitors.

Corporate strategy involves answering a key question from a portfolio perspective: "What business should we be in?" Business strategy involves answering the question: "How shall we compete in this business?" In management theory and practice, a further distinction is often made between strategic management and operational management. Operational management is concerned primarily with improving efficiency and controlling costs within the boundaries set by the organization's strategy.

Strategic planning is an activity performed by the top management of the organization, that helps to relate the organization with the business environment for long term i.e. 5 years. Figure 8.3 depicts the strategic planning process.

Strategic planning starts by asking 3 questions:

Questions	To Obtain Answers
1. Where are you going?	(a) Determine the enterprise mission (b) Determine the scope of operations (c) Establish specific goals
2. What is environment?	(a) Examine the internal conditions of the firm (b) Examine the external environment
3. How do you get there?	(a) Develop Strategies (b) Develop objectives/targets/measures (c) Develop contingency plans

Strategic Planning Process Map

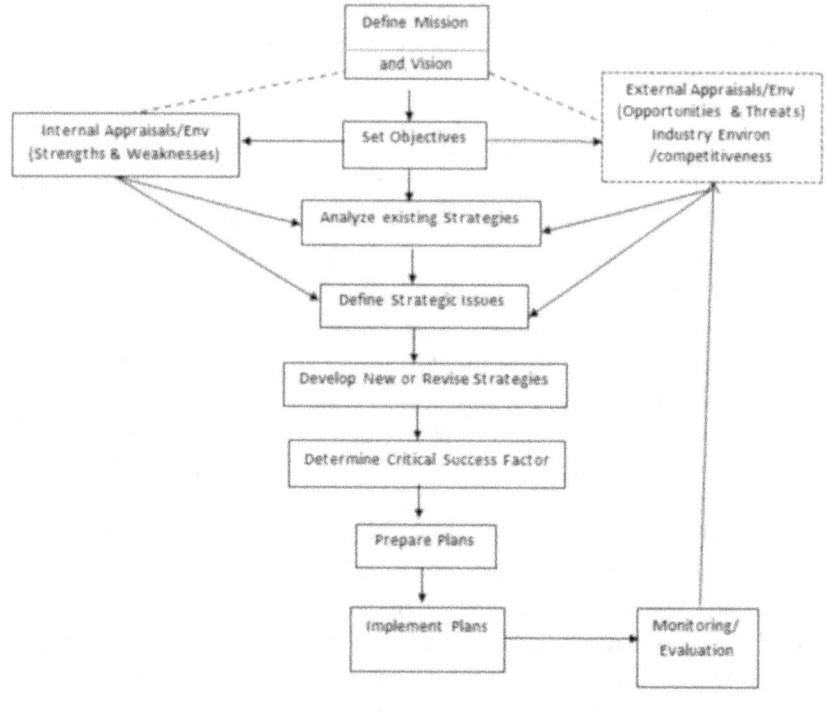

Figure 8.3

8.2.2 An Organization's Mission, Objectives and Goals

To achieve sustainable success, an organization must meet its overarching objectives over the long term while operating in an uncertain world. When developing a sustainability program, it is important to understand the organization's objectives and how they were established. Organization's Mission Statement

The mission statement is widely regarded as an explicit statement of the reason for the organization's existence and what it is meant to accomplish. Mission statements are typically focused on a 5- to 10-year time frame and should

- Separate what is important to the organization's sustainable success from what is not as important
- clearly state the customers, clients, or other persons and organizations that are served and how they are served
- communicate the organization's "looking forward" position to its stakeholders

For a Private business, the mission is focused on its products or services. in the public sector, the mission statement focuses on what the organization is trying to accomplish. Most not-for-profit organizations are established to start something new or stop something that they find objectionable, such as protecting a wetland area or eliminating, the emission of greenhouse gases. In all cases, the mission statement provides the foundation for the strategic planning process and the management of the processes and activities within the organization. A mission statement is very important to an organization because it helps management increase the probability that the organization will achieve sustainable success over time.

A mission statement is different from a vision statement. Most regard the mission statement to be the cause and the vision statement to be the effect. Looking at this relationship in a different way, the mission statement is something to be accomplished and the vision statement something to be pursued for that accomplishment.

Most small organizations do not have a written mission statement but rely on the implicit understanding of what is most important to the organization—what it stands for. Preparing a written mission statement enables the organization to explicitly state its purpose for anyone with interest. Sustainability may be embedded into the operational objectives, along with the organization's values, to become part of how the organization operates every day.

Many larger organizations have written a mission statement. In many cases, the mission statement comes from a parent organization at the top of a hierarchal structure. If there is an existing mission statement, it can be evaluated or revised prior to the process of creating a set of strategic objectives. The mission statement process starts with a review or the drafting of the mission statement to make sure that it addresses four sets of questions:

- Who are we? What is the purpose of our organization? What do we do? What are our products and services?
- Who do we serve? Who finds these products and services of value?
- Why are we here? What value do we provide? What business problem, human need, or desire do our products and services fulfill? Have we identified the most important values?
- Will principles or beliefs guide the organization?

There are many guides to writing mission statements on the Internet. Remember that a well-crafted mission statement

- Expresses the organization's purpose in a manner that inspires support and ongoing commitment to provide the organization with a unique identity
- Is articulated in a way that is convincing and easy to understand

- Uses proactive verbs to describe what the organization does
- Is free of unnecessary jargon
- Is short enough to enable stakeholders to easily recognize it

A well-written mission statement is an important prerequisite for the development of the strategic objectives.

Mission Statements: What you're here to do

Your mission statement is a declaration of an organization's core purpose. A mission statement answers the question, "why do we exist?" They are essential for your strategic plan.

Vision Statements: Where you're going

A vision statement is a declaration of where you are headed – your future state. A vision statement should challenge and inspire employees.

Values Statements: What you will or won't do to get where you want

Your values statement should explain what you stand for and what you believe in.

Dupont's mission, vision and core values:

Mission

To create shareholder and societal value while reducing the environmental footprint along the value chains in which we operate.

Vision

To be the world's most dynamic science company, creating sustainable solutions essential to a better, safer, healthier life for people everywhere.

* *DuPont defines "footprint" as all injuries, illnesses, incidents, waste, emissions, use of water and depletable forms of raw materials and energy.*

Core values

The core values of DuPont are the cornerstone of who we are and what we stand for. They are:

- **Safety and health** - We adhere to the highest standards to ensure the safety and health of our employees, our customers, and the people of the communities in which we operate.
- **Environmental stewardship** - We protect the environment and strengthen our businesses by making environmental issues an integral part of all business activities. We continuously strive to align our actions with public expectations.
- **Highest ethical behavior** - We conduct our business affairs to the highest ethical standards and in compliance with all applicable laws. We work diligently to be a respected corporate citizen worldwide.

- **Respect for people** - We foster an environment in which every employee is treated with respect and dignity, and is recognized for his or her contributions to our business.

Dow's Essential Elements

Taken together, Dow's essential elements of mission, vision, values, and strategy describe why the company exists, who we are, what we intend to do, and how we intend to do it. These essential elements provide insight, offer motivation, and point the way forward as we seek to grow and achieve our goals.

Mission

To passionately create innovation for our stakeholders at the intersection of chemistry, biology, and physics

Vision

Maximize long-term value per share by being the most valuable and respected science company in the world

Corporate Strategy

Invest in a market-driven portfolio of advantaged and technology-enabled businesses that create value for our shareholders and customers
Combination of low-cost and value-add products enables superior value creation throughout the cycle

- Integrated manufacturing positions in chemicals, plastics, key materials and agriculture
- Low cost in all product and asset positions, leveraging integrated sites
- Presence in all growing geographic markets
- Growing downstream specialties for value add to low cost positions
- Will be in some commodities to achieve low cost for our integration, and will run these for maximum cash to reinvest in:
  o Specialty positions (Integrated Plastics)
  o Value-add specialties (Electronics & Agriculture)
  o Reward our shareholders via share buybacks and dividend increases

Values

- Integrity
- Respect for People
- Protecting Our Planet

To publicize your commitment to sustainability, revise your mission, vision or values statements to include principles of sustainability, or write a separate statement. Here are some steps to help you in this process:

- **Encourage participation and input from all employees.** A shared vision helps each employee understand how he/she individually contributes to the company's success, as well as how everyone contributes collectively. This can help your organization create a coherent and congruent message, which will improve the effectiveness of communication with clients. To increase stakeholder engagement, gather a team that represents different levels and departments in your organization, which will help you create a message that resonates with the majority of your employees.
- **Determine what sustainability means to your organization.** Sustainability is a value-based term. No definition can possibly encompass all cultures, nationalities, worldviews, races, businesses, and so on. Really drill down to the core meaning of sustainability, and how that relates to your organization, for each stakeholder participating in the visioning process.
- **Write the statement.** After all, participants have a chance to voice their opinions, use this information to create your organization's sustainability vision statement.

Some Example of Mission statements with sustainability focus are as follows:

- Charter Films will strive to reduce the impact that our internal operations have on the environment through sustainable practices and source reduction initiatives. In addition, we will seek to provide our customers with solutions designed to help them produce products that are inherently more sustainable."
- "LG Electronics' Promise represents the promises made to the people, the Earth, and LG Electronics itself: a society in which LG Electronics' employees, stakeholders, and the entire population can live happily; the Earth which we help make a cleaner, safer place for generations to come by carrying out various environmental activities; and LG Electronics as one of the top international players thanks to its innovative spirit. LG Electronics aims to realize these three dreams."
- "Cisco's commitment to sustainability extends through all phases of our product's life cycle, from design and manufacturing to support and end of life. Our considerations focus on reducing resource consumption in our development process and reducing resource and related emissions consumption by our products."

Many organizations seek to be a good neighbor and a positive contributor to the community. Their work should not cause harm to the neighborhood. Organizations need members or employees to create the products and services associated with their operations and mission. If the community suffers from environmental, social, and economic problems, the organization is likely to have trouble recruiting members and retaining them at this location. It is always easier to attract and retain members in an organization when a community is growing in a sustainable manner. Having a beneficial relationship with the local community is vital to securing and maintaining its "social license to operate." By enabling beneficial collaborations and partnerships with the community and other organizations in that community, it is possible to aspire to values that will set the organization apart from its competitors. Sustainability and social responsibility provide a means for the organization to build long-term relationships with local suppliers and customers while enhancing its reputation as a good neighbor in the community

An organization can use its mission statement to communicate with its internal and external stakeholders a good sense of what it is seeking to achieve in the area of Sustainability. In this manner, the organization can communicate its legitimacy to the community and seek new members, employees, of trusted partners that can identify with its stated purpose. Some organizations use their mission statement on making a profit. This kind of statement may not be viewed favorably by some external stakeholders because it will be seen that organizations place profits above addressing the interests of the stakeholders. A sustainability program helps create responsible mission statements and objectives that demonstrate the value of its environmental stewardship, its focus on social well-being and the shared value associated with these contributions. However, these contributions must not be seen as something that is provided separately by an organization that struggles with coming to terms with its place and role within the community.

Organization's Objectives:

Once the mission statement is explicitly stated, it is important to link the mission to the objectives of the organization. This will help provide the means for accomplishing the mission. At the highest organizational level, strategies objectives are statements of broad intent that are strategically linked to the mission statement. Like the mission statement, these strategic objectives typically have a window of accomplishment of approximately 5-10 years. Ideally, an organization should have between three and five strategic objectives, derived from its mission statement. Each strategic objective should be concise, specific, and able to be understood by the stakeholders. Many involved in the field of organizational development consider objectives to be "continuous," while the goals have a clear beginning and end associated with them. In this way, the objectives provide the bridge between an inspirational mission and the clearly stated goals that will provide a feedback loop from the bottom of the organization Up to provide some proof that the strategic objectives are on target. The objective setting does not end at the strategic level. Objectives must also be prepared for each of the organization's operating levels, local operations, and individual work units. At the operating level, objectives establish the outcomes sought through the processes and operations and explain what the organization is seeking to accomplish at these operating levels. Objective setting; is a top-down process that must extend from the strategy-setting level to the lowest operating levels of the organization (Figure 8.4). The objectives at the lowest operating levels must be linked to objectives in the next higher level and be directly traceable to the strategic objectives. Objectives at the lowest levels of operations help to motivate the members or employees to work effectively to help the organization realize its overarching strategic objectives. The operational objectives are specific and short-term, so they can be used in the operation's day-to-day activities. The relationship between organizations overarching ', strategic objectives and its operational objectives is a key factor in its ability to meet its objectives in an uncertain world. Long-term organizational success is only likely to happen if short-term operational activities are. consistent with the long-term strategic intentions. This is important to keep in mind when embedding the sustainability program into this objective structure. Sustainability objectives must be aligned the operating objectives and directly support the strategies objectives

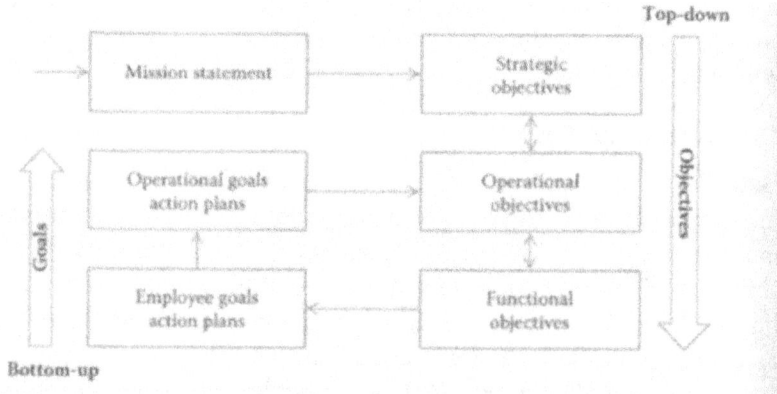

Figure 8.4

A hierarchy of objectives

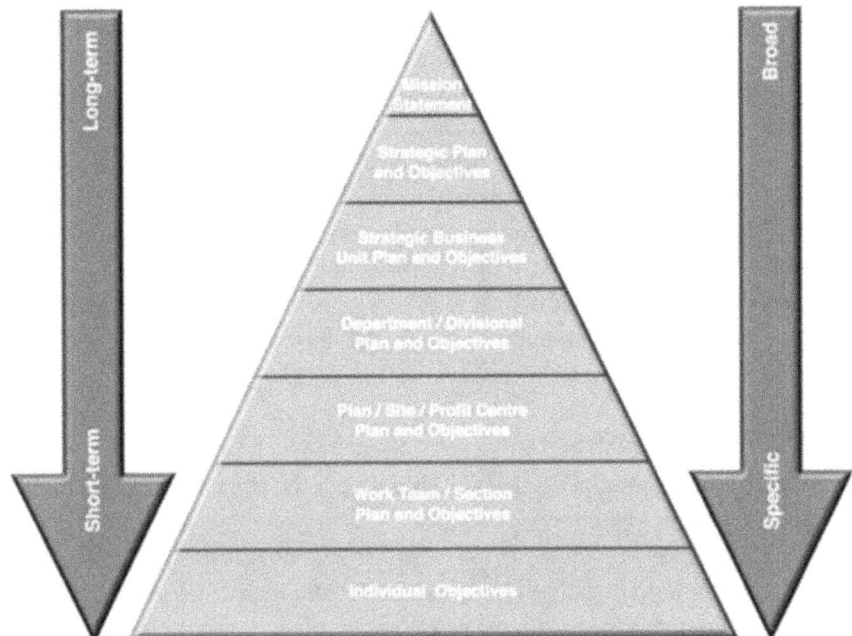

Figure 8.5

8.3 Goal Setting and Operational Execution

An organization's strategy is implemented at the operating level by defining work goals and developing action plans that help people reach these goals. Goals provide a bottom-up feedback loop to test the top-down objectives (Figure 8.5). They state the specific, measurable results that specify how much or what will be accomplished by when. Goals linked to action plans let management know whether operations are meeting their immediate operational objectives. Each work goal is supported by an action plan. These action plans provide a prioritized set of activities that must be achieved in order for the work goal to be realized. Every action is subject to the question, how does this effort help the organization's operational and strategic objectives? This question helps the member or employee think of how the organization operates with its processes and activities. No activity performed within the organization should be a stand-alone effort that is separate from the main activities and processes of the organization.

Every member of an organization, whether in a supporting position or, in an operational role at any level, should have measurable objectives to work toward and defined by KPI and such KPI should be linked to the Mission and Visions statement and objectives and provide sustainability results or meet other needs. It is about setting goals so fundamental to the mission of the organization that achieving them ensures that the strategic objectives will be realized. Once the activity goals are selected, a number of lead and lag measures are used to track the progress following the action plan. The measures are carefully tracked to help the members or employees create a "cadence of accountability."

When considering that the organization is operating in an uncertain world, it is prudent to coordinate the use of objectives and goals with the risk management efforts. The strategy should always be in line with the mission statement and the stakeholder interests. Organizations must be capable of creating an efficacious strategy that is able to effectively address the mission statement through the auspices of its overarching strategic objectives.

Developing the Objectives

To develop the strategic, high-level objectives, the drafting team needs to ask the following questions:

- What are the three to six areas in which the organization will continue to be actively involved over the next 5-10 years?
- What areas need attention to accomplish what is found in the mission statement?
- Do the objectives convert the mission statement into action?
- Do the objectives help to sustain the organization's competitive advantage?
- Is there a risk management program in place for prioritizing the opportunities and threats found in the organization's internal and external operating environment (context)?

The objectives of a parent organization affect the objectives throughout an organization. Business or divisional objectives are derived from the corporate objectives but are specific to these levels of the organization. Department objectives are derived from the divisional objectives so that the linkage back to the strategic objectives can be maintained. This progression is repeated down to the individual member or employee level. It does not matter whether the organization is a business or a not-for-profit. Similarly, the time frame for objectives can range from 5-10 years for long-term strategic objectives to 1 year for an objective at an individual level. Every organization needs to have more than one objective at the strategic level. Objectives are always derived from the mission statement. A sustainability program can set strategic objectives only if there is a focus on sustainability that is embedded within the operational or functional level-, which support the strategic objectives, at the highest level in the organization

The mission and the strategic objectives should not be considered to be unchangeable mission statements from the foundation for objectives, and both can change over time. There are factors in the external operating environment that can create opportunities and threats as the uncertainty of the operating environment is changed.

8.4 Developing Goals and Action Plans

Each member or employee would have one or two goals that are clearly stated and measurable.

There are a number of important questions that must be addressed within this goal-setting process:

- What element of the performance of our work can best help achieve the operational goals?
- What are our greatest strengths that can be leveraged to ensure that the goal is achieved?
- What area of our past performance needs to be improved to ensure the goal is achieved?
- It is critical to identify the goals that promise the greatest positive consequence for the operational objective that supports the strategic objectives which should be SMART:
- Specific
- Measurable.
- Achievable
- Realistic
- Time-based

Once these elements are satisfied, the worker or team can assist the supervisor in defining the goal so that an action plan can be prepared.

The action plan needs to be complete, clear, and current. It should include information and ideas that were gathered during the planning of the goals. The following information is needed:

- Describe the goals to be achieved.
- Describe the specific, measurable, and attainable outcome-based goals.
- What tasks, actions, or activities will occur to accomplish the goal?
- Who will conduct and be held responsible for these actions?
- When will the activity take place? Provide an appropriate timeline.
- Secure the allocation of the resources (e.g., money and people) needed to conduct the activity.
- How will the activity, along with its successes and opportunities for improvement, be communicated within the organization?

Sustainability Goals and Objectives

If the Sustainability program is embedded within the organization, the operational objectives will require Sustainability goals to be established as described above.

8.5 Organizational System of Management:

All organizations use some kind of system for managing their activities.

At the same time, there are services and Products that are using other processes for the operations of an organization. There are a large number of processes involved in a system of management and the operations. The process approach can be used to keep track of processes, activities, products, services, and the overall performance of the organization.

Creating an Aligned Management System

There are three categories of management systems found in organizations today:
1. Financial management and enterprise risk management (ERM)
2. Operating management system (OMS)
3. Functional Management systems (e.g., quality, and environment, and safety)

Role of management systems in an organization:

The system of management is a useful means for helping management tend to the management of organizational risk. This approach may involve the following:
- The application of the quality management system to control the activities involved in the provision of products and services to customers.
- Dealing with operations that are regulated to prevent releases to the the environment in the provision of products and services that may be of interest to external stakeholders
- Provision for the treatment of risk in activities that are managed by a health and safety standard
- Handling security risks associated with a cyber-attack on the organization's information systems
- Managing business continuity risks that provide a faster response to disruptive events
- Establishing controls to protect the organization's assets

Processes in the System of Management

A system of management framework consists of the following documents:

- *Standards:* Sections and descriptions, along with operational definitions
- *Policies:* Statement that provides the rules an organization uses to govern or constrain operations and its activities
- *Processes:* A high-level description of a large task or series of related tasks that describes "what happens" within the organization to create products and services that conform to the relevant standards in accordance with the policies of the organization
- *Procedures:* Detail "who" performs the work, "what" steps are performed, "when" the steps are performed, and "how" the procedure is performed

A standard is an agreed way of doing something. Standards represent a sense of "best practice," as they come from the wisdom of people with expertise in the subject matter who know the needs of the organizations they represent. They prepare standards working with others from all kinds of organizations, including regulators, associations, stakeholders, and customers. Standards are knowledge. They can help organizations meet their objectives.

A basic system of management has the following management processes associated with it:

- Scanning the external operating environment (context)
- Scanning the internal operating environment (context)
- Stakeholder engagement
- Determining the scope of the integrated system of management
- Creating the integrated system of management
- Characterizing the governance of the organization
- Creating the mandate and commitment from the leaders
- Establishing the policies of the component management systems
- Deterring the roles, responsibilities, and authorities of the organization's members
- Using uncertainty analysis to address opportunities and threats
- Defining the organization's objectives and planning to achieve them
- Defining the resources needed to support the system of management

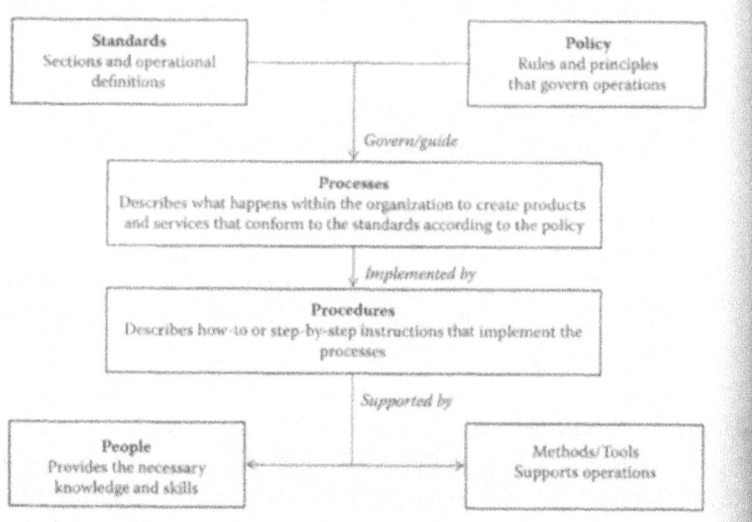

Figure 8.6

Documents of the system of management. (Adapted from ISO (International Organization for Standardization), Guidance on the concept and use of the process approach for management systems. ISO/TC 176/ SC2/N 544R3, ISO, Geneva, 2008, http://www.ios.org/iso/04_concept_ and-use-of-the-process-approach_for_management_systems.pdf, retrieved June 22, 2015.)

- Maintaining competence in all organization members or employees
- Creating an awareness program to keep all people currently on the system of management
- Maintaining a system of internal and external communication
- Maintaining documented evidence necessary to support the system of management
- Developing and maintaining operational planning and control system
- Developing and maintaining monitoring, measurement, analysis, and evaluation of the organization's ability to meet its objectives
- Providing for internal audits, self-evaluation, and maturity measurement
- Maintaining a regular management review processes.
- Maintaining a means for searching for nonconformities and taking corrective action when needed
- Maintaining a program of continual improvement

Using a process approach is a management strategy that helps give effect to the standard. Leaders seek to manage and control processes. The interaction between processes creates a coherent system of management.

All the frameworks in use in an organization should be aligned to facilitate their interconnectivity potential while being available to improve decision making. Organizations should make sure that risk and uncertainty management is never a separate activity. It must be an integral component of the combination of all the management programs.

8.6 Managing for the Sustained Success of an Organization

Sustained success is described as the ability of the organization to achieve and maintain its objectives over the long term. Achieving sustained success should be possible if the organizations follow. the system management for quality, as long as it is used. Based on the quality management principles:

- Maintain a focus on the on the customer's requirements while striving to exceed expectations.
- Leaders need to establish the unity of purpose within the organization while creating and maintaining a work environment in which all people can become involved in helping to achieve the organization's objectives.
- People are the essence of an organization, and their engagement enables their abilities to be used for the organization's benefit.
- Desired results are achieved efficiently when activities and resources are managed using the process approach.
- Managing interrelated processes as a system contributes to the organization's effectiveness in achieving its strategic objectives.
- Continual improvement of the organization's overall performance is treated as an overarching objective.
- Effective decisions are based on facts obtained from the careful analysis of data and information.
- Organizations need to work with members of the value chains through mutually beneficial relationships that enhance the ability to create shared value.

It is easy to see how these principles contribute to sustained success, whether part of a quality program or used as an integral component of risk management and sustainability effort.

An organization can achieve sustained success by paying close attention to its ever-changing external operating environment. Other elements of this approach include the following:

- Creating a strategy and policy
- Managing resources
- Paying attention to people in the organization
- Working closely with suppliers and customers within the value chain
- Maintaining a suitable work environment

213

- Managing knowledge, information, and technology
- Managing processes
- Monitoring, measurement, analysis, and review
- Improvement, innovation, and learning

Many organizations keep their systems of management separate from each other. However, the management of risk and uncertainty along with sustainability should be coordinated so that they can collectively contribute to the organization's core purpose and its strategic objective an organization. should enhance its resilience by ensuring that unnecessary overlap in processes and activities that wastes resources is avoided.

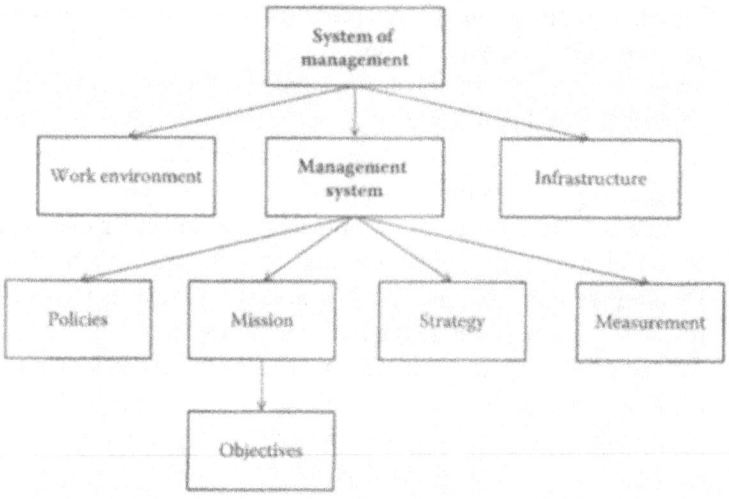

Figure 8.7

Leaders should align operational activities through the achievement of coherence across the various systems of management. This can help an organization build the ability to adapt to changing conditions as they emerge. It can modify its structures, activities, and behaviors to adjust to new conditions while retaining its core purpose and objectives.

8.7 Approach for the management of Organizational processes

The following methodology can be applied to manage the processes of the **organization.** The approach starts with the identification of the processes of the organizations

- Determine the purpose *of the organization:* Create a mission statement.
- Define the policies of organization: These will include- risk management and sustainability

- determine the sequences of the processes' sequence has been proposed above
- *Define the process ownership:* Starts with the leaders and is cascaded down through the organization.
- *Define the process documentation:* This includes the process documentation and procedures.

Next, the organization needs to plan the process. It can do so with the following steps:

- *Define the activities within the process:* These are necessary to achieve the intended outputs.
- *Define the monitoring and measurement requirements:* Provides the control and improvement of the processes and the intended process outputs.
- *Define the resources needed:* Determines the resources needed for the effective operation of the processes.
- *Verify the process against its planned objectives:* Confirms that the processes are consistent with the mission statement and the strategic objectives.

The third step involves the implementation and measurement of the process and its activities. The organization needs to provide the following assistance to the implementation effort:

- Communication
- Awareness
- Training
- Management of change
- Direct involvement of the leaders
- Management review

The fourth step involves the analysis of the process. It is important to compare the results of process performance information with the requirements of the process as defined in the previous steps. This will help identify any need for corrective action. When corrective actions are needed, the method for implementing them must be clearly defined.

These four steps are often referred to as the Plan-Do-Check-Act (PDCA) methodology covered in Section 4.1.4 .

8.8 Organization's Internal and External Context

Management of an organization involves a large number of coordinated activities to control its activities, processes, operations, products, and services as it pursues its strategic objectives.

Risk management is a component of organizational management involving', coordinated activities associated with the effect of uncertainty on those objectives. Effective risk management is fundamental to the

215

success of the organization, as it focuses on its performance against the objectives. An organization's performance in relation to society and the economy, as well as its impact on the environment, has become a critical part of measuring its overall performance and its ability to continue operating effectively. Because risk is the effect of uncertainty on achieving strategic objectives, it is important to examine the influences and factors in the internal and external context that can have an effect on the organization's objectives.

8.8.1 Context of the Organization

Organizations operate in an uncertain world. Whenever an organization seeks to meet: its objectives, there is a chance that everything will not go according to plan. It is possible that the organization will not achieve its objectives even ifthe objectives were carefully planned. What lies between the organization and that leads to an incomplete understanding of what can happen that would either threaten or enhance the organization's ability to meet its objectives. The operating environment within which the organization operates includes many sources of uncertainty. This uncertainty creates "effects. "These effects can be negative or positive. Negative effects are referred to as"threats" Positive effects are- referred to as "opportunities." These effects create positive or negative consequences that affect the organization's ability to meets strategic objectives. Consequences are the outcomes of an event or decision. Affecting the organization's objectives, effective risk management help the organization understands its opportunities and threat. And address them as appropriate to manage the consequences and thereby maximize its chance of achieving objectives by managing the uncertainty.

It is important to remember that risk is associated with the performance of the strategic objectives of the organization.

8.8.2 Internal Context

An organization's internal context is the operational environment within which it seeks to achieve its objectives. The internal context includes anything that the organization has control over or where it has a sphere of influence. The sphere of influence is an important concept. It represents the range and extent of political, contractual, economic, or other relationships through which an organization has the ability to affect the decisions or activities of individuals or organizations. The internal context can include the following:
- Governance, organizational structure (including relationships with a parent organization), roles, and accountabilities
- Policies, objectives, and strategy

- Operational capabilities understood in terms of processes, operations, and resources
- Decision making, knowledge, and sense making
- Engagement with the internal stakeholders
- Relationships with other organizations within its value chain
- Organization's culture
- Standards, guidelines, and operating models adopted by the organization
- Honoring contractual relationships

An organization must consider everything that is internal and relevant to its mission, strategic objectives, strategic direction, processes, and operations. It needs to understand the influence these considerations could have on its sustainability program and on the results that it intends to achieve.

8.8.3 External Context:

The external context includes the broad external operating environment in which the organization operates. Influences and factors in the external context can include the following:

- Cultural, social, political, legal, regulatory, financial, technological, economic, natural, and compelled
- Key drivers and trends exerting positive and negative consequences
- that affect the objectives
- Relationship with external stakeholders, along with their perceptions, values, and interests

Organizations must assess their external operating environment to determine and characterize the crucial influences and factors that might support or impair their ability to manage the opportunities and threats that are identified. These factors are identified by examining the conditions, entities, and events that determine the associated opportunities and threats, and which may influence the organization's activities and decisions.

Because the external operating environment affects the operations, people involved in supporting the operations have an interest in the information that is created in the characterization of the external environment. The following elements are often considered:

- Material resources: Suppliers, real estate, and brokers
- Human resources: Labor market, schools, and unions
- Financial resources: Banks, investors, granting agencies, and contributions
- Markets for products and services: Customers, clients, and users
- (Competitive environment: Competitors and competitiveness
- Technology: Hardware, software, information technology, and production techniques

- Economic conditions: Inflation rate, signs of recession, the rate of investment, and growth
- (Government oversight: Regulations, taxes, services, the court system, and political process
- Sociocultural Demographics, values, beliefs, education, religion, work ethic, and the green movement
- International: Exchange rate, competition, selling overseas, and regulations

An organization needs to consider its relationship to each of these elements, in terms of their strengths, weaknesses, opportunities, and threats.

8.8.4 Scanning the Organization's Operating Environment

Organizations are connected to an outside world with a constantly changing set of influences and factors. There is often a similar change going on within the organization. organizations should monitor the context to identify,

Assesses and manage the opportunities and threats associated with change. If the organization is able to analyze these changes that can affect its performance, it can then begin to make a decision and develop 'a strategy for operating in this uncertain world

Understanding the context of the organization provides insight into the internal and external influences and factors that impact the way organizations operate at the community level and influence the decisions that will be made by leadership at that location.

Scanning the Internal Environment:

Understanding the internal context prepares the organization for managing the opportunities and threats originating within its processes and operations. The internal context is also important to the implementation of any risk management activity by the organization. Most factors associated with the internal context are within the control of the organization or within its sphere of influence.

A methodology widely used in the project management field provides a set of "influences" that are useful for scanning the internal operating environment. This TECOP tool contains the following influences:

- Technical: Information and communications technology (hardware and software), internal infrastructure (including its condition), knowledge sharing, research and development, assets, required skill levels and competency of workers, and innovation efforts
- Economic: Financial management, financing, cash flow, return on investment, capital reserves, taxes, royalty payments, insurance, and the commercial viability of the organization
- Cultural: Demographics, and collective attitudes and behavior characteristics of the organization

- Organizational: Capabilities, policies, standards, guidelines, strategies, management systems, structures, and objectives
- Political: Governance, internal politics, decision-making systems, stakeholders, roles, and accountabilities

There is another version of TECOP that replaces cultural with commercial. However, for the purposes of determining the internal context, the cultural category is of great importance for understanding the influence of people on an organization's operations.

When considering the processes and operations of the organization, SWIFT (i.e., "structured what ifs technique") tool can be used to supplement the characterization of the internal context through the use of the TECOP analysis. SWIFT is a method that enables a facilitator to guide, a team through a systematic valuation using, "prompts" to determine how the processes .and operations could be affected by opportunities and threats found through the use of TECOP analysis deviations processes and operations create additional opportunities and threats that must be considered in the internal context.

Scanning the External Environment

The external context is characterized by conducting a broad scan of the external operating environment. A PESTLE analysis tool is used to systematically assess the influences and factors that create opportunities and threats in the external operating environment that are not. controlled by the organization. The influences associated with the PESTLE analysis include the following:

- Political: Factors include the extent to which governments or political influences are likely to impact or drive global, regional, national, local, and community trends or cultures.
- Economic: Factors include global, national, and local trends and drivers; financial markets; credit cycles; economic growth; interest rates; exchange rates; inflation rates; and the cost of capital.
- Societal: Factors include culture, health consciousness, demographics, education, population growth, career attitudes, and an emphasis on safety.
- Technological: Factors include computing, technology advances or limitations, robotics, automation, technology incentives, the rate of technological change, and research and development.
- Legal: Factors include legislative or regulatory issues and sensitivities.
- Environmental: Factors include global, regional, and local climate; adverse weather; natural hazards; hazardous waste; and related trends.

Gathering the information to prepare the external context can be time-consuming and difficult. Having an independent analysis conducted by a local team under contract could facilitate the ability to determine the opportunities and threats associated with each of the factors. However, the people working within the organization may have some unique perspectives that a contractor might not be able to develop during the life of the contracted effort. Once' there has been some meaningful engagement of the internal stakeholders, it is possible to use their knowledge of the external operating environment to complement this effort.

Adapting to a Changing External Context: Uncertainty in the external context may create a need to make changes in the organizational, behaviors. An organization in a certain external operating environment is managed and controlled differently from an organization operating in an uncertain external context. Organizations need to have the correct fit between the internal structure and the external environment. Volatility, uncertainty, complexity, and ambiguity scanning involves both looking at information (i.e. viewing) and looking for information (i.e., searching) VUCA.

8.8.5 Scanning Methods

One method to help understand the external operating environment is to review a wide range of different sources

- Laws and regulations
- Newspaper
- Electronic media
- Newsletters, magazines, journals, and books
- Reports and presentations
- Interviews

All the information from the strategic planning process should be reviewed. Data from the organization's documented information is quite useful, for both the operations and the supply chain.

Once information from all sources has been reviewed, it is time to start using the PESTLE analysis method. The acronym letters refer to the influences in the external operating environment. Each influence has a number of factors. It does not matter how the factors are allocated to the different influences. The aim of the scanning activity is to identify as many factors as possible.

In order to find out which factors can yield valid opportunities and threats, it is important to have the scanning team to learn how to ask effective questions. Questioning is a vital tool that helps obtain data, information, knowledge, and wisdom. However, the information obtained is only as good as the questions asked. Questions contribute to the success or failure of finding opportunities and threats as the team seeks to understand a complex and changing external context.

Effective Questioning:

The scanning team needs to have a plan to use the questions to catalyze insight, innovation, and action on the part of the organization each of the following steps is of critical importance to the discovery of opportunities and threats:

- Assess the current situation with the influence-factor combination.
- Discover the big questions that can help identify and clarify usage opportunities and threats.
- Create images of possibilities and scenarios of how to organization be affected.
- Evolve and create strategic opportunities and threats.

Many organizations use scanning for marketing as well as for strategy keep in mind that the methods and outcomes are quite different. Sustainability practitioners are usually keen on finding opportunities in both the internal and external context; It is important to engage the sustainability team as part of the scanning effort. If there is no sustainability focus in place, the scanning team needs to reach out to people that are involved in the stakeholder engagement process. It is likely that the external stakeholders are already savvy about what is happening in the neighborhood and the community at large. Exchanging information with the stakeholders will help improve the effectiveness of the engagement process.

The scanning team should consider the following methods to help improve the effectiveness of their effort:

- Engage in shared conversation.
- Convene and host "learning conversations/.'
- Include diverse perspectives in all conversations.
- Foster shared meaning.
- Nurture communities of practice.
- Use collaborative technologies.

All these are important elements of effective questioning in a learning organization.

8.8.6 Sustainability and Context

Organizations operating without a focus on sustainability seek to primarily control internal threats. In an internal context, this is referred to as "operatic controls." Scanning of the external operating environment often involves those who are interested and involved in the organization s Sustainability efforts. These Sustainability efforts focus on effective process and efficient operations within the internal context, but also on searching for opportunities and threats in the external operating environment through their involvement with the stakeholder engagement program. Without a focus on Sustainability, the stakeholders are regarded as "interested parties."

Sustainable organizations where there is a high level of stakeholder engagement tend to be more vigilant about changes in the external context. Moreover, the sustainability program to be continuously vigilant with respect to opportunities and threats with a changing external context.

In some organizations, the information about the internal context can be determined by reviewing existing practices, plans, processes, and procedures. However, many organizations operating at the community level tend to operate informally. Context review team members need to ask questions of the members or employees to determine how they function within the organization. The organization's leader could access the ability of the organization to achieve the identified objectives through some basic level of strategic planning (e.g., strengths, weaknesses, opportunities, and threats). It always helps to see how the organization has dealt with previous failures, incidents, accidents, and emergencies to obtain a complete picture of an informal internal context. Changes in either the internal or external context create uncertainty for the organization. Organizations must manage the effects of uncertainty (i.e., the opportunities and threats) to lower the risk to meet their objectives. An increased level of uncertainty is often associated with the inability of internal decision makers to obtain sufficient information about the context factor and the opportunities and threats associated with these factors. Uncertainty increases the risk of meeting the objectives. Opportunities can contribute to the chances that the objectives will be met. Threats are likely to lead to chances that the objectives will not be met.

A complex external operating environment is one in which the organization interacts or is influenced by many diverse PESTLE influences and factors. In contrast, a simple external operating environment leads to an organization that only interacts with or is influenced by a small number of similar factors as determined using the PESTLE analysis. There is also a stable-unstable dimension associated with the external context In a stable external operating environment, the PESTLE influences and factors remain essentially the same over a period of months or years. During unstable conditions, the PESTLE influences and factors change rapidly. It is very important to constantly monitor the external context under unstable conditions. This is a role that the Sustainability team is particularly suited for.

The context analysis team might consider the following looking forward

- Reviewing or creating the risk management and sustainability policies
- Analyzing the organization's resources (financial capital, human capital etc.)

- Assets, and materials productivity and knowledge management capabilities
- Performing a stress test of the decision-making processes including
- Creating a cohesive set of organizational systems of management for the use of a plan-do-check-act sequence of processes
- Enhancing the organization's contractual and informal relationships that involve adherence to a "supplier code of conduct" as a condition of collaborating at any level with another organization

Organizations will use these actions to protect the operations associated with the internal context and otherwise manage the level of uncertainty to help meet their objectives. To thrive in a world characterized by uncertainty, an organization needs to turn to risk management and sustainability to help take advantage of the opportunities and use them to offset the threats. Treating threats to make them less unacceptable always leads to the creation of additional threats when operating in a system.

Questions:

1. What are the main objectives of an organization?
2. Discuss the importance of the mission statement
3. Explain the processes in the system of management
4. How do changes that occur in the internal and external operating environments affect the ability of the organization to meet its strategic objectives?
5. How is sustainability affected by changes in the internal and| external context?
6. How does the corporate sustainability man-take this into account when preparing the sustainability report? Why is it important for a corporation to understand that all its facilities (i.e., organizations) are different because of the context even if they have identical products and services?
7. How can the PESTLE and TECOP tools help standardize the scanning processes at different facilities to provide consistency within the corporate?
8. Why are Sustainability goals established without regard for the organization's strategic objectives and goals?
9. How can the Sustainability goals be used to influence the organization's strategic objectives? Why are Sustainability goals focused on producing results rather than on helping the organization meet its strategic objectives?
10. How can the stakeholders be affected when the organization meets its strategic objectives?

Chapter 9

Sustainability through Risk Management

9.1 Risk Management

Changes in regulatory, political, financial, stakeholder and other risks have increased the uncertainties in corporate decision making. As such, the materiality of Sustainability Risk Management has increased dramatically.

Probably the most frequently used definition of *risk* is this one:

Risk = the *Probability/likelihood* of something happening *x* resulting Cost/*Consequences*.

A risk is an uncertain event or condition that, if it occurs, has an effect on at least one organization/ *project* objective. *Risk* management focuses on identifying and assessing the *risks* to the *project* and managing those *risks* to minimize the adverse impact of the *project*. This definition covers not only something that might happen but also how it will affect an organization's ability to meet its objectives in an uncertain world. However, the risk is not just confined to harmful events. Instead, risk and its consequences could be positive (upside of risk) or negative (the downside of risk). The risk is always focused on the organization's objectives. Opportunities and threats represent the effects of uncertainty.

Sustainability Footprint:

$$\text{FOOTPRINT} \implies \text{IMPACT} \implies \text{RISK}$$

From the perspective of the organization, all activities, products, and services have a sustainability footprint. This footprint creates adverse impacts to the environment, society, and the economy. Each impact creates risks for the organization and its stakeholders. The organization can mitigate these risks through responsible operation that avoids creating impacts to the extent possible. (Pojasek, 2012).

The fundamentals of risk management are essentially the process corporations use to identify and manage risks that may impact their ability to profit or operate or to meet organizational mission and vision. If you know what your risks are, you can ensure you have plans in place to manage those risks – and make informed decisions. At the heart of the process is the risk register. A risk register is an itemized list of the identified risks an organization faces. These risks, and how they are managed, define the culture, direction, and strategy of the company. The risk register notes, among other things, risks, the significance of the risk, the likelihood/probability of the risk and the actions required to manage the risk as shown in Figure 9.1. All major organization decisions consult the risk register. This helps organizations ensure decisions have considered all material risks – this means that the risk register essentially influences employee, asset, investment and all other major decisions. Clearly, integrating sustainability here can prove to be a very effective influencing device. To govern the risk register, each risk is assigned an owner. That is, a senior executive responsible for direct management of a specific risk or risks. To manage these risks, owners develop risk registers of their own, sometimes referred to as subordinate risk registers, which break the risk into its components, and which can then be assigned to members of their own management or leadership teams. This process may continue with subordinate risk registers devolving into management risk registers, and so on. As this cycle is repeated, risks become more discreet and specialized and spread throughout the organization, which provides for a massive ability to influence.

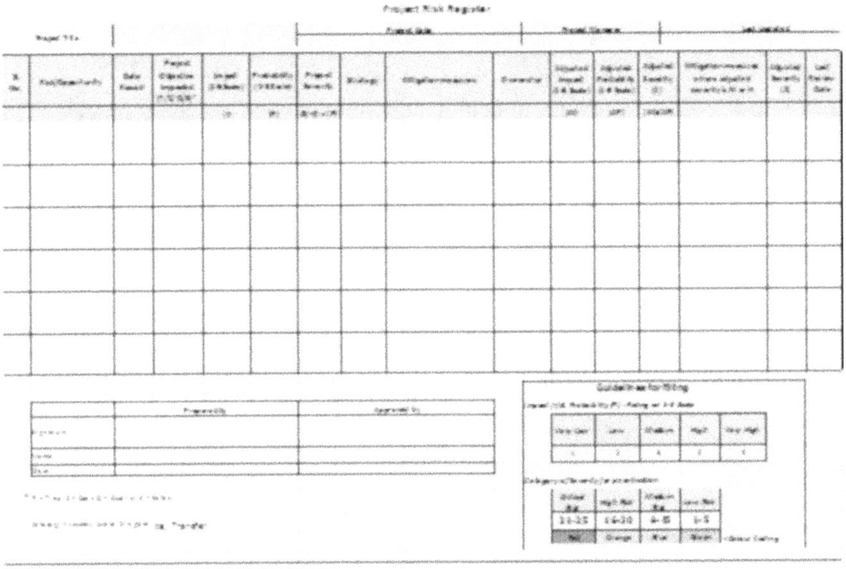

Figure 9.1

Sustainability Risk Management: The materiality of Sustainability Risk Management has increased dramatically. Benefits of Sustainability Risk Management, which refers to the embedding of sustainability risks into the risk register and managing them accordingly, provides a series of highly desirable benefits to corporations. Some of these benefits include Enhanced decision-making capacity, agility, and adaptability of the corporation; Supplying a wealth of insight, knowledge and intelligence on emerging and current risks and opportunities; Managing stakeholder expectations with greater certainty; Providing a framework and principles for innovation.

9.2 Sustainability Risks

Sustainability risks can be broken down into three broad categories. They include existing and emerging environmental, social and governance risks. Also referred to as non-traditional risks, sustainability risks arise when corporate behaviour, or the actions of others in corporations operating environment (e.g., suppliers, media, government), create vulnerabilities that may result in financial, operational or reputational loses in value.

Identifying Environmental Risks:

Value Chain Phase	Sample Questions to Help Identify Environmental Risk
Company Operations	• How big is our environmental footprint? • What resources are we most dependent on(energy, water, materials) and how much do we use? • What emissions do we release into the air or water? • How do we dispose of waste? • How up-to-date is our environmental management system? • What are our chances of a spill, leak or release of hazardous materials? • Have others in our industry had problems? • What local, state, federal, or international regulations apply to our business? Are we in full compliance? Are these requirements getting tougher?
Upstream	• What resources are our suppliers most dependent on? Are they abundant or constrained, now or in the near future? • Does our supplier pollute? Do they meet all applicable laws? Will legal requirements get tighter for them? • What substances go into the products suppliers sell to us? Are they toxic?
Downstream	• How much energy (or water or other resources) does our product require customers to use? • Are there hazardous substances in our products? • What do customers do with our products when they are done with them? What would happen if we were required to take the products back?

Table 9.1

Environmental Risks (examples): Climate change: carbon emissions, Water: drought and flood Biodiversity: constrained resources, Compliance: pollution

Social Risks (examples): Population: diversity and displacement, Community: access to people Change: health, safety, and culture, Resources: availability and access

Governance Risks (examples): Conformance: corporate policy, Finance: compensation and bribery, Information: management and privacy Compliance: regulations

Implementation: It may come as no surprise that embedding sustainability risks into the risk register are not an entirely dissimilar process than including traditional risks. Preparation: As a first step toward Sustainability Risk Management, you will need to 1. Review the existing risk register 2. Review the governance system 3. Interview the risk owners 4. Establish a Sustainability Risk Authority.

Review the existing Risk Register: evaluate the process used by your corporation to manage the risks noted therein and model the Sustainability Risk Management approach in the same regard. Establish Sustainability Risk Authority: ensure that you – or an appropriate agent – are aligned and identified as the go-to person regarding sustainability risks. That means you must understand the aspects and real and perceived consequences of each risk, and be able to provide sufficient insight to those who will become the sustainability risk owners and managers.

Review the governance system: evaluate the methodology used to govern the risk register and determine the most appropriate entry point for sustainability risks. Introducing new risks to the risk register means that someone is about to have a new risk assigned to them to manage, which is never easy to sell.

Interview the risk owners: determine how risk owners manage their assigned risks, how risks are regarded and ensure your proposals fit within their frameworks. Also, use this as an opportunity to find out who among the risk owners would be the most appropriate managers for any of your sustainability risks.

Embedding: Now that you have a better understanding of how your corporation regards and manages traditional risks and have completed your preliminary undertakings, it is time for Sustainability Risk Management implementation. There are four steps to conducting this exercise:

1. Facilitated Risk Discovery
2. Materiality Assessment
3. Facilitated Risk Review
4. Risk Register Incorporation

Facilitated Risk Discovery: convene a panel of internal and external stakeholders who understand the nature and function of your business. That is, those who understand how your corporation makes profit. Task the panel to identify the potential and actual sustainability risks facing your corporation.

Materiality Assessment: analyze the sustainability risks identified by your panel and determine the likelihood of each risk occurring, the significance of the risk to stakeholders and the ultimate and potential impact to the corporation. Note that this process should (at least loosely) match the existing risk register evaluation protocols.

Facilitated Risk Review: Provide the material sustainability risks to the risk management team and determine what sustainability risks, if any, can be absorbed by existing risks on the risk register, and those which will need to be managed as new risks. At this point, potential risk owners should also be identified and consulted.

Risk Register Incorporation: using existing risk management processes, incorporate the sustainability risks into the risk register, ensuring that ownership is clearly outlined.

Once you have successfully completed this implementation, maintain a dialogue with the sustainability risk owners and managers. Provide concise advice such as briefs or updates or any other form that suits each risk owner and manager best.

Sustainability today is not about greenwashing for most corporations; instead, it's about managing risk, according to Peter Graf, Executive Vice President and Chief Sustainability Officer for SAP. But whether the driver is compliance or corporate image, sustainability management is exploding. Not only do companies have to comply with government regulations, such as greenhouse gas emissions reporting mandated by the EPA or disclosing country of origin for wood products under the Lacey Act, but they also have to comply with the best practices established by other companies. If you want to do business with Walmart, you have to comply with any sustainability measurements that they have in place.

Furthermore, the evidence is mounting that there is a strong business case to be made for making the switch. Sustainability practices in large companies can contribute to 38 percent higher profits, according to the National Environmental Education Foundation, and companies listed in the Dow Jones Sustainability Index consistently outperform the general market.

Sustainability risks directly impact a company's long-term financial results and sustainability. Any company operating today will encounter risks relating to sustainability. Environmental protection, human resources, occupational health and safety, local community engagement, infrastructure, and social affairs in the regions of a company's operation directly impact a company's long-term financial results and sustainability.

Risk Management

- Is produced by natural processes that are characterized by inherent variability (e.g., weather)
- Changes over time (e.g., due to competition, trends, new information, or changes in underlying factors)
- Is produced by the perception of uncertainty, which may vary between different parts of the organization and with its stakeholders

Understanding Uncertainty:

Uncertainty originates in the internal and external context within which the organization operates.Uncertainty represents a deficiency of information that leads to an incomplete understanding of what can happen that would threaten the organization's ability to meet its objectives. Think of this as a recession, a severe storm, a devastating legal situation, or any number of things that could happen that would distract the organization from meeting its objectives. Uncertainty exists whenever the knowledge or understanding of an event, consequence, or likelihood is inadequate or incomplete. Incomplete knowledge may involve information that alone or in combination with other Information,

- Is not available
- Is available, but is not accessible
- Is of unknown accuracy
- Is invalid or unreliable
- Involves factors whose relationship or interaction is not known

By working within the risk management program, sustainability can help the organization overcome the effects of uncertainty, thereby enhancing its chance of attaining its strategic objectives.

Members or employees of the organization must have the appropriate competence for managing risk and uncertainty in order to be held accountable for their role in this risk management framework. The framework must be embedded in all the organization's practices and processes while keeping the contents associated with the framework relevant, effective, and efficient. Many organizations have a risk and uncertainty management plan to ensure that the design elements are embedded in all the organization's practices and processes. Often, this plan is part of the strategic plan.

Once the risk and uncertainty framework has been designed, it is time to plan and execute the implementation of the elements so that the risk management process is routinely applied to decision making throughout the organization. When implementing risk and uncertainty management, the organization should do the following:

- Define the strategy for implementing risk and uncertainty management

- Apply the risk management policy, and process to the organization's processes
- Comply with legal and regulatory requirements
- Ensure the decision making is aligned with the outcomes of the risk and uncertainty management processes
- Provide awareness development activities
- Engage the stakeholders to ensure that the risk and uncertainty management framework remains appropriate and effective

Any weaknesses in the design or implementation of the risk management framework can lead to poor performance with respect to meeting the organization's strategic objectives. The framework needs to be monitored and reviewed to determine its effectiveness to support organizational performance in the following ways:

- Measure risk management performance
- Periodically measure progress against the risk management plan
- Periodically review whether the design and its components are still appropriate
- Report on risk and uncertainty management progress and how well the risk management policy is being followed.

Based on the results of monitoring and reviews, decisions should be made on how the risk and uncertainty management framework, policy, and plan can be improved. These decisions should lead to improvements in the organization's management of risk and its risk management culture.

9.3 Embedding Risk Management:

The focus of every organization should be on meeting its strategic objectives. This starts with the setting of responsible objectives that cascade from the top to the bottom of the organization. At this point, goals are set, along with action plans, to make sure the objectives are met. The management of risk should be embedded in the activities to manage the opportunities and threats associated with the effects of uncertainty found in the internal and external operating environment. Objectives need to be established and maintained mindful of those opportunities and threats. The people that are responsible for setting the objectives should also be responsible for managing risk, however, the leaders of an organization know that everyone is responsible for the risk management within the structure of objectives and goal setting. Risk management should be delegated to specialized risk practitioners in separate departments. A risk assessment is used to prioritise the opportunities and threats, based on highest risk or opportunity value in accordance with definition in Section 9.1, in order to ensure action that create an efficacious strategy and strategic decisions that will enable the organization to meet its objectives. When there are frequent changes in the external operating environment, a risk assessment of the strategic options is required. It will facilitate the analysis of the stakeholders interests customer requirements for products and services.

Risk management must be tailored to the organization. Organizations must realize that there are differences in the internal and external context at each of their facilities or operations. Where risk management is embedded within the governance of the organization, the risk management function plays a number of important roles:

- Facilitates proper risk management and internal control processes within all levels of the organization
- Serves as the custodian of the overall risk management and control frameworks
- Provides internal assurance on the effectiveness of risk management and internal control within the organization

9.4 Four Categories of Risk

Risk slip into the boardroom in several costumes. Some are scarier than others. Some may impact the income statement; others may jeopardize multiple aspects of the company's financial performance. Some are more material than others. When performing sustainability risk management (SRM), we pay attention to the same four categories of risks that are assessed in enterprise risk management (ERM) scenarios:

- Strategic risks relate to the company's future business plans and strategies, including reputational risks associated with its markets and demand for its products and services, competitive threats, technology and product innovation risks, and risks arising from public policy.
- Operational risks relate to factors that threaten the effectiveness of the company's people, systems, and processes, as well as external events that could affect the operation of its businesses and its bottom line. They include threats from the supply chain and product life-cycle impacts.
- Compliance risks relate to the possibility that government regulatory actions will impose additional costs on the company or force it to change its business models or practices' in order to be compliant.
- Financial risk relates to the company's ability to meet financial obligations and mitigate credit risk, liquidity risk, and exposure to financial market risks.

Ernst and Young's 2010 Business Risk Report summarized business risks identified by a panel of 70 executives representing 14 industry sectors. Figure 9.2 arrays the report's top 10 risks into the risk quadrants listed above. For the first time in E&Y's annual survey, "social acceptance risk and corporate social responsibility" was a top 10 business risk. "Radical greening" also made the list, suggesting stakeholder demands for more proactive measures to reduce environmental impacts. The report also found that companies are threatened by changes in regulations and carbon trading schemes.

Interestingly, the executives identified 15 "below the radar" risks, in this priority sequence: inability to innovate, emerging technologies, taxation risk, pricing pressures, resource scarcity, shifts in consumer demands, global realignment, reputation risks, energy shocks, supply chain risks, new business models, capital allocation changes, intermediary power shifts, and shifting demographics. .

Sustainability strategies help mitigate risks from all of the above risks, avoiding threats to revenue and increases to expenses.

Top 10 Business Risks of 2010

- (▲) Up from 2009
- (▼) Down from 2009
- (⊖) No change
- (✳) New entry

Social acceptance risk and corporate social responsibility (✳)

Access to credit (▼)
Slow recovery/ double-dip (⊖) recession
Emerging markets (▲)
Radical greening (▼)
Non-traditional entrants (▼)

Regulation and compliance (▲)
Managing talent (▲)
Cost cutting (⊖)
Executing alliances and transactions (▼)

Financial · *Compliance* · *Strategic* · *Operations*

Source: Adpated from "The Top 10 Risks for Global Business," Ernst & Young Business Risk Report 2010, July 2010, p. 3. Based on interviews with 70 industry executives and analysts in14 industry sectors.

Figure 9.2

9.5 Mitigating Strategic Risks That Could Erode Revenue

A business is perceived as legitimate when its activities align with the goals and values of the society in which it operates. In other words, to be legitimate, a business must earn its social license to operate from its important stakeholders. To this end, a company tries to create and maintain its image as a good corporate citizen, or at least a better one than its competitors. Companies may justify their sustainability initiatives as a means of boosting their legitimacy, brand image, and reputation. Strategic risks threaten the company's reputation, which could impact its future revenue and, in turn, its long-term profitability.

Regulatory and litigation risks are usually top of mind when companies think of sustainability-related risks, and most companies have learned how to avoid or manage them. Reputation risk may grow to be the most important for many businesses as big companies are becoming more aggressive with their suppliers and demanding transparency on the energy, carbon, water, material, and social footprints of not only purchased products but also the supplier's whole company.

Walmart led this trend in 2010 with a 15-question survey of its 100,000 suppliers (see Figure 17.2), and now companies like Procter & Gamble are following suit with their supply chains. Other retailers like Safeway and Best Buy are showing interest in adopting similar supplier-rating schemes. A firm's ability to satisfy the sustainability criteria of these big corporations could be a gating factor for its continued income from these business-to-business (B2B) customers. Companies that do not improve their track record and associated reputations could be jeopardizing revenue streams. The bar is being raised. Although it may be shiny today, the corporate image may tarnish from lack of polishing.

Example:

Figure 9.3 summarizes the potential hits to revenue from seven threats from two generic companies, Sam's Solutions and M&D Corp. Five of them arise from potential brand erosion on environmental footprint issues; one is based on lack of action to mitigate escalating energy, water, and material expenses; and the last is the threat of sudden disruption of the company's supply chain or access to customers. There are other potential threats, but this is a reasonable cross-sector starter set. In each case, the risk is calculated by monetizing its potential impact and factoring that amount by the likelihood it will occur within our three- to five-year horizon.

Sam's Solutions' Potential Revenue Loss from Strategic Risks (Base revenue $1,000,000)

	Percent of Revenue at Risk	Percent Probability of Occurring Within 3 to 5 Years	Potential Lost Revenue
Risk to revenue from poor reputation on energy and carbon management	5%	25%	$12,500
Risk to revenue from poor reputation on water management	5%	25%	$12,500
Risk to revenue from poor reputation on materials and waste management	5%	20%	$10,000
Risk to revenue from poor supplier reputation and behaviors	5%	10%	$5,000
Risk to revenue from poor reputation on ecosystem damages	5%	1%	$500
Risk to revenue from less competitive prices	10%	10%	$10,000
Risk to revenue from sudden disruptions in the value chain	2%	5%	$1,000
Potential decreased revenue without sustainability initiatives			**$51,500**

M&D Corp.'s Potential Revenue Loss from Strategic Risks (Base revenue $500,000,000)

	Percent of Revenue at Risk	Percent Probability of Occurring Within 3 to 5 Years	Potential Lost Revenue
Risk to revenue from poor reputation on energy and carbon management	5%	25%	$6,250,000
Risk to revenue from poor reputation on water management	5%	25%	$6,250,000
Risk to revenue from poor reputation on materials and waste management	5%	20%	$5,000,000
Risk to revenue from poor supplier reputation and behaviors	5%	10%	$2,500,000
Risk to revenue from poor reputation on ecosystem damages	5%	1%	$250,000
Risk to revenue from less competitive prices	10%	10%	$5,000,000
Risk to revenue from sudden disruptions in the value chain	2%	5%	$500,000
Potential decreased revenue without sustainability initiatives			**$25,750,000**

Figure 9.3

9.6 Risk to Revenue from Poor Reputation on Energy and Carbon Management

Companies stakeholder concerns about the multiple repercussions of climate change, shown in Figure 9.4. The cumulative impact of employee expectations, investor requests, and customer expectations makes carbon a strategic issue for companies today. As can be seen in Figure 9.4, "brand improvement," "product differentiation," and "risk management" are strong reasons for corporate action on climate change. Not only does a company want to grow its revenue using the sustainability strategies described in Chapter 2 on Benefit 1, but it also needs to protect the top-line growth from climate-related reputational threats.

Corporate press releases almost always accompany announcements of reduced energy use with information about associated carbon footprint reductions, since fossil fuels power a substantial proportion of the electricity grid. In most jurisdictions, carbon reductions do not save the company money, and yet when a price is put on carbon through a carbon tax or

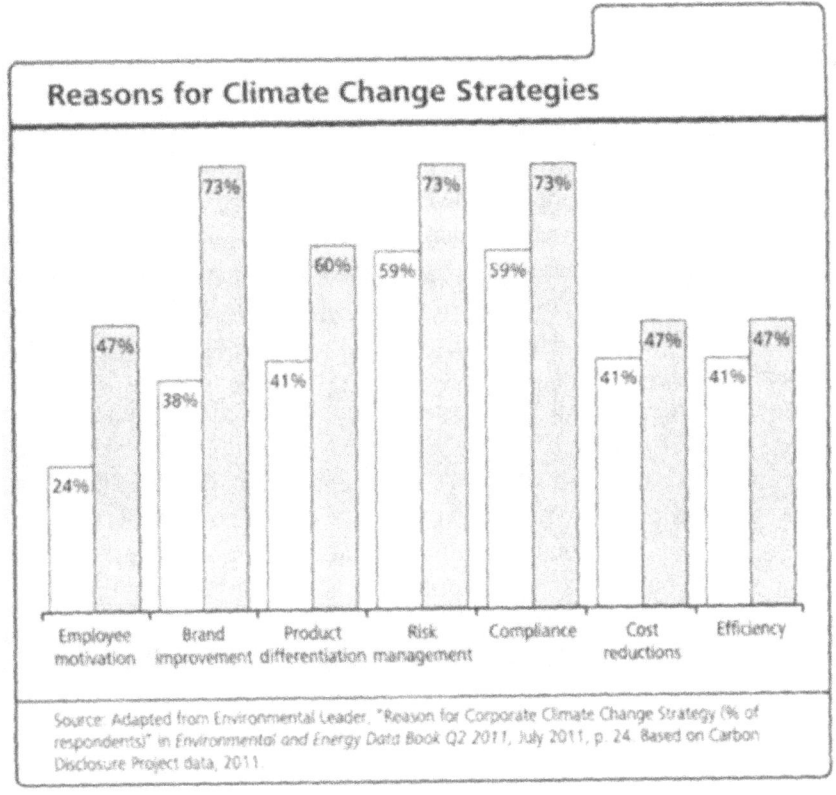

Figure 9.4

a cap-and-trade mechanism, companies will reap financial benefit from their carbon reductions. In the meantime, carbon reductions are a proxy for the company's smart governance — it anticipates a price on carbon and is positioning itself strategically to benefit from it rather than being blindsided by it. Energy conservation saves expenses; carbon management builds a reputation.

How many business-to-consumer (B2C) and/or B2B customers care enough about climate change and carbon footprints to use them as supplier criteria? Increasingly, procurement criteria include a significant weighting for carbon management in B2B transactions. However, it can be assumed that a company could lose 5% of its revenue if B2C and B2B customers are not happy with its action to reduce its carbon contribution to the climate change threat. Further, it can be assumed that there is a 25% chance that customers will vote with their wallets on companies and products that they perceive to be harming the health of the planet.

9.7 Risk to Revenue from Poor Reputation on Materials and Waste Management

We are running out of resources as we eat into our natural capital rather than living off its interest. Our industrial appetite for finite raw materials is not sustainable, and as they become scarcer, increasingly aggressive tactics will be required to find and extract them.

One of the ways in which a company's reputation can be sullied is by direct or indirect involvement in the abuse of people, especially indigenous people, who get in the way of resource extraction. As well, environmental pollution is often a companion of desperate efforts to find, mine, and refine vital materials. Reputation-destroying news stories about these social and environmental impacts can lead to customers going elsewhere for their products and services.

These are the material- and waste-related reputational threats that start at the source of the materials. As discussed earlier that our take-make-waste business model provides two more opportunities for waste issues to damage a company's reputation in the eyes of its customers. It can cause air, water, or ground pollution around its refining, manufacturing, or commercial building site — overflowing tailing ponds are in this waste category. A company can also be held accountable for the responsible disposal of the product after the user is finished with it. Images of full-up landfill sites and of Asian children picking through mountains of e-waste have sensitized customers to these waste issues. Further, hazardous waste is such a concern for companies that they are often quiet about their goals to reduce it, as reduction goals imply that they have hazardous waste in the first place. Sustainability strategies promote responsible material and waste management, closed-loop systems, and product take-back by producers. These material-neutral approaches reduce the need to extract new natural resources and, therefore, reduce the associated waste from exploration, mining and drilling, refining, and processing steps before the raw materials arrive at the company's receiving dock.

Laggard companies are more exposed to hits to their reputation from materials and waste issues. It may be assumed that 5% of the company's annual revenue is at risk if it has a poor reputation on material and waste management, and there is a 20% chance that revenue could be lost in the next three to five years because customers go elsewhere. Most popular sustainability goals are

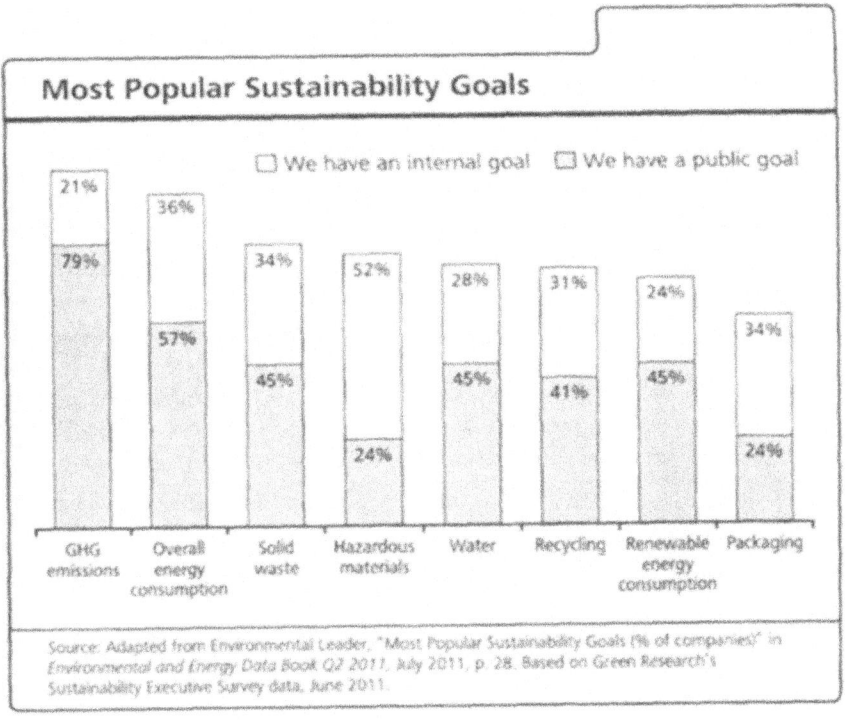

Figure 9.5

9.8 Risk to Revenue from Poor Reputations of Suppliers or Customers

No longer are companies expected to report only on their own operations; now they are also held accountable for the operations of their suppliers. When a company's reputation is only as good as the reputation of the worst-behaving supplier in its supply chain, its executives become very focused on avoiding any guilt by association.

Nike and Gap were the early sacrificial lambs on the altar of corporate accountability when conditions in offshore sweatshops producing their goods caused controversy. Recently, Apple was taken to task for conditions in its suppliers' plants in China as shown in Figure 9.6. In June 2011, Greenpeace accused toy manufacturers such as Mattel and Walt Disney of packaging their Barbie dolls in material from Indonesian rainforests, thereby contributing to the country's rapid deforestation and pushing critically endangered wildlife, including tigers, toward extinction/ In contrast, in May 2011, SC Johnson added its name to the growing list of companies pledging to source sustainable palm oil. Like Walmart, General Mills, and McDonald's, SC Johnson set a goal of using palm oil only from certified sustainable sources by 2015. These companies knew their corporate images would be at risk if Malaysian farmers seeking more land for palm trees destroyed ecosystems and animal habitats.

As Arthur Andersen learned the hard way, the reputation of a significant customer can deal a fatal blow to your revenue stream. When other customers learned about the' accounting firm's involvement in the Enron

Apple in China

In 2011, the Beijing-based non-profit Institute of Public and Environmental Affairs (IPE) accused Apple of ignoring health and environmental concerns at the Chinese factories of its suppliers. In its ranking of 29 tech companies, IPE placed Apple last.

"[Apple] only care about the price and quality [of their products] and not the environmental and social responsibility issues. In some ways they drive the suppliers to cut corners to win their contracts," IPE director Ma Jun told Reuters.

According to IPE, workers at the Wintek plant, where touch-screens for Apple products are produced, became ill from n-hexane exposure. Wintek eventually removed the substance after being sued by workers. IPE said Apple ignored workers' concerns, but the company also did not acknowledge that Wintek was a supplier. By refusing to confirm who its suppliers were, Apple "avoided responsibility for environmental problems in its supply chain."

IPE was also critical of Apple's lack of response to worker suicides at the Foxconn plant. The same month the report was released, a 25-year-old Foxconn employee died, becoming at least the 14th suicide victim at the plant in a 12-month period.

Source: "Apple Ranks Last for Environmental Response" [accessed July 30, 2011], EnvironmentalLeader.com, January 24, 2011

Figure 9.6

fiasco, its income dried up, and it dropped off the corporate landscape.

In many ways, the Internet is responsible for the increased importance of corporate reputation. The Internet makes it easy to communicate internationally and to instantly organize individuals into large and significant global groups. This has dramatically changed the power dynamic between corporations and citizens. Risks related to sustainability are potential flashpoints, as consumers test their new-found ability to rally support for activist causes. A company can lose its reputation overnight as a result of poor reputation management, especially in its supply chain.

9.9 Risk to Revenue from Poor Reputation on Ecosystem Damages

Ecosystem services are the benefits people gain from nature and biodiversity. These include water, crops, timber, flood protection, waste assimilation, carbon sequestration, recreation, and spiritual benefits. What are nature's life-support services worth? In one sense, they are priceless. The Earth's economies would soon collapse without fertile soil, fresh water, breathable air, and an amenable climate. But "priceless" too often translates to "zero" in the equations that guide land use and policy decisions. Ecological economists believe more concrete numbers are required. In one of the first efforts to calculate a global number, a team of researchers from the United States, Argentina, and the Netherlands put an average price tag of $33 trillion a year on these fundamental ecosystem services.

In a groundbreaking corporate environmental profit-and-loss statement in 2011, the shoe and sportswear company Puma estimated it would have to pay $133 million a year to cover its impacts on water and climate, the two largest sources of global environmental costs. Puma's direct operations were responsible for about $10 million; its supply chain was responsible for $123 million. Puma's P&L statement will eventually include other environmental impacts, such as the cost of waste and land use, as well as its social and economic impact in such areas as job creation, taxes, and philanthropy.8 Reporting trends foreshadow regulations. Puma prepared its statement in case such disclosure becomes a requirement.

Accounting standards organizations are discussing new rules that could require businesses to publish information on their environmental and social impacts along with their financial statements. In 2011, the World Business Council for Sustainable Development published a Guide to Corporate Ecosystem Valuation, which would help companies begin to assess the cost of their 'damage to ecosystems. The World Resources Institute published the "Corporate Ecosystem Services Review" as a companion document.

A study from environmental research group Trucost estimated the cost of environmental damage by the 3,000 biggest companies in the world as

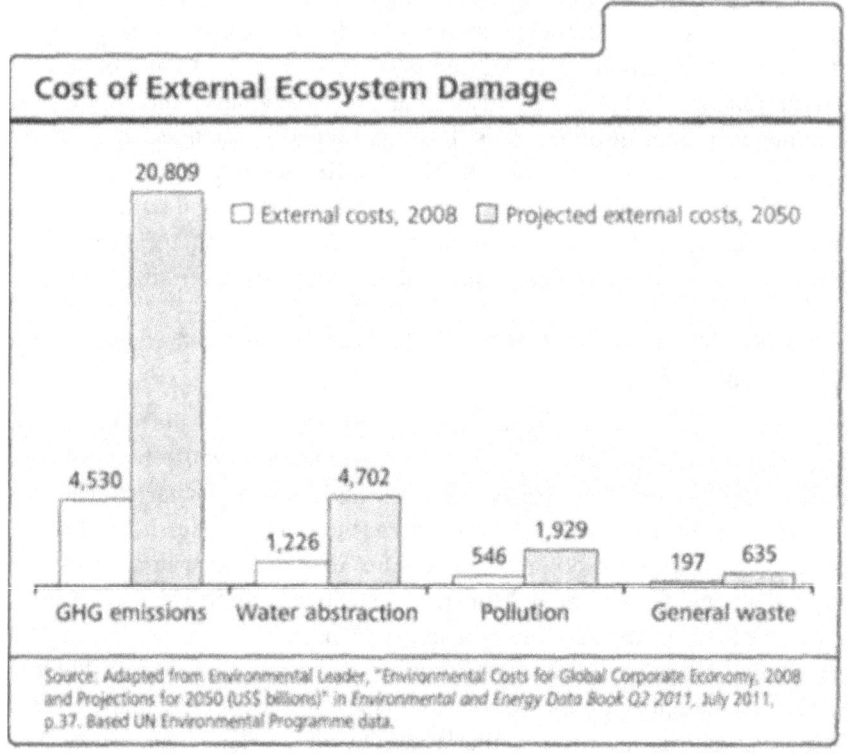

Figure 9.7

about $2.2 trillion in 2008. That figure equals 6% to 7°/o of the companies' average revenue. It may be assumed that 5% of a company's revenue could be at risk when the public learns of its externalized cost of damages to vital ecosystems as shown in Figure 9.7.

9.10 Risk to Revenue from Less Competitive Prices

No margin, no mission. Social responsibility and sustainability include growing sufficient revenue and profitability to sustain the organization's mission. There is nothing wrong with building enough margin into the prices of products to generate healthy profits. However, there are two ways a company could jeopardize its margin.

First, it is one thing to be expensive; it is another to be more expensive than competitors. Pricing worries are behind the top three. If competitors are quicker to harvest the benefits of materials, energy, and water efficiencies, they could gain a price advantage and attract customers away.

Second, there is also evidence in the consumer goods retail sector that a business could be leaving a margin on the table, or on its competitor's table, if it does not invest in a good CSR reputation. A 2010 study of 3,000 grocery shoppers showed that four dimensions of CSR performance positively influenced consumers' attitudes toward a retailer: environmental friendliness, treating employees fairly, community support, and sourcing from local growers and suppliers. Grocers who offered locally sourced products and who were known to pay their employees fairly earned their customers' goodwill and loyalty. If a retailer was able to improve consumers' perception of its fair treatment of employees and its local sourcing by 20%, the amount of business from those customers increased by 1.7% and 2% respectively. These numbers appear small, but they represent a sales increase of 10% to 15% for the average retailer in the study.

The big surprise in the study was that if a retailer chose to leverage its improved CSR perception into higher prices rather than more sales, a 20% increase in customers' perception of employee fairness "translated to a price premium of about 12%, and a similar increase in local product sourcing translated to a price premium of about 16%. Consumers do not just respond to the price charged; they also respond to how fair they think the price is. High prices are considered fairer if they can be attributed to 'good' motives like covering the cost of CSR efforts rather than to 'bad' motives like pure profit-taking.

We conservatively assume that companies not practicing good CSR could find themselves with a price disadvantage that jeopardizes 10% of their revenue.

9.11 Risk to Revenue from Sudden Disruptions in the Value Chain

Every company faces a particular set of physical and operational risks from severe weather, political uprisings, protracted permit delays, or other snags in its value chain.

Extreme weather events are happening more frequently, can damage the company's facilities, and may require extensive time and money to rectify. The homes of employees may be severely damaged, or infrastructure providing access to the company site may be destroyed. Supply chain resilience after severe weather events is a growing issue for companies with far-flung global operations and suppliers. Storms at supplier locations or en route can jeopardize supply and force the company to use more expensive alternative sources. Chiquita's 10-K report provides insights into how adverse weather conditions can severely curtail a food company's supply. Work in process may be destroyed. The supplier's own supply chain may be disrupted. And so on. Weather-related supply chain disruptions cause revenue flow disruptions.

At the other end of the value chain, customers who are affected by weather may be in no position to require further products. They may be just trying to survive and rebuild. If the company has not diversified its revenue streams, prompted by sustainability product and service opportunities, the resulting loss of revenue could be financially catastrophic, even though the company's own facilities are unaffected by severe weather.

9.12 Mitigating Operational Risks Through Sustainability strategies

Most companies are already familiar with operational-risk management (ORM) and are taking steps to ensure company-wide operational continuity. ORM is the systematic process of planning for, identifying, analyzing, monitoring, responding to, and mitigating operational risks. It involves processes, tools, and techniques that help maximize the probability and results of positive events and minimize the probability and consequences of adverse events. Risks associated with sustainability aspects of the company's operations are simply a special subset of operational risks.

Integrating sustainability considerations into an operational risk program enhances an organization's ability to be competitive in the marketplace since it enables management to make strategic business decisions based on a more complete and integrated risk portfolio. In order to maintain a competitive advantage and improve overall performance, organizations seek ways to understand and proactively manage the risks that can impact business expenses. Sometimes a company may decide the cost of taking action to avoid the risk is disproportionate to the benefit it receives. By calculating the size of the hit, it is prepared to absorb, the company determines its appetite for operational risk.

Sustainability strategies can mitigate several types of operational risk as follows:

1. Risk of higher cost of energy
2. Risk of a price on carbon
3. Risk of higher cost of waste
4. Risk of higher cost of water and materials
5. Risk of higher cost of capital for long-term debt
6. Risk of higher voluntary turnover of employees
7. Risk of lower employee productivity

These risks are monetized for Sam's Solutions and M&D Corp. in Figure 9.8. As with the strategic risks outlined above, we first quantify the potential impact of each risk on expenses and then factor that amount by the likelihood it will occur within the next three to five years. The thinking behind the calculation is explained in the following subsections. All assumptions are educated guesses, as with any planning exercise. The beauty of the Sustainability Advantage Simulator Worksheets and Dashboard at sustsinabilityadvantage.com is that executive judgment calls on these factors can tailor the operational risk assessment to each company's situation.

Sam's Solutions' Operational Risk of Escalating Expenses

	Base	Percent Potential Impact	Percent Probability Within 3 to 5 Years	Potential Increased Expenses
Risk of higher cost of energy (Base = Cost today)	$20,000	10%	75%	$1,500
Risk of a price on carbon (Base = $20/T x 300T/$1M revenue today)	$6,000	100%	25%	$1,500
Risk of higher cost of waste (Base = Cost today)	$25,000	5%	75%	$938
Risk of higher cost of water and materials (Base = Cost today)	$50,000	5%	75%	$1,875
Risk of higher cost of capital (Base = Long-term debt today)	$300,000	0.60%	75%	$1,350
Risk of higher employee voluntary turnover (Base = Cost today)	$14,400	5%	25%	$180
Risk of lower employee productivity (Base = Total salaries today)	$300,000	1%	10%	$300
Potential increased expenses without sustainability initiatives				$7,643

M&D Corp.'s Operational Risk of Escalating Expenses

	Base	Percent Potential Impact	Percent Probability Within 3 to 5 Years	Potential Increased Expenses
Risk of higher cost of energy (Base = Cost today)	$10,000,000	10%	75%	$750,000
Risk of a price on carbon (Base = $20/T x 300T/$1M revenue today)	$3,000,000	100%	25%	$750,000
Risk of higher cost of waste (Base = Cost today)	$75,000,000	5%	75%	$2,812,500
Risk of higher cost of water and materials (Base = Cost today)	$150,000,000	5%	75%	$5,625,000
Risk of higher cost of capital (Base = Long-term debt today)	$150,000,000	0.60%	75%	$675,000
Risk of higher employee voluntary turnover (Base = Cost today)	$7,200,000	5%	25%	$90,000
Risk of lower employee productivity (Base = Total salaries today)	$150,000,000	1%	10%	$150,000
Potential increased expenses without sustainability initiatives				$10,852,500

Figure 9.8

Potential Increased Expense = Base x Potential Impact x Percent Probability

9.12.1 Risk of Higher Cost of Energy

When Deloitte polled 400 business decision-makers responsible for their company's energy decisions or energy policy for its resources 2011 survey, 60% thought electricity prices would rise by at least 6% in the next one to two years. In 2011, the Institute for Building Efficiency surveyed 4,000 owners and property managers of commercial buildings on six continents. A full

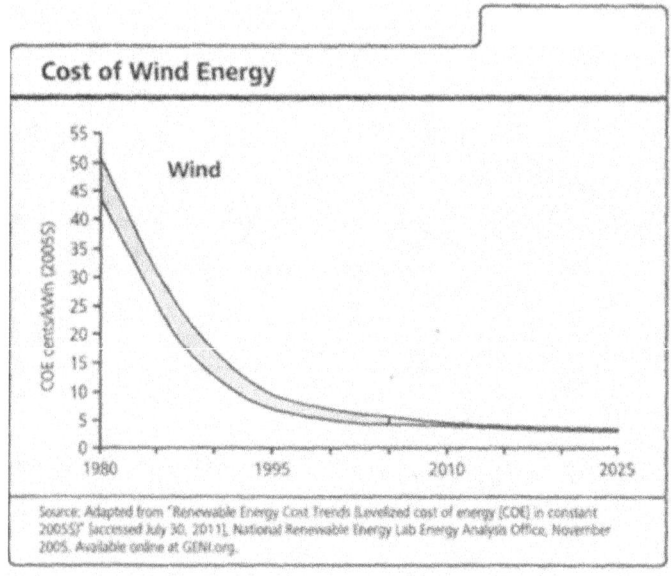

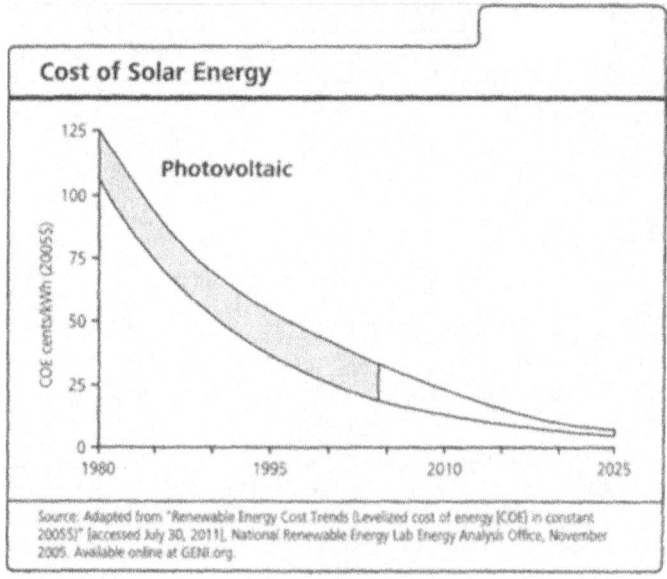

Figure 9.9

80% of respondents expected energy prices to rise 11% in the coming year. Energy prices are going up. The only questions are "How much?" and "How soon?" The cost of non-renewable energy like wind and solar has dropped exponentially since 1980 as shown in Figure 9.9, and that trend is projected to continue. If governments phase out subsidies to the fossil fuel industry, non-renewable prices would soon be at par with fossil fuels. Eco-efficiency reduces dependency on energy from the grid. Generating renewable energy onsite mitigates energy price increases. Companies that are energy neutral, or close to it, are better positioned to weather tumultuous times and energy price volatility. As they reduce their energy use, they offset price increases. As they disconnect from the electrical and fuel grids, they buffer themselves from whatever happens to energy prices. That is sustainability at its best.

9.12.2 Risk of Higher Price of Carbon

Ten years ago, carbon emission and climate change were of little concerns. Today, more than 3000 organizations in over 60 countries measure and disclose their greenhouse gas emissions through the carbon disclosure project, which act on behalf of 551 institutional investors, holding over $70 trillion in assets under management. In 2009, environmental researchers at Trucost analyzed the carbon intensity of the top 500 US companies listed in S&P 500.they found that on average, companies emit 382 tons of carbon dioxide for $1Million of revenue generated

9.12.3 Risk of Increased Cost of Waste

Could a company's cost of waste go up if it does not undertake aggressive efforts to reduce waste as part of its sustainability portfolio of initiatives? The answer is a resounding yes. The costs of each of the four contributors to the total cost of waste could rise. As described earlier, they are:

1. Cost of materials purchased, but later wasted. As we will see in the next section, there is a strong likelihood that materials will become more expensive in the next three to five years. Some resources are becoming scarcer, and it looks like the cost of fossil fuels used in their extraction, smelting, refining, and distribution will continue to rise as well. Since the cost of wasted materials makes up 60% of the total cost of waste, this is a significant contributor to the threat of higher costs if the company does not undertake a waste reduction program.

2. Cost of processing the material before it is wasted. This includes the wasted energy and labor used to work on the material before it becomes scrap. As discussed earlier, energy costs are likely to rise within the next three to five years. Judging by historical patterns, so will labor costs. This component represents 20% of the total cost of waste.

3. Cost of waste prevention and environmental management. The cost of personnel with formal environmental management responsibilities

contributes 10% to the total waste cost. Companies that lack engaged employees may find employees are less committed to mitigating waste, making this a bigger challenge instead of a smaller one.

4. Cost of end-of-pipe waste treatment and waste disposal. Storage, haulage, disposal, tipping, and other fees for treatment and disposal contribute the last 10% to the cost of waste, and there is every sign that these costs will rise in the next three to five years. Historically, tipping fees rise by about 7% a year. In the United States, about 70% of solid waste goes to landfill, but more and more hazardous waste is banned from landfills; the number of landfills is shrinking, and their capacity is strained; and the trend toward privatizing landfills continues.

So, each of the four factors in the cost of waste is destined to continue to rise.

EXAMPLE:

Examples of Eco-Savings through Employee Engagement

Dow. Dow Chemical launched its Waste Reduction Always Pays (WRAP) program in the early 1980s. WRAP challenged employees to propose waste reduction initiatives offering greater than 100% return on investment (ROI) per year. In 1982, the first year, 27 projects met the standard, with a satisfying average ROI of 173%. The traction for the program continued to grow. In 1993, 11 years after the program began, the company adopted another 140 employee WRAP recommendations, with an average ROI of 298%. Over 10 years, Dow implemented 575 employee-suggested projects with an average ROI of 204% and audited cumulative savings of $110 million per year.

Source: Kenneth Nelson, "Dow's Energy/WRAP Contest, A 12-Yr Energy and Waste Reduction Success Story," *Proceedings from the Fifteenth National Industrial Energy Technology Conference*, March 1993, Houston, Texas, pp. 12, 13, and 16.

3M. Through its voluntary Pollution Prevention Pays (3P) program, introduced in 1975, 3M reduced consumption of resources by preventing pollution up front — through product reformulation, process modification, equipment redesign, and recycling and reuse of waste materials. By 2011, 3M had implemented 8,100 employee suggestions with payback periods of under a year and saved over $1.4 billion, as well as eliminating over 3 billion pounds of waste.

Source: "3P — Pollution Prevention Pays" [accessed July 30, 2011], 3M.com.

Interface. Interface began its Quality Using Employee Suggestions and Teamwork (QUEST) program in 1995. It engaged cross-functional teams of about 15 associates each in identifying, measuring, and eliminating waste in its carpet tile manufacturing processes. As a result of their suggestions to minimize material usage and improve the efficiency of equipment and processes, QUEST had achieved a 50% reduction in waste cost per unit by 2011, resulting in $372 million in avoided waste costs.

Source: "Sustainable Carpets, Interface" [accessed July 30, 2011], GreenEconomyCoalition.org.

Figure 9.10

9.12.4 Risk of Higher Cost of Water and Materials

In the discussion of strategic risks, we accounted for the potential revenue a laggard company might lose if it had a poor reputation due to its water, material, and waste management practices. But such a company is not only exposed to a shrinking top line; it is also likely to experience escalating costs for its water and materials, which compounds the risk to the bottom line.

Prices for water worldwide rose 10% in 2010, well above inflation rates, and this trend is expected to continue. Prices for materials are also on the rise worldwide. Escalating material costs are driven by two factors: their increasing scarcity, and the rising cost of oil that provides the energy to extract, refine, smelt, and transport raw materials before their productive use.

Earlier, we discussed four ways that companies on a sustainability journey can reduce their need for new raw materials and water. They can dematerialize their products and packaging — that is, use less material and water to produce a product of equal or better quality. They can substitute more plentiful material for scarce materials. They can separate, purify, and reuse materials and water onsite. Or they can create a closed-loop system in which they reclaim their products when the user is finished with them and remanufacture new products using the parts and materials in the returned products. These strategies enable companies to better control the price of their materials and water. The strategies also buffer them from price swings in the commodity market. None of these are easy to do, but the transformation pays off as the company becomes more independent of escalating material and water costs.

Sustainable Solutions for Water

Sustainable solutions could also be classified as "essential solutions." Fact is, as the population of our nation continues to grow and more pressure is placed on water resources, sustainability must be the rule, not the exception.

A sustainable solution is one that remains productive without exhausting resources or having a negative impact on the environment. When it comes to water, sustainable solutions may be found in technologies such as water reuse, where wastewater is treated and reused for irrigation, energy generation or agriculture.

Advanced leak detection technologies are helping to reduce the volume of water lost to leaky pipes, creating a way to not only reduce waste but bolster supply. Acoustic sensors allow professionals to find leaks with sensitive microphones instead of heavy equipment and torn-up pavement. And with 97 percent of the earth's water taking the form of salt water, there is tremendous opportunity to add to the supply of fresh water through desalination.

The most sustainable solutions can transform the availability and management of resources, especially water.

9.12.5 Risk of Higher Cost of Capital

Managers should make environmental investments for the same reasons they make other investments: because they expect the new equipment or premises to deliver positive returns or reduce risks.

However, access to capital for any investment can be a challenge, especially in a time of tight credit. Lenders are increasing their requirements for loans and asking for more extensive disclosure about applicants' sustainability policies, management systems, track record, and stakeholder relationships to help them assess environmental and social risk. Why? First, environmental practices may expose borrowing firms to expensive legal, reputational, and regulatory risks that could jeopardize their solvency. Second, lenders want to ensure they are not stuck with the borrower's current and past environmental liabilities if the borrower defaults on the loan. Third, lenders are wary of risks to their own reputation if the public perceives they are abetting the borrower's irresponsible corporate behavior. For these reasons, laggard companies with poor sustainability track records may find they pay a higher rate for their borrowed capital.

In "Corporate Environmental Management and Credit Risk," the 2010 Moskowitz Prize-winning paper, the authors analyzed the environmental profiles of 582 US public companies and their associated cost of debt from 1996 to 2006 and recorded these findings:

- Companies with low environmental scores pay a premium for debt financing and have lower debt ratings from agencies like Moody's and S&P.
- Companies with better scores pay less for debt, but they tend not to be rewarded for their environmental performance by the rating agencies. The agencies seem to lag individual bond investors regarding the significance of sustainability metrics.
- Perhaps most intriguing, the link between environmental risk and debt costs has strengthened. For example, bond investors seem to be pricing climate change-related credit risk in anticipation of laws yet to be passed.

So the credit standing of borrowing firms is influenced by legal, reputational, and regulatory risks associated with environmental incidents. Companies with weak environmental performance pay a premium for debt financing, and companies with better scores pay less for debt. The spread can be as much as 64 basis points, and it is growing. It can be safely assumed that sustainable companies realize a 60 basis point reduction in the interest rate paid on their long-term debt.

EXAMPLE:

Sustainability Investments Pay Back

Marks and Spencer. M&S launched Plan A (described in Figure 6.12) in 2007, committing itself to address issues of climate change, waste, sustainable raw materials, "fair partnership," and health over five years. The company expected to invest £200 million in the program, but by 2009–10 Plan A had broken even and was adding £50 million to the bottom line. In response, M&S added another 80 commitments to the original 100 in Plan A.

Source: "How We Do Business Report 2010." Marks and Spencer, 2011, p. 3.

GE. General Electric spent $5 billion on R&D in the first five years of ecomagination, but the program to develop the clean technologies of the future generated revenues of $70 billion in that same period.

Source: "Ecomagination 2009 Annual Report" [accessed July 30, 2011].
General Electric, 2010, p. 3, ecomagination.com.

Figure 9.11

9.12.6 Risks of Higher Voluntary Turnover and Lower Employee Productivity

There are three ways a poor track record on environmental and social responsibility could negatively affect productivity and talent retention: i) the firm could find that its talented employees drift away and productivity reduce due to due to poor sustainability record ii) employees are away from job more and productivity falls due to the company not following the good sustainability practices, iii) or that employee productivity and innovation deteriorate due to the company's neglect of sustainability issues..

9.12.7 Mitigating Compliance Risk

Companies must consider whether the potential impact of pending environmental and social regulations will be material. Fortunately, environmental enterprise resource planning (EERP) systems are available to help companies manage compliance and regulatory requirements. With a good EERP system, firms can quantify financial and economic risks from potential regulations and avoid higher insurance premiums.

One way to mitigate the impact of compliance is to substitute environmentally friendly materials for hazardous substances like pesticides, dioxins, furans, CFCs, lead, and elemental chlorine before the regulations are enacted. It is usually less expensive to make the necessary changes voluntarily than to comply with more bureaucratic terms and conditions from unanticipated regulations.

A company occasionally must pay the cost of cleaning up accidental spills and releases or cover fines and penalties. Most major companies pay for these costs from their operating budgets, but this expense could be mitigated by ensuring against these spills. In February 2011, after five years of investigation and litigation, retailer Target agreed to pay $22.5 million to settle claims that it dumped hazardous and combustible liquids in local landfills for eight years. In July 2011, a jury ordered Exxon Mobil to pay $1.5 billion in punitive damages for a leak of 26,000 gallons of gasoline from a Maryland gas station in 2006.

Finally, forward-thinking companies can design closed-loop systems in which they take back their own products, and even those of competitors, instead of having users throw them away. Planning and implementing the logistics of product collection and disassembly can be cheaper than setting up such a system after it has been dictated by regulations.

Although the cost of the compliance risk could be substantial, we assume it is covered within the operational risk line items outlined earlier, especially the ones associated with energy, materials, and water, so no additional risk is calculated.

9.12.8 Mitigating Financial/Stock Price Risk

If a company does not implement sustainability programs, do investors lose out? The Domini 400 Social Index, Dow Jones Sustainability Index, Sustainalytics' Jantzi Social Index (JSI), and the Financial Times (London) Stock Exchange Index all track companies rated as sustainability leaders. Sustainability leaders do not seem to sacrifice financial market value for their efforts, nor are others missing market gains.

Further, since 2000, academic researchers have conducted several meta-analyses and have found a small positive correlation between sustainability performance and financial/stock market results, and little evidence of a financial downside of having good or bad sustainability performance. In 2008, the Network for Business Sustainability commissioned Dr. John Peloza and Ron Yachnin to do a systematic review of thousands of studies from both academia and the corporate world on valuing sustainability. The two analyzed 159 studies and meta-studies published since 1972 and found that 63% showed a positive relationship between sustainability, which they call corporate social performance (CSP), and stock market performance, which they call corporate financial performance (CFP); only 15% of past studies showed a negative relationship. Still, methodological limitations of past research — such as over-reliance on old data and definitions, sampling problems, concerns about the reliability and validity of the CSP and CFP measures, lack of opportunities to test mediating mechanisms, and a need for a causal theory to link CSP and CFP — could result in either understatement or overstatement of findings. Further research is needed, using more current data.

Intangibles/non-financials/reputation have become a larger part of a company's iceberg of market value in the last 30 years. Corporate attention to sustainability issues may be viewed as a proxy for good governance by financial analysts, but those analysts are still in the early stages of integrating sustainability considerations into their company valuations. Similarly, the increased weight of reputation in market capitalization may soon legitimize sustainability factors as valuation drivers. In the meantime, academic research and the performance of sustainability indices do not provide compelling quantitative support for a stock price benefit for good CSP, nor a risk of a. CFP-downside for companies not embracing sustainability strategies. Therefore, sustainability strategy's effect on share price risks cannot yet be confirmed.

EXAMPLE

However, companies can focus on benefit areas with the fastest payback period first, prioritizing projects that yield the greatest energy, water, materials, and waste savings before the others. The results will build momentum, and some of the returns can finance other sustainability projects via the rotating Sustainability Capital Reserve, creating a multiplier effect. Further, although we assume that it takes three to five years for the potential profit improvement to be fully realized (also outlined in Figures 9.12), aggressive action using best practices could accomplish the improvements in three or four years.

Small and medium-sized enterprises (SMEs), also known as small and medium-sized businesses (SMBs), are important. Their aggregate environmental and societal impact is immense. What they lack in size they make up for in numbers.

Definitions vary between the European Union, the United States, and Canada but, in general, companies with fewer than 500 employees and less than $50 million in revenue are classified as SMEs. Over 99% of the companies in all jurisdictions are medium-sized, small, or even micro (under 10 or 20 employees), and they employ 50% to 60% of the labor force.

What distinguishes SMEs from larger firms? First, their management structures and specialized positions are less well-defined and formal, so environmental and social responsibilities lie with busy staff people who have several other responsibilities. Second, cash flow trumps profit. A positive

M&D Corp.'s Bottom-Line Profit Benefit

	Percentage Improvement in 3 to 5 Years	Annual Benefit	Annual Profit Increase
1. Increased revenue	9%	$45,000,000	$3,150,000
2. Reduced energy expenses	75%	$7,500,000	$7,500,000
3. Reduced waste expenses	20%	$7,500,000	$7,500,000
4. Reduced materials and water expenses	10%	$5,250,000	$5,250,000
5. Increased productivity and innovation	2%	$3,150,000	$3,150,000
6. Reduced employee turnover expenses	25%	$1,800,000	$1,800,000
Improvement in revenue and expenses		$70,200,000	
Impact on profit if sustainability strategies used	81%		-$28,350,000
Plus ...			
7. Avoided risks to revenue and expenses		$36,602,500	
Impact on profit without sustainability strategies	-36%		-$12,655,000
Plus ...			
Sustainability Capital Reserve, for more projects			$12,750,000

M&D Corp.'s Five-Year Build to Full Benefits

	Percentage of Benefit	Annual Savings/ Improvements	Annual Profit Increase	Percentage Profit Increase
Year 1	30%	$21,060,000	$8,505,000	24%
Year 2	50%	$35,100,000	$14,175,000	41%
Year 3	70%	$49,140,000	$19,845,000	57%
Year 4	90%	$63,180,000	$25,515,000	73%
Year 5	100%	$70,200,000	$28,350,000	81%

Figure 9.12

Sam's Solutions' Bottom-Line Profit Benefit

	Percentage Improvement in 3 to 5 Years	Annual Benefit	Annual Profit Increase
1. Increased revenue	9%	$90,000	$6,300
2. Reduced energy expenses	75%	$15,000	$15,000
3. Reduced waste expenses	20%	$2,500	$2,500
4. Reduced materials and water expenses	10%	$1,750	$1,750
5. Increased productivity and innovation	2%	$6,300	$6,300
6. Reduced employee turnover expenses	25%	$3,600	$3,600
Improvement in revenue and expenses		$119,150	
Impact on profit if sustainability strategies used	51%		$35,450
Plus ...			
7. Avoided risks to revenue and expenses		$59,143	
Impact on profit without sustainability strategies	–16%		–$11,248
Plus ...			
Sustainability Capital Reserve, for more projects			$4,250

Sam's Solutions' Five-Year Build to Full Benefits

	Percentage of Benefit	Annual Savings/ Improvements	Annual Profit Increase	Percentage Profit Increase
Year 1	30%	$35,745	$10,635	15%
Year 2	50%	$59,575	$17,725	25%
Year 3	70%	$83,405	$24,815	35%
Year 4	90%	$107,235	$32,905	46%
Year 5	100%	$119,150	$35,450	51%

Figure 9.13

cash flow requires that a company be ruthless with ongoing expenses and minimize upfront costs required to reap benefits, so the business case focuses on benefits from early eco-efficiencies that have quick paybacks and short-term productivity improvements. Third, SMEs do not have the money, resources, or time to contend with environmental and social issues, and they cannot fall back on parent companies for expertise and support with funding. Fourth, SMEs often lump water; waste, and energy costs into "overhead" rather than tracking them in separate accounts, making it harder to identify and meter improvements.

On the other hand, SMEs are more likely to have local roots and to care about stewardship of the local environment and community, since that is where they, their children, relatives, and friends live. They are typically more intimately connected with their employees, investors, suppliers, and customers. They are more agile, and their shorter, less-bureaucratic decision chain allows them to respond quickly to changing market conditions. They can capitalize on the window of opportunity to reduce costs, improve sales, and stay ahead of the curve. When sustainability-strategies are integrated within the overall business strategy in SMEs, they spawn innovative ways to achieve the benefits identified in the simulator and improve cash flow — just what SMEs want.

9.13 Climate Change Related Risks

There are, in broad terms, various different kinds of climate change related risks as shown in Figure 9.14 below. Moreover, climate-related risks can be divided into two interconnected groups: value-chain risks ,and external-stakeholder risks as follows:.

i. Value Chain risks

Physical risks are those related to damage inflicted on infrastructure and other assets, such as factories and supply-chain operations, by the increased frequency and intensity of extreme weather events, such as wildfires, floods, or hurricanes. According to the *New England Journal of Medicine*, the frequency and severity of climate-related disasters like floods, droughts, and storm surges have increased markedly since the 1970s.

This can affect company performance in real and visible ways. In 2012, for example, Cargill, one of the world's largest food and agricultural companies, posted its worst quarterly earnings in two decades, in large part because of the US drought. While no single event can be attributed to climate change, of course, this is an example of how climate can and does affect business prospects. Western Digital Technologies, a major supplier of hard disk drives, posted a sharp decline in revenues in 2011 after flooding in Thailand, where most of its production was located. That loss

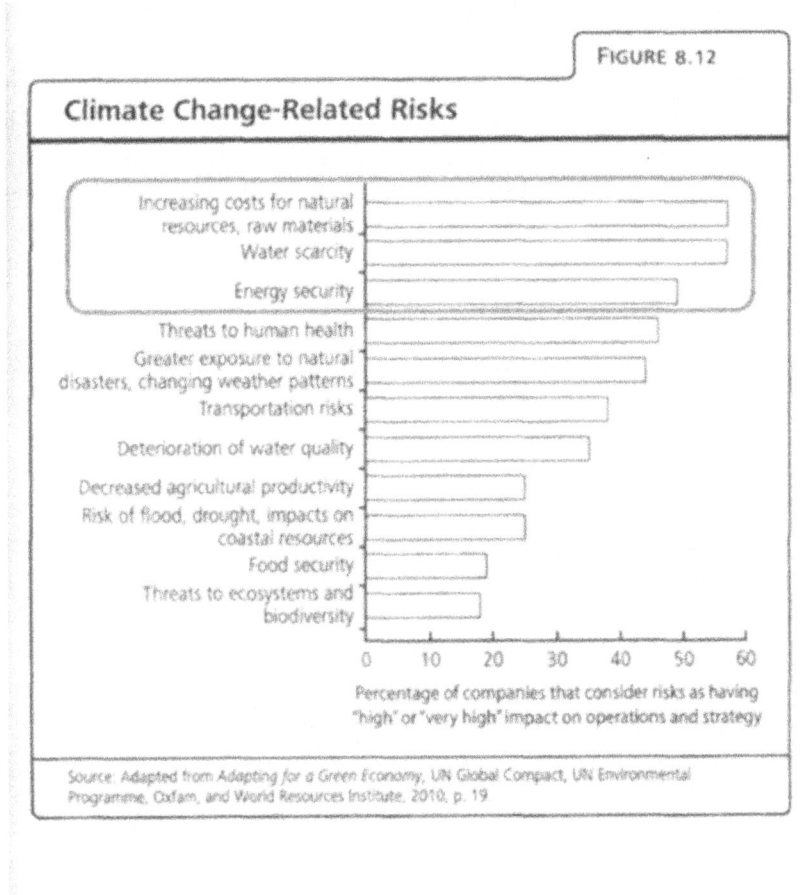

FIGURE 8.12

Climate Change-Related Risks

Percentage of companies that consider risks as having "high" or "very high" impact on operations and strategy

Source: Adapted from *Adapting for a Green Economy*, UN Global Compact, UN Environmental Programme, Oxfam, and World Resources Institute, 2010, p. 19

Figure 9.14

of production meant global supply slumped, with severe reverberations for computer manufacturers.

Such physical risks are impossible to control, but companies can take steps to prepare for the changes that could occur in years and decades to come. First, it helps to forecast a range of reasonable scenarios; doing so may require the help of specialized climate modelers. Climate forecasting can highlight high-level risk probabilities by region, such as for flood, drought, or sea-level rise, and for long-term changes in such factors as temperature, humidity, or rainfall patterns. The scenarios should help reveal which parts of the business are vulnerable. A variety of mitigating risk processes, technical standards, and capabilities can then be put in place. In the long term, risk management could call for changes to supply chains (to build in geographic variability or redundancy), including moving away from suppliers and/or locations that are highly exposed.

i.   *Price risks* refer to the increased price volatility of raw materials and other commodities. Drought can raise the price of water; climate-related regulation can drive up the cost of energy. High-tech and renewable-energy industries, for example, face price risks in the competition for rare earths, which are used in the production of computer hard drives, televisions, wind turbines, solar photovoltaic systems, and electric vehicles.

For more than a decade, the prices of many resources have been both rising and volatile. An unstable climate could ratchet up the pressure further, forcing companies to cope with uncertainty around inputs to production, energy, transport, and insurance.

Some companies are taking significant steps to get ahead of this concern. IKEA is in the process of substituting renewables for conventional sources of energy; in time, it hopes to be largely self-sufficient with regard to power. In that event, the retailer will have a good idea of what price it will pay for power and will insulate itself against global and regional energy price spikes.[4] Volkswagen is doing something similar. To hedge against the possibility of rising fossil-fuel prices, the German car-maker is investing €1 billion in renewable-energy projects and is aiming to power its manufacturing sites mainly through on-site production.[5] These are just two examples: we expect more and more companies to go "off the grid" for both strategic and economic reasons.[6]

iii. Product risks refer to core products becoming unpopular or even unsellable. Effects could range from losing a little market share to going under entirely. Alternative cooling technologies, for example, could conceivably displace air-conditioning systems; ski resorts that no longer can count on snow or cold weather could go under. Regulatory and production costs could raise the price of coal in some markets above that of lower-carbon competition, with ripple effects for mining-equipment manufacturers and related industries.

This kind of risk, of course, is familiar; new products, by definition, displace older ones. The difference is that responding to climate-related pressures can change the entire context in which a business operates, not just a specific segment. It's more like the change from the horse-and-buggy era to the car than shifting from manual to automatic transmission. Utilities, for one, know this; they are seeing their traditional business model threatened in markets where renewable energy accounts for a greater part of a new generation.

On the positive side, however, greener products are emerging in a number of industries. The construction and infrastructure sectors are developing new products and services that cater to cleaner cities, such as electric-vehicle charging infrastructure, renewables integration, smart metering, smart grids, congestion-fee systems, and high-performance building technologies.

In the business-to-consumer sectors, especially retail and consumer products, new segments are making inroads as people make it clear they are willing to pay for greener products. Groceries advertised as sustainable, for example, are growing fast in the United States, and the organic-food sector has seen double-digit growth for the past decade. This is a testament to the emergence of a significant cohort of customers for whom environmental consciousness is a factor in where and what they buy.

How can companies adapt? One approach is to adopt a "design to sustainability" approach, in which new products are designed to minimize waste and to be broken down for reuse or recycling. Another is to redefine corporate strategy to align business interests with climate-change mitigation and adaptation. Siemens, for instance, has developed a dedicated "environmental portfolio" of carbon-efficient products, while Saint-Gobain, the construction and packaging giant, puts sustainable housing technologies at the core of its product-development strategy.

iv. External-stakeholder risks: We define *ratings risk* as the possibility of higher costs of capital because of climate-related exposure such as carbon pricing, supply-chain disruption, or product obsolescence.

While the ratings risk varies widely between and within industries, even companies with carbon-intensive activities can start to manage it. Already, more than 4,000 organizations are reporting their exposure to the CDP (previously known as the Carbon Disclosure Project), a first step in dealing with the issue. A number of oil majors use an internal carbon price to guide some of their strategic decisions.

v. Regulation risk refers to government action prompted by climate change. This can take many forms, including rules that add costs or impede specific business activities, subsidies in support of a competitor, or withdrawal of subsidies. In many industries, government plays a crucial role in setting the rules of the game; with climate change in mind, many of those rules are changing.

Around the world, we see governments respond to the possibility of climate change in ways that necessarily affect business prospects. To cite just a few examples: China is launching carbon-trading programs in seven regions in preparation for a potential national plan by 2020. Most US states have introduced renewable portfolio standards, which require a certain proportion of the state's electricity to be produced from renewable sources. Ethiopia has charted a course to become a middle-income country through low-emissions growth with its Climate-Resilient Green Economy strategy.

One complication is that on the national and international level, climate-change policies often change, sometimes with the speed of an election result. That makes it difficult for businesses to make long-term investment and operating decisions. Businesses can, however, take the initiative in managing regulation risk. The first step in preparing for and helping to shape future regulation is to understand the policy options. The second step is to develop an internal strategy for climate change to put the company in a position to react effectively to regulations and policy changes. The final step is to work with external stakeholders, such as regulators and industry groups, to get their perspectives.

vi. Reputation risk can be either direct, stemming from a company-specific action or policy, or indirect, in the form of public perception of the overall industry. In the climate-change context, reputation risk can be understood as the probability of profitability loss following a business's activities or positions that the public considers harmful. A poor reputation on climate can hurt sales through consumer boycotts or local community protests. It could damage the regulatory environment and investor relationships. And it could make the company less attractive to current or future employees.

This is part of a larger trend: the changing expectations of stakeholders. Investors are asking for disclosure of carbon emissions and starting to lodge concerns about "stranded" assets—those that become unusable due to climate-policy regulation or physical climate change. Many employees want sustainability to be part of the day-to-day operations of their companies. Nongovernmental organizations are getting more prominence when it comes to their ability to measure and compare corporate actions.

In response, some companies have taken very public steps to adopt climate-change strategies. Unilever, for example, leads the FTSE CDP Carbon Strategy risk and performance index and has improved its carbon efficiency by 40 percent since 1995. Its stated goal is to reduce the carbon and water footprints of its products to half of 2010 levels by 2020. The retailer Kohl's has been recognized for its efforts to green its operations and reduce emissions. IBM has also gotten positive attention for its actions on climate, such as setting rigorous greenhouse-gas-emission standards for suppliers. IBM won a 2013 Climate Leadership Award from the US Environmental Protection Agency for supply-chain leadership[8]and was also recognized in 2014 for its greenhouse-gas management. Just about every company in the Fortune 500 touts its commitment to sustainability. There is still a long way to go in many respects, but it can be said that action has well and truly started.

One truth is evident across all these industries: companies that ignore climate-related risks are likely to feel the consequences. Those that identify the most pertinent risks think through how they relate to one another, and then put in place appropriate measures can begin to manage the challenges ahead. These companies will not only put themselves in a position to ride out the storm; they could rise above it.

9.14 Uncertainty

What makes risk management unique among other types of management is that it specifically addresses the effect of uncertainty on objectives. Uncertainty identification process is used to compile a list of opportunities and threats that might contribute to or detract from the achievement of the organization's objectives. For each opportunity or threat, it is important to know the what, where, when, why and how something could happen and the range of possible outcomes that affect the organization's objectives. Uncertainty analysis involves developing an understanding of the opportunities and threats and provides an input to uncertainty evaluation and to decisions on whether threats need to be treated and opportunities need to be embraced and developed. Uncertainty analysis will also shed light on the consequences and likelihood of the uncertainties in terms of highly negative to highly positive and highly unlikely to highly likely.

There are four uncertainty evaluation categories which can be looked at from the perspective of threats:
- *Avoid:* Seek to remove threats to lower or eliminate uncertainty
- *Transfer:* allocate ownership to enable effective management of a threat, often using an insurance company for this purpose.
- *Mitigate:* Reduce the likelihood or consequences of the threat below an acceptable threshold
- *Accept:* Recognize residual risks associated with uncertainty and devise ways to control or monitor them.

Opportunity uncertainty response takes into consideration how to act in order to improve the likelihood and impact of an opportunity. There are four major categories of opportunity uncertainty response as follows:
- *Exploit* identified opportunities, removing uncertainty by seeking to make the opportunity succeed
- *Enhance* means increasing its positive likelihood or consequence to maximize the benefit of the opportunity
- *Share* opportunities by passing ownership to a third party best able to manage the opportunity and maximize the chance of its happening
- *Ignore* opportunities included in the baseline, adopting a reactive approach without taking explicit actions.

Uncertainty response involves selecting one or more significant opportunities and threats and exploiting the opportunities while avoiding the threats.

For both threats and opportunities, the following criteria have been defined to assess the effectiveness of these uncertainty responses:

- *Appropriate*: Correct level of response based on the size of the uncertainty
- *Affordable*: The cost-effectiveness of these responses should be determined
- *Actionable*: Need to identify an action timeline since some uncertainty requires immediate action/attention where others can wait.
- *Agreed*: The consensus and commitment of the stakeholders should be obtained before creating the response
- *Allocated and accepted*: Each response should be owned and accepted to ensure a single point of responsibility and accountability for implementing the process.

Questions:

1. What is the importance and main elements of a risk register? What are the different categories of risk?
2. Describe the steps to implement sustainability risk management
3. Discuss the risk to revenue from disruptions in the value chain
4. What is "Design to Sustainability" approach?
5. Discuss how sustainability strategies can mitigate several types of operational types of operational risk
6. Discuss uncertainty analysis.

Chapter 10
Organizational Sustainability

Sustainability was first proposed as the goal of sustainable development and as stated earlier that 'Sustainability is portrayed as having three dimensions—environmental, social, and economic. These dimensions are mutually reinforcing and inter-dependent. It is considered to be a misunderstanding to limit sustainability to a single dimension, such as climate change, non-sustainable resource depletion, or biodiversity. Sustainability is relevant to all levels of human activity, from the global level to the national, regional, community, organizational, and individual levels. Since organizations are the basic building blocks of society, it is important to see how this perspective is different from the other definitions.

10.1 Determining the scope of sustainability program

The organization determines scope of the sustainability program by establishing its boundaries and applicability. When determining the scope of the sustainability program, the organization considers
- External and internal context
- Opportunities and threats associated with the uncertainty in the context
- Interests of the stakeholders
- Organizational functions and physical boundaries
- Need to obtain and maintain a social license to operate
- Authority and ability to exercise control or influence

The scope should include all activities, processes, products, and services within the organization's control or influence that can pose a significant risk to the organization as determined in the risk assessment process. Some organization's share the scope of their sustainability effort with internal stake-holders and many key external stakeholders as well.

10.2 Context of Organizational Sustainability

As stated before that sustainability refers to a state of the global system with a focus on the environmental, social, and economic subsystems, in which the needs of the present are met without compromising the ability of future generations to meet their needs. From this perspective, sustainability is a characteristic of the planet as a whole and not of any particular activity or organization. Sustainable development addresses the activities and products of particular organizations (or nations, regions/ and communities) and the ability to engage in such development in a manner that contributes to sustainability. Development is needed to meet the needs of both present and future generations and is essential to sustainability.

Social responsibility encompasses an organization's responsibility for the impact of its decisions and activities on the environment, society, and the economy. As such, social responsibility is the organization's contribution to sustainable development and sustainability. Social responsibility is applicable to all organizations (not just corporations) as they recognize that they also have a responsibility to contribute to current sustainable development .and future sustainability.

Sustainability is often described as the goal of sustainable development understanding and, achieving; a balance between environmental, social and economic systems (ideally in mutual supporting ways) is considered essential for making progress toward achieving sustainability.

Achievement of sustainability needs to be recognized as one of the most important considerations in all human activities. To summarize, the term sustainable development is used to describe development that leads to sustainability. The term social responsibility is used to describe how an organization can contribute to sustainable development. It would make sense that as the organization begins to contribute significantly to sustainable development and sustainability,it may be referred to as a sustainable organization.

From the perspective of an organization, sustainability is the capability of an organization to transparently manage its responsibilities for environmental stewardship, social well-being, and economical shared value over the long-term while being held accountable by its stakeholders. This definition is actionable with any organization at the community level. The definition can form the bottom-up feedback loop for any definition of corporate sustainability or corporate social responsibility. In contrast to conventional management approaches, organizational sustainability management requires the integration of both financial and non-financial strategic success factors including environmental and social, into the management system of the company.

Each of the responsibilities can be defined by best practices associated with social responsibility.

Some organizations define responsibilities in general terms:
- Doing what you have committed to do
- Always giving your best effort
- Being held accountable for your choices
- Helping others when they need help
- Being fair
- Helping to make a better world

To reinforce these responsibilities and make them more specific to daily activities, an organization may create a "code of conduct" that outlines expectations of how responsibility will be embedded into what employees do every day. Organizations may also specify responsibility as part of their core values to ensure that "acting responsibly" is part of the organization's culture. These codes of conduct typically state that the organization should

- Be accountable for its impacts on the environment, society, and the economy
- Be transparent in its decisions activities that impact its responsibilities.
- Behave ethically
- Respect, consider and respond to the interests of its stakeholders
- Accept that respect for the rule of law is mandatory

Each organization will have its own list of significant sustainability responsibilities'. While they are often divided up by categories, please remember that each of the responsibilities is interconnected with the other two.

To be effective, the code of conduct should consider a number of items:

- Maintaining evidence of compliance with relevant local, regional, and federal laws
- Understanding the consequences of noncompliance with the laws and regulations
- effectively managing the elements of the code of conduct
- Maintaining the integrity and reputation of the organization
- Adhering to aspirational values in line with sustainability
- dealing with conflicts of interest and confidentiality
- being responsible for engaging with external stakeholders
- Maintaining nondiscriminatory practices
- paying attention to how members or employees are treated
- Conditions of membership or employment
- using and accounting for organizational resources
- conditions within the organization are safe and hygienic
- paying attention to occupational health and safety
- Acting as a steward of the environment and a good citizen of the community

An organization's commitment to the code of conduct should include the benefits and importance of having such a code or honoring a supplier code of conduct. The code needs to be an integral component of the framework developed to manage risk and sustainability within the organization.

For an organization to practice environmental stewardship, its activities, processes, decisions, products, and services should strive to have no net negative consequences to the environment. Environmental responsibility involves the following

- Having effective processes, for all operations associated with products or services. and system of management to provide management oversight of the processes and operations (e.g., environmental, assets, energy management. business continuity and sustainability development
- Enhancing the productivity of natural resources—use only what is needed, use it efficiently with a focus on reducing or eliminating waste, and be aware of issues with the management of waste that is not eliminated, including the reuse of products at their end of life
- Being mindful of energy use and climate change and not simply switching to renewable energy, which has significant Scope 3 greenhouse gas emissions or large amounts of embodied energy in the fabrication, installation, operation, and maintenance of the technology
- Addressing the stewardship of the natural habitat and its biodiversity in the neighborhood, the community, and in areas affected by the value chain partners
- Paying attention to widespread contamination of the environment and in human tissue of large numbers of bio persistent chemicals
- Considering the interests of the organization's external stakeholders identified in its external operating environment

In the case of social well-being, the organization should seek to avoid negative consequences to society as a whole, with particular emphasis on its members, employees, and other people directly impacted by its activities, processes, decisions, products, and services. All its suppliers should be contractually obligated to follow its supplier code of conduct or have systems of management in place to facilitate the progress to sustainable development. Social well-being includes the following:

- Respect for human rights by having the organization exercise due diligence in seeking to determine where human rights issues may arise within its value chain
- Responsibility for its labor practices, both in its own operations and where it has a sphere of influence in the value chain
- Having a system of management (e.g., health and safety; governance, risk, and compliance; social responsibility; and risk management) in place to facilitate the attainment of social well-being
- Adoption of fair operating practices to deal ethically with other organizations, including the prevention of corruption, responsible

participation in the political process, respect of property rights, and promoting responsibility in its sphere of influence

- Involvement in community development and participating in local education and culture, public health, literacy, social investment, and quality of life
- Each organization should use its control or sphere of influence in partnership with other local organizations and its value chain partners to address economic issues and their interrelationships with the other two sustainability responsibilities:
- Employment in the community
- Poverty and similar needs
- Local business climate
- Income levels
- Economic performance and community development
- Use of technology and innovation
- Value and supply chain prosperity
- Maintenance of the social license to operate
- Working with other local organizations to promote the value of organizational sustainability

Here are items that could be included in an organization's list of responsibilities:

- Continually improve the resource productivity of the operations
- Eliminate wastes of all kinds
- Pay attention to the prevention side of the activity rather than using recycling or controls
- Manage energy to respect the need for climate change mitigation
- Protect natural habitats and biodiversity
- Consider environmental impacts in areas under the organization's control and within its sphere of influence
- Protect human rights with an evaluation of the entire value chain
- Ensure fair operating practices
- Assess labor practices, including health and safety
- Evaluate consumer issues associated with products and services
- Optimize community involvement
- Consider social impacts and license to operate in areas under the organization's control and within its sphere of influence
- Contribute to the community's development
- Look for opportunities to share value within the community
- Consider community shared value impacts in areas under the organization's control and within its sphere of influence attention to these items should help an organization operate responsibly

10.3 Motivating Factors why Companies should Invest in Sustainable Development:

A research conducted at Tuft's Fletcher school, funded by Citi Foundation, to understand why companies would even consider investing in sustainable development. Four motivating factors were found:

1. Mitigating business risk from potential disruption of operations, supplies or reputational damage.
2. Adhering to industry norms of transparency, traceability, environmental responsibility and other accepted standards.
3. Winning a share in current markets and establishing a beachhead with future customers.
4. Building goodwill with key stakeholders.

These issues gain even more currency in the developing world, where much of the future market growth resides. Consider the example of Coca-Cola, with 75 percent of operating income from overseas and a heavy reliance on emerging markets. Also, Coke, as a heavy user of both water and plastics, has a giant environmental footprint, which, arguably, is unsustainable. It is not surprising, therefore, that Coke is an active participant in innovating in sustainable development. It shares its logistics capabilities to distribute medicines and supplies to remote African communities. Its Beyond Water partnership with the World Wildlife Fund works to maintain resilient freshwater systems in 50 countries. Its Project Nurture partnership helps farmers in its supply chain identify new opportunities and improve productivity. It has developed the first-ever recyclable plastic bottle, with plans to make the practice universal by 2020.

10.4 Operating Responsibly

The concept of operating responsibly is at the core of an organization's sustainability program. As in the case of risk management, the three responsibilities must be integrated with each other and embedded in the organization's activities, processes, decisions, services, and products. Responsibility is seen as a balanced approach for organizations to address environmental, social, and economic issues in a way that aims to benefit people, communities, and society. Organizations are responsible for the consequences of their activities and decisions through their transparent and ethical behaviors. The responsibility extends to the customers, neighborhood, community, society, and environment. Exercising an organization's responsibility involves many aspects of its operations:

- Contribution to sustainable development, including health and welfare of the community and society
- Active engagement with stakeholders to determine their interests in the organization and its products and services

- Operating in a manner that complies with applicable laws and is consistent with the international norms of behavior
- Integrating sustainability throughout the organization and practicing it in relationships that are within the organization's control or sphere of influence

A number of specific relationships guide the responsibilities of an organization. They include relationships between the organization and society, between the organization and its stakeholders, and between the stakeholders and society. All these relationships affect the operation of organizations at the community level.

First, and most importantly, all organizations should have a relationship with the community. Every organization needs to understand how its activities, processes, decisions, products, and services affect the community. Organizations often support the community as a great place for their employees or members to live. Often, the suppliers have operations in the community as well.

Second, organizations have a relationship with their stakeholders—both inside and external to the organization. Just as each organization engages with the internal stakeholders, it is important to extend the engagement beyond the customer to other external stakeholders. This dialogue with stakeholders should be face to face, and interactive, and occur over long period of time. The interests of the stakeholders need to be understood and acknowledged if there are issues, with stakeholders. Some of the mediation should be considered; this will enable engagement to dominate the agenda with all stakeholders

Third, the organization's stakeholders have a relationship with the larger community (state, province, regional authority, and federal authority). Since stakeholders can be associated with diverse groups, it is possible that some of their interests are not consistent with the expectations of the community at large. Stakeholder interests must be carefully balanced across a broad spectrum of interests. It is important that the stakeholder organizations realize that the interests of other stakeholders may conflict with their own.

Organizations must understand how these relationships can complicate Their ability to maintain their social license to operate. To some degree, local organizations have always conducted their activities with a particular awareness of their relationship to the community. However, with the range of communication methods available today, it is even more important that they pay particular attention to these relationships. The organization must responsibly decide how it will embed sustainability into its operations, rather than focusing on "initiatives" that compete with its core day -to-day operational activity.

10.5 Embedding Sustainability

Just as with risk management, organizational sustainability should be part of what every member or employee does every day. At the parent organization level, claims are often made that sustainability is embedded within the entire organization's structure and functions. The reality is that very few parent organizations have fully embedded or integrated sustainability into the way they operate day in and day out. Sustainability is frequently operated as a separate program with its own goals that are not aligned with the organization's strategic objectives. Many of these goals are designed to appease outside interests and not for the point of operating in a stewardship mode seeking to prevent creating environmental, social, and economic problems.

There are two different means of embedding sustainability. The first involves making sustainability and the responsibilities associated with the sustainability part of the work instructions and operational controls of everyone in the organization. Sustainability would be clearly part of what they do and not practiced solely as a separate activity (e.g., green team initiatives). The second way of embedding sustainability is to make its considerations part of every decision made at all levels of the organization. In either case, there needs to be a close connection between sustainability and the strategic objectives between the stakeholders and the organizations.

The strategy comes from the mission statement in terms of the strategic objectives. These objectives are cascaded down to the lower levels of the organization. Workers have goals and an action plan to achieve the goals using the guidance and structure of the strategic objectives covering their work. The realization of the goals at each level in the organization can be compared with the objectives to see if there is value created over and above the meeting of the objectives. Sustainability would need to be included within the strategic objectives, as well as the focus of the action plans associated with every worker's goals.

It is important that the members or workers in every organization understand their organization's strategic objectives. These objectives need to be transparent to both internal and external stakeholders. When goals are established, many of the responsibilities listed above can be incorporated as a potential means for creating value and ensuring the effectiveness of the stewardship approach. The effects of uncertainty must be dealt with if the organization wants to meet its strategic objectives.

It becomes easier to engage the leaders in sustainability when it is linked to risk management. As described earlier, risk and uncertainty management are almost always embedded in the organizations since meeting the strategic objectives is so crucially important to any organization.

Building the competency for using sustainability can become a part of the organization's drive for effective and efficient processes. Creating a culture of sustainability within the organization is easier when everyone sees it as a way to meet their goals so that their department can meet its objectives. Meeting strategic objectives benefits everyone associated with an organization. Risk management and sustainability contribute to the ability of the organization to have an efficacious strategy.

As risk management and sustainability become embedded in the organization, there may be a need for changes in decision-making processes at all levels of the organization. There may also be some changes in governance that will recognize the positive consequences of embedding risk management and sustainability into the processes used by the organization and its partners in the value chain. There are some that feel that sustainability needs to be integrated into the organization and that this will take a lot of time and effort. By embedding sustainability as described above, it is embraced more effectively and quickly However; this is often threatening to the sustainability manager.

Some compare sustainability to quality. When an organization is recognized for the quality of its products and services, it is not a time to cut back on quality. With a global economy and the need for continual improvement, the lead in quality can be lost suddenly. This is much less likely to happen when all the disciplines are embedded into the processes and operations to help the organization function effectively and efficiently and to maintain its social license to operate.

To be successful, sustainability must be developed from within the organization, by budding on what is already in place. Sustainability should create relationships between processes and operations having regard for the interests of the stakeholders. The organization incorporates sustainability within its system of management to encourage resource productivity, decision making based on factual evidence, and a focus on the customers for its products and services, as well as on the interests of the stakeholders and the community at large. Organizations should seek an appropriate level of sustained success in line with the complexity of the decisions that need to be made. An organization also needs to have a current and comprehensive understanding of its uncertainty (i.e., opportunities and threats) and the risks associated with meeting its strategic objectives.

10.6 Attributes of Organizational Sustainability

There are eight attributes that organizations can use to evaluate the extent to which sustainability is effective and whether it can be improved. Organizations should aim at an appropriate level of performance of their risk management and sustainability programs that is in line with the complexity of the decisions that need to be made. This list of attributes represents organizational sustainability at a high level.

i) Ethical Behavior

An organization should behave ethically. This behavior stressed values of honesty, equity, and integrity. These values imply a concern for people, animals, plants, and the environment, as well as a commitment to address the impact of its activities and decisions in light of its stakeholder's interests.3 This attribute can be tested by examining how the organization defines and communicates the standards of ethical behavior expected from its governance structure, personnel, suppliers, contractors, and owners and leaders. Usually, this information is found in the organization's "code of conduct," (covered in more detail in Section 12.2)or it may be found in the customer's "supplier code of conduct," which is often made part of the purchase order for products and services.

ii) Respect for the Rule of Law

An organization must demonstrate its respect for the rule of law. It is generally implicit in the rule of law that laws and regulations are written, publicly disclosed, and fairly enforced according to established procedures. In the context of sustainability, the organization should take steps to be aware of applicable laws and regulations and to inform those within the organization of their obligation to observe and implement those measures.4 This is tested by determining how the organization keeps itself informed of all legal and other obligations and ensures that its relationships and activities comply with the intended and applicable legal framework. The organization should also conduct a periodic evaluation of its compliance with applicable laws and regulations, including contractual adherence to codes of conduct.

iii) Respect for Stakeholder Interests

An organization must respect, consider, and respond to the interests of its stakeholders. Besides the internal stakeholders, other individuals or groups may also have rights, claims, or specific interests that need to be taken into account. Sustainability also demands that the organization consider the interests of stakeholders who may be affected by a decision or activity, even if they have no formal role in the stakeholder engagement efforts or are unaware of these interests. This is tested by the ability of stakeholders to contact, engage with, and influence the organization. There should also be documented information on the role stakeholders play in the conduct of the organization's uncertainty analysis.

iv) Full Accountability for Opportunities and Threats

Uncertainty analysis includes comprehensive, fully defined, and accepted accountability for testing opportunities and threats for significance and taking the proper response. All members or employees of an organization need to be fully aware of the opportunities and threats, the controls and engagement tasks for which they are accountable. The definition of risk management and sustainability roles, accountabilities, and responsibilities should be part of all the organizations work instructions and operating controls. Many organizations include the performance of uncertainty assessment and sustainability accountabilities in performance reviews.

v) Engagement with Stakeholders

Risk management and sustainability require continual, interactive communications with external and internal stakeholders, including comprehensive and frequent reporting of uncertainty assessments (i.e., opportunities and Threats) and the application of risk management and sustainability to an appropriate degree. Communication is seen as a two-way process, so that property informed decisions can be made about the level of uncertainty and the need for opportunity and threat response in line with properly established and comprehensive uncertainty criteria. This can be tested by looking at the documented information the stakeholder engagement process

vi) Embedding Sustainability in the Organization's Governance

Risk management and sustainability are considered to be central to an organization s system of management, such that risks of meeting the organization's strategic objectives are improved by managing the effects of uncertainty (i.e., opportunities and threats). The governance structure and process are based on the management of risk, uncertainty, and sustainability. Effective management of the opportunities and threats is regarded by leaders as essential for the achievement of the organization's strategic objectives8 in an uncertain world. This is indicated by leaders' language and the written materials in the organization using the term uncertainty in connection with risks to the strategic objectives.

vii) Including Sustainability in Decision Making

All decision making within the organization, whatever its level of importance or significance, involves the explicit consideration of the effects of uncertainty (i.e., opportunities and threats) and the management of risk of meeting its strategic objectives. This can be tested to determine if performance evaluation criteria include sustainability in the decision making of individuals in the organization. There should be documented information to determine whether decision making is expected to include explicit consideration of the organization's strategic objectives, the effects of uncertainty, organizational knowledge, risk management, and sustainability.

viii) Continual Improvement and Learning

An emphasis is placed on continual improvement in risk management and sustainability through the setting of goals and action plans against which the organization's members assess whether the strategic and operational objectives are being met. The organization's performance can be documented and shared with the stakeholders' during the engagement process. Sustainability often has a regularly scheduled management review meeting as a component of its system of management. The learning is expressed as t component of the plan-do-check-act cycle.

10.7 Managing Opportunities and Threats

Every organization operates in an uncertain world. This presents the operations with opportunities and threats (i.e., the effects of uncertainty). The external influences and factors are responsible for creating the opportunities and treats. As part of the goal setting and action planning, any significant opportunity or threat needs to be examined and managed through the action planning process. By controlling the effects of uncertainty, the organization is more likely to be on the upside of risk. This creates value for the organization. If there are unattended threats or unrealized opportunities, the organization is more likely to be on the downside of the risk. Risk management and uncertainty analysis must be a part of the Sustainability program once it is integrated into the operation of the organization.

Organizational Sustainability has a lot of moving parts, but they are much easier to control at the organizational level.

Structure for Planning and Implementing organizational Sustainability:

Most successful organizations use a plan-do-check-act (PDCA) sequence to implement and maintain programs to improve quality; environmental protection, health, and safety; and other functional disciplines. Some PDCA programs are implicitly stated, and some are explicitly defined in a system of management.

10.8 Importance of Organization's Context

To begin the embedding process, it is important to make sure that the mission statement has been converted to a clear set of strategic objectives, and that the cascading of the objectives from the top down is in place. To provide the feedback, the goals and action plans must also be in place. These practices are described earlier in Chapter 8 Once this happens, the organization will have the means for the sustainability program to be embedded in the process for meeting the strategic objectives, rather than having a separate set of "sustainability goals" with supporting initiatives that are not formally coordinated with the organization's objectives.

The scanning of the organization's internal and external context helps identify its opportunities and threats. Sustainability practitioners need to be involved in this search for opportunities to make sure that they are properly identified. This is a key linkage for sustainability to make as it starts the embedding process. The scanning of the external operating environment provides the best view of the social, environmental, and economic requirements of the organization. Examining the legal and other requirements would be a part of this effort. Some organizations have contractual commitments to follow their customers' supplier codes of conduct. There may be other contractual requirements to customers, as well as a parent operation.

Scanning of the internal and external operating environments also helps identify the stakeholders. These individuals and organizations are associated with the opportunities and threats identified in this activity. Sustainability is usually outwardly focused. Now that the opportunities and threats are associated with the uncertainty, there is an internal need for sustainability to help lower the amount of uncertainty so that the risk of meeting the strategic objectives is improved. Sustainability can make sure that the stakeholders are engaged and that there is a proper sense-making effort in place to determine changes in the internal and external operating environments that would dictate when a new scan is needed.

This scanning activity can be expanded within the organization's value chain Suppliers! contractors, customers, and business partners need to be engaged through sustainability to manage uncertainty associated with these relationships. All the members of the value chain need to conduct their own scans of the internal and external operating environments. Uncertainty can come from any point in the value chain. Part of the relationship is to provide some support to value chain partners to help lower the uncertainty of the entire value chain to promote the "upside of risk" where the opportunities are offsetting the threats to manage risk within a tolerable or even beneficial level.

It is also important for an organization to be aware of the level of commitment of the leaders to use sustainability, along with the other organizational risk management methods, to make sure the organization is always in a comfortable position for meeting its strategic objectives. Where there is an active focus on meeting organizational objectives, it is easy for the leaders to recognize the roles played by the different functional units in keeping the level of risk in line with expectations. When sustainability is seen as an active participant in managing uncertainty and risk, it is much easier to obtain the approval of leadership. The contribution of sustainability to meeting strategic objectives becomes clear when it is embedded in these processes.

10.9 Understanding Organizational Sustainability

A key role for sustainability in an organization is participation in the due diligence activities. This is a process to identify the actual and potential positive and negative social, environmental, and economic impacts of an organization's decisions and activities. This happens with the active management of the internal and external context. It is no longer the case of just looking to avoid and mitigate the negative effects (threats), but it is more about using the positive effects (opportunities) to create a positive upside of risk. This due diligence also involves influencing the risk and uncertainty analysis conducted by other organizations in the value chain. With the speed of news in this digital media world, a lot of negative publicity can happen all of a sudden when a supplier has encountered problems. Increased communication and cooperation within the value chain are now seen as critical to the long-term success of any organization, of any size or type.

When the organization conducts its uncertainty analysis, it identifies the opportunities and threats that are most significant to the organization. This is a formal process that can be either qualitative or quantitative. An uncertainty (i.e., risk) map is used to identify the organization's opportunities and threats altogether. Stakeholders need to be involved in this process. If the engagement process is working well, the stakeholders will be a valuable source of information for the organization. They can help alert the organization to changes in the external operating environment and the need for an update of the uncertainty analysis. It is possible that they can help in the offsetting of the threats with the opportunities that have been identified.

In the areas of sustainability and corporate social responsibility, this is often referred to as a "materiality" determination. Rarely do these determinations use uncertainty analysis and tie the results into the way risk is managed within the organization and its value chain So do not confuse the formal uncertainty analysis with a materially determination One area that sustainability programs find to be difficult involves the determination that the organization is in compliance with local, state and order all laws and regulations that govern its operation, A careful review of the opportune and threats often indicates that there are some nuisance areas that involve odors vibrations, light noise, and traffic, among other things. while these might meet the legal tests, the situations can be very irritating to the stakeholders. Likewise, a product sold in a retail store might be made in a country that has serious human rights issues or environmental regulations that are not enforced. These kinds of interests should be found in the scanning activities; however, there is a sense of complacency associated with meeting the requirements. This is just one more reason to have a strong stakeholder engagement program. Stakeholders can help seek opportunities, as well as threats.

10.10 Engagement, Not Simple Communication

Communication must be effective two-way dialogue over a period of time in order to become engaged. Many organizations continue to use traditional means of communication to develop awareness about the role of risk management and sustainability in helping an organization meet its strategic objectives. Frequent conversations on how the organization can improve the use of sustainability in its processes and operations need to be interactive and acknowledged. Digital media is helping make this more effective. The dialogue must be transparent and thoughtful. It is important to have a focus on helping the organization meet its responsibly set objectives over the long term, if objectives need to be changed, there needs to be a dialogue over the pros and cons of such a change and the linkage of the change to risk management and sustainability.

Communication should be part of the processes and used in the operations. It exists to inform people and transmit important messages. Engagement takes place both within the organization and with the external stakeholders. Often, it may be an external stakeholder that starts the engagement with a question, complaint, or suggestion. It could be started by the organization to explain the need to make some changes and by inviting others to participate in the decision-making process.

The people within the organization need to become familiar with the different methods and media that may be used for engagement. Thoughtful answers come from discussions with others before responding. This allows other people to join in the dialogue.

A special form of engagement is with the media. Many organizations that deal with the media on a regular basis get to know someone at the media outlet and invest time to get to know him or her better. The building of trust will help enable some engagement to commence. The focus should always be on how the organization is able to meet its strategic objectives while providing shared value with the external stakeholders. It makes a lot of sense to want a vibrant community and make an investment to see what happens when you know that employees are more likely to remain with the organization when the community is very strong and healthy. In these ways, there is a difference between handling sustainability as a separate program and having sustainability embedded in the organization and made part of what every employee does every day.

10.11 Reviewing and Improving Organizational Sustainability

Effective performance on risk management and sustainability depends on commitment, participation, engagement, evaluation, and review of the contributions to effective processes, efficient operations, and efficacious strategy. Monitoring and measurement related to sustainability will come from the people that are engaged in using them to do their work every day. There will also be a means for collecting the information on how the significant opportunities and threats were managed to enable the organization to be on the upside of risk.

Living in an uncertain world makes it imperative to monitor the external operating environment and the entire supply chain. These numbers are not created for a report. Instead, the measurements are part of the continual improvement, innovation, and learning in an organization.

Contrary to popular thought, one does not just pick processes and operations and measure them. There is a formal process of monitoring and measurement that needs to take place. It will produce information for operating the organization and engaging with the external stakeholders. The information will be transparent, and the organization will be accountable for improving so that it can meet its strategic objectives.

10.12 The Five-Stage Sustainability Journey to a Sustainable Enterprise

As companies progress to become sustainable enterprises, we can position them on the five-stage sustainability continuum shown in Figure 10.1. Their business framework evolves from an unsustainable take-make-waste model in Stages 1, 2, and 3 to a sustainable borrow-use-return model in Stages 4 or 5. Executive mindsets, which in the early stages see initiatives labeled "green," "environmental," and "sustainable" as expensive and bureaucratic impediments to success, also evolve to recognize these initiatives as catalytic investments for competitive advantage.

- **Stage 1:** Pre-Compliance. The company cuts corners and tries not to get caught if it breaks the law or uses exploitative practices that cheat the system. It flouts environmental, health, and safety regulations. This stage is the norm in corrupt jurisdictions. Elsewhere, intelligent companies move quickly to Stage 2 in order to avoid fines, prosecution, and public embarrassment.

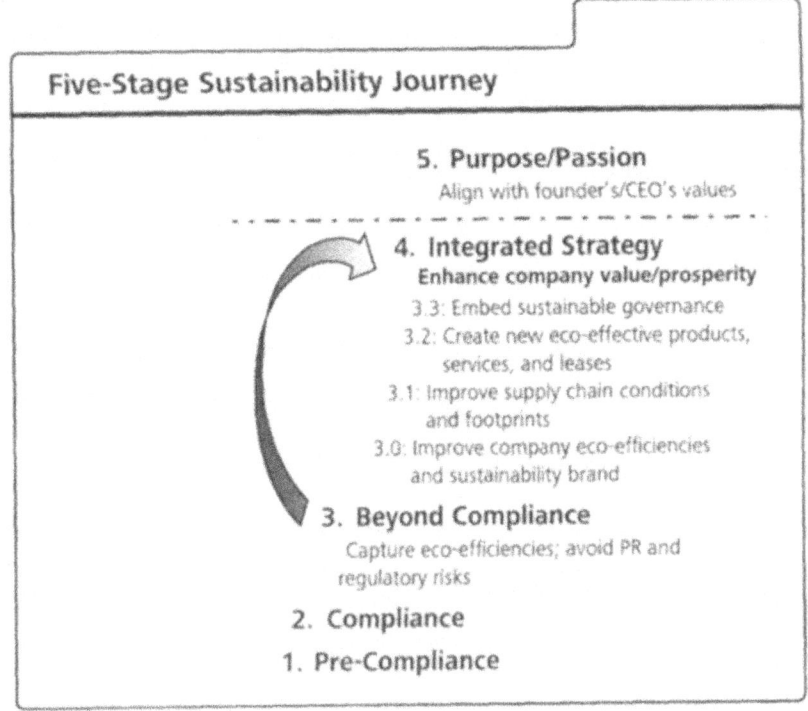

Figure 10.1

- **Stage 2:** Compliance. The business manages its liabilities by obeying labor, environmental, health, and safety regulations in the jurisdictions in which it operates. It has an environmental management system and company policies on environmental protection and human rights. It reactively does what it is legally bound to do while happily externalizing its ecological and social collateral damage. It installs pollution abatement equipment as end-of-pipe retrofits. Therefore, it should avoid fines, prosecution, bad PR. Stage 2 is the baseline.
- **Stage 3:** Beyond compliance. A company voluntarily moves to Stage 3 when it realizes that it can save money with proactive operational eco-efficiencies, or at least avoid a public relations crisis and discourage/avoid the threat of new regulations. It reaps incremental "low-hanging fruit" by saving energy while reducing its associated carbon footprint; saving water; saving materials in its products and packaging; and saving waste costs.

Stage 3 companies focus efforts where they can generate big results, fast. In Stage 3, sustainability initiatives are usually marginalized within specialized departments. They are tacked on as green housekeeping, rather than being institutionalized in the company's governance systems.

Companies in Stage 3 are not sustainable; they are just less unsustainable. Many Stage 3 companies have annual targets for further waste and electricity reduction and for the further elimination of toxic substances used in manufacturing, but the goals are increasingly difficult to meet. The law of diminishing returns inhibits further savings from eco-efficiency programs. A new phase must be entered. That is why companies aspire to Stage 4.

Stages 4 and 5: Similar Behaviors, Different Motivations

About 90% of the behaviors of Stage 4 and Stage 5 companies look the same. Companies in both stages adopt a cyclical, borrow-use-return model of sustainable capitalism. They inject sustainability principles into their cultural DNA. Companies in both stages deploy business strategies that respect the environment, the community, and the ongoing business health of the firm. They unleash the untapped creative energies of all employees and managers, empowering them to suggest and implement sustainability-oriented expense-saving and revenue-growing opportunities. Sustainability expectations are aligned within the organization and across the entire value chain. Instead of seeing green costs and risks, companies in both stages see investments and opportunities. They make cleaner, greener products, and they embrace eco-effectiveness and life-cycle stewardship. They are sustainable enterprises doing no harm, doing good, and making more profit.

It is the motivations of companies in these two stages that differ, as represented by the dotted line between Stage 4 and Stage 5 in Figure 10.1. The means and the ends — the benefits and the co-benefits — of companies in the two stages are flipped. Think of Stage 4 companies as publicly traded companies that are chartered to put their shareholders' interests first and ensure they reap competitive advantages from their Sustainability initiatives. Think of Stage 5 companies as founder-owned companies with a priority on values-based corporate citizenship.

Many Stage 5 companies do not go through the first four stages. They start and end in Stage 5. Many of them are in the 98% to 99% of companies in the world that are small or medium-sized businesses. Their company values mirror the values of their founders. If you were to congratulate CEOs of small Stage 5 companies for being sustainable enterprises, many would have no idea what you were talking about. They do not frame their strategies and behaviors in those terms. They just do it. Publicly traded companies may evolve to Stage 5 once the legitimacy of social and environmental purposes is embraced in the business community.

Does it matter whether a company is in Stage 4 or Stage 5? We would all like companies to do the right things for the right reasons. Our priority is to quickly reach the tipping point of a critical mass of sustainable firms to ensure a sustainable planet. Whatever convinces Stage 3 companies to aspire to Stage 4 will do. At Stage 4, they can see the wisdom of transforming to Stage 5 later

The Four-Step Transformation from Stage 3 to Stage 4

Is it really possible for a for-profit company to become a sustainable enterprise — to make the radical leap from Stage 3 to Stage 4 on its sustainability journey? Yes, but it requires a significant transformation. Each of the four intermediate stepping-stones between Stage 3 and Stage 4 (shown in Figure 10.1) is designed to produce real business benefits.

- Stage 3.0: Improve company eco-efficiencies and sustainability brand. In this stage, the firm captures the energy, water, materials, and waste handling eco-efficiencies within the company's current internal operations and processes. Carbon footprint reductions usually accompany energy reductions in anticipation of a government-imposed price on carbon emissions. The company produces the same products and services and uses the same processes, but it does these more efficiently, passing the savings straight to its bottom line.

- Stage 3.1: Improve supply chain conditions and footprints. Acknowledging responsibility for the environmental and social impacts of its products throughout their life cycles, the company implements sustainable procurement practices. It works with suppliers to help them achieve the same eco-efficiencies that the company itself realized in Step 3.0. Suppliers are encouraged — or coerced — to clean up their acts or else risk losing the firm as a business-to-business (B2B) customer.

- Stage 3.2: Create new eco-effective products, services, and leases. The company redesigns its products and reengineers its processes to be radically more eco-effective, rather than simply eco-efficient. It co-creates new green products and services by collaborating with diverse stakeholders. Innovation abounds. The company reinvents itself, providing useful products and services in existing markets and in new, strategic markets. It leases products instead of selling them, and takes them back at the end of their useful life.

- Stage 3.3:Embed sustainable-governance. The firm bakes sustainability into its decision making, its policies, and its culture. The company embeds sustainability-principles in its financial measurement and management systems. It aligns its recognition, reward, evaluation and remuneration systems to ensure everyone understands that sustainability considerations are important.

279

Executive teams and boards revamp the company's governance system to assess — and transparently report on — how the firm is contributing to a sustainable global economy, society, and the environment.

The four stepping-stones may be taken serially or in parallel. They may be looped, with more being accomplished on each step during each pass. The speed and sequence of the steps will vary. But they are all touched sooner or later.

10.13 Sustained Success of an Organization

To achieve sustained success, leaders should adopt a risk management and sustainability approach. The organization's system of management should be based on the sustainability principles found discussed earlier. These principles describe concepts that are the foundation of effective risk management and sustainability program.

The organization achieves sustained success by consistently addressing the interests of its stakeholders, in a balanced way, over the long term. An organization's internal and external operating environment is ever changing and uncertain. To achieve sustained success, the organization's leaders should

- Maintain a long-term planning perspective
- Constantly monitor and regularly analyze the organization's operating environment
- Identify all stakeholders and assess their potential impacts on the organization's performance
- Engage stakeholders and keep them involved in the review of the organization's management of its significant opportunities and threats
- Establish mutually beneficial relationships with members of the organization's value chain
- Conduct uncertainty assessments as a means of identifying and managing the significant opportunities and threats
- Anticipate future resource needs and the overall resource productivity of the organization
- Establish processes appropriate to achieving the organization's strategic objectives
- Establish and maintain processes for continual improvement, innovation, and learning

These processes for sustained success are applicable to any organization, regardless of size, type, and activity. Attention should also be paid to a number of important risk management and sustainability approaches to different elements found in organizations.

Risk management and sustainability are critical components of an organization's sustained success.

These practices should be embedded in the Organizational Sustainability decision-making process by including them in the knowledge policies, organizational culture strategies, and operations. The organization needs to build internal competency for sustainability undertake engagement on sustainability with all stakeholders and regularly review its actions and practices using the attributes of organizational sustainability.

10.14 Sustainable Business Model Innovation

The inner workings of a business model – its products and processes, its interactions with stakeholders, what and how it measures, the transactions it requires – influence a company's ability to thrive in the future and shape its impact on people and planet. But many existing business models are predicated on the assumption that vital, non-financial resources – i.e., natural, human and/or social capital – are in virtually limitless supply. Societal benefits, if considered at all, is often an after-thought. To truly create a sustainable world that can thrive over time, we need business models that operate within planetary limits and are sensitive to their roles as economic, social and environmental linchpins. Nowadays many companies have realized the merits of modifying their products and processes to become more sustainable. Some have revamped their offerings to be more effective, more efficient and produced with safer and greener materials. Other companies have rethought their processes such as by utilizing renewable energy sources in production or enhancing performance and trust through various certifications such as LEED for 'green' buildings. But these innovations will only get us so far. What we need are not just better products and processes but fundamentally different business models.

Definition of business model

This describes the method or means by which a company tries to capture value from its business. A business model may be based on many different aspects of a company, such as how it makes, distributes, prices or advertises its products.

The business model concentrates on value creation. It describes a company's or organization's core strategy to generate economic value, normally in the form of revenue.

The model provides the basic template for a business to compete in the marketplace, it provides a template on how the firm is going to make money, and how the firm will work with internal players (firm's employees and managers) and external players (stakeholders such as customers, suppliers, and investors).

The business model indicates how the firm will convert inputs (capital, raw materials, and labour) into outputs (total value of goods produced) and make a return that is greater than the opportunity cost of capital and delivers a return to its investors. This means that a business model's success is reflected in its ability to create returns that are greater than the (opportunity) cost of capital, invested by its shareholders and bondholders. Business models are an essential part of the strategy – they provide the fundamental link between product markets, within the industry, and the markets for the factors of production such as labour and capital.

Any resilient business model must be able to create and sustain returns for its investors over time. Otherwise, it is likely to go out of business or fashion.

Example

The 'razors and blades' model used by companies such as Gilette, in which a basic product (the razor) is sold cheaply, but an essential add-on or consumable (the blade) is sold at a high price once the customer has been lured in.

Another example is a mobile phone company may sell handsets (the bait) at a reduced price while signing up customers to buy calls over the period of a contract (the hook).

This is not to say that products or process innovations are not needed or useful – in fact, in some cases, they may even support or lead directly to a significant change in a model.

Business model innovation ultimately involves a novel form of exchange at some point along a company's value chain. When that exchange sometimes completely new, other times just different creates new social and environmental value and/or distributes economic value more equitable for more stakeholders, then it may be considered business model innovation for sustainability.

Examples

The most straightforward exchange is one between a company and its customers. The development of power purchase agreements (PPAs) for solar projects, pioneered by SunEdison, provides a good example of a change in how a solar provider, in this captures revenues from its customers. Using PPAs has lowered the barrier for commercial and industrial customers to adopt solar because there is no upfront cost. SunEdison's customers get cleaner energy at lower rates than commercial power while also taking advantage of renewable energy credits. The use of PPAs helps spread the use of renewable energy and lower costs, providing more value to customers and the system at large.

Other examples of novel exchanges that provide value to more stakeholders and shift incentives can be found in interactions between a company and its suppliers (e.g. the SABMiller sourcing from disadvantaged cassava farmers), a company and its employees (e.g. the cooperative ownership structure at Ocean Spray) or a company and its community (e.g., 2 Degrees providing a meal to a hungry child for every health bar sold). In each case, the value created in the transaction is no longer concentrated among the company's owners or shareholders, but it is distributed more equitably, usually shifting social and environmental outcomes along the way.

Another useful illustration of the power of the business model to illustrate is LifeStraw, which has a growing foothold in the developing world. LifeStraw's product – a personal use straw designed to remove bacteria and parasites from water – is certainly innovative. But the product is only successful if it gets into the hands of people who need it, particularly those with less access to clean water. This is where LifeStraw's innovative product financing business model comes in. Its unique approach to financing relies on funding from a carbon credit market, allowing the company to offer products at low to no cost in certain areas. It earns carbon credits by eliminating the need for families to cut down trees for firewood to boil and purify water. According to the MIT report *Creating Value Through Business Model Innovation*, it is important to innovate in areas where the competition is unable or unwilling to act. The classic example is Apple – the iPod would not have been the game changer that it was without the ecosystem created by iTunes. The resulting system dramatically changed how we acquire, store and listen to music, and made Apple the go-to provider of this new and better experience.

Examples of Innovative Sustainable Business Models for:

1. Environmental Impact:

(i) Closed Loop Production: In a Closed-Loop production model, the material used to create a product is continually recycled through the production system. Every effort is made to reduce waste in the production system, and those elements that can not be eliminated are recaptured and reused or biodegraded and composted. Few, if any, outside inputs are needed.

Therefore, it is a sustainable system in which a product is created using renewable energy, with no pollutant output and no waste-the materials used in production are recycled and reused rather than discarded. Ingenious. Therefore, closed-loop production is good for the world because it creates new products with no pollution and with recycled products.

(ii) Physical to Virtual: The consumer market-place at one time was almost exclusively comprised of brick and mortar stores – the corner store, the grocery store, big box store or shopping mall. That model of erecting a store on every corner or in every town provides convenience but can be resource-intensive and expensive as well as create environmental pollution. The physical-to-virtual model eliminates brick and mortar infrastructure to dramatically reduce the resources needed to supply a product to a customer. It changes how and where a transaction happens. As consumers become more comfortable with virtual shopping, we will likely see fewer retail outposts and more on-line only bands, like Flipkart and Fresh Direct, the grocery-delivery company.

Some companies in the category such as Netflix, achieved greater environmental sustainability through this innovation. It is important, however, to note that in augmenting some environmental elements of sustainability, this business model innovation may eliminate jobs, thereby creating questions about social sustainability.

2. Social Impact: 2 Degrees:

(i) This company sells nutrition bars direct to consumers and through retail outlets. For every 2 Degrees bar purchased, the company provides a meal to a hungry child. The company does this by forming partnerships with nonprofit organizations that provide food assistance through health clinics, schools, and community groups in areas where children are suffering from malnutrition or chronic hunger.

(ii) Walmart: For several years, Walmart has had a plan in place to source food directly from farmers, cutting out middlemen and enabling farmers to boost their income and in some countries, this has meant fresher, more local produce for customers. Part of Walmart's plan includes providing training to one million farmers and farm workers in crop selection and sustainable farming, as well as a goal to increase small and medium-sized farmer income by 10-15%. By sourcing directly from farmers, Walmart aims to strengthen local farms and economies.

3. Financial Innovation/Impact:

(i) Freemium: In this business model, a proprietary product or service (often software, media or web services) is provided free of charge, but money(premium) is charged for "premium" features., functionality or virtual goods. A freemium model is sometimes used to build a consumer base when a critical mass is needed to make the product valuable to consumers. Social network sites like Twitter, Facebook and LinkedIn all use this model to build a user base, and only in later stages or beyond the basic package do they offer paid services or advertising opportunities.

(ii SolarCity designs, installs, finances and maintains solar systems; in 2013 they started offering Energy Explorer software to customers for free so that they can pinpoint home inefficiencies and understand possible cost and savings improvements.

10.15 Example of a Sustainable Organization

Let us use an example of sustainability of a Pizza restaurant. The operation of the Pizza restaurant will be sustainable (or close to it) when the following factor happens:

- **Materials:** All your produce, pizza boxes, cleaning products etc. came from sustainable/green/animal product free/ socially responsible resources. You buy organic tomatoes from farmers who provide good working conditions and wages for their migrant workers. Your pizza boxes could be made from 100% recycled papers or pulp from certified forests and cleaning products will be environmentally benign.

- **Energy:** All your energy for cooking, transportation and space heat came from renewable sources. (You could buy 'green power' from your utility and your delivery vehicles could run on biodiesel. You could even consider cycling for delivery instead of using fuel.)

- **Process:** Your cooking and other processes are as efficient as possible (You could use non-disposable tableware and capture the waste heat from you oven.)

- **Product Design:** Your main product is biodegradable, even edible, so it is quite benign. Do the ingredients come from local or sustainable or organic sources? You could vary the menu to take advantage of seasonal availability. What about packaging? Could you invent a reusable pizza box?

- **Waste:** All your waste products can either be reused, recycled or composted.

(You could choose biodegradable serving items, eliminating plastics drink covers or polystyrene cups).

- **Industry influence**: You apply your leadership and buying power to drive the rest of the industry towards sustainability. (To have an affordable and adequate supply of organic produce, you might help set up a cooperative)

- **Community Contribution**: You have a programme to help solve a pressing social problem that relates in some way to your business. You might work on migrant labour issues and/or hunger, for example. If you serve beer, then drunk driving may be an issue to address.

Questions:

1. Discuss the motivating factors why companies should invest in sustainable development.
2. How do you embed sustainability in an organization?
3. Discuss the attributes of organizational sustainability
4. What is the importance of an organization's context?
5. Describe the 5-stage journey to a sustainable enterprise
6. Discuss sustainable business model innovation.

Chapter 11

Stakeholders and Social License to Operate

Every organization comes face-to-face with a wide variety of stakeholders as it begins to develop sustainability by characterizing the internal and external operating environment. A stakeholder is individual or organization that has an interest in a decision or activity of an organization; Interest refers to the actual or potential basis of a claim or demand for something that is owed or to demand respect for a right. The claim does not need to involve a financial demand or legal right Sometimes; it is the simple request to have the right to be heard. This interest gives them a "stake" in the organization. However, this relationship is usually not formal or even acknowledged by the stakeholder or the organization. Stakeholders are also referred to as "interested parties." The relevance or significance of an interest is determined by the principles of risk management and sustainability.

The three responsibilities of sustainability require the willingness of an organization to operate in a transparent and accountable manner and in compliance with all applicable laws and regulations. It is expected that the organization practices its three responsibilities within its activities, processes, and operations while taking into account the interests of its stakeholder.

11.1 Stakeholders

Identification of and engagement with stakeholders is fundamental to the practice of sustainability by an organization. Every organization should determine who has an interest in its activities, processes, decisions, products, and services. It needs to determine the consequences of its activities when conducting the internal and external operating environment scanning exercises While an organization is usually clear about the interests of the owners, members, customers or other constituents of the organization, often people and organizations outside of the control of an organization that have rights claims, or other specific interests that need to be addressed that are not being addressed.

Many organizations are not aware of all their stakeholders and may not be aware of the potential of an organization to affect interests. To address these conditions, an organization should

- Create a means of identifying its stakeholders and keep that list current

- Recognize and have due regard for the interests and other legal rights of its stakeholders and engage with them regarding their interest
- Assess and take into account the ability of stakeholders to engage with, and influence the organization
- Take into account the relation of its stakeholders' interests to the organization's risk management and sustainability programs, as well as the nature of the stakeholders' relationship with the organization
- Consider the views of stakeholders whose interests are likely to be affected by activity, process, or decision even if they have no formal role in the governance of the organization or are unaware of these interests

An organization needs to understand the relationship between the various stakeholders' interests that are affected by the organization, while also considering the interests of society as a whole-starting with the community. Although stakeholders are a segment of the larger society, they may have an interest that is not consistent with the expectations of society.

An effective means for an organization to identify its sustainability responsibilities is to become familiar with the practice of scanning its internal and external operating environments while realizing that the stakeholders are the face that can be put on the opportunities and threats that have been identified.

In order to continually improve its sustainability performance, the organization determines

- How it will satisfy its environmental, social, and economic responsibilities within the sustainability program
- How it will embed this framework into its operations—part of how the organization operates each day
- The influence of its stakeholders and their interests

Sustainability needs to be included within the scanning of the external operating environment and in the uncertainty analysis activity through the use of stakeholder engagement because:

- The interests of internal and external stakeholders are important to an organizations ability to meet its objectives
- People will need to take (or not take) actions in order for sustainability to be managed effectively
- People have some of the knowledge and information upon which effective Sustainability management relies (i.e., obtaining the social license to operate).
- Some people might have a right to be informed or consulted about the activities and decisions of the organization.

Stakeholder engagement (i.e., communication and consultation with a two-way dialogue) is a key supporting activity for all processes and decisions within the sustainability and risk management processes.

The organization should develop and implement a plan as to how it will communicate with the external stakeholders. This plan should include

- Engagement of the appropriate external stakeholders and ensuring effective exchange of information
- External reporting to comply with legal, regulatory, and government requirements
- Providing feedback and reporting on communication and consulting as part of the stakeholder engagement program
- Using engagement communication to build confidence within the organization
- Digitally communicating with stakeholders to make it convenient for them

These planning elements should include processes to consolidate risk management and sustainability information from all available sources.

Remember that engagement, communications, and consultation are processes, not outcomes. They normally take place with stakeholders. The beneficial effects of these processes are based on the transparent exchange of information and persuasion. Decisions are always improved by engagement of stakeholders and keeping them digitally engaged. Stakeholder engagement is what separates sustainability from "business as usual."

In view of the above, stakeholder engagement is an essential and helpful component of every sustainability program. Failure to develop stakeholder engagement within the sustainability program can lead to the loss of the organization's social license to operate. An effective stakeholder engagement process can help to reduce the effects of uncertainty (i.e., opportunities and threats) caused by the external operating environment.

It is worth reiterating the importance of a robust stakeholder engagement effort, especially when there is a good deal of change in the organization's context. Identifying and engaging stakeholdersis how the organization manages its uncertainty so that it can meet its strategic objectives. With this understanding, the organization can seek alignment with its stakeholders' interests while demonstrating how its activities, processes, decisions, prod-acts, and services can be of benefit to these people and their organizations. An organization never deals with all the stakeholders at the same time, but by following the VOC procedures with the stakeholders, the engagement will be separate and specific to certain interests. Some of the engagement will be driven by the stakeholders, while other elements of the engagement will be initiated and maintained by the organization itself.

Stakeholder engagement needs to be documented as part of the organization's knowledge management effort. This documentation should be maintained to help improve decision making and help determine the degree to which sense making needs to be actively scanning the external operating environment.

11.2 Internal Stakeholders

Some stakeholders are involved within the organization. They include members, employees, leaders, and owners. These stakeholders have an interest in the mission and the strategic objectives of the organization. However, this does not mean that all their interests will be the same. Competent empowered and engaged people at all levels in the organization are critical to the success of the organization meeting its objectives in an uncertain world.

It is important to remember that internal stakeholders are also connected to external stakeholders through their family and friends in the community. Since everyone belongs to multiple organizations, it is important to have the members or employees assist with the monitoring of the external operating environment and identify which key external stakeholders are known to them.

Another point to remember is that the parent organization is linked to all its organizations through the internal context and reporting structure. This provides some consistency throughout a corporation, but the individual facilities are still all different from one another because of context.

11.3 External Stakeholders

All the organizations that are identified in the scan of the external operating environment have people that become external stakeholders. The organization and its parent organization may have a sphere of influence on some of the external stakeholders.

Some organizations consider their value chain organizations as internal stakeholders since there are often contractual arrangements or other factors that create a sphere of influence. However, the level of influence is reduced in the second and third tiers of the value chain.

11.4 Identification of Stakeholders

An organization should determine what other organizations or individuals have an interest in its activities, processes, decisions, products, and services While this is often accomplished as a component of the scanning of the internal and external operating environment, extra effort is warranted to enable the organization to understand the relevance of its opportunities and threats and the consequences of these effects of uncertainty on the stakeholders. Putting a "face" on these opportunities and threats helps the organization when it conducts the uncertainty analysis. Identification of stakeholders does not replace the considerations of the broader reach of society in determining norms and expectations of the organization's activities and decisions.

Parent/large organizations (e.g., corporations) will have global stakeholders such as the major nongovernmental organizations (NGOs), and multilateral groups, such as the United Nations and the International Labor Organization. Organizations at the community level will deal with local environmental official's community government departments, local community board members, neighbors, local advocates of various cases and people involved in community services. Many people in a community have an interest in what an organization is seeking to accomplish with its strategic objectives.

To identify stakeholders beyond its scan of the external operating environment, an organization should consider the following questions:

- To what organizations are there legal obligations?
- Who might be positively or negatively affected by activities, processes, decisions, products, and services?
- Who might express concerns about these activities, processes, decisions, products, and services?
- What involvement have other organizations or individuals had in the past when similar concerns needed to be addressed?
- Typically, who helps the stakeholder organization address specific consequences?
- Which stakeholders can affect the ability of an organization to meet its responsibilities?
- Who would be disadvantaged if excluded from engagement?
- Who in the community or value chain is affected?

Some sustainability practitioners refer to interest as an "issue." An issue is defined as a point or matter in question or in dispute, or a point or matter that is not settled and is under discussion or over which there are opposing views or disagreements. When stakeholders have issues rather than interests, the organization has waited too long to engage with them. Learning about an issue signifies that an impasse has been reached and that mediation may be necessary to get past this impasse. By not choosing to deal with stakeholder issues, an organization could jeopardize its social license to operate.

To be sure that an organization has satisfactorily dealt with the identification of its stakeholders, it should consider each of the following tasks:

- Have a process for identifying both its internal and external stakeholders while considering the process for conducting the internal and external operating environment scans

- Recognize and have due regard for the interests, as well as the legal rights, of its stakeholders and engage with them to better understand their interests
- Recognize that some stakeholders can significantly affect the level of uncertainty of an organization and keep it from achieving its strategic objectives
- Assess and take into account the relative ability of stakeholders to engage with and influence the organization
- Take into account the relation of its stakeholders interests as well as the nature of the stakeholders relationship with the organization
- Consider the views of stakeholders whose interests are likely to be affected by a decision or activity—this is a perspective view that comes from an effective stakeholder engagement process

Stakeholder identification and engagement are critically important in addressing an organization's three responsibilities of sustainability—environmental stewardship, social well-being, and the sharing of value between organizations in the community.

11.5 Stakeholder Engagement

Stakeholder engagement is defined as "activity undertaken to create opportunities for dialogue between an organization and one or more of its stakeholders, with the aim of providing an informed basis for the organization's decisions."

It is important that the employees know that they contribute to their organization's success and the achievement of the strategic objectives. External to the organization, engagement can involve similar activities:

- face-to-face meetings with active listening on both sides
- involvement taking place over time
- Seeking to monitor the effectiveness of the engagement process

As in the case with employees, effective engagement with external stakeholders also involves a strong emotional bond to the organization. Uncertainty, few stakeholder gather information from internal and external stakeholders. The use of surveys does not meet any of the three elements of engagement mentioned above.

Digital media is changing the way we engage with stakeholders. Being digital enables an organization to evaluate how its engagement with external stakeholders may present opportunities and threats. This means understanding how stakeholder behaviors and interests are developing outside of the business, which is crucial to getting ahead of trends that can deliver or destroy value. Digital tools also contribute to rethinking how to use new capabilities to improve how stakeholders are engaged. Data and metrics can focus on delivering insights about stakeholders that in turn drive the ability to understand their interests. Digital tools enable an organization to constantly engage its stakeholders as part of a cyclical dynamic where internal processes and changes in the external operating environment are constantly evolving based on direct inputs from the stakeholders, fostering ongoing engagement and empowerment. Being digital is about using data to make better and faster decisions and moving those decisions lower in the organization. The use of digital tools also speeds the engagement process, enabling fast-moving, stakeholder-facing interactions over time. Many very small organizations are beginning to use digital media in their marketing efforts. They will learn how to extend it to stakeholder engagement.

Another means for improving stakeholder engagement is borrowed from the more traditional voice of the customer (VOC) method. A VOC program is defined as a channel for acquiring business insight about customers and what is important to them. Capitalizing on customer feedback requires a strategic and ongoing dedication to hearing, active listening, understanding, and acting on the customer's "voice: through a formal program built on:

- Active listening: A mechanism providing all customers the opportunity to share their compliments and comments about their experiences with an organization's product or service.
- Pulse monitoring: A recurring and systematic means of tracking changes in business outcomes, their leading indicators, and the influential drivers by periodically contacting and talking to a statistically representative sample of customers. This is now done digitally instead of using polling.

Listening to customers is now starting to include the remainder of the external stakeholders. This needs to be a central element in the scanning of the external environment as well. Many organizations are beginning to use these VOC techniques with members or employees.

11.6 Putting Engagement into Practice

Some actions for engaging members or employees of the organization:
- Recognize that sustainability is embedded in the work that they do
- Promote collaboration through the organization to ensure the organization meets its three responsibilities of sustainability.
- Communicate face-to-face with people to promote understanding of the importance of their individual contributions to sustainability and to assess their satisfaction with the working environment that enables them to realize their commitments.
- Facilitate open discussion and sharing of knowledge and experience between members or employees.

- Recognize and acknowledge people's contribution and learning, as well as the improvement that comes from their efforts.
- Enable their self-evaluation of performance against their personal objectives for sustainability within their control.
- Communicate the results of sustainability and recognize all significant contributions.

When an employee is engaged with an organization, operational friction are reduced while an emotional bond is created. However, employee engagement must be self-motivated rather than simply participating in random sustainability initiatives.

A VOC-type program is much more than the use of an occasional survey. It is recognition of the importance of customers (and employees) to an organizations success and a commitment to include stakeholder perspectives in decisions being made in every part of the operations. Essential questions for addressing sustainability as a critical component for stakeholder engagement, and the maintaining of the organization's social license to operate is given below. It begins with the opportunities and threats gathered in the internal and external context scans, continues with the practical and insightful analysis of stakeholder feedback (i.e., interests), and concludes with the creation of activities guided by the analysis to demonstrably impact the manner in which the organization engages all its stakeholders. This is the way to embed stakeholder engagement into the organization's culture.

Within a sustainability program, employees are engaged, informed, incentivized, motivated, and rewarded for their contributions to the organization's sustainability program. This effort is often operated as a "behavioral change" program with a wide variety of different tools, techniques, frameworks, and approaches.

11.7 Social License to Operate

The social license to operate is defined as existing when an organization has the ongoing approval within a community and from other internal and external stakeholders to continue its operations. This can also be expressed as having broad social acceptance or ongoing acceptance. Social license to operate is rooted in the beliefs, perceptions, and opinions of the external stakeholders. While the "license" is intangible to a great extent, an organization recognizes the importance of earning the acceptance or the highest level of approval from its stakeholders. This represents the greater community accepting the organization and its projects into their collective identity.

A social license to operate is usually granted by the stakeholders in the community. Similar organizations might have a social license in one application and not have it for a similar application in the same area or neighborhood. Generally, the more expansive the environmental, social, and economic impacts of an organization and its activities, products, and services, the more difficult it becomes to get the social license.

The critical components of the social license to operate are

- Legitimacy: This is based on the norms of the community, which may be legal, social, and cultural, as well as formal or informal, in nature. Organizations must clearly understand the community's "rules of the game." Failure to do so risks rejection. In practice, the social license to operate comes from a program of stakeholder engagement. Nothing should be left to chance. There must be a transparent exchange of information about the activities, decision, product, or service.

- Credibility: The capacity to be credible is created by consistently providing accurate and clear information and by complying with any and all commitments made to the community in the process of the stakeholder engagement. Documenting the understandings helps manage expectations and reduces the risk of losing credibility by being perceived as creating a breach of promises. Many experts offer the advice of not making a verbal commitment since, in the absence of a permanent record, there are always areas open to reinterpretation at a later date.

- Trust: Trust, or the willingness to be vulnerable to the actions of another, creates a very high-quality relationship and one that takes both time and effort to create. Trust comes from shared experiences gained in the stakeholder engagement process. The challenge for the organization is to go beyond a traditional stakeholder engagement process and create opportunities to collaboratively work together and generate the shared value- within which it can prosper.

Gaining and maintaining a social license to operate is complex, to say the least. Difficulty arises when organizations are unable or unwilling 'to make the nominal investment of time to make things work well. There is a number of common problems associated with obtaining a social license to operate:

- An organization sees the social license to operate as a series of tasks, while the stakeholders and community grant the license on the basis of the quality of the relationship. A cultural mismatch often results in failure.

- The organization mistakes acceptance for approval, cooperation for trust, and technical credibility for social credibility.

- The organization does many of the following actions:

- Fails to understand the local community's local rules of the game and is unable to establish social legitimacy
- Delays the start of the stakeholder engagement process when there has been a significant change in its internal and external context
- Fails to allocate sufficient time for relationship building
- Undermines its own credibility by failing to give reliable information or failing to deliver on promises made to the key stakeholders or the community
- Underestimates the time and effort required to gain a social license to operate
- Overestimates the quality of the relationship with the key stakeholders or the community

While the term community is used when talking about a social license to operate, it is really about the interests of the key stakeholders, especially when they are in line with the norms of the community and embrace its principles. It is definitely more difficult to create a relationship with stakeholders when their interests are not in line with others' in the community. It is important for organizations to have the ability to use techniques for capacity building at the local level. This is often accomplished with outside consulting help.

There are some cases where it is difficult to achieve a social license to operate. Similar to the practice of sustainability, there is no "one-size-fits-all" activity for either effort. It is always prudent to seek the counsel of people that understand the social structure and let them guide the organization as it performs its analysis of the external operating environment and as it applies this information within the context of its risk assessment process to rank order its opportunities and threats. A risk assessment process can be a valuable asset when an organization is involved in obtaining its social license to operate. Finally, it is important to remember that the quality of the license to operate is dynamic and responsive to the changes in perceptions regarding the organizations and its activities, decisions and, influences. The organization has to be diligent to work hard to maintain its social license to operate over time once it is obtained

There are many useful publications dedicated to the social license to operate. Many of them are written for large corporations for use with operations that extract resources from the ground. Be careful that the information used by a specific organization is tailored to that organization and its stakeholders.

Internalizing Stakeholder Interests in an Organization

Organizations of all sizes and types can use risk management to help embed the determination of the internal and external context in the way they operate every day. Here is an example of how the context can be addressed in a sustainability management framework.

Understanding the Needs and Interests of the Stakeholders

The organization determines the internal and external context using the influences determined by the PESTLE and TECOP analysis methods. Context factors must be relevant to its purpose and affect its ability to achieve its responsibly set objectives. Furthermore, the context factors include conditions addressed by the three responsibilities within the organization's sustainability policy. The knowledge gained by understanding the context is considered when establishing and maintaining the organization's sustainability program.

11.8 Understanding the Interests of the Stakeholders

The organization must determine the
- Stakeholders that are relevant to the achievement of its responsible objectives
- Relevant interests of the stakeholders
- Need for a social license to operate any portion of its operations, products, or services

The knowledge gained is considered when establishing and maintaining, the organization's three-responsibility sustainability program. An effective stakeholder engagement process provides the lookout function, which in turn monitors context so that objectives can remain responsible and the social license to operate can be maintained.

Questions:

1. How are the stakeholders identified by the scanning of the external operating environment?
2. Why is it so important to engage the external stakeholders as the means for discussing their interests in the organization's Sustainability efforts?
3. How does true engagement differ from other tools (e.g., surveys) used to understand the stakeholders' interests?
4. Discuss the significance and critical components of social license to operate.

Chapter 12

Leadership, Board's Role and Governance for Sustainability Change Management

12.1 Nature of Organizational Governance

Organizational governance is the system by which an organization makes and implements decisions in pursuit of its objectives. Governance system varies with the size and type of organization and the environmental, economic, political, cultural, and social context associated with its location.

Governance from the perspective of an organization is not to be confused with corporate governance, which focuses on governing bodies (e.g., the board of directors). Instead, it is a system that has a person or a set of trustees that have the authority and responsibility for realizing the organization's objectives. Organizational governance can be applied in either a formal or informal manner.

Organizational governance is present in every organization as one of its core functions. It provides the framework for decision making at all levels of the organization. The decision making is usually influenced by the leadership of the organization. Governance enables the leadership to take responsibility for the risks associated with its activities and make decisions to embed sustainability into the organization. Responsibility can be extended when organizations and its leaders commit to relationships with other organizations and the community at large.

Corporate Governance Structure

Effective leadership is critical to the success of the governance system. This is true not only for decision making but also for the effective motivation of the internal stakeholders to make sustainability part of what they engage with every day. Governance seeks to make sustainability part of how the organization operates.

Organizational governance provides the framework or rules, relationships, systems, and processes that enable the authority to be exercised and controlled within an organization. This includes the manner in which the organization and those people that lead it are held accountable. If the governance is effective, it is more likely that the organization will be able to meet its objectives in an uncertain world. Governance enables to direct and control the uncertainty associated with the organization's opportunities and threats. Effective governance must be carefully

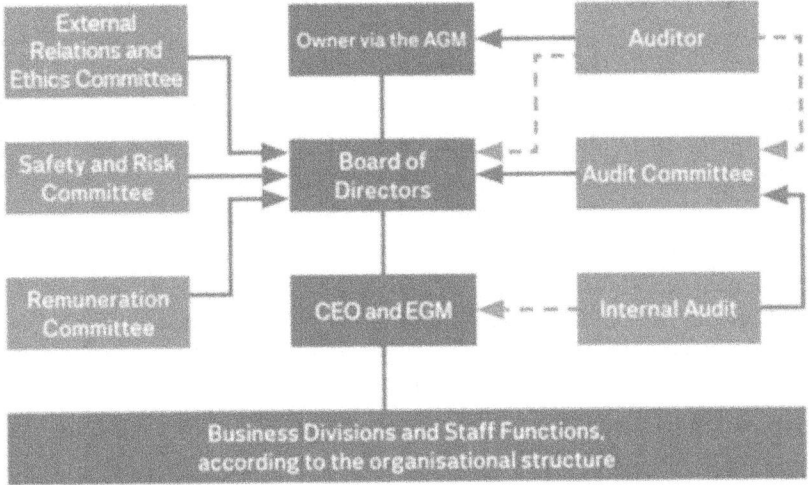

Figure 12.1

monitored to be able to determine its effectiveness while committing the resources necessary to continually improve. As an organization grows in size, it needs to review the elements of governance on a regular basis. Partnerships and other relationships, formal and informal, are informed of the results of any reviews that take place.

Organizational governance is an important factor in enabling an organization to embed Sustainability. Organizational resilience is an outcome of organizational governance.

12.2 Organization's Code of Conduct

A code of conduct is a document that can help shape the Sustainability culture of an organization. This document sets the standards of behavior expected of all members or employees in an organization. It also helps them deal with the ethical dilemmas they experience while serving in the organization. The code of conduct is used by the organization to

- Effectively deal with compliance with relevant laws and other rules
- Help management be more effective in monitoring the culture of the firm and its interactions with a wide range of different stakeholders
- Maintain the integrity and reputation of the organization and its members or employees

By establishing a culture of compliance, the organization can be effective in limiting its liability both in penalties and with its reputation.

A code of conduct should include a clear statement of the organization's commitment to comply with laws and regulations. It must promote an internal culture of fair and ethical behavior and report matters that could prove to be detrimental to the organization's reputation. This commitment can be quite informal in the case of small organizations. A code of conduct is an important element in an organization's risk management program.

The code of conduct applies to all the internal stakeholders. External stakeholders are often asked to comply with the code as a condition of their engagement with the organization, particularly when there are matters that could impact the organization's compliance status or reputation. Many of the operational elements in the governance program should also be applied to the use of the code of conduct. Typically, the code of conduct covers environmental, social, and economic responsibilities to maintain a clear linkage with the sustainability program.

In the true meaning of embedded sustainability, the governance, code of conduct, and three responsibilities of sustainability (environment, social, and economic) are linked within the organization with the engagement with stakeholders Sustainability is informed by the risk management process the management of the uncertainty(i.e. the opportunities and threats),and a number of principles and processes, the long-term viability of an organization. Without all these elements present and aligned with each other, it would be difficult to fully embed sustainability, governance, and the code of conduct into a uniform decision-making framework used at every level of the organization.

12.3 Leadership

Effective leadership is critical to the success of the governance system and the ability of the organization to meet its strategic objectives. Leaders need to address the following actions:

- Develop the mission, vision, values, and ethics while acting as a role model
- Define, monitor, review, and drive the continual improvement of the organization's processes and operations
- Engage directly with all stakeholders
- Reinforce a culture of operational excellence with the organization's members or employees
- Ensure that the organization is resilient in order to manage to change effectively
- some of the personal traits of leaders are as follows:
- Ability to communicate a clear direction for the organization with a defined strategic focus

- Understand the management of uncertainty in order to enable achievement of the strategic objectives of the organization
- Ability to be flexible in adapting and realigning the direction of the organization in light of changes in the external operating environment
- Recognize that sustainable success relies on continual improvement, innovation, and learning
- Ability to use knowledge management and sense making to improve the reliability of derisions at all levels of the organization
- Inspire while rivaling a culture of engagement, ownership, transparency and accountability
- Be the role model for integrity, sustainability, environmental stewardship, social-well-being and shared value both internally and in the community in a manner that develops, enhances and protects the organization

Leaders are responsible for creating the mandate and commitment to sustainability.

Mandate and Commitment:

Leaders of organizations need to demonstrate their commitment to governance with the following actions:

- Ensuring that the risk management and sustainability policies are established in accordance with the organization's objectives, context, and strategic direction
- Ensuring that all the structural elements in this book are addressed with processes in all the operations of the organization
- Taking accountability for the effectiveness of the processes used and the efficiency of the operations associated with the organization's products and services
- Ensuring that risk management and sustainability are embedded in the process approach to the operations
- Communicating the importance of risk management and the responsibilities associated with sustainability to all stakeholders within the engagement process
- Ensuring that risk management and sustainability effectively contribute to enabling the organization to meet its objectives

The purpose of the mandate is to ensure that the organization clearly understands the benefits of risk management and sustainability and will embrace the change involved by embedding these practices into the manner in which the organization operates each day. It is necessary for the leader to be deeply involved in these programs in order to establish credibility with the external stakeholders.

301

Each organization should consider the following questions when establishing its mandate and commitment to risk management and sustainability:

- How is sustainability embedded in the objectives of the organization, and what goals and action plans are in place to help ensure success?
- Is the leadership clear about the significant opportunities and threats associated with the internal and external context and willing to engage with all stakeholders to make sure the organization can effectively manage the effect of uncertainty?
- Does the leader need to make changes to the prevailing risk attitude that will facilitate the embedding of sustainability in the organization's activities, processes and decision making.
- Does the form of the policy that provides for the embedding of risk management and sustainability support the other policies that direct the way the organization is operated?

Leaders must reinforce the organization's commitment and mandate through the following actions:

- Make sure the risk management and sustainability objectives are carefully linked to the objectives derived from the mission statement
- Make it clear that risk management and sustainability is about effectively delivering the organization's strategic objectives with a uniform program of top-down objectives and a feedback loop of employee goals and action plans
- Ensure the risk management and sustainability activities required by the mandate are fully integrated into the governance and the organization's processes at the strategic, tactical, and operational levels
- Make the commitment to make the necessary resources available to assist those accountable and responsible for managing risk and sustainability
- Require regular monitoring and measurement on the risk assessment and sustainability processes to ensure that they remain appropriate and effective
- Monitor to ensure that the organization has a current and comprehensive understanding of its opportunities and threats and that they are within the determined risk criteria
- Initiate corrective actions when threats are deemed to be unacceptable when they are not able to be offset by the opportunities
- Lead by example
- Review the commitment to the mandate as time, events, decisions, and the external operating environment conditions create change

Meeting the organization's objectives is considered to be essential to the organizations. Operating in an uncertain world makes it more important that the leadership is committed to risk management and sustainability, and that these practices are explicitly recognized in everything the organization does.

12.4 Sustainability Policy

Once the mandate is in place, it is important for leaders to make the mandate explicit through the issuance of risk management and sustainability policy. The purpose of this policy is to provide an effective means to clearly express the organization's intentions and requirements. The effectiveness rests on the expression of the organization's motivation for managing risk and sustainability and explicitly establishing what is required and by whom. Leaders must set the proper tone by emphasizing the necessity of using risk management and sustainability to help manage the opportunities and threats that define the uncertainty within which the organization operates. It goes without saying that short policies have a tendency to be more effective. The policy should be succinct, as well as short in length.

Effective communication of the policy also requires confirmation that the information has been understood by the stakeholders inside and external to the organization. Stakeholders must truly believe that the policy reflects the organization's intent to embrace risk management and sustainability as part of how it operates. To secure appropriate buy-in, the leader will need to produce tangible objective evidence that the organization has adopted changes in the way it has operated prior to the adoption of the risk management and sustainability policy, and that those changes are able to persist over time. The organization's reputation and the credibility of its risk management and sustainability management efforts are dependent on its success in meeting the commitments embodied in the policy.

A risk management and sustainability policy is established, reviewed, and maintained by the leaders of an organization. Generally, it must meet the following requirements:

- Be appropriate to the purpose and context of the organization
- Provide a framework for setting and reviewing objectives affected by the risk management and sustainability contributions
- Include a commitment to satisfy all applicable legal and other requirements
- Include a commitment to effective processes, efficient operations, and efficacious strategy
- Include a commitment to continual improvement, innovation, and learning
- Be maintained as documented information
- Be communicated within the organization
- Hold a key part of the engagement with the external stakeholders

All reviews of the risk management and sustainability processes begin with the examination of sustainability policy it is the keystone element of all activities, processes, decisions, products, and services associated with the organization,

12.5 Organizational Roles, Responsibilities, and Authorities

As required by the organizational governance, leaders must ensure that the responsibilities and authorities for relevant roles are assigned, communicated, and understood within the organization. Leaders need to assign responsibility for the following:

- Ensuring the risk management and sustainability processes are established with a reference or benchmarked to "best practice" for the organization
- Ensuring that the processes are effectively delivering their intended outcomes
- Reporting on the performance of the risk management and sustainability processes, on opportunities for improvement, and on the need for change or innovation
- Ensuring the promotion of risk management and sustainability throughout the organization
- Ensuring the integrity of the risk management and sustainability processes when changes are planned and implemented in the organization it is important to have a process focus for the management of risk and sustainability that goes beyond the preparation of a sustainability report. The focus must be on the identification of processes and operations that must be controlled to maintain and improve the organization's risk management and sustainability performance.

12.6 Organizational Strategy

At the organization level, it is important to set a strategy to meet the strategic objectives typically in a 5- to 10-year time frame. The effects of uncertainty (opportunities and threats) must be managed in order for the strategy to be executed in the most effective manner. With this in mind, a strategic plan provides a set of processes that are executed within the organization in order to meet the overarching objectives of an uncertain world. The focus is on developing strategies that will drive the organization in achieving the objectives that have been derived from the mission of the organization to create benefits for their internal and external stakeholders. This strategy also helps the leaders make decisions that support its execution by binding together the governance and the Strategy links governance and leadership in an organization. Leadership, the organization is prepared for execution (Figure 12.2). Most strategic failures are commonly failures of execution.

Figure 12.2

A strengths, weaknesses, opportunities, and threats (SWOT) analysis helps organizations use their strength to take advantage of the opportunities and overcome the threats. This analysis also helps organizations in minimizing the weaknesses that are subject to the threats.

Strategic planning must account for the effects of uncertainty and how they affect the future. A scenario is an internally consistent view of the future. Scenario planning is the process of generating and analyzing a set of different futures. The results from building scenarios are not an accurate prediction of the future; rather, they provide better thinking about the future. Scenarios are used in strategic planning to provide a context for decisions. As events incidents unfold in the external operating environment, it is necessary to continue to review whether plans fit the realities of the PESTLE analysis results. If they do not, the planning team needs to revise its scenario analysis. Execution of the strategy is a process and requires more people involvement than strategy formulation.

12.7 Sustainability Leadership:

Sustainability leaders/champions promote the dialogue that creates the culture change and governance transformation necessary for a company to be truly sustainable. They are change makers and transform their companies into more sustainable corporate citizens with better products, more sustainable and responsible services and more inclusive governance approaches.

The Five-Stage sustainability journey has to be followed by the leader as discussed in Chapter 10, section 10.6 (Figure 10.1)

12.8 Community-based Social Marketing for behavior change:

Community based social marketing tools can be used for behavioral change towards sustainable behavior among staff and customers.

When members of a community use resources wisely – by turning off idling engines, for example – it moves toward sustainability. To promote a more sustainable future, it is essential to know how to encourage individuals and organizations to adopt activities that collectively promote sustainability.

Increasingly, those who develop and deliver programs to promote sustainability are turning to community-based social marketing for assistance. This kind of marketing emphasizes direct, personal contact among community members and the removal of barriers (i.e., "roadblocks" to more sustainable actions and behaviour) since research suggests that such approaches are often most likely to bring about behavioural change.

Community-based social marketing also uses tools that have been identified as being particularly effective in fostering change. Although each of these tools on its own is capable of promoting sustainable behaviour, the tools can often be particularly effective when used together. Key community-based social marketing tools include:

- Use prompts – remind people to engage in sustainable activities (e.g., a vehicle window sticker indicating that the driver does not idle);
- Get commitments – have people commit or pledge to engage in sustainable activities (e.g., signing a pledge card to avoid unnecessary idling);
- Use social norms – develop community norms that a particular behavior is the right thing to do;
- Use incentives – Incentives, primarily that of appropriate recognition and awards can be considered.
- Make it convenient – All notice boards and placards containing instructions and information on sustainable behavior should be conveniently located and in popular languages.
- Persuasive communications strategies with engaging messaging and images.

Community-based social marketing is also pragmatic. It involves:

- Identifying the barriers to a behavior;
- Developing and piloting a program to overcome these barriers;
- Implementing the program across a community; and
- Evaluating the effectiveness of the program.

To promote activities that support sustainability, barriers to these activities must first be identified. Community-based social marketers, therefore, begin by conducting the research that will help them identify these barriers. It is not unusual for this research to uncover multiple barriers that are quite specific to the activity being promoted. For example, barrier research on the issue of vehicle idling suggests that an effective social marketing strategy would:

- Remind drivers to turn their engines off; clarify the brief length of time that a vehicle should be idled before being turned off (10 seconds);
- Address the myths about vehicle idling; develop community norms that support turning off an engine as "the right thing to do"; and be delivered during the warmer months, since comfort and safety are important reasons why idling occurs in colder months.

Once the barriers have been identified, community-based social marketers develop a program that addresses each of them. Personal contact, the removal of barriers and the use of proven tools of change are emphasized in the program.

To ensure that the program will be successful, it should be piloted in a small segment of the community and refined until it is effective. The program is then implemented throughout the community, and procedures are put in place to continually monitor its effectiveness.

The steps that make up community-based social marketing are simple but effective. When barriers are identified, and appropriate programs are designed to address these barriers, the frequent result is that individuals and organizations adopt more sustainable activities, which is the cornerstone of healthier, more sustainable communities.

Community based social marketing tools have been applied in Case Study No. 2.

12.9 Organizational Change Management Process: Identifying Important Elements to Successful Organizational Change for sustainability implementation:

Kotter (1995) summed up what he perceived as the essential 8 step process for successful organizational transformation which can be applied for sustainability-related change implementation.

Kotter's defined 8-step process is as follows:

1. Establish a sense of urgency

- Examine market and competitive realities.
- Identify and discuss crises, potential crises or opportunities.
- Create the catalyst for change.

2. Form a powerful coalition

– Assemble a group with enough power to lead the change effort.
– Develop strategies for achieving that vision.

3. Create a Vision

– Create a vision to help direct the change effort.
– Develop strategies for achieving that vision.

4. Communicating the Vision

– Using every channel and vehicle of communication possible to communicate the new vision and strategies.
– The guiding coalition teaching new behaviors and leading by example.

5. Empowering others to act on the vision

– Removing obstacles to change.
– Changing systems or structures that seriously undermine the vision.
– Encouraging risk-taking and nontraditional ideas, activities, and actions.

6. Planning for and creating short-term wins

– Planning for visible performance improvement
– Recognizing and rewarding employees involved in these improvements.

7. Consolidating improvements and producing still more change

– Using increased credibility to change systems, structures, and policies that don't fit the vision.
– Hiring, promoting, and developing employees who can implement the vision.
– Reinvigorating the processes with new projects, themes, and change agents.

8. Institutionalizing new approaches

– Creating the connections between new behaviors and corporate successes.
– Developing channels to ensure Leadership development and succession.

12.10 Definition and Practices of Sustainability Champion

12.10.1 Definition of Sustainability Champion

An individual who seeks to lead change in an organization to transform that organization into a smarter, more successful, and more sustainable enterprise. This individual may exist at any level within an organization and in any type of organization, from the Chief Executive Officer to administrative assistant, from Mayor to city staffer, from the university president to student leader.

Sustainability Champions are most effective when they: establish personal credibility about sustainability; pursue dialogue; seek collaborations and networks; meet people where they are; piggyback sustainability initiatives on existing processes; influence the influencers; and practice "planful opportunism."

12.10.2 Practices of the New Sustainability Champions

Sustainability Champions exhibit three broad sets of characteristics. They:
1. Proactively turn constraints into opportunities through innovation
2. Embed sustainability in their company culture
3. Actively shape their business environments

Each category comprises specific behaviours and merits a closer look.

12.10.2.1 New Sustainability Champions proactively turn constraints into opportunities through innovation. Their approach involves pragmatic adaptation of existing technologies and delivery mechanisms. They eschew expensive research into new technologies to make current products cheaper, more widely available or better suited to local production processes. The Champions stand out for their ability to turn constraints in delivery channels into opportunities. For instance, they may identify alternative production methods to get products to market more directly.

To innovate effectively, New Sustainability Champions focus attention on these key points:

12.10.3 They address lack of resources.

One response to a current or future shortage of a particular resource is to find ways to reduce the amount used. While this often makes sense from an efficiency viewpoint, it also increases the longevity of the business by preserving a critical resource. Importantly, Champions recognize that the reductions need not be limited to their operations but can, and should, apply to their suppliers and users.

Two noteworthy examples of Champions successfully addressing resource shortages are Shree Cement, an Indian cement producer, and Manila Water, a water utility in the Philippines.

Faced with limited access to low-cost energy, Shree Cement developed the world's most energy-efficient process for making its products. The company has become the global benchmark: leading cement companies from around the world visit Shree to learn from its innovations. Shree Cement Sustainability Report can be viewed from the following website: https://www.shreecement.in/pdf/Shree%20CSR%2004-05.pdf

For its part, Manila Water drove down its levels of non-revenue water (NRW – water that does not reach the customer due to leaks or illegal tapping) from 63% in 1997 to 12% at the end of 2010. This was achieved partly by providing affordable supply to low-income areas, which turned probable NRW perpetrators into partners who now help prevent illegal tapping.

Another way in which New Sustainability Champions turn resource constraints into opportunities is by exploiting the by-products of other companies' outputs or processes. China offers two illustrations of this approach. For instance, Broad Group, a large producer of air chillers, uses alternative energy sources such as waste heat from buildings to power its range of non-electric air-conditioning units. This accommodates a key constraint in China: many people still live "off-grid" in China, and for those who do use electricity, grid supplies are not always reliable.

Zhangzidao Fishery Group is another example. The company practices integrated multi-trophic aquaculture (IMTA), a more sustainable form of biodiverse fish farming that uses the waste of one species to feed another. IMTA aquaculture techniques allow Zhangzidao to increase production and economic diversification while reducing waste by converting by-products and uneaten fish feed into harvestable crops, reducing the need to introduce artificial feeds into the system.

12.10.4 *They educate their customers.*

A new product or service, no matter how well conceived, cannot succeed unless consumers are convinced of its benefits for them. Lack of knowledge and limited awareness constitute barriers to adoption that the New Sustainability Champions must work hard to circumvent, often in creative ways. For example, Jain Irrigation uses dance and song to explain the benefits of drip irrigation to local communities. With this innovative way of marketing, the company can convince and educate potential customers about its products. Not only does this approach help Jain to sell successfully, but it helps the company work collaboratively with local communities to improve its services and products.

12.10.5 *They provide customers with appropriate financing.*

Another major constraint is a lack of financial assets with which to make necessary capital investments, even when positive returns are expected in the long run. This is particularly true of the rural poor in emerging economies, where banks have limited presence. Kenya's Equity Bank uses mobile phone technology to enable it to reach small farmers in rural Kenya, something that branch-based banking cannot do economically. Equity Bank partnered with Safari.com, leveraging the Kenyan mobile-services provider's M-Pesa financial services platform to launch and provide financial services to its customers.

Suntech, a solar power company in China, cut the costs of its products to make them affordable to customers of limited means. Suntech also provides financial solutions that enable low-income customers to structure payments for its equipment. And when its photovoltaic cells reach the end of their life, the company takes them back for recycling.

12.10.6 Embedded Sustainability

The Sustainability Champions embed sustainability in their company culture. They are aware that deep and sustained impact requires demonstrable commitment from the entire organization – not only from the top management team and certainly not solely from the chief executive. The best intentions can flounder, or be subverted if they are implemented by a skeptical or indifferent team. Conversely, an engaged and proactive staff can be a constant source of new ideas for products, services, delivery mechanisms, talent development, supply sources and more.

New Sustainability Champions put in place the mechanisms that make sustainability an integral part of their business fabric. In particular:

12.10.7 They define a bold sustainability vision.

Champions stand out for the ways in which they define clear aspirations and goals for sustainability and use them to galvanize the entire organization. They move beyond incremental change to create a vision capable of inspiring their staff – and external stakeholders. Sekem, an Egyptian organic food producer, took a holistic view of environmental and social development. The company wanted to use organic farming as a way to reclaim desert land, producing food for the local market and reinvesting the profits in the community. Sekem also has a highly unusual business model. While it is a profit-making enterprise, its aim is not profit maximization. Through a profit-sharing methodology, it shares its prosperity with the smallholder farmers in its network.

In 2008, at the height of the global financial crisis, the chief executive of Florida Ice & Farm in Costa Rica announced a dramatic change in business strategy to make the food and beverage company more sustainable. The company has set the goals of becoming water- neutral by 2012, achieving carbon neutrality by 2017 (a target even more ambitious than Costa Rica's national goal of carbon neutrality by 2021) and becoming a "zero solid waste" company by 2012.

12.10.8 They integrate sustainability into operations.

At the same time, pragmatic business leaders recognize that inspiration alone is rarely enough to produce the desired outcomes, so they develop the appropriate incentives and metrics. Florida Ice & Farm exemplifies this approach. The company spent four years developing a balanced scorecard which measures non-financials such as the number of community service hours that employees spend on watershed-related activities. Remuneration is linked to such performance indicators. For example, 60% of the CEO's salary is linked to the triple bottom line of "people, planet, profit."

Masisa, a wood products manufacturer in Chile, developed a balanced scorecard on sustainability that measures performance in all dimensions, including non-financial indicators. The scorecard's inputs and outputs cascade down to each worker and are tracked over time.

In Hong Kong, train operator MTR Corporation has made a clear link between sustainability and risk management. The company built a sophisticated framework – a Sustainable Competitive Advantage model – to guide its actions. One example of the framework in practice: eight environmental impact assessment reports are mandatory for every project to develop a new rail line. MTR Corporation also measures the impact of these projects on biodiversity both before and after the construction stage – an approach that is rarely found in its industry.

12.10.9 They engage the workforce in sustainability.

Aside from setting out a bold vision and integrating sustainability into everyday operations, it is necessary to fully engage the workforce. Natura, a Brazilian cosmetics company, invests heavily in training its managers to identify socio-environmental challenges and turn them into business opportunities. Natura's staff is also motivated by bonuses based on environmental and social performance as well as on economic measures. And Woolworths, a South Africa- based retailer, works to boost employees' pride in their jobs, ensuring they are rewarded for contributing ideas that improve the business. The success of this approach can be seen in the fact that many of its best new initiatives do not come from senior management.

12.10.10 Sustainable Business Environments

The New Sustainability Champions actively share their own business environment. They recognize that maximum impact cannot be achieved solely within the boundaries of their own organizations. They understand that engagement with the wider business ecosystem of regulators, competitors, suppliers, customers and other stakeholders is required. They actively engage with these entities to shape the outcomes they envision for themselves.

12.10.11 They influence policies and standards.

Companies operating in weak regulatory regimes have the opportunity – and, arguably, the obligation – to define the standards to which the industry should aspire. While it is true that such companies benefit directly from the policies, they are also effectively using policy as a multiplier to augment the impact of higher standards across their industries. This can be achieved through direct discussions with policy-makers, or through associations and trade bodies.

One strong proponent of this approach is Brazilian organic sugar producer Grupo Balbo. The company aims to help turn the entire sugar industry into an organic sector. It is now collaborating on the creation of Brazil's first national organic certification system. Balbo is in discussions with environmentally-minded politicians in Germany and Brazil to promote incentives such as tax breaks for organic production. The company has partnered with a governmental environmental research, department to conduct more than 1,600 biodiversity field studies.

In India, Suzlon, a wind power producer, uses its knowledge and experience to educate citizens and policy-makers. The company faces the challenge of getting the right policies in place to foster the development of renewable power, particularly in the United States. Internationally, Suzlon helps shape the debate on sustainability and renewable power through organizations such as the European Union Commission, the World Economic Forum, and the United Nations, as well as through an active outreach programme to the media.

12.10.12 They partner to achieve mutual goals.

Partnerships with organizations that share similar goals can potentially generate far greater impact than if each were to work in isolation. For example, depending on their mandate and focus, NGOs could be potential allies with which for-profit businesses could collaborate.

Kenya's Equity Bank has adopted this strategy. The bank has a host of partnerships that range from links to agrochemical manufacturers such as Agmark and trade bodies such as the Eastern Africa Grain Council to not-for-profit organizations such as Millennium Promise, aid agencies such as the German government's GTZ and the United Nations World Food Programme. Equity Bank also has strategic partnerships with organizations such as the Alliance for a Green Revolution in Africa and The International Fund for Agricultural Development, a United Nations agency that provides cash guarantees that reduce the bank's risk when lending to smallholder farmers who have little or no collateral.

New Britain Palm Oil, operating in Papua New Guinea, worked closely with local NGOs to engage with local communities. The connections helped to smooth negotiations involving land rights – a critical issue since conflicts with suppliers and landowners are the largest barriers to palm oil operations in the region.

12.10.13 They build awareness of the importance of sustainability

Customers are among the key stakeholders who should be engaged to maximize the impact of sustainability initiatives. By educating customers about issues such as pollution, depletion of water or climate change, companies can help put pressure on industry to improve sustainability practices and on the government to improve standards and enforcement.

In Brazil, sugar producer Grupo Balbo runs awareness-building campaigns targeting grocery shoppers as well as students and local communities. The company publishes data, including its sustainability report, to increase transparency and establish confidence among stakeholders as well as to spread knowledge and understanding of the organic cultivation of sugar cane.

In China, Broad Group has developed a miniaturized device for measuring air pollution that can fit inside a mobile phone. The device can help boost awareness of air pollution issues and even empower citizens by putting knowledge about air quality in the palms of their hands.

12.11 Board Roles and Responsibilities in Sustainability

A board's responsibility for sustainability can be categorized in three ways: traditional duties adapted for a world in which sustainability is ever more important, explicit responsibilities for activities related to sustainability performance, and implicit responsibilities related to prioritization and agenda-setting.

Traditional activities adapted for a new world: Boards generally focus on core activities: overseeing business strategy, selecting and overseeing the chief executive and determining executive compensation, and ensuring legal compliance.

Given this, the integration of sustainability and governance is, in part, about the application of traditional governance activities to a 21st century operating environment. Over the past two decades, company leaders have learned that topics not previously considered relevant to business, such as human rights and climate change, can shape business success. Many have seen the hardwon reputations of their businesses damaged by campaigns led by an increasingly vigorous civil society that is now fueled by social media. And many leaders have found it difficult to maximize the value of core assets when social and environmental questions can affect the legal license to operate. Moreover, the primacy of shareholder value, especially in the context of publicly traded companies, is subject to increasing debate.

In this context, directors' traditional responsibilities are being redefined to include ESG considerations. This is seen through the rewriting of charters for boards and board committees to include these topics.

Specific sustainability related activities: Boards are also undertaking several specific activities related to sustainability, including the integration of strategy and sustainability, a focus on stakeholder perspectives, the approval of sustainability reports, and the oversight of executive accountability and compensation for sustainability performance. In contrast to what is described in the previous section, these activities generally go beyond legal requirements.

As boards undertake these activities, new questions arise, and new sources of information grow in importance. The already complex subject of executive compensation has become more challenging for company leaders aiming to integrate sustainability factors into decisions about rewarding senior management.

Approval of sustainability reports also illustrates changing dynamics. Many boards now sign off on their companies' sustainability reports before publication. These reports do not raise the same kinds of legal attestation requirements associated with financial reports—yet. The Johannesburg Stock Exchange, for example, now requires listed companies to report on sustainability considerations, and China's Stateowned Assets Supervision and Administration Commission now expects the largest state-owned companies to report as well. These developments coincide with a rising interest in "integrated reporting." As this movement gains steam, it's possible boards will devote more attention to how their companies report on energy use, water use, labor issues, and other topics directly related to Global Compact principles.

Implicit responsibilities: Directors also undertake informal activities that have a high degree of relevance to sustainability performance, such as setting agendas, raising questions, and shaping mindsets.

It is possible to reduce effective governance to the concept of stewardship, and good stewards of corporate assets ensure that management considers all relevant risks and opportunities. Doing so effectively means that the board takes a close look at topics such as societal and regulatory acceptance of new technologies and business processes, entry into new markets, and the impact of "externalities" on business success. Over the past two decades, there have been multiple examples of the risks incurred when boards overlook such questions. In many cases, the ability of company leaders to bring their companies' innovations to market can rise and fall based on how well they anticipate whether society is prepared to accept those innovations.

Board Structure: According to 2010 research by the UN Global Compact, 39 percent of 1,300 surveyed companies have boards that "routinely address corporate sustainability issues." But the mechanism used by companies varies widely, with three models appearing most frequently: full board oversight, dedicated sustainability committees, and existing committees taking responsibility for sustainability.

Board committees: While an increasing number of large companies are giving their boards responsibility for oversight of sustainability, there is no current consensus about the best model to apply. In a 2009 Deloitte survey of 220 directors of American companies with more than US$1 billion in revenues, 37 percent of respondents said some committee should oversee sustainability responsibilities. When asked which committee should have oversight, 24 percent of respondents chose risk and governance committees, 22 percent chose the strategy committee, and 15 percent chose the audit committee. These figures suggest that the future may deliver not a single model but rather a range of options for companies.

Committee mandates: A 2010 BSR survey revealed that, regardless of whether they are focused on sustainability in whole or in part, board committees today generally define their sustainability mandate broadly, shifting away from a more narrow focus on single issues or topics. Typical mandates include a review of policies, practices, and positions; a review of performance against sustainability goals; and a review of trends in legislation, regulation, and public debate.

Company leaders implement these responsibilities through a mix of activities broadly related to overall board responsibilities, such as the dual purposes of advice and oversight. The most common activities include auditstyle reviews of commitments and data in sustainability reports, annual reviews of performance and goal-setting, and frequent and informal engagements on strategy development.

External advisory panels: In addition to the formal committees comprising company directors, one more model merits attention: external advisory panels. These bodies are growing in number, and while they do not qualify as formal governance mechanisms, they represent an interesting development. In cases where they serve in an advisory role and/or provide a public oversight mechanism, they create a "soft-governance" model. Over the coming decade, it is possible that this mechanism will develop further, and some companies have begun experimenting by melding the "soft governance" of external panels with the "hard governance" undertaken by the formal board of directors.

Board Composition: One of the core questions relating to boards and sustainability is who sits on the board. While not yet widely adopted, the notion of the "stakeholder director"—a director elected to a board specifically to represent the perspectives and/or interests of key stakeholders and to provide the overall direction of the company—is a logical development for companies that see sustainability as a strategic imperative. If the shift in thinking described above, from a "pure" focus on shareholder value to one that aims to balance the interests of multiple stakeholders, takes hold, then it stands to reason that boards would evolve in a manner that ensures that stakeholder perspectives—indeed, that the stakeholders themselves—are in the room when decisions are made.

This shift has not yet occurred, but it will likely get more attention in the years ahead, especially if public policy makers redefine fiduciary responsibilities to include material sustainability matters.

One can imagine four possible futures for board composition:

- Status quo: In this model, we would see a slow but steady effort to increase board diversity, with a focus primarily on gender and global representation, but with little change to existing governance models.

- New voices: Governance models would remain very similar to what they are today, but with a rapid diversification of board composition to include directors chosen in whole or in part because of their knowledge, networks, and perspectives on material sustainability issues. This model integrates the "stakeholder director" concept described above.

- Formalizing the advisory panel: One could also see the maturing of the external advisory panel as a parallel body that maintains existing governance models with a formal channel to expertise that would enrich the board's ability to anticipate and manage key sustainability questions. This hybrid model might represent the "path of least resistance" to progress.

- Bicameral models: As in Germany and some other jurisdictions, a dual board structure could emerge to balance shareholder and stakeholder interests in a more formal way than the hybrid advisory panel model described above.

Over the long run, the best solution is to integrate sustainability into all board activities so that it becomes "mainstream." This mirrors the indispensable effort of many company leaders over the past decade to integrate sustainability into business strategy and operations. Ideally, dedicated board committees would be seen as redundant in a decade's time, but they might be needed now to catalyze the transition.

Questions:

1. Why is leadership a process rather than a personal trait or characteristic of a person who is a leader? Discuss the role of leadership in an organization.
2. What is the purpose of organization's code of conduct?
3. What is the purpose and role of sustainability policy?
4. Discuss the practice of a sustainability champion.
5. Discuss community-based social marketing for behavior change.
6. Describe a process for organizational change management.
7. Discuss the Board's role in implementing Sustainability in a company.

Chapter 13

Monitoring and Measuring Sustainability

Understanding monitoring and measurement is critical to the success of sustainability and a key component in helping an organization meet its strategic objectives. Measurement also supports the organization's pledge to continual improvement.

The organization needs to evaluate the performance and effectiveness of its sustainability program. Measurements are relevant and critical to major organizational decisions and help the organization track its progress toward meeting its strategic objectives. Therefore, there should be practical means to conduct the relevant monitoring and measurement tasks in a sustainability program. Sustainability practitioners are focused on gathering available data and reporting the information to interested stakeholders in the external operating environment.

13.1 Deciding What to Measure:

Organizations need to have effective systems and processes for determining what data and information should be collected, and how they are handled, stored, analyzed, and interpreted. This information is used to increase the organization's understanding of the internal and external operating environment within which it operates. Data and information need to be continually reviewed to ensure they remain current, meaningful, and effective.

Sources of data need to be reviewed on a regular basis to monitor their effectiveness and continual improvement in meeting changing organizational requirements. Based on the scanning of the external operating environment, a wide range of stakeholders are involved in determining what data should be gathered.

The measures or indicators selected should best represent the factors that lead to improved customer, operational, financial, and societal (i.e., external stakeholders) performance.

Sustainability managers need to figure out what sustainability is supposed to do when it is embedded within an organization. What does sustainability mean to processes and operations, and why does it matter? Sustainability is a vague concept to many people that need to be associated with what is actually expected to be observed. Once everyone is familiar with the answers to these questions, the situation starts to look more measurable. The decision-making for sustainability would progress as follows:

- If sustainability matters, it is likely to be detectable and observable.
- If it is detectable, it can be detected as an amount or range of amounts.
- If it can be detected as a range of possible amounts, it can be measured.

It is also important to state why it is important to measure sustainability in order to understand what is really being measured. Understanding the purpose of the measurement is often the key to defining what the measurement is really supposed to be. Some things seem to be "intangible" only because people have not defined what they are talking about.

13.2 Measurement Methods

Measurement involves using different types of sampling and experimental controls. This involves taking small random samples of some activity.

Think of measurement as iterative. Start measuring what sustainability is contributing to the organization. You can always adjust the method based on the initial findings.

There is much interest in the topic of sustainability results, but there is less written on how the results must be linked to help the organization meet its strategic objectives: All KPIs should be linked to the organization's success factors that will help meet the strategic objectives. These factors may be core values, technical competence of the workers, or marketing success. These links will help the leaders know how close the organization is to its strategic objectives. Sustainability results must be linked to activities, processes, systems, products, and services associated with the operation of the organization.

An organization needs to have effective systems and processes for determining what data and information should be collected. The core practices include many of the following, whether formal or informal in nature:

- Planning of data collection and linking it to the strategic planning
- Analyzing and interpreting data to learn and inform strategic planning
- Sharing the data among those who can use it to improve performance
- Ensuring data integrity (i.e., valid, relevant, timely, secure, and sound)

Some organizations use measures from the past. How did the costs today compare to the same location's costs a year ago? We do this when we look at our electricity bills. Measuring the current performance is critical to any organization, even though the moment it is measured, that result is in the past (i.e., lag measures). Past and present metrics are the easiest to come up with because we typically have data on these types of measures and these results have actually happened. It is important to have lead measures in the measurement system.

Selecting the right metrics or measures is actually much more than simply deciding what to measure. It is a key part of the organization's strategy for success. Selecting the wrong metrics will put a strain on the success of the organization. Many small businesses are using a generic "balanced score-card" method so they can have fewer measures and still be able to drive success. Organizations are learning that success is about balance, not a dependence on any fixed set of measures.

Like objectives, metrics need to be set at the highest levels of a hierarchical organization and followed down to all levels and functions. Metrics at one level should lead to metrics at the next level of the organization. Defining key performance measures based on SMART in this manner ensures that there are no disconnects or inconsistencies in how the parent organization measures performance.

One way of reducing the number of measures to a reasonable number is to assign a weight to each individual measure in a family of metrics and develop an -index" that is an aggregate statistic.

13.3 Strategic Measurement Model

While measurement may be easy, it is difficult to measure the right things and learn to ignore other interesting data that does not help the organization become more sustainable. There have been a number of different approaches

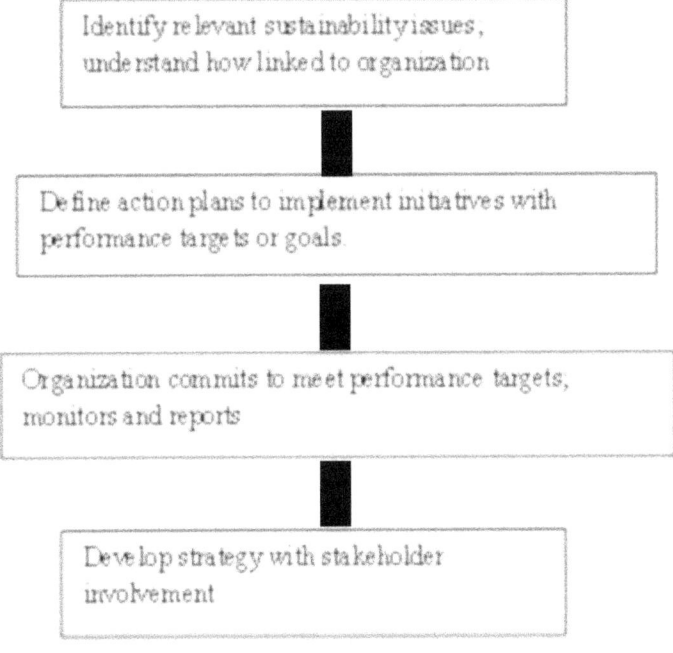

Figure 13.1

on how to select and use metrics in an organization. Larger organizations and parent organizations use externally derived collections of sustainability metrics to guide the development of their strategy (Figure 13.1).

It is possible to take a more internal view by looking at metrics from the internal perspective (Figure 13.2). In this model, the organization determines what it stands for and its vision of the future. Obviously, its external impacts and stakeholder engagement will shape the vision. Next, the organization focuses on what it needs to do in order to maintain its competitive advantage, as well as its social license to operate. This would involve understanding its internal and external context. Usually, the organization will start by determining its lead indicators and determine how they can be measured

Sustainability reporting as a management process. (Adapted from GRI IFC, Getting more value out of sustainability reporting, 2010, https://www. globalreporting,org/resourcelibrary/Connecting-IFCs-Sustainability-Ferformance-Standard-GRI-Reporting-Framework.pdf.)

Strategic measurement model. (Adapted from Brown, M.GV *Keeping Score: Using the Bight Metrics to Drive World-Class Performance,* Quality Resources, New York, 1996.)

Figure 13.2 shows a means of assessing how effectively the lead indicators are working to influence the sustainability results (i.e., lag indicators). It is important to remember that results are merely the outcomes

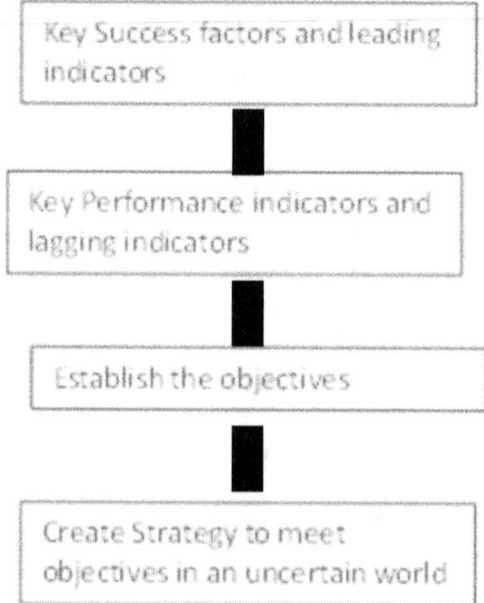

Figure 13.2

of performance. It is important to create the results that are keeping score so that changes can be made in the support activity that is the focus of the lead indicators.

Objectives should be set only after there has been some experience with the determinations of the critical success factors. Often, there is a rush to set the strategic objectives. This leads to objectives that are surpassed with little effort or objectives that cannot be reasonably achieved. Neither of these extremes is helpful for driving an organization to meet its strategic objectives over the long term. Metrics are the tools used to monitor the progress of meeting responsibly established strategic objectives. This reminds us that the sustainability strategy should be prepared after the measurement system is already in place. One should never start with the strategy and derive measures that measure the progress on that strategy.

13.4 Roles of Monitoring and Measurement

When any kind of determination is needed, there is a need for monitoring and measurement.

Monitoring can determine the status with observations or measurements There are relationships between all these different practices as they work together to make important determinations. In an organization, monitoring and measurement are not conducted for the sole purpose of addressing the interests of stakeholders. The stakeholders are interested in an outcome and want evidence of what is actually happening in that regard.

Monitoring, measurement, and review are activities that are used to determine the suitability and adequacy of processes and operations, and how the achievement of effectiveness and efficiency enable the organization to meet its objectives in an uncertain world.

Monitoring

Monitoring involves the routine surveillance of actual organizational performance in order to create an accurate comparison with the expected or required performance. This activity involves continual checking or investigating, supervising, critically observing, and determining the process or system status to identify these changes, as well as changes in the context of the organization. The main purpose of monitoring is to generate information needed to ensure that opportunities and threats are managed effectively.

Monitoring requires a systematic approach that involves:
- Establishing a procedure for continual checking, supervising, critically observing, or otherwise determining the status of information or systems
- Developing a means of detecting change from what has been assumed or is expected

- Incorporation of the organization's performance indicators and the interests of the stakeholders
- Determining how resulting information can be captured, analyzed, reported, considered, and acted upon
- Providing the necessary resources and expertise for these activities
- Allocating responsibilities for various risk management and uncertainty monitoring activities and incorporating those responsibilities in the member's or employee's performance review criteria

Monitoring is an aspect of effective *governance* to make sure that uncertainty is managed effectively. The selection of things to be monitored should be focused on the significant opportunities and threats.

Next, it is important to determine *what* needs to be monitored. Here are some typical monitoring examples:

- Key characteristics of operations that have significant impacts on the environment, society, or the local economy and meeting the organization's three responsibilities
- Processes in place that ensure compliance with legal and other compliance obligations
- Key characteristics associated with the interests of stakeholders
- Significant organizational opportunities and threats
- Operational controls associated with the system of management
- Value chain controls associated with suppliers, customers, and stakeholders
- Interactions found in the value chain model
- Determinants of progress toward the organization's strategic objectives

Documented information is needed to review the results of the monitoring activity. Included in these records are the following:

- Information on how monitoring decisions were made.
- Information regarding the interests of stakeholders.
- Controlled records for any reporting that is required for
- Assistance to the organization in the review of its activities, processes, and systems
- A demonstration of whether the process has been conducted in a planned and systematic manner
- Enabling of information about the process to be shared through engagement with internal and external stakeholders
- Provision of objective evidence for internal and external process audits

Leaders need to establish and maintain processes for monitoring and collecting and managing the information obtained from the monitoring activities.

Measurement

All organizations collect different types of data. Trying to track too much information is a big problem in the sustainability arena. It is important that the organization measure the activity associated with the significant opportunities and threats, the effectiveness of the processes, and the efficiency of the activities, processes, and systems. These measurements provide critical data about key processes, outputs, results, and other outcomes. Measurement focuses on the past, present, and future (i.e., looking forward results) and may be based on the needs of employees, management, customers, and stakeholders. The key to a successful measurement program is pinpointing the vital few key measures

Measurement is a process for determining a value. Measurements should be either quantitative or semi-quantitative. It is important that measurements be conducted under controlled conditions with appropriate processes and procedures for ensuring the *validity* and *traceability* of the results. These processes include adequate calibration and verification of monitoring and measurement equipment, use of qualified people, and use of suitable methods and quality control procedures. Written procedures for conducting measurement and monitoring are necessary to provide consistency m measurements and enhance the reliability of the data that is produced

Leaders need to assess the progress of the organization in achieving planned results against its strategic objectives, at all levels and in all relevant processes and functions. A measurement and analysis process is used to gather and provide the information necessary for performance evaluations and effective decision making. The selection of appropriate key performance indicators (KPIs) and measurement methodology is critical to the success of the measurement and analysis process.

We have previously discussed lead and lag indicators. Here in below provides a more detailed discussion based on measurement system.

13.5 What are Leading and Lagging Indicators?

As described above that leading and lagging indicators are two types of measurements used when assessing performance in a business or organization. A leading indicator is a predictive measurement, for example; the percentage of people wearing hard hats on a building site is a leading safety indicator. A lagging indicator is an output measurement, for example; the number of accidents on a building site is a lagging safety indicator. The difference between the two is a leading indicator can influence change, and a lagging indicator can only record what has happened.

All too often we concentrate on measuring results, outputs and outcomes. Why? Because they are easy to measure and they are accurate.

If we want to know how many sales have been made this month, we simply count them. If we want to know how many accidents have occurred on the factory floor, we consult the accident log. These are **lag indicators**. They are an after-the-event measurement, essential for charting progress but useless when attempting to influence the future.

To influence the future, a different type of measurement is required, one that is predictive rather than a result. For example, if we want to increase sales, a predictive measure could be to make more sales calls or run more marketing campaigns. If we wanted to decrease accidents on the factory floor, we could make safety training mandatory for all employees or force them to wear hard-hats at all times. Measuring these activities provides us with a set of **lead indicators**. They are in-process measures and are predictive.

Lead indicators are always more difficult to determine than lag indicators. They are predictive and therefore do not provide a guarantee of success. This not only makes it difficult to decide which lead indicators to use, but it also tends to cause heated debate as to the validity of the measure at all. To fuel the debate further, lead indicators frequently require an investment to implement an initiative prior to a result being seen by a lag indicator.

What has become clear over years of research is that a combination of lead and lag indicators result in enhanced business performance overall. To provide a couple of specific examples; "satisfied and motivated employees" is a (well-proven) lead Indicator of "customer satisfaction." "High-performing processes" (e.g., to 6 Sigma levels) is a good lead indicator for "cost efficiency." When developing a business performance management strategy, it is always good practice to use a combination of lead and lag indicators. The reason for this is obvious; a lag indicator without a lead indicator will give no indication as to how a result will be achieved and provide no early warnings about tracking towards a strategic goal.

Equally important, however, a lead indicator without a lag indicator may make you feel good about keeping busy with a lot of activities, but it will not provide confirmation that a business result has been achieved. A 'balance' of lead and lag indicators are required to ensure the right activities are in place to ensure the right outcomes.

There is a cause and effect chain between lead and lag indicators; both are important when selecting measures to track toward your business goals. Traditionally we tend to settle for lag indicators, however, do not underestimate the importance of lead indicators.

Lag Indicators

Lag indicators are measures that focus on the outcomes or results of planned initiatives at the end of a time period. Results or KPIs largely indicate historical performance. There are large numbers of targeted sustainability indicators and KPIs available in the literature. However, the challenge in using them includes the fact that these results do not reflect current activities. They lack predictive power. There is a caution in the investment world that states, "Past performance offers no indication of future results." Past performance is useful in valuing the sustainability program only as far as it is indicative of what is to come in the future since sustainability is always defined as happening over the long term. Many sustainability practitioners regard past performance as being able to at least provide an idea of the direction in which the organization is headed. However, a performance trend is not considered to be a leading indicator.

Although sustainability practitioners and stakeholders tend to focus on results (lag indicators), these lagging indicators may not provide enough information to guide actions and ensure success. There are some good reasons why lag indicators may not always be sufficient for measuring sustainability:

- Lag indicators often provide information too late to enable sufficient response.

Outcomes are the result of many factors. Lag indicators may tell you how well you are doing, but may not give information as to why something is happening and where to focus any corrective actions that may be necessary to improve performance.

- When the outcome rates are low, there may not be sufficient information in the measures to provide adequate feedback for effective management of the process.
- When the outcomes are so threatening that you cannot wait for it to happen before the process is upset.
- Lag indicators may fail to reveal latent threats that have a significant potential to result in disaster.

Lag measures tell you if you are going about your success in terms of achieving the strategic objective as a "work in progress" measurement. It is difficult to do anything about a lag measure once it is reported because lag measures have already happened when you measure them. You are always referring to the past when talking about a result (lag measure). Yet despite the problem of not possessing a looking forward capability, lag measures are believed to be a sign of succeeding with a strategic objective by getting the results to demonstrate this achievement.

Lead Indicators:

A lead performance indicator is something that provides information that helps the user respond to changing circumstances and take actions to achieve desired outcomes or avoid unwanted outcomes. The role of a lead indicator is to help organizations improve future performance by promoting action to correct or avoid potential weaknesses without waiting for something to go wrong. The *ability to* guide actions to influence future performance is an *important characteristic* of lead indicators.

There are two forms of lead indicators. One form of a lead indicator involves providing information about the current situation that will affect future outcomes. A second form of lead indicator involves the measurement of processes involving people that can make a process more effective and connected to meeting the organization's strategic objectives.

A good *example of* the former lead indicator is when an economist uses certain lag indicators, such as "new housing starts," that foretell of the demand for goods necessary to build and furnish those homes. This reinforces the *tendency of* finding patterns with results (lag indicators).

The latter form of leading indicator involves the measures of activities connected to meeting the organization's strategic objectives. These measures are within the control of the organization. This lead measure (e.g., leadership) *is different since it* can foretell the result. You can recognize lead measures because of the following characteristics:

- A lead measure *is predictive-if* the lead measure changes, you can predict that the lag measures associated with the lead measure willalso change.
- A lead measure is *influenceable-it* can be influenced by the organization that seeks to manage the activities connected to meeting the organization's objectives.

For many people, lead measures seem to be counterintuitive. For example, we know that leaders and sustainability practitioners always focus on the lag indicators, even though it is not possible to act on a lag measure since it is always in the past. There is a feeling that lead measures are hard to keep track of since they measure behaviors and behavior change. Finally too many people, lead measures often look too simple. Since lead indicators focus on behaviors such as leadership, employee and stakeholder engagement, those that are not involved with these activities directly think that they are not as important as a measure for sustainability.

In the fields of organizational development and risk management, we are focused on behaviors (i.e., positive effects) that help the organization achieve its strategic objectives. The information on lead indicators makes a difference and enables the organization to close the gap between what the organization should do and what it is actually doing. Risk managers often describe lag indicators as driving an automobile with the front windshield painted black, moving forward by navigating with the three rearview mirrors. So how does an organization prepare for creating lead indicators to drive the lag indicators over the long term?

Lead Indicators and the Process

Processes always present some challenges since people are focused on results

- Is the process producing good results?
- Are people carefully following the process?
- Is the process effective with efficient operations?

The process focus element of performance frameworks looks for leverage points in the process. These are those critical steps in the process where performance can falter. Lead indicators are linked to these points to improve the results using leadership, strategic planning, employee engagement, stakeholder engagement, information and knowledge management, and process focus.

The trick is to use the leverage of the people support processes in the Porter value chain model to trigger the improvement of the results (lag measures) over time. The approach, deployment assessment, and refinement (ADAR) approach is used to accomplish this. Once you have a goal to meet an objective, there is a need to look to the performance area that would be responsible for providing the leverage factor, as shown in Figure 16.1, The process focus category in the performance framework can be used to guide the development of the approach. This is followed by a plan to deploy the process focus approach to guide the improvement of the lead measure. When this combination works well, the lead measure will be predictive and influence the lag measure. The lag measures that are attached to each lead measure should vary in the same manner.

13.6 Performance Frameworks

Performance frameworks which have been used in many countries provide the foundation for what are referred to as national quality award programs. Performance excellence programs were introduced in the late 1980s to spur the competitive advantage of businesses in those countries. In the United States, the Baldrige Performance Excellence Program has been in continuous use since 1987. This program has developed a set of criteria for performance excellence to be used by participating organizations, which include large and small businesses, government, nonprofits, schools, and healthcare facilities. There is a scoring method that enables the assessors to score the applications and grant the award to those who perform best.

Many organizations have learned to use the performance frameworks as a means to improve their competitiveness without applying for the award. Because the frameworks are updated on a regular basis to reflect changes in the best practice for each of the categories, they provide a useful means for looking forward and driving performance. This, in turn, helps improve the results. The developers of these frameworks noted that *results are merely the outcome of performance* and do not measure performance directly. What is different with the performance frameworks is their focus on driving performance in each of the following areas:

- Leadership
- Strategic planning
- People and employee engagement
- External stakeholder engagement (including customers)
- Information and knowledge management
- Process focus

Each of these areas can be scored and act as a lead indicator. Each lead indicator is associated with results (lag indicators) to see if the lead indicators are influencing and predicting the lag indicators. By measuring the inputs to a process, lead indicators can complement the use of results (lag indicators) and compensate for some of their shortcomings. Lead indicators of this nature can also be used to monitor the effectiveness of process controls giving advance warning of any developing weaknesses before problems occur.

Using a Performance Framework

A performance framework contains information on what is recognized as a best practice in each of the categories. To keep current, the framework must be continually modified to reflect current best practice. Any organization can use these descriptions to benchmark against and make corresponding improvements in its processes and operations.

The documents are prepared by the organization for each of the performance categories selected to help guide the efforts to attain the level of performance that is sought. These documents include an *approach*, the means of *deploying* that approach, and the manner in which the organization will *assess* and *refine* (ADAR) the approach and the deployment of the course of the implementation period—usually one year.

A description of how to prepare each of these documents is provided below. This is followed by a description on how to score them so they can act as a semi-quantitative measurement. These measurements will become the lead indicators for the sustainability program.

Approach

To create lead indicators that drive performance for each of the sustainability indicators, an organization needs to create its strategy. The approach of the ADAR cycle is basically the planning stage of the sustainability process. An organization must establish the strategic and operational objectives and the processes necessary to deliver sustainability results or KPIs.

The approach identifies the organization's intent to become sustainable and to measure its progress. In other words, the approach is the way by which something is made to happen. It consists of processes and actions that take place within a framework of principles and policies.

In order to create the approach for each category, it is important to answer the following questions:

- What is the organization seeking to achieve for each category? What is its intent?
- What strategic and operational objectives and worker goals and action plans have been established?
- What strategies, governance, and processes have been developed to achieve the intent? How were these items chosen by the leadership of the organization?
- What indicators or KPIs have been designed to track the progress of the organization's performance?
- How does the approach provide alignment with the strategic objectives established by the organization?

The approach should not only specify *what* an organization is planning to accomplish, but also include the reason *why* it is planning to do this. In order for the approach to be sound, the organization should consider many of the following:

- Interests of the stakeholders as determined in the engagement process
- Alignment with the organization's strategic objectives and strategy
- Appropriateness for the organization's internal and external context
- Links to other approaches, if appropriate
- Sustainability principles
- Whether it enables the organization's approach to continual improvement, innovation, and learning
- Consideration for the scoring matrix used to create the semi-quantitative score

By addressing the information provided above, the approach will ensure that organization's sustainability strategy correlates with a planned and strategic cycle of improvement. The stronger the adherance to these items, *the higher the score that will be given to* approach. When items are not addressed affirmatively the score will be lower. .A weak approach typically addressed what was to be accomplished not how or why. A well-defined approach that is supported by some benchmarking information tends to score higher using the scoring matrix.

Deployment

The deployment of the approach identifies how an organization plans to implement those processes and activities to create this lead indicator component. Successful deployment involves embedding the approach into the activity and full acceptance of the process steps and activities found in the approach. The deployment goal is to achieve the intent that was stated in the approach.

To successfully implement the approach, the organization should consider preparing a draft action plan. Essentially, the action plan heading should describe the area being addressed (i.e., leadership, strategic planning employee engagement, and so forth). It should also include the purpose of the action or the intent, and state the expected benefits. Next, each of the tasks should be outlined by assigning them to individuals, providing a timeline, and highlighting the anticipated performance improvements required for completing the item. The tasks will be the key process steps and procedures outlined in the approach. Usually, the first task of the action plan should describe what is being measured during the deployment, and the last step should recap the lessons learned by the employees and leaders as a result of the deployment of the approach.

To assess the success of the deployment (i.e., implementation plan), organizations should be able to describe the following:

- How have the strategies, processes, and activities been executed with the employees? What is the effectiveness of their implementation throughout the organization? To what extent have they been accepted and embedded as part of normal operations?
- Has the approach been implemented across all relevant organizational areas to its full potential and capability? Do the planned implementation activities support operations and sustainability improvement?
- Has the deployment of the approach been executed in a timely fashion and structured in a way that enables it to adapt to changes in the internal and external operating environment?
- Is the deployment of the approach achieving the planned benefits?
- Is the deployment of the approach understood and accepted by the internal and external stakeholders?

A written action plan will facilitate the evaluation of the deployment and enable the organization to address each of the questions that are posed during the scoring of each approach and deployment.

Assessment and Refinement

Assessment and refinement provide a process of improvement that enables the approach and deployment statements to be reviewed and modified to achieve the best possible result. Through monitoring and analysis of these results, the level of effectiveness of the sustainability program can be measured. An efficient and highly rated organization will conduct learning activities in the organization in order to prioritize, plan, and promote creativity, innovation, and improvement. This leads to three categories of an assessment and refinement: measurement, learning and creativity, and innovation and improvement.

13.7 Measurement

The approach and deployment must be regularly monitored and measured to ensure efficiency and the implementation of processes. Monitoring and measurement enable the organization to indicate that the results indeed stem from the deployed approach. The organization should be able to answer the following questions to assist in the assessment and refinement:

- What processes are in place to review the appropriateness and effectiveness of the approach and deployment?
- How do the results of the approach and deployment compare with benchmarks or previous levels of performance?
- How do you communicate, interpret, and use these results?

Learning and Creativity

In a learning stage, an organization identifies the best internal and external practices so that it will be able to recognize improvement opportunities in its sustainability program. Through the use of creative measures, the organization can then refine the approach and deployment by encouraging continual improvement and innovation. Answers to the following questions are addressed by learning and creativity:

- What have you learned?
- How have you captured this learning?
- How can you use the learning to improve the approach and deployment?

Improvement

Finally, the organization should use the results from the measurement, learning, and creativity to plan and implement the identified improvements. These refreshments and innovations should be shared across all relevant approaches for consistency and continual improvement. At this point in the process, the organization can state how it has used the learning to improve the approach and deployment.

13.8 Scoring the ADAR Categories

Performance frameworks score the ADAR categories using a special scoring matrix (Table 13.1). The approach is analyzed to determine its soundness in providing a clear rationale, defined processes, and a focus on stakeholder interests. It should have strong ties to the sustainability and the organization's efficacious strategy. The deployment is analyzed to determine whether it is systematic and effectively implemented. It is important to ask whether it.

Score	Approach	Deployment	Assessment and Refinement
0	No evidence that the approach has been considered and there is a reactive attitude to performance	Anecdotal information on how the approach has been deployed. No evidence that a deployment action plan has been used.	Anecdotal information on how the approach and deployment have been addressed. No results shown and no improvement activities in place.
1-2			
3-4			
5	Approach has a rationale and is proactive with defined processes. May not address strategy and recognition of stakeholder interests. No improvement from assessment and refinement.	Approach is applied to many areas and activities. Approach is becoming part of operations and planning with formal action plans and accountability. Evidence that results are caused by approach in some areas.	Positive trends in many areas. Results are comparable with benchmarked findings in many areas, Evidence that results are caused by the approach and deployment is subject to ad hoc review. Evidence that some improvements are implemented.
6-7			
8-9			
10	Approach is accepted as best practice and is benchmarked by other organizations seeking to improve, All items in the guidance are evident.	Approach is deployed to all areas and activities. Approach is totally integrated into normal operations and planning.	Results are clearly caused by the approach in all areas. There is a proactive system for regular review and improvement of the approach and deployment.

Source: Adapted from EFQM, EFQM excellence model, EFQM, Brussels, 2010

Table 13.1

Performance Scoring Matrix was conducted on time and in a structured way. The scoring of the approach and refinement is threefold, beginning with the measuring of the effectiveness and efficiency of the approach and deployment, and then learning and creativity, and improvement and innovation.

When scoring each ADAR category, the assessor should start by reading the information in the middle row (i.e., 5 points). If the evaluation is deemed to be better than that description, the assessor looks at the low and high side of the next higher row (i.e., 6-7 points). On the other hand, if the evaluation is deemed to be less positive than the middle row, the assessor looks to the wording in the next lower row (i.e., 3-4 points). The movement continues until the assessor is comfortable with the evaluation in the scoring matrix as a reasonable explanation of what was observed. The assessor scores each of the ADAR categories in order, from right to left in the scoring matrix. Typically, the deployment lags the approach, and the score is typically at least 1 point lower. The assessment and refinement lags the approach and the deployment, so the score is typically 1 point lower than the deployment score. It takes a little practice to use the scoring matrix.

Remember that the leadership is using the scoring sheet when preparing the approach, deployment, assessment, and refinement documents. Some organizations start with a modest approach in the range of 5 points. If successfully put into use, the approach will generally score between 4 and 6 points. The scores get higher when the organization has more experience with this process. As mentioned, there are typically up to six processes that are implemented as leading indicators, as found in the top section of the Porter value chain diagram. No organization is equally proficient in the ADAR of the six lead indicators. You may see some approaches in the 8-9 scoring range and some in the 4-5 scoring range. As the best practices improve, it becomes more difficult to get the same score as the year before with the same amount of effort. On the contrary, the organization must improve its ADAR methods to maintain its score as a result of the improvement in best practice.

13.9 Transparency, Accountability and Sustainability Performance

At the organization level, information and stories are transmitted to the parent company for inclusion in a sustainability report. When operating separately, the monitoring and measurement activities that take place at the organizational level let the leader know whether there are effective processes and efficient operations. Some of this data and information is shared within the stakeholder engagement program or with customers that request information.

No matter where the sustainability program is located, attention must be paid to the concepts of transparency and accountability. In any organization, *transparency* provides a sense of openness about decisions and activities that affect the environment, the community, and the economy, as well as a willingness to communicate this information in a clear, accurate, timely, honest, and complete manner. *Accountability* is all about being responsible for decisions and activities to the organization's governance, legal authorities, financial authorities, and more broadly, the stakeholders. The *performance* of the organization is measured relative to the achievement of its strategic, operational, and tactical objectives. Organizations seek levels of performance that deliver ever-improving value to all stakeholders, thereby contributing to organizational sustainability. The quest is always for effective processes, efficient operations, and efficacious strategy. Having examined the monitoring and measurement tasks, we will now explore some of the outcomes of these efforts, and perhaps discover even more sustainability measures or disclosures that need to be made to different stakeholders.

Transparency

In the practice of sustainability, an organization is expected to be transparent in its decisions and activities that have impacts on the environment society, or the economy. As such, a local organization is expected to disclose a clear, accurate, and complete manner, and to a reasonable and sufficient degree the policies, decisions, and activities for which it is responsible. This disclosure should include information on the known and likely impacts that the organization may have on the local environment, the people in the community, and its shared values.

Until the organization has secured its "social license to operate/' stakeholders may expect the organization's information to be readily available, directly accessible, and understandable to those who have been or may be affected in significant ways. Information should be timely and factual and presented in a clear and objective manner. This should enable the outside stakeholders and the organization to engage in discussions about the impact that title organization's decisions and activities have on their respective interests. Under the best of conditions, much of the disclosure takes place within an established stakeholder engagement process.

The principle of transparency does not require that proprietary information be included in the disclosures. Furthermore, transparency does not involve providing information that is privileged or would breach legal, commercial, security, or personal privacy obligations. Often, there is a contentious time in the process of stakeholder engagement when the organization has not built a sufficient level of trust in the view of the stakeholders. The information is used to determine the organization's performance until trust is established.

Many organizations find themselves in a situation where the more information that they provide to the stakeholders, the more information that the stakeholders may demand to have provided. This can be remedied by using a risk assessment method to examine the failure modes (i.e., the impacts) and find a way to address the root cause of the situation referred to as the "impact" so that the stakeholder engagement process can focus more on whether the organization is meeting its strategic objectives and whether these objectives will have positive effects for the stakeholders as well. Failure mode effects and analysis has been adapted to manage all three responsibilities of sustainability.

There are a number of other things an organization should consider when seeking to become more transparent:

- Explaining the purpose, nature, and location of its activities at the community level
- Identifying people with a controlling interest that are involved in the organization
- Manner in which decisions are made, implemented, and reviewed, including the definition of the roles, responsibilities, accountabilities, and authorities across the different functions in the organization
- Standards and criteria against which the organization evaluates its own performance relating to sustainability
- Performance on relevant and significant interests of the stakeholders in the area of sustainability
- Sources, amounts, and application of its funds
- Known and likely impacts of its decisions and activities on the stakeholders, society, the economy, and the environment
- Stakeholders and the criteria and procedures used to identify, select, and engage them

The use of such an extensive list would be difficult for most organizations at the community level. For large hierarchical organizations, people would have to be hired just for the purpose of fulfilling the demand for transparency in a sustainability program.

Accountability

In the practice of sustainability, an organization is expected to be accountable for its impacts on the environment, society, and the economy. This suggests that an organization should accept appropriate scrutiny and a duty to respond to this scrutiny. Sometimes this concept moves away from engagement with stakeholders and assumes that there will be watchdog organizations that are looking to see what organizations are creating impacts. Would not this definition be more consistent with the transparency definition if the accountability were to engage stakeholders directly and discuss the information that was provided in a transparent manner?

It is well accepted that accountability involves an obligation of the organization to be answerable to legal authorities with regard to laws and regulations. However, the concept of accountability is expanded by sustainability to include a similar obligation for an organization's overall impact of decisions and activities on the environment, society, and the economy to those affected by its decisions and activities, as well as to society in general.9 Accountability also includes accepting responsibility where wrongdoing has occurred, taking the appropriate measures to remedy the wrongdoing, and taking action to prevent it from happening again.

Many believe that organizations should base their behavior on standards, guidelines, or rules of conduct that are in accordance with accepted principles of doing the right thing or practicing good conduct in the context of specific situations, even when these situations are challenging. Finally, organizations are expected to respect, consider, and respond to the interests of their stakeholders. The process of engagement helps establish an understanding where both parties would be expected to do the same. This is one of the outcomes when the organization is granted its social licensees to operate. It is easy to see that we have a long way to go in how these very important principles are used to get parties to engage with each other just as the word is meant to convey.

13.10 Organizational Basis for Disclosures

An organization seeks to meet its strategic objectives in an uncertain world. Let us use a concept that is often used for businesses to look at how organizations seek to disclose information on what they are doing to achieve these objectives. There is a continuum in all organizations that move from the mission to strategic objectives, to strategy, to execution and the determination of the organization's performance. Each organization should pay attention to the "voice of the customer and stakeholder" in each step along the way, The outcomes of the well-executed continuum include engaged stakeholders (internal and external to the organization) and effective processes and efficient operations. Within a sustainability program, the internal and external performance is usually disclosed both within the organization and external to the organization. If there is an emphasis on engagement of stakeholders throughout the continuum, the disclosure of performance is generally not found to be contentious. It is rather a statement on how well the organization and stakeholders are engaged.

The economic disclosures come from the realization of the first principle of sustainability management:

Our organization exists to create and protect value for our members, employees, customers, and stakeholders.

Sustainability contributes to the demonstrable achievement of objectives and improvement of organizational performance.

The society perspective represents the successful realization of stakeholder engagement—to both the internal organization and the external stakeholders and society in general. There are different levels of engagement that the organization must navigate in this perspective:

- Identify stakeholders during the scanning of the internal and external operating environments
- Begin communicating with the stakeholders
- Seek engagement with the stakeholders
- Grow relationships with stakeholders
- Every organization has a broad range of stakeholders. The organization's operations can be divided into a number of processes that are important in the environmental perspective:
- **Develop and sustain the** organization's niche in important value chains
- **Produce** products and deliver services in an efficient manner
- **Distribute and deliver** products and services stakeholders (e.g.customers)
- **Manage** the organization's risks associated with these processes

The process and activity of the organization are focused on the effective and efficient conservation of resources used in services and products that can pose threats to the environment if the organization does not manage its operations, customers and stakeholders, and three responsibilities, and take advantage of innovation associated with its performance improvement.

The learning and growth perspective is clearly driven by the sustainability management principles as they are applied to the sustainability program. Many of the value chain illustrations benefit from the judicious application of these sustainability principles.

13.11 Context and Performance Measurement

When an organization has a sustainability program with an *inward-focused perspective,* it is dealing with stewardship of the three responsibilities of sustainability, value chain management, quality management, availability of people that can accept the organization's culture, and a system of management. There is a focus on efficiency, growth, financial structure, and other operational attributes. Much of the monitoring and measurement is focused on meeting its strategic objectives over the long term, and successful engagement with the stakeholders. Sustainability can be embedded in the way the organization operates every day.

When an organization has a sustainability program with an *outward-focused perspective,* it begins to demonstrate its awareness of how environmental, social, and economic factors affect the operation of the organization. There is a focus on meeting objectives by managing the positive and negative effects (i.e., opportunities and threats) of uncertainty. It will begin to quantify the threats and opportunities related to environmental, social, and economic factors. The organization will start to quantify the threats and opportunities related to its three sustainability responsibilities. This begins to demonstrate through stakeholder engagement that sustainability is part of the internal strategy and will lead to performance that recognizes both the internal and external context.

Trust is what sustainability disclosure is all about. Transparency and accountability help the organization establish credibility. They demonstrate the effectiveness of stakeholder engagement both to the internal organization and with external stakeholders. The organization begins to see transparency as allowing the will of the stakeholders to play its part in monitoring the trustworthiness (i.e. validity) of the sustainability disclosures. Organizations with an internal-only focus are much less likely to share information from the management of the internal context. The major disconnect between the three-responsibility performance and internally focused performance is the latter's focus on impacts and regulations, which are seen as a cost center instead of a value center. Many of the sustainability measures currently in use are not designed to optimize three-responsibility performance or to understand the long-term impacts of organizational decisions. Most of the metrics currently in use focus on one responsibility and are internally focused.

13.12 Materiality and Performance Measurement

The corporate sustainability practitioners use a sustainability management method referred to as "materiality." This is a financial term that is being applied to all the organization's nonfinancial metrics. The materiality matrices in use today have the external context (interest to the stakeholders) on the y-axis and the internal context (interest to the organization and its operations) on the x-axis.

In the materiality determination, the y-axis on the grid has one of the following labels:
- Importance to external stakeholders
- Community, neighborhood, or society concern

These concerns constitute the external context of the organization. The x-axis or the materiality plot consists of one of the following different labels:

- Likelihood of an impact to an organization
- Influence on the organization's objectives
- Current or potential impact
- Significance to the organization

These concerns constitute the internal context of the operation.

In order to engage with stakeholders and improve the operation, it seems to make more sense to discuss the uncertainty (both opportunities and threats) of the organization and how uncertainty is being addressed through the uncertainty assessment and response efforts, The metrics would include the lead indicators to show how management is dealing with the effects of uncertainty through the efforts of the people support activities.

Found in the top half of the value chain model, the lag indicators or the results of those efforts are reflected in the suppliers ,inputs, process, outputs and customers (SIPOC) diagram at the bottom half of the value chain model (See Figure 4.4). Just like the monitoring and measurement done with the process, it is best to select a few very important areas to focus on. By using the uncertainty assessment, an organization can talk about the approach to identify the effects of uncertainty and can then show how it plans to manage the significant opportunities and threats, along with the risk of achieving its strategic objective.

This is a more effective approach to sharing of sustainability information within the engagement of stakeholders process as long as the organization examines all its significant opportunities and threats, rather than selecting from an established list of sustainability results (i.e. lag indicators) and putting them on a materiality plot. The organization's reporting should involve presenting a clear picture of how dealing with the effects of uncertainty can help improve its ability to meet its strategic objectives. By focusing on the strategic objectives, it is possible to manage the expectations of the organization and drive the optimization of the results that are needed to demonstrate progress. Managing the results will involve balancing the response to the internal and external contexts by dealing with the significant opportunities and threats.

13.13 Designating the Lag Indicators

All organizations analyze and evaluate appropriate data and information from their monitoring and measurement activities. These results (lag indicators) are used to evaluate many of the following:

- Conformity of an organization's products and services
- Degree of customer satisfaction
- Performance and effectiveness of the system of management
- Degree to which the strategy is efficacious

- Effectiveness of actions taken to address the effects of uncertainty
- Performance of the value chain suppliers
- Need for improvement, innovation, and learning
- Organization may receive requests for specific results (i.e. lag indicators) from parent organizations as part of the sustainability reporting effort or from suppliers banks and other organizations that are dealt with on a regular basis. The requested results are not currently collected as a part of the monitoring and measurement effort; it is useful to engage the parties in a discussion of the process used to gather these results. The organization should seek to:
- Measure aspects of the value chain process that create value
- Measure the activity outcomes that set the organization apart (i.e., competitive advantage)
- Measure what other similar organizations are measuring since this ensures that focused metrics are harmonized
- However, the measures need to be mindful of stating the creation of value. The methods used by the organization to monitor and measure, analyze, and evaluate these results should ensure that
- The timing of monitoring and measurement is coordinated with the need for analysis and evaluation of the results
- The results of monitoring and measurement are reliable, reproducible, and traceable
- The analysis and evaluation are reliable and reproducible, enabling the organization to report trends
- Each of the lag indicators can be judged for *significance* on the basis of the following:
- Is the result important or significant to the organization?
- Is the result associated with an action plan already in use?
- Is the result regularly tracked with the organization's leaders following its trends?
- Does the organization actively benchmark this result with others?

Positive answers to these questions show that this process of tracking results is improved by the attention given to the performance management process.

By engaging external stakeholders in this process, it should be possible to provide them with results that are more useful while not creating an extra effort within the organization. The obvious exception to this is the information that is needed to measure the regulatory compliance, along with other similar contractual obligations.

What about the accountability associated with the engagement with other external stakeholders associated with a parent organization? There may be requests for results that are not routinely collected; it is important that these requests be discussed within the engagement process since an investment will be necessary to collect that information. The external stakeholder needs to understand the full mechanism of monitoring and measurement, while the organization needs to understand whether an interaction with external stakeholders requires such measurement. Within the organization, goals and action plans are set in the lowest levels of the operations. It is important to have activities where the people involved only have one or two goals. The success of the action plan is based on the ability of the people that work with a process to meet these goals. Remember that the lag indicators are the tracing measurements used to determine whether the goals are being met. It is important to keep score. The strategic objectives are achieved through successfully meeting the operational objectives. This process of requesting results is cascaded all the way to the bottom of the organization. Results must be kept at each level in the operations and then in the organization as a whole. Since the connection between levels is created at the initiation of the scoring dashboard, it is important that each level only views what is important to them. The leaders of the organization will manage the progress for achieving the strategic objectives and will communicate that information to the entire organization and external stakeholders—all at the appropriate time.

The results of the sustainability program can also be scored using the four attributes of lag indicators mentioned earlier. It is possible to score the 15 or 20 key performance indicators (KPIs) or other results and then aggregate those scores to a single lag indicator score. More information will be provided after looking at the lead indicators.

13.14 Designating the Lead Indicators

Based on the available performance frameworks, it is possible to create a number of leading indicators representing the support that people provide in the top half of the value chain model. Here is an example of these lead indicators:

- The leader embraces accountability for the organization's sustainable success.
- The organization's strategic plan is instrumental in mainstreaming sustainability.
- Engaged employees embrace sustainability as part of their daily work.
- Engaged stakeholders provide value through sense making and process improvement.
- The organization participates in partnerships when collaboration can further improve sustainability,

- A sustainable organization is created through effective processes and efficient operations and planning This helps secure support of the organizational strategy and supporting policies.
- People in the organization are encouraged and supported in developing their knowledge and capabilities.
- People are aligned, involved, and empowered to meet the strategic objectives and the Sustainability policy as part of what they do every day.
- People must communicate effectively throughout the organization.
- People are rewarded, recognized, and cared for within the organization.

13.15 External Stakeholder Engagement Process

The organization will identify its stakeholders in its process of scanning its external operating environment and seek to engage with them to help manage uncertainty in line with the organization's Sustainability program.

The organization will seek to obtain and maintain the social license to operate that is granted by the external stakeholders in the local community by sharing interests and building relationships.

The organization will design and tailor processes for building and managing customer and stakeholder relationships to suit markets with the aim of acquiring new customers, retaining existing customers, and enveloping new market opportunities in line with the organization's sustainability program.

Finally, the organization will measure customer satisfaction and loyalty; compare the results with those of the competitors and use the information to improve internal processes, products, and services; and deliver increasing value for customers, markets, and other external stakeholders.

13.16 Partnerships and Resources Process

Partners and suppliers are managed for sustainable benefit by building relationships based on mutual trust, respect, and openness.

Finances are managed to secure sustainable success by developing financial strategies to support the organization's Sustainability programs strategy.

Buildings, assets, infrastructure, materials, and natural resources are managed in a sustainable way.

Technology is managed by involving internal stakeholders and other stakeholders in the development and deployment of new technologies to maximize the benefits.

Information and knowledge are managed to support effective decision making and sense making, and to build the organization s capability to continually improve within its Sustainability process.

13.17 Using Effective Processes and Efficient Operations

Processes are designed and managed to optimize stakeholder value, clearly linking the outcome measures to the organization's strategic objectives.

Products and services are developed to create optimum value for the customer while taking into account any impact the products and services may have on environmental, social, and economic responsibilities in the sustain-ability program-Products and services are produced, delivered, and managed by involving people, customers, partners, and suppliers in optimizing the effectiveness and efficiency demanded by our sustainability program-Products and services are effectively promoted and marketed without making any claims that are not clearly supported by our sustainability program.

Customer relationships are managed and enhanced by informing them of our sustainability program to build and maintain an open dialogue based on openness, transparency, and trust.

Measuring Performance of the Lead and Lag Indicators

There is a reliable way to measure the performance of an organization that has been widely used around the world. It is often referred to as performance excellence. The way it scores the lead and lag indicators is presented below. The organization carefully gathers the data and information on each of the lead indicators, including documented information derived from the system of management, internal audits, management reviews, stakeholder engagement, and benchmarking efforts. Typically, a team of assessors will be trained on how to evaluate the information and score it using the scoring matrix. Everyone on the assessment team needs to be familiar with the information on approach, deployment, assessment, and refinement (ADAR) that is presented here in order to use the scoring matrix and review this data and information.

If the assessors score the components of each lead indicator, the scores are added to provide a score for each lead indicator. The scores of the lead indicators can be aggregated and divided by the number of indicators to provide a single lead indicator score. The score is usually adjusted for reporting on a 1000-point basis.

Next, the lag indicators are measured against results scoring matrix. The Baldrige scores are provided in the following results categories: "Products and Processes, "Customers," "Employees, Leadership, and Governance," and "Financial and Market. The European Foundation for Quality Management (EFQM) has four result categories: "People," "Customer," "Society," and "Key Performance." All the results in a category can be scored and aggregated as a score for that category. Independent KPIs without an assigned category can also be scored. Because scores have no units of measure associated with them, it is possible to aggregate all the scores and divide by the number of indicators included to produce a single score for the lag indicators, usually presented on a 1000-point basis.

The two scores can then be combined (one of the performance excellence programs combines them at 60% lead indicators and 40% lag indicators based on almost 30 years of experience) to give the sustainability program a single score This can be done on a quarterly, semiannual, or annual basis. This single performance can then be tracked over time to measure the continual improvement of the organization.

Improvement and Innovation:

Organizations need to meet their strategic objectives in an uncertain world. Improvement is essential for an organization to maintain its operational performance and react to changes in the organization's internal and external operating environments. As such, improvement is essential for an organization to exploit in order to maintain current levels of performance. It is a key part of the "act" component of the plan-do-check-act (PDCA) cycle—taking actions to continually improve.

External change is a driver for innovation. Changes in the organization's external operating environment could require innovation in order to address the interests of the stakeholders. An organization needs to identify the need for innovation and establish an effective innovation process.

Organizational learning includes both continual improvement of existing operations and significant change or innovation often leading to new objectives, products, and services. Through learning, an organization enhances, captures, and formulates the knowledge, skills, and experience of its members. This learning can be integrated into what is known as organizational wisdom, which is shared and used by the organization to support and enrich its improvement and innovation processes.

Organizations that are embedding sustainability should be able to balance and increase the satisfaction of the full range of stakeholders. These organizations need to continuously develop their capabilities to improve, innovate, and embed these activities into their products, processes, operational structures, a way of operating in their context, and system of management. The foundation for effective and efficient improvement and innovation processes is learning.

13.18 Continual Improvement

An organization defines its strategic objectives to seek improvement of processes and products, and services based on information it receives from the following activities:

- Monitoring, measurement, and analysis of feedback its full range stakeholders

- Monitoring, measurement, and analysis of its operations and supporting processes
- Internal audits and self-assessments
- Suggestions from stakeholders and partners
- Management reviews at the operational and strategic levels

It is also possible for continual improvement to be initiated through collecting data, analyzing information, setting operational and tactical objectives, and implementing corrective actions associated with any nonconformities in the system of management.

Continual improvement is a result of a set of recurring activities that are conducted to enhance the operational performance of an organization. Improvement activities can range from small-step, ongoing improvement to more important breakthrough efforts. An emphasis is placed on continual improvement in an organization through the setting of worker goals at the tactical level that helps meet the tactical objectives, thus beginning the feedback loop toward meeting the organization's strategic objectives.

The terms *continuous improvement* and *continual improvement* are frequently used interchangeably. The American Society for Quality is always reminding people that there is a difference. *Continual improvement* is a broader term referring to general processes of improvement and encompassing many different approaches, covering different areas at different times. *Continuous improvement* is a subset of continual improvement with a more specific focus on linear, incremental improvement within an existing process. Continual improvement is not limited to quality initiatives. Improvements can be made in organizational strategy, results, and customer, employee, supplier, and stakeholder relationships. It means "getting better all the time." Improvement is a result. It can only be claimed after there has been a beneficial change in an organization's performance.

Improvement can be effected reactively (e.g., corrective action), incrementally (e.g., continual improvement), by step change (breakthrough), or pro-actively (e.g., innovation). Improvements can be focused on a program (e.g., environmental management), in a process (e.g., resulting in a product or service), or in results. It is common for people to look for areas of under-performance or opportunities to improve that can be addressed by the practice of continual improvement. When an improvement project begins, it is possible to track, review, and audit the planning, implementation, completion, and results of these initiatives. To address these widespread improvement activities, the quality management system of operation has raised improvement to a *principle* seeking to create a quality culture that leads to

- Employing a consistent organization-wide approach to continual improvement

- Making continual improvement *of* products, services, processes, and systems an objective for every individual in the organization (i.e., embedded in the work)
- Providing people with training in the methods and tools of continual improvement
- Ensuring that people are competent to successfully promote and complete improvement projects
- Establishing goals to guide, and measurements to track, continual improvement
- Recognizing and acknowledging the improvements that result from these activities

In practical terms, some improvements take time to achieve. Some may require allocations for a budget or careful planning for a consistent rollout of the results. Plans for improvement should consider priorities and relative benefits and should allow for the monitoring of progress. Continual improvement of the organization's overall performance should be a strategic objective of the organization. It is widely believed that organizations that have an ongoing focus on improvement are successful in many of the ways that such success is measured.

The leaders of the organization need to ensure that continual improvement becomes established as part of the organization's culture through a number of directed efforts by

- Providing opportunities for the internal stakeholders to embed improvement in their work
- Providing the necessary resources for this to happen
- Recognizing and rewarding successes
- Continually seeking to improve the effectiveness and efficiency of the improvement process
- Breakthrough projects can be conducted using a combination of project management methods and approaches for the management of change while seeking to introduce these methods into the culture of the organization.

It might help to look at the basis for determining the maturity of an organization's continuous improvement process:

- *Level 1:* Improvement activities are ad hoc and based on customer or regulatory complaints,
- *Level* 2: Basic improvement processes based on corrective and preventive actions, are in place. The organization provides awareness for its members to help understand the concept and practice of continual improvement.
- Level 3: Improvements efforts can be demonstrated in most of the processes, products, and services of the organization. The focus of

the improvement process is aligned with the strategy and the strategic objectives. Recognition systems are in place for members that are generating strategically relevant improvements in their work. Continual improvement processes work at some levels of tin-organization and with its suppliers and partners.

- *Level 4:* Results generated from the improvement processes enhance the performance of the organization. The improvement processes are schematically reviewed. Improvement is applied to processes, products, services, organizational structures, the operating model, and the organization's system of management and supporting processes.
- *Level 5:* There is evidence of a strong relationship between improvement activities and the achievement of above-average performance for the organization determined in benchmarking activity. Improvement is embedded as a routing activity across the entire organization, as well as for its suppliers and partners. The focus is on improving the performance of the organization, including its ability to learn and change.

13.19 Innovation

Changes in the organization's internal and external operating environments may require innovation in order to address the interests of the stakeholders and continually improve its ability to meet its strategic objectives. Leaders should identify these changes and initiate the impetus for innovation through the refinement of the strategic plan so that it continues its efficacious ways. Innovation can be applied within the organization through changes in:

- Technology, product, or service do not only respond to the changing needs and interests of stakeholders, but also to anticipate potential changes in the organization's external operating environment and product and service life cycles
- Processes that improve cycle time, stability, and variation
- The organization itself through innovation in organizational structure and governance
- The organization's system of management that ensures the competitive advantage is maintained and new opportunities are realized when there are emerging changes in the organization context that are needed for this purpose. The resources that the organization should consider include:
  - i.   Creative ideas from all the engaged stakeholders
  - ii.   Results from management reviews of its strategy
  - iii. Results of activities to improve its system of management and supporting processes
  - iv.   Organization's performance

    v.   Results of assessments commissioned by the leaders

    vi.   Evaluating the threats, as well as the opportunities for innovation

    vii.   Internal skills and knowledge, as well as assistance from suppliers, partners, customers, and stakeholders

    viii.   Availability of scientific or technical information

    ix.   Products and services that are approaching the end of their productive time and the need for replacement product and service offerings

    x.   Availability of methods for innovation while considering both the opportunities and threats

The design, implementation, and management of processes for innovation can be influenced by

    i.   The urgency of the need for innovation

    ii.   Innovation objectives and their impacts on processes, products, services, and the organization's structure

    iii.   Understanding of the organization's current situation and current capabilities in relation to its innovation objectives

    iv.   The leader's commitment to innovation

    v.   Willingness to challenge the status quo

    vi.   Availability and emergence of new technologies

    vii.   Identification of the threats associated with innovation

    viii.   Successful exchange of knowledge and expertise internally and out side the organization

The timing for the introduction of an innovation process is usually a balance between the urgency with which it is needed and the resources available for affecting change. Innovation that is based on the organization's learning ability is essential for long-term success of its sustainability program. The organization should use a process that is in alignment with its sustainability strategy to prioritize innovations in conjunction with its uncertainty assessment process, innovation must be supported with the resources necessary or appropriate.

Innovation has become an imperative for any organization operating in the changing world. Since almost all organizations are dealing with frequent and significant changes, they need a defined process for developing and maintaining innovation across everything that they do every day.

It might help to look at the basis for determining the maturity of an organization's innovation process:

- *Level 1:* There is limited innovation. New products and services are introduced on an ad hoc basis with no planning for innovation in place.
- *Level 2:* Innovation activities are based on data concerning the needs and interests of customers and other stakeholders.

- *Level 3:* The innovation process for new processes, products, and services is able to identify changes in the organization's external operating environment in order to initiate the planning for innovation.
- *Level 4:* Innovations are prioritized using uncertainty assessment based on the balance between their urgency, the availability of resources, and the organization's strategy. Suppliers and partners are involved in the innovation processes. The effectiveness and efficiency of the innovation processes are assessed regularly as a part of the learning process (see the next section, "Organizational Learning"). Innovation is used to improve the way the organization operates.
- *Level 5:* Innovation activities anticipate possible changes in the external operating environment. Preventive plans are developed to avoid or minimize the identified opportunities and threats associated with the innovation activities. Innovation is applied to processes, products, services, organizational structures, the operating model, and the organization's system of management, as well as it supporting processes.

Many consider the embedding of sustainability into the organization an important part of the innovation process. The new work items for the organization may include

- Facilitate reflection on the consideration of sustainability interests in the innovation process
- Assess the level of embedding of these interests in the innovation process
- Identify points of vigilance, key points to facilitate the embedding of interests at each stage of the process
- Propose an evaluation system that is consistent with sustainability interests

Innovation is essential in today's world for all organizations. This globalized context implies that the implementation of partnerships and the sharing of a common vocabulary and practices have become essential to sustainable development.

13.20 Organizational Learning

The organization should encourage improvement and innovation through learning. In this way, the organization can enhance, capture, and formulate the knowledge, skills, and experience of its members, and integrate them into organizational wisdom, which can then be shared and used by the organization to foster its improvement and innovation processes.

Development of the organization's learning ability depends on its ability to collect information, analyze, and gain insights from various activities in its internal and external operating environments, as well as its ability to integrate the knowledge and thinking of its members into the value system of the organization.

To be successful, organizational learning is embedded in the way an organization operates, just like sustainability. This means that learning is

- Part of what members and employees do every day
- Practiced at personal, work unit, and organizational levels
- About solving problems at their source (i.e., root cause analysis)
- Focused on building and sharing knowledge and participation in sense making
- Driven by opportunities to create significant and meaningful change and to innovate

Learning is achieved through research, evaluation, and improvement cycles; ideas from employees and external stakeholders; sharing of best practices with partner organizations, and benchmarking. Learning contributes to the organization having a competitive advantage and sustainability.

Organizational learning can result in the following:

- Enhanced value to customers through new and improved products and services
- Development of new organizational and business opportunities
- Development of new, improved, or disruptive processes or business models
- Reduced errors, defects, wastes,
- Improved process responsiveness and the cycle time required for products and services
- Increases in resource productivity resulting in requirements for less resources as inputs
- Enhanced performance in fulfilling the organization's sustainability policy

Learning that integrates the capabilities of the organization and its members can be achieved by combining knowledge, thinking patterns, and behavior patterns of people with the values of the organization. This involves the consideration, of

- The organization's mission, vision, values, and strategy
- Supporting efforts in learning and demonstrating the leaders' involvement
- Stimulations of networking, connectivity, interactivity, and sharing of knowledge both inside and outside the organization
- Maintaining systems for learning and sharing of knowledge
- Recognizing, supporting, and rewarding the improvement of people's competence, through processes for learning and sharing of knowledge

- Appreciation of creativity, supporting the diversity of opinions of the different people in the organization

Rapid access to and use of this knowledge can enhance the organization's ability to manage and maintain its sustainability program.

It might help to look at the basis for determining the maturity of an organization's learning process

- *Level 1:* Some lessons are learned as a result of complaints and the difficulty of maintaining the social license to operate. Learning is on an individual basis without the sharing of knowledge.
- *Level 2:* Learning is generated in a reactive way from the systematic analysis of problems and other data. Processes exist for the sharing of information and knowledge,
- *Level 3:* There are planned activities, events, and forums for sharing information. A system is in place for recognizing positive results from suggestions or lessons learned. Learning is addressed in the strategy and policies.
- *Level 4:* Learning is recognized as a key process. Networking, connectivity, and interactivity are stimulated by leaders to share knowledge in the organization. Leaders support initiatives for learning and lead the process by example. The organization's learning ability integrates personal competence and organizational competence. Learning is fundamental to the improvement and innovation processes.
- *Level 5:* The culture of learning permits the taking of risks and the acceptance of failure, provided this leads to learning from the mistakes, threats, and opportunities that are identified. There are external engagements for the purpose of learning.

Essential questions for improvement, innovation, and learning can be found in the following box:

Questions:

1. What needs to be measured? What methods should be used for monitoring, measurement, analysis, and evaluation to ensure valid results?
2. What are the differences between lag and leading indicators? Explain with examples. Why does an organization monitor and measure to support its sustainability program? What is the difference between monitoring and measurement? Why do you need both? Describe the Performance framework and the ADAR process.
3. Why is it important for an organization to seek continual improvement of its processes, products, and services?
4. What is the key driving force that creates the impetus for an organization to improve its innovation process?

353

5. What is the relationship between improvement, innovation, and learning, and why is this relationship important to the development of effective learning? How do the lead indicators associated with an embedded sustainability program influence and predict the lag indicators that are selected for disclosure by the organization? How does the scoring method common to the major performance frameworks provide meaningful information for disclosure while protecting sensitive information associated with some of the sustainability initiatives?

Chapter 14

Developing Sustainability Metrics

Sustainable metrics and indices are measures of sustainability and attempt to quantify beyond the generic concept.

Sustainability reports need to be reframed as a metrics-driven transparency tool that can help businesses both internally and externally. Externally, reporting metrics will help to increase transparency for stakeholders and dispel any suspicions of green-washing. Internally, tracking and reporting sustainability metrics ensures results. Whether or not a company chooses to publish a sustainability report, everyone needs to track all of these metrics to achieve cost savings and reduced environmental impact. Without comprehensive internal reporting on metrics, companies do not have a clear picture of how they are performing over time. They lack the information they need to evaluate and improve their practices. And metrics-driven sustainability is smart business. By tracking and reporting data on internal resource usage and costs, companies can focus in on the green initiatives that will deliver the biggest bang for the buck. Recent surveys on green building and corporate spending both confirm that for most CEOs and facility managers alike, saving money on energy and other operating expenses is the number one reason why they pursue any green initiative. Comprehensive metrics that make the business case for sustainability initiatives help to build internal buy-in as well.

14.1 Comprehensive and Effective Metrics

Combine leading and lagging metrics. As explained earlier that lagging metrics measure past performance, and leading metrics help you to measure the future efforts/plans and drive lagging indicators. Example: GHG emissions vs. Reduction plans. Energy use is a lagging metric, but investment in energy conservation is a leading indicator.

Effective Indicator Sets/metrics must be:
- Mix of leading and lagging indicators
- Must be relevant and tied to system – one measure looking at all three responsibilities
- Must be representative, understandable, relevant, comparative, quantifiable, Time-based and normalized and unbiased and validated and SMART (Specific, Measurable, Achievable, Realistic/reliable and Time-bound).

Define ongoing and project-specific metrics: Some of your metrics should be tracked over the long term so that you can compare results year after year. Others may only be tracked for a short period to assess the effectiveness of an initiative. Many organizations, for example, should track greenhouse gas emissions year after year. Often, shorter-term metrics are tied to specific projects. For example, if you have a paper reduction goal for the year, you'll want to report against your baseline.

Draft your sustainability report before gathering data. It will save you a lot of wasted time if you mock up your sustainability report before you begin gathering data. Figure out what charts you'll want to include, including the chart type and legend. Do you just want to show solid waste or do you want stacked bars showing the different types of waste m the waste stream? Figuring this out now will ensure that the data you do gather can actually produce the information you want.

Review the Global Reporting Initiative (GRI). Large publicly traded corporations consider following the GRI.

Should targets be realistic or audacious?

There are two schools of thought about setting targets. The first is that goals or targets should be realistic and based on what is possible. For example, by upgrading lighting and improving insulation, we should expect to get X percent improvement, so that is our goal. The advantage of this approach is that it is often easier for people to support because they can envision the steps necessary to accomplish it. The downside is that it only usually achieves incremental improvements.

To reach full sustainability, though, a quantum leap in performance is necessary, so some long-term radical stretch goals are needed. If you choose 'zero waste' as a goal, for example, this will often generate more radical innovations than if you just strive for a 5 percent reduction in waste every year. You often can't get there just with incremental improvements. You have to rethink the design of the product or call into question your existing business model.

Radical stretch goals can lead to employee cynicism if the goals are not based on an external standard (e.g. the requirements of performance of the industry leader). But when presented well, radical stretch goals will often produce more significant improvements.

So think about your situation. Chances are, you'll need some of both. With an existing facility or manufacturing process, you'll probably mostly strive for incremental improvements. But whenever you design a new building or product or spend significant capital, this is the best time to set radical stretch goals.

Linking your metrics to your framework

Your sustainability framework(s) should influence your choice and organization of your metrics, as well as the type of work you do. Tables 14.1 list recommended metrics associated with two of the more common frameworks: The Natural Step and triple bottom line.

Common Metrics Tied to the Natural Step Framework

System Condition (In a sustainable society, nature is not subjected to systematically increasing):	Reworded as 4 sustainability Principles (To become a sustainable society we must eliminate our contributions to):	Possible Metrics
1. Substances extracted from the Earth's Crust	the systematic increase of concentrations of substances extracted from the Earth's crust (for example, heavy metals and fossil fuels)	Greenhouse gases; metric tonnes of CO2 equivalent (will necessarily include energy use by type); may be measured over a baseline such as Kyoto Protocol Metals; recycling rate and also recycled content
2. Human-made substances produced in society	the systematic increase of concentrations of substances produced by society (for example, plastics, dioxins, PCBs and DDT).	Persistent bio-accumulative toxins: volume used Cleaning products: percentage of green cleaning products
3. Productivity of nature/degradation by physical means	the systematic physical degradation of nature and natural processes (for example, over harvesting forests, destroying habitat and overfishing);	Natural resources: percentage from a certified sustainable source (including paper and other wood products, agricultural products, fish etc.)
4. Human Needs	Conditions that systematically undermine people's capacity to meet their basic human needs (eg, unsafe working conditions and not enough pay to live on)	Water: conservation measured by reduction of use over baseline. Employee satisfaction: measured by annual or biannual survey International labour standards: measured against SA 8000 or social audits

Table 14.1

Common Metrics tied to the triple bottom line

	Environmental	Social (system condition 4)	Economic
Internal	Energy conservation (system condition 1) Green Cleaning products (system condition 2) Water conservation (system condition 3) Green Purchasing (system condition 3)	Employee satisfaction Employee retention	Profitability Living wage
External	Greenhouse gases (system condition 1) Toxic emissions (system condition 2)	Labour practices of suppliers Customer satisfaction Charity(hours & dollar)	Sales of green/ certified products(system conditions 1 to 4), local purchases, Investment in sustainable businesses

Table 14.2

General Sustainability Metrics

Area	Metrics
Energy/climate	Greenhouse gases - climate neutral
Energy efficiency	greenhouse gas (GHG)/$
Materials	Percentage of purchases from sustainable source
Major processes	Percentage of employees paid living wage and benefits
New buildings/remodels qualifying for Leadership in Energy and Environmental Design (LEED)	Silver or better as a function of existing building/floor space
Products/services	Percentage of sales from sustainable/green products/services
'Residual products'/waste	Percentage solid waste diverted from landfill
Recycling rate	as a percentage of total waste
Strategic/supply chain partners	Percentage of major suppliers who have sustainability efforts underway
Community	Profits and time donated
Local sourcing	as a percentage of total purchases

Table 14.3

Examples of Specific Measurements for Tracking Sustainability

Category	Description	Specific Measurement to be tracked
Social	Actions that can affect all members of society; category includes poverty, violence, injustice, education, health care and labor and human rights	• Accidents per hour of work • Product safety ratings • Anticorruption practices • Performance on transparency in labelling, as determined by outside rating agencies
Economic	Actions that affect how humans meet their basic needs; category includes employment opportunities, access to health care and safe housing	• Revenue growth • Margin percentage • Revenue per employee • Reserves for future expenses • Customer satisfaction
Environmental	Actions that affect earth's ecology; category includes climate change, preservation of natural resources, carbon footprint and conservation	• Materials used by weight or volume per dollar of revenue • Percentage of recycled input materials used • Energy use per unit of revenue • Percentage of locally customized products or service offerings • Energy saved from conservation and efficiency • Total water use • Percentage and total volume of water recycled and used • Total direct and indirect greenhouse gas emissions by weight • Negative effects on biodiversity • Annual transportation cost
Cultural	Actions through which communities manifest identity and preserve and cultivate traditions and customs from generation to generation	• Visits to suppliers • Hours of training and development per employee per year • Percentage of products bought from within 500 miles of locations • Employee retention • Percentage of employees covered by excellent health care benefits • Cultural diversity of workforce • Distinctly cultural traditions

Werbach, Adam, "Strategy for Sustainability," 2009, Boston, Harvard University Review

Table14.4

14.2 Metrics based on Mission and Values

Mission statement	What they measure
To serve as a model that environmentally and socially responsible businesses can also be profitable.	Resource use (solid waste, wastewater, packaging) pesticides and toxics. Energy use and global warming for facility and supply chain Acidification
To educate consumers and proudest about the value of protecting the environment and of supporting family farmers and sustainable farming methods.	The proportion of organic sales organic acres supported a number of small dairy farms supported a proportion of milk from small family dairy farms price to farmer (milk)
To provide a healthy, productive and enjoyable workplace for all employees, with opportunities to gain new skills and advance personal career goals.	Lost workday illness/injury rate compensation, holidays, vacation turnover, etc. as compared with national benchmarks education and training; tuition reimbursement as compared with national benchmarks employee climate survey
To recognize our obligations to shareholders and lenders by providing an excellent return on their investment	Net sales, gross margin, share price, earnings before interest and taxes, net income, overheads, market share, earnings before interest, taxes, depreciation, and amortization.
To produce the very highest quality all natural and certified organic products that taste incredible	Quality checks, consumer complaints, shelf-life studies; chill cell compliance, sanitation.

Table 14.5

14.3 Metrics Based on Triple Bottom Line

	Environmental	Social	Financial
Internal	Energy reduction Waste reduction The proportion of sustainable materials in museum exhibits	Employee satisfaction Turnover	Net operating dollars Net margin percent. Museum attendance
External	CO_2 emission reduction	Scoring of sustainability content in educational programmes and exhibits	Scholarships

Table 14.6

Metrics worksheet (area: greenhouse gases and energy use)
How to Obtain the Data:

Metric	Ultimate Goal	Baseline	Sources of Data	What to track separately	How to Compute
Percentage reuction of GHG from baseline	80% reduction by 2050	Zero (10 million tonnes a year in 2008)	Electricity bills Fleet records Expense report Airline miles and personal autos)	Electricity Natural gas Auto airline Commuting	Use climate Trust factors to obtain CO_2 equiv-alent
Greenhouse gases by source				Building energy Process energy Transportation	

Table 14.7

14.4 Responsibility and Frequency for Sustainability Metrics

Who	What	When
Facility manager	Enters electricity and natural gas usage numbers in to spreadsheet	Monthly, when bills arrive
Human Resources Manager	Conducts and compiles commuting survey	Annually, in January
Clerical team	Tracks and reports on air miles of everyone in their respective departments, entering data in the spreadsheet	Monthly, after time sheets are submitted
Board of Directors	Decides on the amount of carbon offsets we can afford or need to purchase	Annually, in February
Sustainability Director/ Champion	Compiles data and produces report	Annually, in February finalizes metrics in March after board decisions on offsets

Table 14.8

14.5 A short list of critical metrics

The following list of sustainability metrics can be followed:

- *Climate neutral*: Show greenhouse gases at least for your own operations. You may also choose to also include impacts associated with employee commuting, embodied energies in major purchases and the customer use and disposal of your products.
- *Zero toxics*: Often the simplest way is to show volume of persistent bio-accumulative toxins purchased or in use. If you don't use any, the you can show the percentage of green cleaning products or landscaping products
- *Zero Waste*: Measure waste diverted from landfill and total waste (including recycling)
- *Sustainable natural resources*: If you use significant amount of natural resources (e.g. water, wood products, fish and agricultural produce), show the percentage coming from sustainable sources.
- *Social impact (Internal)*: Have some measure of the quality of work life. Depending upon your situation, this may be the percentage of employees paid a living wage, the ratio of highest to lowest paid worker, average wages by gender or race, employee satisfaction results, etc.
- *Social Impact (External)*: Depending on the nature of your business, this may include metrics related to international labour practices (e.g. SA 8000 results), local purchasing, and/or charitable endeavors (time and money donated).

14.6 Categories of Leading Indicators:

- Leadership/Social Responsibility
- Strategic planning
- Stakeholder engagement
- Employee involvement
- Knowledge management and innovation
- Process management and system

Examples of Leading Indicators:

- Put effective and visible systems and processes of sustainability leadership in place at all levels of the organization
- Use systems and processes to strategically plan for sustainable success and to align the sustainability program to its core purpose
- Use knowledge to support decision making, stimulate innovative thinking, and to ensure organizational success and sustainability
- Determine what stakeholders and markets want now and what they will want in the future

- Continuously improve products and services based on determinations of how they perform against stakeholder expectations.

Examples of Lagging Performance Indicators: Economic

- Economic performance
    - EC1: Direct economic value generated and distributed
    - EC2: Financial and other risks and opportunities due to climate change
    - EC3: Coverage of defined benefit plan obligations
    - EC4: Significant financial assistance from the government
- Market Presence
    - EC5: Ratios of standard entry wage compared to local minimum wages
    - EC6: Policy, practice, and proportion of spending on local suppliers
    - EC7: Procedures for hiring from the local community (incl. senior managers
- Indirect Economic Impacts
    - EC8: Infrastructure investment and services primarily for public benefits
    - EC9: Significant economic impacts and their extent

Examples of Performance Indicators: Environmental

- Materials
    - EN1: Materials used by weight and volume
    - EN2: Percentage of materials used that are recycled input materials
- Energy
    - EN3: Direct energy consumption by primary energy source (clean energy, fossil fuels)
    - EN4: Indirect energy consumption by primary source
    - EN5: Energy saved by conservation and efficiency
    - EN6: Initiatives to provide energy-efficient or renewable energy-based products and results (energy efficiency, renewable products)
    - EN7: Initiatives to reduce indirect energy consumption
- Water
    - EN8: Total water withdrawal by source
    - EN9: Water sources significantly affected by withdrawal of water
    - EN10: Percentage and volume of water recycled and reused
- Biodiversity
    - EN11: Land owned, leased, or managed in/near protected areas or areas of high biodiversity
    - EN12: Significant impacts on biodiversity in protected areas or areas of high biodiversity

- EN13: Habitats protected or restored
- EN14: Strategies, actions, and plans for managing impacts on biodiversity
- EN15: Number of species affected by operations
- Emissions, effluents, and wastes
  - EN16: Total direct and indirect greenhouse gas emissions
  - EN17: Other relevant Indirect Greenhouse Gas emissions
  - EN18: Initiatives to reduce greenhouse gas emissions and results
  - EN19: Emission of ozone-depleting substances
  - EN20: NO, SO, and other significant air emissions
  - EN21: Total water discharge by quality and destination
  - EN22: Waste by type and disposal method
  - EN23: Number and volume of significant spills
  - EN24: Hazardous waste (Basel convention) transported, imported, exported or treated
- Impacts of Products and Services
  - EN26: Initiatives to mitigate environmental impacts of products and services (Biodegradable products)
  - EN27: Percentage of products sold and their packaging that is recycled (Recycling, packaging)
- Compliance
  - EN28: Fines and non-monitory sanctions for noncompliance with environmental regulations
- Transport
  - EN29: Environmental impacts of transporting products, materials used and members of the workforce
- Overall
  - EN30: Total environmental protection expenditures and investments

Examples of Performance Indicators: Social

Labor Practices

- Employment
  - LA1: Workforce by employment type, contract, and region
  - LA2: Employment turnover by age group, gender, and region
  - LA3: Benefits to full-time employees not provided to temporary or part-time employees
- Labor and Management relations
  - LA4: Percentage of employees covered by collective bargaining agreements
  - LA5: Minimum notice period on significant operational changes

- Occupational health and safety
  - LA6: Percentage of workforce represented in management-worker H&S committees
  - LA7: Rates of injury, occupational disease, absenteeism, and work-related fatalities
  - LA8: Education and Risk Control programs for employees, their families, and community on serious diseases (Employee/family well-being)
- Training and education
  - LA10: Average hours of training per year per employee
  - LA11: Programs for skill management that supports continuous employability and managing career endings
  - LA12: Percentage of employees receiving regular performance reviews
- Diversity and Equal Opportunity
  - LA13: Breakdown of governance bodies and staff by gender, age, minority groups membership etc.
  - LA14: Ratio of basic salary of men and women by employment categories

Social -Human Rights

- Investment and Procurement
  - HR1: Percentage of significant investment agreements that have undergone human rights screening
  - HR2: Percentage of significant suppliers and contractors that have undergone human rights screening
  - HR3: Total hours of employee training on human rights relevant for operations
- Non-discrimination
  - HR4: Total number of incidents of discriminations and actions taken
- Freedom of Association and Collective Bargaining
  - HR5: Operations in which right to freedom of association and collective bargaining may be at significant risk
- Child labor
  - HR6: Operations with significant risk for incidents of child labor and measures taken
- Security practices
  - HR8: Percentage of security personnel trained in operationally relevant human rights aspects
- Indigenous Rights
  - HR9: Incidence of violations involving rights of indigenous people, OBCs, SCs and STs and actions taken.

Social –Society

- Community Impacts
  - SO1: Programs to assess and manage impacts of operations on communities (entering, operating, exiting) (community impact/ outreach)
- Corruption
  - SO2: Business units analyzed for risks related to corruption
  - SO3: Percentage of employees trained in organizations anti-corruption policies and procedures
  - SO4: Actions taken in response to incidents of corruption
- Public policy
  - SO5: Public policy positions and participation in public policy development and lobbying
  - SO6: Total value of contributions to political parties, politicians and related institutions
- Anti-competitive behavior
  - SO7: Legal actions for anti-competitive behavior, anti-trust and monopoly practices and their outcomes
- Compliance
  - SO8: Fines and non-monetary sanctions for non-compliance with laws and regulations

Social – Product Responsibility

- Customer health and safety
  - PR1: Life cycle stages in which H&S impacts are assessed for improvement
  - PR2: Incidents of non-compliance with regulations/codes concerning H&S impacts of products and services
- Product and service labelling
  - PR3: Type of product and service information required by procedure, percentage of products and services subject
  - PR4: Incidents of non-compliance with regulations/codes on product and service information and labeling
  - PR5: Practices related to customer satisfaction, including results of customer satisfaction surveys
- Marketing Communications
  - PR6: Programs to adhere to laws/standards/codes on marketing communications
  - PR7: Incidents of non-compliance with regulations/codes on marketing communications

- Customer Privacy
  - PR8: Substantiated complaints regarding breaches of customer privacy and losses of customer data
- Compliance
  - PR9: Fines for non-compliance with laws/regulations concerning provision and use of products and services

Questions:

1. Provide examples of Environmental, social and economic sustainability indicators

Chapter 15
Sustainability and Resilience

15.1 Strategic Purpose of Resilience

Knowledge about resilience is an important aspect of sustainability management. Resilience is the key for any business wanting to thrive in an ever-changing world. Climate change, economic crises and consumer trends are just some of the pitfalls that can dramatically affect the way an organization does business and survives. Organizational resilience is a company's ability to absorb and adapt to that unpredictability, while continuing to deliver on the objectives it is there to achieve. When studying sustainability, one learns about resilient ecosystems, resilient infrastructure, resilient individuals, resilient communities, and resilient value chains. There has been a growing body of knowledge on resilient organizations. Every day, the sustainability of an organization is tested in a world that constantly changes. Resilience is characterized as a strategic objective that is intended to help an organization survive and prosper. Highly resilient organizations are more adaptive, competitive, agile, and robust than less resilient organizations. These organizations can anticipate, prepare for, and respond and adapt to everything from minor disruptive events to acute shocks and other effects of uncertainty.

Resilience is a dynamic concept without a fixed endpoint. It is a never-ending journey that operates within a risk landscape and is conditioned by people, knowledge, and technology, as well as their interactions. Resilience is enhanced by integrating and coordinating the various operational programs that are commonly found in a sustainability program. Resilience is built not only within the organization, but also across its value chains and the larger web of interactions with other organizations.

15.2 Dimensions of Organizational Resilience

The study of resilient organizations suggests that this resilience is a function of three interdependent attributes:

- *Leadership and culture:* The adaptive capacity of the organization
- *Networks:* The ability to leverage the internal and external relation ships that have been developed
- *Change readiness:* The results of planning and direction that helped establish the ability of the organization to be change-ready

The core strategic purpose of resilience is to enable an organization to prepare itself to be able to survive and prosper. These purposes include the following:

- *Competitiveness:* Being able to continue past, recover, and learn from, and even capitalize on, opportunities presented by disruptions in a way that increases value that exceeds that of the competitors who are less resilient.
- *Coherence:* Aligns strategic objectives with operational resilience measures, such as the alignment of organizational silos to become more integrated and interoperable.
- *Efficiency and effectiveness:* Creating a framework to mesh together diverse components, while allocating resources to improve overall resilience.
- *Reputation: A* coherent framework helps build trust among the various operating units and outside allies helping to manage and enhance the organization's reputation.
- *Community resilience:* Organizational resilience helps to enhance community resilience by being able to provide assurance to stakeholders (e.g., regulators, government, customers, partners, and families) of its ability to provide vital products and services to the public in times of need.

Every organization is subject to the effects of uncertainty, and resilience thinking must embrace learning. Achieving favorable outcomes in the face of uncertainty requires creativity and innovation. An organization must be able to overcome strategic barriers to answer three basic questions after experiencing a disruptive event:

1. What have we learned?
2. How did we learn?
3. How can we integrate what we learned to understand complex, interrelated events; engage in reflective conversations; and cultivate shared aspirations for the future?

As organizations build on the past to expand their ability to act, they are developing new ranges of possible actions that will enable them to meet threats posed by disruptive events. They are even looking for opportunities that are often masked by the threats that demand immediate action. Responding without hesitancy to unexpected events is now considered an organizational perspective.

Organizational Foundations for Resilience

In order to build resilience into the operating structure of an organization, it is necessary to create a foundation that helps define the attitudes that affect organizational decisions and actions. This foundation should support the further development of resilience in organizations

Organizations need to have the ability to detect, assess, prevent, and respond to and recover from disruptive events and challenges of all types. However, organizational resilience differs significantly from the more traditional concepts of business continuity. Resilience seeks to create critical thinking, learning, and capabilities not just to bounce back (as with the practice of continuity), but also to bounce forward. This requires a combination of continuity and adaptability. The concept of adaptability includes a strong sense of social security where pre-established relationships, learning, flexibility, and a sense of a new normality are built into the organization so they can participate in this new focus on continuity and adaptability. After all, the organization is the basic building block of society.

It would be instructive to take the framework for sustainability and see how it can be adjusted and adapted to include this continuity-adaptability perspective.

A new standard, ISO 22316, *Security and resilience – Organizational resilience – Principles and attributes*, provides a framework to help organizations future-proof their business, detailing key principles, attributes and activities that have been agreed on by experts from all around the world.

15.3 Resilience in the Structural Operating Framework -Mission Statement and Strategic Objectives

The organization needs to have a common vision and purpose (included in the mission statement) for the future (included in the sustainability program). This enables the organization to build resilience into the strategic objectives so that challenge, change, and opportunity are assessed against the vision and mission and can be acted upon accordingly.

Leaders of the organization need to understand how the organization's, efficacious strategy as created for the sustainability program can address the needs of resilience development. This understanding starts with knowledge of the current level of resilience.

The organization needs to promote and create universally shared expectations that strengthen its resilience. This may be reflected in one of the strategic objectives. It can be accomplished by developing and promoting cultural norms that value openness in review and evaluation of the organization's resilience and how resilience will be addressed in the feedback loop to ensure that the strategic objectives are met in an uncertain world.

For resilience to be effective, the organization must be highly informed about its internal and external operating environments which is discussed earlier. There is a new focus on influences, factors, opportunities, and threats that might influence or compromise the organization's resilience. Sometimes, this is referred to as situational awareness in the resilience literature.

In addition to the scanning performed as part of the sustainability program, the organization needs to pay attention to methods designed to identify opportunities and threats that fall within the resilience realm:

- Identifying what values and purpose that it wants to protect and any threats that could impact those set of values and purpose
- Looking for emerging factors, along with the other scanning targets, to find new opportunities and threats affecting resilience
- Drawing upon sense making with the assistance of the stakeholder engagement process and the knowledge management function that is constantly examining opportunities and threats both from the context and from the literature
- Using uncertainty assessment and response to help puse the opportunity response to offset the threats before they contribute to the level of uncertainty that lies between the organization and its ability to meet its strategic objectives

It is also important to scan for the kinds of events that might be expected to *affect* the organization. An *event* is defined as an occurrence or change of a particular set of circumstances and the effect they can have on the organization. That event could have one or more occurrences and several causes. An event could also consist of something *not* happening. Some events do not have consequences and are referred to as a "near miss," "incident," or "close call." Environmental management and health and safety management have preparedness and emergency response programs to deal with events. There are also management programs for business continuity. All these programs will be included within the organization's response to resilience.

Stakeholders and the Social License to Operate

The stakeholders are also dealing with uncertainty. They understand how it can affect their organizations. They may not understand the power of resilience to help deal with uncertainty. Sharing information on resilience within the stakeholder engagement process will truly be valued. The ability of the stakeholders to assist with a lookout for change in the external operating environment and with sense making will provide the organization with their eagerness for advice on using the adaptive capacity of resilience By being transparent on the topic of resilience within the stakeholder engagement process. The organization can help build a greater level of trust. This should help the organization secure and maintain its social license to operate from the stakeholders.

Leadership and Commitment

Leaders need to consider the impact of their decisions and the sustainability strategy on an ongoing basis. They need to create a culture in which it is essential to consider resilience within the decision-making process. This culture of trust, openness, and innovation will empower the members or employees in an organization to assume ownership of and address uncertainty as the scans of the external operating environment note new opportunities and threats. Authority and responsibility are delegated by the leaders to the individuals best able to make the decision for the organization, both under normal operations and in crisis.

The leaders are responsible to lead the engagement with all stakeholders. The engagement process needs to foster transparency that enables information to be proactively shared across internal boundaries with independent partners and other key stakeholders.

Effective governance enables the organization to exploit the results of the uncertainty assessment and response. This should direct the internal stakeholders to make decisions in accordance with the knowledge and sense making that has been increasingly involved in assembling knowledge on resilience. Effective governance also enables the organization to encourage improvement and innovation to help continually improve the knowledge system. Resilience will succeed when the governance is coherent, transparent, and "forward-looking" and is embedded in a culture that is supportive of the continual enhancement of organizational resilience.

The leaders are accountable for ensuring that an appropriate level of resilience is achieved by the organization. This accountability will begin with a resilience policy that is embedded in the sustainability policy and coordinated with other important policies. This provides the leaders' commitment to all the outcomes important to the organization, including sustainability and resilience.

15.4 Managing Uncertainty and Organizational Planning

The organization needs to adapt to changing conditions as they emerge in the internal and external operating environments. The organization may choose to accept that some disruptions cannot be prevented and will still occur. It can plan, implement, test, and review a range of measures that will help the organization prepare to deal with disruption, possibly arising from unforeseen events or effectively adapt when the established plan discover what is being experienced. It is important that the people responsible for uncertainty assessment have open communications with the people responsible for operations, supporting processes and innovation, along with others that need to respond to the changes leadership must be involved in this effort to ensure the ability to take timely and informed actions to intercept and contain adverse events, both foreseen and unforeseen, such as to effectively respond to the uncertainty, including overwhelming crises that threaten the continued existence of the organization.

15.4.1 Organizational System of Operating

Perhaps the most important element of resilience is the need to develop coherence in the organization's operations that provide its products and services. When an organization has coherence, all its activities and processes work well together. Even simple organizations have a large number of processes to manage. The systems of management now have a harmonized structure that makes it easy to add various operational components in a freestyle, mix-and-match manner. On the other hand, it is also easy for an organization to remove operational elements that are no longer being used. Leaders need to align operational activities within this structure to achieve coherence and build resilience. To ensure that organizational silos support resilience, the organization needs to embed sustainability and risk management activities and operational disciplines as a means to drive integration. Knowledge also needs to be actively shared across internal organizational boundaries so that opportunities and threats are addressed coherently by all parts of the organization.

Sustainability and resilience draw on a large list of different processes. For many organizations, these processes are operated in silos. Leaders should find a way to create bridges between these operating silos through the use of the process approach.

It is important to understand the interdependencies with other organizations, including suppliers, contractors, outsourcers, and competitors. There is a greater need for interdependencies when developing resilience methods.

The organization needs to adapt its operations to changing conditions as they emerge in the internal and external operating environments. This may involve switching between preplanned responses to events and adaptive actions as necessary, and modifying its governance structures, operations, and behaviors to adjust to new conditions. The planning for the operations focuses on normal situations. There must be a link between the uncertainty assessment and response efforts in the planning and emergency planning for abnormal events in the operations. This will allow the organization to respond to change in a resourceful manner as the support processes help operations adjust to the new conditions.

In order to strengthen the operations of the organization, specific measures need to be implemented to address disruptive events, emergent risks, and changes in the external operating environment. This can be addressed by ensuring that the employees understand the importance of considering resilience during decision making and other instances of change management. All employees may need to take actions to prevent or reduce the likelihood of disruptive events or disruption to protect people, physical assets, financial value, reputation, and social capital.

15.4.2 VUCA (Volatility, Uncertainty, Complexity, and Ambiguity)

To help meet its objectives in an uncertain world all operations of the organization should consider VUCA (Volatility, uncertainty, complexity, and Ambiguity) which are potential risks to the operations.

For resilience is a never-ending journey that uses risk management focus an organization – its people, knowledge, technology, finance, sense making and decision making which will help to survive and thrive in turbulent times. If we do not adapt to changes in the external context, it will not meet their objectives. By creating an organization that is adaptable, competitive, agile and robust, we are creating its ability to anticipate, prepare for, respond and adapt to sudden and gradual change in its external environment (context) including with respect to community satisfaction and to obtain Social License to Operate.

Volatility

Volatility refers to the propensity for changing from one state to another. Under certain conditions, volatile materials can dangerously explode, changing rapidly from stable to disordered. This provides another implication that volatile conditions are dangerous conditions.

Another example of volatility is found in financial markets, and it the concept of volatility expresses the rate and amount of change from buying to selling and the changing interest (in terms of numbers of contracts/ shares) in any given market.

The interesting thing about volatility is that even though it might represent danger, it can also represent opportunity. Let's return to the financial market situation: many market traders make excellent money by trading on volatility (making an informed bet on the movement of a financial instrument) such as trading options on a company that is making a scheduled earnings announcement. The point is this: volatility is a good if you are seeking opportunities and bad if you like predictability.

Uncertainty

Uncertainty refers to the lack of specific information, which can be found by answering specific questions. Asking "What is the probability that it will rain today?" is a question that is an attempt to characterize uncertainty.

Complexity

Complexity refers to the number of components, the relationships between the components. The normal layperson's usage of the complexity tends to oversimplify the scope of practical problems facing leaders in organizations. Complexity differs from "complicated." A complicated issue can be understood by analysis and investigation beforehand.

Ambiguity

Ambiguous language is language that can be interpreted differently. Ambiguity is a cause of stress for many people (especially those who work in well-structured organizations) as the disorder implied by ambiguity is not comfortable. People tend to avoid, ignore, or minimize ambiguity.

VUCA is a condition that calls for questions — lots of them. Penetrating questions that ferret out nuance. Challenging questions that stimulate differing views and debate. Open-ended questions that fuel imagination. Analytical questions that distinguish what you think from what you know. The only thing you know with certainty about your strategy is that it's wrong. Persistent probing will help you discern if it's off by 5 percent or 95 percent before events swiftly reveal the answer to you. Agility is critical because strategic adjustments must be made continually.

15.4.3 Organizational Supporting Operations

Organizations need people who are competent in resilience and adaptability through education, training, and experience to develop and implement uncertainty assessment and business continuity plans. Employees need to be able to identify significant threats and opportunities associated with their work and to apply procedures to reduce the consequences of a disruptive event. Because many organizations will not experience major disruptions, experience can be achieved through exercise and rehearsed drills. The exercises need to be modified regularly to take into account new information in the knowledge management system. However, organizations and their members must be able and willing to adapt to change in order to become resilient. When a significant disturbance strikes, continuity plans may need to be radically adapted to reflect the new circumstances. In some cases, the business continuity plans will need to be discarded to ensure that appropriate and considered action is taken.

The organization needs to create the means, incentives, and imperatives to communicate information on how resilience is a unifying factor in the organization's system of management. These messages will create a need for engaged employees and outside stakeholders who want to know more. Changes associated with resilience will lead to collaboration between those involved in these stakeholder engagements, as well as collaboration across the value chain and even among competitors.

The importance of building adaptive capacity must be included in the awareness program that is operated by the supporting operations. They need to disseminate and oversee the implementation of good practice for dealing with resilience identified from within and outside of the organization. It is useful to have an effort to share information on errors, failures, and mistakes in a transparent manner so that all the internal stakeholders are aware and learn how to avoid these issues. Many organizations share information through trade and professional associations to gain valuable lessons on how to deal with uncertainty and improve operations. This activity helps all organizations improve. Finally, the adaptive capacity can be improved by developing the internal stakeholders to get involved in the innovation process and to know that there is a need to be flexible during times of change.

15.4.4 Resilience in Organizational Performance Management

The organization needs to include efforts to address resilience when it audits its system of operation in a way that demonstrates the efficacy of the program. The resilience measures need to be tied to the capacity of people to learn and adapt when required. This information should inform the organization understanding of its resilience capability and may be used to prompt strategic change to further enhance how resilience will drive strategic change. As part of these efforts, the organization should verify that it is complying with legal and regulatory obligations.

Monitoring and Measurement of Performance

The organization must define the transparency and levels of accountability by which individual and collective decisions and actions on resilience are related to the norms, expectations, and obligations of the organization, its partners, and its stakeholders. There needs to be a means of measuring the performance of the resilience efforts within the framework of measuring the normal operations, products, and services.

- There should be a self-assessment and maturity matrix for resilience. This would enable the leaders of the organization to determine the level of resilience that is already in place and how new efforts to enhance resilience are leading to an increase in resilience maturity. Toeffect this assessment, the organization should identify. What needs to be monitored and measured
- The methods for monitoring, measurement, analysis, and evaluation, as applicable, to ensure valid results
- How to provide a continuous assessment of resilience

- The thresholds at which the output from measurements will be considered acceptable
- How measurement and monitoring arrangements will work along side, support, or integrate into existing monitoring processes
- How the results from monitoring and measurement will be analyzed and evaluated

The organization needs to understand what evidence it requires to support its assessment of resilience and ensure there is an evaluation process that is developed to support the evidence.

Based on the Case Study No.2, the following maturity matrix is presented:

15.5 Maturity of the Sustainability Program: Conducting Self-Assessment

Approach to self-assessment should be comprehensive and systematic review of the organization activities and its sustainability performance in relation to its degree of maturity. The results of the monitoring and measurement should be input to the self-assessment.

Approach to Maturity Plot:

Upon completion of self-assessment done in Chapter 5, DKCCDC (organization in Case Study No2), can decide how to characterize the five maturity levels as follows:

1. Beginner 2. Proactive 3. Flexible 4. Innovative 5. Sustainable or level 1 to 5 can be used.

These are used to identify the maturity level for each of the organization's individual structural levels/elements. For DKCCDC to start at level 1 and progress to the higher maturity levels to maximum 5 is more appropriate as it addresses DKCCDC maturity aspects better.

Maturity Spider Matrix for DKCCDC:

The maturity spider matrix of DKCCDC is as follows which visually reflects the maturity of various elements for sustainability

Organization and setting responsible objectives	3
Understanding the internal and external context	2
Engaging with stakeholders and maintaining the social license to operate	3
Governance and leadership –sustainability policy	2
Risk Assessment	2
Resources and Operating System	3
Sustainability/Financial	1
Value Chain Model to Scope Measurement	1
Monitoring and Measurement	3
Transparency and accountability	2
Maturity process	1
Improvement and Innovation	4

Note: 5 being the most matured whereas 1 being least matured

Questions:

1. Describe the purpose and attributes of resilience
2. Discuss the dimensions of organizational resilience

Chapter 16
Sustainability Marketing

16.1 What is Sustainability Marketing?

Sustainability marketing also referred to as green marketing, is when a company focuses social and environmental investments as a marketing strategy. Companies are often criticized for waste, price markups, and misleading advertising. To counteract this type of publicity, more companies are turning to sustainability marketing. Since conventional marketing is considered mainly responsible for continuously increasing consumption, the goal of sustainable marketing is to promote sustainable consumer behaviour and offer suitable products, with the aim of economic, social and environmental sustainability. Green and environmental marketing emerged due to increasing concerns of consumers for the environment. Sustainable marketing is a holistic approach. A company's mission and vision has to support sustainable marketing, which can be found in the core values of a company. Designing, producing and delivering a sustainable product is not only the responsibility of the marketing department but requires the collaboration between all departments in a company. Otherwise, a company cannot be truly sustainable. Furthermore, consumers increasingly expect not only the company to be sustainable but the whole supply chain. Many companies outsource production to developing countries, which legally frees them of any responsibility. However, in some of these countries, child labour and sweatshops are common practice, which reflects badly on the company. The aim of sustainable marketing is to add value to the consumer and satisfy the customer's wants and needs but in a sustainable way. Therefore, sustainable marketing can be defined as a holistic approach with the aim of satisfying the wants and needs of the customers while putting equal emphasis on environmental and social issues, thus generating profit in a responsible way. In order for sustainable marketing to be successful, consumer behaviour and consumption patterns have to be reconsidered.

Societal Marketing:

Social marketing is the use of marketing theory, skills and practices to achieve social change. It has the primary goal of achieving "social good." It is a principle of sustainable marketing that holds a company should make marketing decisions by considering consumers' wants, the company's requirements, consumers' long-run interests, and society's long-run interests.

Societal marketing is a concept in marketing that emphasizes social consciousness as part of the overall marketing plan. Societal marketing is when a company markets a product not only with consumer and company needs in mind but also the long-term well being of society as a whole and that is true example of sustainable marketing. Companies that produce effective social marketing campaigns incorporate social and ethical considerations into the marketing plan. There are many ways a company can accomplish this goal.

Societal Marketing Purpose and Strategy

The purpose of societal marketing is for a company to meet its needs and the needs of a consumer while considering the long-term good of society. In this type of marketing, a company uses its socially conscious stance as a way to attract consumers who may appreciate the company's desire to market its products with consideration for society. As a result, the company's concern for society, seemingly over profit, positions the company in a favorable light and may help sell more products.

Consumer Health

Marketing campaigns that emphasize consumer health are campaigns that fall into the societal marketing strategy. Companies that market organic ingredients or no chemicals or additives in their products consider consumer health in making their products. This concern for consumer health becomes a strong point in the marketing process. Products that place a high value on consumer health fulfill the societal marketing criteria of meeting consumer needs, company needs and the long-term benefit of society or its members. Labelling on Cigarette package that smoking is dangerous for health is another example.

Eco-Friendly Marketing

Companies that place an emphasis on recycled products and organic products that aren't going to damage the ozone layer fall under the societal marketing strategy. Companies that make products from recycled materials can market themselves as a company concerned about the long-term impact on society. This doesn't just apply to the materials used for producing products. Some companies market themselves as "green" and emphasize that it uses all recycled products in day-to-day operation of the business, as well. Bodyshop do not produce any product with animal products and bans testing on animals and enforces this in its supply chain too.

Supporting Farms and Local Business

Companies that don't import raw materials practice a more contained form of societal marketing by marketing products made with materials obtained from local sources. This type of marketing takes into account the well-being of a local social structure. A company that purchases raw materials from local farmers or other businesses can market its products using this fact as a key part of its marketing strategy.

16.2 The Sustainability Marketing Matrix

The marketing mix, of four Ps broadly details the activities the marketing manager needs to consider to achieve the organization's desired market offering: product, price, promotion and place which are discussed more in detail below. Sustainability challenges include: altering the way things are done, that is, the way value (harm) is created; clearly demonstrating to stakeholders the firm's sustainability stance and values; collaborating with other individuals and organizations to achieve sustainability-related synergies, and ensuring employees and customers are included and supportive of the drive toward greater sustainability. These challenges are addressed through, respectively, processes, physical evidence, partnerships, and participants. They are added to the traditional four Ps to expand our understanding of what needs to be in a more sustainability-relevant marketing mix, and then these 8 elements are cross-referenced against the TBL's (Triple Bottom Line) planet, people and profitability measurements to form the Sustainability Marketing Matrix. Before discussing the TBL, we might draw on services marketing explanations in explaining these additional mix elements.

Process: describes how the service is assembled, the 'actual procedures, mechanisms, and flow of activities by which the service is delivered – the service delivery and operating systems.'

Physical evidence: refers to the tangible clues that assist consumers' evaluations of products. In service contexts, such evidence might include elements of design and furnishing, employee appearance, and communications. Manufactured products might make use of evidence as product packaging and labelling information, distribution, e.g. use of low-carbon transportation modes, and architectural design (passive building design, solar-energy cells). Walmart, for example, planned to generate solar energy at more than 130 of its Californian stores by 2012. When complete, this solar commitment was expected to generate up to 70 million kilowatt hours of clean, renewable energy per year, the equivalent of powering more than 5,400 homes; avoid producing more than 21,700 metric tons of carbon dioxide emissions per year, the equivalent of taking approximately 4,100 cars off the road; and provide 20 to 30 percent of each facility's total electric needs.

Partnership: refers to the cooperative efforts of sustainability outcome-enabling individuals and organizations in the realization that one organization cannot stand alone in the struggle to achieve sustainable development. Productive partnerships include employees and the organization's customers, captured under participants, as described below, and other stakeholders and even competitor organizations. Firms' partnering with universities' research centres to innovate around sustainability performance metrics is an obvious choice. The concept of partnership is also important in instances of co-production, which, in terms of service-dominant logic, is a potentially significant market.

Participants: include 'all human actors who play a part in service delivery and thus influence the buyer's perceptions: namely the firm's personnel, the customer, and other customers in the service environment.' This element highlights the role of human resource management and customer management, as key ingredients in the service offering. For sustainability marketing, employees and customers are equally important. Employees should be committed to the sustainability ethos, and be committed to continuous sustainability performance improvement. Global carpet tile manufacturer, Interface, for example, is, 'creating a culture defined by engaged employees with a shared vision for the sustainable business. The inspired employees are taking the mission outside the company walls, improving the communities and redefining how business should be done.' Customers too can be included in continuous-improvement efforts and suggestion systems. Customers are not merely targeted to consume the outputs of the organization in the general marketing sense, but are also to be included in the co-production of sustainability achievements as much as possible through, for example, product use, servicing and disposal, recycling, and future product purchase. Each of these additional ingredients can and needs to be effectively managed by the marketing manager in the pursuit of sustainability outcomes. The inclusion of participants, physical evidence, process, and partnership is recognition that the traditional sense of the marketing mix, that is, that which is controllable by the organization, must be seen more comprehensively. Each of these, now eight, marketing mix elements can be managed against assigned sustainability performance indicators by simply cross-referencing each mix element against the TBL's pillars, Planet, People, and Profit, to form the Sustainability Marketing Matrix. The purpose of this matrix is to raise the following questions:

- Planet: How does our (marketing mix element) make optimal use of environmental resources, maintain essential ecological processes and help to conserve natural heritage and biodiversity?
- People: How does our (marketing mix element) demonstrate respect for individuals and the socio-cultural authenticity of communities? and

- Profitability: How does our (marketing mix element) ensure our viable, long-term economic operations, and provide long-term socioeconomic benefits to all stakeholders that are fairly distributed, including stable employment and income-earning opportunities to communities

The Sustainability Marketing Mix

Marketing Mix Element	Sustainability Consideration
Product	Is it sustainable? Impacts of its use & disposal, social and environmental impact
Price	Cost of production, social and environmental costs, cost savings, eco-efficiency
Place	Social and eco aspects of the distribution channel, minimize impacts
Promotion	sustainability claims encourage sustainable behavior, impact of marketing methods, sustainability report for accountability and trust
Physical Evidence	Avoid unnecessary use of physical evidence, use eco-friendly materials
People/ participants	Treat them fairly, ethical practices internally, uphold international laws
Process	Designed to respect and enhance natural and HR, reduce impacts along the process
Partnership	Collaboration among stakeholders such as customers, employees, competitors and other stakeholders towards sustainable consumption and promotion of sustainable behavior

Table 16.1

Another model that can be looked at is from customer's perspective whereas traditionally, marketing has 4 elements namely, Product, Price, Place, and Promotion which represent the seller's viewpoints and offer opportunities to influence consumers. By contrast, Lauterborn (1990) has developed the 4Cs, namely, - customer solution, customer cost, customer convenience and customer communication - which represent the consumers' view of the market mix. Here in below, both the traditional and customer's view is presented.

The 4P's are converted to 4C's to include sustainability criteria into a marketing strategy.

Traditional Sustainability		Sustainability Marketing Mix
Product		CustomerSolution
Price	Transformation	Customer Price
Place	→	Convenience
Promotion		Communication

Table 16.2

Product: No product can have zero impact on the environment. Life-Cycle-Assessment (LCA) is a tool that helps companies to analyze the environmental impact of a product during its life. The LCA of a product from cradle-to-grave is shown below:

Raw Material Extraction → Processing & Production → Packaging → Distribution → Product Use → Disposal → Recycle → Disposal

The starting point is to source depleting raw materials more efficiently or even use recycled materials as input. However, if raw materials are needed, it is important that they are sourced from sustainable sources. One such sustainable source is Forest Stewardship Council (FSC) certified wood, which comes from sustainably managed forests but also protects the right of the workers and indigenous populations . The production process itself is energy-efficient and minimizes emissions. A further step toward sustainability is the use of renewable energies instead of conventional energy sources. Another side effect of production is waste. Resource efficiency reduces waste, and the remaining waste can often be useful in some other way, which saves waste disposal cost. An increasingly important role plays the packaging of a product. More and more packaging is made of recyclable material. Smaller packaging has the advantage that increased freights reduce the number of shipments.

From the customer's solutions perspective, a product should offer a complete package to consumers, which satisfies their wants and needs, provides a solution to their problem while being sustainable in use and disposal. The environmental component focuses on energy-efficiency and durability. For instance, energy-efficient cars and home appliances offer consumers personal benefits in the form of reduced electricity bills and gas costs. On the other hand, durability has declined, and instead products become more easily obsolete, either because they are unfashionable, or their usability is limited on purpose. Planned obsolescence needs to be reversed and products' lifetimes need to be lengthened again. Besides environmentally-friendliness, products have to be safe to use for the customers and pose no health threats. At the end of the product's lifecycle, the aim is that products are recyclable but at least should not be dangerous when ending up in a landfill. Increasingly important is the take-back of products. Partly, companies have already implemented reverse logistics, which can be applied to packaging, used products and other materials which are then reused in some way. This is a step towards closed supply loops and cradle-to-cradle. All this comes at a price, which has often been higher than that of conventional products and is a major decision-making factor for customers. However, pricing of conventional products has to be rethought in terms of externalities and depleting raw materials, as well as how to price sustainable products accurately.

3.5.2 **Price:** Often the price of a product can make or break a purchase. Prices are not only what customers pay but can communicate quality or exclusivity to consumers, be part of market segmentation, reflect demand and supply of products, be part of competitiveness and include costs of production and profit margin. However, environmental and social costs caused by production are usually not included in the end price. Instead, these are treated as externalities, which are costs that are shifted on to society. Internalized costs would take these costs into account, though hardly any producer internalizes costs on a voluntary basis. Sustainable pricing is affected by many factors, and different strategies can be applied. We will look at value- and cost-based pricing. Consumers tend to believe that sustainable products are more expensive. This is usually a misconception which might still stem from the times of green/environmental marketing. This is not to say that sustainable products cannot have a higher price compared to conventional products. However, the question is if those higher prices are a mark-up for sustainability or have another reason. Premium prices often reflect pricing strategies but also production costs can be behind higher prices. Value-based pricing looks less at costs of production and instead of how much the consumers are willing to pay for a product, based on the perceived value. Premium prices can be based solely on the fact that the production process is sustainable, which usually aims at a niche market willing to pay more for sustainably manufactured products. As mentioned before, this does not appeal to the bulk of the market because there is a value-action gap towards sustainable products. If prices are higher than those for competitors' products but with the same features, customers inevitably choose the competitors' lower prices products. Therefore, higher prices are more sensible when the product excels in performance or quality or some other way, such as energy saving light bulbs which not only lower energy costs but have a considerably longer lifetime. Value-based pricing does not necessarily mean premium prices but depends on the business' strategy. On the other hand, cost-based pricing takes the costs of production into account and adds a profit margin to calculate the end price. Higher prices based on cost-based pricing can stem from high costs due to change towards sustainable production processes, initial low production volumes or internalizing costs. Sustainable production processes usually pay off in the long-term because they lower costs over time, which then allows the reduction of prices. However, the costs for the consumers include more than just the purchase price. A survey in Finland shows that the price is the most important evaluation criteria, even if a product can bring in long-term savings.

Place: One aspect of the total customer costs is the distribution intensity and convenience. For customers, it is important that a product is easily available but distribution, retail stores and the purchase of products have environmental impacts as well which have to be considered. Products need to be conveniently available for consumers to purchase. Sustainable products do not only have to be at the right place, at the right time but also the impacts of their distribution have to be taken into account. Distribution's main environmental impacts are packaging, waste, emissions, and use of fuel. How much fuel is used depends on where the product is manufactured, purchased and used. Due to globalization these distances have grown, which can bring products halfway around the world. It is likely that production, distribution, and consumption will become partly more local again, to shorten distances and reduce fuel consumption. More fuel-efficient and low emission trucks can address two issues at the same time. Tesla car is an example of that. Another factor concerning the environment is the mode of transportation. Air freight has by far the highest environmental impact in terms of greenhouse gas emissions, followed by road transport. However, air freight is the least used mode of transport due to costs, whereas road transport is mostly responsible for inland transport. Whenever possible a shift from air to sea for international transports and from the road to rail for inland transports would help to reduce emissions. In recent years, retailers have become more interested in making their stores more sustainable. Through energy-efficient fridges, freezers and lightning retailers can save costs, but they also address water efficiency and waste reduction. However, retailers' role goes beyond these efforts and are responsible for supplying sustainable products to customers. Retailers decide whether or not sustainable products get shelf space. It could be said that they act as 'gatekeepers' between producers and consumers. Accessibility and availability of products in major retail stores and online retailers is indispensable to be successful with the mass market. Although customers would be interested in buying sustainable products, low availability would prevent most from doing so. For that reason, eco-oriented stores emerged in the 1980s and 1990s, to supply a niche market with sustainably-oriented products so that retailers have the possibility to educate their consumers about sustainable products and offer return systems for certain materials. In many countries, the prices at the shelves of sustainable product are labelled 'organic,' 'environmentally-friendly' or 'fair.' Furthermore, organic vegetables and fruits have their own corner in the vegetable and fruit section, which is indicated by a big sign reading 'organic.' Used batteries can be disposed of in stores which sell batteries. Although specialized eco-stores offer a great opportunity for niche products and market entries, sustainable marketers have to aim at conventional market channels to reach the biggest possible market. Additionally, big retailers are able to provide products at a lower price than eco-stores. Even when sustainable products are available in supermarkets, companies need to communicate their products and services to the consumers, as well as educate them about sustainability.

Promotion: Marketers have been faced with environmental and social criticism over the years. Marketing is, at least partly, regarded as responsible for the current condition the planet is in, by constantly creating demand and encouraging consumption. Social criticism involves creating unrealistic desires and images of people, as well as targeting children. Therefore, sustainable marketers have the difficult task of communicating their sustainability agenda to consumers, without attracting the same criticism. Sustainable marketing communication is about communicating solutions products have to offer to consumers as well as communicating to all stakeholders about one's company. The objectives of sustainable marketing communication can be numerous and are as follows: • Raising the mass market's awareness of sustainable products. Coverage of sustainability in the media, such as reports about climate change or endangered species, additionally helps to create awareness. Informing about the product or company. Information should be clear and easily understandable to avoid information overload and instead help to compare products. Company information furthers transparency. • Reminding consumers either about the product itself, sustainable use or post-use behaviour, such as recycling or take back possibilities. • Persuading consumers to purchase sustainable products or services. This can mean to try a new product or a change of brand for the consumer. • Rewarding customers for buying a product, engaging with the company or other behaviours which motivates and helps to build customer loyalty. In order to achieve one or more of these objectives, the right promotion mix out of advertising, personal selling, direct marketing, sales promotion, e-marketing and PR has to be found. All of these marketing methods are open to sustainable marketers. However, they have advantages and disadvantages but can also be prone to criticism. For instance, direct marketing in the form of mail is often perceived as junk mail and criticised for the amount of paper it uses. Another common approach, of which many consumers have tired, are advertisements with vague claims concerning sustainability. Maybe even more important than the promotion mix, is the content of what businesses communicate to consumers and how they do it – in other words, what appeal the product has for the consumers. Iyer and Banerjee (1993, 497) have identified six appeals, which are described in Table 16.3, of how green products are communicated in print advertisements. These appeals can also be applied to sustainable products.

Six appeals of communicating sustainable products
(Iyer & Banerjee 1993, 497).

Zeitgeist Appeals	- Portraying sustainability as a trend of the times - Companies portray their products as sustainable, communicating that they are part of this trend
Emotional Appeals	- Tending to make the consumer feel fear or guilt but also empowered
Financial appeals	- Emphasizing the savings consumers can make with a product - Sales discounts - Donations to good causes
Euphoria Appeals	- Highlighting the well-being of consumers: health benefits or natural ingredients of a product
Management Appeals	- Company is working towards sustainable development, not contributing to social and environmental problems
Other Appeals	- Testimonials - Celebrity endorsement - Comparative advertising

Table 16.3

Particularly negative emotional appeals by communicating global sustainability issues are considered as preventing consumers from buying sustainable products. Confronting consumers with the threat of climate change or loss of biodiversity can be intimidating and cause guilt or fear, which does not necessarily lead to a change in behaviour. Although consumers might feel guilty, they might also feel that the claims are false or at least exaggerated, as well as being manipulated. Consumers are more receptive to change when communications appeal to their self-interests or focus on their benefits. Although consumers do care about the environment and social issues, they want to know what is in it for them when they use sustainable products. Therefore, communicating self-interests and benefits through efficiency and cost-savings, health and safety, performance, symbolism and status, or convenience can give, etc. Popular examples for efficiency and cost-savings are home appliances, such as refrigerators and washing machines, hybrid cars, LED or CFL bulbs. At the same time, efficiency can also mean convenience because hybrid cars have to be refilled less frequently and LED or CFL bulbs have to be changed less often. Organic food is an example for health and safety. In times of genetically-manipulated food, the use of pesticides and diseases, organic food seems to an increasing number of consumers as a safe and healthy option. However, often consumers do not buy organic food because of these reasons; instead, they perceive organic food to be better in taste. Performance is a very typical communication tool for products and something many consumers do not associate with sustainable products, as mentioned earlier. Nevertheless, high-performance products can be sustainable without the consumer being aware of it. Symbolism and status is often driven by celebrity endorsement or simply when celebrities are seen with sustainable products, which then becomes fashionable. For the marketers, it is important to know their customers in order to be able to provide them with relevant information. However, the most important factor for sustainable marketing communication to be successful is credibility. Although many claims of companies are true, consumers are skeptical and do not take their word for it. Not unlike in the 1990s, companies want to offer their customers sustainable products but make untrue, unverified or unethical claims either intentionally or unintentionally. Although greenwashing was originally meant for deceiving environmental practices, it has since then also been applied to false sustainability claims. The sustainability and marketing consultancy TerraChoice (2007, 1-2) found during a study conducted in North America that out of 1,018 examined products, all but one made at least one unsubstantiated or misleading claim, with a total of 1,753 claims. They identified six 'sins' of greenwashing, into which the claims could be categorized: hidden trade-off, no proof, vagueness, irrelevance, fibbing and lesser of two evils. Over 80% of the claims were hidden trade-offs or had no proof. Most commonly used to display credibility are labels by third-parties. Due to the great number of labels available, companies have to choose carefully. Most preferable are well-recognized and credible labels. Moreover, companies' self-declaration claims alone can make consumers mistrustful but combined with official labels and transparent behaviour they can support credibility. Furthermore, a company needs to follow through with its commitments, provide stakeholders with information not only about products but the production process and the company itself, as well as being consistent in one's actions. As part of the major sustainability promotion, some companies have already started indicating GHG emission for the production and consumption of that product in the product package labelling. Carbon Trust's provides guidance on this issue. Code of Good

Practice for Product Greenhouse Gas Emissions and Reduction Claim is given in the following link: https://www.gasnaturalfenosa.es/servlet/ficheros/1297092546661/698%5C1016%5CCode_Good_Practice_Espa%C3%B1a_GrandesClientes_ES.pdf

16.3 Benefits of sustainable marketing for companies:

As we have seen that sustainable marketing can bring benefits to customers in many different ways. However, sustainable marketing can necessitate great organizational changes for companies, a rethinking of current marketing practices and require sometimes costly modifications of production processes. Thus, there have to be benefits for companies as well, in order for them to pursue sustainable marketing.

1. Cost savings can be one of the biggest motivators for companies. Actions taken are usually easily realizable but save costs only in the short term. Sustainable marketing offers both easily realizable and low-cost actions, as well as more comprehensive and cost-intensive changes, both leading to long-term cost savings. It would be unrealistic to expect companies to make their production more sustainable all at once. A step-by-step approach is sensible, starting with easily realizable actions which pay off quickly before realizing more cost-intensive changes. Common cost benefits are achieved through energy, material and waste efficiencies.

2. Reputation has to be earned and being sustainable can earn companies a good reputation. A company does not necessarily have to demonstrate their sustainability in so many words but rather through their actions. Word of mouth or endorsement from reputable NGOs is more powerful than something which comes from the company itself. If sustainable marketing is practiced in the right way, the company or brand image can only benefit, and it earns the company the trust of their customers.

3. New markets can open up through sustainable marketing. Environmental and social sustainability, as well as different sustainability issues, such as cruelty-free products, appeal to consumers. Often a product is not only purchased for the product's sake but also for the company or brand image the product represents. When a company is renowned for being sustainable, this can lead to new customers. Besides gaining new customers through being sustainable, innovation can result in new products and services which can attract new customers who otherwise might not have bought the company's products. In any case, sustainability can be something with which a company can differentiate itself from its competitors.

4. Reduced risk is another benefit of sustainable marketing. Some natural resources will become scarce in the future; their prices will rise as a

consequence and supply becomes uncertain. This can limit a company's production and increase product prices. Proactive companies mitigate these problems and gain a competitive advantage over competitors by switching to alternative energy sources, becoming more resource efficient or finding alternative resources.

5. Attracting and retaining employees can be easier for a company by practicing sustainability. A survey in Finland revealed that graduating students believe that a company is accountable for their impact on society and the environment and half of the respondents would take a lower salary to work for a sustainable company. Furthermore, working for a sustainable company can enhance current employees' innovativeness, motivation, and productivity.

6. Leadership can be either gained or maintained through sustainable marketing. By making sustainability part of the business, the company can enhance their image and gain a competitive advantage. By implementing sustainable solutions now, companies can leave the competition behind because it can take years to make up leeway concerning sustainability and gaining the reputation.

16.4. Sustainability marketing strategy- issues and challenges

The goal of sustainability marketing strategy is changed to attain competitive advantage through a position that is desirable, different, and defensible. But practically, it is not easy to design these kinds of marketing strategies because of the related issues and challenges. In addition to this, according to sustainability principles there is need to conserve the resources and to consume less, while on the other hand, the principle of marketing says to sell more, which means more production, hence more consumption of resources. Therefore, the need is to strike a balance between the two, which means that the strategy should be formulated in such a way, so that profits can still be earned even after reduced impact on environment and society. No doubt that problems and solution go hand in hand because if someone finds a solution for one problem, then other problem arises.

Sustainability in marketing strategy not only helps in competitive advantage but also opens door for cost savings and innovation. It is rightly said that companies cannot stay for longer in the market if they will not become truly sustainable. But, there are limited companies which are trying to adopt sustainability in their marketing strategy. Moreover, they also have unsustainable products in the market. Therefore, first of all, the consumer segments which are early adopters and ready to buy sustainable products should be targeted and positioned. In addition to this, the future goal of sustainability marketing strategy should be focused on segmentation, targeting and positioning customer on the basis of sustainability criteria along with designing sustainability marketing mix for better products and services, better prices, better distribution and better promotion.

16.5 Sustainable Consumer Behavior

Sustainable consumption is necessary due to increasing resource depletion and other environmental problems. Although sustainability marketing's goal is to satisfy consumer's needs, the consequences for society and environment, caused by production and consumption are equally important. Similarly, sustainable consumption is about people's ability to satisfy their needs without compromising the ability of others to do so in the future. More sustainable consumption calls for change in consumer behavior. Sustainability adds a new dimension to the information search besides traditional criteria such as price and place. More often than not, consumers are overwhelmed by the amount of information about sustainability. Additionally, consumers are often less knowledgeable about sustainability, and the information search turns into a learning process. When evaluating alternatives, consumers look at the benefits and attributes the different products have to offer. Sustainability is only one of these attributes and is not seen as a benefit by all consumers. Other attributes and benefits are price, performance, and status which can outweigh sustainability. Post-purchase behaviour includes the use and disposal of the product. Sustainable use of the product means efficient usage but also maintenance in order to prolong the product's lifespan. Sustainable post-use behaviour is about recycling, reusing or remanufacturing products in order to reduce waste which goes to landfills. Another post-use possibility is to resell the product to someone else. Consumers tend to focus on single sustainability issues and buy products which respond to these issues, such as Fairtrade products or cruelty-free products. Therefore, the main challenges are to include all ranges of sustainable products into sustainable consumption and that the mass market consumes sustainably.

Sustainable marketing strategy

Making sustainability part of the business can be an initiative from the company itself but also a reaction to consumer pressure or changes in competitors' strategies. In the future, companies may be forced to change their behaviour due to consequences of climate change or impending raw material shortages. In any case, marketing objectives and strategies need to be adapted to the sustainability agenda. Typically, economic objectives are about profits and market shares. Instead, economic objectives in sustainable marketing can be set for increasing the revenues and market shares of sustainable products and services. Environmental and social objectives have been often ambitious and published in CSR reports but have been ultimately not followed through. Environmental objectives should not only concern the production process, such as lowering emissions but the whole life-cycle of the product. Therefore, environmental objectives can aim at lower energy consumption during the use phase or 100% recyclability. Social objectives are about making the products as healthy and safe as possible when used. However, the safety and health of employees as well as workers within the supply chain, has gained increasing attention, which is why social objectives are now also set for health and safety in factories and in the supply chain.

16.6 Segmentation

One of the most important decisions to make is who to target. It would be fatal to repeat the mistake of green and environmental marketers to target only a niche segment of green consumers. The focus of sustainable marketing needs to be on the whole market and not only 'sustainable consumers.' Thus segmentation has to move away from traditional characteristics, such as demographics, and divide segments according to their attitudes towards sustainability. Due to inconsistent consumer behaviour and the need for behavioural change segmentation is done according to consumers' current behaviour and their willingness to act more sustainably. Current behaviour looks at how sustainably consumers behave already and how existing sustainable consumption patterns can be deepened. Furthermore, reasons for or against sustainable behaviour need to be identified. Segmentation helps marketers to identify potential target groups, which can then be offered products in a suitable way. The British government's Department for Environmental, Food and Rural Affairs (2008, 42-45), has divided the British population into seven segments, which reach from very engaged to extremely disinterested. Positive Greens, Waste Watchers, and Concerned Consumers all show sustainable behaviour at home and in purchases to a different extent. Positive Greens have integrated sustainability into nearly all of their lifestyles, whereas Waste Watchers are mostly focused on avoiding waste. Sideline Supporters, Cautious Participants and Stalled Starters have pro-environmental attitudes in varying degrees, but actual sustainable behaviour is low to non-existent, but at least recycling is practiced. The Honestly Disengaged have no interest in the environment whatsoever. Table 16.4 shows the segments' ability and willingness to act and what restrains them from behaving more sustainably. The more the ability and willingness decreases, the more barriers arise.

16.7 Positioning

Positioning is about how the target market perceives a product and what position it takes in consumers' minds, also compared to competitors' products. A well-positioned product should communicate its essence, what it does for the consumers and how it distinguishes itself from other products. In the case of sustainable marketing, the emphasis can be put on sustainability in different ways. An environmentally and socially sustainable product can be positioned as the most sustainable product, which does not appeal to the mass market but only a small niche. If only part of the production is environmentally sustainable or social sustainability is neglected, this strategy is to be avoided. In times of the internet, these practices are quickly revealed and spread, which can ruin a company's reputation for good. Instead, products can be positioned by highlighting single sustainable benefits such as benefits to human health or cost savings. As explained earlier, the aim of sustainable marketing is that the mass market consumes sustainable products throughout all product ranges. Therefore, the main emphasis is not necessarily sustainability alone but is seen as an additional benefit. Instead, a product is positioned according to other primary benefits, in order to reach consumers who are not concerned with sustainability and which represent the greatest part of the market. For instance, clothes are usually positioned as fashionable but behind these fashionable clothes can stand a sustainable company, with good working conditions, environmentally-friendly sourcing, and materials as well as production processes. Thus, sustainability itself can be a competitive advantage.

16.8 Competitive advantage

A competitive advantage is gained when a company is able to perform better compared to their competitors. Companies can gain a competitive advantage through enhanced environmental and social performance, which is usually expressed through a specific attribute, such as being organic, local or Fair Trade, among others. Globally, the sales of organic and local food have grown, and the demand is expected to grow. Equally, Fairtrade certified products have grown in popularity worldwide. Also, energy efficiency is an attribute of enhanced environmental performance. However, the competitive advantage is not necessarily the environmental performance but durability, cost-savings, convenience or all three together. More sustainable production processes, products or services can be accomplished through innovation. In the 1980s and 1990s, companies were unwilling to change their production and pointed to increasing costs, which would lead to higher prices and destroy competitiveness. However, innovation towards more environmentally-friendly production can gain companies a competitive advantage. Instead of increasing costs, costs could actually be reduced through innovations in production processes, packaging or distribution. This brings the company a cost advantage, which would allow them to lower their prices while sustaining or increasing their profit margin. As a result of the improvement of the production process, the quality of a product can be increased, too. This is only one approach companies can take to gain a competitive advantage through innovation.

Possible sustainable segmentation

Segment	Ability/ Willingness	Barriers
Positive greens	High	None to little
Waste watchers	Medium/low	Think they are doing enough/ skepticism
Concerned consumers	Medium	Think they are doing more than they actually do Difficulty adapting lifestyle/ skepticism
Sideline supporters	Low/Medium	Low knowledge about sustainability Difficulty in changing habits and adopting lifestyles
Cautious participants	Medium/low	Difficulty in changing habits and adopting lifestyles Losing self-identity Low priority Do not want to be identified as green Not the social norm
Stalled starters	Low	Low priority Skepticism Low knowledge about sustainability Inconvenience, costs Difficulty in adapting lifestyle Losing self-identity Do not want to be identified as green
Honestly disengaged	Low	No opinion about or interest in sustainability, not the social norm/ Low priority

Table 16.4

Questions:

1. Define sustainability marketing and its benefits.
2. What are the sustainability marketing mix and marketing matrix? Provide examples
3. Discuss sustainable consumer behavior.
4. Discuss sustainability marketing positioning and segmentation.

Chapter 17

Sustainable Procurement and Supply Chain

17.1 Traditional vs. Sustainable Procurement

Sustainable Procurement means taking into account economical, environmental and social impacts in buying choices. Sustainable procurement, therefore, means making sure that the products and services your organization buys are as sustainable as possible – with the lowest environmental and most positive social impact. This includes optimizing price, quality, availability but also environmental life-cycle impact and social aspects linked to product/services origin.

Therefore, Sustainable Procurement consider the environmental, social and economic consequences of Design, Renewable material use, Manufacture and Production methods, Logistics, Service Delivery, use, Operation, Maintenance, Re-use, Recycling options, Disposal, and supplier's capabilities to address these consequences throughout the supply chain resulting in:

(i) Energy efficient and greenhouse-friendly products

(ii) Products that are water efficient and reduce water use

(iii) Less toxic products to reduce health effects

(iv) Products using less packaging or with a provision for packaging take-back

(v) Products that use fewer resources or in other ways create reduced environmental impacts throughout their life cycle

(vi) Products made from recycled materials, such as recycled road construction materials

(vii) Recycled green organics and recycled plastics products

- Traditional procurement focuses upon value for money considerations. The aim of sustainable procurement is to integrate environmental and social considerations into the procurement process, with the goal of reducing adverse impacts upon health, social conditions and the environment, thereby saving valuable costs for organizations and the community at large.

- Sustainable Procurement comes at 2 levels: Product and Supplier. Procurement can make a significant contribution to the policy goals of sustainable development and efficient resource usage by ensuring that the suppliers, contractors and the goods and services purchased achieve optimum environmental performance.

- British Standard – BS 8903:2010 Principles and framework for procuring sustainably, CIPS Sustainable Procurement Guide
- United Nations and major Oil Companies practicing it, e.g., Exon/Mobil, BP

17.2 Benefits/Business Case of Sustainable Procurement

- Reducing the harmful impact of pollution and waste & reducing greenhouse gas emissions and toxic materials in the environment that harm environment and people.
- Reducing waste and landfill through purchasing recycled content products and products that creates less waste
- Saving water and energy and Preserving the natural habitat
- Reducing costs through greater energy efficiency, and disposal cost
- Most businesses spend high proportions of their total cost of operations with external suppliers, 65-85% in some estimates
- Generating financial savings through greater energy efficiency; reduced waste and disposal (including reduced packaging); reduced water use; and reusing and recycling materials and products, thereby lowering the cost of a product over its life cycle
- Design/Procure products/service which has the least environmental and social impact
- Procuring sustainably helps organizations to eliminate waste, become more energy efficient and save money. As well as, use renewable energy as much as possible to reduce GHG emissions and cost.
- Savings on disposal costs

17.3 Key Objectives for Sustainable Specifications

- Cost-effective alternatives to unsustainable resources
- Minimising waste
- Maximising recycling of materials
- Ensuring ethical and responsible trading and employment practices throughout the supply chain
- Maximising access to contracts for SME's, local suppliers
- Maximising resource and cost efficiency throughout the supply chain

Sustainable Procurement Policy Guide

- Identify whether there is a need for the good or services
- Understand the potential environmental and social impacts and risks of the goods and services to be procured

- Consider alternatives to purchasing – reuse, recycling, and hire of the goods and services
- Research alternatives that may offer reduced environmental and social impacts
- Carry out whole life cycle costing
- Include sustainability specifications in contracts management and reporting process

17.4 Cases of Sustainability Cost Reduction Initiatives Through Sustainable Procurement:

i)   Reduced internal costs

ii) Savings of €1 million 2007: A mail and logistics company saved €1M by replacing air transport with train transport for the Paris-Bordeaux route, reducing cost and CO_2 emissions simultaneously.

iii) Savings of US $200 million 2008: By driving fewer miles in its fleet, Wal-Mart reduced CO_2 emissions by 200,000 metric tons. These efficiency improvements also resulted in fewer trucks on the road, less wear-and-tear on roads, highways and bridges, as well as a savings of nearly US $200 million in 2008.

iv) Savings of US $8 million 2007: UPS, whose trucks drive 4 billion kilometres a year, achieved annual savings of around 48 million kilometres and 14 million liters of fuel by implementing its Route Optimization programme. This equates to 1,100 fewer trucks per day sent down the road. The results were no less than US $8 million in fuel procurement savings and a reduction of 32,000 tons of CO_2 emissions year on year.

v)   Savings of US $12 million 2008: Water conservation, energy efficiency, green building projects and other eco-friendly initiatives yielded Baxter International Inc. a total of US $11.9 million in environmental income, savings and cost avoidance.

vi) Savings of US $1 million 2008: An Italian multi-utility company concluded that public lighting by CFL bulb lamps would result in annual savings of €1 million and 6,500 CO_2/tons. 2009: Accor Hotels. The use of energy-efficient lights in 2,300 hotels yielded savings of 72 million kWh of electricity in one year and the use of tap nozzles resulted in a 4 million m3 reduction in water consumption in one year. (1) Most of the data in this report were based on publicly available information and were not verified independently

vii) Cost Reduction through Reduced Specification N.A. 2004: Lafarge introduced one-ply cement bags instead of the standard double- or triple-ply bag, reducing the cost of materials used in production.

viii) Savings of US $3.4 billion 2007: Wal-Mart launched "CO_2 Scorecard" aimed at saving 0.6 million tons of CO2 and US $3.4 billion in costs through reduced packaging content. €100 million 2009: Finnish mobile phone giant, Nokia, saved more than €100 million by placing a greater emphasis on the reduction of packaging.

ix) Savings of €2.5 million 2010: Danone France removed the outer cardboard packaging of Activia and Taillefi ne yoghurt saving €2.5 million. €54,000 Alter Eco, a French fair-trade company, also reduced cardboard packaging of its chocolate bars from 220 g/m2 to 205 g/m2 (a 7% reduction). Saving 1.5 Euro cents per bar, amounts to a significant saving considering that the company is selling around 3.6 million units per year. N.A. 2010: PUMA launched the "clever little bag" reducing paper consumption by 8,500 tons, saving 20 million Megajoules of electricity, 1 million litres of fuel oil and 1 million litres of water. During transport 500,000 litres of diesel is saved and lastly, due to the replacement of traditional shopping bags with the lighter built in bag the difference in weight can save up to 275 tons of plastic. Reduced compliance costs €3.2 million (2) In France, disabled people must represent 6% of the workforce of companies employing more than 20 people. Companies that do not comply with this law must pay an annual tax to a public agency. Half of this quota can be fulfilled by working with social and solidarity organizations. Therefore, procurement departments can play a key role in reducing the amount of this specific social tax. Example of cost reduction for a company with 20,000 employees (3): Number of disabled employees required in the workforce: 1,200 - Tax reduction if the company works with social and solidarity organisations and provides work to 600 full-time equivalent.

Therefore, when we think of valuing the benefits of Sustainable Procurement, most of us immediately

- Think of cost reduction initiatives, such as:
  — The savings resulting from energy-efficient lighting,
  — The impact of reducing packaging by 20%,
  — The cost-benefit impact of providing the truck fleet with a new ultra-efficient engine resulting in a 35% reduction in fuel consumption.
- As we can see, these examples are easily quantified and clearly show how initiatives typically aim at improving a company's EBIT. But is this all that Sustainable Procurement stands for? Is this the only factor that could directly or indirectly impact an organization's performance? Two other areas have been identified in this study as having a significant impact on a company's valuation: (i)risk reduction and (ii)revenue growth. Unlike cost reduction, these other two factors are not as straight-forward or easy to quantify.

1) Cost reduction

Among the three factors mentioned, cost reduction is perhaps the first thing that comes to mind when thinking about the benefits of Sustainable Procurement. As illustrated in the table below, sustainability initiatives can result in the reduction of costs (in particular total cost of ownership [TCO]) in different ways:

- Reduced internal costs: Two main drivers can be considered to reduce internal costs:

Procurement of more efficient products and the reduction of consumption. For many products sustainability can lead to investments in more efficient products (lower energy consumption, longer lifespan, lower maintenance cost) where higher investment cost will be offset by lower operating costs, resulting in a lower TCO. Sustainability can also drive changes in behaviours by reducing the consumption of non-production related product categories such as paper, energy for buildings, business travel, etc.

- Reduced specifications/demand: Sustainability analysis can push customers to reduce over-specification (a famous example being over-packaging) for many products and services, resulting in lower costs.
- Reduced environmental and social compliance costs: social and environmental taxes can take various forms and represent significant expenses for companies. The Waste Electrical and Electronic Equipment (WEEE)and Packaging taxes in the European Union paid by producers are essentially calculated based on weight and product category.

However, eco-design criteria are progressively being taken into account in the calculation of the quantitative model was created by the analysis of the three main drivers and their respective impact on a company's annual procurement spends, market cap and revenue. Their impact was then compared to the implementation cost of a Sustainable Procurement programme.

Based on research carried out at MIT, the following impact was found in sustainable procurement:

1. Cost reduction: Reduction in total cost of ownership linked to reduced energy costs, reduced over-specification, reduced consumption and reduced social and environmental compliance costs 0.05% of total revenue per project (1)
Up to 6 times payback
Implementation Probability: High

2. Risk reduction Financial impact on brand value from bad supplier practices (e.g., child labour, local pollution); economic cost of supply chain disruptions
(e.g., noncompliance with environmental regulations)
Additional direct costs as a 0.7% of total revenue
Up to 85 times payback
Decrease of
12% in market
capitalization
Implementation Probability: Low
3. Revenue growth
Additional revenue through innovation of eco-friendly products/services, price premium or income from recycling programmes
0.5% of total revenue
Up to 58 times payback
Implementation Probability: Medium

Using procurement to deliver sustainable outcomes

The document should consider procurement as a strategic process and a way of delivering business objectives through a supply chain. The standard needs to set out how sustainability objectives of an organization are addressed at the early stage of the procurement process through strategic procurement techniques such as market analysis, forward commitment, life cycle assessment, risk management, whole-life costing, scenario modelling, social return on investment and more.

Focus on impacts material to the procurer

The sustainability requirements of an organization need to be clearly defined and materiality understood in consultation with stakeholders. This aligns well with the GRI reporting process.

'Sustainable supply' not 'sustainable supplier'

The focus of the standard should be on sustainable supply, not sustainable supplier. This means using procurement techniques to deliver the outcomes required by the buying organization's corporate responsibility objectives or policy outcomes for the public sector. It should not primarily focus on the sustainability practices of the supplier in their own organizations unless this represents a risk to the purchasing organization (e.g. labour standards).

However, most ESG investors demand that suppliers use ISO 14001:2015 and OHSAS 18001 (now ISO 45001:2018). The suppliers can use these programs to manage the sustainable development program using the harmonized high-level structure. This method replaces "sustainability" with sustainable development and resilience.

Not one-size-fits-all

Prioritisation should be of the essence to the standard. Sustainability impacts and risks should be mapped against categories of supply and high priority impacts/categories should be addressed first. This should be done with a wide range of internal stakeholders, also taking into consideration corporate policy and external stakeholder requirements. This is clearly set out in BS 8903.

Manage demand

Demand management should be key to the standard. The most sustainable way to procure is not to buy at all or to keep demand to a minimum by operating the business more efficiently. There needs to be an organizational link between procurer and user of goods, works and services.

Embedding sustainability into current procurement practice

It is important for the standard to address achieving more sustainable outcomes through the current procurement practices of an organization. It is not telling you to buy better, it should set out how to deliver sustainability through a variety of procurement processes for all sizes and types of organizations.

Tier one is not the only one

The standard is not just about the first tier of suppliers. It must refer to the management of the overall supply chain where there are often significant risks (such as labour standards) or opportunities (for example positioning local SMEs in lower tiers of the supply chain).

Encourage innovation

The process should encourage innovation related to more sustainable goods, works, and services, through effective market research and use of outcome specifications.

Develop a competitive, sustainable supply chain

There should be emphasis on maintaining or improving the competitive market. For example, if a supplier with lower sustainability capacity is selected for other commercial or technical reasons, they should be required to develop a programme of work to improve during the contract. This will improve the pool of competitive suppliers who can deliver sustainable outcomes.**Following is a questionnaire that Walmart uses to gauge its Supplier Sustainability Index**:

A. Energy and Climate

1. Have you measured your corporate greenhouse gas emissions (GHGs)?
2. Have you opted to report your GHGs to the Carbon Disclosure Project (CDP)?
3. What is your total annual GHGs reported in the most recent year measured?
4. Have you set publicly available GHG reduction targets? What are they?

B. Material Efficiency

1. What is the total amount of solid waste from facilities that produce product(s) in the most recent year measured?
2. Have you set publicly available solid waste reduction targets? What are they?
3. What is the total water use from facilities that produce product(s) for Walmart?
4. Have you set publicly available water use reduction targets? What are they?

C. Natural Resources

1. Have you established public sustainability purchasing guidelines for your direct supplier(s)?
2. Have you obtained third-party certifications for any of the products that you sell to Walmart?

D. People and Community

1. Do you know the location of all the facilities that produce your product(s)?
2. Do you evaluate the quality of, and capacity for, production at all supplier facilities?
3. Do you have a process for managing social compliance at the manufacturing level?
4. Do you have a process for managing social compliance with your supply base to resolve compliance issues?
5. Do you invest in community development in markets you source from/ operate within?

Gaining B2C and B2B revenue from a more responsible brand is the first of three ways that sustainability strategies bolster revenue. Next, we'll look at new revenue from new green products.

Full and fair opportunity

Local procurement, minority businesses, SMEs etc. are often significant stakeholder priorities and should be supported through the supply chain where appropriate. However, this needs to be set in the context of full and fair opportunity and not positive discrimination.

Production and Process Methods:

When procuring products Purchasing/Contracts Depts. can also set criteria based on specific materials that should or should not be included in them, as well as the process or production methods of the products provided. The Purchase Dept. can indicate the materials that are preferable or alternatively specify that none of the materials or chemical substances should be detrimental to the environment. For example, a common approach for the environmental procurement of cleaning products is for the business unit to provide an indicative list of hazardous substances harmful to the environment or public health (on the basis of an objective risk assessment) that it does not wish to have present in the product. For example, Purchase Dept. can require that:

- Paper is produced without the use of chlorine (TCF)
- Food is organically produced (without the use of chemicals pesticides and fertilizers)
- Electricity is generated from renewable sources only. For example, for an Electric car, the electric charge stored in the battery should be from renewable energy sources such as solar and not from gas turbine or coal plant.

17.5 Sustainability Intervention in Procurement Cycle

Sustainability intervention in procurement cycle is depicted in Figure 17.1.

Supply chain sustainability is the management of environmental, social and economic impacts, and the encouragement of good governance practices, throughout the lifecycles of goods and services. The objective of supply chain sustainability is to create, protect and grow long-term environmental, social and economic value for all stakeholders involved in bringing products and services to market. By integrating the UN Global Compact principles, as stated in 3.9.7 herein, into supply chain relationships, companies can advance corporate sustainability and promote broader sustainable development objectives. Supply chain sustainability is important because by managing and seeking to improve environmental, social and economic performance and good governance throughout supply chains, companies act in their own interests, the interests of their stakeholders and the interests of society at large. Environmental, social

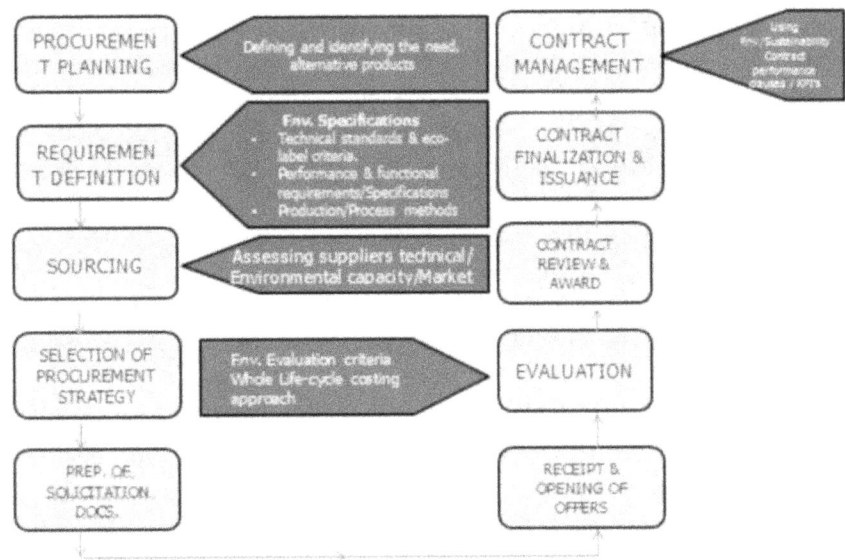

Figure 17.1

and economic Impacts exist throughout every stage of supply chains. At every stage in the life-cycle of specific products, there are social and environmental impacts, or externalities, on the environment and on people. In addition, governance, or the accountability of organizations to their stakeholders for their conduct, is important at every stage throughout the supply chain.

Companies also realize that sustainability issues are no longer confined to supply chains but have gone beyond and are currently being seen through the lens of the value chain, keeping into account public disclosures and reporting mechanisms being demanded by key stakeholders including the civil society, consumers, lenders and governments at federal and sub-federal levels.

17.6 Common business case/drivers for supply chain sustainability

i. Managing business risks: ■ Minimize business disruption from environmental, social and economic impacts ■ Protect the company's reputation and brand value

Companies can protect themselves from potential supply chain interruptions or delays associated with suppliers' practices with regards to human rights, labour standards, environment, and anti-corruption by ensuring suppliers have effective compliance programmes and robust management systems covering all the areas of the UN Global Compact

Ten Principles. For companies who have single sources for key inputs, managing risks is also critical to ensuring continued access to those resources. Increasingly, customer and investor expectations and overall society are driving companies toward more responsible supply chain management. Strong management of social and environmental issues helps companies avoid and address adverse impacts to stakeholders, which can in turn help ensure that companies maintain their social license to operate by taking into consideration risks to surrounding communities. Effectively managing social and environmental risks can also help companies avoid potentially costly operational delays from conflicts with local communities and can help companies avoid reputational risks. Furthermore, companies now face a growing expectation to disclose information related to their supply chain as well as an emergence of legal requirements.

ii. Realizing efficiencies ■ Reduce cost of material inputs, energy, transportation ■ Increase labour productivity ■ Create efficiency across supply chains.

A focus on sustainability-driven productivity in the supply chain can reduce a company's procurement costs while also reducing the environmental footprint of the supply chain, such as energy, water and use of natural and synthetic materials. This may also reduce the harm to worker health and safety and improve worker motivation, productivity and cost efficiency. Other benefits include: • Increased understanding of key processes in the supply chain, including natural resource management and extraction, logistics and manufacturing and enables better management and stewardship of resources • More efficiently designed processes and systems which reduce required inputs and lower costs. Productivity and efficiency initiatives require a full understanding of the different steps of the supply chain and the key social and environmental impacts and cost drivers. By addressing the root causes of issues through strong communication capabilities, in-depth understanding of business drivers and sustainability trends and shared assessments and priorities for improvement, companies can drive improvements and derive the benefits.

iii. Creating Sustainable products: ■ Meet evolving customer and business partner requirements ■ Innovate for changing market.

Collaboration with suppliers on sustainability issues can foster product innovation. Companies embarking on such initiatives have added new features and performance characteristics to existing products and even generated new products. For example, sustainable products may result in reduced negative environmental impacts compared to traditional products or have improved end of life collection and disposal options. It is also possible for the sustainability of products to be a differentiating factor and to lead to increased sales for some companies.

Incorporating sustainability into a company's supply chain is complex but the failure to act may be the biggest risk of all. Companies can take several initial steps to move toward sustainable supply chains.

17.6.1. Map your supply chain

Many companies do not have a comprehensive understanding of the sustainability impacts of their supply chain. An early step is to inventory suppliers, identify the most significant environmental and social challenges they have, and prioritize efforts with suppliers.

New Balance Athletic Shoe Inc. reduced the number of suppliers it does business with, in part based on performance against sustainability criteria. The company reduced its footwear supply chain by 65 percent and is focused on forming strong, positive partnerships with its suppliers. Some criteria that may be helpful for prioritizing suppliers include the level of spending, importance to business continuity, and geography as a proxy for risk.

CH2M HILL established a supply chain sustainability strategy for evaluation and election of products, complete with procedures, tools, communications, training, and metrics for reporting implementation progress. Since 2010, CH2M HILL has identified suppliers with strategic or preferred status based on volume and business impact. Tier 1 and Tier 2 suppliers are required to provide information about their sustainability programs and demonstrate continuous improvement. Suppliers are classified into four groups of environmental performance, with each incorporating specific key performance indicators (KPIs). CH2M HILL's direct procurement organization has begun incorporating sustainability into the design, procurement, and construction of projects by promoting the selection of suppliers and subcontractors that value sustainability.

17.6.2. Communicate expectations

Focusing on sustainability within your supply chain is a great way to communicate corporate values and culture to your suppliers and customers. Establishing and communicating expectations through a supplier code of conduct is a critical step in involving suppliers in your sustainability efforts.

Many resources and tools have been created to assist companies with the development of a supplier code of conduct. For example, the United Nations Global Compact publication, "Supply Chain Sustainability — A Practical Guide for Continuous Improvement" has guidelines and tips for writing and adopting a successful supplier code of conduct. A new tool developed by the Global Environmental Management Initiative (GEMI) helps companies prioritize where in their organization's value chain they may have opportunities to improve supply chain sustainability, and then provides case studies of companies that have leveraged these opportunities.

17.6.3 Baseline supplier performance

Once you know who your target suppliers are and have set compliance standards, collecting data from suppliers through a simple benchmarking questionnaire or self-assessment will provide you an understanding of your starting point.

Many organizations, such as retailers, major brands, and the U.S. Federal Government, have started evaluating the performance of their suppliers through questionnaires and surveys. Increasingly, organizations incorporate all areas included in their code of conduct with special focus and weight in the self-assessments related to areas that are important to their business. Our client work shows that more companies are aligning the content of their assessments with the GRI guidelines and CDP questionnaires. Some sectors, such as the electronics (Electronics Industry Citizenship Coalition Self-Assessment Questionnaire) and pharmaceutical (Pharmaceutical Supply Chain Initiative Self-Assessment Questionnaire) industries, have developed industrywide surveys to reduce the burden on suppliers of responding to multiple requests for information that varies in content and format.

The baseline assessments form the starting point for future programs to improve supply chain sustainability and help assess where the greatest need for improvement exists. For example, Pacific Gas and Electric (PG&E) uses the response from the Electric Utility Industry Sustainable Supply Chain Alliance survey to gauge the performance of its top-tier suppliers on important aspects of environmental performance, including greenhouse gas emissions, energy and water usage, and waste generation. The information is used to compile the environmental metric in the annual scorecards for top-tier suppliers and to identify opportunities to partner with suppliers to advance business practices in target areas

Communicating back to suppliers in a constructive way is critical for future engagement and provides encouragement for improvement.

17.6.4. Develop training and capacity building programs

This is an important step in improving sustainability and driving behavioral changes throughout your supply chain. Many external resources are available to support these efforts, and some are tailored to specific sector needs.

One effective way to transfer knowledge across the supply chain is to leverage the best practices and case studies from top-performing suppliers at annual vendor conferences, via online training modules, and through capacity building campaigns. By showcasing the success stories of selected suppliers, companies not only recognize their efforts but also demonstrate the practical benefits of sustainability initiatives to others in the supply chain. For example, HP has established supplier- and peer educator-run programs that have provided training to a large number of workers. Since the start of their capacity building program in 2006, HP has carried out 22 training programs in 12 countries on topics such as anti-discrimination, energy efficiency, labor rights and women's health. Through programs conducted jointly with its first-tier suppliers, HP has already trained 155 second-tier suppliers, leveraging the investment and knowledge-sharing efforts dedicated to Tier 1 supplier capacity building.

17.6.5. Drive performance improvement

Once supplier baseline performance is understood, an audit program can measure performance improvement over time. While in many cases, the self-assessments are completed by a corporate group, such as EHS, procurement or marketing, onsite audits can reveal local practices, behavioral challenges and practical opportunities for improvement that are difficult to identify through questionnaires alone.

Once your organization implements an audit program, be prepared to act on the findings by developing and executing corrective action plans by clearly communicating the results and your expectations to suppliers, developing a capacity-building program and, if necessary, terminating suppliers if non-compliance persists.

Assessments and audits paired with incentive programs that reward sustainability efforts have a greater ability to drive sustainability performance. Encouraging transparency and selecting or awarding more business to suppliers with stronger sustainability performance can be very effective in driving improvement. Where this is not possible, incentives — greater access to your value chain, such as access to customers or clients — also can be effective.

In an effort to avoid audit fatigue and to provide a common framework for evaluation, some industries have developed common auditing and assessment tools. For example, the Sustainable Apparel Coalition developed the Higg Index, a performance assessment tool for the apparel and footwear industries. The Electronic Industry Citizenship Coalition has developed the validated audit process that covers both social and environmental performance and includes an auditor certification program to drive for further consistency in audits. Chemical companies have formed a joint initiative called Together for Sustainability (TfS), with the mission of developing and implementing a global supplier engagement program that assesses and improves sustainability sourcing practices.

17.6.6. Join industry collaboration

Many companies recognize that complex supply chain challenges cannot be solved by individual efforts and that industrywide collaboration is required. Working in a pre-competitive environment, peer companies that share similar supply chains can set common standards and best practices for sustainability performance and allow suppliers to be evaluated on the same metrics. These collaborations help prevent audit fatigue, training redundancy and mountains of paperwork for suppliers working to meet similar requirements from their customers. Working with your industry peers is a great way to share knowledge about the sustainability performance of your suppliers.

The Zero Discharge of Hazardous Chemicals Programme (ZDHC), the Sustainable Apparel Coalition, the Outdoor Industry Association and the American Apparel and Footwear Association are a few examples of industry collaborations in the apparel and footwear sector. CH2M HILL is the program manager for the highly ambitious ZDHC Joint Roadmap, which has grown from six founding brands (Adidas Group, C&A, H&M, LiNing, Nike Inc., and Puma SE) into a coalition that includes Esprit, G-Star Raw, Gap Inc., Inditex, Jack Wolfskin, Levi Strauss & Co., Limited Brands, Li Ning, M&S, New Balance Athletic Shoe, Inc., PVH Corp. and United Colors of Benetton. These brands are working together to integrate higher standards of environmental and business practices for their industry by eliminating the use of 11 classes of hazardous chemicals from textile production by 2020.

If you have a more mature supplier sustainability program, your company can do even more:

- Develop and/or deploy robust tracking tools, including software solutions, to monitor supplier performance and improvement over time
- Perform a logistics assessment to determine where sustainability improvements can be made
- Integrate supply chain sustainability criteria into the procurement process
- Create a shift towards supply chain sustainability by leveraging your buying power and influence
- Expand your sustainability goals beyond your direct operations across your supply chain
- Encourage innovation

But don't get caught by the biggest risk of all: not acting.

17.6.7 Ten Principles of United Nations Global Compact and Supply Chain Sustainability

Human Rights Principle

Principle 1: Businesses should support and respect the protection of internationally proclaimed human rights; and Principle

Principle2: make sure that they are not complicit in human rights abuses.

Labour Principle

Principle 3: Businesses should uphold the freedom of association and the effective recognition of the right to collective bargaining;

Principle 4: the elimination of all forms of forced and compulsory labour;

Principle 5: the effective abolition of child labour; and

Principle 6: the elimination of discrimination in respect of employment and occupation.

Environment Principle

Principle 7: Businesses should support a precautionary approach to environmental challenges;

Principle 8: undertake initiatives to promote greater environmental responsibility;

and Principle 9: encourage the development and diffusion of environmentally friendly technologies.

Anti-Corruption Principle

Principle 10: Businesses should work against corruption in all its forms, including extortion and bribery.

Questions:

1. Discuss the benefits of sustainable procurement
2. Discuss strategies for a sustainable supply chain.
3. What are the principles of UN Global compact and supply chain sustainability?

Chapter 18
Sustainable Finance

18.1 Definition of Sustainable Finance

The purpose of finance is to allocate scarce resources to productive uses with the goal of benefiting society and its progress. In the process, finance is responsible for helping individuals and businesses reduce risk through diversification and insurance thus creating value, both tangible and intangible, in stable markets. Growing awareness of the global problems of anthropogenic climate change and poverty has raised questions regarding finance's contributions to society's welfare. The urgent need to reduce the risks of extreme weather, a changing climate, social unrest and violence, which threaten our lives and ecosystems, has motivated the search for a more responsible and holistic approach to financial analysis and practice.

In addition to the economic and financial dimensions, business professionals are increasingly expected to consider and incorporate environmental and social dimensions into their decision-making processes. In a finance context, this implies a need for internalizing externalities through awareness and valuation, regulation or taxation. Consistent with "corporate social responsibility" and the "triple bottom line," finance professionals are analyzing the environment, social and governance (ESG) factors and recognizing and assessing the value of our environmental and social capital in addition to our financial capital. Asset valuation and capital budgeting, financing, investing, financial intermediation and insurance, as well as foreign direct investment.

Green finance, social business, social impact bonds, socially responsible investing—Sustainable finance touches many different aspects of society and takes on several forms. This is a major trend that responds to investors concerned about sustainable growth.

Sustainable finance refers to any form of financial service integrating environmental, social and governance (ESG) criteria into the business or investment decisions for the lasting benefit of both clients and society at large.

A sustainable financial centre is a financial marketplace that, as a whole, contributes to sustainable development and value creation in economic, environmental and social terms. In other words, one that ensures and improves economic efficiency, prosperity, and economic competitiveness both today and in the long-term, while contributing to protecting and restoring ecological systems, and enhancing cultural diversity and social well-being.

Activities that fall under the heading of sustainable finance to name just a few, include sustainable funds, green bonds, impact investing, microfinance, active ownership, credits for sustainable projects and development of the whole financial system in a more sustainable way.

The first step in sustainable finance is that financial institutions avoid investing in, or lending to, so-called 'sin' companies. These are companies with very negative impacts. In the social domain, they include, for example, companies that sell tobacco, anti-personnel mines, and cluster bombs or that exploit child labour. In the environmental field, classic examples of negative impacts are waste dumping and whale hunting. More recently, some financial institutions have started to put coal, and even the broader category of fossil fuels, on the exclusion list because of carbon emissions. These exclusion lists are often triggered under pressure from non-governmental organizations, which use traditional and social media for their messages.

The issuance of socially- and environmentally-focused fixed-income securities has been growing in recent years. The instruments are termed sustainable bonds, socially responsible bonds, green or climate bonds and may be issued by municipalities, non-profits, public-private partnerships, or corporations. In 2013, $14 billion in green bonds were issued, and forecasts for 2018 range from $50 billion to $100 billion. Uses for the funds from socially- and environmentally-focused bonds include, for instance, affordable housing, community and economic development, renewable energy and climate change action, natural resource conservation and management.

In 2014, a group of financial institutions created voluntary process guidelines for issuing green bonds, the "Green Bond Principles." Key recommendations stress the need for transparency and disclosure to ensure integrity to facilitate market transactions. Specifically, the guidelines address the use of proceeds, a process for project evaluation and selection, the management of proceeds, and reporting practices.

A very good example of financial sustainability application can be seen from "Fundamentals of NGO Financial Sustainability" from the following link:

file:///C:/Users/deb/Desktop/Fundamentals_of_NGO_Financial_ Sustainability.pdf

Meaning of "sustainable finance."

Sustainable finance is anchored in a long-term ethical vision of financial investing. It seeks to reconcile economic performance with positive social and environmental impact, by funding companies that actively contribute to sustainable development. Different models exist—some of which overlap.

1. **Socially Responsible Investing (SRI).** This approach has gained the largest following. SRI involves integrating environmental, social and corporate governance (known as "ESG") criteria, in a systematic and traceable manner, into decisions on financial management and investment. It favors a responsible economy by encouraging portfolio-management companies to consider extra-financial criteria when selecting asset values. In 2016, the sector reached a total balance of 22.89 trillion dollars, up 25% from 2014.

2. **Green Finance.** Generally seen as an arm of SRI, it combines all financial transactions that favor the energy transition and fight against climate change. Almost nonexistent in the early 2010s, the market is expected to exceed a value of 100 billion dollars per year by 2020. One of its main tools is **green bonds**, issued with the aim of financing ecological initiatives. A complementary approach in green finance is the decarbonizing of investor portfolios, by financing companies that limit their ecological footprint.

3. **Social Finance.** This includes savings and assets invested in social finance products. Representing 10 billion euros in France in 2016, the sector offers to fund to projects that do not fit into classic financing circuits, such as businesses tied to employment (28% of capital), social and housing (31%), international solidarity (5%) and the environment (36%). In France, the specialized organization Finansol certifies certain social finance products (including SRI products) and monitors trends in social finance.

4. **Social Business.** This refers to businesses whose ends are not only lucrative but primarily social in nature. In addition, they also follow viable economic models. Profits are reinvested in order to combat exclusion, protect the environment or promote development and solidarity. Social business comes in three main forms:

   (i) Generic term for financial services related to mitigation of and adaptation to climate change. It specifically refers to investments in greenhouse gas emission reduction projects and the related creation of CO_2-certificates, financial instruments that are tradable on carbon markets. (ii)Carbon Neutral: this occurs when an organization's net carbon emissions are equal to zero. The process requires measuring organization's total CO_2 emissions, taking active steps to reduce emissions where the company can, and then purchasing CO_2 certificates to offset CO_2 emissions that can not be eliminated from a company's operations. The CO_2 certificates contribute to financing projects reducing CO_2 emissions (i.e., by replacing fossil power generation with renewable projects).

(iii) Corporate Social Responsibility (CSR): This term refers to the commitment of an organization, beyond what is required by law, to ensure that the social, economic and environmental impacts of their actions create a net benefit to communities and society. This is already covered in Chapter 1. This is founded on the belief that all corporations have a 'duty of care' to all their stakeholders in every area of their business operations and that being a responsible citizen improves the long-term business success of a company. This term refers to the commitment of an organization beyond what is required by law to ensure that the social, economic and environmental impact of their actions creates a net benefit to the community and the society.

5. **Microfinance**, a solution that facilitates access to credit for the most disadvantaged populations (132 million customers worldwide for a total balance of 102 billion dollars in 2016).

   — **Impact Investing**, which refers to investing one's savings in companies with a strong social or environmental impact.
   — **Social Impact Bonds (SIB),** which are bonds repaid to investors upon maturation only if the project's social objective is met.

18.2 Everyone has a role to play in Sustainable Finance

Encompassing individual investors, investment funds, institutions, and companies of all sizes, sustainable finance applies to capital from a wide range of origins.

Who invests in Sustainable Finance?

1. **Investors** who want to take part in financing companies and organizations involved in projects with a high social or environmental value, whose impact they may experience directly.

2. **Investment funds**. Institutional and private investors can enrich their asset portfolios substantially with SRI funds. In France in 2016, the 122 SRI conviction funds listed by Novethic posted growth in total investments of 20%.

3. **Pension funds**. Despite a long period of reticence, pension funds from many countries (United States, Japan, etc.) have begun to integrate sustainable finance criteria into the way they manage capital.

4. **Private banking and wealth management**. Over the next 30 years, 41,000 billion dollars in capital will be transferred from Baby Boomers and Generation X to Millennials, who have shown a firm commitment to effecting positive social change through their investments. According to EY, 17% of Millennials prefer to invest in companies that meet the highest ESG standards, compared with just 9% among older generations. That means demand for green financial products has only one direction to go: up!

18.3 Sustainable Asset Valuation and Capital Budgeting

Conventional net present value analysis focuses on forecasting initial cash outflows associated with installation or project set-up, and present values of future net cash flows associated with operations or project termination, calculated with rates of return required by investors. A more comprehensive measure would be the Net Present Sustainable Value. This concept estimates the net present value added across financial, environmental and social dimensions using a required rate of return that considers not only investors' opportunity cost for their financial capital, but also the opportunity costs of the environmental and social capital inputs. It is no longer uncommon for analysts to recognize incremental savings of water, energy, and waste in capital budgeting processes. Beyond that, emerging methods of ecosystem valuation, estimates of the social cost of carbon, the social cost of atmospheric release, a living wage, and broader awareness of the connection between productivity and work-life balance are resulting in more comprehensive estimates of the incremental cash flows associated with individual projects. The value that previously had been considered "intangible" and arbitrarily set to zero is now receiving more attention. While the accuracy of any given estimate may well be debated, at least attempts are made to produce dollar estimates based on the best information that is available without simply ignoring variables that are "too difficult to measure."

Awareness of ESG factors is an absolute necessity for the more comprehensive and more detailed analysis that is required by the increasing complexity of issues in all of our critical industries. In energy production, distribution and conservation, value comparisons need to be made between renewable sources of energy and various fossil fuels. New alternatives in distribution are emerging centered on a "smart grid" that is distributed (decentralized) and allows for two-way power flow. In food production and distribution, local and fair trade sources of food are increasingly preferred over alternatives, while the environmental and health benefits of organic production are receiving greater attention. In agriculture, research is ongoing regarding the costs and benefits of GMO versus non-GMO crops while, in farming, consumers seem to increasingly demand the humane treatment of animals. The commercial and residential real estate and related industries are focusing on the value of LEED certification in new construction and retrofits, while healthcare providers are asked to consider alternatives, whenever possible, that go well beyond pharmaceutical products and include healthy food, exercise and therapy. In the transportation of people and freight, a ranking of costs would prioritize rail/ship/barge over truck/bus and then plane. But, of course, the best possible solution would have to be identified on a case-by-case basis.

Beyond costs and benefits at an individual firm level, investors are also increasingly interested in assessing risks in global supply chains. This requires transparency and value creation at all stages of the production and distribution processes, and strong relationships with suppliers and vendors all over the world. Innovation in finance is accompanied by innovation in the collection, storage and interpretation of "big data," which adds to the complexity but also raises the possibility of better solutions. In response to financial decisions that increasingly reflect value previously considered intangible and ignored, market prices and cash flows will change and further facilitate better decision-making in the future.

18.4 Sustainable Investing

Sustainable investing is not new. It has previously been referred to as socially responsible investing (SRI). An article by Dale Wannen in the Winter 2015 issue of the Conscious Company Magazine describes three main areas of activity: ESG screening, shareholder activism, and impact or community investing.

Databases that help identify high performance along ESG dimensions include, for example, Bloomberg, KLD, and Sustainalytics. Examples of environmental variables include greenhouse gas emissions, energy and water consumption, hazardous waste, number of chemical spills, climate change policy, biodiversity policy, green building and sustainable packaging. Examples of social variables include the percentage of employees that are minorities, accidents per 1000 employees and number of fatalities, employee training on corporate social responsibility, fair remuneration policy, and health safety policy. Examples of governance factors include financial ratios measuring profitability, financial leverage and asset utilization, as well as measures of the effectiveness of the Board of Directors. Companies that disclose and measure their ESG performance and perform at the top of the range, not surprisingly, turn out to provide financial returns that are at least as good as the performance of companies in control groups of samples examined by academic researchers. In other words, firms that manage their financial resources in a responsible and productive manner will do the same with their non-financial resources. Also, these firms are most likely to be more resilient during financial crises and recessions.

Shareholders are taking a more active role in holding directors accountable as reported by an article in the Wall Street Journal on shareholder activism by Vanguard and BlackRock on March 4, 2015. Shareholder resolutions have also led companies to integrate more sustainable practices into their business operations. Examples are the recycling program started by Best Buy, the use of cage-free eggs at Denny's restaurants, and Dunkin'

Donuts' decision to stop using a whitening agent in some of their sugars – all in response to shareholder proposals.

Impact and community investments are initiatives that allocate resources to projects that are intended to have a positive impact on our infrastructure, our communities and society at large. Examples are investments in the education sector, agriculture, clean transportation, clean energy and ecological stewardship. Investment vehicles come in a wide variety of forms from all over the world and include equity, debt, lines of credit, or loan guarantees. Institutional investors often wish to align their missions with their investments, while individual investors select investments consistent with their personal values. An overriding goal may be to exclude greedy, destructive and criminal market participants from access to funding, which would help public law enforcement and the judicial system accomplish their objectives and make the world a better place.

Great improvements have been made in recent years, and promise to continue, in the area of transparency and disclosure. The CDP (formerly, Carbon Disclosure Project) has operationalized reporting and performance evaluation for action on climate change risk, water, forests, and supply chain management. The Sustainability Accounting Standards Board (SASB) is currently in the process of defining reporting standards for each individual industry sector. Firms' efforts in this area are currently voluntary but may become mandatory at some point. For the companies that have participated on a voluntary basis, initial research suggests that valuation effects have been positive. This holds great potential for improving valuations for participating firms in the future.

Given the lack of a common definition of the term sustainable finance, there are many different forms and approaches to it. If we focus on the investment side, for instance, the Global Sustainable Investment Alliance distinguishes between

- Screening
- Integration
- Sustainability-themed investing
- Impact or community investing
- Corporate engagement or shareholder activism

18.4.1 Screening refers to the technique of restricting the investment universe according to predefined criteria. For example, screening could consist of refraining to invest in companies or assets that relate to specific activities (e.g., coal production, tobacco, alcohol, military) or that do not meet certain environmental or norms-based standards. Screening is not necessarily negative, that is to say exclusionary, but can also be positive in the sense of overweighting assets, companies, sectors or projects based on their environmental or social characteristics and performances. Such positive screening is also sometimes referred to as *Best in Class*.

18.4.2 Integration is the systematic and explicit inclusion of environmental, social, and governance (ESG) criteria into traditional financial analysis and decision making. An integrated investment approach would consist of deriving investment and financing decisions from the joint evaluation of both ESG criteria and more traditional financial criteria.

18.4.3 Sustainability themed investments are typically defined as investment strategies that address specific sustainability issues such as climate change, food, water, renewable energy, clean technology, or agriculture. Examples of such strategies would be investment funds that invest in assets related to energy efficiency, clean water or sustainable agriculture.

18.4.4 Impact investments are investments made into projects, companies, organizations, and funds with the intention to generate social and environmental impact alongside a financial return. Such impact investments often occur in private markets. For more information, see the Global Impact Investing Network.

18.4.5 Community investing is similar to impact investments and as such also aimed at solving social or environmental problems, where capital is specifically directed to traditionally underserved individuals or communities. To some extent microfinance can be regarded as a form of impact and community investing.

Finally, **Corporate engagement and shareholder action** refer to the technique of using shareholder power to change and influence corporate behavior. Such corporate engagement typically occurs through directly engaging with the managers of companies (i.e., communicating with senior management and/or boards of companies) or through the filing of shareholder proposals, and proxy voting that is guided by ESG criteria.

Insurances companies, in particular, could be exposed to the threat of fossil fuel and related assets becoming "stranded" or unusable, if regulations were to change in response to climate change, as recently pointed out by the Bank of England. The property-casualty industry is preparing for these risks with the Actuaries Climate Index Research Project that was recently introduced to the Saint Joseph's University community by Mike Angelina, Director of the Academy of Risk Management and Insurance. The actuaries are planning to provide an internet-based index to provide information on climate risks and serve as a monitoring tool for all affected parties as well as the public.

18.5 Sustainable Foreign Direct Investment

In the area of international finance, sustainability becomes very important when firms consider investments in developing countries. Projects need to be profitable enough to allow firms to continue operations while simultaneously producing net benefits for the host countries' long-term development goals. A recent guidance paper on evaluating a sustainable foreign direct investment by John Kline of Georgetown University suggests that sustainable projects will meet goals that span economic, environmental, social and governance categories. Examples of goals in the economic category are capital and technology transfers, employment, taxes, infrastructure, and exports. Goals in the environmental category may include pollution controls, water usage, carbon footprint, and waste reduction. Examples of social goals are labor rights, skills enhancement, public health, and non-discrimination. And in the governance area, sustainability would require external transparency, local management, supply chain standards and stakeholder dialogue. Firms that endorse international standards, such as the Global Reporting Initiative, the UN Global Compact, or Principles for Responsible Investment, tend to have priority during a search for a good company – host country match.

18.6 Sustainability plan for Funding

A Sustainability Plan is often required for funding agencies. A large number of factors affect project sustainability.

The Matrix below identifies the sustainability factors and sustainability objectives that projects need to target in order to build the potential for sustainability into their projects and improve the probability to receive funding.

Project Design and Implementation		
Sustainability Factor	**Sustainability Objective**	**Sustainability Actions**
Employing a change theory For sustainability, clear definitions of the target population, the needs to be met by the project, the expected outcomes of the project, and the interventions employed to attain them should be clear.	• Design project using evidence-based change theory or strategy	• Use evidence-based strategies • Adopt a theory of change or logic model for change • Utilize community-based participatory principles in choosing strategies and approaches

Demonstrable Effectiveness		
Sustainability Factor	**Sustainability Objective**	**Sustainability Actions**
To mobilize resources required to sustain the project beyond its initial grant, it is not enough that the project attains its objectives. The project must be able to document its success (and failure) and disseminate the evidence among stakeholders. The advertisement of the project's effectiveness not only to its stakeholders but also to the general public serves as a meaningful predictor of the sustainability of the project in that it enhances community support. (i.e., social marketing).	• Evaluate project effectiveness • Disseminate results to the community	• Design and implement a comprehensive evaluation plan to assess the impact of the strategies implemented • Hold regular dissemination meetings with the stakeholder community and professional conferences to dissemination the results of the project and build recognition for success.

Project Flexibility		
Sustainability Factor	**Sustainability Objective**	**Sustainability Actions**
The ability of a project to change in accord with changing circumstances can significantly affect its chances of survival and success. The projects that underwent changes and modifications in the course of their implementation had better chances of being sustained than projects that stuck to their original pattern.	• Maintain project flexibility to adjust to project challenges and barriers	• Get regular feedback from key stakeholder about progress and strategies • Develop a list of alternative strategies and plan to implement them if chosen strategies do not work out.

Human Resources		
Sustainability Factor	**Sustainability Objective**	**Sustainability Actions**
Staff training or expertise building in a range of matters, including strategic planning skills, knowledge of needs assessment and logic model construction, and leadership skills and fundraising expertise, is important to project sustainability. The chances of sustainability increase where staff and other stakeholders feel that they or their clients can benefit from the project.	• Provide staff and community stakeholder training to support strategic planning skills, knowledge of needs assessment and logic model construction, leadership skills and fundraising expertise,	• Hold regular comprehensive staff training and preparation on key sustainability factors • Conduct regular coalition training on key implementation and sustainability factors

Financial Resources and Financing Strategies		
Sustainability Factor	**Sustainability Objective**	**Sustainability Actions**
Sustainability increases when projects have multiple sources of funding when financing strategies are in place, and when these strategies are implemented early on. Postponement of efforts to obtain funding to later stages of the project can be a major obstacle to project sustainability.	• Attain multiple sources of funding • Develop fundraising strategies with partner organizations and coalition members	• Work closely with community partners and coalition member organizations to assist them in writing grants to fund companion efforts. • Recruit and engage Community Champions or community volunteers who are receiving training in PSE approaches.

Project Evaluation		
Sustainability Factor	**Sustainability Objective**	**Sustainability Actions**
Ongoing project evaluation is viewed as a valuable tool to promote sustainability. In addition to achieving alignment of the project's characteristics with the needs of its stakeholders, project evaluation can help in the development of strategies for sustainability, to follow up their implementation, and to evaluate their effectiveness. Similarly, evaluation can be useful in identifying problems in the project and in facilitating flexibility.	• Develop and conduct a comprehensive project evaluation	• Design and implement a comprehensive evaluation plan to capture the effectiveness of the project.

Organizational Setting: Organizational stability and flexibility		
Sustainability Factor	**Sustainability Objective**	**Sustainability Actions**
Stability of an organization and its ability to integrate new elements into its structure and culture contribute significantly to the sustainability of new projects. Sustainable projects are a result of a dynamic process of organizational change, consisting of changes in the organization's structure, approaches, and values.	• Implement the existing structure of the host organization and community infrastructure.	• Assess organizational readiness for change, culture and climate-related to the adoption of innovations and projects • Implement organization development and change interventions as needed.

Project Champions		
Sustainability Factor	**Sustainability Objective**	**Sustainability Actions**
Project champions, who promote the project in the organization and the community, can contribute to project sustainability and such champions should have a relatively high position in the organization, the ability and authority to make necessary compromises, and negotiating skills.	• Recruit, train and engage community champions	• Recruit and engage Community Champions at targeted organizations

Managerial support and flexibility		
Sustainability Factor	**Sustainability Objective**	**Sustainability Actions**
Management's openness to new ideas and readiness to take risks for the project increase the project's chances of survival in the organization.	• Gain the endorsement and support of collaborative organizational managers	• Assess leadership support and implement a change process as needed • Recruit organizational leaders for coalitions • Disseminate program impacts to leaders and educate them on the project's importance in meeting the organizational goals

Integration in the organization		
Sustainability Factor	**Sustainability Objective**	**Sustainability Actions**
Self-contained projects are less likely to be sustained than projects that are well integrated with existing systems. The development of organizational policies and procedures that will assure that projects still remain part of the routine activities of the organization even after the departure of persons who were originally responsible for creating and implementing the project. One way of attaining this aim is to integrate the goals of the project with the goals of the host organization.	• Integrate the goals of the project with the goals of the host organization	• Integrate project activities into the structure of the organization. • Building project responsibilities into job descriptions for existing and ongoing funded staff

Broader Community: Community support for the project		
Sustainability Factor	**Sustainability Objective**	**Sustainability Actions**
Community support for a project, as manifested in the cooperation of community bodies (e.g., schools, community organizations, government agencies, etc.) with the project implementers is a major predictor of its sustainability. Therefore, is the importance of strengthening the sense of ownership among those who benefit from the project in the community to increase their motivation to sustain it.	• Develop community support and ownership for the project in the targeted communities.	• Recruit the cooperation of community bodies (e.g., schools, community organizations, government agencies, etc.) and engage them in the project implementation

Political Legitimation		
Sustainability Factor	**Sustainability Objective**	**Sustainability Actions**
Another factor that has been advanced as promoting project sustainability is political support. Given the power and perseverance of institutional routines it is viewed as important to adapt projects to the policies and regulations of the relevant government bodies or, alternatively, to exert pressure to amend the policies to better accord with the project.	• Attain political support for the activities by influencing policy	• Through grassroots advocacy efforts the coalitions can work to exert pressure on local and state legislative bodies to adopt or amend policies.

18.7 Sustainability and Return on Investment

The evidence is mounting that there is real ROI advantage to companies that include ESG / Sustainability as an integral part of competitive, capital and operational strategy.

- Corporate Responsibility (a.k.a. ESG and / or Sustainability) can help to increase sales revenue by up to 20% and affect variations in customer satisfaction by 10% or more. It can also reduce the company's staff turnover rate by as much as 50%, as found in the Project ROI study sponsored by Campbell Soup and Verizon
- 43% of US-based company finance executives have indicated that revenue growth is a key driver for their actions on sustainability, of which 87% have experienced some level of revenue growth over the past 12 months, based on recent interviews of 210 executives conducted by ING.
- 66% of consumers have reported that they are willing to spend more for goods and services that have a positive impact on the world around them, as Nielsen found in a study of 30,000 consumers in 60 countries. Nielsen concludes that "committing to sustainability might just pay off for consumer brands
- Even Barron's has noticed the ROI connection and, in its February 2018 issue, published the first ranking of *Barron's 100 Most Sustainable Companies in the U.S.* In compiling their list, Barron's found the 2017 share price performance of these 100 companies as a whole returned 29%, compared with 22% for the S&P 500 Index, and observed that "... what began as an expression of values is finding wider currency as good corporate practices.

One can infer the ROI for the following investment stories as embedded in their P&L:

- UPS is saving $400 million annually from its investment in its proprietary sustainability-focused logistics software tool, ORION, that helps delivery trucks significantly reduce miles driven. Since initially deployed in 2013, UPS has avoided driving 210 million miles, saved 10 million gallons of fuel and reduced CO_2 emissions by 210,000 metric tons. Going forward, UPS expects to see annual reductions of 100 million miles and 100,000 metric tons in CO_2 emissions.
- W.W. Grainger has over 72K environmentally preferable products from which it realized $532 million in 2017 sales revenue (or 5% of total company 2017 sales revenue).
- Kellogg's indicates it has saved $28 million over ten years (2005-2015) by reducing energy and water consumption.

Two financial sector institutions, Northern Trust and State Street, advertised new ESG investment products and / or tools launches over the last two years and, in an April 2017 press release, State Street shared results of its global survey of investment institutions:

- 68% found the integration of ESG in investment strategy has significantly improved returns
- 78% of asset owners have some level of ESG engagement with the companies in which they invest, taking ESG investment beyond negative screening
- 80% of asset owners now have an ESG component in their investment strategies
- 84% of respondents are satisfied or very satisfied with the financial performance of their ESG strategy

Financial sector companies provide an interesting double-sided vantage, both as the beneficiary company for their own ROI and for a glimpse at related institutional investor returns.

- Starbucks has issued press releases that indicate they have been clearly including the issuance of corporate sustainability green bonds, both in the U.S. and internationally, in capital financing strategy.
  - SAWK has stated that [ESG] is a huge benefit for employee attraction and retention as employees really believe strongly that our company can make a difference in the world. Many people come to the company and say, this is one of the reasons that I joined
- Starbucks has issued press releases that indicate they have been clearly including the issuance of corporate sustainability green bonds, both in the U.S. and internationally, in capital financing strategy.

Questions:

1. Define sustainable finance.
2. Provide examples of sustainable finance
3. Discuss sustainability and ROI

18.8 Further Examples of sustainable finance practiced by financial organizations are given in Appendix 3.

Chapter 19
Sustainability Reporting

19.1 About Sustainability Reporting

The history of reporting process starts with financial reporting. Although the annual reports in which companies report their financial indicators are the first examples of the process, the reporting of only the positive (or negative) developments in financial indicators are not sufficient for investors or stakeholders. Issues such as the increasing depletion and price of natural resources as well as the increasing importance of human rights in the business world caused companies to be more sensitive to such matters. In parallel, after the United Nations developed the notion of sustainable development, leading companies started to report their work and performance concerning sustainability starting from the 1990s. Basically, including data on consumption of resources such as power and water as well as emissions, these reports also provide information on employee rights and social responsibility projects.

Sustainability reporting started through the individual efforts of companies and complied with various international standards and specific norms today. The most widely accepted standard in sustainability reporting around the world, the Global Reporting Initiative (GRI) is implemented through the up-to-date G4 methodology. GRI G4 reduces sustainability reporting down to economic, environmental and social dimensions, the three main pillars of sustainability. The Global Reporting Initiative is the most widely used global framework for the standardized reporting of economic, social and environmental performance. The GRI guidelines are created through a multi-stakeholder, consensus-seeking process that involves an international network of business, civil society, labour and professional institutions. www.globalreporting.org. The Global Reporting Initiative is the most widely used global framework for the standardized reporting of economic, social and environmental performance.

A sustainability report is a reporting system that is accepted worldwide and has an extensive field of practice. According to the GRI reports database, 24,018 out of 34,726 reports published worldwide are GRI approved as of August 2016.

A sustainability report is a most important communication channel that an organization has with its internal and external stakeholders. It should be considered a very valuable tool which a company can use to share its environmental performance and environmental activities, the opportunities it offers for employees and the social benefit it creates, in addition to sharing its financial performance. However, it should be remembered that sustainability reports are never tools for promotional activity. The goal of a sustainability report is to identify the priorities of the company under the main headings that matter to both itself and its stakeholders, report the work it carries out in the light of these priorities and in view of its key performance indicators (KPIs), and make such reporting available for readers in a way to allow comparison with previous reports.

A sustainability report is also a reporting tool that publicly shares the data demanded by the sustainability index, the performance standards of the leading international financial institutions, and other international organizations such as the UN Global Compact.

Any company deciding to prepare a sustainability report will need to establish a structure for the provision of environmental data (energy consumption, emissions, amount of savings, environmental benefits from company operations, etc.) and social data (educational and gender breakdown for employees, total hours of training they receive, settlement rate for customer complaints, benefits from corporate social responsibility projects, etc.). Companies and relevant company departments may consider this structure to be an additional workload, but the collection of such data is crucial for the company to review and assess its own performance. Therefore, once a company decides to engage in sustainability reporting, it should also design and establish a holistic management system structure which defines processes relevant to the company's operations, allows for communication among all processes, systematically provides data and ensures periodic data flow. Already implemented worldwide and also a growing trend among the leading domestic companies, such structures develop a methodology in which sustainability is managed within the company and address the requirements of international criteria and various reporting standards such as CDP, only if they are designed accordingly in advance. The company provides data for different processes and reports at one go and with minimal effort, thus improving the efficiency of the process.

Sustainability reporting enables organizations to consider their impacts of a wide range of sustainability issues, enabling them to be more transparent about the risks and opportunities they face. A sustainability report is an organizational report that gives information about economic, environmental, social and governance performance.

Sustainability reporting is not just report generation from collected data; instead, it is a method to internalize and improve an organization's commitment to sustainable development in a way that can be demonstrated to both internal and external stakeholders. Organizations can improve their sustainability performance by measuring (EthicalQuote (CEQ)), monitoring and reporting on it, helping them have a positive impact on society, the economy, and a sustainable future. The key drivers for the quality of sustainability reports are the guidelines of the Global Reporting Initiative (GRI). The GRI Sustainability Reporting Guidelines enable all organizations worldwide to assess their sustainability performance and disclose the results in a similar way to financial reporting. The largest database of corporate sustainability reports can be found on the website of the United Nations Global Compact initiative. www.globalreporting.org

There is now a new guidance for companies to report their impact on the Sustainable Development Goals published jointly by Global Reporting Initiative (GRI) and United Nations Global Compact on 1st August, 2018. The new publication, *Integrating the SDGs into Corporate Reporting: A Practical Guide*, helps companies of all sizes to prioritize SDG targets to act and report on, set related business objectives, and measure and report on progress. Following link provides the details:

https://www.unglobalcompact.org/docs/publications/Practical_Guide_ SDG_Reporting.pdf

19.2 What is Sustainability Reporting?

A sustainability report is a report published by a company or organization about the economic, environmental and social impacts caused by its everyday activities. A sustainability report also presents the organization's values and governance model and demonstrates the link between its strategy and its commitment to a sustainable global economy.

Sustainability reporting can help organizations to measure, understand and communicate they're economic, environmental, social and governance performance, and then set goals, and manage change more effectively. A sustainability report is a key platform for communicating sustainability performance and impacts – whether positive or negative.

Sustainability reporting can be considered as synonymous with other terms for non-financial reporting; triple bottom line reporting, corporate social responsibility (CSR) reporting, and more. It is also an intrinsic element of integrated reporting; a more recent development that combines the analysis of financial and non-financial performance.

19.3 Importance of Trust

Building and maintaining trust in businesses and governments is fundamental to achieving a sustainable economy and world. Every day, decisions are made by businesses and governments which have direct impacts on their stakeholders, such as financial institutions, labor organizations, civil society and citizens, and the level of trust they have with them. These decisions are rarely based on financial information alone. They are based on an assessment of risk and opportunity using information on a wide variety of immediate and future issues.

The value of the sustainability reporting process is that it ensures organizations consider their impacts on these sustainability issues and enables them to be transparent about the risks and opportunities they face. Stakeholders also play a crucial role in identifying these risks and opportunities for organizations, particularly those that are non-financial. This increased transparency leads to better decision making, which helps build and maintain trust in businesses and governments.

Who Should Report?

Sustainability reports are released by companies and organizations of all types, sizes, and sectors, from every corner of the world.

Thousands of companies across all sectors have published reports that reference GRI's Sustainability Reporting Guidelines. Public authorities and non-profits are also big reporters. GRI's Sustainability Disclosure Database features all known GRI-based reports.

Major providers of sustainability reporting guidance include:
- GRI (GRI's Sustainability Reporting Standards)
- The Organisation for Economic Co-operation and Development (OECD Guidelines for Multinational Enterprises)
- The United Nations Global Compact (the Communication on Progress)
- The International Organization for Standardization (ISO 26000, International Standard for social responsibility)

One reason for the popularity of sustainability reporting is that transparency not only helps companies tell their story, it also drives improvements in performance. Because of this success, multiple sustainability reporting frameworks have emerged. Companies complain of an increasingly fragmented and burdensome process. Part of this discussion is whether companies should use the standards from the Global Reporting Initiative (GRI) or the Sustainability Accounting Standards Board (SASB). This is often framed as a competition; a choice between rivals.

At a time when we are confronted with existential threats such as climate change, as well as egregious issues such as human trafficking, we don't have the time or resources to waste on such false distinctions.

Rather than being in competition, GRI and SASB are designed to fulfill different purposes for different audiences. For companies, it's about choosing the right tool for the job. The following Table shows the comparison between different framework/standards:

19.4 The Top Five Sustainability Frameworks You Should Know

STANDARD	FOCUS	WHY REPORT	SCORING	WHO REPORTS	REPORTING PERIOD
CDP Driving Sustainable Economies	Primarily GHG emissions, but has grown to address water and forestry issues as well.	CDP holds the largest repository of corporate GHG emissions and energy use data in the world and is backed by nearly 800 institutional investors representing more than $90 trillion in assets. Its transparent scoring methodology helps respondents understand exactly what's expected of them. CDP was regarded as the world's most credible sustainability rating in 2013.	Companies receive two separate scores for Disclosure Leadership Index (CDLI).	Public and Private companies, cities, government agencies, NGOs, supply chains.	• Climate Change Program: Feb. 1 – May 29 • Supply Chain Program: April 1 – July 3 • Cities Program: Jan. 1 – Mar. 31 • Water and Forestry Programs: Feb 1 to June 30
Dow Jones --- Sustainability Indexes	Industry-specific criteria considered material to investors. Equal balance of economic, social and environmental indicators.	Membership in the DJSI is prestigious as it represents the top 10% of the 2,500 largest companies in the S&P Global Broad Market Index. The Corporate Sustainability Assessment (CSA) brings a sector-specific focus and need-to-know simplicity to disclosure for public companies. The index was regarded as the world's second most credible sustainability rating after CDP.	Companies receive a total sustainability Score is between 0-100 and are ranked against peers; includes a Media and Stakeholder Analysis; those scoring within the top 10% are included in the index.	The 2,500 largest public companies in the world.	April 3 – May 28

433

Global Reporting Initiative	Corporate Social responsibility with equal weight on environmental, social and governance factors. Heavy on stakeholder engagement to determine materiality.	GRI was announced as the official reporting standard of the UN Global Compact, making it the default reporting framework for the compact's more than 5,800 associated companies. It's among the oldest , most widely adopted and most widely respected reporting methodologies in the world. Its thorough focus on social and governance aspects of ESG is unparalleled.	The focus is on transparency so no true scoring methodology; new G.4 framework requires entity reporting to choose "Core" or "Complete" reporting.	Public and private companies, cities, government agencies, universities, hospitals, NGOs.	Anytime, but typically integrated into a company's traditional annual report.
GRESB	Environmental, social and governance performance in the global commercial real estate sector only. Includes asset- and entity-level disclosures.	Private and public institutional investors look to GRESB's annual survey as the barometer of sustainability performance in the commercial real estate industry. Its niche target audience allows it to give deeper and more accurate insights into industry performance and reveal "investment grade" results.	Responses scored out of a possible 140.5 points distributed across two categories of data. Heavy weighting placed on implementation and asset-level performance.	Commercial real estate owners, asset managers, and developers.	April 1 – June 30

SUSTAIN-ABILITY ACCOUNTING STANDARD(SASB)	US public companies only. Industry-specific issues deemed material to investors.	SASB's standards enable comparison of peer performance and benchmarking within an industry. Studies by Goldman Sachs and Deutsche Bank have shown the stock of companies who disclose on sustainability outperforms that of companies who do not. SASB is backed by the likes of Bloomberg LP and the Rockefeller Foundation, giving it extra clout with capital markets.	No scoring system. Instead, SASB is a standardized methodology for reporting sustainability performance through the Form 10-K.	No one yet – they've just released their first sector reporting guidelines.	Integrated into quarterly 10-K filings.

Established in 1997, GRI developed the first corporate sustainability reporting framework. Today, GRI's standards are used by the majority of companies reporting sustainability information. The standards are designed to provide information to a wide variety of global stakeholders ranging from civil society to investors. Consequently, the GRI standards include a very broad scope of the disclosure. Typically, companies use them to develop and design their sustainability or corporate responsibility reports.

SASB, established in 2011, develops standards for the disclosure of material sustainability information to investors in mandatory filings (financial disclosures). SASB standards, available for 79 industries, identify material sustainability factors that are likely to impact financial performance.

Investors have their own unique needs, different from those of suppliers, customers, communities, interest groups and other stakeholders. They demand reliable and comparable sustainability information with clear links to financial performance. Focused on this need, SASB standards identify the subset of sustainability issues that are reasonably likely to be material to investors. In order to preserve a focus on financial materiality as well as to attain comparability among peers, SASB standards are industry specific.

Different audiences, unique needs

As you can see, GRI and SASB are intended to meet the unique needs of different audiences. The GRI standards are designed to provide information to a wide variety of stakeholders and consequently, include a very broad array of topics. SASB's are designed to provide information to investors and consequently, focus on the subset of sustainability issues that are financially material.

As such, deciding between GRI and SASB is a false choice. Companies that produce a sustainability report also should (and in many cases must, when required by law) disclose financially material sustainability information in their mandatory financial reports, such as a 10-K. Conversely, companies that only disclose sustainability impacts that meet a financial materiality test are potentially ignoring issues critical for sustainable development.

Truly sustainable companies do both. They identify sustainability impacts that are financially material (and therefore compelled to be disclosed to investors) as well as the impacts relevant to a broader range of stakeholders. They communicate their story to investors and other stakeholders in the appropriate reporting channels and ensure consistency.

The bottom line is that the GRI and SASB standards are not mutually exclusive; they are mutually supportive. Transparency is still the best currency for creating trust among investors and other stakeholders, but companies should focus on which stakeholders need which information in which format.

19.4 Material indicators

The materiality of information is at the center of sustainability reporting.

GRI's definition of materiality: The materiality principles of GRI's guidelines defines materiality in the context of the sustainable report.

The report should cover aspects that:

- "Reflect the organization's significant economic, environmental and social impacts; or
- Substantively, influence the assessment and decision of stakeholders."

Materiality is the threshold at which aspects become significantly important that they should be reported. Beyond this threshold, not all aspects are of equal importance, and the report should prioritize the relative priority of these material aspects.

For example top 10 GRI aspects reported in the Technology Hardware and Equipment sector are:

1. Emissions, effluents, and waste
2. Products and services
3. Training and education
4. Employment
5. Community
6. Energy
7. Economic performance
8. Materials
9. Occupational health and safety
10. Diversity and equal opportunity

Top 10 GRI aspects recorded in the Banks and Diverse Banking Sector are:

1. Community
2. Training and education
3. Product and service labeling
4. Product portfolio
5. Economic performance
6. Employment
7. Emissions, effluent, and waste
8. Diversity and equal opportunity
9. Compliance
10. Customer privacy

The world needs corporations to understand, reflect and act on a broader range of concerns than those raised by financial stakeholders. Stakeholder concerns are often leading indicators of what may become financially material to a company in the future.

Investors need standardized, high-quality information on material factors that can affect price or value. When sustainability disclosure distinguishes between that which is material to the investors (because it may affect price or value), and that which is of interest to stakeholders (because it describes company's impacts and could affect the company trajectory in the long-term), all stakeholders benefit. SASB and GRI are designed to meet these respective needs.

Actions driven through the financial markets and actions driven through a wider range of stakeholders are important in different ways. Both SASB and GRI recognize this, and we pledge to support one another in this common quest for improving corporate performance on sustainability issues.

19.5 Sustainability Reporting Guidelines:

The GRI sustainability reporting guidelines can be found from the following links:

https://www.globalreporting.org/resourcelibrary/GRIG4-Part1-Reporting-Principles-and-Standard-Disclosures.pdf

https://www.globalreporting.org/resourcelibrary/G3.1-Guidelines-Incl-Technical-Protocol.pdf

Examples of Sustainability Reporting

Sustainability Reporting Examples of Companies from various sectors and industries can be found from the following link:

https://www.icas.com/technical-resources/sustainability-reporting

Sustainability Reporting in India:

A recent incisive study of 46 companies on the quality of India's corporate sustainability reporting shows significant progress. Yet, it rues lack of seriousness of senior management to sustainability and the lack of will to create greater value

GRI Regional Hub South Asia, Indian Institute of Management Bangalore and TCS Ltd jointly released a study in November 2016 titled 'Sustainability Integration – Corporate Reporting Practices in India.' It found that the level of disclosure by Indian companies has gone up indicating a greater understanding of the links between sustainability practices, corporate performance, and competitive advantage.

It also explores the level of disclosure among Indian reporting organizations. It focuses on understanding the qualitative aspects of the disclosure in the area of sustainability strategy, and its potential connection to senior decision-makers' commitment, materiality, risks, and opportunities.

To the authors of the report, 'Integrating sustainability' implies incorporating sustainability issues (environmental, social, and broader economic factors) into an organization's decision-making process, actions, and performance management.

It is to be noted that a lack of an integrated approach limits an organization's abilities to thrive in the future. Integration of risk arising out of material aspects allows organizations to move sustainability from a stand-alone initiative to an embedded consideration – part of the larger picture.

Companies and stakeholders have realized that greater transparency fosters stronger relationships, which is essential for building long-term trust.

India's stock market regulator Securities and Exchange Board of India (SEBI) has so far asked only top 500 companies listed on Indian stock exchanges to include business responsibility reports in their annual reports.

Of the 46 companies included in this study, 34 preferred reporting 'in accordance' with the GRI's G4 Sustainability Reporting Guidelines' core option, rather than the comprehensive option.

Most, especially small and medium-sized enterprises (SMEs) prefer to gradually step-up the level of their reporting, beginning with the core option and eventually moving on to the comprehensive option.

Key Findings

- Only 39% of the firms in this study provided a comprehensive description of the risks and opportunities arising from sustainability trends. There is an urgent need for the management to pay greater attention to this aspect
- Over 93% of the firms studied identified and disclosed material aspects. These material aspects often have a significant financial impact in the short term or long term on an organization.
- While senior decision-makers generally articulate key events and achievements, few have started disclosing challenges such as accidents, fatalities, or workforce unrest.
- Due to GRI reporting requirements and the evolution of regulatory bodies on mandatory reporting, Sustainability is now entrenched in the boardroom; leading to improved governance of sustainability impacts.

The Flip Side

- Reporting is often seen as an exercise in public relations rather than a tool for corporate transformation which can contribute to a sustainable economy.
- Many companies claim that 'sustainability is in their DNA' but fail to create value, indicating the lack of integration in their core business strategy.
- While many corporate sustainability programs have achieved success on initiatives like optimizing energy use, reducing CO_2 emissions, water conservation, and managing labor conditions, few have broken out of the sustainability silo and embedded this practice in the overall organizational strategy for business value creation.
- Even leaders in reporting are still cautious about disclosing sustainability aspects.
- Very few companies demonstrate senior management involvement and leadership
- The absence of proactive interest from users of the sustainability-related information such as consumers and governments
- Dependency on a regulatory regime of disclosure rather than business case driven voluntary approach

Questions:

1. What is sustainability reporting?
2. Discuss the Top 5 sustainability reporting framework.

PART III
Cases

Case Study 1
Marti Uday Case Study

Abstract

The present era of globalization, modernization and development is the result of the extreme exploitation of natural and human resources in developed as well as developing countries. But the scarcity of these resources leads the business or corporate world to explore the methods of handling and exploiting them to fulfill the current and future needs without any compromise. Therefore, being sustainable is becoming the most important factor for any developmental process. As manufacturing is also viewed from the broader perspective of sustainability these days, so manufacturing companies are also pushing them to achieve various dimensions of sustainability, such as social, economical and environmental. Sustainability, in the case of a manufacturer, is measured by evaluation of products, processes or systems that effect its operations. It requires an assessment of all the factors that affect the manufacturing facilities and then developing strategies to reduce their impact. Therefore, the manufacturing companies are always under pressure to develop strategies to allocate their resources efficiently, because of increasing prices and competition. As traditional approach related to quality and price cannot be ignored, the manufacturers are intensely focused on areas like energy, water, emission, waste, production, awareness, etc. This paper reviews sustainability manufacturing practices and initiatives were taken by Maruti Udyog Limited in this field.

Keywords

Sustainability, resource allocation, and manufacturing.

I. Introduction

Traditionally, the manufacturing system was assumed to be sound if it can provide an opportunity for continuous improvement, hence results in an increase in production and operational quality. In such a system, the production system was designed to improve process capability and operational performance. However, the proper attention was paid towards product nonconformities and process off-specifications . The reason behind was, this kind of system resulted in lesser waste and emissions due to the reduction of rejected parts . The manufacturing companies

443

were only emphasizing on good quality in lesser price and optimal use of resources. As it is rightly said, for these kinds of manufacturing units by David C. Korten that Economists know the price of everything and the value of nothing .

Therefore, nowadays, manufacturing system is viewed from a different perspective. Revolutionary production-systems thinking directed at the identification and elimination of all forms of non-value added activity, or waste, from an organization. The manufacturing systems need to be designed for value creation. As said by Henry Ford, "If it doesn't produce value, its waste." So, it directs an organization towards the waste elimination from all the sources. Because, manufacturing industries are additionally under the economic pressure to compensate for increasing cost and create adding value . So, it has become necessary to design products as well as processes for value creation.

Besides value creation, the manufacturing systems are viewed from the broader characteristic of sustainability these days. The idea of sustainability has come to represent the rising expectations not only from an economic viewpoint but also from social and environmental performances of the manufacturing system . So, the manufacturing system is not only limited to value creation but to sustainable value creation. That means the manufacturing companies are finding their way to sustainable development by using methodologies of increasing the efficiencies (economic, ecologic, social) into the production system by producing products with less energy, less material, and less pollution . Some of the objectives of a sustainable manufacturing system can be,

Improving resource efficiency and waste management
- Examining the product lifecycle involved in manufacturing.
- Trying to ensure economic growth minimizing environmental pollution.
- Examining how to stimulate innovation and investment to provide cleaner technology
- Providing awareness and training to employees.

This paper compares quality with sustainability and reviews the concept of sustainability in reference to manufacturing and concludes with the sustainability practices adopted by Maruti Udyog Ltd.

II. Quality Vs. Sustainability

According to Caplan (1990) "Quality is process dependent" which means that the quality can be attained by effective product and process design. Deming, Juran, and Crosby made the claim that quality programs would increase efficiency, rather than just raise costs. Crosby's famous words that "Quality is free." made the important point that businesses can make breakthroughs by seeking quality . According to Feigenbaum (1991), "Quality is the most cost-effective, least capital-intensive route to productivity." . Thus, quality and productivity objectives are not different according to the traditional view. But sustainability takes quality thinking to the next level to include creating a healthier, safer society by integrating environmental concerns into manufacturing and design efforts .

III. Sustainability

World Commission on Environment and Development defined sustainable economic progress as "development that meets the needs of the present without compromising the ability of future generations to meet their own needs." Elgin also observes, "if we do no more than work for a sustainable future, then we are in danger of creating a world in which living is little more than 'only not dying." It has been said because; our ecological demands already exceed what nature can supply. This "ecological overshoot" means the stock of natural environmental capital is depleting. Therefore, business enterprises need to grow at least enough to keep pace with the economy, but defining growth and the ways & means of growth need to change .

Earlier, the industries were only limited to environmental laws and regulations set by Government bodies. The traditional understanding of environmental management was limited to "cleaning up the mess" after production is completed. Environmental management in many companies is oriented to compliance, remediation of contaminated land, and reduction of targeted hazardous materials . Then, they start talking only about the green production which was only limited to eco-friendly products and processes. It is a very proven fact that eco-factories are not only the solution if they are producing the unsustainable products . Therefore, companies are proactively coming forward to develop sustainably. Many of these companies are now going beyond environmental performance and are now beginning to discuss sustainability. Sustainability pushes the environmental envelope and challenges companies to consider issues such as the environmental impact of the materials they select, the social implications of their products and operations, and in some case the need for their product at all . However, successful sustainability initiatives often require fundamental product redesign and operational rethinking. Therefore, achieving solutions to environmental problems that we face today requires long-term potential actions for sustainable development. In the long term, sustainable enterprise resilience can be defined as the "capacity for an enterprise to survive, adapt, and grow in the face of turbulent change," and at the same time, "to increase shareholder value without increasing material throughput." Sustainable enterprise resilience within the framework of industrial ecology creates multiple business opportunities through green technologies, reduction of raw material and energy use .

In Fig. 1, the holistic view of the production system has been given. If the overall effectiveness of the industry has to be improved, then the company has to pay proper attention towards economic, ecological and social factors of production, which in return result in sustainable production.

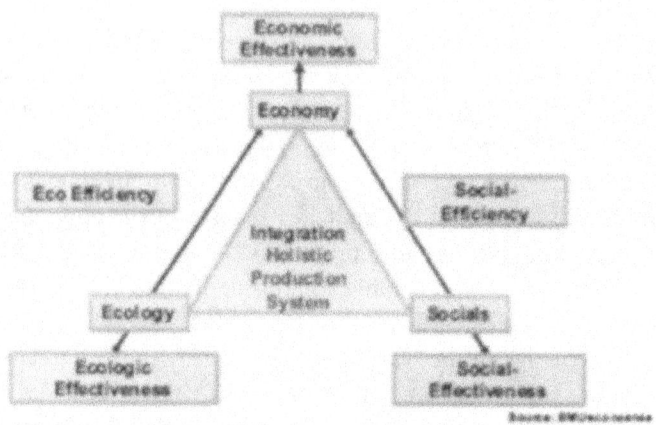

Fig.l: Efficiency and sustainability.

Concepts that are discussed above guide sustainability practices at multiple levels. Firms use these frameworks to motivate sustainability initiatives, to educate employees, and in decision-making. Viewed together, these frameworks can guide firms in encouraging and launching sustainability initiatives, in evaluating their success, in integrating environmental considerations into the allocation of resources, and in designing products to gain competitive advantage from a sustainable business

IV. A case study of Maruti Udyog Ltd.

The products of automobile industry touch daily lives by providing personal mobility for millions. But there are some challenges that are faced by the industry such as deterioration of local air quality, global warming and the treatment of the scrapped vehicle. Every automaker has worked in the direction to save the environment, and the considerable improvements are also made in this direction. As there are competitive pressures to reduce cost, the automakers are driven towards resource productivity and the minimization of waste to achieve economies of scale . A recent World Energy Council (WEC) study found that without any change in our current practice, the world energy demand in 2020 would be 50-80% higher than 1990 levels .

Maruti Udyog, India's leading automaker whose parent is Suzuki from Japan, has also paved its way towards sustainable development by incremental changes in few things that resulted in big savings. Last year Maruti ran a program to reduce part of each component by 1 gram. Interestingly, Maruti has reduced its electricity consumption per vehicle by 20 percent in the last nine years, water consumption by 46 percent, and landfill waste by 67 percent. The carbon dioxide emission has declined 27 percent in seven years. It has become a zero discharge company and recycled all its water. The small car named 'A-Star,' which is the global car of Maruti is designed in such a way that 87 percent of the car can be recycled as explained by European regulations about the concept of end-of-life-vehicles (ELVs) .Therefore the company bagged an order of 35000 A-star from Nissan in Europe recently . In this direction, Maruri has taken some other initiatives towards sustainability, which are,

- When the Indian market was offering only two tube light configurations, i.e., 42 watts and 36 watts, Maruti tied up with a small manufacturer for 28-watt tubes. In the factory, there is provision for three CFL lamps and company managers realized that the room would have enough illumination with two lamps of 36 watts in each holder. So the third lamps were taken out. This seems to be a small step but if we look towards energy savings in a year time, and then they are huge.

- In the assembly line, where axles are installed, the components are placed on an inclined bar on which they slide towards the worker due to gravity which helped in eliminating the use of conveyor belts.

- Water pumps in cooling towers were made to consume less electricity by slightly reducing the size of the impeller.

- The power supply of machines that run intermittently was cut to save energy.

- The compressed air used to run various tools used to go into the shop floor at 28-29 degrees centigrade allowed to raise its temperature to 32 degrees because of no harm.

- Earlier waste water from all sources was dumped into Government sewers, for which company was paying Government. But now after the improvements in treatment processes, no sewer is discharged into Government sewers and all waste water is recycled by the company.

- The company has used steel crates rather than wooden or board packaging for storage and transport of components coming from Japan. After using the steel crates are folded and sent back for reuse. The thousand of parts coming from Indian vendors are supplied in reusable plastic bins to avoid wastage.

The steps put forward by Maruti Udyog not only resulted in economic growth but also in environmental and social progress. It is quite obvious that if a company wants to exceed in future than it has to look its present. Maruti Udyog realized the importance of being sustainable in the present. The company is proving that the journey starts with the small initiatives, but they result in big savings. No doubt, it is not easy to bring change for sustainable development. To implement sustainability principles, firms need clear objectives . It is a fact that only those programs that are implemented effectively and communicated to all employees result in value for the organization. So this study reveals that by combining sustainability in a manufacturing system, how a company can reduce water, electricity, and general energy usage, and lowered waste disposal costs. Hence, all these activities can take a company towards sustainable value creation.

V. Conclusion

The automobile sales are increasing in India and today there is a challenge before manufacturing industries to become sustainable. It clearly shows that the raw materials are finite and there are increasing demands. Therefore, companies are moving towards a change in product designs, various stages of processing, consumption, and use of raw materials so as to encourage optimum reuse and recycling, thereby avoiding wastage and preventing depletion of the natural resources stock. But there is nothing special that has to be created; therefore the change begins with little transformations in a manufacturing system. There is no single formula which can be applied to make a company sustainable immediately. Sustainability is temporal and deals with continuous advancement in all areas. Also, sustainability is not forced, but it depends upon the will of the organization for a change. To protect, maintain and improve present lifestyles and preserve them for the future, companies are voluntarily coming forward to become sustainable. Thus, sustainability in the manufacturing system is the key to address various problems of the production and operations in the industry. Maruti Udyog Ltd took some steps forward to make its products sustainable. Therefore other companies should also come forward to adopt sustainable manufacturing practices so as to secure the future of coming generations.

Case Study 2

Sustainable Organization and Social and Environmental Impact – A Case Study

Abstract

This article on organizational sustainability is divided into three parts: PART I discusses the problem of how sustainability approach helps an organization to meet its mission and objectives efficiently and effectively based on the various sustainability criteria. PART II discusses how the operation of an organization affects the three major sustainability areas of environmental, social and economic aspects. This article discusses the concept of sustainability through a case study of a non-profit organization called DKCCDC, based in Santiniketan, West Bengal, India of which the author is the founder and director which has helped him to conceptualize and organize the data and implement the sustainability concepts in greater detail on a first-hand basis. The concept detailed here is equally applicable for both profit and nonprofit organizations. It also discusses the problem of how to calculate Green House Gas Emissions and carbon footprint and how to mitigate the impact of Carbon and Green House Gases as well as consider renewable energy towards carbon reduction strategies and convert footprint into handprint. Ultimately, it addresses the problem of how to make an organization sustainable in terms of reaching its goals as well as meeting operational sustainability requirements. PART III discusses the sustainability change management issues leading to practicing change management by the staff in my NGO. This article is based on a study the author of this book conducted as part of his sustainability certification of Harvard University, USA.

Keywords

Sustainability, Social License to Operate, Carbon Footprint, Green House Gases, Hand Printing

PART I:

Organizational sustainability refers to achieving organizational missions and objectives efficiently and effectively with due consideration to stakeholder interests. Following method describes how this can be achieved:

449

Section 1: Introduction:

The sustainability initiative that I have introduced, since the beginning of this course, is in my own NGO which is located in a large town, named Bolpur, in India. The NGO has a clinic for providing free quality health care to the poor, a school for providing free education from Grade V to Grade XII as well as a vocational training center for skill development training for employment generation. Poor and underprivileged students and patients are the main customers of my NGO. They do not pay any money whatsoever for the service they receive. I am the founder and director of the NGO and completely finance the operation of the NGO.

The sustainability method is presented here through 16 elements/sections namely: Organization and Internal context, setting objectives, Understanding the external context , Engaging with stakeholders , Social license to operate , Governance and leadership –sustainability policy, Risk Assessment, Financial sustainability, Resources and Operating System, Sustainability Program, Value Chain Model to Scope Measurement, Monitoring and Measurement, Transparency and accountability, Maturity process and Improvement and Innovation are the comprehensive and good way to implement sustainability as these elements cover all possible scenarios and situations and risks to ensure a sustainable organization. However, wholehearted implementation of these elements is essential together with self-assessment and PDCA to check at what level of sustainability maturity the organization is and continuously improve to reach the highest level (level 5) of maturity, to achieve full-scale sustainability. Through this approach, sustainability can be built into the process of an organization and not as a separate activity.

Section 2: Organization and Internal Context

Approach to overview of the organization will include the name of the organization, where it is located, its purpose, mission , the services it offers, its assets, employee make up, facilities, core competencies, organization structure and governance, its key stakeholders, its competitive environment and strategic context, operating environment, organizational relationships and sustainability environment.

Overview of the Community will include the demographic nature of the community in terms of location, male/female ratio, literacy rate, climate, economic status/wealth, main industries, income distribution and equality, no. of schools and hospitals, as well as the political, social, economical, technological environmental and legal environment.

Approach to internal context is as follows:

Internal context include a mission statement, objectives, leadership styles, and its organizational culture, organization's operating environment, as well as

- Policies for sustainability
- Capabilities – resources and knowledge (e.g., capital, people, processes, and systems)
- Decision-making processes including sense making and knowledge management
- Systems adapted by the organization centered on the plan-do-check-act model
- Organization's contractual relationships that involve adherence to a supplier code of conduct as a condition of doing business with another organization determine all the activities, products, and services, apply SWIFT (Structured What If Techniques) and SWOT analysis.

Therefore, the factors associated with the internal context should be identified, and then SWOT will be used to find the opportunities and threats. Thereafter, the risk assessment process is to be used to find the opportunities that need to be embraced and the threats that need to be avoided.

The aforementioned is implemented in DKCCDC as follows:

a. Organizational Operating Environment	**DKCCDC** is located in a small town of about 0.5 million people called "Bolpur" in the State of West Bengal in India. It has a literacy rate of 60%. Male literacy rate is 60% and female literacy rate is 40%. Male to female ratio is 50:50. In economics term, about 10% of the population is considered to be rich, 50% Middle class and 40% poor.
1) Product/Service Offerings[1]	DKCCDC offers health care services including free consultancies, medicines and diagnosis, Mobile Medical unit, education (coaching school of Grade V to XII) and vocational training for employment, who come to DKCCDC completely free of cost. DKCCDC also does environmental protection and civic works through its customers(i.e. students of the school) for a better and greener environment.
2) Vision/Mission/ Core Values/ Purpose/Core Competencies[2]	The **mission** of DKCCDC is to improve health care for the poor, help eradicate illiteracy and reduce unemployment in the community. DKCCDC **core value** is to uplift the condition of the poor and bring them at par with the mainstream of the population in terms of health, education and financial condition and empowerment of the poor to improve the overall sustainability of the community. Its Values are: • Compassion • Innovation • Empowerment and Equality • Opportunity to all

3) Staff/Volunteer/ Member Profile[3]	There are about 50 staff working in DKCCDC. There are no volunteers among the staff. The staff consists of 10 Physicians, 20 teachers, 12 trainers for vocational training and 6 administration staff including accountant.
4) Assets – Facilities, property, equipment, technology	DKCCDC operates in 3 separate buildings one each for health clinic, education and vocational training. It has all the modern equipment for vocational training and computers for education as well as a vehicle for Mobile Medical Unit
5) Regulatory Requirements[4]	DKCCDC operates under the legal requirement of Govt. of India and has the necessary legal license to operate.
b. Organizational Relationships	
1) Organizational Structure/ Governance	The organization structure is according to the Memorandum of Association of DKCCDC which includes President, Vice President, Treasurer, Secretary and 5 Members and is according to the legal requirement. The owner is also the President of DKCCDC and completely funds the full operations of DKCCDC.
2) Stakeholders (including customers)	Main Stakeholders are: 1. Customers i.e. the poor and destitute who come for service to DKCCDC 2. Neighbors in the community where DKCCDC operates 3. Suppliers: Mainly medicines suppliers, computer and book suppliers as well as suppliers of clothes for tailoring school. 4. Government who audits the operations of DKCCDC to ensure they are in line with DKCCDC Mission 5. Employees and staff 6. Towns outside Bolpur 7. Other NGOs/Competitors 8. Volunteers
3) Suppliers and Partners	1. Mainly medicines suppliers and book suppliers as well as suppliers of clothes for tailoring school. 2. Medical equipment suppliers 3. Computer suppliers

Organizational (strategic) Situation for DKCCDC is as follows:

a. Sustainability Environment[1]	
1) Competitive Position	There are many Non-Government organizations in Bolpur. But the competitive position of DKCCDC is very good as it offers services with highly qualified staff and very good facilities all at free of cost.
2) Comparative Data	Comparative data is available on competitors' websites. There is no direct comparative data though as DKCCDC always has the competitive advantage over others as it provides all services completely free of cost to its customers and not dependent on outside funding which no other NGO in the area does.
3) Strategic Context	Strategic context and advantage of DKCCDC is based on providing high-quality service free of cost to the underprivileged of the society on a continuing basis.
4) Sustainability Program	Main sustainability program of DKCCDC is continuous improvement of its services through improved quality, new services, improved relationship with its stakeholders to ensure customers (poor patients and students) keep taking the services of DKCCDC as well as ensuring long-term availability of finance so that DKCCDC can continue operating for a long time to come.

Section 3: Establishing Objectives

Overarching and operating objectives of DKCCDC are as follows:

DKCCDC's overarching and operating objectives are stated below:

1. Overarching objective: Reduce illiteracy

   Operating objectives:

   1.1 Build coaching centers to provide study support to students from Primary to Higher Secondary (Grade I to XII) to improve their learning abilities as well as grades

   1.2 Coach senior students to impart education on basic mathematics and language to small poor children in their community

   1.3 Invite poor adults to school to take training on reading and writing skills after their working hours

2. Overarching objectives: Reduce Poverty

   Operating objectives:

   2.1. Provide vocational and skill training to the poor unemployed people to improve their possibility of getting jobs

   2.2. Collaborate with other organizations to employ students of DKCCDC upon their successful completion of the training programs

   2.3 Help to form Self Help Group (SHG) for women and give them loans to start small businesses

2.4 Help to provide nutrition to the poor by providing meals once a day. Give free books and other stuff for learning.

3 Overarching objective: Improve Healthcare

Operating Objectives:

3.1 Build a hospital with modern facilities and General and Specialist doctors

3.2 Provide medical services free of cost or minimal charges to the poor including consultancy, medicines, and diagnosis

3.3 Advocate the need of health and hygiene and good living to the poor

3.4 Operate mobile medical unit equipped with modern equipment and medicines and visit poor communities to render health care and those who can not visit DKCCDC facility.

   a. Provide basic medical training such as nursing so that the number of medical practitioners can increase to provide health care services.

4. Improve Community living and environment protection Plant trees, clean schools and roads, etc. for better environmental protection and better living.

Section 4: External Context

Approach to External Context is as follows:

External contexts are Conditions, entities, events, and factors surrounding an organization that influences its activities and choices, and determine its opportunities and threats. It may also be called the external operating environment and includes the following:

- Use PESTLE analysis
- Identify the external factors
- Each factor has positive and/or negative effects on the organization
- The focus is on the organization
- Use the SWOT analysis on each element
- Identify all the opportunities and threats

The External Context of DKCCDC:

Political: DKCCDC is established under the Societies Registration Act of 1861 of Government of India. This Act is a tool for the Government to help establish non-Government and Non-profit organizations with the purpose of channeling aids to these organizations to help in projects related to removing illiteracy, better health care, flood relief, etc.

Opportunities: It is easy to establish NGOs and so, the owner of DKCCDC has started his NGO with his own funding with a view to fulfill the purpose of DKCCDC.

Threat: There are many political parties vying for votes in Bolpur. it has become difficult for DKCCDC to remain neutral without supporting any political party. Sometimes, opposite political parties create problems in program implementation, if they don't receive votes in their favour.

Economic: The town of Bolpur is economically asymmetric meaning that though there are many rich people, however, the majority are poor. Therefore, Govt. aid is not always sufficient to help the cause of the poor.

Opportunities: Due to many underprivileged people in Bolpur and surrounding areas, there is clearly long-term opportunities for serving these people according to DKCCDC's goals. Therefore, DKCCDC has made many capital expenditures and built school, hospital and other infra -structure.

Threat: DKCCDC is totally funded by its sole Owner/Founder. Therefore, the main threat is that how long he can continue to fund it. Secondly, even if he has funds, how he can ensure sustainability of DKCCDC after his death. He is now 60 years of age. Further, job opportunities in Bolpur is primarily in the agricultural sector. Therefore, students may find it difficult to find jobs even after being trained and may need to migrate to bigger towns for jobs.

Social: The citizens of Bolpur welcome the idea of NGOs operating in their communities as it also helps in improving the well being of the poor people in their community and builds a healthy and prosperous image of the town.

Opportunities: Due to the conducive environment in terms of support from the local community, it is easy to run a NGO in Bolpur.

Threats: Many poor and sick people line up for free healthcare which sometimes spread disease in the community. Further, due to lack of sanitary facilities, they defecate on the roads and make the roads dirty. Therefore, neighbours of DKCCDC often threaten with closing down DKCCDC.

Technological: Bolpur is well equipped with internet facilities and technology enabled learning for imparting education. However, medical facilities are not always modern and sometimes good doctors are not available.

Opportunities: DKCCDC is currently offering many IT courses and can expand into more web-based education. This will enable the underprivileged students to access to the internet and global exposure to possibilities in education, knowledge, and jobs and will truly enable them to change their lives and empower them to be social change agents.

Threats: Offering proper health care to the underprivileged is a major problem due to insufficient healthcare facilities as well as inadequate advanced equipment.

Environmental: There are no environmental regulations that are in force in Bolpur.

Opportunities: There is a lot of opportunities for improving the environment, and DKCCDC is involved in a lot of environmental work such as planting trees, cleaning roads, schools, etc. These work are done by the students themselves under leadership as part of their learning to serve the society.

Threats: The main threats are of the spread of disease due to a high level of pollution and filth in the town due to poor environmental care and protection.

Legal: DKCCDC is legally constituted.

Opportunities: DKCCDC has employed its own security due to the uncertain legal environment to protect its infrastructure. DKCCDC is also offering courses on security and private defense to bolster the safety of the citizen and enforcement of laws.

Threat: Due to the uncertain legal environment and ineffective law enforcement, DKCCDC sustainability has become rather precarious.

Section 5: DKCCDC Stakeholder Engagement

How Stakeholders were engaged:
- Staff and employees were asked about what is their understanding of environmental sustainability and how it can be improved. Therefore, teachers, administration staff, doctors, and nurses were approached and they responded in writing
- From the patients and students, the same questions were asked but their responses were recorded or noted down on the paper.
- Staff and customers were told about the NGO sustainability targets
- Review the engagement plan at regular intervals, i.e., weekly
- Check the progress against the goals on a fortnightly basis
- Identify specific metrics to measure the progress (such as reducing water usage, reducing electricity consumption, reducing waste generated, etc.)
- Use the metrics to determine the effectiveness of the efforts.
- Internal Board: They are involved in strategizing and developing Mission of DKCCDC.
- Management and Employees: They operate DKCCDC and ensure quality and customer satisfaction
- Donor: Directly involved and is the founder, director, and financier of DKCCDC
- Customers (Students & Patients): They are the raison d'taire for the organization as DKCCDC exists to serve them

- Suppliers: High level of involvement as they ensure supply of books and branded medicines at a discount.
- Community members and neighbors: Their involvement is limited but their support is essential for the continuity of DKCCDC and to get "License to Operate." Therefore, fortnightly I take feedback from my community members about the improvements we are making.

TABLE – 1 below depicts the stakeholder engagement

TABLE – 1 (Stakeholder Engagement)

Stakeholder Group	Involvement	Influence	Contributions	Method of Engagement/ Frequency	Interests
Internal: Board	They are involved in strategizing and developing Mission of DKCCDC.	High level of influence as they determine the direction of DKCCDC.	Develops objectives of DKCCDC and monitors and controls its activities.	Meet quarterly	High level of interests as they determine and guide the strategic objectives of DKCCDC and ensure that DKCCDC is sustainable on a long-term basis.
Management/ Employees	They operate DKCCDC and ensure quality and customer satisfaction	Involved in the selection of suppliers and customers. Often affordable customers try to receive services of DKCCDC as it is free of cost and high quality. So, proper screening is done to ensure only truly needy avails the services of DKCCDC.	Participates in the day to day operations of DKCCDC.	Direct contact with the customers and suppliers on the Daily basis	High level of interest as they ensure DKCCDC operates according to the mission of DKCCDC and monitors and controls the activities of DKCCDC.
Volunteers	No direct involvement	None	Insignificant	Word of Mouth to Customers about DKCCDC	Insignificant

Donor	Directly involved and is the founder, director, and financier of DKC-CDC	He is directly involved in both strategizing and operations of the NGO	He makes the full financial contribu-tions for the oper-ations of DKCCDC	He is directly involved all the time.	Have a high level of interest and drives DKCCDC and its goals.
External					
Customers (Students and Patients)	They are the raison d'taire for the organi-zation as DKC-CDC exists to serve them	Have a high lev-el of influence as their satisfaction of services pro-vided by DKC-CDC bring them to DKCCDC	Financial contribu-tion is nil as they don't pay for the services. Main con-tributions are their opinion of the nature and quality of services provided	1. Survey on a monthly basis 2. Feedback after services provided on the weekly and random basis 3. Continuously and as re-quired basis 4. Quarterly parents/teach-ers meetings are held to learn about customer's needs and if services can be improved within the available budget.	Have a high level of interest in the service of DKCCDC as without it poor patients cannot get medical treatment, and poor students may not get education or skills for em-ployment
Suppliers	High level of involve-ment as they ensure supply of books and branded medi-cines at a dis-count.		High level of contri-butions as they ensure supply of medicines and books and other materi-als are delivered on time, at high quality and competi-tive price	Direct and via telephone and emails on daily and as required basis	They have a high level of interests in the success of DKCCDC as DKCCDC contributes to their business-es through purchasing from them.

Local Profitable Businesses (who are offering similar services at cost)	Limited involvement	Limited influence. However, they sometimes complain that due to the free service provided by DKCCDC, their business sometimes suffer. Therefore, they do not support DKCCDC services.	Has no contributions	There is no engagement	They have interests in a negative way as they do not want DKCCDC to succeed as it affects their businesses to some extent.
Community members and neighbors	Limited involvement	They have a good level of involvement in terms of passively supporting the activities of DKCCDC and not openly complaining against it.	They have contributions in terms of supporting the activities and tolerating the activities of DKCCDC without any direct benefits to them.	Adhoc. DKCCDC members sometimes visit community members for communicating their gratitude for the support given by the community members for DKCCDC to continue their services in the neighborhood.	They have interests in terms of their areas not being dirtied by the customers and also noise created by the customers.
Competitors, i.e., other NGOs	Limited involvement	Limited influence	There is no contribution, but sometimes they refer customers where they don't offer similar services.	On ad-hoc basis as sometimes, they do refer some potential customers to DKCCDC where they are not offering services that DKCCDC provides	No direct interests in DKCCDC

Media	Limited involvement	Limited influence	Sometimes they broadcast and air DKCCDC services through television and newspapers because of the high-quality free services provided by DKC-CDC as information and to motivate the public for doing similar work.	ADHOC basis and when media is called by DKCCDC to cover certain project activities that they are carrying out.	They don't have any direct interests in DKCCDC.
Local Government/Municipality	Limited involvement except to attend DKC-CDC functions occasionally	They have a moderate influence for DKC-CDC to continue its activities as they fully support it due to a large number of poor customers being benefitted which improves the health and educational environment of the community for which the local government is responsible to a large extent. As a result of this, neighbors and community members do not openly oppose DKCCDC activities.	There is no direct contribution apart from openly supporting DKCCDC activities	Half yearly when invited by DKCCDC to attend DKCCDC activities	They have a good level of interest in the success of DKCCDC as it projects a healthy and developed community.

Section 6: Social License to Operate

Approach to securing the organization's social license to operate:

The social license to operate exists when the activities of an organization or a specific project has the ongoing approval within the local community and other stakeholders. In order to achieve the social license to operate, an organization needs to adopt the following approach:

- Understand the community's interest/disinterest in the operation of the organization
- Understand the community's convenience/inconvenience in the operation of the organization in the community
- Understand the legitimacy, credibility and trust components of the Social License to Operate so that the risks attached to it can be addressed and mitigated considerably, if not completely eliminated.
- Allocate sufficient time for relationship building with the community
- Do something of interest to the community even if it is outside the main activities of the organization to get the community buy-in of the organization's activity, i.e., to get SLO.
- Be aware of the techniques for capacity building at the local level
- Appreciate that the quality of the social license to operate is dynamic and responsible to changes in perceptions regarding the organization and its activities, decisions, and projects. It is also susceptible to outside influences. The organization has to be diligent to work hard to maintain its social license to operate over time.

DKCCDC can ensure social license to operate by keeping the community members and local council/government happy so that they allow DKCCDC to operate. Though DKCCDC is a Govt. registered organization and licensed to operate, its customers create a lot of filth, noise, and even disease to some extent in the community as it treats very poor/unhygienic people as well as teaches and trains poor children who create lot noise and sometimes lack proper mannerisms. It may be emphasized that the community itself has no particular interest for DKCCDC to operate as it is a well to do community where DKCCDC operates as the Owner's house and facilities are located there

Meeting the community members and local council regularly, getting them engaged and developing good relationships, reducing their perception of risk, reducing conflict, address their concerns, advocating the need of DKCCDC activity to them on the importance of this social good and social work for overall community development are the best ways to maintain social license to operate.

Section 7: Organizational Governance and Leadership and Sustainability Policy:

Governance supports the organization's ability to meet its objectives in an uncertain world. Governance supports the organization's leadership as it seeks to address the organization's ever-changing external context and seeks to continuously improve the internal context so the organization can meet its objectives. The governance provides the mandate and commitment for sustainability and makes sure that the provisions of the sustainability policy become part of what every member does every day. Organizational governance is the system by which an organization makes and implements decisions in pursuit of its overarching objectives. Organizational governance is the most crucial factor in enabling an organization to take responsibility for the consequences of its decisions and activities and to integrate the three responsibilities (environment, social well-being, and shared value) throughout the organization and its engagement with the internal and external stakeholders. One of the responsibilities of DKCCDC is to communicate with the external stakeholders about the approach the organization is using to manage its risk.

The sustainability policy serves as the foundation for the QEH&S management system and provides direction for the entire organization. The policy lets people in the organization know what's important to management. The policy should not be too specific or lengthy, but it should be meaningful to employees as well as customers, suppliers, contractors, and other stakeholders.

The content of the policy is up to the organization. However, DKCCDC must specifically address the following commitments:

- Compliance with all relevant EH&S legal requirements, customer, and product
  requirements, and any sector guidelines maintained by associations, and any other QEH&S commitments made by the organization
- Prevention of workplace injuries
- Continual improvement
- Prevention of pollution
- Other sustainability commitments, especially to stakeholder engagement.

Sustainability Policy of DKCCDC:

1. **Vision:** DKCCDC should make sure to build a strong argument for the reasons why DKCCDC is needed. Accordingly, the first rule for risk and sustainability is to have a clear vision,
2. **Finance**: DKCCDC needs to guarantee a future for DKCCDC, it is crucial to develop a strong financial plan for long-term sustainability of DKCCDC

3. **Community Support**: DKCCDC needs long-term support of the community to run its operations in the community successfully and peacefully.
4. **Quality of Service**: Though DKCCDC offers free service to the underprivileged, they will not come to DKCCDC unless they perceive a benefit to come to DKCCDC. So, DKCCDC need to maintain a high quality of service
5. **Motivation**: As DKCCDC is primarily driven and financed by its owner/founder, he needs to ensure that his motivation and willingness to serve the underprivileged of the society is always intact.
6. **Environmental, social and economic accountability: DKCCDC** needs to ensure that these areas are addressed properly for a sustainable operation which will also benefit the community at large.

Section 8: Risk Policy and Risk assessment of DKCCDC

From the perspective of the organization, all activities, products, and services have a sustainability footprint. This footprint creates impacts on the environment, society, and the economy. Each impact creates risks for the organization and its stakeholders. The organization can mitigate these risks through a responsible operation that avoids creating impacts to the extent possible. (Pojasek, 2012).

Risk Assessment:

FOOTPRINT =====➔ IMPACT =====➔ RISK

Risk Policy of DKCCDC:

The approach to risk assessment is about the overall process of risk identification, risk analysis, and risk evaluation.

1. DKCCDC needs to define the purpose of risk management and how it links to DKCCDC vision and mission.
2. DKCCDC should identify and assess risks to its operations on a regular basis (i.e., quarterly) for smooth operation.
3. DKCCDC should allocate appropriate resources for risk management, i.e. insurance policies to protect its assets, appropriate staff who will be responsible for developing and implementing risk management policies, i.e. accountabilities and responsibilities for managing risks.
4. DKCCDC should reassess its risk management strategies/policies as new risks occur or where risk mitigation strategies are not working
5. Establish and maintain rules governing appropriate risk behavior and practices. This should include how its patient and students, who are the main customers will behave to avoid risk of spreading the disease to the community as well as the acceptable level of noise.

6. Be compliant with local regulations for environmental, safety and law enforcement.
7. DKCCDC should have a risk monitoring and control procedure with KPIs for measuring risks to ensure risks are properly managed.

Major Risks of DKCCDC are:

1. Complaint by community members of increased traffic of patients and students which is creating nuisance related to noise and filth and consequently, risking losing the license to operate
2. DKCCDC customers are not attracted to DKCCDC service and do not attend to/visit DKCCDC services
3. What if the owner who funds DKCCDC lose his motivation to serve the society or can not arrange sufficient funds in future or dies

DKCCDC Risk Assessment and Potential Mitigations for Major Risks

TABLE 2

Risk Type	Risk Event	Risk Consequences (Opportunities/Threats)	Risk Controls	Effectiveness	Likelihood	Consequences	Priority for RiskMitigation	Risk Action
Community/ Neighborhood	Complain by community members of increased traffic of patients and students	Threat. Risk of spread of disease by the patients as well as increased traffic and noise and filth generated by the customers, i.e. patients and students Community may not allow continuity of services by DKCCDC ii)DKCCDC will not be able to fulfill its mission iii) Poor customers will lose the benefits of free services and may not get health care, and students will not get education or training	i)Employ guards by DKCCDC to control noise and filth by controlling the customer behaviour. ii) Talking to customers about the need to behave appropriately including not spitting, littering or urinating openly. iii) Leaving the DKCCDC premise as soon as they are done with their business. iv) Employ some community members in DKCCDC which will create jobs in the community and reduce resistance to DKCCDC operations	Customers become more organized and create less nuisance. But unless such controls are strictly followed, the problem continues	8	The community will be more tolerant towards DKCCDC and better see the need for the services provided by DKCCDC.	2	DKCCDC needs to boost its relationship with community members thru advocacy on the need of DKCCDC operation so that there will be less resistance as well as improve the control on the customer as well as lecture them on the need for positive behaviour to ensure they cooperate and behave in a sustainable manner for DKCCDC

465

Customers	DKCCDC customers are not attracted to DKCCDC service and do not attend to/visit DKCCDC services	**Opportunity** More customers are likely to visit DKCCDC and more poor will be benefited which is the core objective of DKCCDC.	DKCCDC can consider implementing ISO 9000 and ISO 26000 quality control which will help them be more responsible to customers and better customer control	Implementing of ISOs is likely to give a boost to DKCCDC operations	6	More customers are likely to visit DKCCDC and more poor will be benefitted which is the core objective of DKCCDC.	3	DKCCDC should look for continuous improvement in services through customer survey and improvement of facilities
		Threat If customers don't turn out and receive DKCCDC services this will ultimately lead to non-fulfillment of DKCCDC mission. Moreover, the poor will lose the benefit of free education and health care which is the degradation of society.	i) DKCCDC works with communities, schools and other stakeholders such as schools and hospitals to send their patients/students to DKCCDC for better services ii) Advocate the customers on the need of education for personal and social development and remove illiteracy. iii) continuously improve its services by offering higher quality and customer oriented services	The effectiveness of this approach is high. However, the biggest challenge is to motivate the students to come to school and make them see the need for schooling in life	8	More customers are likely to visit DKCCDC	2	DKCCDC should strongly advocate in community centers, schools and even through TV advertisement the need for an educated and skilled under-privileged workforce as well as a healthy citizen and welcome the underprivileged to avail the free services offered by DKCCDC

| Finance/Funding | What if the owner who funds DK-CCDC lose his motiva-tion to serve the society or can not arrange suf-ficient funds in future or dies | Threat | DKCCDC operations will close, and a large section of the underprivileged people will stop receiving the free services | DKCCDC owner is making a trust for continuity of services beyond himself. HE is also looking for an association with other NGOs/Govt. agencies for funds in the event his funds run out. | This is an effective measure. However, the new trustee should have sufficient interest to run DKC-CDC. | 2 | DKCCDC will continue for a long time to come. | 1 | DKCCDC owner should ensure conti-nuity of DKCCDC through trust and other mechanism such as proper succession planning who can take over from him as well as Govt. support for financing if needed. |

Note: "Likelihood of Happening": 10 = Highest, 1 = lowest   "Priority": 1 = Highest, 10 = Lowest

467

Section 9: Financial Sustainability

Financial sustainability refers to the ability to maintain financial capacity over time. Regardless of an organization's for-profit or nonprofit status, the challenges of establishing financial capacity and financial sustainability are central to organizational function. However, maintaining the ability to be financially agile over the long term may be especially important for nonprofits, given that many of them serve high-need communities that require consistent and continually available services. With this in mind, the goal of financial sustainability for nonprofits is to maintain or expand services within the organization while developing resilience to occasional economic shocks in the short term (e.g., short-term loss of program funds, monthly variability in donations). For most nonprofits, such as DKCCDC, a core challenge is balancing (1) the need to maintain financial sustainability and (2) the pursuit of organizational mission and maintenance of consistent and quality programming over time.

DKCCDC's main financial support and resource are through philanthropic donations from its founder and director. The positive side of this is that DKCCDC is highly focused in achieving its mission as its objectives are not dependent on the donations from others. However, the negative side is that this total dependence on one individual for its financial resource makes DKCCDC vulnerable for its operations in the future . Therefore, DKCCDC needs to strengthen its financial sustainability by arranging other sources of finance through other individual, institutional or governmental support though this may be at the risk of diluting DKCCDC's objectives and values. Therefore, the founder is now in the process of forming a trust which will enable the long-term financial sustainability and continuity of DKCCDC and also try for collaborations with like-minded philanthropists for funding where the fund does not have to be refunded which is called a Big Bettor strategy for funding(Foster, 2009).

Section 10: Resources, Operating System, and Processes

Operating System/Processes: Following is the process for DKCCDC

DKCCDC Mission

SCS mission is to reduce poverty and illiteracy as well as improve health care of the poor and underprivileged and improve the wellbeing of the poor in its community and District by providing free of cost and good quality services

Overarching Objectives:

1. Reduce illiteracy
2. Reduce Poverty
3. Improve Health Care

Operating Objectives - Reduce Illiteracy

1.1 Build coaching centers to provide study support to students from Primary to Higher Secondary (Grade 1 to XII) to improve their learning abilities as well as grades.

1.2 Provide training on social value and improving self-confidence and self-image

1.3 Coach senior students to impart education on basic mathematics and language to small poor children in their community

1.4 Actively search and scout for poor students in the communities and advocate the

Operating Objectives - Reduce Poverty

2.1 Provide vocational and skill training to the poor unemployed people to improve their possibility of getting jobs

2.2 Collaborate with other organizations to employ students of SCS upon their successful completion of the training programs

2.3 Help to form Self Help Group (SHG) for women and give them loans to start small businesses

2.4 Advocate the need for healthy living and knowledge

2.5 Help to provide nutrition to the poor by providing meals once a

Operating Objectives - Improve Health Care

3.1 Build hospital with modern facilities and General and Specialist doctors

3.2 Provide medical services free of cost or minimal charges to the poor including consultancy, medicines and diagnosis

3.3 Advocate the need of health and hygiene and good living to the poor

3.4 Start mobile medical unit equipped with modern equipment and medicines and visit poor communities to render health care and those who cannot visit SCS facility.

Resources	Goals/KPI's	Resources	Goals/KPIs	Resources	Goals/KPI's
i). Fund: $1 M, 2. ii) Manpower: 10 teachers, 2 administration staff, 2 Guards iii) 2 Buildings iv) 20 Computers	i) 60% students passing exams and promoted to next grade each year ii) 50% adults learning to read, write and do arithmetic's each year iii) 50% of senior students participating in teaching children in their own communities each year iv) 10% student growth rate each yr	i) Fund: 0.5 M ii) Manpower: 8 multi-disciplined Trainers,iii) Breakfast meals iv) Training equipment and materials v) 2 administration staff	i) Minimum 2 SHGs formed each year ii) Conduct at-least 4 quarterly meetings each year for advocating need for healthy living and knowledge iii) Provide 10% extra nutrition and free books each year iv) At least 2 collaborations each year with other organizations for employment v) 10% student growth rate each year	i). Fund: $1 M , ii) Doctors: 10 Nos., iii). Nurse: 2 Nos. iv). Administration Staff : 3 Nos v) Ambulance 2 Nos. vi). Trainers: 2 Nos vii) Cleaner: 1 No. viii) Guard: 1 No. ix) medicine x) surgical items xi)medical equipmt e.g. x-ray machine	i) Building hospital within a year ii) 10% increase in no. of patients treated each year iii) Conduct at least 4 quarterly meetings each year in communities for advocating need for healthy living and knowledge iv) 10 % increase in medicines and diagnosis each year v) Nursing training to commence within a year vi) Mobile Medical unit has commenced

The above process has proved itself to be highly effective as the Mission is linked to the goals through overarching objectives, operating objectives, resources, and KPIs. The process is also efficient as the process activities, and amount of resources required is optimized.

Responsibility and authority for this process: The Owner/Founder

For full implementation, Plan-Do-Check-Act (PDCA) should be applied to control and ensure that the Activities and goals are proceeding according to the Performance Measures and corrective measures are taken where it is not.

Section 11: Sustainability and Resilience

The approach is on helping meet its objectives in an uncertain (VUCA – Volatility, uncertainty, complexity, and unambiguity) world and this is sustainability. Therefore, all operations at DKCCDC must consider VUCA which are potential risks to the operations.

For, resilience is a never-ending journey that uses risk management focus an organization – its people, knowledge, technology, finance, sense making and decision making which will help to survive and thrive in turbulent times. By creating an organization that is adaptable, competitive, agile and robust becomes able to anticipate, prepare for, respond and adapt to sudden and gradual change in its external environment (context), particularly with respect to community satisfaction and to obtain Social License to Operate. If we do not adapt to changes in the external context, it will not meet their objectives. By creating an organization that is adaptable, competitive, agile and robust, we are creating its ability to anticipate, prepare for, respond and adapt to sudden and gradual change in its external environment (context).

Section 12: Scoping with Value Chain Model

Approach to the value chain is based on the process view of organizations, the idea of seeing manufacturing (or service) organization as a system, made up of subsystems each with inputs, transformation processes, and outputs. Inputs, transformation processes, and outputs involve the acquisition and consumption of resources - money, labour, materials, equipment, buildings, land, administration and management. How value chain activities are carried out determines costs and affects profits. These activities can be classified generally as either primary or support activities that all businesses must undertake in some form.

DKCCDC value chain fits well into the above Porter's Model. However, I will make the following changes to the Porter's model to fit DKCCDC situation:

i) Under Primary Activities, instead of "Marketing & Sales," I will apply the term "Advocacy and Promotion" as DKCCDC being a nonprofit organization, is not involved in any marketing and sales. Further, DKCCDC conducts various levels of Advocacy and promotion of its services to its internal and external stakeholders.

ii) There is no outbound logistics for DKCCDC as such. However, cured patients or educated children may be considered

iii) Under support activities, I will add "Innovation."

iv) Lead measures for support activities and lag measures for primary activities

v) The concept of shared value within the context of DKCCDC may be less appropriate as DKCCDC is already in the business of serving the community. However, the value can be shared with suppliers.

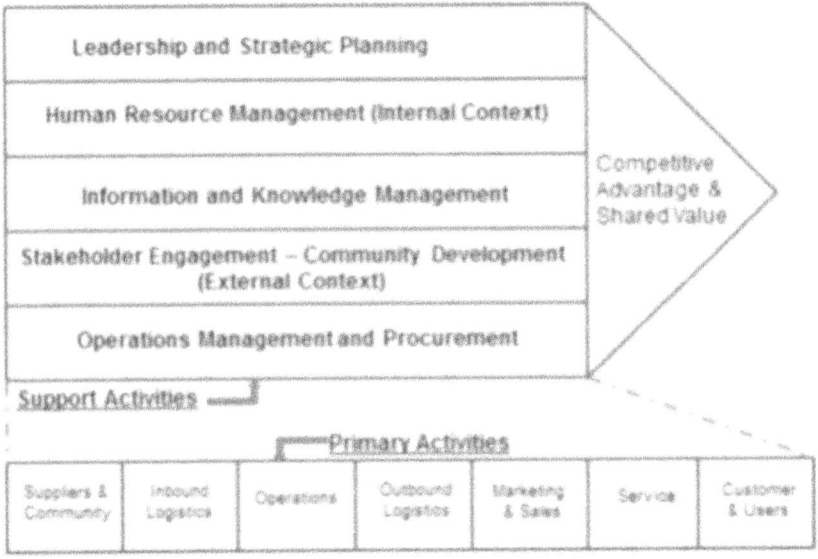

Section 13: Monitoring and Measurement

Approach to Monitoring

Monitoring involves the routine surveillance of actual performance against a target so that there can be an accurate comparison with the expected or required performance.

DKCCDC needs to determine the method used for monitoring that is consistent with the measurement method selected. DKCCDC can use the Plan-Do-Check-Act model against target KPIs to monitor how well it is doing against the objectives and what actions to be taken where DKCCDC is not meeting the objectives.

Approach to Measurement

The primary use of monitoring and measurement is the linkage of the support elements at the top of the value chain with the operations at the bottom. Therefore, the value chain model is useful in scoping the monitoring and measurement program for DKCCDC.

Lead and Lag Measures are as follows:
Lead measure are about strategic or future whereas lag measures are of what happened in the past.
Lead and Lag Measures for DKCCDC are as follows:
The following lead and lag measures have been developed from the Value Chain above

Lead Measures:

Hospital:

i)New medicines introduced each quarter, ii)new medical services introduced every quarter, iii)extent of engagement of the community members, iv)amount of community support service carried out each year, v)new investment made each year on medical program and infrastructure vi) level of customer engagement in DKCCDC vii) Implementing lead measures on operations of DKCCDC as indicated

School/Training Center:

i)No. of new courses and vocational training introduced each year ii) extent of engagement of the community members iii) amount of community support service carried out each year, iv)new investment made each year on school program and infrastructure, v) level of customer engagement, vi)promotional expenditure yearly to promote DKCCDC to its customers vi) innovating new ways to propagate education in poor areas of Bolpur e.g. snr. DKCCDC students are teaching basic mathematics, English and environment care to small needy students in their neighborhood/community and making their community a literate one. Vi) No. of new advocacies carried out to retain good teachers at less than market rate salary

Lag Measures:

Hospital:

No. of patients treated per week, How soon patients return after treatment, weekly expenditure on medicines, customer satisfaction rating, staff expenditure monthly, diagnostic and laboratory expenditure per month, No. of staff leaving DKCCDC each year.

School/Training Center:

Attendance record of students, Examination passing rates of students, No. of students getting jobs after vocational training, customer satisfaction rating, staff expenditure monthly, No. of staff leaving DKCCDC each year

Section 14: Transparency and Accountability

Approach to Transparency:

In the practice of sustainability, DKCCDC is expected to be transparent in its decisions and activities that impact on the environment, society or the economy. As such, DKCCDC is expected to disclose in a clear, accurate, and complete manner, and to a reasonable and sufficient degree, the policies, decisions and activities for which it is responsible to its stakeholders, society, the economy and the environment. DKCCDC is currently doing this in an inconsistent manner without complying to any specific requirements.

Accountability:

In the practice of sustainability, an organization is expected to be accountable for its impacts on the environment, society and the economy. It is well accepted that accountability involves an obligation of the organization to be answerable to legal authorities with regard to laws and regulations. However, the concept of accountability is expanded by sustainability to include a similar obligation for the overall impact of decisions and activities on the environment, society and the economy to those affected by its decisions and activities, as well as to society in general. DKCCDC does take accountability by engaging the neighbors in the community where it operates through satisfaction surveys and complying with their requirement in these three areas.

Section 15: Maturity of the Sustainability Program: Conducting Self Assessment

Approach to self-assessment should be a comprehensive and systematic review of the DKCCDC activities and its sustainability performance in relation to its degree of maturity. The results of the monitoring and measurement should be input to the self-assessment.

Approach to Maturity Plot:

Upon completion of self-assessment, DKCCDC can decide how to characterize the five maturity levels as follows:
1. Beginner 2. Proactive 3. Flexible 4. Innovative 5. Sustainable or level 1 to 5 can be used.

These are used to identify the maturity level for each of the organization's individual structural levels/elements. For DKCCDC to start at level 1 and progress to the higher maturity levels to maximum 5 is more appropriate as it addresses DKCCDC maturity aspects better.

Maturity Spider Matrix for DKCCDC:

The maturity spider matrix of DKCCDC is as follows which visually reflects the maturity of various elements for sustainability

Organization and setting responsible objectives	3
Understanding the internal and external context	2
Engaging with stakeholders and maintaining the social license to operate	3
Governance and leadership –sustainability policy	2
Risk Assessment	2
Resources and Operating System	3
Sustainability/Financial	1
Value Chain Model to Scope Measurement	1
Monitoring and Measurement	3
Transparency and accountability	2
Maturity process	1
Improvement and Innovation	4

Note: 5 being the most matured whereas 1 being least matured

Section 16: Improvement and Innovation

Continuous improvements and innovations are required to meet the external and internal threats of the organization as well as meeting mission of the organization. In DKCCDC various innovations have been made such as:

i. Peer learning among students to help them learn faster as well as developing their personality

ii. Training senior students in the school to teach basic math, language and hygiene to their neighbors where they live so that they can be change agents from an early stage in their lives as well spreading education to an illiterate population.

PART II

PART II discusses how the operation of an organization affects the three major sustainability areas of environmental, social and economic aspects and ways to calculate the environmental impacts and mitigate such effects. From the perspective of the organization, all activities, processes, products, and services have a sustainability Footprint (i.e. adverse impact). This footprint impacts the environment, society, and the economy. Each impact creates risks for the organization and its stakeholders. The organization can mitigate these risks through responsible operation that avoids creating adverse impacts to the maximum extent possible.

Sustainability's Three major Responsibilities areas are as follows (Pojasek, 2012):

Environmental Stewardship:
- Reduce the use of all resources.
- Eliminate waste.
- Pay attention to the prevention of pollution.
- Respect the need for climate change mitigation and adaptation.
- Protect natural habitats and biodiversity.
- Consider each of these items throughout the value chain.

Social Well-Being:
- Protect human rights.
- Ensure fair operating practices.
- Assess labor practices, including health and safety.
- Evaluate consumer issues associated with products and services.
- Optimize community involvement and awareness.
- Consider each of these items throughout the value chain.

Economic Prosperity:
- Create top-line growth (brand).
- Ensure bottom-line growth (profits).
- Improve governance and maintain the organization's "license to operate."
- Contribute to community development.
- Consider each of these items throughout the value chain.

1. DKCCDC's Sustainability Impact are as follows:

1.1 Economic Impact and benefits of Service:

DKCCDC employs qualified but poor people without jobs. Therefore, it creates employment in the town. It also offers vocational training to poor unemployed students which helps unemployed people to get jobs and helps in income generation for the town and surrounding communities which helps in poverty alleviation.

1.2 Social Impact and benefits of Service:

Social impact of service is that more poor patients and students will get free medical care and education free of cost making my community literate and healthy who can also contribute to the welfare of the community. In the process, the community also becomes free from crime and social degradation.

1.3 Environmental Impact and benefits of Service:

Environmental impact of service is that the community is becoming cleaner with more trees and greeneries as well as less polluted. For environmental impact, I have analyzed the current emissions at DKCCDC and how to reduce the environmental impact of DKCCDC as detailed below.

To help delineate direct and indirect emission sources, improve transparency, and provide utility for different types of organizations and different types of climate policies and business goals, three "scopes" (scope 1, scope 2, and scope 3) are defined for GHG accounting and reporting purposes.

Scope 1 emissions: Direct GHG emissions occur from sources that are owned or controlled by the company, for example, emissions from combustion in owned or controlled boilers, furnaces, vehicles, etc.; emissions from chemical production in owned or controlled process equipment.

Scope 2 emissions: Scope 2 accounts for GHG emissions from the generation of purchased electricity consumed by a company. Purchased electricity is defined as electricity that is purchased or otherwise brought into the organizational boundary of the company. Scope 2 emissions physically occur at the facility where electricity is generated.

Scope 3 emissions: Scope 3 is an optional reporting category that allows for the treatment of all other indirect emissions. Scope 3 emissions are a consequence of the activities of the company, but occur from sources not owned or controlled by the company. Some examples of scope 3 activities are extraction and production of purchased materials; transportation of purchased fuels; and use of products and services

2. **With reference to 1.3 above, A description of DKCCDC's emissions Scope 1, 2 and 3 are as follows:**
   I. Direct Emissions: Scope 1: Petrol for back-up generators, diesel for Medical Mobile Unit. Direct emissions from school buildings and equipment including furniture as well as from goods and services consumed in the school such as books, computers, cleaning materials, electrical wirings, waste generated etc.
   II. Indirect Emissions: Scope 2: Electricity

III. Indirect Emissions: Scope 3: Use of software, employee commuting, Projector, Supply chain activities of companies producing goods and services procured by schools

The major Green House Gas Emissions are: Carbon Di Oxide (CO2), Methane (CH4) and Nitrogen Oxides (N2O). Carbon dioxide equivalent is a measure used to compare the emissions from various greenhouse gases based upon their global warming potential. For example, the global warming potential for methane over 100 years is 25. This means that emissions of one million metric tons of methane is equivalent to emissions of 25 million metric tons of carbon dioxide.

3. A calculation of emissions for the school and training center (Scope 1 and 2 and Scope 3 emissions source

Ans: The calculation of major emissions for Scope 1, Scope 2 and Scope 3 are as follows:

TABLE - 3

Major Emission Areas in School	Quantity/ Month Used	Emission Factor(CO2)	Emission Factor (CH4)	Emission Factor (N2O)
Petrol/Gasoline (Scope 3)	50 litres (470 Kwh)	0.269 kg/kwh	0.00024 kg/kwh	.0000051 kg/kwh
Diesel (Scope 1)	8 litre (88.8 Kwh)	0.276 kg/kwh	0.000012 kg/kwh	.000036 kg/kwh
Kerosene (Scope 2)	20 litre (196.42 kwh)	0.25884 kg/kwh	.0000036 kg/kwh	.000000216 kg/kwh
Waste* (Scope 2)	100 Kg	0.8421* kgCO2e/kg	-	-
Electricity (Scope 2)	200 Kwh	0.926 kg/kwh	0.0000068 kg/kwh	0.0000087kg/ kwh

*Waste: Due to mixed nature of Waste, there is no specific emission factors for waste for India except for CO2equivalent as indicated above.
GWP for CO2 = 1, GWP for CH4=25 and GWP for N2O = 298

TABLE - 4

	Quantity Per month (i)	CO2 Total Emission = Emission factor (Kg CO2/KWh) x Quantity(kwh) (ii)	CH4 Total Emission = Emission Factor (kG CH4/kwh) x Quantity(kwh) (iii)	N2O Total Emission = Emission Factor (kG N2O/kWh) x Quantity (kwh) (iv)	CO2e Kg (GWP = 1) x (ii)	CO2e(CH4) (GWP = 25) x (iii)	CO2e(N2O) (GWP = 298) x (iv)	Total CO2e (Kg) per month
Scope – 3 Petrol/gas-oline for employee commuting (For motor cycle)	50 litre = 470 Kwh	0.269 kg/kwh x470 kwh = 126.43 kg	0.00024kg/kwh x 470 kwh =0.115 kg	.0000051 kg/ kwhx470= 0.0024 kg	126.43 kg	0.115 kgx25 = 2.875 kg	0.0024x298 = 0.7152 kg	130.02 kg
Scope – 1 Diesel (Motor-Tra-nsport)	8 litre = 88.8 Kwh	0.276 kg/kwh x 88.8 kwh =24.50 kg	.000012kg/ kwhx88.8 kwh = .0010 kg	.000036kg/kwhx-88.8kwh=.003199 kg	24.5 kg	.0010x25 =.025 kg	.003199x298 = 0.95 kg	25.47 kg
Scope – 1 Kerosene (for domestic power use i.e. diesel generator)	20 litre = 196.42 kwh	0.25884 kg/kwh x196.42 kwh= 50.88 kg	.0000036 kg/ kwhx196.42 kwh=.00070	.000000216 kg/ kwhx196.42 kwh=.0000424	50.88 x 1= 50.88=50.88	.00070x25 = .0175	.000424x298 = .1263	51.02 Kg
Scope-1 Waste	100 Kg	-	-	-	0.8421 kgCO2e/kg x 100= 84.2 kg	-	-	84.2kg
Scope – 2 Electricity	200 KWh	0.926kg/kwh x 200 kwh = 185.2 kg	0.0000068 kg/ kwhx200 kwh= .00136 kg	0.0000087kg/ kwhx200 kwh=.00174 kg	185.2x1 = 185.2 kg	.001366x25 =.034 kg	.00174x298 =0.518 kg	185.752 Kg
Total CO2e emissions (Kg) per month for Scope 1+Scope2+Scope3								476.46 Kg/ Month

Total emission (Kg) = Quantity of fuel x emission factor x Global Warming Potential (GWP). For CH4 and N2O, total emissions for these elements were multiplied by the Global Warming Potential (GWP) to come to CO2equivalent (CO2e) values for comparison of all emissions on equal basis.

4. A detailed description of the firm's largest sources of emissions are, and the best way they could reduce them.

Ans: Based on the TABLE-4 above, it is clear that the largest source of emission of DKCCDC is electricity (Scope 2) at 85.75 Kg CO2e (42% of total emission) per month followed by employee commuting (Scope 3) at 130.02 Kg CO2e (30%) per month.

Therefore, the emission reduction strategies are prioritized based on the source that is emitting the largest amount of CO2e in descending order.

The reduction strategy can be based on the following approach:
1. Behavioral Change
2. Conservation
3. Efficiency
4. Process Change
5. New Technology

A. Reduction in electricity use (Scope 2) in the School:
The above approach can be used to **reduce electricity use as follows:**

i) **Behavioral Change:**
- explaining the need for energy savings and efficiency
- top down mandate for less electricity use
- bottom up approach leading to feeling of ownership with support from management
- appointing energy 'champions', who are responsible for spotting energy waste and promoting energy efficiency
- seeking input to the energy plan and rewarding feedback
- celebrating achievements
- keeping people informed about new ideas
- making it fun by having activities or competitions around saving energy.
- Understand energy bill and how much energy is used in school for monitoring and control of energy
- Use renewable energy as much as possible
- Share information with people and staff

ii) Conservation:
- Educate the staff and children to turn off energy-using appliances and lights when not in use
- Draught strip windows and doors
- Reducing consumption of electricity
- Reusable serving ware
- Not using air conditioning
- Use less hot water

iii) Efficiency:
- Use energy efficient lighting such as LEDs
- Manage ICT (Information and Communications Technology) loads
- Use building systems properly to save energy
- Efficiency upgrade for equipment
- Replace regular light bulbs with compact florescent light (CFL) bulbs.

iv) Process Change: Demand management by having more classes in the day light where electricity will not be required. Most electricity demand is at night.

v) New technology:
- Install smart metering
- Use renewable energy as much as possible such as wind and solar
- Upgrading heating control
- Increasing insulation:

B. Reduction Strategy for Petrol/gasoline use for Employee Commuting (Scope 3)
   1. Encourage cycling by providing secure bike storage and lockers.
   2. Set up a 'walking bus' or an alternative scheme
   3. Incorporate sustainable travel activities across the curriculum
   4. Hold special promotions for active travel and exercise opportunity
   5. Arrange training for walkers and cyclists on independent travel
   6. Spread the message to pupils and parents
   7. Liaise with feeder schools to agree guidance for new pupils and employees on sustainable travel
   8. Find ways to involve pupils obliged to travel by car
   9. Work to improve bus provision and behavior on school transport

10. Work with local authority to identify safer routes and possible highway improvements
11. Reduce emissions from school business journeys
12. Telework and alternative work schedules
13. Driving an alternative fueled or hybrid vehicle
14. Participating in rideshare, carpool or vanpool programs
15. Using public transit such as buses, Metro, and commuter rail
16. Biking or walking to work if possible.

It is expected that there can be 20% reduction in CO2e as a result of approaching the above strategies. However, the main constraint is extra time required for travelling when using alternative transport such as cycling or pooling with others or public transport instead of using their own motorcycles (main means of transport).

C. Reduction Strategy for Waste (Scope 1)
- Work with students to carry out a school waste audit to find out how much waste is produced, then classify the types of different waste and identify waste 'hot spots' within the school.
- Develop an action plan on how to tackle waste in the school. Track the progress by undertaking regular measuring and monitoring.

Waste reduction can be achieved through the following schemes and processes:

Reuse – (i) Encourage pupils to use reusable bottles and flasks for drinks. This can easily be done by installing water fountains around the school and encouraging pupils to drink tap water.
ii) Printer cartridges: get the old cartridges refilled and use them again (it may take 1000 years for cartridges to decompose in landfill, and it is often cheaper to refill them than buy new.
iii) Stationary: reuse old envelopes for internal mail or by sticking a new label over the previous address. The same can be done for old paper or plastic folders.
iv) Furniture: repair or repaint items of furniture to prolong their life.

Recycle – recycling old products into new ones saves raw materials and energy

Recycling helps save energy and tackles climate change, and can save your school money on rubbish collections. The types of materials that can be recycled and the cost savings to the school will depend on the local authority or other waste services provider.
- Find out from the waste services provider what recycling services they offer.

- The services offered may either be co-mingled (all items in one container) or collected in separate streams.
- It can be started with the biggest or most popular streams like paper, cardboard,
- cans, glass containers, plastics bottles and cartons. This can also start with schemes for smaller, more specialized streams like ink cartridges, light bulbs, batteries and CDs.
- Make it easy to recycle by placing recycling bins in sensible areas, such as next to printers and photocopiers, classrooms, and in the staff room. These areas can be identified from a waste audit.
- Use clear posters and signs to encourage everyone to use recycling bins, and use
- them correctly, so this becomes second nature

Swap or give it away
- We can donate them to a local charity shop, advertise on Freecycle, or exchange them in 'swap shops' or 'give and take' days.
- Set up a scheme to collect old ink cartridges and mobile phones from the local community —some charities are keen to accept these to help raise funds
- Make it easy for pupils and their families to swap, donate and exchange second hand uniforms.
- Contact local charity shops or Freecycle to find a new home for other unwanted items such as furniture, books etc.
- Old books and computers can be sent abroad though donation schemes, but check there are procedures in place for maintaining the equipment and disposing of it correctly at end of life

Reduce paper and card waste
- Paper and card contributes around one third of all waste in schools. It is easy to make more efficient use of paper and card, and to recycle it when you're done. It saves money too.
- Put scrap paper trays in each classroom, and in the reception office, the copier room and other places where lots of paper is generated.
- Make double-sided printing and photocopying the default, or add clear instructions next to printers on how this can be done manually. If need be run short training sessions for staff so this approach becomes routine.
- Keep boxes from deliveries if they are suitable for use in storage.

- When recycling cardboard boxes to make sure to flatten them first so they do not occupy a lot of space in the recycling bins and/or feed cardboard into your compost bins.

D. Reduction Strategies for Kerosene (Scope 1)

Kerosene is used primarily to run the Diesel Generator for generating electricity when there is no electrical power available in school and this is unavoidable. This is a small duration run during emergency with small emission and reduction strategy is not required for it.

E. Reduction Strategy for Diesel (Scope 1)

Diesel is used to run the Mobile Medical Unit to provide health care services to old and disabled patients in villages who can not visit my hospital. There is no alternative to it and hence reduction strategies are not required. However, we are taking most optimum routes to villages to reduce diesel consumption.

5. A suggested GHG reduction goal that DKCCDC can reach:

GHG emissions goals can be set not only in terms of emissions reductions targets and dates for achieving them but also in terms of the categories of GHG emissions to be reduced. Therefore, emissions reduction goals can be established separately for Scope 1, 2, and 3 categories of GHG emissions.

Based on the above, my suggested GHG reduction goal is as follows:

Reduction goals can be on short term (Monthly), Medium terms (6 months) and on long term basis (1 year).

Scope 2: 10% reduction in GHG emissions can be achieved in 1 month compared to TABLE-3 due to reduced electricity uses through the **strategies described above. 15% in 6 months and 20% in one year.**

Scope 3: 5% reduction in GHG emissions can be achieved in 1 month compared to TABLE-3 due to reduced use of Petrol/gasoline for employee commuting. Staff can be persuaded to use renewable or alternative transport such as cycling or walking.10 % in 6 months and 15% in 1 year. This is because habit takes time to take effect.

Scope 1: 5% reduction in GHG emissions in 1 month can be achieved compared to TABLE-3 due to reduced use of kerosene and diesel as well as reduced waste generation through re-use and recycling of waste as well as buying stuff with less packaging. Further, 20% waste can be reduced in 6 months and it is expected that up to 40% reduction in waste can be achieved in 1 year as this is very much within the control of DKCCDC, primarily through behavioural change and process change, as discussed above.

The above proposed reduction is a bit conservative considering that due to their low socio- economic background the children in my school and staff are less likely to adopt and adapt to this new requirement of GHG reduction.

6. Energy Audit and Reporting Requirements

Annual energy audits would provide the relevant information from which students, faculty, and staff can make informed choices and prioritize projects that will improve energy efficiency.

7. Supply Chain

Emissions from Supply chain activities of companies producing goods and services procured by schools, Scope-3 emissions, were not immediately available as suppliers are not keeping record of emissions in India.

Linking action to reduce emissions with the school curriculum
Linking what is taught in the classroom to carbon reduction activity underway in the wider school environment can build momentum for change through pupil leadership and involvement.

8. Making Sustainable purchasing in schools

1. Develop procurement expertise – nominate and train someone to coordinate everything centrally
2. Plan ahead: identify what is needed early to get the best deal
3. Buy energy efficient and sustainable consumer goods
4. Don't buy unless needed – does anyone have a spare?
6. Look for alternatives to branded products
7. Think sustainably about the paper school buys and uses
8. Buy food locally and seasonally
9. Improve buying power and work collaboratively
10. Share best practice – if a good sustainable deal is made let other schools know about it is doing.
11. Work with suppliers for less packaging for the goods they sell.

9. Hand printing:

Many companies are already changing the world for the better—by greening their products, launching programs for sustainability in their communities, or improving the lives of employees and their families. Each of these initiatives is a positive business impact—what is called a "handprint." We compare a company's handprint to its footprint (which is an adverse impact of an organization's operations), and when its handprint is larger than its footprint, the company becomes a *Net* Positive Enterprise.

Hand printing at DKCCDC is two pronged namely Social and Environmental as follows:

i)   Social Hand printing:

I find it difficult to spread education beyond those who come to my school to study in other words, I am not able to touch those who are not coming to my school. Therefore, I am now training higher grade students in my school e.g. grade X, XI and XII on teaching techniques and inculcating social values in them and the need for social service in their lives. Therefore, they have now started teaching primary students in their villages on language and mathematics and hygiene and making their villages free from illiteracy. This has been very successful as higher grade students are taking responsibility for their communities through teaching from an early age and getting self confidence and have become change agents from a very early stage in their lives and in the process they are creating social capital. For me, this has been a very good social innovation and a prime example of social hand printing. These students are also actively trying to enroll more students in their communities in my school so that more poor kids can be educated and take advantage of our free education.

ii)   Environmental Hand printing:

Students and staff in my NGO have started planting trees in their communities that can reduce the amount of carbon dioxide in the air, reduce soil erosion and improve the environment collectively – slowly and surely.

10. Sustainability Impact Assessments and Performance Measures/ KPIs:

10.1 The method that I have used to evaluate the environmental sustainability impact of my NGO (i.e. DKCCDC) is that I have measured the total emissions generated by the NGO in CO2equivalent (TABLE-3 and TABLE -4). Regarding, social and economic sustainability, logging and recording of increased **number of patients and students are done on daily and monthly basis.**

10.2 Key Performance Indicators (KPIs) for measurement:
  * Energy used such as Electricity (KWH/Day) and renewable energy used

- Water (liter per day) used and water pollution
- Medical, toxic and general waste (Kg. /day) generated
- Diesel (liter/day)
- No. of trees planted
- Amount of garbage dumped on the ground (Kg/day)
- No. of New patients and students being served
- Type and quantity of green house gas Emissions released in the air

1. Introduction and Objective

Currently, environmental sustainability is not well practiced in my organization and awareness about sustainability among the NGO staff, students and patients are also inadequate. Moreover, as the patients and students generate lot of nuisance and garbage in the community there is resistance against the operation of the NGO from the community members where it is located.

The objective of this project is to introduce environmental sustainability awareness as well as start practicing environmental sustainability among my NGO staff and customers. It is hoped that this will also significantly reduce community resistance against my NGO due to improved livability and make my NGO operation lasting and trouble free.

2. Brief Explanation of the Environmental Impact of the Project

The following is expected as environmental impact of the Project in my NGO:

- Less use and wastage of water
- Less use of energy, particularly, electricity
- Cleaner school and hospital belonging to my NGO
- Cleaner environment where my customers and staff live (i.e. away from my NGO)
- Generation of less waste and toxic/infected substance
- Cleaner air for breathing
- Healthier and safer community and environment
- Less polluted water, air and ground/ soil
- Greener environment through more trees plantation and vegetation
- Solar energy for lighting and heating instead of current conventional energy leading to sustainable environment such as cleaner air and less pollution
- Clean community where my NGO is located without filth and garbage and noise

3. Organizational Assessment – Current Practices, Barriers to Change, Key Stakeholders and How they were engaged

Current Practices:

The current practices related to environmental sustainability in my NGO is rather insignificant. As shown in the APPENDIX that the current maturity level of the environmental sustainability program in my NGO is around 2, which is at the Development stage. Before, the start of this project, the only environmental care that was done is cleaning schools and public facilities as well as planting trees throughout the town by the students of the NGO.

Barriers to Change:

- Lack of awareness about environmental sustainability and its benefits
- Apathy towards the environment as people are more interested in their daily lives rather than the environment. Therefore, it is not a priority.
- People are not interested to make life style or behavioral changes which will bring about positive changes towards environmentally sustainable behavior.
- People are more engaged and interested about the present than being concerned about the future generation and the state of the planet
- Lack of Education and understanding in the area of sustainability
- Resources – time and money required to implement environmental sustainability

Main Stakeholders are:

- Customers i.e. the poor and destitute students and patients who come for service to the NGO
- Neighbors in the community where the NGO operates
- Suppliers: Mainly medicines suppliers, computer and book suppliers as well as suppliers of clothes for tailoring school.
- Employees and staff of my NGO

How Stakeholders are engaged:

- Staff and employees were asked about what is their understanding of environmental sustainability and how it can be improved. Therefore, teachers, administration staff, doctors and nurses were approached though survey and they responded in writing
- From the patients and students i.e. the NGO customers, same questions were asked but their responses were recorded or noted down in paper.
- Staff and customers were told about the NGO sustainability targets
- Review the sustainability engagement plan at regular intervals i.e. weekly
- Check the progress against the goals on a fortnightly basis
- Identify specific metrics to measure the progress (such as reducing water usage, reducing electricity consumption, reducing waste generated etc.)
- Use the metrics to determine the effectiveness of the efforts.

4. Project Implementation and Narrative:

Being the sustainability champion/leader in my NGO, I thought that the best way to implement the sustainability project in my NGO is to use a model as follows:

Step 1: Make the Commitment
Step 2: Create a Structure for Supporting Environmental Sustainability
Step 3: Support and Finance Environmental Sustainability
Step 4: Set goals and measure, report and evaluate change
Step 5: Celebrate and share Successes
Step 6: Continue to assess and identify new Opportunities

Step 1: Make the Commitment

The first step toward any change is making a commitment. NGO management and trustees have considered the drivers behind their decision to pursue environmental sustainability. Reasons for deciding to implement sust*ainability initiatives are:*

i)   Saving money for the NGO through less usage of resources such as water, energy and generating less wastage
ii) Demonstrating social responsibility
iii) Contributing to community health by reducing pollution, filth and waste
iv) Making NGO operations more efficient
v)   Increasing employee satisfaction, engagement and retention
vi) Fostering a positive public imagery
vii) Meeting compliance or regulatory requirements
viii) Improving the customer experience
ix) Less resistance to the NGO from community members and ensuring long term survival of the NGO
x)   Bring environmental sustainability awareness and educate them about the benefits among my NGO staff, students and patients and so that they start behaving in an environmentally sustainable manner while they are at my NGO. I also hope that they will also so behave at home or in public. Accordingly, I have solicited commitment from staff and customers on sustainable behavior.

Step 2: Create a Structure for Supporting Environmental Sustainability

I have created a Environmental Sustainability Plan (ESP) for my NGO. Currently I have designated one of the senior science teachers as the Environmental Sustainability Coordinator who heads the Environmental sustainability program and directly reports to me. Further, the hospital and school each have a Sustainability Champion who will review and monitor the environmental sustainability plan implementation and report to the Environmental Sustainability Coordinator.

Step 3: Support and Finance Environmental Sustainability

Some fund has been budgeted and created for sustainability implementation such as, purchase of more garbage cans, hiring more cleaners, cost for purchasing posters and placards for advertising about sustainability, purchase of plants for increased plantation of trees in the community, purchase of solar plant/panels for introducing solar energy etc. My goal is eventually to set off the cost of sustainability implementation with the savings generated due to such implementation such as: less use of water and energy, more re-use, better recycling etc.

Step 4: Set goals and measure, report and evaluate change

The main goals and measures that have been targeted for this fledgling program of about 3 months is: reducing water and energy consumption (in litres) by 10% by the year end 2015 as well as reduction of waste (in Kg.) by 10% by the year end, as detailed below. There is also a goal of planting 20 new big trees in the community by the end 2015. At the end of 2015, an assessment will be done on what has been achieved against the above target. We have however, started collecting data and as of now, i.e. end of November, 2015, we have been able to reduce water and energy usage by 5% and less generation of waste by 5% and have also planted 8 new big trees in the community.

Step 5: Celebrate and share Successes

It is too early for this at this stage for my NGO. But certainly, successes will be celebrated. However, I have not yet determined how and in what form. But the small achievements that we have achieved to date have been communicated to all concerned stakeholders for encouragement. Appropriate non-monetary award will be considered in due course.

Step 6: Continue to assess and identify new Opportunities

Sustainability is a journey of continuous performance improvement. In addition to improving on the target levels of the existing targets, new opportunities for improvements will be sought, implemented and measured.

Further, I found through the Survey (See TABLE 2) that most participants consider that the biggest blocks for environmental sustainability change are the change in behavior required for full sustainability thinking and implementation as well as poor sustainability awareness.

Therefore, I used Community Based Social Marketing Tools for behavioral change implementation towards sustainable behavior among the staff and customers as follows:

i)   Get commitment : To get the commitment I made the sustainability practice requirements in writing and actively involved the customers in taking oath to follow the sustainability practices. I also made one Champion for school and one champion for the clinic who all report to the Overall Sustainability Coordinator.

ii) Use prompts: All over the hospital and school and in key locations across the roads where the NGO is located, close to the point of action I put up notice boards and placards which are eye catching and noticeable, with clear instructions on following sustainable practices. Weekly meetings are also being held among the champions and sustainability coordinator for follow up and to learn about extent of compliance and take appropriate actions where such compliance is not happening.

iii) Use Social Norms: For encouraging sustainable behavior, it was important to highlight to the NGO customers that if they don't observe sustainable practices, the NGO may be shut down by the community members as they are making the community undesirable for living and property prices there may also come down. Since they get lot of free and important services from the NGO it is vital for them to ensure through their sustainable behavior that the NGO operates with the support of the community. List of sustainable behavior and the current status of implementation is detailed in the TABLE 2 below. Therefore, their sustainable behavior should be visible to the community, personally motivated, community oriented, and encourage positive behavior for others too.

iv) Use incentives: The main incentives used for the customers are non-monitory in nature. For the patients, those who are following the sustainability requirements, are placed in the beginning of the queue for receiving medical treatment and medicines. For staff, higher and leadership positions are considered whereas, for students, Class champion for sustainability is considered. Therefore, these incentives are based on competition among peers. In the annual school functions, they will be honored with achievement certificates for being sustainable champions.

v)   Make it convenient: All notice boards and placards containing instructions and information on sustainable behavior are conveniently located and which are easily accessible in various local languages. NGO staff has also been trained to communicate with the poor patients in a professional and patient manner.

vi) Persuasive communication strategies: I am trying to use language that my customers understand, make the message vivid to capture attention as stated in (ii) above and framing my message by what is being lost in terms of living in an unhealthy and poor environment due to unsustainable practices instead of discussing about the future generations as sometimes people have difficulties in appreciating about next generations when their present is not a happy one. I am also getting involved at a personal level as a founder and director of my NGO, so that the customers can appreciate the need for sustainability and also trust the whole sustainability implementation process and participate in it . I am also using community level outreach by engaging my neighbors and community members to encourage the NGO customers towards sustainability practices. However, I find that approach to patients who are mostly illiterate needed to be different than staff and students and so, communication approach needed to be tailored according to the type of customers. For example, with patients, more direct approach is used in terms of directly talking to them and explaining how sustainability practices can reduce their ailment. Active listening was very useful to listen to their understanding about environmental sustainability and influence them towards environmentally sustainable behavior. Finally, feedback is being collected from the customers whether their understanding of the message is clear and correct. For students and patients and staff, we are advocating environmental sustainability practices not only in my NGO premises but also where they live.

Other Implementation Areas:

1. Based on the data collected in TABLEs 1 and 2, I decided that those suggestions with highest frequency in terms of causes of environmental degradation and ways to improve environmental care and sustainability, should be given first priority for implementation as people are already aware of what is needed to be done though no concerted action has been taken in that direction. Accordingly, I have already started implementing in some of those areas as indicated in TABLE 2. Where not yet implemented, the implementation schedule is mentioned in TABLE 2.

2. Sustainable purchasing is an area that is not yet considered but I plan to implement this in the 1st Qtr. of 2016.

3. Started environmental sustainability education in my school

4. Discussion has started with the local authority such as the Municipality to collect the garbage and cleaning the road on a daily basis as well as treatment/recycling of the garbage.

5. We have not yet started monitoring air or water quality as such quality is also affected by neighboring communities. However, once we

start implementing the sustainability improvement program in many communities, we will start monitoring air and water qualities too.

6. Install a solar plant for energy savings which will be more environmental friendly as well as save energy cost in the long term say, in 1 year from the date of installation. I plan to install the solar plant within the next 1 year.

7. Though this project is primarily concerned with environmental sustainability, a major issue for my NGO continuity is support of my community members. Therefore, I conducted a survey among the community members about what will make them support my NGO activities and all of them said that if my NGO become environmentally sustainable particularly, with respect to waste and filth elimination and noise free, they will not have any problem with my NGO operating in the community.

5. Areas of School and Hospital Environmental Sustainability

How School can be environmentally more sustainable through the following process:

1. Reduce Carbon generation in School
2. Reduce energy and water use in school
3. Increase sustainable purchasing and supplier in school
4. Increase sustainable school travel
5. Reduce waste in school
6. Use solar energy instead of conventional energy
7. Develop the global dimensions in school through education
8. Schools to engage in Biodiversity
9. Incorporate sustainability in design for new and existing buildings

How Hospital can be environmentally sustainable:

1. Reduce energy and water usage in hospitals
2. Increase sustainable purchasing and suppliers
3. Reduce waste and proper treatment of toxic and infected waste without damaging the environment i.e. without incinerating which can release toxins in the air
4. Reduce carbon generation in clinic
5. Incorporate sustainability in design for new and existing buildings
6. Plant more trees and vegetation in and around my NGO
7. Use solar energy instead of conventional energy

Key Performance Indicators (KPIs) for measurement for the NGO:

- Electricity (KWH/Day)
- Water (liter per day)
- Medical waste (Kg. /day)
- General waste (Kg. /day)

- Diesel (liter/day)
- No. of trees planted
- Amount of garbage dumped on the ground (Kg/day)

Monitoring Schedule to track the implementation of Sustainability is shown in TABLE 3.

6. Discussion of My results, grounded in the Change Theories discussed in the Course

1. Though environmental sustainability is in the development stage in my NGO, all the stake holders openly discussed about how to improve from the current state of sustainability (Maturity level of 1 to 2) to an Accomplished level (Maturity Level 3) and even Maturity Level 4(See APPENDIX). Therefore, there was a high level of psychological safety. However, motivation and accountability of the stakeholders were rather low. Therefore, my NGO is in the comfort zone in terms of learning. I think this can be developed to a learning zone through more education and advocacy on the necessity and benefits of environmental sustainability.

2. Lot of the open discussions on the causes of low level of the sustainability in my NGO and suggestions for improvements were possible because I allowed an Adaptive Operating System to operate and everyone freely gave their ideas without going through any hierarchical structure with full psychological safety. Even doctors freely interacted with school teachers and senior staff with junior staff across functions. AOS also allowed people to connect and innovate with new ideas, such as, through group intelligence, on sustainable operation and even sustainability development became an intrinsic motivation.

3. Not everyone at this point is equally motivated to implement environmental sustainability. Therefore, through the AOS system I have mobilized the early adopters for such implementation particularly, few motivated doctors, teachers and students. Patients, being mostly illiterate were more difficult to convince.

4. The change agent or in my case, the designated Change Coordinator tried to reduce the risks across all the four spheres of the organizational ecosystem namely: individual system, social system, organizational system and infrastructural system. I can also say that he has been partially successfully in his effort to date and as this process wears on, he will be more successful. Infrastructural system have also seen improvement in terms of lesser use of water and electricity and lesser generation of waste in both the clinic and the school.

5. Many discussions have taken place in groups where each class has been used as a group and Group intelligence has been used for

brain storming and coming up with new ideas for sustainability implementation.

6. Negative social dynamics have been largely eliminated and positive social dynamics has been used to reduce resistance to sustainability introduction in my NGO and towards full implementation of environmental sustainability with full engagement of all staff and students. People have been treated with respect and credit have been given to those who are contributing. However, I have been less successful with patients due to their apathy towards sustainability but continuing effort is made to improve on this. I feel that more active listening is required so that they develop trust and I can eventually influence them to adopt sustainable behavior.

7. Engagement Maturity Model is being used by the change Coordinator through awakening (getting to the agenda),pioneering (piloting, pivoting, growing champions), integration(to existing organizational system/structure) and Transformation (changing existing organization system, structure and processes) to create sustainability awareness and start implementing sustainability related changes as well as bring stability and equilibrium to the forces of change so that change can be sustainable and stable.

8. I found that lot of behavioral change is required across the stakeholders for them to part away from the old habits and adopt sustainability. The tool I used for behavioral change is Community Based Social marketing (CBSM) which I discussed as part of my project implementation plan. Learning by doing is also essential as the project progresses and in some cases, staff and customers are practicing environmental sustainability at home and those learnings they are applying in the NGO.

9. I had to apply the Zone of Proximal Development by placing scaffolding for growth and development in the area of practicing sustainability for staying on course and growing through the learning zone as it is a long haul for full implementation of sustainability in my NGO. The primary scaffolding I am using is advocacy and training and some incentives such as recognition and promotion, albeit non-monetary once the full implementation is over successfully.

10. The main pivot I used for implementing sustainability in the NGO is Zoom out pivot and Project pivot as environmental sustainability implementation is itself a project.

11. Life Cycle Costing or NPV analysis was not carried out as the focus of the project is on environmental sustainability development and implementation and not financial sustainability issues. Further, it is also a little premature to do LCC as the sustainability project has started just 3 months back.

7. Conclusions and Recommendations:

1. Contrary to my expectations, I found that generally people want positive environmental sustainability related changes as they see many benefits in doing so including better and healthier living

2. I found that though people want changes as they see benefit in it, they don't want to change themselves and behavioral changes take time.

3. Implementation is easier when groups are formed as groups learn from each other and success at one group level induces and leads to success in other groups.

4. Improvements in environmentally sustainable behavior improved community perception of my NGO which is leading to lesser resistance and greater acceptability of the NGO.

5. Sustainability projects do make a difference towards bringing positive changes to the environment and also cause better living for the community as well as can lead to cost savings.

6. When we work across the organizational ecosystem (i.e. individual systems, social systems, organizational systems and infrastructural systems) and remove risk and foster stability as change agent, any change is possible and this approach should be used for all types of change management. In fact, over the past 3 months, we have been able to reduce energy and water use by 5% and reduced daily waste generation by 2 Kg. as well as have planted quite a few trees. Therefore, it is already giving positive results.

7. It is important to bring equilibrium among the forces of change, during the change management process, else change will be unstable and unsustainable. Therefore, I am always trying to bring stability to this new change related to environmental sustainability implementation in my NGO through continuous engagement with the stakeholders as explained in 6.7 above through Engagement maturity Model. In fact my hypothesis is that Engagement Maturity model can bring about equilibrium in change management process.

8. Based on the sustainability tools discussed above, it is clear that an organization can become sustainable operationally as well as in terms of its impacts in the society in which it operates. An organization can self monitor its maturity level for sustainability as well as check how to adjust the environmental, social and economic impact of its operations with the best interest of its stakeholders. Ultimately, the article addressed the problem of how to make an organization sustainable in terms of reaching its goals as well as meeting operational sustainability requirements.

9. Finally, I can confidently say that the approach and strategy I have adopted and the course concepts/learnings I have applied in bringing

about environmental sustainability related changes in my NGO is working and I did not have to change my approach or course so far and I am optimistic that it will give me the intended results in the end i.e. full implementation within a year. Indeed, my journey as a change agent has been very productive and fruitful so far.

(TABLES AND ANNEXURE ARE in PAGES BELOW)

Survey Results among the Staff and Customers on Reasons for environmental degradation and ways to improve environmental protection and sustainability.

Total No. of people sampled is 30 which includes staff and customers.

TABLE - 1:

S. No.	Causes of Environmental degradation	Frequency*
1.	Cutting of trees is reducing oxygen level and increasing pollution	20
2	Greenhouse Gas generation	10
3	Water is highly polluted as people bathe and clean in ponds and underground water also not very clean	10
4	Air is highly polluted and toxic	20
5	Ground and soil are toxic and polluted and harmful	17
6	Industrial pollution which cause water, air and ground pollution	20
7	Increase in pollution and environmental damage due to increase in population and transportation and vehicles	12
8	Apathy among population regarding environmental sustainability and protection and dumping garbage or filth anywhere or generating toxic gases	20
9	Lack of awareness and education in environmental sustainability	25
10	Lack of recycling of waste and improper handling and removal of waste	16
11	Excessive waste generation by public	10
12	Lack of adequate sanitation facilities	14
13	Wastage of Water during daily use	19
14	Wastage of energy through use of inefficient energy devices or negligent use of energy	24
15	Lack of adequate garbage dump areas or facilities or toilets	24

TABLE - 2

S. No.	How to improve Environmental Care and Sustainability	Frequency*	Action Taken Since Course Start
1	Planting more trees and vegetation	20	Planting of trees started
2	Less Waste generation and treatment and waste generated in environmentally friendly manner to prevent water and air borne diseases and infestation of mosquitos	22	Less waste being generated but no treatment started
3	Recycling of Garbage and Waste	10	No recycling started. Expected to start after 2 months
4	Reuse of packaging, paper, bottles/ containers, waste products instead of throwing away	8	Started
5	Composting	1	Not started yet. Expected to start after 1 month
6	More garbage bins and waste baskets in the community	20	Construction started
7	More education and awareness about environmental protection and sustainability	24	Has started through conducting classes
8	Conservation of and less Wastage of energy	12	Have started
9	Conservation and less Wastage of Water	22	Have started
10	Adequate sanitation Facilities	20	Under construction
11	Behavioral Change towards sustainable practices	25	Started but slow in Progress
12	Care of ground and soil to restrict contamination of ground including not dumping waste on the ground	14	Action started
13	Environmental law and legislation and enforcement for environmental protection	5	Not started. Will approach Municipality within a month
14	Regular garbage collection, cleaning and disinfection of roads and drains	17	In progress
15	More use of alternative transport such as bicycles by the customers which will reduce carbon emissions in the community	5	Has started
16	Engage with local Govt. for waste collection & treatment	0	Process Started

17	Put notice board and placard in school and clinic so that the customers will not dirty the roads and clinic and/or clean up before they leave the NGO premises which will also improve relations with the community/neighbors	20	Process started
18	Avoid use of plastics and polythene bags .Use jute or paper more.	15	Process started
19	Avoid using coal or wood as fuel but use clean gas such as LPG	5	started
20	Avoid using too much pesticide and chemical disinfectant which poisons the ground and the water underneath	8	started
21	Introduce Sustainable Purchasing	0	Not started. Expected to start after 2 months

*Frequency: Number of Suggestions in the Survey

TABLE-3

I am using the following Monitoring Schedule to track the implementation of sustainability in NGO :

What	How	How often	Records	Who
Energy use	Meters to monitor energy/electricity usage	Fortnightly	Meter data	Concerned Champion
Waste	Waste monitoring checklist	Fortnightly	Spreadsheet	Concerned Champion
Water use	Meters to monitor water usage and peaks	Fortnightly	Meters data	Concerned Champion
Fuel use	Monthly bills and vehicle fleet log records	Fortnightly	Spreadsheet	Concerned Champion
No. of trees planted	Counting	Monthly	Record Book	Sustainability coordinator

ANNEXURE

The current **status/indicator and maturity level of environmental sustainability in terms of water, electricity, waste and ground in the past 3 months (since the project started) in my NGO is as follows:**

Water

	Exemplary (Maturity Level 4)	Accomplished (Maturity Level 3)	Developing (Maturity Level 2)	Beginning (Maturity Level 1)
• Extent to which water consumption has been reduced in KL per annum from baseline date and since implementing water conservation initiatives.	The NGO has exceeded the targets set for water conservation	The NGO has met the targets set for water conservation.	The NGO has not yet reached targets set for water conservation.	The NGO is not yet undertaking water conservation initiatives.
• Extent to which the staff and students have adopted water conservation practices within the NGO	The whole NGO community is informed about water conservation practices and implements them consistently.	The NGO community is informed* about the set procedures for water conservation (*eg. signs, posters, newsletter articles, announcements).	The NGO has established set procedures for water conservation.	There are no accepted practices for water conservation in the NGO
• Extent to which the NGO has been able to carry out a water conservation refit to NGO facilities.	The NGO has implemented all possible options for water conservation.	The NGO has developed a comprehensive plan for water conservation and is successfully implementing that plan.	The NGO has begun to implement individual, small scale projects designed to conserve water.	No water conservation works have been undertaken at the NGO
Electricity				
• Extent to which electricity consumption has been reduced in kilowatt hours per annum from baseline date and since implementing energy efficiency initiatives	The NGO has exceeded the targets set for energy efficiency.	The NGO has met the targets set for energy efficiency.	The NGO has not yet reached targets set for energy efficiency.	The NGO is not yet undertaking energy efficiency initiatives.

Extent to which the staff and students have adopted energy efficiency practices within the NGO.	The whole NGO community is informed about energy efficiency practices and implements them consistently.	The NGO community is informed about the set procedures for energy efficiency (*eg. signs, posters, newsletter articles, announcements).	The NGO has established set procedures for energy efficiency.	There are no accepted practices for energy efficiency in the NGO
• Extent to which the NGO has been able to carry out an energy efficiency and renewable energy refit to NGO facilities.	The NGO has implemented all energy efficiency enhancement projects as planned (eg: expansion of PV capacity, lighting retrofit of school).	The NGO has developed a comprehensive plan for energy efficiency (beyond EQ expectations) and is successfully implementing that plan.	Energy efficiency projects funded by EQ or other government sector/s have been completed.	No energy efficiency retrofit, or installation of a renewable energy system has been carried out at the school.
Waste				
• Extent to which waste to landfill has been reduced from baseline date and since implementing waste management initiatives.	The NGO has exceeded the targets set for waste management.	The NGO has met the targets set for waste management.	The NGO has not yet reached targets set for waste management.	The NGO is not yet undertaking waste management initiatives.
• Extent to which the staff and students and patients have adopted waste management practices within the NGO.	The whole NGO community is informed about waste management practices and implements them consistently.	The NGO community is informed about the set procedures for the management of waste (*eg. signs, posters, newsletter articles, announcements).	The NGO has established set procedures for the management of waste.	There are no accepted practices for the management of waste in the NGO.

501

• Extent to which the NGO has been able to develop facilities to assist in waste management.	The school has developed all of the facilities planned to manage all aspects of waste.	The school has developed a comprehensive plan for waste management infrastructure and is implementing that plan.	The school has begun to develop some facilities for waste management	The school has not developed any facilities for waste management.
NGO Grounds				
• The extent to which the NGO has increased the variety of habitats in the school ground.	The NGO has developed all possible areas as sustainable habits to increase biodiversity.	A landscaping plan increasing the variety of natural habitats has been developed and is being implemented.	There have been only limited activities to increase natural habitats within the NGO grounds.	No work has been carried out to increase habitats within the NGO ground.
• The extent to which the area of local native vegetation and local native habitat has increased since participating in the initiative.	There has been a major increase in local native vegetation / habitat area.	There has been some increase in local native vegetation / habitat area.	There has been limited increase in local native vegetation / habitat area.	There has been no increase in local native vegetation.
• Extent to which landscape design has reduced the consumption of resources (eg shade trees planted near buildings, mulch added, or drip irrigation installed).	The NGO has completed all landscaping projects as planned, resulting in a saving in resource consumption.	A landscaping plan with elements to decrease resource consumption has been developed and is being implemented.	Isolated landscaping projects resulting in a reduction in resource consumption have been carried out.	No landscaping has been carried out within the NGO grounds.

502

• Extent to which food gardens and their programs have been established and utilized to engage NGO community and students in tangible environmentally sustainable learning linked to water, waste, energy, soil & plant health (including the role of beneficial insects)	Productive food gardens/ programs supplying food to members of the school community and strong student learning outcomes associated with the gardens via links with the curriculum	Productive food gardens/programs present in NGO grounds with active involvement of many members of the NGO community	At least one food garden/ program has been established in the NGO grounds	No food gardens/programs have been established in the NGO grounds

As can be seen from above, that the current maturity level of the environmental sustainability program in my NGO is around 2, which is at the Development stage.

PART IV
Appendix

Appendix 1

India Community Protocol for Accounting & Reporting Greenhouse Gas Emissions

The text below was extracted partially from the following site:
http://www.environmentportal.in/files/file/IPC_draft_03.10.12.pdf
Readers who are interested to read in detail, is requested to follow the above site.
Version 1.1 - December 2012

Abstract:

This document is prepared by: ICLEI Local Governments for Sustainability-South Asia Secretariat, in collaboration with ICLEI World Secretariat, Bonn, Germany

Basis: Global Protocol for Community - Scale GHG Emissions (GPC) prepared by C40 Cities Climate

Leadership Group and ICLEI Local Governments for Sustainability in collaboration with: World Bank, UNEP, UN-HABITAT, World Resources Institute

India Community Protocol is prepared with support from British High Commission (BHC), India under project titled "Integrating urban climate guidelines through clean technologies (RE&EE) at the state and city level to build sustainable low carbon cities" in Rajasthan & Tamil Nadu States.

Local governments are invited to use this Protocol Pilot Version 1.0 to conduct their community GHG inventories. Other stakeholders are welcome to give their comments. All feedback should be sent to iclei-southasia@iclei.org

Table of Contents

Abbreviations and Acronyms

AFOLU	Agriculture, Forestry, and Land Use
CO	Carbon monoxide
CC>2	Carbon dioxide
CO2e	Carbon dioxide equivalent
FOD	First-order decay
g	Gram(s)
GHG	Greenhouse gas
GWP	Global warming potential
HCFC	Hydrochlorofluorocarbon
HFC	Hydrofluorocarbon
HV/AC	Heating ventilating, and air conditioning
ICP	Indian Community Protocol for Accounting &Reporting GHG emissions
IPCC	Intergovernmental Panel on Climate Change
IPPU	Industrial process and Product Use
ISO	International Organization for Standardization
J	Joule
Kg	Kilogram(s)
kWh	Kilowatt-hour(s)
LHV	Lower heating value
LPG	Liquefied petroleum gas
MSW	Municipal solid waste
mt	Metric ton(s)
N2O	Nitrous oxide
NOx	Oxides of Nitrogen
PFC	Perfluorocarbon
SF6	Sulfur hexafluoride
UNFCCC	United Nations Framework Convention on Climate Change
UN- HABITAT	United Nations Human Settlements Programme
UNEP	United Nations Environment Programme
WRI	World Resource Institute
WBG	World Bank Group
TPD	Tonnes Per Day
VKT	Vehicles Kilometer Travelled
VMT	Vehicles Miles Travelled
IPPU	Industrial Process and Product Use Emissions

Acknowledgement

ICLEI South Asia wishes to thank British High Commission for providing the support for the development of the India Community Protocol for Accounting & Reporting Greenhouse Gas Emissions (ICP). This Protocol could not have been produced without their generous support. Additionally, ICLEI SA is grateful to all of the individuals and organizations that have provided their valuable comments on the draft versions of the ICP.

1. Introduction & Background

Cities are rapidly growing as centers of innovation, energy consumption, population, and sources of global greenhouse gas (GHG) emissions. As a major source of emissions, cities also have a huge potential to drive emission reductions. To effectively manage emissions, cities must first measure and report them publicly. Planning for climate action at the city level starts with developing a GHG inventory. An inventory allows local policy makers and community members to understand which sectors are responsible for the highest level of GHG emissions in their city or community, and respond by developing action plans for those sectors.

Although many Indian cities have conducted a GHG inventory and set voluntary emission reduction targets, there is currently no consistent global guidance for conducting a city-level inventory. The resulting inconsistent inventories cannot be easily communicated between local, sub-national and national governments, financing institutions and the private sector. The lack of a common approach also prevents comparison between cities over time, and reduces the ability of cities to demonstrate the global impact of collective local actions.

The India Community Protocol for Accounting & Reporting Greenhouse Gas Emissions (ICP) is an ICLEI South Asia's initiative with support from Cities Climate Centre, ICLEI Local Governments for Sustainability, World Secretariat, Bonn, Germany. ICLEI South Asia has developed this protocol under the project titled "Integrating Urban Climate Guidelines through Clean Technologies **(RE & EE) at the State and City Level to build sustainable low carbon cities" in Tamil Nadu and Rajasthan states. The project is supported by British High Commission India, Department of Local Self Government, Government of Rajasthan and Commissioner of Municipal Administration, Government of Tamil Nadu.**

The ICP has been developed in line with the Global Protocol for Community-Scale Greenhouse Gas Emissions (GPC), which is developed by ICLEI - Local Governments for Sustainability and C40 Cities Climate Leadership Group as part of their agreement to develop a standard approach for accounting and reporting GHG emissions that will boost cities ability to access funding and implement actions. Other core partners that participated in the development of GPC include the World Bank Group (WBG), United Nations-HABITAT (UN-HABITAT), United Nations (UNEP), the Organization for Economic Cooperation and Development (OECD), and the World Resources Institute (WRI).

1.1. Purpose of ICP

This Protocol provides requirements and guidance for Indian cities on preparing and publicly reporting their a GHG emission inventory. This is the first such document available for local governments in any developing country which will present standard pathways for Indian Cities on measuring, analyzing and reporting GHG emissions in an effective and transparent way. The planning of climate action at the city level starts with developing of a GHG inventory, which allows local policy makers and residents to understand, which sectors drive GHG emissions in their city or community, and respond by developing action plans that address those sectors.

The primary goal of ICP is to provide a standardized step-by-step approach to help cities quantify their GHG emissions in order to identify measures to manage and reduce their GHG impacts.

The ICP was developed with the following objectives:
- Help cities prepare a comprehensive and credible GHG inventory;
- Help cities develop effective strategies for managing and reducing their GHG emissions through a thorough understanding of GHG impacts from their human activities;
- Support consistent and transparent public reporting;
- Harmonize existing international protocols and standards for city level GHG inventories;
- Support cities ability to demonstrate the global impact of collective local actions, and to measure collective progress credibly over time.
- Support GHG accounting, reporting, and trading schemes at the local/sub-national/national level; and
- Facilitate access of local governments to climate finance opportunities.

1.2. Target Users

The ICP is intended for adoption by local authorities or city governments who exercise jurisdiction over a defined geographic area. Local authority, as defined by 1SO/TR-14069, is a public body recognized as such by legislation or by the directives of a higher level of government to set general policies, plans or requirements. Academics, NGOs, or other parties representing the local authority may also use the ICP. In the context of this document, local authority is used to represent any and all of these relevant audiences.

ICP can also be useful for sub-national entities such as towns, districts and states pursuant to appropriate modifications.

Indian Urban Governance Structure

The Indian administration system is a three-tier system where the control flows from upward to downward, from Central government to state government, from state government to local government. The central government is the repository of maximum power, the laws and rules passed by center are implemented by the state and state is accountable to implement these rules with the help of local governance. The constitution divides areas for action in central, state and concurrent lists to define primary action responsibility.

The local governance performs at two levels at city level and rural level. At city level we have Municipal Corporation and Municipal Council depending upon population and area.

The main responsibility of all these government institutions is to provide better public amenities to its citizen and to maintain law and order in the state. Most attention is required by the local governance for delivering better amenities to its citizens.

1.3. Relationship to other Protocols/Standards

The ICP is building upon the knowledge, experiences, and practices defined in previously published protocols and standards. These include the International *Local Government GHG Emissions Analysis Protocol1, the International Standard for Determining Greenhouse Gas*

Emissions for Cities2, the GHG Protocol Standards3, the Baseline Emissions Inventory/Monitoring Emissions Inventory methodology4, and the Local Government Operations Protocol5.

1.4. India's Actions on Climate Change

The Indian Government attaches significant importance to climate change issues, and signed the United Nations Framework Convention on Climate Change (UNFCCC or Convention) in 1993. The first GHG emission estimates for India were made in 1991 and an update was prepared in 1992. Other important milestones are presented in the Table 1 in Chronological **order:**

2. Accounting and Reporting Principles

Accounting and reporting for community scale GHG emissions shall be based on the following principles:

Relevance: The reported GHG emissions shall appropriately reflect emissions occurring as a result of activities and consumption from within the city's geopolitical boundary. The inventory shall also serve the decision-making need of the local authority, and take into consideration relevant local, sub-national, national, and regional regulations. The principle of relevance should be applied when determining whether to exclude any emissions. Local authorities should also use this principle when selecting data sources and deciding on the data quality.

Completeness: All emission sources within the inventory boundary shall be accounted for. Any exclusion of emission sources shall be justified and clearly explained. Notation keys should be used when an emission source is excluded, considered not relevant, and/or not occurring.

Consistency: Emissions calculations shall be consistent in approach, boundary, and methodology. Consistent methodologies for calculating GHG emissions will enable meaningful trend analysis over time, documentation of reductions, and comparisons between cities. Accounting of emissions should follow the standardized, preferred methodologies provided by the ICP. Any deviation from the preferred methodologies should be justified and disclosed.

Transparency: Activity data, emission sources, emission factors, and accounting methodologies should be adequately documented and disclosed to enable verification. The information should be sufficient to enable individuals outside of the inventory process to use the same source data and derive the same results. All exclusions need to be clearly identified and justified.

Accuracy: The calculation of GHG emissions should not systematically overstate or understate actual GHG emissions. Accuracy should be sufficient to give decision makers and the public reasonable assurance of the integrity of the reported information. Local authorities should reduce uncertainties in the quantification process to the extent that it is possible and practical.

Measurability: The data required to support completion of an inventory should be readily available or made available within reasonable time and/or cost. Any exclusion of emission sources shall be justified and disclosed. The use of proxy data and estimated figures should be justified and clearly disclosed.

In the practice of completing an inventory, sometimes conflicts may be encountered among these six principles, and tradeoffs between them may, therefore, be required. For example, achieving complete inventories may at times require using less accurate data. On the other hand, achieving the most accurate inventory may require excluding activities with low data accuracy thus, compromising overall completeness.

In these or similar scenarios, local authorities should strive to achieve an appropriate balance among the principles and objectives of conducting a GHG inventory. For instance, tracking performance towards a specific reduction target may require more accurate data. Over time, as both the accuracy and completeness of GHG data increase, the need for tradeoffs between these accounting principles will likely diminish.

3. Boundary Setting

The inventory boundary shall be set according to the geopolitical territory, where the respective local authority (or local government) has full jurisdictional authority (generally speaking the city or community's boundary). One of the main challenges of this approach is that some activities within the boundary may result in emissions outside the city. To manage this, direct and indirect GHG emissions of communities should be addressed first:

- Direct emissions are emissions from sources within the city boundary.
- Indirect emissions are emissions that are a consequence of the activities within the city boundary, but occur at sources outside the city.

To help delineate the distinction between direct and indirect emissions, ICP adopts the GHG Protocol's scope framework, which is also elaborated in the *International Local Government GHG Emissions Analysis Protocol*, as such:

- Scope 1: All direct emissions from sources within the geopolitical boundary of the community.
- Scope 2: Energy-related indirect emissions that occur outside the community boundary as a consequence of consumption/use of grid-supplied electricity, heating and/or cooling within the community boundary.
- Scope 3: All other indirect emissions that occur outside the boundary as a result of activities within the community's geopolitical boundary, as well as trans-boundary emissions due to exchange/use/consumption of goods and services

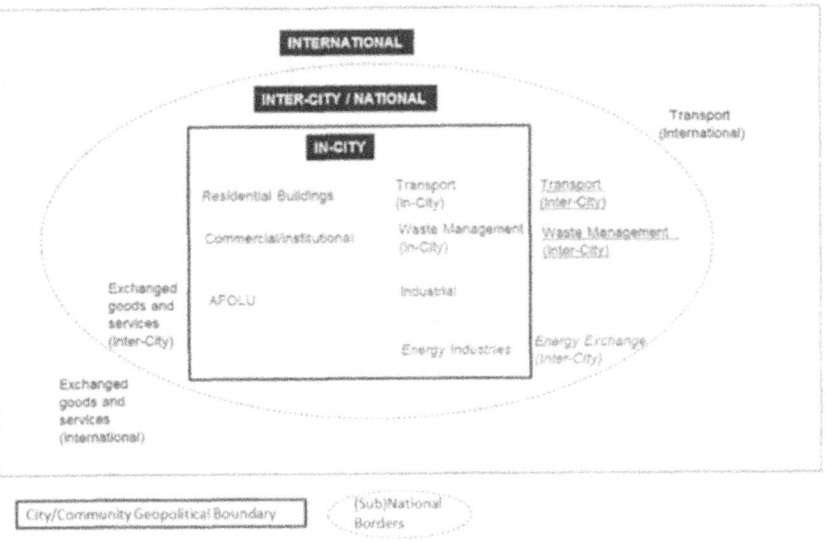

Figure l. Sources and boundaries of community-scale GHG emissions

*Figure 1 above illu*strates the concept of direct and indirect emissions, and the relationship between a city inventory and a national inventory. Direct emissions (scope 1) include sources located within the city boundary (solid red-lined box). These include sources such as in-city transit systems, energy use from buildings, and emissions from industrial activities. The hashed-line represents the regional boundaries, such as state or provincial borders. Some activities in the city transcend the city boundary into other communities. Regional transportation systems, electricity generation and use, waste disposal, and exchanges of goods and services are examples of activities that may be shared between cities. These activities are indirect emissions (scopes 2 and 3) outside of the city boundary, but within the country boundary. The solid line black box indicates international boundaries, or global emissions. Activities indicated here could also be driven by a city, and may include international air or marine transportation and the import or export of goods and services.

4. Reporting

Reporting by Sources

ICP 2012 BASIC: Covers all scop*e 1 and scop*e 2 emissions of stationary units, mobile units, wastes, and Industrial Processes and Product Use (IPPU), as well as scope 3 emissions of waste sector. Dark green cells in the ICP 2012 Framework indicate these sources. In reporting the total by BASIC, Scope 1 emissions from Energy Generation (ICP 1.3.1) are not included in order to prevent double counting since the total BASIC figure also includes Scope 2 emissions. However in reporting by 'Scopes', total Scope 1 emissions must also include Scope 1 emissions from energy generation (ICP 1.3.1).

TCP 2012 BASIC+: Covers TCP 2012 BASIC as well as agriculture, forestry and land use (AFOLU) and scope 3 emissions for mobile units.

ICP 2012 EXPANDED: Covers the entirety of scopes 1, 2, and 3 emissions including trans-boundary emissions due to the exchange/use/consumption of goods and services.

Reporting by Scopes

Regardless of whether local authorities choose to report BASIC, BAS1C+, or EXPANDED, the GHG data shall be aggregated and reported by scope 1, scope 2, and scope 3 separately.

4.1. ICP 2012 BASIC Reporting

Local authorities wishing to comply with the ICP pilot framework are required to account and report at least in the ICP 2012 BASIC and scopes 1 and 2 categories. In order to ensure compliance with ICP 2012 BASIC, it is recommended that Notation Keys be used as appropriate, so that a lack of quantified GHG emissions in the respective source is justified.

The selection of sources that are included in ICP 2012 BASIC is based on the analysis of current best practices in different regions and the availability of internationally accepted GHG accounting methodology. There are readily available methodologies for all ICP 2012 BASIC categories and sources included in the table, as noted in the references to the IPCC Guidelines for National GHG Inventories, 2006 or are included in other published documents.

In order to report through ICP 2012 BASIC+, further guidance is needed for accounting and reporting of agriculture, forestry and land use in urban spaces, as well as appropriate accounting and allocation of GHG emissions due to inter-city and international transport. These sources require further clarification and international consensus, which will be addressed in a future ICP update.

Reporting through ICP 2012 EXPANDED includes all scope 3 categories based on full consumption-based and production-based accounting. This is a new area of work where accounting methodologies are either not available or require further development.

4.2. Required Information

Emissions by Sources: Total GHG emissions (in tCO2e). For sources included in ICP 2012 BASIC; if quantification is not possible, Notation

Keys should be used. The total number of occurrences of each Notation Key and relevant ICP reference number should be indicated. If ICP 2012 BASIC+ or EXPANDED is chosen, sources that are included should be clearly indicated.

Emissions by Scopes: Indicate the scope of each emission source, and separate total emissions by scope 1, *scope 2, and sc*ope 3. It is noted that in reporting by 'scopes', complete Scope 1 emissions must be reported, including emissions from Energy Generation (ICP 1.3.1).

Gases: Data for CO2, CH4, N2O, HFCs, PFCs, and SF6 in metric tons and in tons of CO2 equivalent should be reported.

Data quali**ty: High (H): localized em**ission factors and detailed activity data

Medium (M): national emission factors or generic activity data

Low (L): international/national emission factors and generic activity data Year: Year of inventory or emission data Quantification: Report source or sector-specific quantification methods used

4.3. Data Sources

In developing an emissions inventory, all emission sources should be considered in accordance with the principles of relevance, completeness and consistency. Although this should be interpreted within the context of each local government, this section provides guidance regarding an acceptable approach to inventory compilation. Table 2 gives a picture of the various sources of data and the data requirement for developing the emissions inventory for Indian ci**ties.**

**Table 2 Community Scale-GHG Emissions
Inventory Data Sources in Indian Context**

Inventory	Concerned Person/Office
1. Residential/ Commercial	
Electricity	Executive Engineer (State Electricity Board/DISCOM/ Electricity Distribution utility/Agencies/Power Departments)
LPG Distributor	Individual agencies [Indian Oil Corporation Limited(IOCL), Bharat Petroleum Corporation Limited (BPCL), Hindustan Petroleum Corporation Limited (HPCL), etc]

Petrol/Diesel	Individual agencies [Indian Oil Corporation Limited(IOCL), Bharat Petroleum Corporation Limited (BPCL), Hindustan Petroleum Corporation Limited (HPCL), etc]
Kerosene	City distributor/ civil supply departments, and Individual agencies [Indian Oil Corporation Limited(IOCL), Bharat Petroleum Corporation Limited (BPCL), Hindustan Petroleum Corporation Limited (HPCL), etc]
Coal	Individual agencies/distributor
Fuel Wood	Individual agencies or any other fuel distributor, secondary source: public govt. reports, research papers.
2. Industrial	
Type & Nos. of Unit.	Industrial Development Corporation/ Pollution control Department
Electricity	Executive Engineer (State Electricity Board/DISCOM/ Electricity Distribution utility/Agencies/Power Departments)
Fuel Consumption	Industry associations/oil distribution companies
3. Transportation	
Type & Nos. of Vehicles	Development Authority/ Town and Country Planning Organization (TCPO) / Regional Transport Office (RTO)
Vehicles Kilometer Travelled Engineering	Research institute/ transport department or any College (Department of Civil Engineering)
Inventory	**Concerned Person/Office**
Fuel Consumption [Motor Spirit (MS), High Speed Diesel (HSD), Compressed Natural Gas(CNG)]	Regional Transport Office (RTO)/ oil and gas distribution companies.
4.Waste	
Solid Waste Generation	City Health Officer, Municipal Corporation and Urban Development departments
Management System	City Health Officer/Public health Engineering department
5. Others	
Public water Supply and sewage/Public lighting etc	Municipal corporation /Utility/Jal Board/Public Water Works etc
Buildings and facilities	Municipal Corporation/Public Works Departments

4.4. Data Requirement

4.4.1. Stationary Units

Stationary units refer to the emissions from energy consumption in buildings (residential, commercial and industrial) and sedentary (e.g., non-mobile) equipment or machinery. Emissions in this category can be produced directly from consumption of fuels combusted on-site or indirectly through consumption of grid-delivered electricity, heating and/or cooling.

Stationary combustion refers to the burning of fuels (solid, liquid or gaseous) in buildings or by any equipment or machinery that is in a fixed location. Sources of stationary combustion are located in all sectors of the economy (e.g., residential, commercial, industrial, etc.) and typically account for a large percentage of community GHG emissions. One of the most common sources of stationary combustion is the use of a boiler or furnace that is fueled by coal, natural gas, biomass or furnace oil. These devices consume carbon-based fuels on-site, resulting in direct emissions of carbon dioxide (CO_2), methane (CH_4) and nitrous oxide (N_2O). Stationary combustion can also include a variety of industrial equipment, including kilns, ovens, generators, turbines and incinerators, or any other stationary equipment that burns fuel.

a. Electricity consumption

Sectors	Year 1 Consumption (kWh)	Year 2 Consumption (kWh)	Year 3 Consumption (kWh)	Year 4 Consumption (kWh)
Residential				
Commercial				
Industrial				
Street Light Water Pumping Facility				
Sewerage Treatment facility				
Others (Agriculture etc.)				

b. Fuel Consumption

Fuel consumption under different sectors has a major share in overall city emissions, therefore, fuel consumption data is required for the last four to five years to represent trend and compile inventory of the base year.

Fuel

Sectors	LPG	Kerosene	Coal	Biomass	Others	Wood
Residential						
Commercial						
Industrial						
Others						

Note: (a) Data required for last four to five years for showcasing trend and growth; (b) Consumption unit may vary fuel to fuel, (c) In case of electricity and LPG -write the total numbers of connection & please specify the unit for -which you have filled the rate.

4.4.2. Mobile Units

Mobile combustion refers to the burning of fuels by transportation devices and mobile equipment or machinery. Please note aviation sector is not covered here. Sources of mobile combustion include on- and off-road vehicles, as well as rail, air and water transport systems. Emissions from these sources can be produced directly from fuel consumed by vehicles or indirectly through utility-delivered electricity.

a. **Number of vehicles and VKT**

Type of Vehicles	Number of Vehicles	Annual VKT
Motorcycles/Scooters		
Cars/Jeep		
Light-duty vehicles		
Heavy-duty vehicles		
Buses		
Fire Fighting Trucks		
Waste collecting dumpers/trucks etc		
Others		

b.   Fuel consumption in vehicles

Type of Vehicles	Fuel Consumption (KL, MT etc.)				
	MS	HSD	CNG	Auto LPG	Others
Motorcycles/Scooters					
Cars/Jeep					
Light-duty vehicles					
Heavy-duty vehicles					
Buses					
Fire Fighting Trucks					
Waste collecting dumpers/trucks etc					
Others					

4.4.3. *Waste Emissions Inventory Data requirement:*

Community-generated waste can encompass a variety of waste types (e.g. household waste, industrial waste, construction and demolition waste, agricultural waste, etc.). This section focuses on the data required to estimate GHG emissions associated with the disposal of municipal solid waste (commonly known as trash or garbage) and wastewater handling and treatment.

Similar to inter-city issues associated with transportation, waste and wastewater emissions are complicated by the fact that in some communities waste and wastewater are treated both at facilities within the community and facilities located outside of the community's geopolitical boundaries. Further, other communities (located outside of the jurisdiction) may dispose of their waste and/or wastewater at facilities located within the community.

a. Waste generation and composition

Total waste generation from all concerned sectors of community scale and its composition of last four to five years were accounted to calculate GHG emission and showcase trend & growt**h in waste quantity generation.**

Waste Compositio**n Delivered to Site**

Solid waste				Other
	Paper	**Plant**	**Wood/**	**Metal**
Year Generated	**Organic**			**Waste**
Year 1				
Year2				
Year3				
Year 4				
Year 5				
(Latest year)				

b. What is the system of solid waste disposal?

City specific solid waste disposal system need to be examined along with different attributes like unit capacity and area covered etc.

S.N.	Type	Yes**/No**	**C**apacity
1	Small Open Dump		
2	Sanitary Land Filling		
3	Composting		
4	Incineration		
5	Any other		

4.5. Emission factor and Energy density

Emission factors are used to convert energy usage into the associated emissions and so are central to the emissions analysis. They are usually expressed in terms of emissions/energy used (e.g. tonnes CO2/GJ). The energy density of fuels used is also required where the quantity of fuel used is expressed in mass or volume. The conversion to emissions follows the simple approach of:

Fuel consumed (activity data) x emission factor = GHG emissions

There are a variety of emission factors available from numerous sources. The reliability and accuracy of various sources of emission factors from different sources is an important consideration. Common sources are listed below.

- National Government agencies;
- Sub-national (state, county, etc) Government agencies;
- International agency (e.g. IPCC Tier 1);
- Universities or other research institutions;
- Non-government organizations;
- Corporate/industry associations

Table below provides the information on the available values for India specific energy density and emission factors. The information was collected from the various agencies and research organizations.

4.5.1 Energy Density

A		Fuel	Unit	Value
	Stationary	LPG	Gj/t	47.31
		Kerosene	Gj/t	43.75
B	Mobile	Gasoline	Gj/t	44.79
		Diesel	Gj/t	43.33
C	Waste	MSW	Gj/t	11.00
D	IPPU	Naphtha	Gj/t	45.01
		Propane	Gj/t	46.10

4.5.2. Emission Factor

The emission factors used are a mix of default emission factors available in IPCC publications (1997, 2000, 2003 and 2006) and country specific emission factors referred from 'India: Greenhouse Gas Emissions" INCAA, 2007 (http://moef.nic.in/downloads/public-information/Report INCCA.pdf). Default emission factors have been used for gases and categories where country specific factors are not available.

4.5.3. Emission Factor-Electricitv

Emission Unit: Grams/kWh	Year/Gas	CO_2	N_2O	CH_4	NOx	SOx
NEWNE Grid Average electricity	2010-11	830	0.0087	0.0068	2.7666	2.2286
Southern Grid Average electricity	2010-11	760	0.0097	0.0076	3.2016	3.1589

4.5.4. Emission Factor-Fuels

Sector	Fuel	Carbon Dioxide CO_2	Nitrous Oxide N2O	Methane CH_4
Residential	Kerosene	71900 kg/TJ	0.6 kg/TJ	10 kg/TJ
	Liquefied Petroleum gas	63100 kg/TJ	13 g/GJ	5 kg/TJ
Industrial	Charcoal	112000 kg/TJ	4 kg/TJ	200 kg/TJ
	Furnace Oil	42.79 TJ/KT	0.6 kg/TJ	3 kg/TJ
	Petroleum Coke	97500 kg/TJ	0.6 kg/TJ	3 kg/TJ
	Natural Gas	56100 kg/TJ	1 kg/TJ	240 kg/TJ
	Jet Kerosene	71500 kg/TJ	0.6 kg/TJ	10 kg/LTJ
Commercial	Anthracite Coal	98300 kg/TJ	1.5 kg/TJ	10 kg/TJ
	Charcoal	112000 kg/TJ	1 kg/TJ	200 kg/TJ
	Motor Gasoline	69300 kg/TJ	0.6 kg/TJ	10 kg/TJ

Sector	Fuel	Vehicle Type	Model / Standard	CO_2 (kg/GJ)
Transportation	Gasoline	Passenger Vehicle	Bharat IV	74.82
	Diesel	Passenger Vehicle	Bharat IV	76.8
	CNG	Passenger Vehicle		51.85
	LPG	Passenger Vehicle		59.03
	Diesel (ULSD)	Passenger Vehicle		74.1

Sector	Category	Methane CH_4
Waste*	MSW	0.0182

*Waste Emission Unit: tonnes/tonnes

5. Accounting and Reporting Pilot Framework

The ICP 2012 Accounting and Reporting Pilot Framework given in the Annexure presents a complete list of sources for a community scale GHG inventory and includes options for aggregation and reporting by sources, namely, ICP 2012 BASIC, ICP 2012 BASIC+ and EXPANDED and by Scopes namely Scope 1, 2, and 3.

In order to meet these requirements, local authorities may need to consider using a sub-set of BASIC sources or a combination of the BASIC and BASIC+ sources (see Section 4 Reporting for further details on these reporting options).

In these cases, however, local authorities are encouraged to include an additional set of results according to the ICP's requirements to ensure international comparability and to ensure full compliance with the ICP BASIC inventory.

Local authorities may also find that some of the emission sources indicated in the ICP do not exist within their defined community boundary, or that the emissions are not significant. Water-borne transport, for instance, does not exist in some inland cities. In such contexts, excluding or omitting emission sources that are not relevant to the objectives of the inventory should apply the principle of relevance. Notation keys should be appropriately used.

When local authorities encounter tradeoffs between principles or between the ICP and local/ sub-national/ national/regional requirements, they should revisit their objective of conducting a GHG inventory. Generally, local authorities should prioritize the city's inventory needs based on key objectives and significance of GHG emissions. While fulfilling minimum needs or requirements, local authorities should aim to improve completeness and accuracy over time to ensure full compliance with the ICP.

A credible GHG inventory report presents information based on the principles of relevance, completeness, consistency, transparency, accuracy, and measurability. To ensure comparability between cities, ICP requires local authorities to report their GHG emissions based on the ICP 2012 Accounting and Reporting Framework that is presented in Annexure along with the guidance provided under key accounting principles in Section 2.

Considering both local decision-making needs and the IPCC Guidelines for National GHG Inventories, the ICP 2012 Accounting and Reporting Framework includes six main categories: Stationary units, Mobile units (in the IPCC Guidelines these two categories are grouped under 'energy'), Waste, IPPU (industrial process and product use), AFOLU (agriculture, forestry, and land use), and Other indirect emissions. These emission sources are further categorized by scopes *(see Section 3 Boundary Setting)* to distinguish direct and indirect impacts.

For each source, the corresponding IPCC classification number is also provided. This enables local authorities to have a more active collaboration with their national governments in the preparation of national GHG inventories for submission to UNFCCC.

In order to ease the reporting process, and following the practice used by national governments in the IPCC and UNFCCC processes, ICP enables the use of Notation Keys. These are:

- IE- Included Elsewhere: Emissions for this activity are estimated and presented in another category of the inventory. The category where these emissions are included should be noted in explanation.
- NE- Not Estimated: Emissions occur but have not been estimated or reported; justification for exclusion should be noted.
- NA - Not Applicable: **The** activity occurs but does not cause emissions; explanation should be provided.
- NO - Not Occurring: **An activity or process does not occur or exist wit**hin the community.

Annexure: ICP 2012 Accounting and Reporting Pilot Framework

ICP No.	IPCC Class	Scope	GHG Emissions Sources	Accounting Approach	IE	NE	NO	NA	CO₂	CH₄	N₂O	HFC	PFC	SF₆	CO₂ e	H	M	L
					Notation keys				GASES						Total GHG Gases	Data Quality		
L.			**Stationary Units**															
L1			Residential Buildings															
L1.1	1A4b	1	Direct Emissions (Scope1)	In-Boundary Fuel Combustion														
L1.2		2	Energy Indirect Emissions (Scope2)	In-Boundary Energy Consumption														
L2			Commercial/Institutional Facilities															
L2.1	1A4a	1	Direct Emissions (Scope1)	In-Boundary Fuel Combustion														
L2.2		2	Energy Indirect Emissions (Scope2)	In-Boundary Energy Consumption														
L3			Energy Generation															
L3.1.	1A1	1	Direct Emissions (Scope1)	In-Boundary Fuel Combustion														
L3.2		2	Energy Indirect Emissions (Scope2)	In-Boundary Energy Consumption														
L4	1A2~1A5 +1A4c		Industrial Energy Use															
L4.1		1	Direct Emissions (Scope1)	In-Boundary Fuel Combustion														
L4.2		2	Energy Indirect Emissions (Scope2)	In-Boundary Energy Consumption														
L5			Fugitive Emissions															
L5.1	1B	1	Direct Emissions (Scope1)															
H.			**Mobile Units**															
H1			On-Road Transportation															
H1.1	1A3b	1	Direct Emissions (Scope1)	In-Boundary Fuel Combustion														
H1.2		2	Energy Indirect Emissions (Scope2)	In-Boundary Energy Consumption														

Appendix 2
Sustainability Frameworks and Tools
Overarching Principles

Framework/Tool	Comments
The Three Es: This is based on United Nation's work regarding what is needed for sustainable development. The Three Es are usually referred to as Economy, Environment and Social Equity	This framework gives no guidance about what to do but can help you organize your thinking. Social equity is only part of the social aspect of sustainability. Compare this with Triple Bottom line which has a broader interpretation of the social element
The Triple Bottom Line: Somewhat used interchangeably with the Three Es but different in subtle ways. Basically, the same framework as Corporate Social Responsibility: often framed as Social, Economic and Environment or People, Planet and Profits.	This framing of the social component allows for the inclusion of other social issues such as human health, governance etc. business for social responsibility is probably one of the best sources for this approach.
The Natural Step Framework: This provides a planning framework in the form of four 'system conditions' or principles based on science that guide decision-makers of an organization or governmental body systematically towards sustainability. For society to be sustainable nature must not be subject to increasing concentrations of human made substances; its functions and diversity must not be impoverished (displacement, over-harvesting etc.) and resources must be used fairly and efficiently in order to meet basic human needs globally. (See the Natural Step, www.naturalstep.org)	Because the framework is derived from fundamental scientific principles, it has more face validity than some of the other frameworks. The framework does an excellent job of describing the environmental aspect of sustainability, but it is often criticized for not adequately addressing the other two areas of sustainability namely social and economic elements.
CERES Principles: Created in response to the Exxon Valdez disaster, CERES offers a code of conduct and a credo for organizations to adopt. The principles address issues such as energy conservation, waste reduction and disposal, and management commitment: www.ceres.org	CERES and other sets of principles like it, are arguably not sustainability frameworks because they don't overtly recognize the limits of nature.

Conservation Economy: Eco-trust has put together a website that documents best practices for social, economic and environmental practices. They have identified 'patterns' (e.g. Certification, labelling) that have application in many situations. www.conservationeconomy.net	Based on three legs of sustainability, the web tool is useful
Natural Capitalism: A book of the same title lays out a set of principles for a sustainable economic system. The main principles involve dramatically improving the productivity of natural resources, redesigning production around biological models (biomimicry), rethinking business as a service and reinvesting in natural capital. www.naturalcapitlism.org	
Six Es: Trade Unions in Europe are developing a working model that will support companies and organizations that wish to change their operations on the basis of goals set for Agenda 21. This model is called 6E and stand for ecology, emissions, energy, ergonomics, efficiency and economics.	This includes more quality of life issues than other frameworks

Industry-Specific Framework

Framework/Tools	Comments
Agenda 21: Created at the Rio Earth Summit through the UN, this lays out actions needed at a national and international level to reach sustainability.	Talks about what needs to happen but provides no accountability to make it happen.
UN Global Compact: Created by the UN to foster corporate citizenship. www.unglobalcompact.org.	Puts forth ten principles for business in three areas – labour standards, environment and anti-corruption in support of the Agenda 21 goals.
Talloires Declaration: A set of principles for colleges and universities. Provides ten principles signed by universities from all over the world. Created by the University Leaders for a Sustainable future.	Like CERES, provides no clear targets
Equator Principles: Similar to Talloires but for financial institutions.	Like CERES, provides no clear targets
Leadership for Energy and Environmental Design (LEED): Provides a scoring system for evaluating the sustainability of buildings. Certification is possible. See the world green building council (www.worldgbc.org) or the US Building council (www.usgbc.org).	Used in the US and a number of other countries. LEED does not define a fully sustainable building but it is the intent of the US Green Building Council to slowly raise the bar as practices and technologies improve.
Environmental Management System/ ISO 14001: International guidelines for environmental management systems and their certification. Most often used by manufacturing and to a lesser extent, government.	Can provide a process for managing your sustainability effort but by itself does not provide sustainability targets. Can easily be dovetailed by other frameworks.
Smart Growth/New Urbanism: Provides guidelines for land use planning	Provides important guidelines for the development of liveable communities.
Hanover Principles: Developed by William McDonough Architects for EXPO 2000, held in Hanover, Germany (For a complete list of the principles, see www.virginia.edu/-arch/pub/hanover_list.html)	The nine principles focus on the design of 'green' buildings or the 'built environment' and stress the interdependent relationship human society has with nature.
huna	
human	

Biomimicry: Using nature as inspiration for human designs. Most useful for research and development.	Co-opted by Natural Capitalism as one of their principles, this is also practice unto itself.
Zero Waste: One approach to sustainability is to eliminate all form of waste, turning our linear economy into a cyclical one, like nature's, where waste from one process becomes input to another. The Zero Waste Alliance has assessments and services to help you implement this approach. (See www.zerowaste.org or the Grassroots Recycling network at: www.grrn.org)	Can seem more tangible than some of the other frameworks but people often interpret it as only dealing with solid waste.
Industrial Ecology: Designing manufacturing systems so that waste of one process is input to another.	In Eurpoe the focus has been on co-locating facilities (sometimes called eco-industrial parks). This has been less successful in US.
Green Chemistry: Designing chemical processes to eliminate hazardous by-products and improve the efficiency of the processes themselves.	An emerging practice with lot of promise for product development.
Product stewardship, Extended producer responsibility, Extended product responsibility (EPR): These three terms are roughly synonymous with subtle distinctions about who should bear responsibility. The concept is to make manufacturers responsibility for their products for their entire lifecycle, including end of life.	While many efforts here are end-of-life (ie. Taking back products at the end of their useful life), they necessarily deal with the entire life cycle.

Measurement-related Tools

Framework/Tools	Comments
Global Reporting Initiative: Standards for sustainability reports. www.globalreporting.org	Created by CERES. It is intended to provide consistency across organizations but to date some organizations find difficult to implement
Bellagio Principles: Provide criteria and guidelines for the selection of metrics	Useful when creating metrics
Genuine Progress Indicators: Gross National Product adjusted so that spending on 'bad things' like prisons and environmental clean-up are deducted.	Useful for economists
Greenhouse Gas Protocol: A standardized method of reporting climate impacts.	Important to follow if you plan to trade carbon credits or make public claims about reduction in greenhouse gases.
Lifecycle Assessments: A method of examining the impacts of a product or decision over its entire life cycle (from raw material and manufacture to transportation, use and disposal)	Can be overwhelming to do a thorough job.
Lifecycle coting: A method of examining the cost of financial decisions (eg. Construction of buildings) over their lifetime (versus first cost)	This is a small financial practice that may already be standard practice in your organization.
Ecological Footprint: if you put a bubble over your city, it would quickly die because there would be no place to get raw materials or dispose of wastes. So the ecological footprint of our cities are much bigger than the area within the city limits. The Ecological Footprints approach shows you how to estimate the land needed to sustain way of life. For example: an average American needs30 acres, the average Italian less than half that.	Interesting concept but can be overwhelming to try to compute

Appendix 3

Mainstream Financial Institutions involved in Sustainable Financing

1.YES Bank:

Sustainable Financing:

Sustainability has been a core value proposition to YES BANK since inception, weaving sustainability into its operations as well as creating stakeholder value through positive impact business solutions. The central Responsible Banking team holds the mandate to set and drive the bank's strategy based on a triple bottom line of financial, social and environmental returns.

While India continues to account for a very low per capita emission level, over the past five years, overall CO_2 emissions have risen. Climate change could result in huge economic losses accounting to over 1% of India's GDP. It is estimated that an investment of over USD 2.5 trillion will be required for India to achieve its emission intensity-reduction targets and adaptation to climate change by 2030. This makes it critical to align the growth agenda with addressing climate change, and for financial institutions to bring their expertise, to the task at hand of integrating sustainability in financing.

Sustainability in Operations

YES BANK having realized sustainability as the future of business has focused on developing a knowledge driven approach to banking, and is striving to drive it through its sustainable finance interventions.

Establishing a framework to recognize, evaluate, monitor and manage the environmental and social facets in day-to-day decision-making process has assumed critical importance for banks. It has become imperative for banks to consider the triple-bottom-line approach in making credit decisions.

In line with its Responsible Banking strategy and practices, YES BANK takes a holistic risk management approach through consideration of environmental and social impacts of its lending activities. YES BANK, since 2006, has implemented an Environment and Social Policy through which, the Bank integrates environmental and social risks into its overall credit risk assessment framework. The Bank has voluntarily adopted this policy which is based on international frameworks such as the Equator Principles and IFC guidelines.

First bank globally to migrate to the latest environment management system

In 2017, YES BANK successfully completed ISO 14001:2015 recertification for 444 metro urban branch locations by implementing the globally recognized Environmental Management System. With this, YES BANK continues to set a benchmark in the industry for environmental sustainability.

Focus on Renewable Energy

The Bank signed an agreement with the Indian Renewable Energy Development Agency (IREDA) to foster renewable energy (RE) development in India, at the Make in India Week at Mumbai in February 2016. The MoU will boost green energy financing, strengthen the Bank's efforts towards meeting the COP21 commitment of mobilizing USD 5 Billion for climate action by 2020 and help forge a close partnership between both institutions to create a supporting framework for funding of renewable energy and energy-efficient projects.

Focus on Energy Efficiency

The Ministry of Power and Bureau of Energy Efficiency (BEE) have constituted Partial Risk Guarantee Fund for Energy Efficiency (PRGFEE) for providing financial institutions (Banks/NBFCs) a partial coverage of risk involved in extending loans for energy efficiency projects. Under this program, YES BANK participated in the Energy Efficiency Services Ltd. (EESL) organized roundtable meeting with Banks/Financial Institutions/ ESCOs in October, 2015 in Mumbai. At the meeting, YES BANK signed a charter with BEE for empanelment of Participating Financial Institutions (PFIs) under PRGFEE, which is expected to set the tone for other Banks/ NBFCs to join this league and contribute in promoting Energy Efficiency in India.

Strategic Approach to Sustainable Financing

YES BANK believes in a knowledge driven approach to banking and has deployed a strategic four-pronged, approach to its sustainable financing work. The following attributes of the bank's financing mechanism make it a winning strategy:

Genuine intent to contribute

The bank believes that to achieve any strategic outcome, short, medium and long term goals are important. Aligned to this thought, YES BANK has announced many targeted commitments towards sustainability and climate action.

The bank on the occasion of Conference of Parties (COP) 21 climate summit in Paris, has targeted to mobilize USD 5 Billion from 2015 to 2020 for climate action through lending, investing and raising capital towards mitigation, adaptation and resilience will holistically impact and aid India's target of meeting its Nationally Determined Contributions (NDCs).

The other commitments of the bank including the target finding of 5,000 MW of clean energy and the planting of 2 million trees by 2020 shows the unfeigned attempt the bank is making towards sustainable development.

Strict adherence to policies

The bank in a structured way puts in place relevant policies and processes that help achieve the aforementioned targets. YES BANK accordingly has in place a detailed set of internal guidelines for its green bonds to be Green Bond Principles compliant. The bank also instituted an Environmental & Social policy to guide its lending decisions, while its resource management is upheld by an Environmental Management Policy

This policy-led approach substantiated with clear procedures has not only made the strategy self-run, but has also helped the bank reach its leadership position in this space in India.

Collaborative leadership

To further bolster its approach to sustainable finance, the bank has become an active member of some highly credible coalitions. YES BANK, as the first Indian signatory to the UNEP FI, a global partnership between the UNEP and financial sector, continues to play a leadership role at the platform. Namita Vikas, Group President and Global Head – Climate Strategy & Responsible Banking, is the current Asia-Pacific Chair of the UNEP FI.

YES BANK's membership with the Natural Capital Finance Alliance (NCFA), which "seeks to increase awareness of the natural capital risks to which financial institutions expose themselves through loans and investments" and the bank's association with the Green Bonds Principles (GBP) is a testimony to the bank's sincerity towards the making of a new benchmark for sustainable financing.

These memberships not only are the conduits of international best practice, but also strengthen the sustainable finance operations in the bank.

YES BANK also focuses on internal capacity building in the environmental sustainability domain by creating a learning environment for its employees. Among many other initiatives towards climate change mitigation, the bank has also taken considerable steps to reduce its own carbon footprint. To achieve this, the bank has designed a series of e-learning modules which each employee has to attend mandatorily. The modules educate the employees as to how they can make environmentally responsible decisions in their daily activities like reduction in paper consumption, using clean water wisely etc. For successful integration of environment and social risks under YES BANK's risk management framework, the bank employs focused workshops and e-learning modules. This equips the employees with relevant skillset and tools to recognize, evaluate and, to the highest degree possible, manage the relevant environmental and social risks. Other initiative like knowledge sessions by reputed industry leaders and intra knowledge transfer sessions within teams also help the bank move towards a common goal of mitigating environmental risks.

2. BANK OF AMERICA www.bankofamerica.com Bank of America financially supports efforts to promote "Smart Growth", a collaborative regional planning program that brings together community stakeholders to create integrated regional growth solutions. The goal is to produce sensible growth – growth that plans for jobs and economic development, while respecting the natural environment. Smart Growth examples include: • Mixed-use developments • Mixed-income housing • Redevelopment on contaminated property • Protection of open space and ecologically valuable lands • Redevelopment in city-center areas that have been abandoned or fallen into disrepair. Two of the bank's Smart Growth initiatives include: • A partnership with the Urban Land Institute that fosters informed and collaborative efforts among stakeholders, supports national policy forums, and increases community outreach initiatives. • An investment in the California Environmental Redevelopment Fund that helps provide debt financing for the investigation and cleanup of contaminated properties. Bank of America has issued a company-wide policy to pay special attention to businesses that play a positive environmental role and to caution against doing business with companies whose environmental performance is unacceptable.

3. CITIGROUP www.citigroup.com Citibank, a subsidiary of Citigroup based in the US, has established a Non-Profit Financial Services Group, specializing in financing and cash management services for non-profit organizations. In its aim to provide an integrated approach to supporting non-profit organizations that transcends philanthropy, it offers a Citibank Community Building Tool Kit, including: • Customized Financing Solutions • Business Services • Management Expertise and Technical Assistance • Financial Education Programs • Employee Volunteers • Charitable Contributions. Some specialist services include construction/ rehabilitation financing for commercial owner occupied properties,

special needs housing and facilities, and operating lines of credit and term loans which include interim financing against foundation and government contracts and commitments. The bank has established a National Community Development Group to address the needs of national community development intermediaries and non-profit organizations and local opportunities that fall outside its 10 prioritized regional markets. This National Community Development Group provides non-profit and for-profit developers and businesses financing packages for their projects in low and moderate-income areas. For example, Citybank offers national warehouse facilities and lines of credit to support affordable housing, social services and business entrepreneurs. It also has established a "Partners in Progress Fund for Innovation", providing below market-rate financing to established community development corporations. Additional community development investments include a partnership with the YWCA of USA to establish Financial Empowerment Individual Development Account(IDAs) Programmes for low-income women; founding sponsorship of Together in America, a national membership association for immigrants of every ethnic background in the US in which Citibank is expanding access of its products and services at discounted and advantaged rates; Community Summer Intern Program which awards salary grants to 100 community development organizations so they can hire university students to grow the next generation of community leaders; and the Community Development Institute, which covers costs for non-profit professionals to attend workshops to help them strengthen their organizations. The Institute also offers Citibank Nonprofit Days that include capacity-building sessions and networking time for hundreds of nonprofits a year. It also has commitments to invest in sustainable forestry and renewable energy including financing for social panels, residential wind turbines and fuel cells.

4. HSBC PLC www.hsbc.com. Individual Development Accounts help low-income people achieve asset wealth and financial stability through savings matched by a philanthropic program, financial education and a connection to community resources. IDAs help people to reach their goals of home ownership, self-employment or a college education with the necessary capital, information and support. In 2003, the board of HSBC Holdings plc established a CSR Committee, responsible for overseeing HSBC's CSR policies and advising the board on CSR. In late 2004, this UK company committed itself to a carbon neutral target across its operations. To achieve this goal, the company plans to plant trees, reduce energy use, buy green electricity and trade carbon credits to cut carbon dioxide flows. The move will cost up to USD 7m in 2005, less in future years, representing 0.004% of the bank's market value. In addition to the carbon-neutral plan, the bank is investing £650,000 in environment research at two UK universities,

researching climate change and society's awareness of the issues and developing technologies to overcome some of the problems identified. HSBC has a clear business objective for its commitment, expecting to gain a deeper insight into the emerging low carbon economy and to be well placed to understand the needs of, and opportunities for, its clients. This thinking is premised on the overarching HSBC belief that corporate social responsibility underpins sustained earnings growth. To this end, the bank is also developing a range of socially responsible investment funds. In addition to helping its institutional clients with their investment decision-making by providing environmental and social, as well as financial, analysis, it provides opportunities for institutional investors to meet and question companies on their sustainability progress and plans. A few other noteworthy initiatives include: • ATM users in Mexico are given the opportunity to make a donation to several national and regionally recognized charities after withdrawing cash. This facility helped customers to donate over 24 million pesos to help children with healthcare, education and nutrition in 2003. • It is in the middle of implementing "Investing in Nature" a USD 50-million, 5-year programme to support 3 leading environmental charities: Botanic Gardens Conservation International, WWF and Earthwatch, which are focusing on saving endangered plant species, helping to restore 3 of the world's major rivers, and sending 2,000 HSBC staff to work on conservation research projects around the world, respectively.

5. MORLEY FUND MANAGEMENT www.morleyfm.com Based in the UK, Morley is the largest fund management company owned by Aviva , with over £128 billion under management, 981 staff and 9 international offices. Its overall vision is to fully integrate corporate responsibility in the way it runs its business, enabling it to act as a responsible investor in the interest of Morley's long-term prosperity. It is committed to applying the same sustainability standards it requests of its investee companies to its own business, driven by its belief that companies most likely to grow consistently over the next few decades will be those that are promoting or benefiting from sustainable development. Morley's CSR committee of 8 staff takes responsibility for implementing Aviva Group's CSR policy, reporting to the Managing Director for Human Resources. In 2003, it levered their purchasing power with brokers, encouraging them to take SRI seriously and incorporate sustainability criteria into their research and analysis. Morley participates on the United Nation's Environment Program (UNEP) Asset Management working group and through this medium has been encouraging brokers to undertake work on sustainability issues. As a result of its efforts and those of others, a number of papers exploring the links between social and environmental issues and business performance

were published. Further, Morley is a participant in the United Nations Environment Programme's (UNEP) initiative to develop a set of globally recognized principles for responsible investment by September 2005. Since its launch in 2002, the Morley Fund Management FTSE100 Sustainability Matrix has been rating FTSE 100 companies according to social and environmental criteria with the purpose to: • Encourage companies to improve their social and environmental performance • Protect and increase shareholder value by adding another tool for company analysis • Provide transparent analysis of companies' social and environmental policies • Stimulate debate and raise awareness of CSR. It offers 10 screened SRI funds covering a broad range of global bond and equity markets, including the Igloo Regeneration Fund, a specialist property fund with a balanced and diversified investment portfolio of urban regeneration development and investment projects, the first of its kind in the UK. Offering direct real estate regeneration investment opportunities to socially responsible investors, the fund targets investments into environmentally sustainable, well designed real estate development that contributes to the regeneration of the local area.

6. ROYAL BANK OF SCOTLAND GROUP www.rbs.co.uk. In 2003, The Royal Bank of Scotland Group board of directors adopted a Corporate Responsibility policy for the Group and a Corporate Responsibility Working Group was established, involving all divisions to manage implementation of their CSR policies. One of the Group's priorities is community investment in which it is focused on 4 key components, achieved by developing long-term partnerships with charities and government: • Matching the support of their people • Financial education and inclusion • Education and employment • Enterprise and regeneration In each of the projects it supports as a Group, it looks to create opportunities for its employees to play a role, combining staff expertise with financial support. In one such national initiative, for example, each employee volunteering opportunity is mapped to the Group's competency framework and linked to the employee's personal development plan. It has identified that a common barrier preventing community volunteering is the difficulty people confront in finding suitable opportunities. To assist its staff in the UK, it operates a program called Give A Little, an on-line database that holds detailed information about volunteering and fund-raising opportunities for over 1,600 charities. The service, which also enables on-line payroll giving to be set up, is available free of charge to any registered charity in the UK. The following additional community investment initiatives were reported on in 2003: • The Group has a leading 45% market share in lending to businesses in the 5% most deprived postal codes. In these disadvantaged areas a Community Development Banking Team supports a range of initiatives

providing loan finance to individuals, community businesses, social enterprises and other not-for-profit organizations. • The RBS group is the lead relationship bank to both the education and charity sectors in the UK, banking more than 1 in 3 charities and higher educational establishments in this market. Its goal is to continually develop its offerings to this sector, aiming to provide the most efficient use of treasury and deposit products, payment products, campaign management services, electronic banking and other e-charity solutions. • The Group believes that, as levels of consumer borrowing rise, it is increasingly important for people to know how to manage their personal finances effectively, which is only possible if consumers have a good understanding of financial issues and access to free, independent financial advice. Committed to playing a significant role in this field, the Group provides the UK's most widely used corporate financial education programme for schools and is the leading corporate supporter to the money advice sector – helping people, the self-employed and small businesses in greatest need to better understand their finances and manage their debts. • The Group runs programs to support enterprise development and regenerate local communities. In addition to its lending in the most disadvantaged inner city areas, it also sponsors the annual Inner City 100 Awards, presented by the Chancellor of the Exchequer. The Inner City 100 Index is a register of the 100 fastest growing businesses located in the most disadvantaged inner city areas. It also works to redevelop sites for business or community use through the 1997 initiative "Priority Sites", a public/private sector property joint venture with a target of creating 1 million square feet of new industrial and business premises on brownfield land in areas affected by industrial decline. • Its US subsidiary, Citizens Bank, sets its own community investment priorities, one of which is its Community Champions programme in which a new champion is selected each quarter from a range of social service areas including health care, hunger, homelessness, youth services and affordable housing. Each agency receives USD 25,000 in unrestricted funds, extensive public relations and promotional support as well as volunteer support from Citizens and from employees of its local media partner in each market.

7. SWISS RE www.swissre.com Swiss Re is one of the world's leading reinsurers. Given the long-term nature of its business, identifying long-fuse risks early and learning how to deal with them is critical for the company. Correspondingly, it has named Sustainability as one of Swiss Re's 4 core values, along with excellence, efficiency and integrity. Swiss Re believes that Sustainability leverages 3 domains (society, environment, economy) to create a forward-thinking business model that addresses the fundamental drivers of the world economy in the 21st century, namely: • Rapidly growing global population which relies on resource-intensive

lifestyles; • Future valuation of vital yet endangered natural resources; and • Risks from newly emerging social and ecological issues. Given Swiss Re's mission to anticipate, identify and understand the developments which are shaping the future risk landscape, the company has established a formal "Top Topics" process to help answer fundamental questions on the key market, regulatory, scientific and social trends shaping the future business environment. This in turn helps the company anticipate potential sources of future losses resulting from changes to the risk landscape. The company shares information on its "Top Topics" through stakeholder dialogues, participation in international fora and publications on topical environmental and societal issues. As part of this effort it funds the Centre for Global Dialogue which hosts international and regional conferences to address global risk issues and facilitate new insights into future risk markets. Two sustainability "Top Topics", identified in 2002, are Climate Change and Water, around which the company is implementing a program to build issue-specific awareness among major climate and water stakeholders and to foster dialogue. Products and services The company seeks to provide best practice in environmental underwriting. Its group-wide Environmental Risk and Underwriting Knowledge Network and obligatory Environmental Management Guidelines contribute to this effort, as do the following: • The Greenhouse Gas Risk Solutions unit offers various financial solutions in the area of emissions reductions and is developing products in greenhouse gas synergy areas such as green certificates and renewable energy. • Swiss Re provides advanced concepts in environmental impairment liability insurance and participates in European pool solutions. • It developed Contingent Gap Forward Insurance to facilitate emissions trading by covering counter-party and delivery risks faced by buyers of emissions reduction credits. • Swiss RE also offers a reduction in its premiums to companies with good environmental performance. Further, Swiss Re targets its sustainability asset management efforts in 3 areas: 1. Eco-portfolio including direct investments in solar energy, recycling and waste disposal, integrated raw material production and organic pest management, and indirect investments via 2 funds which screen investments on the basis of their sustainability profile. 2. Carbon disclosure project, a joint effort with over 30 large institutional investors asking all Fortune 500 companies to disclose their climate change policies. 3. Real estate, where buildings in Swiss Re's real estate portfolio are increasingly meeting national energy efficiency and user comfort standards. Technical training modules in environmental management are offered to employees and Swiss Re's clients. In 2002, it launched a 10-year programme to become fully carbonneutral, the world's first major financial institution to do so.

8. ALTERNATIVES CREDIT UNION www.alternatives.org Alternatives Credit Union in Ithaca, New York, is dedicated to building wealth and creating economic opportunity for underserved people and communities. Its mission is to provide: • Access to transactional services • Savings and community investment opportunities • Capital investments to individuals, small businesses and non-profits • Education about capital In its efforts to help members move along the continuum between poverty and self-sufficiency, it sees its job as helping members move along that continuum by empowering them to make decisions, and offering opportunities that will move them towards financial self-sufficiency. It created a Credit Path model to provide alternatives with guidance in designing products and services to meet members' needs at different points along the path, helping them to progress towards successful asset ownership. It sees its members moving along the Credit Path in stages: Transactor: For the poorest members, those who are new to the banking system, immigrants, and others who need access to basic financial services. Transactors need to cash cheques, purchase money orders, get change, or wire money to others. As banks charge more for these services, transactors turn to fringe financial providers, such as cheque cashers, and pay high fees. Alternatives prices these services to be affordable to members, but sustainable to the credit union. In 2003, it added a free tax preparation service for low-income earners, with the hope of introducing previously unbanked people to the credit union's services. Saver: Alternatives provides incentives for this traditional credit union market by paying interest on all accounts with a $5 minimum balance and charging no monthly fees. It offers special Savers Certificates with a minimum of $100. Also offered are Individual Development Accounts (IDAs) which significantly expand the likelihood of success at this stage by providing both a savings match and financial education. Borrower: Responsible borrowing is a financial tool that can lead to greater wealth. Alternatives helps its members develop good credit records by offering several "starter" loans, including the Alternatives Debit Card, Credit Builder Loan and Community Partnership Loans. It also offers a short-term loan for those who used Alternatives' free income tax preparation services and wanted quick access to their tax refund. One of Alternatives' goals is to help members avoid the high rates and endless refinancing of predatory lenders. Much of the lending at this stage is consumer lending: cars, personal loans, VISA cards and lines of credit. As members handle these loans successfully, they can build up to larger amounts. Owner: Learning to save and developing a good credit record help people move towards becoming owners of homes or businesses. Alternatives offers a variety of home and business loan products, many to members who started at the beginning of the Credit Path. Alternatives also

offers Business CENTS (Community Enterprise Networking and Training Services), a small business development program providing a "how to" business training course, seminars, one-on-one business counselling and marketing support for people interested in starting or expanding a business. To further help its business members and support the economic resiliency of the community, Alternatives offers Business Yellow Pages to its members, putting them in touch with the credit union's business members and Business CENTS graduates. Round off is another Alternatives' initiative, allowing members to donate "spare change" to local community organizations. A checkoff box on deposit forms lets members make small donations to the non-profit member organization of the month every time they make a deposit.

9. CHARITY BANK www.charitybank.org Based in the UK, Charity Bank is a not-for-profit national bank that offers retail savings and deposit accounts, which are on-lent to charity and non-profit organizations. In addition to providing affordable financing for charities and community groups to build new facilities, renovate buildings, purchase equipment or extend their services, Charity Bank also offers advice and assistance services to this market. It normally provides financing if other financial institutions will not do so or will only provide loans on unaffordable terms. Charity Bank gives depositors the option of withdrawing their interest, reinvesting their returns in Charity Bank, directly donating their returns to the depositor's choice of charity, or a mix of any of these options. The Charity Bank Community Investment Tax Relief Account is one of the deposit accounts that provides savers the following returns: • 5% per year tax relief for the account holder (equivalent to a gross return of 8.33% a year for higher tax rate payers or 6.4% a year for standard rate tax payers). • An additional 2% annual interest on all deposits. This interest can be kept by the depositor or given to a charity of their choice (donated interest can be uplifted by 28% for the charity through the UK's Gift Aid scheme, creating a double tax break). • A social return in which their money is making a difference to charities and disadvantaged communities across the UK, while still remaining theirs. Given its charitable nature, the bank has received donations from unclaimed funds in dormant accounts of banking and broker organizations, allowing the bank to leverage this equity to generate over £100,000 of additional funding for the voluntary sector.

10. ECOLOGY BUILDING SOCIETY http://www.ecology.co.uk/ The Ecology Building Society, based in Yorkshire and offering services (savings and mortgages) throughout the UK, was founded in 1981. A mutual organization, it uses savers' deposits to grant mortgages on properties and projects that help the environment. With a mission to

improve the environment by promoting sustainable housing and sustainable communities, savings placed with the Ecology fund mortgage lending on: • energy efficient housing • ecological renovation • derelict and dilapidated properties • small-scale and ecological enterprise • low-impact lifestyles Its AGMs are held in a different part of the country each year, at a venue of environmental interest, thereby enabling attendance from members around the country.

11. PERMACULTURE CREDIT UNION www.pcuonline.org Based in New Mexico, US, Permaculture Credit Union members are dedicated to the following ethics of Permaculture: • Care of the earth • Care of people • Reinvestment of the credit union surplus to benefit the earth and its inhabitants. • It offers their members a Sustainability Discount Program, which provides a 0.75% interest rate discount for projects that can be certified to be for one of the following purposes: • home energy efficiency upgrades • renewable energy generation • permaculture landscaping • water catchment and delivery • farm machinery • fuel efficient automobiles (0.75% for vehicles that achieve 35mpg average and 1.5% discount for vehicles that exceed 45 miles per gallon average.)

PART V

BIBLIOGRAPHY

1. Pojasek, Robert **B. ,(2017), Organizational Risk Management and Sustainability – A** Practical Step-by-Step G*uide, Boca Raton,* Florida, CRC Press
2. Esty, Daniel C., Winston, Andrew S., (2006), Green to Gold, Hoboken, New Jersey, Wiley
3. DE*FRA.(2008).* A Framework for Pro-environmental Behaviours. London: Department for Environmental, Food and Rural Affairs.
4. Hi*tchcock, Darcy and Wi*llard, Marsha, (2006), The Business Guide to Sustainability – Practical Strategies and Tools for Organiza*tions, New York, New Y*ork, Earthscan,
5. McDonough, William and Braungart, Michael, (2002), Cradle to Cradle, New York, New York, North Point Press,
6. Martin, Dean and Schouten, John, (2014), Sustainable Marketing, Essex, UK, Pearson
7. W*illard, Bob, (200*9), The Sustainability Champion's Guidebook, Gabrioala Island, BC, Canada ,New Society Publishers
8. Avlonas, *Nikos a*nd Nassos George, P.,(2014), Practical Sustainability Strategies – How to Gain a Competiti*ve Advantage, Hoboken, New Jersey, Wiley*
9. *Turan, Fikret, Korhan, (2010), Organizational Sustainability – A Quantitative Decision Model Towards Maximizing Organizational Sustainability, Saarbrucken, Germany, VDM*
10. *Willard, Bob, (2012), The New Sustainability Advantage – Se*ven Business Case Benefits of a Tr*iple Bottom Line, Gabriola Island, BC, New Society Publishers*
11. *Ernst, Dorothy, (2016), Personal and Org*anizational Transformation Towards Sustainability – Walking a Twin Path, *New York, New York, Bu*siness Expert Press,
12. Belz Frank Martin and Peattie Ken, (2009), Sustainability Marketing, Sussex, UK, Wiley
13. Vi*ctor, A. Peter,(2008), Managing Without Growth, Cheltenham, UK, Edward Elgar*
14. **Hitchcock, Darcy,E.** and Willard, MarchaL., (2008), The Step-by-Step Guid*e to Sustainability Planning: How to Create and Implement Suatainability plans in any Busines or organization, London, Earthscan*
15. Choudhury, Dr.Deb Prasanna, (2011), Strategic Planning and Management of Nonprofit Organizations and NGOs – T*heory, Practice, Research and Cases, , New Delhi, India, Asian Books Private Limited*
16. Werbach, Adam, (2009), Strategy for Sustainability – A Business Man*ifesto, Boston, MA, Harvard* Business Review Press
17. Sharp, Leith (2015), Put simply, we are in the wrong organizational vehicle for the 21st century, LEED Block, Peter, (2009), Community : The Structure of Belonging, San Francisc*o, CA Berrett-Koehler* Publishers Inc

18. "Community Based Social Marketing - Fostering Sustainable Behavior: Community Based Social Marketing" (Doug McKenzie-Mohr)

19. Victor, A. Peter,(2008), Managing Without Growth, Cheltenham, UK, Edward Elgar

20. Winston, Andrew, S., (2014), The Big Pivot – Radically Practical Strategies for a Hotter, Scarcer and More Open World, Boston, MA ,Harvard Business Review Press

21. Pojasek, R. B. (2010). "Quality toolbox: Sustainability: The three responsibilities". Environmental Quality Management,19(3), 87–94.

22. Pojasek, R.B. (2012). "Quality Toolbox: Understanding Sustainability: An Organizational Perspective". Environmental Quality Management, 93-100.

23. Easwar Iyer and Bobby Banerjee (1993) ,"Anatomy of Green Advertising in NA - Advances in Consumer Research Volume 20, eds. Leigh McAlister and Michael L. Rothschild, Provo, UT ": Association for Consumer Research, Pages: 494-501.

24. Socolow Robert and Pacala Stephen, et al (2004) "Solving the Climate Problem – Technologies available to curb CO2 emissions", ENVIRONMENT, Volume 46, pp. 8-10.

25. Identifying and Analyzing Stakeholders and Their Interests. (n.d.), Community Toolbox, Retrieved from: http://ctb.ku.edu/en/table-of-contents/participation/encouraging-involvement/identify-stakeholders/main

26. B.Klaus, (September, 2012), Building capacity in NGO Risk Management, Retrieved from:
http://www.thesustainablengo.org/improving-capacity/building-capacity-in-risk-management

27. India Community Protocol for Accounting & Reporting Greenhouse Gas Emissions(December, 2012), ICLEI- Local Governments for Sustainability, South Asia. Retrieved from: http://urbanlowcarbonfinance.iclei.org/resources/ICP-Draft_Dec_2012.pdf

28. Sustainability Trends in 2018 and Questions you should ask https://www.terrafiniti.com/sustainability-trends-in-2018-and-the-questions-you-should-ask/

29. Rocamora, Alexis and Amellin, Areyani, IGES List of Grid Emission Factors(2018), Institute for Global Environmental Strategies, Retrieved from http://pub.iges.or.jp/modules/envirolib/view.php?docid=2136

30. Regional and Sectoral Assessment of Greenhouse Gas Emissions in India. Atmospheric Environment, Vol. 35/15, pp. 2679-2695 Retrieved from http://www.decisioncraft.com/energy/papers/ecc/ei/ghgei.pdf

31. India Specific Road Transport Emission Factors(2015), India GHG Program. Retrieved from: http://indiaghgp.org/sites/default/files/Road%20Transport%20Technical%20Paper.pdf

32. Calculations and Emission Factors. Retrieved from: http://www.carbonneutralcalculator.com/Carbon%20Offset%20Factors.pdf

33. Easwar Iyer and Bobby Banerjee (1993) ,"Anatomy of Green Advertising in NA - Advances in Consumer Research Volume 20, eds. Leigh McAlister and Michael L. Rothschild, Provo, UT ": Association for Consumer Research, Pages: 494-501.

34. The C*limate Registry. Retrieved from:* https://www.theclimateregistry. org/wp-content/uploads/2015/04/2015-TCR-Default-EF-April-2015-FINAL.pdf

35. Aashe: Setting Emissions Targets and Measuring Progress. Retrieved March 19, 2016 from http://www.aashe.org/wiki/cool-campus-how-guide-college-and-university-climate-action-planning/7-setting-emissions-target

36. INCREASING ENERGY- AND GREENHOUSE GAS-SAVING BEHAVIORS AMONG ADOLESCENTS: A SCHOOL-BASED CLUSTER-RANDOMIZED CONTROLLED TRIAL . Retrieved from: http://web.stanford.edu/group/peec/cgi-bin/docs/behavior/research/highschoolcurriculum/curriculum%2045%20final%20.pdf

37. Summary of Emissions Factors for the Guidance for Voluntary Corporate Greenhouse Gas Reporting – 2015. Retrieved from: https://www.mfe.govt. nz/sites/default/files/media/Climate%20Change/voluntary-ghg-reporting-summary-tables-emissions-factors-2015.pdf

38. GHG Inventory report for Electricity generation and consumption in India 2009-10. cBalance Solutions Private Balance Ltd. Retrieved from: http:// cbalance.in/wp-content/uploads/2013/01/cbalance_white-paper_Electricity-emission-factors_28Dec2012_revised_V2.pdf

39. Parikh, Jyoti and Manoj Panda et al (2009), CO2 emissions structure of Indian economy, Energy. Retrieved *from* http://www.irade.org/egy_2307-with-corrections.pdf

40. India GHG Program: India Specific Road Transport Emission Factors, (2015) Retrieved from: http://indiaghgp.org/sites/default/files/Road%20 Transport%20Technical%20Paper.pdf

41. Calculations and Emission Factors. Retrieved from http://www. carbonneutralcalculator.com/Carbon%20Offset%20Factors.pdf

42. The Climate Registry. Retrieved from: https://www.theclimateregistry.org

43. Aashe: Setting Emissions Targets and Measuring Progress(March 19, 2016): Retrieved from http://www.aashe.org/wiki/cool-campus-how-guide-college-and-university-climate-action-planning/7-setting-emissions-target

44. Increasing Energy- and Greenhouse Gas-Saving Behaviors Among Adolescents: A School-Based Cluster-Randomized Controlled Trial (March, 2016), Retrieved March 17, 2016 from http://web.stanford.edu/group/ peec/cgi-bin/docs/behavior/research/highschoolcurriculum/curriculum%20 45%20final%20.pdf

45. Summary of Emissions Factors for the Guidance for Voluntary Corporate Greenhouse Gas Reporting (2015). Retrieved from: https://www.mfe.govt. nz/sites/default/files/media/Climate%20Change/voluntary-ghg-reporting-summary-tables-emissions-factors-2015.pdf

46. Cagnnin, CH, Loveridge, D, and Bulter, J. (2005). Business sustainability Maturity Model. Retrieved from http://www. crrconference.org/previousconferences/bse2005/proceedings/ cristianohugocagnindenisloveridgeandjeffbu.html

47. What is the Social License to Operate? Retrieved from: (2015) http://www. miningfacts.org/Communities/What-is-the-social-licence-to-operate/

48. Foster, William; Kim, Peter & Christiansen, Barbara, Ten Non-Profit Funding Models, Stanford Social Innovation Review, (Spring, 2009), Retrieved 04/11/2016 from http://ssir.org/articles/entry/ten_nonprofit_funding_models

49. Serrat, O., From strategy to practice, Knowledge Solutions, Asian Development Bank, Manila, 2009c, (2015) Retrieved from: http://digitalcommons.ilr. cornell.edu/cgi/viewcontent.cgi?article=1154&context=intl,

50. Sustainable Marketing – The Importance of being a Sustainable Business (2012): Retrieved from: https://www.theseus.fi/bitstream/ handle/10024/50565/Reutlinger_Janina.pdf

51. Majumdar, Utkarsh; Rana, Namrata; Sanan, Neeti, India's Top companies for CSR and Sustainability (2015), Retrieved from: https://www.iimu.ac.in/ upload_data/main_containts/about/Social-Responsibility/IIMU_CSR_REPORT.pdf

52. The Carbon Footprint of 5 diets compared, Retrieved from: http:// shrinkthatfootprint.com/food-carbon-footprint-diet

53. Werbach, Adam, (2009), Strategy for Sustainability, Boston, Harvard University

Review

54. Wollmuth, Jessica and Ivanova, Velislava, 6 Steps for a more sustainable supply chain (2014), Retrieved from: : https://www.greenbiz.com/ blog/2014/01/24/6-steps-more-sustainable-supply-chain

55. http://asherleaf.com/wp-content/uploads/2011/05/asherinnovation. Sustainability-Risk-Management.May-2011.pdf

56. A Brief Overview of Sustainable Finance. Retrieved from: https://www. ignited.global/publications/crimson-financier/brief-overview-sustainable-finance

57. Strandberg, Coro, BEST PRACTICES IN SUSTAINABLE FINANCE , Retrieved from: https://www.luxflag.org/media/pdf/SustainableFinance Best_Practices1.pdf

58. Supply Chain Sustainability – A practical guide for Continuous improvement (2000) , By United Nations Global Impact, Retrieved from: https://www.bsr.org/reports/BSR_UNGC_SupplyChainReport.pdf

Clancy, Heather (2018, May), Why biotech innovator Novozymes uses the SDGs as a catalyst for growth. Retrieved from: https://www.greenbiz.com/article/ why-biotech-innovator-novozymes-uses-sdgs-catalyst-growth,

60. Burrows, Tim (2008), Corporate Climate Change Management and the Strategic Advantage of Companies Integrating a Climate Change Strategy. Retrieved from: https://www.azocleantech.com/article.aspx?ArticleID=121

61. Dhanjode, Chetan, Ralegaonkar R.V., Dakwale Vaidehi, DESIGN AND DEVELOPMENT OF SUSTAINABLE CONSTRUCTION STRATEGY FOR RESIDENTIAL BUILDINGS: A CASE STUDY FOR COMPOSITE CLIMATE (2013)" International Journal of Sustainable Construction Engineering & Technology (ISSN: 2180-3242) Vol 4, No .1 :Universiti Tun Hussein Onn Malaysia (UTHM) and Concrete Society of Malaysia (CSM) 12, Retrieved from: http://penerbit.uthm.edu.my/ojs/index.php/IJSCET

62. Top Businesses reveal climate change strategies, (27.01.2012), Retrieved from: http://www.climatechangenews.com/2012/01/27/top-businesses%E2%80%99-reveal-climate-change-strategies/

63. Haanes, Knut, Michael, David, et al (March, 2013), Making Sustainability Profitable, Retrieved from: https://hbr.org/2013/03/making-sustainability-profitable

64. Rohm, Howard and Montogomery, Dan (2011), Link Sustainability to Corporate Strategy Using the Balanced Scorecard: , Retrieved from: http://www.balancedscorecard.org/portals/0/pdf/linkingsustainabilitytocorporatestrategyusingthebalancedscorecard.pdf65. ESG/Sustainability – Are Companies Realizing Real ROI,(May 22, 2018), Retrieved from: https://www.alpha-sense.com/blog/esg-sustainability-are-companies-realizing-real-return-on-their-investment-2551

Index